WHITE HYENA

First Edition

ISBN: 979-8-365-66514-9

This book is dedicated to Zewdie.

Proceeds from the sale of this book will be donated
to projects supporting the health, welfare and livelihoods
of rural women traders in Ethiopia.

Map of Ethiopia, 1980s

Eritrea *

Red Sea

10

Sudan

9

Djibouti

•8

5• •6

Addis Ababa ★
•2
1• •3 •4

7

11

Somalia

Kenya

1. Alem Tena
2. Debre Zeit
3. Nazareth
4. Tinsay Berhan

5. Debre Berhan
6. Ankober
7. Harar
8. Ataye

9. Gondar
10. Masawa
11. Yabelo
* Independence 1993

Preface

This is Bedilu's story. The project to write this book began in 2005 with the words: 'You should write your story.' Without him, this story could not be told, the original structure and outline of the story are his. With Bedilu's agreement, I took over the stories and characters to create the fictionalised account told here.

Countless phone calls, questions and note-taking, research and chatting on visits to Ethiopia over many years, have informed this book. We have travelled together to the highlands of northern Shewa to film interviews with rural women, men and families to promote the agro-forestry work of an Ethiopian/British NGO. In 1999, I led an Oxfam research team to better understand the barriers to accessing health and education services in four of the poorest parts of Ethiopia, including Wollo Delanta in the northern highlands. Some of my observations from these trips, of the women and men, girls and boys we met, and the villages and landscapes they lived and survived in, have fed into the telling of this story.

The parallel stories of Ashebir and Izzie, while based on lived experiences, have been fictionalised. Names have mostly been changed, some people have been amalgamated. Online research, a rich body of literature by Ethiopian, Nigerian, Kenyan, African American, Ghanaian, British Caribbean and Tanzanian authors, as well as my own letters from the time I lived and worked in Ethiopia, have all helped to inform the craft of writing and the storytelling.

Care has been taken to be as accurate as possible regarding historical events, but this is not a history book.

Fra von Massow
London, December 2022

List of Characters

The Orphanage
Ato Habtamu "the fat Uncle"
The fat Uncle's wife
The Boys: Desalegn, Sammy, Wef
and Theodros "Tedi"
The Finnish Women: Laine and
Taimi

Alem Tena
Zewdie Tamru and Lakew Tamru
Emet Hawa
Boleke

Ataye Market
Wozeiro Etalem
Comrade Abebe

Debre Berhan Camp
Mesfin and Daniel
Belaynesh
Dawit
Gwad Tadele

Tinsaye Berhan
Haile Tesfaye
Genene Haile
Ade Senbeta and her son

The Village Outside Ataye
Temima and Mohamed Ahmed
Their children Mohamed Abdu,
Aminat and Konjit
Mohamed Bilal from Albuko
Selam and Mohamed Shinkurt
Their children Yimam, Nuru
Ahmed and Fahte
Ali and Yishaereg
Their two brothers
Their mother
Emet Fahte Ibrahim
Wozeiro Zeineba

Debre Berhan
Wozeiro Tsehai
Her daughter Wubit

Ankober
Ato Tadesse
Mama Turunesh

Malawi
Sam Brown

London
Izzie's sisters Helen and Kate

Addis Ababa

Piazza
Negisst
Girma
Awgucho
The Street Boys: Hailu, Mekonnen,
Biniam and their mother, Abebech

Moe's Office
Fasika
Mulu
Mr. Robert Riley Jr.
Kidist
Amari

*Agency for Disabled, Children and
Destitute*
Uschi
Comrade Aklilu
Gezahegn
Simaynesh
Genet
Desta
Elsabet
Wozeiro Meheret
Ato Solomon
Ato Embaye
Comrade Adugna

Friends and Expats
Moe Bellamy
Booker Keyes
Leila
Tom
Sheila and Brian
Aster
Hiwot
Alessandro
Ingo
Susan
Matt
Duncan
Solomon

Relief Council
Wondwossen

RAF Guys
Scud
Andy

Prologue

August 1997, Addis Ababa to Ataye

It was cold and the night unusually still. He had been sleeping restlessly. Memories and half sleep interrupted by the high-pitched whine of mosquitoes around his head. There were at least two circling his room and he simply could not see them. The walls were bare, white emulsion on smooth plaster. He had painted them himself. But could he spot a single mosquito to squash satisfyingly against the wall? Never.

He had had that dream again and his heart was strumming uncomfortably in his chest. Reluctant to put on the light, he felt around the end of his bed until his fingers found his soft gabi.[1] He wrapped it round his shoulders. The matches were on the small table next to his bed. He struck one. He liked the flash and smell of sulphur. He lit the white candle in the wrought iron holder Sammy had made for him. Candlelight was better. Every minute of electricity was another five centimes he couldn't afford. The evening before, he had gone around switching off all the lights as usual. The electricity bills were high. He and the boys never had enough money to cover them.

He sat hugging his knees, resting his chin on top. Who he was and where he came from was the problem. He even had difficulty with his name. It had started on his very first day in school. The day after the fat Uncle's wife had given him a pair of shoes. The day after he had met Desalegn.

The misery whirled around in his stomach as he remembered the teacher asking: "What is your name?"

"My name is – " he remembered the words coming out in a whisper, his mouth too dry to speak.

They sat row upon row on the schoolroom's earthen floor, staring at the teacher and the large blackboard. There must have been at least sixty

---

[1] Locally woven white cotton shawl.

1

of them in First Grade. Many of the other children were smaller than him.

"Stand up, boy. We can't hear you." The teacher had persisted. "What is your name?"

"A – A – A – " he remembered stammering, as he pushed himself up onto his feet, trying to avoid the curious eyes looking up at him. He could hear their whispers and snuffled giggles.

"He can't say his name!"

Some were holding two hands over their mouths trying to stifle their laughing, exchanging wide-eyed looks with their friends.

He had been so alone.

"Can't you even pronounce your name for us?" The teacher continued, his face protruding from the end of his long thin neck at Ashebir.

Like a vulture, he remembered thinking.

"Are you a donkey?" the teacher said loudly.

The class exploded.

Ashebir's chin hung close to his chest. He could see his shorts billowing round his skinny legs, his feet enclosed in the new shoes. They dug into his skin and he shifted uneasily from one foot to the other. His feet were used to bare feet. The soles were hard and flattened. His toes spread wide, a large space between the big one and the next. He lifted his head to find the teacher's small gleaming eyes staring at him, obviously enjoying himself.

Anger for the small boy welled up inside him. How dare he? How could a teacher behave like that?

He remembered trying to swallow. Avoiding the children's stares, his eyes had gone from the teacher's triumphant face to his new pinching shoes. He remembered his heart pounding in his ears and the fear creeping over his body. He had wished so badly that his mother were waiting outside for him. He did all he could to stop the tears welling behind his eyes, from pouring down his cheeks.

He could hear his mother's voice, "Be strong, yeney lij.[2] We have to be strong and work hard. This is our life."

"Ashebir. Ashebir Lakew," a quiet voice said.

Ashebir had glanced behind him, then up at the teacher.

"What was that?" the teacher's eyes veered sharply towards the voice. "Stand up, boy."

---

[2] My child.

It was Desalegn. He stood up and cleared his throat. "His name is Ashebir Lakew, Sir." His voice faltered. "He is new at the orphanage, Sir."

Whispers spread across the class.

"Sit down," the teacher said. "Both of you."

Ashebir sat down, quickly wiping his eyes. He had wanted to turn and smile his gratitude, but dared not move. That was brave of Desalegn. The boy was slender, pale and serious. He was not particularly outspoken.

Ashebir remembered whispering in his mind, over and over: Ashebir Lakew Tamru. My name is Ashebir Lakew Tamru. He curled up on his side, hugging himself against the chill. The tears rolled down his cheeks. He let them fall. If only the morning would come.

He knew now why the name had been painful as a child. He was alone. The people who had named him were gone. But there was something else. Why did Zewdie and Lakew have the same surname, Tamru? That's just not possible. There was an unusual coincidence in his parents' names. They both had the same surname, Tamru. But husband and wife do not share the same surname. Your father's first name is your surname, followed by your grandfather's first name. It would certainly be a coincidence if both his parents' fathers had been called Tamru. He had pushed the doubt to the back of his mind for a while. Now he needed to know.

Did he resemble Lakew? Ashebir wondered if anyone had ever looked at him as a child and said: "Ashebir Lakew, don't you look like your father." There was no one who could tell him.

He tried to evoke his mother's face. As a child he would comfort himself every morning when he woke by conjuring up her face in his mind. Of course, he had no photos from that time. He would get flashes of her smile, or the shape of her head, her hair soft to touch, her hands, the way she laughed. But he had to admit, he could not see her clearly anymore. His father Lakew's face had vanished long ago. He had rarely seen him.

Lakew Tamru and Zewdie Tamru. Were they brother and sister? He rubbed his hands backwards and forwards over his head, his body tingling with agitation. He felt like he was being attacked by a thousand mosquitoes.

If I cannot be sure of their names, how can I be sure of who I am? Clasping his hands behind his head, he let out a long sigh. If Lakew was not my father, then who was? Hot tears stung his eyes.

After that first miserable day in school, he had grown more confident with the help of Desalegn and the other children at the orphanage. He had replied, "Ashebir Lakew Tamru," when asked for his name. He had given this response with the certainty of a trusting child.

He wished now more than ever that his mother were there to answer his questions. Whose past did he belong to?

The candle lit up a small circle of light, its brightness flickering. Every now and then it threw a pale light into the dark nooks and crannies of the room. There would be someone who could shed light on his story.

Finally, morning dawned. The neighbour's cockerel competed with the sing song call to church from the priest on top of the hill behind the house. He heard the hollow rush of water into their large kettle. Ayene had arrived and soon there would be tea. He pulled on his jeans and t-shirt and wrapped his gabi round his shoulders. It felt soft and warm. Outside was still fresh from the night, the sky a vivid pink red. The sun's rays were still low and as yet only sent a little warmth into the garden.

His compound was blooming with the flowers he had planted after the renovations had been completed. The grass now grew thick and green. The palm tree in the middle of the lawn was still short and stubby. The individually placed boulders he had painted gave the compound an artistic flare and the whole was pleasing to his eye. One of the rock paintings was of a gojo-bate,[3] a round mud and thatch house, standing in the shade of a tall warka tree,[4] another was of a waterfall. His favourite was the one of Muletta mountain. For as long as he could remember, he had sketched and painted.

He went and sat in a huddle on the veranda step by the front door, drawing the gabi close around himself. The weight of his night-time thoughts still had not lifted.

"Tenasteling[5] Ashebir. Did you not sleep well? You are up early for a Sunday. It's barely sunrise."

"Tenasteling Ayene. How are you?" He turned to look at her, too tired to get up and greet her properly. "How is the family?"

"I am fine, we are all fine, Egziyabher yimesgen,[6]" she sucked her teeth, like Zewdie used to. It meant that not everything was as 'fine' as she would have wished.

Ashebir smiled.

---

[3] A round, village cottage made of mud and thatch.
[4] A sycamore-fig tree found in Ethiopia and Yemen.
[5] Hello, Good day.
[6] Thanks be to God.

"Do you want breakfast? I've made tea."

Ayene Abeba was their maid. She stood expectantly in her long dark red skirt, black plastic shoes on her feet. She wore an old jumper and a black scarf wound tightly round her head. She was like a mother to them. She cooked for them, and washed their clothes. The boys living with him liked her and so did he. Her fingernails, clipped short, had blobs of leftover red varnish on them. She was slightly plump; her food was good. He was sure she liked to taste it as she cooked.

"Yes, I would love some tea," he said.

She looked at him again, "You look bothered, Ashebir. Are you worrying about the bills again?"

"No, no. It's nothing," he said.

She took another look at him, and went back inside the house. Ayene lived in the neighbourhood with her sister's family. She had moved there with her son. Her husband had been killed in the fighting in Eritrea. Working for the boys meant she could pay her way, and when she cooked for Ashebir and the boys she always made enough to take some home for herself and her son. Ashebir shook his head thinking life was not easy for anyone.

Moments later she was back with hot tea and a piece of fresh ambasha.[7] He bowed his head towards her, as he took the food, both hands outstretched. He closed his eyes and whispered thanks to God. Ayene went back into the house looking satisfied.

He took a tiny sip of the hot tea with a loud slurp. That felt better. While chewing on his bread his thoughts went to his grandmother, Emet Hawa. She was a very old woman. Everyone called her Emet out of respect. He had been fond of her.

He closed his eyes and could see her sitting on a low wooden stool preparing coffee. She wore her traditional, long white dress, made from hand woven cotton. The one she always wore for prayer. Her hut filled with the aroma of fresh coffee mingled with sweet smoky itan.[8] A basket of fluffy white fendisha[9] sat on the floor next to a tray of tiny white coffee cups. In his mind's eye he could see the shadow of a small boy framed in the doorway, the brilliant sunlight streaming in behind. He must have been about five years old. Children were not allowed to take part in the coffee ceremony, but he remembered how he

---

[7] Homemade thick bread.

[8] Incense made from tree sap.

[9] Fresh hot popcorn, always eaten with coffee.

5

had always laid hopeful eyes on the fendisha.

If he was honest, he could only vaguely see his grandmother Emet Hawa. When she said her prayers, she used to make coffee and chew khat,[10] always wearing that soft white handwoven gown of hers.

**

Today was Sunday. He would ask Ayene to prepare traditional coffee for them all. Just the way Emet Hawa used to do.

"More tea, Ashebir?" Ayene called out softly, interrupting his thoughts.

"Ishi[11] Ayene, thank you," he said.

"Are you feeling better now?" She asked coming out with the teapot and filling his glass again, a bowl of sugar in her other hand.

"Yes, I'm fine. Thank you."

"You worry me today, yeney lij," she said.

That was her way of inviting him to unload his heart.

"Ayene," he said, "Would you prepare buna[12] for us today?"

He put a hand up to stop her, "Only one sugar Ayene, egziersteling.[13]"

"Yes of course. We can have coffee in the garden this afternoon. I can make it after lunch."

"That would be great. Thank you," he said. "You know why I don't take much sugar?"

"No, why is that?"

"My mother was a trader."

"Enday?[14] Really?" Ayene said, putting the tea pot down. She gathered her skirts around her knees and sat down on the step next to Ashebir with a grunt.

He had never talked to her about his mother before. She sat looking at him sideways, cupping her cheek in her hand.

"My mother used to store goods for the market in our gojo-bate. One evening when she was preparing injera[15] over the fire, I crept behind the mud partition to where she kept her stocks for the market."

"How old were you?"

---

[10] A bush, its fresh green leaves chewed for its stimulant properties.
[11] OK.
[12] Coffee.
[13] Thank you.
[14] Expression of surprise.
[15] Flat bread made from teff, an Ethiopian staple.

"About five, I suppose."

"Naughty boy!"

They chuckled together.

"I found the white sugar and carefully tucked one packet into my pocket."

"E-ssay," Ayene hissed, shaking her head and smiling.

"Early the next morning I took off into the hills as usual with our animals."

"Enday!" she sat up straight, looking at him. "You, a shepherd boy?"

"Yes, I was a shepherd boy."

"God be praised indeed, and look at you now!"

"So, I was up in the hills and I found a large round stone to sit on, like this, Ayene." Ashebir got up to demonstrate, sitting on his haunches on the lawn. "I gently pulled the small packet of sugar from my pocket." Ashebir made as if to take something from his pocket. "It was plastic. I bit a corner off and slowly poured it into my mouth."

"Weyne, poor thing, miskin."

"It was so sweet," Ashebir licked his lips, exaggerating. "So I wanted more. There was a small stream nearby. I went and filled the packet with water and drank down the last grains."

"In heaven's name it was a happy morning for you, Ashebir."

"Not quite," Ashebir chuckled. "I'd barely finished drinking, when I threw it all up again."

"Oh my God."

"I had never eaten anything sweet in my life."

Ayene giggled, sliding the small metal cross she wore round her neck back and forth absently. "When the price of sugar goes up again you will not suffer as much as the rest of us."

"Too right."

"Well, I better get back to the kitchen," she said, pushing herself up with a grunt, more from her weight than her age. She disappeared into the dark interior of the bungalow.

"Thank you for the tea," he called quietly after her.

The other boys were still sleeping. Ashebir could sit for a while in peace.

The six of them had grown up at the orphanage in Debre Zeit together, and now they were living in this bungalow on the outskirts of Addis Ababa. Some were studying, others, like Sammy, were doing vocational training, like metal work at Hope Enterprises. Late teens, early twenties, all grown-up orphans without a home, too old for the orphanage, too young to look after themselves. They were lucky to have this place and Ayene. The house snuggled amongst a few others below the hills in a new, sparsely populated, suburb to the south west of the city centre. Everyone said it would grow and become part of Addis one day. It lay almost in the countryside on a dirt road, heading for Jimma. Each main artery leaving the capital carried the name of its destination: the Jimma Road, the Debre Zeit Road, the Asmara Road, the Ambo Road. He was yet to travel all of them. The houses in his neighbourhood were connected by rough rocky pathways and dirt roads wide enough for a small Isuzu truck. Many of the bungalows, like theirs, were tucked inside their compounds behind pale grey breeze-block walls. He was glad they had built the wall; it was high with a large corrugated iron gate. It made him feel cocooned, and at the same time he could still look out and beyond to the surrounding countryside. There were no shops, only tiny hole-in-the-wall suks,[16] like Alemu's, selling a few basic items. For most of their provisions it was necessary to go to Mercato, the large market in the centre of Addis, a few miles away.

For the time being, Ashebir joined the throng of night school students, walking through the University gates every evening with bags of books over their shoulders, studying their way to a better life. He was taking a diploma in educational administration, all the time wishing he had a small shop. At around five o'clock, at the end of the working day, there was a buzz of activity around the cafés and bars near Arat Kilo before night school started. This country is not only hungry for food, he thought. It's also hungry for learning.

He and Desalegn had already started talking about the shop idea.

Zewdie's trading skills must be in my blood. I'm no academic. I'm a villager, the son of a highland trader. He was proud of feeling her influence in him.

He could hear the familiar early morning murmur of voices, and the intermittent clang of metal pans being washed up, sending out dampened echoes. A radio crackled out one of the latest songs. He was happy here; despite the restless undercurrent in his mind.

Someone was having eggs. The smell of frying onions and green chilli peppers made his mouth water. It reminded him of the rare times they had had eggs at home. Zewdie most often had to sell them.

He returned to thoughts of his grandmother, Emet Hawa. She had had a ram. A ram that she loved. He was fat from all the food she gave him.

---

[16] A small shop.

For some reason she always wanted to have that ram near her, maybe it was something religious, he thought. Sometimes she used to go out into the fields with Ashebir when he was tending his mother's few sheep and goats, and the ram would follow. One day she was sitting on a rock having a rest. That ram came right up to her and butted her off. Ashebir smiled as he remembered how they had laughed together. The ram used to tease him too, playfully pushing him around.

One day he found some branches of her khat. He tried chewing the fresh green leaves, imitating his grandmother's prayer-time habit. It was so bitter he had to spit it out. She gently reprimanded him, "Ashebir. My child. Stop it. Stop it. Khat is not for you, yeney lij. It is not good for you and it won't help you. You are with us, but you don't belong to Islam. You came from a Christian family."

You came from a Christian family. The words suddenly struck him. He now remembered her telling him this, and how he had stood, a few of the bitter khat leaves still in his mouth, wide-eyed, and not understanding the secret. At that tender age, if his grandmother said that she and his mother belonged to one religion, and he to another, how could he find it strange? He knew God and Allah and prayed to them, but he had been too young to really know what 'religion' was. He had accepted God and Allah just like he had accepted that he was not allowed to take part in the adults' coffee ceremonies. Just like he had accepted that his mother and father had the same name.

Now he was puzzled. What had she meant by that? he wondered. How could it be that my mother and grandmother were Muslims and I a Christian? That's just not possible. Am I imagining Emet Hawa saying that?

But Zewdie was a Christian. She took him to church, gave him a godfather. When he was very small, they used to meet a tall man wrapped in a thick white gabi, whom Zewdie called Ato Baruda.

"He is your godfather, Ashebir." Zewdie would tell him; and he would have to go and shake the man's hand, looking up at the dark distant face.

He felt his heart quicken. He took another sip of tea and lifted his face to warm it in the gentle morning sun, a slight frown on his brow. He opened his eyes deliberately slowly, playing with the light between his lashes. He looked for a while at the largest stone on which he had painted the thatch roof gojo-bate. He remembered Lakew coming to their gojo-bate in Ataye from time to time. And the feeling of excitement at seeing him.

Deep inside he knew there must be an explanation and he had to find it. He sat for a while looking up towards the hills. From the veranda he could see the low mountains which changed colour throughout the day like the foothills around his old home. He could just make out the church on the top of the hill behind his house, surrounded by juniper and tall eucalyptus. He liked to walk up there with his friends. He felt as if he was still in the countryside.

**

After his graduation from school, he had desperately wanted to return home. He had set off, accompanied by Sammy. Sammy was a warm-hearted boy with a round face that was always smiling. He made a good travelling companion. And Sammy had been excited to go on a journey along the Asmara Road, into the countryside way to the north of Addis. He had never been that far before.

It had been a disaster. He and Sammy had taken a bus headed for Dessie early one morning. They reached the town which he had known as Ataye. It was now called Epheson. They found a simple roadside hotel and had eaten a lunch of injera and sherro wot.[17] Then they took a walk through the town, which was much bigger than Ashebir remembered, and around the market where Ashebir and Zewdie used to go. The first night they spent talking. Each time they fell silent, they heard the town dogs barking and the eerie but familiar whooping and chuckling noises of hyenas on the mountainside.

The next morning, they'd walked along the road towards the stone-built bridge which crossed the Ataye River. Ashebir immediately recognised the path running along on the other side leading to his home. They set off along the mountain track in the direction of his old village. They met with some village women, making their way home with their donkeys. Large sacks of grain strapped to the donkeys' backs, and the women bent double, carrying long bundles of firewood. They stopped, as was their custom, to enquire after and greet the young strangers. They shook hands with Ashebir and Sammy. They were gentle people.

Ashebir did not know these women. He had introduced himself and Sammy, excitedly explaining that he had once lived in Sudan Sefer with his mother Zewdie. Did they perhaps remember her? He told them about how they had left because of the drought.

---

[17] A spicy sauce made with ground chick peas to accompany injera.

One woman said, yes, she remembered talk of them. Hadn't his mother passed away?

"Yes, my mother died at the time," he said.

The women shook their heads, clicking their tongues, and saying sorry.

Another woman said, "People said her boy must have died too."

They praised the wonder of Allah in all his mercy for keeping him alive, and began greeting him all over again. He was no longer a complete stranger. They shook his hand again and greeted Sammy with the same warmth.

"Are you married?"

"Do you have children?"

"Did you get accustomed to the city life?"

They held onto his hand. Theirs rough and bony, looking into his face, their dark eyes sparkling with curiosity.

They suddenly seemed like black crows, hopping back and forth to peck at a piece of carrion, taking another look, another peck. He was a novelty. He looked about him, feeling uncomfortable and struggling not to cry. Standing in this place surrounded by so much that was familiar to him, and yet strangely distant, had deeply saddened him. They said they knew that many children had lost their families because of the wars and the famine. They were sorry, sorry for all the lost children.

It had been a strange experience. It was as if he had returned from the dead. He had wanted to get away. It turned out that they had not been his neighbours. They were villagers from the surrounding area who had only heard of him and his mother. They told him they did not think he had any relatives in the village.

That is when the nausea had overcome him and he thought his legs would give way. He thanked them, and indicated to Sammy to go back down the path they had come on. His eyes streamed with tears as soon as he turned to walk away. Sammy had walked alongside in silence, an arm around his shoulders, as they headed back along the river to the bridge.

So he never made it to his village. He had been too overwhelmed to continue along the path into his past. He had felt close to his mother for the first time in years. But she was dead. And there he had stood, on the path with those simple women who so resembled her, struck by an enormous sense of helplessness. The city boy, estranged and apart, bound as if by an invisible twine to these women, the aura around them, the strong warm smell of their animals, the familiar trees and shrubs, the mountains beyond. It was home. But he was a stranger.

It was better to return to Addis. He was just out of school and lacked the confidence. He had been puzzled and upset to hear that he had no family, no answers left in the village. His life in the city seemed very far from this place. Circumstances had taken him away and he could not imagine returning to that life again. He would try and get on with his life, with the friends he had made in the orphanage and in school. They had become his family.

Now, as he sat looking up at the church on the hill, he knew it was time to go home again. Perhaps this time he would be strong enough to find out more about Zewdie and Lakew.

Ashebir went inside, leaving an invisible imprint, a warm patch on the concrete step where he had been sitting, the shadow of a moment.

**

Two days later, Ashebir left for the bus terminal carrying a small canvas bag. His neighbour's cockerel had not even cleared its throat to break the silence of the night. On his way out of the house he had passed the kitchen, taken a chunk of Ayene's ambasha bread and popped it in his bag for the journey. She had baked extra the night before, and it was sitting in the large round breadbasket, carefully covered in a cotton cloth. He was full of expectation and purpose. When had he last felt like that? He closed the front door quietly not to wake the others. Even his fingers tingled with excitement. He wanted to jump and run like a goat up the mountain. He chuckled.

This time he would not turn away emotional and afraid. Whatever happened, he would keep going along the path. He shut the tall corrugated iron gate to his compound with its usual clanking, jarring noise. He passed Alemu's small suk in the wall, its metal shutters closed.

Most of his friends knew something of their past. They had relatives who could tell them stories. His friends from Akaki School knew who they were, and their families' origins. They were Oromo or Gurage or Eritrean. They were Amhara or Tigrayan. He was not even sure if he was a Muslim or a Christian. As he watched his step over the rocky pathway, he shook his head with a wry smile at the thought.

On the main road he climbed into an old VW taxi-bus which took him into town. The driver had a charm hanging from the rear-view mirror, and a black and white passport photo of a young woman, eyes lined with black kohl, stuck to the dashboard. He wondered if it was a wife or a girlfriend.

The main bus terminal for regional travel was in Mercato. It was the biggest market in Africa, if not the world. By the time Ashebir arrived to look for a bus, the day was warming up. Mercato was already heaving with traders and shoppers, the roads jammed with taxis, cars, battered pick-ups, donkeys and people criss-crossing in all directions. There was the smell of crowded humanity in the air, of livestock, ghee and spices. The odd pile of dark and rotting rubbish shrivelled his nostrils for a moment as he passed. Women working for the municipality, in their long dirty khaki dresses and wide straw hats, had already begun clearing the roadside gutters and paths of the debris. The municipality waged a constant war against rats. There were plenty of them in Mercato. A large white municipal truck passed through to collect the waste.

Ashebir was always drawn to the women traders with their children. They reminded him of his mother and himself. They would never guess looking at him that he had once been like them. A part of him, in his longing, was still one of them. The women had set out neat piles of vegetables. Long colourful rows of onions, potatoes and tomatoes, dark green and red chilli peppers, and bundles of green leafy vegetables laid out on sack cloths. They sat on stumpy stools beside their produce under large black umbrellas, their long skirts falling to the ground around their feet, scarves wrapped around their heads.

Street boys, their clothes in tatters, pushed their way through the shoppers, looking for something to carry, hustling for a job, or hawking boxes of cigarettes, soft tissues, chewing gum and caramella.

Clothes and t-shirts hung in rows outside shops with dark interiors. Hardware stalls displayed aluminium and metal kitchenware, suspended in rows above the open entrance, glinting in the sun. Red, yellow and green plastic buckets had been stacked into each other at the entrance and hand-bound brooms, made from long spindly branches, leant against the walls. Ashebir loved Mercato. Maybe he really would open a shop. One day soon. He would much prefer that to his night school. He wanted to work, to be a trader.

**

He found his bus and climbed on board. There was a wait until it was full and the rack on top loaded with bags and baskets of live chicken. The driver shouted instructions at his ticket tout: "Mamoosh, get that woman's bag up on top. Look out. There are people waiting over there. See if they are heading for Kombolcha. Let's get this bus full and on the road."

Finally, they were off. Ashebir settled into his seat. He leant against the window with his chin cupped in his hand and sought distraction in the world passing by. The bus passed through all the hubbub, noise and hustle of the market. The driver manoeuvred them through the city and headed for the Dessie/Asmara road. As the bus left Addis, there were fewer vehicles. They passed trucks billowing black smoke, buses travelling north, and the odd Land Rover. On the outskirts of town, he spotted the area where the Selam Vocational Centre was, up on the left-hand side of the road, on a steep hill behind a wall of tall eucalyptus. He had been sent there for a test when he failed his 11th grade exams. His school, and Laina and Taimi, the women who ran the Boys' Home, thought he should take up vocational training.

"You won't make 12th Grade Ashebir, and you are good with your hands," they'd said.

He shuffled in his seat a little, remembering how he had believed them. They sent him there to spend a week and see if it suited him. He had enjoyed it, and to his surprise came top of his group of forty. They were kept busy. They produced boats, grinding mills and brick making machines. The teachers were kind and enthusiastic. He had been tempted to leave school and enrol at Selam; and they had encouraged him to join them. But Izzie said it was important to complete 12th Grade. He knew she would be proud if he finished school. But it was tough and the maths impossible. He had written to her in England to let her know what was going on and ask for her advice.

Izzie had come with her smiles, laughter and energy, her insistence. She had talked to them all. To him, to Laina and Taimi, to the school, to his maths teacher.

"No wonder you can't do your maths," she had laughed. "How can you possibly put a hand up and ask a question with ninety in your class? I wouldn't."

In the wake of her whirlwind visit, like dust clouds spinning and dancing on the plains of Senbatey, he had gone back to school, extra maths tuition in place. Laina and Taimi nodding heads with no choice but to agree. Izzie disappeared again like the shimmering mirage of women on the horizon, returning home from market in the glow of the evening sun.

"And I made it," he thought, feeling proud of himself. "I got my 12th Grade. I did it."

She was the one who had put him in the orphanage in Debre Zeit. The small town surrounded by mountains and blessed with lakes. His favourite was Lake Bishoftu, where they used to swim. While she was still in Ethiopia, she used to come most weekends. She used to say, "Ashebir, whatever I do for you, imagine it is your mother doing it, ishi?" She wished she could have met Zewdie. "She must have been a very good woman, Ashebir."

Tears welled in his eyes as he remembered Izzie looking down at him with a smile. "Look at you," she would say. "You always do your best. Betam gobez lij neh,[18]" She would shake her head and suck her teeth like an Ethiopian. "Zewdie taught you so much; how to be strong, how to work hard, how to play and laugh, even if things are a total bummer."

She used to call him her 'gift from God'. She made him feel safe and cared for, even if she was far away in a place he could barely imagine.

How many times had he wished he could have lived with her as her son, go to school and come home to her?

"It's better for you to grow up an Ethiopian, knowing your culture, language and food, having friends and people here, Ashebir, yeney lij," she used to say. "Who knows? Maybe one day you might even find your relatives?"

As he got older, he understood her ideas better, and had agreed with her, albeit reluctantly. Nevertheless, when she left Ethiopia to work in Zaire, years back, she took with her his only chance of growing up in a family.

**

They were well out of town by now. He had secured himself a seat on the right side so he could look out over the countryside. The valley suddenly appeared bathed in sunshine, wide open and breath-taking, from behind the eucalyptus trees lining the road. Deep slopes fell away to the right and flowed into the open plain, stretching to the mountains beyond. To their left a hillside climbed up, covered in brush and eucalyptus. The air was filled with the warm, fresh scent from the trees. They were not indigenous. People said they came from a place called Australia, bahir zaf, trees from across the water. They grew fast. In the village they had used them to build their homes, for fences, switches and brooms, walking sticks and firewood. Zewdie used to boil eucalyptus leaves. He could remember the smell filling their gojo-bate. She said the steam was good for colds.

The bus slowed down behind a large truck. A man walked behind his donkey, two fat black rubber sacks filled with water slung on either side of the animal's stocky frame. Three women were bent over, rummaging amongst the trees further below, collecting branches for firewood.

Just like Zewdie. How she used to ache when she got home at night

---

[18] You are a very good boy.

after collecting and carrying firewood. He shook his head.

The landscape was made up of golden squares of farmland under different crops or lying fallow. Small groups of thatched mud huts huddled together. His stomach churned at the thought of home. He felt as if underground hot springs were bubbling up inside him. From his seat near the back, he wondered what thoughts, worries and fears the other passengers were carrying inside them. It's incredible how people can keep their faces still, not giving away the turmoil inside.

His fellow passengers sat, eyes slightly screwed up against the sun and dust, staring out of the open windows. The dirty curtains were drawn back, flapping in the wind, where the catch had broken. Some slept, heads lolling forward on their chests, occasionally jolting into semi-wakefulness, before falling asleep again. One well-dressed woman had fallen asleep with her mouth wide open. He was sure she would not be as amused as he, if she could see how she looked.

The sun was now almost overhead. On the wide open country road, with nothing to shelter them, it was getting hotter in the bus. To the kites and buzzards, floating up there in the blue, wings spread, warm currents of air sending them higher and higher, they must have looked like a tiny speck.

Towards heaven, towards Zewdie. Is she watching me? Sometimes I really feel she is there. Ashebir sat up, trying to pull himself together. Come on, Ashebir! He heard the sound of Desalegn's voice, urging him to cheer up. The thought of his friend made him smile.

**

It was his intention to look for Zewdie's older brother Mohamed Shinkurt.[19] His uncle was nicknamed Mohamed Onion because he grew fields of onions as well as other crops. Was he still alive? If so, he would be an old man by now. Ashebir already thought he was old back then. He had been a 'Big Man' in the village. Ashebir had been afraid of him, but he was his only connection to Zewdie and their story.

He closed his eyes and asked God's help, to be with him, and direct him. He accepted that God's will would be done. It was always so, Egziyabher yawkal.

The bus drew to a halt at the bus station in Debre Berhan. They had covered two hundred and fifty kilometres of tarmac. Ashebir knew this

---

[19] Onion.

road well, the bus station, the market. Tears welled up and his throat felt tight.

"Debre Berhan! Debre Berhan!" young Mamoosh shouted, flinging the front door open. "Everyone can get down. We leave again in fifteen minutes."

Ashebir moved to the front with the others and got down reluctantly. He needed to stretch. It all looked so normal. People going about their business, traders with their donkeys carrying large sacks of produce, women with huge bundles of firewood, others with small children on their way to market, goats chewing on vegetable leftovers, bleating sheep, a baby's cry amidst the murmuring of many voices, movement and bustle. The smell of roasted corn, barley, and groundnuts, ready to tempt hungry travellers. He could hardly bear it.

He looked over to the bus shelter where, thirteen years before, Zewdie had lain, wrapped in her earth coloured gabi. His eyes settled on the spot. He bit down on his lip to stop the feeling of helpless desperation welling inside him, just as it had done then. He turned away. The sun shone down. The deep blue sky carried traces of soft clouds. Despite the heat of the day a shiver of cold ran through his body as he moved slowly back to climb on the bus. He wrapped himself into the gabi he had brought with him for the journey. Covering his head, he sank into his seat, hugging himself tight. Uttering no sound, he let the tears pour down his cheeks.

"Let's go. Let's go," Mamoosh called out, banging the side of the bus with his hand. He was hanging and swinging from the short ladder at the back of the bus.

A large woman with a bulky bundle in her arms, manoeuvred herself around the metal bar of the seat in front to sit down next to him. She brought a waft of Omo and the more pungent smell of ghee with her. She must have washed and scrubbed her clothes, and buttered her hair for the trip. He nodded his head to her politely and shifted himself closer to the window pulling up a corner of his gabi to cover his mouth and nose. She held her bundle as she might hold a child on her lap, her heavily hennaed fingers interlinked. Her thin shema[20] was drawn over her bulky hair. She adjusted it carefully over her shoulder. Finally, the boy slammed the door shut. The driver put on the same Aster Aweke cassette they had been listening to since they left Addis, and the bus was on its way again with a jolt and a loud fanfare from its horn. It continued for

---

[20] Thin hand-woven cotton shawl, often with colourful designs woven along the edges.

some way on up the mountain road. Ashebir fell asleep. The warm smell of the woman next to him, the bus droning, changing notes with the gears, the heat.

Eventually they came to the long tunnel on the northern side of Debre Sina. Known as the Italian Road. Every inch, Zewdie used to say, dug through the mountain with Ethiopian sweat and lives. The tunnel was eerie, dingy and damp, with its earthen walls. It was strange to imagine the weight of that huge mountain above them. Aster Aweke's voice took on a slightly hollowed tone, and the woman next to him whispered prayers, making quiet hissing sounds through her teeth. It was not long before the bus drove through the semi-circle of light at the end and descended down the steep escarpment on the other side of the mountain. The tarmac road, crumbling at the edges, was steep and winding with sharp bends and tremendous views across the valleys and mountains.

By lunchtime they stopped in Debre Sina. Ashebir went in search of hot tea. His anticipation, the smell of the woman's ghee and the lurching of the bus had made him feel nauseous. Children ran around selling rough, hand woven, woollen hats. They were in natural sheep's wool colours with cleverly interwoven designs. Other boys sold short fat bananas, a speciality of that area. One boy insisted he try one to tempt him to buy. It was sweet and delicious. He bought a few for the rest of the journey, and because he knew the boy had to sell. He walked down the road to a small tea house. Metal tables and chairs were loosely arranged on the roadside. He sat at one and ordered a chai. He would not sit for long. It was too hot out in the sun.

After his tea he wandered back up the hill. A few passengers were back on board. He noted with mild relief that the woman with the hennaed hands, and heavy odour had gone. He leant his head against the window, ignoring the greasy imprints left behind by other travellers.

Finally, he heard Mamoosh's sing-song voice, "We are leaving. Next stops: Senbatey, Epheson, Kombolcha, Dessie," he called out. "There's room for more passengers. Come on. Let's go."

The boy was hanging out of the front door, swinging himself to and fro; jumping down each time a passenger arrived to let them on.

"Senbatey, Epheson, Kombolcha, Dessie. Let's go."

As soon as everyone was on board, the bus edged its way down the hairpin bends into the lowlands. The driver rode the straining engine, as if he was holding back a horse that wants to gallop home. Every now and then he honked his horn sending out a short loud tune, warning oncoming drivers that they were coming.

Ashebir watched him and the road intently. He would like to drive one day. The plateau stretched out into the distance in front of them in wonderful patterns, clay browns, ochre yellows and musty greens. Maybe he should have brought his paints.

Senbatey market was around here somewhere. He looked out not to miss it. It would be to the left of the road. People came to it from all over. It was the biggest market in the region and widely known as the camel and silver market. Ashebir remembered going there with his mother. It was a long walk from their village. They used to sell different items depending on what Zewdie had. Sometimes they would sell kid goats from their small stock. Other times they would sell onions or natural powders, made from a plant called Adess, which was mixed with ghee to make hair ointment. It was used by many girls and women because of its rich aroma. Ashebir had never liked the smell of ghee.

Suddenly he saw the market on the left-hand side of the road. He got up and peered through the window opposite, leaning across a man of middle age.

"Senbatey market," the man said with a friendly smile.

Ashebir nodded. "I used to come here some years back."

"Do you come from round here?" The man was clearly looking to pass time.

Ashebir responded briefly, not wanting to be drawn in. "My home used to be near Ataye. I think they now call it Epheson."

"I am going further north to Kombolcha. My brother runs a hotel there."

Ashebir bent forward again to look out onto the wide expanse of dry desert on the valley floor. He recognised the small hill dotted with acacia trees, which provided patches of shade for the traders. The market was full of people, livestock, piles of firewood, and women sitting kutch-kutch on low stools under black umbrellas.

All the movement created dust clouds which hovered in the air. Camels, piled high with white hessian sacks of grain, large bundles of firewood and eucalyptus poles for construction, walked slowly along the road towards the market. They were linked one to the next with a length of rope, the first led by a small boy. Their soft faces looked above and beyond it all with that aloof look Ashebir had always loved. He and Zewdie had never had camels, but others in the village had used them for transporting goods.

Ashebir sat back in his seat and returned to his own thoughts. The women in that area wore thick silver Marie Theresa coins, or Axum crosses round their necks on thick strands of interwoven black threads. When they had run out of food, he had gone to Senbatey with Zewdie to sell two pieces of Emet Hawa's old silver. He could see himself standing by his mother's side. She was sitting on her cot, tutting and shaking her head, turning the soft pieces of silver around in her hands. Those hands, worn from hard work, but always gentle.

"Emet Hawa said we should sell her silver if ever we were in difficulty," Zewdie had said. "And now here we are. We have nothing to trade and nothing left to eat."

He had put his hand on her shoulder, not knowing what else to do. The sadness he felt then, touched him now. He wiped his eyes, sniffed and cleared his throat. He looked out of the window to watch the small groups of women, men and children, driving their jogging livestock in front of them. They looked just like him and Zewdie.

The landscape was still dry with scattered thorn bushes and acacia. There were fewer trees and bushes than he remembered. The heat in the bus was stifling even though all the windows were open. The temperature seemed to have silenced everyone except for Aster Aweke and the baby in the third row. Her mother fanned her to no avail. He closed his eyes and willed time to pass.

**

Eventually the bus came to a standstill on the open roadside. Mamoosh swung open the front door. Passengers collected their luggage. Ashebir peered through the window onto the row of mud huts lining the road.

"Have we reached Ataye?" he asked. "Is this Epheson?"

His neighbour across the aisle said, "You're here. This is your home, Epheson. You don't remember it?"

Ashebir nodded thank you to the man. He hesitated. A part of him seemed to want to hold on to the security of his seat on the bus. He got up, and hooking the little bag over his shoulder, descended onto the tarmac.

Further up the main road he saw a sign: Werku Buna Bate, Hotel. It was a small coffee shop and restaurant with rooms at the back. It looked clean and they had a room to spare. It had an iron bed and a light bulb hanging on the end of a thick wire from the centre of the ceiling. When he flicked the switch, nothing happened. It had no sink or shower, but a large, well-used, red plastic bowl and jug of water by the bed. There was a box of matches and two inches of candle in a cracked china saucer on the windowsill. He was glad he had remembered his torch. Having secured his room, he went and sat on the veranda under the Werku Buna Bate, Hotel sign, overlooking the silent road, and ordered chai. He was glad to see that he could eat his evening meal there.

**

The following morning Ashebir sat on the hotel veranda; its plain concrete floor and black wrought-iron railings the uncluttered stage to many a tale and travellers' gossip. Three well used steps led down to the verge of the road, a jumble of stones and dry grass, meeting the uneven edge of tarmac. The early morning movement of people and straggles of children in blue cotton shirts heading for the first shift of school was already in motion. The sun was still low in the sky and the air fresh. His bread and tea arrived. The chai was especially good, hot and well spiced. He watched the grains of sugar fall slowly through the copper coloured liquid to the bottom of the glass and stirred. What to do. Would he head for the market first, or for the Ataye Bridge, and follow the path towards his old village?

He slurped his tea loudly. It dawned on him that he was watching a young man with a familiar step, walking along the tarmac towards him. It could not be. He had not even thought about Theodros. Of course, he lived in Ataye. Ashebir jumped up, almost knocking over the light metal table.

"Tedi, Tedi," he called out, jumping down the steps waving his arms. Theodros stood there, a look of disbelief on his face.

"Ashebir. Be Egziyabher, what in God's name are you doing here?"

They shook hands, looked at each other, laughed, touched shoulders and cheeks, left and right and over again. People stopped to look at them.

"I forgot you came from Ataye," Ashebir said.

"When did you arrive? What are you doing here?"

"Yesterday evening. Come. Let's have tea. Let's chat."

They walked to the hotel, holding hands, looking at each other and laughing in disbelief.

"It's great to see someone from our old Boys' Home. Do you hear from Desalegn? Are Laina and Taimi still in Debre Zeit? What about Izzie? How is she?"

Ashebir laughed. "Questions, questions, we have time to chat, Tedi, right?"

"You're still a bit skinny, but you look good, Ashebir."

"You look well too. We are the lucky ones."

"Sure. Sure. God has been on our side."

"How long since you came back?" Ashebir said.

"I came after ninth grade. Didn't want to carry on in Akaki school. I wanted to be home with my mother."

"Then it's about three years since I saw you, is it?"

"I guess so. Seems like a long time since I saw anyone from the orphanage. I miss you all, really."

They sat at Ashebir's wobbly table under the Werku Buna Bate, Hotel sign. Tedi stretched out his legs. He was taller than Ashebir and of a slightly heavier build. He wore his hair longer and a black cap with a band of black, red, yellow and green stripes around the edge. His cloth jacket was worn and repaired around the pockets and cuffs, and on his feet the typical barabasso sandals, made from old tyres, that Ashebir remembered Ataye townspeople wearing.

"Remind me how you came to live in Ataye," Ashebir said. "We were too young at Bethlehem to think about these things, isn't it?"

"That's right. We used to play and run," Tedi clapped Ashebir's shoulder. "No time to talk serious then."

"So?"

"My family came from Dessie, originally."

Ashebir nodded encouragement.

"After my parents married, they came to Ataye. My father's uncle was a trader here. They came to join him. They were not doing that well really, just getting by. Then my dad got sick and passed away. I was about six."

"Sorry Tedi, really," Ashebir said. "But you didn't stay with your mother when he died?"

"There were four of us. Without my father she couldn't manage," Tedi said. He shook his head. "To be honest, I don't think they were managing before he died."

The chai had arrived. Tedi put one spoon of sugar in after the next and stirred vigorously. "She kept my baby brother with her."

"Sorry Tedi," Ashebir put a hand on his friend's shoulder. "But Debre Zeit is a long way from here."

"My mother, God knows it broke her heart, sent me and my younger brother and sister to our uncle in Debre Zeit. She didn't know what else to do." Tedi slurped his tea loudly. "My uncle put us all in the orphanage. Bless him. I think he wanted to help but he was too poor. It was difficult for everyone then. Mengistu's time, the hunger, the wars, teff was expensive…"

"It must have been hard to leave your mother."

"Yes, I always dreamt of coming home. But we had a good time at the Boys' Home, didn't we? So many children to play with."

Ashebir nodded. "Remember that boy we called Wef?[21] He always had a small bird or a tiny mouse hidden somewhere. Laina and Taimi could never find his hiding places."

Tedi laughed. "You remember the time when the fat Uncle kept all the boxes of biscuits in his house? We were hungry and we knew the biscuits were for us."

"And they were tasty biscuits too," Ashebir laughed. "We all shouted outside his house. That song we made up about his family. How did it go?"

Tedi started singing and Ashebir joined in,

Abera ibdwa
Kasiti fendwa
Werkenesh tcheberey bontu
Ayele Gambella
Mebrete tchalla tchalla
Mebrete tchalla tchalla
Tsige shenkutey
Habtamu Kusir melata
Birtukan ina Salana menta menta
Birtukan ina Salana menta menta[22]

They sang, laughing and holding their bellies, until they couldn't breathe.

Ashebir kipped his chair back, "Ooooo-wi!" he exclaimed.

"We sat outside their house singing that song every morning and every evening," Tedi said.

"How did we dare? You remember how they all came out. Angry and shouting. Except Kasiti and Mebrete, they always cried."

"They wanted to be our friends," Tedi said. "Miskin."

"The angrier they got, the louder we sang," Ashebir swung his arms as if he were marching energetically.

---

[21] Bird.

[22] Abera is mad, Kasiti's bottom is big, Wekenesh's hair is wild, Ayele is black, Mebrete is dumb, Mebrete is dumb, Tsige is stupid, Habtamu is fat and bald, Birtukan and Salana are twins, Birtukan and Salana are twins.

"Until the kids threw stones at us. I am surprised fat Uncle's wife didn't stop them," Tedi said. "We made a run for it, right? Ha-ha."

"We scattered all over the compound," Ashebir shot his hands out in all directions. "Piaow-piaow. Over there and over there – stirring up the dust until it hung in the air."

"Fat Uncle came out with his whip. He could never run fast enough to catch us."

"I remember laughing and screaming with excitement," Ashebir said, feeling the exhilaration in his body right then and there. "I was terrified," he chuckled.

"Me too," Tedi said. "But we wouldn't give in. They were our biscuits!" He slammed his fist down on the metal table making the tea glasses jump and clatter.

"Then those guys from Finland came to build a new home. You remember that hole they dug? For the foundation?" Ashebir said.

"That was just before Laina and Taimi came to live in the Boys' Home, wasn't it?"

"You remember the night a few of us crept out and climbed down into the hole," Ashebir said. "We flung stones and soil from the bottom up onto fat Uncle's tin roof. Kishh Kishh Kwaa...Kishh Kishh Ko-ko. It made such a racket. It must have been loud inside." He flicked his fingers, "Phew."

"Yes," Tedi said. "And when fat Uncle flung open their front door, holding his flashlight, we ducked down inside the hole. They searched everywhere for the culprits."

"As soon as they went back inside, we started again, Kishh Kishh Kwa Kwa Kwa Kishh, flinging pebbles and soil at their roof. They came out again and again. They couldn't spot us. Oh my God, when they finally saw us there was trouble. He came after us with his horse whip. We all scattered. I ran to my dormitory and scrambled onto the very top bunk bed. Fat Uncle pulled me down and gave me a good hiding. Befitsum.[23] I really felt that. Awa, Awa."

"But next morning, breakfast-time, we were out there again, singing that song," Tedi said. "Honestly, can you imagine. We were tough."

"We were hungry and we knew we were right."

"He gave in, in the end. We got our biscuits."

They slapped hands in the air. High-five.

"You know, Tedi, fat Uncle, Ato Habtamu was his name, right? He knew

---

[23] Honestly

the father of one of our boys, Samson. We heard that he had been renting out Samson's father's house in Addis after the man died. Habtamu tenquolenya neow – he was a wily old fella. He collected enough money in different ways over the years. And you know what? He and all his family are in the USA now. It's incredible how some people manage. "Issu betam adegengna neow", we all used to say. "He's a clever one. He can do something good for himself – but it might not be good for you."

They sat quietly for a moment. It was good to be sitting with Tedi reminiscing. He was lucky to have his brothers from the Boys Home. They had been through a lot together.

"Remember making those cardboard and wire Land Rovers, Ashebir? With biros for the steering column and wheel axles, and cut-out old flip-flops for the wheels. You were really good at making those. And at painting. In fact, you were our very own artist."

"I don't know. We all made them together. It was fun and a good time pass." He sucked his teeth. "So many of my paintings went to Finland with Laina and Taimi's visitors. I sometimes regret that. But I suppose it was a way of repaying them."

"What about you, Ashebir? You also came from around here," Theodros said. "What happened that you came to be in Bethlehem?"

"I lived in Sudan Sefer with my mother. We had a few animals and collected firewood to sell. I was happy. And then we ran out of food." Ashebir looked at his friend. "It was that time, you know. Now I want to go back to my village and see if my Uncle is still alive."

Tedi put a hand on Ashebir's shoulder. "Let me help you. You come stay with us at home. We can go to your village together."

"Thank you, Tedi. That would be great. I asked God's help on the way. Looks like he sent you."

"For sure. It's funny. I don't usually come this way."

Tedi suggested they go to his house first. They would go to Ashebir's village in the early evening, when it was cooler. They would be more likely to find people at home. People who might remember him. Now they would all be out at the market, in the fields or collecting firewood.

Ashebir collected his bag from the room and settled his bill for the past night. They left some coins on the table and took off.

Epheson, his old Ataye, was a more substantial small country town than he remembered. It was still made up of the traditional round mud and thatch gojo-bate, but now there were many more modern style square-built bungalows, their corrugated iron roofs glinting amongst the trees. It stretched out along the main road and into the valley surrounded by mountains. It was busier than before, many more school children than in his day. And so many shops and buna bate. Each with a small veranda, and light metal tables and chairs out front, the inviting smell of freshly made coffee hanging in the air outside.

Tedi's house was a small square mud hut with a corrugated iron roof. It was tucked in amongst others, off the road up a narrow path. A wire, attached to a creosoted pole outside, hung in a loop and disappeared into the house through a hole under the eaves. They had electricity. A low fence surrounded it and a small mimosa tree, shaped like an umbrella, stood nearby, giving the narrow compound some shade. Everything was neatly swept, wide semi-circular marks from the brushing still visible in the grey dust around the entrance. No one was home. Theodros unlocked the padlock and pushed open the door. It was dim and musty inside. A shaft of light shot across the floor and grew wider as the door opened. He motioned for Ashebir to put his bag on a low wooden cot on the opposite side of the room.

"We all sleep in here. It's our living room and sleeping room. There's a kitchen out the back and a small room we use for storing things."

They lived not far from the market and Ashebir wanted to go and have a look.

The market was already full of people, the old familiar raw dusty earthen smells. The warmth of animal hides and strong aromas of spices and eucalyptus.

"Look Tedi, we used to sit under those trees. It was a good spot in the shade. Towards the end we mostly only sold firewood."

"It must have been tough. I feel sorry for the children from the villages," Theodros said. "They work early mornings, going into the deep gorges to collect firewood. And then they carry it home, before coming into school in the afternoons. And I think the difference now, between us in the town, and the children in the villages, is even greater than it was before. I feel sorry. Sometimes the town children laugh at the villagers. They say they smell bad."

"It's an honest smell," Ashebir said, feeling a shot of anger through his belly, "of working the earth, and living close to the animals. It's a warm natural smell. Look at these villagers. They are like me and Zewdie, hardworking, and providing the people in town with everything they need. Townsfolk should not laugh and complain."

"You're right, my friend. You're right."

**

Later that afternoon they walked along the road. Turning a wide bend, he saw it. Ataye Bridge, looking majestic with the mountains behind. It was built from large, soft, grey-white stones and concrete, and made a wide arc over the river, carrying the main Dessie road across it. Ashebir had painted it from memory many times. They reached the bridge and stood leaning on the wall looking down into the clear, fast-running water. The river cut a path through fields of sorghum and millet, its wide black sandy shores covered in white and grey stones, scattered shrubs and thorn bushes.

"Look how it flows, and so deep in the middle." Ashebir said, picking up a handful of pebbles and throwing them one after the next into the water below. "The river was a shallow stream by the time Zewdie and I left."

"Let's go down." Tedi said, going on ahead.

They reached the shore where girls were collecting the washing they had spread out on the banks and thorn bushes to dry. One called out to a little girl crouching half naked in the shallows, her hair plaited into spikes sticking out at comical angles all over her head. She had a sandal in her hand and was patting it in the stream.

"We have to go now, Yeshi."

The child looked up, hearing her name, and then turned back to the water and carried on making small splashes with the sandal.

"Yeshi!" the older girl stood up, one hand shading her eyes, the other on her hip bone, like a mother, her patience clearly running out. Her long skirts had an even wet line round the bottom from the river water. She had wound a pretty green scarf loosely around her head. One piece of it flopped on her shoulder. She called again as she turned to lift a sizeable gourd of water onto her shoulder, green leaves stuck out of its narrow spout on top.

"We are going home now," she called again. She set off over the stony beach towards the sorghum fields on the other side of a raised bank. Her friends piled large mounds of washing into round plastic bowls. They took it in turns to lift them onto each other's heads, and held them in place, their fingers hooked into the rim on either side.

"Come on," they called out as they walked slowly in the direction of the path.

The little girl cried out, "Wait!" She jumped up and ran after them, hopping on and off the larger rocks as she went.

Ashebir laughed, as she came past him. "Hijee, hijee. Go, Yeshi, go," he said.

Further upstream four large zebu cows stood in the shallows, taking a long drink. Two small boys sat perched on grey boulders talking, dangling their fingers in the passing water.

"We used to come here all the time with our animals, Tedi. We used to play on the banks and swim. I had forgotten how peaceful it is here."

The girls were not the only ones heading home. Some women, their backs bent double under large bundles of firewood strapped to their shoulders, were making their way along the path beside the sorghum field. Several goats scampered on ahead, bleating. Three children followed behind with a small herd of zebu cattle and three creamy white sheep with thick fluffy tails. The children carried sticks, or a length of sisal rope, which they occasionally used to flick at the animals' haunches, keeping them together.

Ashebir and Theodros took the same winding path, with the river on one side, the fields on the other. They reached a spot where the land stretched out in front of them. To the left, steep paths climbed up towards higher mountains. It was August, the time of waiting for crops to grow. Ashebir was struck by the beauty of it. This year the fields looked healthy. Teff growing green and feather-like, and different types of sorghum, with bamboo-like stalks and long green leaves, the tiny buds of yellow grains starting to appear.

"You see the sorghum, Tedi?" Ashebir pointed at the field. "If you cut the stem into pieces you can eat it like sugar cane. It's very sweet. Sometimes we used to cut pieces off with our sickles to take with us into the mountains."

"Makes my mouth water. I could eat some now."

Ashebir looked towards Muletta mountain. It towered in the distance to the east, the chain of the Rukessa mountains to the west. This felt more like home than Debre Zeit and the orphanage, than the Akaki school, where he had spent so many years. Tears of sadness, or joy, he didn't know which, poured down his face. He let it come.

"Ashebir…"

Ashebir motioned with his hand, no, no. A young acacia tree bowed across the path further up. He went and sat under it, facing the mountains. He leant against its spindly trunk. Tedi came and sat, his wrists resting loosely on his bent knees, their shoulders touching.

Ashebir let the feelings run through him. It was up on the Muletta mountain that he used to go with his friends to watch over the animals and play. And with his mother he used to go beyond those mountains. They descended into the deep gorges to collect firewood, his machete hooked over his shoulder. It had been a good life. But his recollections were clouded by the struggle they had endured towards the end. The painful hunger in his belly and the journey when he lost everything. Maybe they should never have left this place.

He remembered how, when there was a harvest, they had stored the grains in large holes dug in the ground, covered with a wide flat stone. By the end though, their store was empty, except for the ants.

"Tedi," Ashebir said, getting up, wiping his nose on his green khaki jacket sleeve. "Let's go. My village is over there."

They followed the narrow path round and up the hill, with people behind and ahead of them. The soft murmur of their voices and tread of their feet. An occasional dry branch cracked in the brush. Goats bleated as they jogged past impatiently. The more disdainful zebus uttered the odd, long, full sound of objection, which echoed in the evening air.

The thatched gojo-bate were built in small clusters up the hillside and scattered in ones and twos down into the valley on the other side. There were more than thirty dwellings. Shrubs with pink, yellow and white flowers; acacia and eucalyptus trees grew around and between the houses and along the small paths joining them. Some people used the thick prickly cactus, flowering deep orange and yellow, as fencing around their compounds. Those which had a small plot boasted a few stands of green maize at the back. Little seemed to have changed though it was all much greener and more abundant than the time he had left. He recognised the welcome home-coming smell from the wood fires burning inside the thatched huts. The sign of evening meals being prepared. A thin strand of smoke poured from each of the blackened tin chimney pots, which poked out through the top of the cone-shaped thatch roofs. Ashebir looked to his left and right, not to miss anything. Here he was, heading for his old home perched on the side of a hill up in the mountains of northern Shewa. He could hardly believe it, nor the contrast with his home in Addis.

Ashebir finally spotted the gojo-bate where he used to live with his mother. Wings of anticipation strummed inside his belly and his heart beat a bit faster. A simple fencing of long criss-crossed sticks and twigs, green bush and shrubs covered in yellow flowers, encircled the small compound. It was all thicker and greener than he remembered. He carefully opened the wooden gate, looking back at Tedi, who motioned with his hand to go on. They went into the compound. The papaya tree had become tall. Its fruits hung right up at the top in the shade of leafy fronds.

"I planted that papaya."

"Listen," Tedi said. "I think there's someone inside – "

"Tenasteling," they called out tentatively. "Hello," they called again, to alert the occupants that visitors had come.

"Who's there?" came voices from inside.

"Inya negn. Inya negn." Ashebir and Theodros called out in unison. "It's us. We are here."

"Yigibbu," an elderly woman said, as she lowered her head to emerge through the narrow doorway, leaving the dark interior behind. "Please come in!"

Ashebir recognised her immediately. It was Emet Temima. She had been their neighbour and Zewdie's closest friend. She was his own best friend's mother. She had grown old. Zewdie would look as old as she, he thought.

"Who are you looking for?" Emet Temima said.

"It's me, Emet Temima," Ashebir said, tears clouding his eyes. He wiped them away. "I used to live here many years back, with my mother Zewdie." He reached both hands out towards the old woman, bowing his head as he spoke.

"Ashebir? Is that you?" She moved closer, looking at him intently. Her eyes were clouded with a thin blue-white haze. "Let me see your face my child." She wiped her eyes on the cotton shema which hung limply around her shoulders and peered into his face. Her eyes were watery, her skin soft and deeply lined.

"Ashebir, in Allah's name, it is you." She started to cry and opened her arms to take him in.

"Weyne, weyne," she cried out. "My friend Zewdie's boy is back. We thought he died, and he is back." She wailed. "Weyne, weyne."

His nose buried in her warm shawl, he breathed in the familiar thick smell of her cooking over the wood fire.

Three children appeared from inside the hut and stood close to her skirts, looking up, with large round eyes. A taller girl leaned against the door frame, chewing the edge of her headscarf, looking worried.

Remembering his mother more clearly than for a long time, Ashebir felt the deep sadness from his old wound welling up. He could not stop himself joining her wailing.

"I'm so sorry. I'm so sorry," he sobbed. "The almighty Amlak be with us. May Zewdie rest in peace," he wept as he spoke. "She was my mother. She died so pitifully. Egziyabher inya gar yihun, God stay with us and keep us." He cried into the old woman's shoulder, as she held him to her and sobbed.

Theodros had taken his black cap off, sniffing into his sleeve he stepped forward and put a hand on his friend's shoulder. "Ashebir, Ashebir. Please try and calm yourself. Aysoh, aysoh. It's alright. It's alright."

Neighbours came out of their houses and gathered round.

An elderly man came towards them. "Are you not the child of Zewdie? I think you are." He looked carefully at Ashebir before embracing him, kissing him on one cheek then the other, over and over. "Ashebir. Are you still alive, my son? Wonderful is the work of Allah."

"Yes, I am Zewdie's son, Ashebir," he said, his eyes full of tears. Someone knew him, here were his roots. It was too much. The tears poured down his cheeks.

"As the old saying goes," the old man said, stretching his arms to the sky, "Those who are not deceased do meet finally." He praised Allah in all his goodness and embraced Ashebir again. "It is I, Mohamed Ahmed," he said. "Your friend Mohamed Abdu's father." His declaration over, he looked around for a place to sit, his old eyes watering in his deeply wrinkled face.

The girl stopped chewing her scarf and went inside. She came back with a low wooden stool for Mohamed Ahmed. The old man wore a traditional gildim[24] and a dark green blanket over his shoulder. He adjusted the white turban wrapped around his head, as he lowered himself to sit.

"Is it not a miracle, Ahmed, after all these years?" Emet Temima looked at him shaking her head. "My poor Zewdie, my poor Zewdie."

Nodding agreement, the old man said, "We heard about the death of your poor mother after some time, Ashebir. We were devastated. She was a good woman. A hard-working woman. She was our friend."

Emet Temima nodded in agreement.

The neighbours who had gathered around were softly clicking their tongues, and murmuring: "Weyne, weyne."

"We were worried about what would happen to you, a small boy all alone," Mohamed Ahmed continued. "We thought maybe you died too. Now thanks to Allah, we see you are alive." After saying all this, he softly wiped away the tears with his blanket, stroking his face as he did so, as if comforting himself.

"You are Mohamed Ahmed, I know your face now," Ashebir said. He crouched down, placing a hand on the old man's knee. "I remember

---

[24] A long cloth wrapped around his waist.

31

you tried to help us. Zewdie always said she did not know what we would have done without you."

Mohamed Ahmed bent his head into his hands. "It was not enough. It was not enough."

"Ashebir," Tedi said. "It's getting dark. We should make our way home soon. We can come again tomorrow."

Ashebir would have loved to stay longer. But he could see that the old people had taken a shock. "We should leave you in peace," he said.

It was amazing. This world he had inhabited had continued without him and Zewdie, day in day out. He had almost lost it, except the parts he had kept alive in his paintings and in the stories and images hovering at the back of his mind, appearing and whispering in his dreams. And now here he was, standing on the firm soil outside his old home.

"You are right, Tedi, we should go," Ashebir said, standing up.

"You must come tomorrow, you must." Emet Temima said.

"Do not leave us waiting to see you," Mohamed Ahmed said. "You must come tomorrow. We will be here, waiting for you."

"Tell me, I am also looking for Mohamed Shinkurt, my Uncle." Ashebir paused, hoping to hear that the old man was still alive.

"You will find him and your aunt, Selam, at their place. We will send word that you are coming tomorrow, shall we?"

"That is very happy news indeed," Ashebir said, relief spreading across his face. "Yes, let him know we will come in the morning."

They took their leave of each other, shaking hands, embracing and bowing heads.

"Be sure and come tomorrow," the old man said again.

Ashebir reassured them he would return the next day; that he was as intent on hearing their stories as they were to hear his.

Tedi pulled on his cap again. He shook hands with the old man, with Emet Temima and the children who came forward shyly one after the other. He had a broad grin on his face as he promised to be there the next day with Ashebir. There was nothing he liked better than a good story.

Ashebir walked shoulder to shoulder along the path with his old friend.

"What a day," Tedi said.

"I know, I know. So much, so much."

"I can't believe we just met this morning."

"Tedi, I can't go back to your place without first stopping to see my old friend Mohammed Abdu."

"He is living just here, isn't that what Emet Temima said?" Tedi said, looking towards a neighbouring gojo-bate.

"Yes, that's their old house. They were our closest neighbours. He's still living in their old house."

They walked up the hill towards the house and saw a young man at the entrance to the hut.

He wore the traditional long gildim. He was standing on one foot under the thatched eaves, using a muddy-yellow gourd to pour water over his other foot, washing the dirt away thoroughly with his free hand. He looked up.

Ashebir could see it was his old friend and that he was puzzled seeing them, two strangers, approaching his compound.

Mohamed Abdu straightened himself. He wiped his wet hands on the cotton shawl over his shoulder and looked at them.

He put out a hand. "Tenasteling," he said. "How are you both? Do we know each other?"

"I am Ashebir, Mohamed Abdu," Ashebir said, eyes shining, laughter bubbling in his throat. He took Mohamed Abdu's hand. "You remember me?"

"In Allah's name. I thought you were dead," Mohamed Abdu said, pulling Ashebir to him.

Ashebir looked over his friend's shoulder to the doorway of the familiar homestead. His old friend. Holding him. The years that had passed. It was unbelievable.

Ashebir stood back and looked at Mohamed Abdu. "God has watched over us. Allah has seen us grow. Look at you. You are a real man, a farmer."

Mohamed Abdu's face lit up with his smiling dark eyes. "Allah is great. Only He knows how I missed you. You were like my own brother. But I see you now. You have become an educated man." Then he laughed out loud, his head thrown back. "You wanted to learn then. You remember our Koran lessons? You were so afraid of being beaten."

Ashebir chuckled, "You told me it would happen once only."

"You were so small, innocent."

They clapped hands in the air. Held each other again.

A child appeared in the doorway and ran to hide behind Mohamed Abdu's legs. The child stared up at them with a face just like Mohamed Abdu's.

"He is yours Mohamed Abdu. I can see that," Ashebir laughed, putting a hand out to the child. "I am your Abba's old friend, don't be afraid." He turned to Tedi, putting a hand on his shoulder. "Mohamed Abdu, this is my friend Theodros. He is from Epheson. We grew up together in an orphanage in Debre Zeit."

Tedi stepped forward and shook Mohamed Abdu's hand. "How are you?" he said. "How is your family?"

"We are all well, Allah be praised," Mohamed Abdu said. "We are happy. The harvest will be good."

Mohamed Abdu bent down and picked up his son, hooking him onto his hip. "Come, come," he said. "We will make coffee."

"We just stopped to find you on our way back to Epheson." Ashebir said. "It is getting dark now. We will come tomorrow."

"When you left, I did not imagine it would be for good," Mohamed Abdu said. "Then one day they told me that Emet Zewdie had died."

"It was a bad time. Egziyabher yawkal, God knows."

"I was scared for you," Mohamed Abdu hugged his child closer. "We did not know what happened to you."

"I ended up in Addis," Ashebir said. His sadness fell like a raven's shadow passing over his head, tightening his throat to a whisper. "I didn't know how to come back. And without Zewdie."

"Aysoh, aysoh, take it easy," Mohamed Abdu laid a hand on his shoulder. "My old friend Ashebir is still in there, I can see that. You remember our days as shepherd boys, don't you?"

Their eyes met. They stood quietly for a moment.

"My friends," Tedi said softly. "We better get going before it becomes completely dark."

"Come, let me accompany you a little," Mohamed Abdu said, slipping his feet into his barabasso sandals. "Though you know your way, I am sure. The path has not changed."

"You are right," Ashebir set off down the path, laughing, his arms swinging. "But I still need you to protect me from the hyenas."

A short way down the path Mohamed Abdu waved them off. Ashebir looked back at his tall, proud friend, his child curled securely in the crook of his arm. "Be sure and come tomorrow," he heard him call out.

As he went on his way with Theodros, Ashebir wondered at the fact that Mohamed Abdu had a family, a wife and two children. He most likely would have as well, had he stayed.

"So, you really grew up here, a shepherd boy?" Tedi said. "Such a hard life."

"Yes," Ashebir said. "It was tough. But it was also wonderful. We were free. It was all we knew."

"What happened to your father?"

"I don't know. He disappeared. He was a daily labourer, a migrant worker. He used to come and see us sometimes. My mother had to manage on her own. It was difficult for her without a man, or land to work."

"And you had no brothers and sisters?"

"No, only me. Funny, I never really thought about it. I was quite happy like that. I always had Mohamed Abdu and our neighbour's children."

The two walked on as it grew dark around them. The air was slightly cooler and laced with wood smoke pouring softly like steam from the thatched roofs. The evening injera was being prepared over large fires inside the small round gojo-bate.

That night Ashebir could not sleep. He lay in the dark on the floor next to Tedi, his eyes wide open and staring. Rustling night-time noises, creatures scrabbling about, the branches of the mimosa tree stroking the corrugated iron roof. Maybe now he would be able to piece his story together. He was never sure whether he came from Ataye, or another place somewhere further south. He hoped tomorrow he would find Zewdie's brother, Mohamed Shinkurt. He hoped the old man would know the story.

1

Zewdie could hear them coming. The child was running ahead of his friend Boleke with the animals. He was shouting and laughing.

"Zewdie I am home. Zewdie are you there?"

She smiled. "There you are my boy. I have missed you all day. Did you bring kindling for the fire? Are you hungry?"

"It is there in a small pile, mother. Do you see it?" He said out of breath. "I want to help Boleke." And he was gone.

Boleke was shooing the animals into the small enclosure behind the house and throwing heaps of hay into one corner.

Zewdie picked up the pile of twigs and took them into the house to get the fire going.

She could hear the boys securing the animals for the night.

"See you early tomorrow," Boleke called.

Then came Ashebir's small high voice, "Bye, bye."

She heard him coming. He always kicked up stones on the way into the gojo-bate. "Can I help you with the fire?" he said.

"Are you not tired, little one?"

"No. I am fine. I want to help."

"You can fetch water for the cooking then."

The boy took the jerry can and left the house with a slight bounce in his foot.

Shortly he was back. This time one arm hanging long, the full can of water dragging on the dusty floor, the other arm up in the air to balance the weight. His mouth was pulled in a grimace of concentration.

Zewdie got up laughing. "Look at you. Let me help you. It is too heavy."

She took the can from him. "That should be the last task of the day," she said as he joined her by the fire.

She loved how he sat near her, watching her prepare their evening

36

meal. As soon as he had eaten, he curled up on his cot and fell into a deep sleep.

Now Zewdie's mind could return to her mother. Her mother's illness would not be leaving her. Every day Hawa seemed a little weaker. She spent a lot of time in prayer and when she was not praying, she was sitting on the small wooden stool in the shade of the mimosa tree outside their house, spinning cotton. Hawa wanted to return home to die. She wanted to make the journey before she was too weak. They originally came from Albuko in Wollo, but Zewdie's older brother, Mohamed Shinkurt, had moved them a little way south to live in the highlands of northern Shewa. That is where they would go. Zewdie had already started making preparations. They would leave soon, with just a few belongings.

When it was quiet and the boy fast asleep, Zewdie heard the old woman's voice calling from her cot.

"Let us go soon, Zewdiye? I feel weaker every day. Let us go to Mohamed's place."

"I will take you Hawa. Don't worry." Zewdie said. "We will be ready to go any day now."

Zewdie sat by Hawa's cot for a while.

"What shall we do with Ashebir, mother?" She said quietly, so as not to wake the boy. "It is too far for him to travel. He is so small."

"Maybe we can leave him here with Boleke's mother. You can come back for him?" Emet Hawa suggested. "Boleke is like an older brother to him."

"I will talk to him in the morning when he wakes."

"He is such a good boy. You will look after him, won't you Zewdiye?"

"Of course, mother, of course," Zewdie said, stroking her mother's hair gently.

"We will have to go soon, Zewdie."

"I know. I know. Tomorrow I will go with Ashebir to the market. There's not much left to sell. We will need money for the journey and for when we get there."

The two women settled for the night. Emet Hawa was coughing badly. Zewdie put eucalyptus leaves in a pot of steaming water by her mother's cot, filling their small home with the woodland scent.

They would go as far as Addis Ababa, spend a night, then continue the following day, she thought. Hawa would not make the whole journey in one day.

She packed a few cooking utensils, and some items of clothing. She carefully wrapped and packed their well-worn jabena coffee pot and the fendisha basket Hawa always used when they had coffee. The large worn zip bag had brought her things from Wollo down to Mojo and then here to Alem Tena. Now it would take their things all the way back again. She would take her mother home to her brother Mohamed Shinkurt, and then return for Ashebir as soon as she could. Thinking the practicalities spared her the unbearable thought of her mother's death. She was her closest companion.

It was still dark when Zewdie rose the following morning. Ashebir could help her take the three sheep and Emet Hawa's ram. That would be a hard parting. She pushed the thought to the corner in her mind where all her sadness was stored. She dreaded the boy's reaction to selling the animals, especially the ram. He would be heart-broken.

Her immediate worry was livestock prices. She hoped she would get a good enough price.

She kindled the remains of yesterday's coals to boil up their tea and took bread from the wicker basket in the corner of their gojo-bate.

"Is that you Zewdie?"

"Yes mother. How are you today?"

Coughing came in response.

"Rest yourself a while. Tea is almost ready. It will sooth your throat."

Ashebir looked beautiful, calm and innocent in his sleep. So trusting. How could she tell him they would be leaving without him?

'Egziyabher yawkal,' she thought, 'He will guide us.'

"Ashebir, Ashebir," she said quietly. "Wake up. Don't allow the cockerel a moment of pride, that he was up before you."

"I am awake, I am," the boy sat up, rubbing his eyes. It was still gloomy in their small home and filled with smoke from the crackling fire.

"Come and have your tea and then we are going to the market."

The boy let his legs down onto the floor from his cot and walked outside. She could tell he was still half asleep. As usual, he went round the back to relieve himself and wandered in again to pour water from the gourd into the plastic jug before going outside again. She could hear him washing his face and hands. He came in to take his place close beside her by the fire, his face dripping, his eyelashes wet. She smiled and gave him a cloth to dry himself and put an arm round his shoulder.

"How are you today, little man?" she said.

"I am fine Zewdie," he said, in his quiet early morning voice. A high whisper.

"Ashebir, I have something to tell you," Zewdie said, giving him a mug of hot tea and a small piece of bread.

He bowed his head in thanks and whispered, "Thanks to God."

"Ashebir, yeney konjo. Your grandmother has not been well these past weeks," Zewdie said in a low voice, not wanting Hawa to hear everything she was about to say.

"I know," Ashebir whispered back. "Let's take her to the healer, Zewdie?"

"The healer has been," Zewdie said. "She is just old and wants to return home to your uncle Mohamed's house in the mountains."

"Why don't we take her then?" the boy looked up at her, his eyes shining.

Zewdie swallowed and took a breath. "She wants to go Ashebir, my sweet. You know what that means, don't you?"

She watched him as he thought it through. "She's missing her home, isn't she?"

"Yes, she is. But it is more than that. She wants to die there, yeney konjo, my lovely. She does not want to be buried here, in a strange place."

"No, no," he said, his eyebrows drawn together, frowning. "No, no. That's not right. She has to see the healer again. Or do you think, if we take her home, she will feel better?"

Zewdie was taken by the boy's ideas beyond his age, his assumption they would all go together. "Yeney lij, I think we have to accept that soon it is time for her to rest in peace."

Ashebir began to whimper. He looked up at Zewdie, his eyes clouded with tears.

She took his head and laid it gently in her lap, stroking his cheek. She felt awful. "You are a good boy, Ashebir, and she loves you very much and so do I, you know that. But I have to do this journey with her alone. It's very far. We think it's better for you to stay here with Boleke. I will come back for you –"

The boy sat up suddenly and shouted, shattering the whispering quiet, "No. No. No. I won't stay here without you!" He was up. Jumping and shouting. Tears streamed down his face.

"Hush, hush, aysoh, my sweet," Zewdie reached out to catch the boy's arm. "God only knows I did not want to upset you."

Hawa appeared, wrapped in her gabi, "In Allah's name, my child. Calm yourself." She sounded quite stern. She began coughing, taking in deep rattling breaths. Zewdie got up and led her to the fire.

"Hush, mother. Hush. Come sit here."

Ashebir continued crying and shouting, "I won't stay. I want to come too."

He jumped up and down in front of them, tears pouring down his face.

The dawn crept under the door. Outside the cockerel struck up his morning chorus.

In between sobs and short breaths, Ashebir carried on, "If you leave without me, I'll follow you. I'll climb on top of the bus. I'll jump on a camel. I'll crawl inside your luggage."

"Ashebir. Ashebir. Quieten yourself." Zewdie was taken aback by his outburst.

The boy, still shuddering from his tears, now sounded frightened, "I want stay with you. Don't leave me. Please -"

Zewdie held him close. "Aysoh, hush Ashebir, my child. God forgive me. I did not imagine you would be this upset. You can come with us, can't he Hawa? You can come. Don't be afraid. We won't leave you behind."

He held her tight, crying and crying.

"God only knows I love you, my child. Stop crying, please." She took a corner of her shema and wiped his face. "There, there. Hush now. Aysoh." Zewdie turned to Hawa. "Mother, Ashebir can help us on the journey, and who knows, maybe we will all stay there for a while. I would like to be nearer the family."

"You're right," Hawa said, breathing deeply. She looked exhausted. "We will all go together. It must be Allah's will."

Zewdie felt relief. This was the right decision. She could not bear the thought of leaving Ashebir behind. She only hoped taking him was the right thing to do.

"Ashebir, go and call Boleke. Tell him we are going to the market to sell the animals. I need you both to help carry our other things. We must sell everything we can. Tomorrow we will leave for the highlands."

**

It was a late afternoon. They were on the bus to Ataye. Megabit was one of the toughest months of the year in the highlands. Ashebir heard the talk about the rains. The lack of them. The dry ground. He had looked from one to the next, listening intently.

"The small rains have been good -" the woman sitting next to Ashebir said.

"Yes, Allah be praised," an old man in front of them said without turning round. He cleared his throat after he spoke.

Ashebir wondered if he was going to spit it somewhere. Zewdie always said to be careful where you spit.

"We started planting seeds in our village last week," another said, turning to the woman.

"We are still ploughing," a woman across the aisle said.

"If Allah is merciful, we'll have a good harvest," the old man said, his voice grating as if the spittle were lodged in his throat. "Just now there is too little food."

Ashebir noticed the old man's skinny hand holding onto the metal bar of the seat in front of him, the skin stretched thinly over his finger bones and the veins sticking out like worms.

"Too many people in our village are suffering from mogne bagegne," another said, turning in the direction of Ashebir and the woman.

"The healer is doing a good business," Ashebir's neighbour said, tutting softly.

"No one can pay her until after the harvest."

"We wanted to sell one of our goats, to take my daughter-in-law to the clinic," the old man said, finally turning his head towards them. His eyes watered constantly, like Emet Hawa's. "But the price is too low."

Their voices had rumbled on into the low sound of the engine and his head had dropped onto his chest. When he woke, he was leaning against his neighbour. Who looked down at him with a smile.

Two days after they left Alem Tena they finally arrived. Zewdie called for the ticket boy to get her old zip bag from the roof. As Emet Hawa climbed down the steps to the tarmac, Ashebir stayed in front of her, holding her hand. Zewdie nodded thanks to the driver, a friendly man with a large belly. The back of his seat was covered in a bright red, green and yellow cloth. He sat on an embroidered cushion which lifted his short stocky body level with the window.

Ashebir looked up at the man, squinting in the sun, and thought how when Zewdie saw a belly like that, she always said: "He knows where to find a good meal."

The kindly driver bowed his head at Emet Hawa and said, "God be with you."

Ashebir caught the sad look in the man's eyes. It seemed as if everyone knew her time had come.

The bus took off with a low roar of engine, a puff of black smoke and a tuneful blast of the horn, bidding them farewell. They stood on the road, preparing themselves for the walk to the village.

"I liked the driver," Ashebir said.

"Yes, he was a good man. He knows were to get a good meal, by the look of that belly – "

Hawa and Zewdie laughed.

Ashebir looked at them, happy to see Hawa laughing. Familiar words in a strange place made it feel like home.

Zewdie looked down at him as she lifted the heavy zip bag onto her shoulders. "You take that Ashebir?" she said pointing to the bulging white cloth in which she had wrapped some clothes. "Let's go, it's this way." She started walking on up the road. "Are you alright, mother?"

"Just keep going, I will follow." Hawa replied.

Zewdie turned to her mother. "Did you hear them talking on the bus, Mother?"

"Yes, I did. It is never easy at this time of year. It is always the same."

Ashebir remembered his neighbours' conversation. "Zewdie, what is that? Mogne bagegne?"

"It's a disease people get when they eat rotten maize," she said. "When they have nothing left, people are forced to eat bad food. I was thinking, Mother," Zewdie continued, "Mohamed may not be so happy to see us at this time of year."

"Why won't he be happy to see us?" Ashebir looked up at Zewdie, worried.

"That child has ears like an elephant's," Hawa said with a chuckle.

"Maybe he won't have enough food for three extra mouths," Zewdie said.

"I am sure he will manage," Hawa said. "He has plenty of land and he grows vegetables as well as the usual crops. He should have enough for a sick old woman and her small grandchild. You do not eat very much, Zewdie. It will be fine." She stopped, out of breath. "I don't know how far I will be able to walk, my dear."

"Can you just get to the pathway over there, Mother, and then we'll take rest?"

"But Zewdie," Ashebir said, "In your stories he is a rich man. He has many cows, and fields of onions, teff and sorghum."

"It's the end of the small rains, Ashebir. There is not usually much left from the last harvest. Everyone is busy working, ploughing the land and preparing the fields for the next crop. There is not so much food to be had. With those ears of yours you must have heard them talking on the bus?"

"We can help him, Zewdie." Ashebir felt excited at the thought. "I can work with Uncle Mohamed and his sons."

"You know about Mohamed Shinkurt, but he knows nothing of you yet," Zewdie said. "I hope he will see what a good boy you are."

Hearing the hesitation in her voice, Ashebir fell silent. He had questions but now he did not feel like asking. They walked along the path by the river. He turned to wait, putting out a hand towards his grandmother.

The old woman smiled.

From a nearby field, they could hear the sharp clack of a farmer's whip against the ground. The oxen were drawing the plough through the heavy soil. Ashebir peeked through the bushes to watch. The farmer called out instructions to his animals in low sounds. They seemed like one; man, plough, oxen, all heaving together.

Zewdie put her bag down. Emet Hawa went towards her and sat, letting out a soft grunt, in the shade of the trees lining the field.

"Are you alright, Mother?"

The old woman looked up, her face tired. Ashebir noticed the shadows under her eyes. They seemed darker than ever. Maybe the journey was too much?

Hawa nodded, obviously making an effort to smile but began coughing again.

Ashebir joined Zewdie by Hawa's side, to comfort her.

"Here, drink some water, Mother," Zewdie said.

Two women were coming towards them up the path, laden with firewood. As they came close, they stopped to greet them. Yes, they knew Zewdie's brother, Mohamed Shinkurt. They were his neighbours and were themselves on their way home.

"It is too far for her to walk," they chided Zewdie, tutting and shaking their heads, looking at Emet Hawa.

"Ato Mohamed Shinkurt is a big man. He can surely send one of his mules to bring her. His own mother -"

"- yes, you wait here," the other interrupted. "We will tell Ato Mohamed to send his mule."

"Thank you," Zewdie said. "You are right. Egziyabher yawkal, it is a long journey for our mother."

The women nodded and walked slowly on up the path.

Ashebir saw his mother was tired too. She sat down by Hawa under the trees to wait. It was quiet except for the heavy movement of the oxen in the field behind, the deep furrowing plough drawing up waves in heavy chunks through the soil. On and on the farmer's soft deep voice rang out and the whip went clack into the soil or against the animal's soft rump.

"Tell me again why he is called Mohamed Shinkurt, Zewdie?" Ashebir said.

"Like the women said, he is a big man. He has a lot of land and a few cattle. But he is also known for his onions. He grows and sells a lot of onions. So they call him Mohamed Shinkurt. Mohamed Onion." They laughed softly together. Hawa had fallen asleep. They took a gabi out of the old zip bag to cover her.

"So why doesn't he have enough food, Zewdie?"

"After the last harvest he will have stored some and sold some. He may only have enough left now for his own family," Zewdie said. "He did not plan to feed us too. What he stored will have to last them until the next harvest."

"I am hungry now, Zewdie."

"I wondered why all this talk about food," she said, smiling.

She took a chunk of bread out of her bag and gave him a piece.

He took it gratefully and after whispering a short prayer of thanks he ate. He stopped chewing, "Maybe we should save some for Mohamed Shinkurt?"

"No, eat, dear child. You are growing. You with your elephant's ears, you need it."

**

It was dark by the time they reached Mohamed Shinkurt's compound. He had a large thatched gojo-bate on a low hill just above the river, well covered by trees and brush. Tall cactus plants surrounded the house making a fence, which had a large korkorro corrugated iron gate in it. It wobbled and grated, sounding: korkorro, as they passed through. Someone was carrying a kerosene lantern to help them see their way in. Emet Hawa's mule snorted softly as if it knew not to make too much noise at this hour. Ashebir watched sleepily as the lamp threw lights and shadows across the compound. Once inside, he crawled into the far corner of a cot, curled up and fell into a heavy slumber, leaving the movement of bodies and shadows in the dim lamplight to fade with the murmuring of voices.

He woke the next morning to hear voices. He could see Zewdie talking to an older man, his face furrowed like the fields, his hands strong and cracked. It must be his uncle, Mohamed Shinkurt.

"But I want her to see a doctor," Zewdie was saying. "I did not have enough money to take her in Alem Tena. Surely you can persuade her?"

"Zewdie, I have spoken with our mother. She is tired. She does not want to see a doctor." His voice sounded gruff, a voice that had to be heard and probably obeyed.

"That is what she kept saying. But please, in God's name, try to persuade her Mohamed. I can't bear the idea of her dying."

"We have to respect her wishes. Allah knows best my sister. She is tired. She is near the end of this journey."

Ashebir's heart beat faster. He was afraid without knowing the reason why. He sat quietly, watching and listening. His mother was crying softly. He felt sad for her. Even riches were not going to save his grandmother's life.

"So, who is this boy, Zewdie?" He heard the man say.

"Ashebir Lakew," Zewdie said, sniffing into her shema. "My son."

Ashebir held his breath and crept from his cot to sit beside his mother.

"So, you have given him Lakew's name?" Ashebir could not work out if the man was cross, accusing or maybe he always spoke in this serious tone.

"That's right."

"Do you have any children?" Ashebir asked his uncle in a quiet voice.

"Yes, Allah is great. I have four sons and one daughter. The boys are already out working in the fields. You will find my daughter Fahte outside with her mother. They are grinding millet for our injera."

He felt Zewdie gently push him towards the door. As he went outside, Ashebir heard his uncle say, "So what will you do with the boy? There is not enough room and food for you all here."

It was as Zewdie had said. There was not enough food. There was intense discussion that morning, which continued in the evening. He knew from the tone of their voices that brother and sister were not united. Zewdie did not want to lose the boy. His uncle was not happy about keeping him. He began to be afraid. What would they decide? Where could he go? Would Zewdie come with him?

Finally, the uncle decided. The boy should be sent to a homestead in the mountains. He knew someone on a farm about a day's ride away who was looking for erregnya. That man would be in the market on Friday and he would take Ashebir with him to offer him to the man.

"Zewdiye," Ashebir whispered that night. "What is erregnya?"

"Erregnya are children who look after the animals for farmers in exchange for food. Sometimes they just go for the day and come home in the evening, sometimes they live with the farmer and his family."

"I don't want to go, Zewdiye. I am afraid. I can look after uncle's animals here. I am not very hungry. I will not eat too much. Please Zewdie."

"Ashebir, I cannot argue with my brother. We are in his house. He will decide. That is how it is."

"I heard him say it is a day's ride away." Ashebir felt the wings of fear fluttering in his belly. His throat tightened, making his voice small and high.

"Yes, dear child, it is far. You will have to live there for a while."

Ashebir felt his lips go wobbly. He started whimpering, "No, no, please, Zewdie. Please. I don't want to leave you."

"I cannot go against his word, my child. I promise I will work hard and make our own home so that you can come soon," Zewdie said.

Their lives had been taken over by a might beyond his mother's control. Until now she had made the decisions. That felt safer. She listened to him, she listened to Emet Hawa. Here there was no choice. The uncle's gruff voice was final. His strong hands cracked the whip. They steered them all as they steered the oxen, with a power beyond them.

Friday came. Zewdie gave him a small ox-skin basket filled with injera and 'kollo[25] to eat on the journey.

"You know how to look after animals, boy. Isn't that right?" Mohamed Shinkurt said. Only a 'yes' would do for an answer.

Ashebir was used to looking after the sheep and goats and Emet Hawa's ram with Boleke. He was too small to look after cows and oxen on his own. "Yes, uncle," Ashebir said. He looked up at the man, trying to read his face. It was a broad open face, darkened from the sun and the highland wind and rain. His eyes were not unkind, but his mouth was a firm thin line drawn down at the edges. He knew the man could not be argued with. Neither were emotional outbursts of any use. His uncle did not care for him, he thought. He could not understand what wrong he had done.

"We will look for Ali Yusuf in the market," he was telling Zewdie. "You might remember him. He comes from our place, Albuko, on the other side of the Muletta mountain. He is not a bad man. I am sure he has work for the boy and a place for him to sleep."

---

[25] Roasted barley.

"Please, Mohamed," Zewdie started begging her brother again. "Can't we keep him here? He will be no trouble. He can help look after your animals. He is so small, his appetite is not big for his age."

Ashebir looked from his mother to his uncle. Her face beautiful, soft, pleading; her brother's unyielding, firm. He moved to stand closer to her skirts, grasping the cloth in his fist.

"It is impossible. The boy has to go. There is no place for him here," Mohamed Shinkurt said.

"God only knows we are grateful to you, Mohamed, my brother. We are dependent on you. But please think again. It is hard enough for the boy, so far from his home. To send him away on his own – "

"There can be no more discussion on the matter," Mohamed Shinkurt said. He flung his shawl over his shoulder. He was obviously growing impatient. His mule stomped a hoof and blew sneezes through his wide nostrils. He was also ready to leave.

"Come Ashebir," his uncle said. "Let's go."

Ashebir felt his knees go weak. "I want to say goodbye to Emet Hawa," he said in a quiet voice. "Can I?"

"Be quick now, boy."

Ashebir went with small steps to her bedside. "Emet Hawa, I am leaving with Uncle Mohamed for the market today. I do not know when I am coming."

"Yeney lij, I will wait for you. Allah give you strength. You will come soon."

He buried his face in her warmth, smelt the oil and eucalyptus in her soft gabi and wept as quietly as he could. Where had they come? A place where it was forbidden to weep. Where his mother and even his grandmother had no say.

"There, there, aysoh Ashebir," she whispered. "Allah is great. He watches over all children. I will pray for you. Have no fear."

He stood up, wiping the back of his hand across his dripping nose. He walked slowly out into the sunshine. He ran to Zewdie and wrapped his arms round her, burrowing his face into her soft body. He felt her strong arms holding him tight for a moment. She knelt down, and as she held him back, her hands on his shoulders, he looked into her eyes.

"Ashebir, God is with you," she said. "It will only be a short while."

He could see she was struggling not to cry. He put his hand on her shoulder, biting his lip until it hurt.

"I will send for you as soon as I can," she said. "Be a good boy, remember all the things I have taught you. Be strong and work hard."

His uncle had already turned to walk off down the path. He slipped in just behind him, turning once to look at his mother. She was standing there with the corner of her white cotton shema drawn across her mouth. She always did that when she was worried. She raised a hand and waved.

**

The following weeks passed with an intensity of worry Zewdie could only bear through the ritual of daily routine. There was her mother to care for and income to be earned. Her mind was constantly with Ashebir. She was still angry with her brother for sending him away. He was too small, she had argued. If there was not enough room in Mohamed's house for all of them, the boy could sleep in a corner on the floor. If there was not enough food, she could eat less and he could have her share. But Mohamed had not been interested. He was her older brother and it was his house. She had to resign herself to his will. She prayed to God to help her forgive him and to be grateful for all that he was doing for their mother. Zewdie still wished her mother would go to a doctor, or the local healer, but her mother would not contemplate either. She would have fetched holy water for her mother, but being Muslims they did not believe in the power of holy waters from the Orthodox Church. So Zewdie prayed for Emet Hawa at night and in the moments when she woke before dawn. As for Ashebir, she prayed for him in everything she did. She worked hard so that she could bring him back and look after him herself.

Emet Hawa spent most of her day resting on the cot inside. In the mornings and late afternoons Zewdie took her for a short walk. She wanted to see the mountains. She never complained and said she was happy to have the movement and noises of family life and daily work around her. Her coughing slowly became worse and Zewdie thought each day might bring her last breath on this earth. She prayed to God not to let her mother suffer too long.

Mohamed Shinkurt gave Zewdie one bag of millet. From this she made the local tella beer, and their staple food injera to sell in the market and from those beginnings she started to pick up her trading again. Zewdie was a hard worker and liked nothing more than to bring in her own income, to be independent. During the months of March and April, business was typically slow in the highlands. No one had much money. People were working the fields, ploughing and planting and praying for rain, hoping to secure a Belg season crop. They sold livestock to buy food and pay for medicines, so the price of goats and sheep was low. Some days she went far into the ravines with the other women to collect firewood and carried it on her back to market. She cooked food for her mother and helped her sister-in-law, Selam, and her niece Fahte, grinding the grains and cleaning the house and compound. Her brother and his sons were in the fields ploughing and planting the new crop. The youngest boy was out on the mountains tending their cows, sheep and goats. Not a moment passed when she did not wish Ashebir could have stayed to work with them.

Early one morning Zewdie was up. She could hear the animals rustling in the stall at the back. Her mind was busy with thoughts of Ashebir. Was he getting up now, was he warm at night, did he have enough to eat, was his hair full of lice? She could hear the cockerel outside crowing and thought he was as proud as her brother ruling over the roost. She felt a little guilty for her thoughts. She rubbed her hands and blew softly on them. The air was chilly. She was trying not to feel bitter. It was in God's hands and she had to reconcile herself to the fact that He knew best. She fetched water from the gourd standing in the corner and brought the kindling to a crackling fire so that she could make tea for her mother and for the rest of the house before they left for the fields. The wood smoke stung her eyes but had a comforting aroma which spread softly filling the dark interior. The beginnings of morning light filtered through the open door. She could hear the others stirring to get up. Two of Mohamed's boys Yimam and Nuru Ahmed, went out to wash, greeting their aunt in sleepy voices on the way. Leaving the pot over the fire she went to her mother's cot and placed her hand on the old woman's forehead. She stood still, her heart beating, she could hear and feel the beat, she breathed quietly and then she heard the loud wail. Her own mouth, open and crying. She sank to her knees beside her mother and buried her face in her mother's chest. Her mother's loud breathing and wheezing had stopped. She had been too preoccupied blaming her brother for sending Ashebir away to notice it when she first rose. The two boys ran in from outside, their shocked faces dripping with water.

"What is it?"

"Is it our grandmother?"

"What happened?" Mohamed was by her side. He cried out too. Zewdie was taken aback by her brother's outburst.

"Our dear mother, Hawa," he sobbed. "Allah in his greatness has taken her to Him."

His wife and the other children joined them and began wailing and crying. The noise brought their neighbours, still in their early morning dress, wrapped inside white gabis against the mist and chill which hung softly around their mountain village. Emet Hawa was delivered from her long illness and the life she had enjoyed, with its hardships, love for her family, rituals. Zewdie was glad she had brought her mother's round-bellied jabena coffee pot, made from the soil her mother would return to, the small basket she used for fendisha, and the soft white gown her mother used to wear when she made coffee and prayed. Her beloved Allah, who had been her guide in all things, who decided the rhythm of her days, and now the time of her dying, had taken her to Him.

2

Zewdie had come from selling injera in the market. "Peace be with you my sister," she said as she entered the darkness of the gojo-bate, glad to find Selam there.

"Peace be with you, dear Zewdie," her sister-in-law replied. "How was it in the market today?"

"Everything was fine, as fine as can be." Zewdie put her things down and went to kiss Selam on both cheeks. "I bought the coffee beans -"

"Thank you Zewdie," Selam said, taking the packet from her. "Mohamed wants us to prepare coffee. He has some things he would like to discuss."

It was as Zewdie had thought and she could not help feeling uneasy.

"Don't worry, Zewdie. It will be alright, Insha'Allah," her sister-in-law said.

Zewdie was fond of the woman. Selam had never reprimanded Zewdie for anything and had always managed to be quietly by her side, without contradicting her husband. Over the years Selam had pursued and refined the art of treading a delicate path between the brother and sister, and Zewdie was grateful to her for that.

"He just wants us to have coffee, and talk," Selam said with a smile.

"Yes, of course," Zewdie said, knowing there would be more to it, and that Selam knew that too. "I will go and call him."

Selam put pieces of wood on the fire, rekindling the still warm embers from the early morning tea. "You will find him outside – and call Yimam too. Mohamed wants him to be there."

"I think you know something I don't, Selam." Zewdie said softly, looking at her sister-in-law's back, now bent over the fire. She left to look for her brother and his eldest son, bracing herself.

By the time she came back, Hawa's basket was full of freshly made fendisha, her jabena was standing beside it and the small red clay bowl

Hawa always used for burning itan. It contained a few hot coals and a scattering of itan which had started to burn, sending thin whisps of smoky incense into the room. Selam had scattered fresh grass on the ground. Seeing these things, Zewdie felt Hawa's reassuring presence.

Her brother and Yimam came in bowing their heads, greeting them both: "As-sallamu aleykum," they said in chorus. "Peace be with you."

Zewdie noticed how deep her nephew's voice had become and wondered how it would be when Ashebir was older.

They sat around the fire, thoughts transfixed by the flames, slowly eating the fendisha. All had been working since dawn, they were tired, Zewdie thought. She watched the movement of Selam's hand as she pushed the green coffee beans around with the long metal mequiya, roasting them until they turned dark brown. It was quiet in the dim interior except for the crackle and hissing of the fire and the beans rattling back and forth across the fire-blackened metal dish. She wondered what Mohamed had in mind. She only had one wish, to have Ashebir with her again.

When Selam finished the roasting, she held the dish of steaming dark coffee beans in front of each of them in turn, wafting the smoke towards them, so they could appreciate the full flavoured aroma. Then she poured the beans into a wooden mortar, which she passed to Zewdie. "Please Zewdie," she said. "Can you?"

Zewdie got up and took the beans outside to pound while Selam set a pan of water on the fire to boil.

"Selam," Zewdie said as she went outside, "I am happy to see that you are using Emayey Hawa's jabena for the coffee."

"For sure, Zewdieye, of course," Selam replied.

It was some weeks since Emet Hawa had passed on. She prayed her mother rest in peace. She missed her, their chatting and secrets, and above all their shared love for Ashebir. Once outside, she could hear the muffled tones of her brother's voice and of Selam's soothing responses.

So, Mohamed Shinkurt did have matters to discuss. She knew it. Her brother was the head of the house and strong-willed. She had stood up to him before. She would have to be firm now.

The sun had passed its highest point in the sky. She looked up into the blue and took a deep breath. On the way to the market, she had seen how the tiny green shoots in the fields were growing into plants. They needed water. Everyone in the market had been talking about the rains. They were all praying for more, but not too much and then again, Insha'Allah, not too little.

When she finished pounding, she went back inside. It was dark and cosy in the gojo-bate. Her sister-in-law made the coffee and poured a thick black stream into the little cups, stirring in spoonfuls of sugar. She handed one to each of them and they bowed their heads muttering, "Bismillah,[26]" and, "Shukran,[27]" in turn as they received the hot drink in two hands.

Her brother was talking. She could hear him but felt detached. Her small family had so suddenly been torn apart. Her mother gone and Ashebir given to Ali Yusuf. She did not have news of him, and if he was suffering. She wished she had left him in Alem Tena, with Boleke and his mother. It was worse for him to be on the other side of Muletta mountain.

Before he left, she had changed his name. "I will give you the name Siraje," she had told him, looking into his eyes in all seriousness. He had listened, looking at her, searching for answers. She could see he was afraid, without knowing what he was afraid of.

"It is a Muslim area, Ashebir," she said. "You cannot go there with a Christian name."

His chin quivered a little, and large tears had fallen from those deep brown eyes she loved. "Ishi, Zewdie," he had whispered, and she had not been able to hold back her own tears.

She hoped he had remembered to use the name Siraje and not mistakenly said his own name, Ashebir.

Since he left, she had looked out for women in the market who came from that area, who might have news of him.

"As-sallamu aleykum, sisters," she would start. "Are you coming from near Albuko? Do you know Ali Yusuf? Do you know a boy by the name of Siraje? He is six years old and – "

But no one had heard of him. Some would say: "There are so many erregnya in our area – "

Another would say: "He probably spends most of his time in the open pastures looking after the animals -"

Another would nod in agreement: " – and then sleep in a corner at night. How would we see him and know him?" they said, shaking their heads, knowing how a mother suffers.

The women could only describe the existence of an erregnya child, and how hard that might be. But they knew nothing of her child. So she was

---

[26] In the name of Allah.
[27] Thank you very much.

constantly pushing her worst imaginings to the edges of her mind. It was too late for regrets or recriminations. Now it was time for her to re-assert herself.

"Zewdie," her brother's voice broke through her thoughts.

She felt his hand touch her shoulder.

"I am talking to you."

She looked up at him.

"Now that you are alone, we have to think of your future."

She was dismayed by her initial sense of relief that someone was thinking of her future. But what might he have in mind for her? Would he decide she should stay in their house, or that she should return to Alem Tena? Worse still, was he thinking of finding her a husband?

"My future?" she echoed his words.

"Yes," he said. "We need to decide whether you will settle here with us, and if so where you can live. We might even think of marriage."

She could hear him taking in a breath.

"You are not too old. And time has passed since -"

"Mohamed," Selam broke in.

Zewdie had rarely heard that hint of warning in her sister-in-law's voice.

He took a loud slurp of his coffee, his eyes still on her, ignoring Selam. He continued: "I know a man,"

"Mohamed, please," Selam tried again.

His words: "I know a man," had a familiar ring. Hadn't her elder brother said that when she was a girl, and married her to a man she didn't know? And hadn't he used those words a few weeks ago, and sent her boy away?

Had she lost so much of her strength since leaving Alem Tena? If she wanted Ashebir and her own life back, she would have to wake up.

She cleared her throat. "No, Mohamed," she said. She tried to smile at him, but knew the look was bitter.

"What do you mean, 'No'?" he said.

"No, I don't want you to find me a husband." She put the tiny white coffee cup, with a trace of green and gold decoration, down on the floor in front of her. She squeezed her hands between her knees to stop them shaking and stared at the earthen floor to gather herself.

**

She had been married before. She and her other brother, Ali, had grown up on Mohamed Shinkurt's farm, watching over his animals and threshing the harvest. They had been happy together and it was a good life. She and Ali were inseparable. So near in age and height that people used to joke that they were twins, good-looking twins. Then at the age of eighteen, Mohamed decided to marry her to a much older, local man, bringing her contented life with her brother Ali to an abrupt end. It was not a bad marriage, but after two or three years she was still not happy. Not only did she miss her brother, but she wanted to be a trader. Her husband was not in favour.

The siblings made a plan. Early one morning when her husband left for the fields, Zewdie firmly shut the door to their gojo-bate and ran away to Addis Ababa. There she met Kassahun, a tall, handsome man. He was a driver with one of the government ministries and was frequently on the road. As their love grew, they decided to marry, and it was then that she converted to Christianity and changed her name to Zewdie.

Since Kassahun was often away, they decided to move to Alem Tena near Mojo, south of Addis Ababa. Mojo had a large central market and sat on a crossroads. To the east lay Awash, Harar and the border with Somalia, to the south Awasa, Moyale and the Kenyan border and to the north Addis Ababa. Kassahun often passed through Mojo, so living near there in Alem Tena they could see each other more often. The two were happy and Zewdie built up her trading business.

Then one day, everything came to an abrupt end. Just before dawn, when the Awash road was still wide open and empty, the air fresh and the sun creeping up on the horizon, Kassahun had left to pick up an official from the Awash National Park. The story was that he had been stopped on the road by common bandits, shiftas. They had robbed him and killed him.

Zewdie was devastated. She did not like to think back to that time. Her brother, Ali, had accompanied her to collect Kassahun's body from the Awash police station. Thanks to God she had him by her side.

The fat-bellied officer had told them how dangerous the road had become. "The shiftas usually stand in a line across the road," he had said. "They stop the vehicle by holding up their guns. There is little we can do."

Zewdie and her brother knew about shiftas, everyone did. They were nasty individuals, bandits, often armed with old Italian rifles. They were poor and needy, but they had no mercy.

The officer told them that Kassahun must have put up a fight. The men had beaten him and left him on the roadside to die, "in a pool of blood", he had said. The officer then lit a cigarette, and she remembered how he had drawn on it deeply and blown out a long stream of smoke towards the open door where the sun was shining in. The smoke had hung in the stream of light.

When she identified Kassahun's body, she saw the bruises around his eyes and mouth. She could see the determination to survive in his face. He had not been ready to go to the grave. She had looked at him all over, whimpering softly, her hands shaking, touching him gently here and there.

Whoever had done this, had stripped him of his watch, the new leather shoes they had just bought and which had still been a bit too tight on his feet, his gold wedding band and the small silver cross she had given him on their first anniversary. His shabby black leather wallet containing his I.D. card and driving license, a few notes – he never carried much – and a black and white photo of her was also missing. That those scavengers, those shiftas, those hyenas, had set their eyes on the picture of her, smiling for Kassahun, had filled her with revulsion. In the photo she had been standing at the entrance to their house. Their home.

The clerk, a skinny man with an earnest look, had sat at his metal desk, typing information in triplicate on an old machine, layers of thin paper and blue carbon flapping over the back, slowly eaten up as he typed and swung the return with a 'ting!

Finally, the fat-bellied officer, standing behind a thick well-thumbed ledger, had said, "Sign here please." He had coughed a strong smell of stale cigarettes. "When the clerk is finished, you can take him. You have a vehicle?"

It was all in a day's duty for them. They showed little consideration.

In the following days and weeks their small house had been filled with mourners. She lost interest in life, and her business declined.

"I cannot stand by and watch you fade away Zewdie," her brother had said. "I am going to send for Mother."

Her older brother, Mohamed Shinkurt, had never been able to accept his sister's flight from the first husband, much less the marriage to a Christian in the second. But her mother, Hawa, loved her and had willingly come to help her rebuild her life and her trading business little by little. And so it was that Emet Hawa Jafer came to be living with Zewdie in Alem Tena.

**

Those shiftas, preying mercilessly on my Kassahun. Zewdie stared into the coals burning red and blue. The value of the things they had taken from Kassahun at that time was nothing compared to her overwhelming loss. They had robbed her very soul.

She picked up her cup and took a sip of the strong sweet coffee. It was the first pouring. Selam had refilled the jabena with boiling water and set it on the hot coals again to draw the flavour for the second round.

"No, you say?" Mohamed Shinkurt's voice pierced her thoughts. "What makes you so sure you can manage without our help, without a husband?"

"I am saying no, I do not want to be married again," she said, trying to hold her voice steady. "I am not saying, 'No', I do not need help."

There was silence.

Selam sucked her teeth. "We were thinking maybe you could settle here with us, Zewdie," Selam said. "I know trading is slow at this time of year, but everyone talks about your injera, and the tella is selling well -" She looked at her husband. Selam, as ever, was trying to smooth things.

Mohamed Shinkurt slurped his coffee, staring into the fire with that look on his face. He was listening, thinking, deciding.

"I have been thinking too, my sister," Zewdie said, her heart pounding. "It would be good for us, Ashebir and me, to stay here, near you."

She did not want Mohamed to decide her future, however important he had become. She was sure she would not be marrying any man he might have in mind for her. But she had to tread carefully not to speak too far out of place. Her throat tight, she took another sip of the hot coffee. Coffee, the life force of Ethiopia, green-gold. Hawa had always believed in it. It would give her strength too.

"Yes, the boy," Mohamed Shinkurt sat up, stretching his back, as if waking. He sighed.

Was he softening, did he even feel a little guilt for banishing the boy to Albuko?

"I want him back with me, Mohamed," Zewdie said, fighting the tears. "I do not know how he is, whether he is getting enough food."

"Maybe he can come after the harvest," Mohamed said.

"Why not now?" she could not stop from blurting out. "Why not he come and help with the harvest?" she said more quietly. "Do you have news of him, my brother?"

"I hear he is fine. No better no worse than other erregnya," he said. "But Zewdie, first you need a home."

"How will I get a home?"

"I have been talking to the Chairman of the Peasant's Association," Mohamed Shinkurt said.

This came as a surprise. She looked towards Selam, who nodded almost imperceptibly back.

Her brother had connections. He could talk to important people, eye to eye, and get things done. Despite all his anger against her, and the shame she had brought on the family, he was trying to help her. Maybe something in him had softened since Hawa's death.

"They have agreed to give you a small plot for a house," he said.

"Is that possible?" Zewdie looked from Mohamed Shinkurt to her sister-in-law.

"Have you forgotten the great uprising of the masses, how our beloved Emperor was disposed of?" He spoke, with a fierce look in his eyes. "It was not all for nothing. You know that the land has been redistributed?"

She had heard the rumour, like others, that the old man had been murdered in prison and disposed of under a toilet in one of his palaces. However much they hated him, if it was true, she could not understand why they had done that.

"I am sure you saw enough upheaval down south, but a lot has changed here, too," he said.

Of course, the famine and the revolution had affected her too. There had been no teff to trade, they were also hungry and frightened, she and Hawa.

"He was beloved of the people," Mohamed Shinkurt said. "But he made mistakes. The tax on poor tenant farmers was too high, there was no food. We, his people, were starving, suffering terribly. They did nothing. It was the students, and then the farenj,[28] who raised the alarm that we need food."

"Land to the tiller! Land to the tiller!" Yimam suddenly chanted.

"Yimam," his mother hushed him.

The young man laughed, shaking his head. "You are right, father," he said. "They did not care about the people. Not at all. Mengistu's government makes sure the people get land and can grow food."

"The plot will not be yours to own, but to use," Mohamed Shinkurt said. "You have family here, Zewdie, this is your home. That gives you the right to a small plot for a house with enough to grow a few vegetables at the back."

"I am amazed," Zewdie said. This was a big change. She never got involved in all the political talk and had avoided demonstrations and

---

[28] Foreigner/s.

meetings as far as possible. But this would save her life, a small plot for a house.

"Thank you, Mohamed," Zewdie said. She knelt in front of him. She took his hand and kissed it, bowing down to kiss his feet.

"No Zewdie," he said. "Stop."

"Allah will reward you for looking after your poor sister," she said, looking up at him, careful not to inflame him by saying, 'God bless you'.

"Come, come, aysosh,[29] Zewdiye," Selam said. "Come, come. Let's have another coffee. We'll have the second round, give me your cups." She sighed and tutted, sucking her teeth, "Allah is the greatest and will look after us all. He alone knows what is good and what is not."

Selam took the cups back. She poured the coffee from Hawa's jabena, lifting it high above each cup, making a splashing gurgling noise as they filled. The plume of smoke rose from the itan in Hawa's ochre red pottery dish.

"Our poor mother is barely in the grave and we are making plans in excited voices," Zewdie said.

"She would like the plan, I am sure," Selam said. "Hawa will rest in peace knowing you are settled with us. She worried about you and Ashebir being left alone." Her sister-in-law passed her a cup. "Come, aysosh, drink, drink. Don't fill your head with sad thoughts."

"There is a plot near your old friends, Temima and Mohamed Ahmed," Mohamed Shinkurt said, in his matter-of-fact way. "We will discuss the matter with the village head and the Chairman of the Peasant's Association in the next few days. Now is a good time. The fields are prepared and the crops are growing. People have more time on their hands."

"Zewdie, you should come to the Women's Association meetings," Selam said. "They will see you are an active -"

"Revolutionary Motherland or Death!" Yimam interrupted, lifting a fist in the air and laughing again. "You will have to become a revolutionary, Aunty."

Zewdie shifted in her seat. Yimam's outbursts were disturbing.

"Hush Yimam," his mother said. "That's enough."

"Only joking," he chuckled, without much humour. He turned to Zewdie and said: "Mother is afraid they will come and take us to the front, Aunty." He was quiet for a moment. "What can we do? It is all in Allah's hands."

---

[29] Hush, take it easy.

"That is true enough, my son," Mohamed Shinkurt said, shaking his head a little. "I am too old for them to take. We can only live in hope that they do not send you."

Maybe her brother was not so politically involved, Zewdie thought, maybe they all did just as much as was necessary.

"Let's think about Zewdie's house," he said, coughing into his gabi.

Her brother had aged. There were grey tips in his hair and his face was drawn with the deep lines of his worries and smiles, which seemed more seldom than ever.

"We will try and secure the plot and then we will have to collect materials and ask for help from our friends, and these boys," he cuffed Yimam's shoulder. "You will have to help build your Aunty's house, Yimam."

The boy's face lit up. "I can manage it, Father. I will organise everything. Don't you worry. Aunty, we will do everything."

"I have already talked with Temima and Mohamed Ahmed," Mohamed Shinkurt said. "They will be very happy to have you as their neighbour, Zewdie."

"Praise Allah," Zewdie said looking at her brother. "Thank you for your kindness."

Hawa's jabena was steaming with the third round ready to pour. Zewdie exchanged a small smile with her sister-in-law as Selam shook Hawa's basket and passed more fendisha around.

**

The plot allocated to Zewdie was, just as Mohamed Shinkurt had said, down the hillside from Temima's gojo-bate. The area had been levelled by her nephews and their friends. Under Yimam's instruction the young men gathered, stripped and cut, moulded and shaped the necessary elements, and the small round gojo-bate slowly emerged from the soil, trees and grasses around them. Mohamed Shinkurt came now and then to supervise the overall progress. She was glad of her brother's intervention. It would be a solid house.

Zewdie continued building up her trade, baking and selling injera, brewing and selling tella. She went into the ravines to collect firewood and carried it to the market to sell. She saved as much as she could so that she could buy a few hens for eggs, or if she was lucky, a pair of goats. That was her plan. To build up her reserves so that Ashebir could come and join her. She went to watch the progress on her house and helped whenever she could.

Yimam had told her they would be coming with the grass for the roof the next day. So she hastened back from the market to be there when the camel came with the grass. It was stacked up in a large cradle strapped to its back. Large bundles of grass bulged out high above and on either side of the animal.

Yimam called out instructions to the two boys who lead the camel on a long rope: "Let her come down. Over here. Slowly, slowly."

Once the camel had been led to the right spot, the taller boy cracked his whip on the ground and let out clicking noises. The camel first buckled one spindly front leg and then the other, collapsing forwards to the ground, the back knees quickly followed, folding underneath her. She then settled herself quietly on the ground, still ruminating.

"Take the grass. Pile it over there," Yimam called out. "Yes, over there. Hold the animal still. Watch it, watch it."

The animal let out a long moan, like an ox.

Commotion and excitement. Zewdie felt the thrill.

"Look. The camel is not at all impressed with our work, Aunty," Yimam called to her, laughing.

Zewdie looked at the camel. It was true. The camel was sitting there, her long thin neck sticking up high out of the bulky mass of grass. She turned slowly this way and that, chewing. She looked about her with utter disdain. Zewdie smiled. She appreciated the camel's soft proud face.

She laughed and called to her nephew, "But I am impressed with your work, Yimam, Praise Allah, I am."

The boys had been to Molu Lake, a six hour walk to the north of Ataye. It was there that they collected the grasses for the thatch. Zewdie knew the place herself. It was a long way. They would have set off before dawn to reach in time to cut the grasses and return. She had prepared injera and sherro wot[30] for the boys to eat after the long journey.

The week before, she had been at the house and watched as Yimam instructed his friends: "Cut to size, cut to size. They have to be all the same length," he had told them, as they stripped and cut long poles of eucalyptus for the frame of the gojo-bate.

"This will be the most beautiful house in the village Aunty," he had said proudly.

Everything came from the land around them. She worked with them the day they mixed cow dung and water and painted the walls and the cots, which were also made of mud. Temima and Selam had been there,

---

[30] A sauce made with chick peas and *berberri* – hot chilli spices – to eat with injera.

61

working alongside them too.

"This will stop the dust and keep the house clean, Zewdie," her sister-in- law had said.

She knew, but she nodded her head happily. "Allahu Akbar, Selam, Allah is the greatest," she said, thankful for the older woman's presence.

3

Finally, it was time for Zewdie to move into her new home. She was touched by the joy and celebration around her and wished Hawa could be there to see, and that Ashebir were by her side. She had few belongings. In preparation for the move, she had bought basic cooking implements, a large round clay plate for preparing injera over the wood fire, a pot for boiling water and another for cooking wot. She had the tin cups and plates she had brought from Alem Tena, and Emet Hawa's jabena and fendisha basket and the small clay dish for the itan. She had built an extra partition inside from chikka,[31] behind which stood her cot. She wanted some privacy and a place to store her goods for trading, and for the millet she used for making injera and brewing tella beer.

There was one strong eucalyptus pole in the middle of the hut. It supported the whole structure. Zewdie patted it with the flat of her hand and smiled. It was the backbone of her house.

"This is where I shall hang the new lamp, Temima," she said. She banged a nail in the pole.

Temima passed her the brand-new kerosene lamp and Zewdie hung it up. They both stepped back to look and then laughed, clasping each other's hands.

"Temima, another two months have gone by without Ashebir," Zewdie said when their laughter ebbed. "It's nearly the end of June. Mohamed Shinkurt has been busy with the harvest. I did not want to disturb him."

"Yes, yes, you are right." Temima nodded. "It is time he came."

"My tella sales are going well. I'm making enough money to live day by day. I don't need my brother to look after us anymore."

"The men are thirsty for your beer, Zewdie," Temima said. "Its taste

---

[31] Mud.

is good and loosens their tongues for good chatter," she laughed.

"People seem to be satisfied with the harvest Temima, don't they?" Zewdie said, hoping that to be true. "The price of millet for brewing the beer and making injera is not too high. I can still afford to buy."

"Yes, Mohamed Ahmed says we can't complain. The harvest is not very good but also not very bad."

"We seem to learn to be content with what comes," Zewdie muttered.

"How right you are, how right," Temima shook her head.

The women had been friends since childhood. Zewdie felt lucky to have Temima close by again. Temima knew her story, so she could talk freely.

"The rains will be coming soon, Temima." Zewdie said. "I want him home before then. Mohamed said by harvest time, but that has come and gone."

"Let's see," Temima said. "We'll talk to Mohamed Shinkurt. Maybe he will agree to let the child come, Insha'Allah."

**

The next day Zewdie went far into the ravines with other women from the village to collect firewood. She collected a heavy load and managed to sell it all in the market. She bought green coffee beans and maize corns to prepare fendisha. It was her turn to invite. She would ask Mohamed Shinkurt and Selam, Temima and Mohamed Ahmed, and her friend, Mohamed Bilal from Albuko, who had also settled in Ataye, to come and drink coffee in her new home. She needed to talk about bringing Ashebir home.

She laid fresh grasses on the floor and made the fendisha, the kernels cracking and banging against the lid as she shook the pot.

Her visitors arrived exchanging greetings, shaking hands and kissing each other on both cheeks saying: "As-sallamu aleykum," bowing as they did so.

Zewdie watched her brother carefully. He was looking at the craftsmanship of the roof, nodding his approval. She was determined to say what she needed to say, even if she was a woman. She would phrase her words carefully.

"Come, come, sit down," she said, trying to hide her nerves.

"Mohamed Shinkurt, you and the boys have done a good job," Selam was saying. She looked at Zewdie, smiling. "Look how smooth and clean the walls are -"

"- and a good strong roof, Mohamed Shinkurt," Mohamed Ahmed said, looking up into the dome, a neat structure of thin eucalyptus branches and freshly bound grasses. It was not yet blackened by smoke from the fire.

Zewdie had laid kindling in the small round fireplace which served as her stove in the centre of the room. It was already crackling for the coffee ceremony. Zewdie sat to roast the green coffee beans.

"That is the work of the roofer from Somali Sefer," Mohamed Shinkurt was telling Mohamed Ahmed. "He is a good man."

Zewdie walked round with the dish of hot roasted beans, inviting her guests to savour the aroma. She went to pound the coffee outside, the neighbours' children gathering round while she worked.

"You will soon have a new friend to play with," she told them.

They looked at her shyly. A little girl had come closer to lean on the smooth mud wall under the thatch. She watched Zewdie, chewing on the black thread round her neck.

"My son Ashebir will be coming," Zewdie said. "He will live here with us." She smiled at them with the thought of seeing him again.

A little boy, not more than two years old and wearing only a torn t-shirt, ran to Zewdie's side. He crouched on his haunches next to her. His belly was distended, round and soft between his knees and his whole body was covered in a fine layer of dust. He must have worms, she thought.

He looked up at the little girl and they both giggled, their eyes sparkling.

"When is he coming?" the girl asked, her voice low and husky.

"Soon, soon," Zewdie said, "Insha'Allah." She looked up into the sky for a moment then carried on pounding until the coffee was a fine soft powder. It smelt good.

"When he comes, we'll take him to the river and play," the girl said. "My big brother, Ali, can show him where the boys wash and swim."

Zewdie smiled at the girl, how kind. "Thank you," she said. "I am sure he will be happy with friends like you."

The pounding finished, she stood up. "What's your name?" Zewdie asked, thinking how pretty the girl was. She must be about the same age as Ashebir, six or seven.

"Yishaereg," the girl said.

"Yishaereg," Zewdie repeated. "My name is Zewdie." She held a hand out. The girl's hand was thin and light in hers. It will get stronger with the pounding, cooking, sweeping, carrying, and cutting of firewood,

Zewdie thought with a sigh. She went inside to finish preparing the coffee. Hawa's fendisha basket was already being passed around. White fluffy balls she had tossed with salt. She imagined Ashebir hanging around the doorway expectantly, hoping for a handful.

"In the name of Allah, we have to be thankful," Mohamed Shinkurt said.

"Indeed," Mohamed Ahmed agreed. "And it is good to have you here as our neighbour, Zewdie."

"Thank you, thank you," Zewdie bowed her head.

"There is something I would like us to talk about," Zewdie said, when everyone was sipping coffee.

Mohamed Shinkurt slurped his loudly. "I know," he said. "You want the boy home."

"As soon as possible, Mohamed," Zewdie said, trying to keep her voice respectful but firm. She glanced at Temima before looking down into her coffee cup, her heart beating, her face flushed.

"Maybe it is time the boy came home to his mother, Mohamed Shinkurt?" her friend Mohamed Bilal from Albuko said in his gentle voice.

The others nodded, waiting for the brother's reply.

"Thanks to your kindness, brother, I have a home," Zewdie said. "I am earning a little every day, enough to feed both of us." Much as she tried to stop it, her eyes filled with tears.

Mohamed Shinkurt cleared his throat. "I have been thinking about it." His gruff tone signalled a change of heart. "I will send a message to Ali Yusuf asking him to bring the boy next time he comes to Ataye."

Zewdie fell at her brother's feet and made to kiss them. "Praise Allah," she said. "Praise Allah."

"Zewdie, please," he stopped her.

"Don't Zewdie." She felt Selam's hand on her back.

Zewdie got up. She brushed her long dress down, feeling conscious of herself in the room. She went to sit on the low wooden stool behind Hawa's steaming jabena coffee pot. She wiped her eyes and nose on the corner of her white cotton shema.

"Praise Allah," her friend Temima said. "It will be a good day. Indeed, it will." She smiled at Zewdie. Whenever she smiled, the marks of habitual worry left Temima's face and she became the beauty Zewdie could still remember from their childhood.

"Come. Let's have the second round," Zewdie said quickly, taking their cups back she poured steaming hot coffee into each.

"Praise Allah, indeed," Mohamed Bilal from Albuko agreed, smiling.

"We will all be happy to see him home, Zewdie," her sister-in-law said, as she laid her hand softly on Zewdie's knee. Turning to her husband, she said, "It is a good decision, Mohamed Shinkurt, Allahu Akbar."

**

Finally, the day came. Zewdie had saved enough money to buy two chickens so she could sell their eggs in the market. Today she had put one egg aside for Ashebir to eat that night. She followed the track her brother had taken on horseback to the market, carrying the jerry can full of tella strapped to her back. It was still early and a fresh breeze accompanied her. The sun was beginning to warm the mountain slopes. Children ran behind small flocks of sheep and goats, bleating and stumbling towards the riverbanks below. Others walked more slowly behind large oxen, flicking a switch of sisal rope at their haunches. The children called out, "Good morning", to each other: "Tenasteling!" and to neighbours passing on their way into town.

This is a peaceful place for Ashebir to grow up, Zewdie thought. We will be fine here. Maybe one day we'll have an ox and some goats.

She was eager to reach the market and for the long-awaited moment, when she set eyes on her boy again. She did not expect he would reach the market until at least midday. When she arrived, the market was already busy. Strong smells of the animals, spices and ghee filled the air. Zewdie loved the colour and bustle, the chance to hear news and exchange gossip. Increasingly, however, the chatter wore a more sinister garb. There was whispering of disappearances, talk of the war in Eritrea and Tigray, of sons who were lost, wounded or dead. These days political cadres came to the market with loudspeakers calling out slogans and animating 'the people' to back the Red Star Campaign against the rebels in the north. It made her feel uneasy. The cadres used strange language, calling the people 'the masses', and exhorting them to donate to the cause, to 'the revolution'. At the same time, she and everyone else prayed desperately that their own husbands, sons and nephews would not be sent to the front. More and more people knew someone who had gone and who had never come back.

Zewdie found her spot under the acacia tree, its branches spread like an umbrella. It was just beside the local arake-bate. They brewed and sold arake, a strong liquor. Men who drank it regularly over years were known to die of its effects. She set up her tella stall. Her neighbour, Wozeiro Etalem, had already displayed her onions and potatoes in neat piles on an outspread hessian sack. Three-onion piles, five-onion piles, three-potato piles, five-potato piles.

Zewdie bowed, "Tenasteling," she said, and shook her friend's hand. Before she could sit down and rest her feet, she had to ask after the woman's family. She took her wooden stool and sat, looking out across the market, keen for the morning to pass quickly. She sucked her teeth.

As the sun moved across the sky towards its highest point, she became nervous. Time was drawing closer to the hour Ashebir should arrive in the market with Ali Yusuf. She squinted against the sun, her hand raised to shade her eyes. She looked over to the far corner of the market where the livestock were bought and sold. He would be there somewhere soon.

Unable to contain herself she said, "Wozeiro Etalem? Could you look after my tella for a short while?"

"You want to see if the boy has come?" The woman smiled. Etalem was older than Zewdie and had six children. To her utter dismay, her two eldest sons had joined the army. They had been keen to get an education, a smart uniform, boots and food, they had said. Both had been sent to the front and she had not heard from them since. She awaited news of them every day. "That loudspeaker is like a cockroach in my ear," she was known to say. "Only pain and bad news for us mothers."

"Go Zewdie. I'll keep an eye on your tella, maybe I'll even make some sales for us while you're gone, Egziyabher sifeked, if God permits." Etalem was an Orthodox Christian. Zewdie liked her for this. She felt an affinity to the woman and a connection to Kassahun, and the days in Alem Tena.

"Thank you, Etalem. God bless you," Zewdie said, smiling at her neighbour as she stood up, brushing the dust from the back of her long skirt. She adjusted the black scarf she had wound tightly round her head in the morning and threw her white cotton shema over her head and across her shoulders.

"Enjoy him while he is still small," Etalem said. She shook her head and flicked a black horsehair fly whisk across her vegetables. "You never know what monster is waiting to eat him up when he grows tall."

"Egziyabher yawkal, my dear friend, God only knows," Zewdie said and bent to touch Etalem on the shoulder. "God protect them all."

"Go well and return with him by your side," Etalem said, smiling up at Zewdie.

Zewdie was glad to stand and move about after sitting under the tree for so long. She kept her eyes open, scanning each small ragged boy she passed, for ragged he would be. She walked past makeshift stalls selling butter and oils, spices and herbs. A group of women were making and selling brightly coloured woven baskets which caught her eye, but she continued on her way. The warm smell of their fresh, dried grasses filled her nostrils. The sun was streaming down on them all, releasing the strongest scents and odours, and sharpening the colours of the day.

Finally, she found herself amongst the animals, with their agitated hooves and warm breath, soft noses rubbing against neighbouring hides. Goats and sheep were bleating, some hysterically, as if a knife were already at their throats. There was an excitement and tension in the air which matched hers. She was in the thick of it, herd and flock snuffling on all sides. She stood on tip toes in her black plastic slippers, searching over the tall backs of the oxen for Ashebir's face and then peering down through the bony restless legs of goats, donkeys and sheep for his familiar feet, the wide space between the big toe and the next.

Has he grown? she wondered, still looking with a mad intensity at everything small and human.

Finally, she spotted her brother, Mohamed Shinkurt. He was standing with a group of similarly clad men of middle age. They all wore shirts and shorts or trousers, a white cloth wound loosely round their heads and a dark green or red woollen cloth draped over one shoulder. They were talking, dealing, negotiating. And when all that was done to their satisfaction, they would be going to the local arake-bate, near her spot under the acacia tree, for a drink or two. Some would come to her first and refresh themselves with a drink of her tella beer.

She made her way towards him, weaving in and out of the animals, trying to catch his eye, raising her hand intermittently.

"Wozeiro Zewdie," the men greeted her in turn, putting out both hands to shake hers and bowing their heads politely.

"As-sallamu aleykum. How are you?"

She returned their greetings, but was eager to find out from her brother whether he had seen Ali Yusuf.

"Ali Yusuf is just arriving, Zewdie," Mohamed Shinkurt answered her thoughts. "I can see him coming with his cattle. He will be hoping to sell some this afternoon."

She shaded her eyes from the sun and stood on the tips of her toes, scanning minutely the far edges of the market. People were descending the rocky slopes on the other side coming towards the market, donkeys laden and stumbling over rocks. Small groups of men and women, carrying bundles on their backs and shoulders, shooing their animals on ahead of them, were arriving from the north. A few were on horseback, the saddles and reins decorated in reds, yellows and greens.

She was thinking how colourful they looked, when she heard herself, "Is that them? Mohamed Shinkurt, is it?" She glanced quickly at her brother and the group of men for confirmation, before turning to scan the hillside again. Her eyes focussed on a grey mule in the distance, carrying a small figure, a tall man walking alongside.

"I believe it is," Mohamed Shinkurt said in his low husky voice. He coughed to clear his throat.

Zewdie walked towards the oncoming groups of people and animals, increasing her pace, running a little, breathing hard and then slowing down, walking a little, all the time looking ahead, shading her eyes with her hand. She tripped, looked down and walked on. She was out of breath.

As she got a little nearer, she slowed down and called out, "Ashebir! Ashebir!"

She raised an arm to wave, hesitating. "Is that you, my son?"

She carried on, half walking, half running. Now she could only see the grey, carrying a small figure, swaying to the mule's rhythm. A boy was sitting on top, holding on to the saddle with both hands.

"Zewdie!"

She heard a small high voice calling on the wind. Or was it one of the large brown kites circling for pickings playing a trick on her?

She could see the boy bending down to talk to the man. He was trying to get down from the horse. It was Ashebir. It was him. She was certain.

The man and horse came to a standstill. The man helped the boy down. Barely had he touched the ground when he ran, stumbling and falling towards her.

"Ashebir."

"Mother, mother, Zewdie!" he shouted. His voice high.

She could hear him clearly now. The next moment she was on her knees. Her arms outstretched to take the full impact. She was holding the child to her. He was skin and bones, his hair long and bushy. She buried her face in it, he smelt of days long unwashed laced with a child's sweetness, of cattle hide, sheepskin oils, the deep countryside.

He stood up, his eyes shining. He was out of breath, panting and laughing.

"Zewdie."

"Ashebir. Look at you. You have grown and your hair is so long."

Zewdie could feel the tears in her eyes. She brushed them away to see his face clearly. "How many families of bugs are you housing in there?" She sniffed against her shema. Wiping her eyes, she laughed, ruffling his thick dusty hair.

He clutched his head comically, "All friends. They're all my friends."

A shadow passed between them and the sun. Zewdie looked up to see the tall man and his mule, the grey. She had completely forgotten about Ali Yusuf. She got up hurriedly, adjusting her shawl around her head and shoulders.

"Ato Ali Yusuf, Ato Ali Yusuf. May Allah reward you," she said. She put out her hand to greet the man, bowing her head as she did so. "You brought my son safely home."

"Wozeiro Zewdie," the tall man said. "How are you? How is Mohamed Shinkurt? I hope the family is in good health?"

"We are all well. Praise Allah," she replied, taking Ashebir's hand firmly in hers.

The grey blew a loud sneeze and shook its head, the bells on its reins jingling.

"Let's go," Ato Ali Yusuf said, setting off again.

They walked together making as few polite comments as customarily necessary, while Zewdie exchanged smiles and shining eyes with Ashebir.

Oh God forgive me, he looks so thin, she thought. Hawa forgive me. She looked up at the blue sky, at the kites circling. She had never seen him so skinny. The boy looked up at her, on his face the largest smile she had ever seen.

**

The following morning Zewdie and Ashebir were sitting in the sun outside their new home. The night before, after eating his egg and a few mouthfuls of injera, the boy had fallen into a deep sleep. In the early morning he was up and running from one corner of the house and garden to the next, inspecting everything, much to Zewdie's delight.

She watched him. In disbelief. He was there. She had seen his ribs protruding over his slightly swollen belly. How dirty his clothes. How thick his hair. And the stream of snot running from his nose, congealed with the dust, staying there. He was coughing now and then, deep in his chest. But all the while he was smiling and laughing, looking up at her full of love and trust.

71

How can he trust me after what has happened? She wondered, thanking God in his grace.

She bade him sit on the ground in front of her. She began to chide him gently, "Your hair has become too thick," she said, pulling his head towards her to have a closer look. He leant against her as she rummaged her fingers through his hair.

"Yeney lij," she said as he leant closer against her. "I can see small animals living in the undergrowth."

She ruffled his hair. "They've already built their gojo-bate in there," she said, pushing him softly and laughing. She got up to go to Temima's to ask for their razor.

"Ashebir, you have seen where everything is. Go and fill the plastic bowl with water from the insera,[32] fetch the soap and I am coming!" she called as she went.

Zewdie had an earthen insera for storing water. That morning as Ashebir wandered everywhere in excitement, she had watched as he ran his fingers over the smooth, bulbous, clay pot. It was the colour of the earth and red sherro, the colour of ox hides, and had an opening at the neck. It held about twenty-five litres of water. When it was empty it made a deep hollow sound. Zewdie could lift it onto her back alone when it was empty. She would carry it strapped round her shoulders with long strips of old tire rubber. She would cup her hands behind her, holding its curved base, as if she were carrying a child, and walk along the narrow path to the river, sometimes alone, sometimes with other women. The walk home was harder and she always needed someone to help lift the full insera onto her back. It would last four or five days before she had to make the trek to the river again. Now with Ashebir there she would have to go more often, or send him with a small jerry can. The insera always stood on one spot against the mud wall of the gojo-bate.

As she came back with the razor, Ashebir was coming out of their front door. He was holding the small plastic bowl full of water in one hand and the remaining soap, which had washed down to the size of a smooth pebble, in the other.

"The soap will not last much longer, Zewdie." Ashebir showed her the shining white blob in his outstretched palm. "We will have to buy a new bar."

Zewdie looked at him puzzled. "There's still enough left for your hair, your body and your clothes," she said. Then she remembered how

---

[32] Large gourd for carrying and storing water.

he had always loved it when they got a new bar of soap in Alem Tena. It looked like half a mud brick, but white and shining.

"We will buy some next time we go to Ataye," she said, laughing. She always bought the cheapest soap she could find from the suk on the main road into Ataye. "Ishi. Ashebir. Let's get started." She gathered her long skirt around her and sat down on the small wooden stool she used when she was cooking or making coffee. "Sit here," she said pointing to the ground in front of her. "Where's that soap?"

He sat on the ground with his back to her and passed the soap back in his cupped hand. She was thrilled, it was unbelievable to have him there, still beyond her prayers. But God had answered them, in His grace.

She wet his hair, took the soap and ran it over his head in vigorous circular motions, his head jiggling back and forth as she did so, until it was a mass of white froth. She looked down at his protruding shoulder blades, saddened for a moment. I will feed this boy up again, God willing, she thought.

"When will we get the soap?"

"This one will be finished up first, Ashebir."

"I know. But I like the new soap."

She laughed as he turned his head to face her and pulled a grimace, his mouth pulled down and eyebrows frowning.

"Shemagele,[33]"she cried out, laughing. "You always look like an old man when you pull that face."

"Raarrrh!" he growled at her. His face broke into a wide grin and he let out a chuckle, which broke into that heavy cough again.

She would have to take him to the village healer, Emet Fahte Ibrahim, she thought. Emet Fahte will know how to get rid of that, Egziyabher sifeked. "Keep your head looking forward, I don't want to cut you," she said.

He turned to look at her again then made a large movement to face the front as if in a big huff and shuffled his bottom into the earth to get comfortable. He was obviously so pleased to be home.

"Sit still now. Naughty boy," she said laughing again and gripped his too skinny, pointed shoulders between her knees to keep him in place. She had thanked Ali Yusuf profusely, but the man and his wife had not fed and cared for her son. They had not seen the child. They saw only the herd boy.

She took the razor and carefully drew neat lines, the width of the

---

[33] Old man.

razor, through the thick mud-brown mass of soap and hair, from his forehead to the nape of his neck. Little by little his curved brown head appeared beneath, as the layers of matted hair fell by the side in clumps. Her neighbour's two small boys came scampering around to watch, followed by their sister Yishaereg. They were still too small to go with the animals. They spent their days playing in the dust near their gojo-bate, watched over by Yishaereg.

"How are you today, children?" Zewdie asked them.

"We are fine," they chorused. "We are fine."

"How are you, Yishaereg?" Zewdie asked the girl. "Look, this is Ashebir."

The children just looked at each other.

"My son," she went on. "Ashebir, that is Yishaereg, she's our neighbour."

The two put out their hands shyly to greet each other, making Zewdie laugh in delight.

The two little ones ran about naked with their skinny, dusty legs and round bellies. They came and crouched next to her. Zewdie noticed their tiny fingers and the dirt caked under their nails. They wore black threads round their necks holding little parcels of worn leather, containing a magical mix of herbs to protect them. Their mother must have taken them to Emet Fahte, Zewdie thought. So many small children got sick and died before they were old enough to go out with the cows or collect firewood.

"Ashebir, you are done," Zewdie announced. She rubbed her hand gently over his head. "As smooth as the insera."

He rubbed both hands back and forth over his scalp, looking at her with mock sadness. He bent to gather up the fallen clumps of soapy hair and threw them into the bush.

Suddenly the two boys, who had been quietly sitting on their haunches beside her, jumped up, shrieking out: "Melata![34] Melata!" giving her a shock. They danced around Ashebir, shouting with laughter, their eyes bright and mischievous, legs ready to dart away.

She watched smiling while Ashebir made as if to chase after them, pulling a face.

He shouted, "I will get the razor to your heads. Then you will be bald too."

The boys, their bottoms bare to the world, ran in all directions,

---

[34] Bald! Bald!

shrieking and laughing.

Their sister Yishaereg, her hair long and matted, just leant quietly against Zewdie's gojo-bate, watching and smiling shyly.

"Come, Yishaereg. Yeney konjo.[35]" Zewdie motioned to the girl. "Let me wash your hair. I have water and soap left."

"Ishi, Zewdie. Thank you," the girl said in her quiet voice.

Zewdie got up from her low wooden stool, put her hand on the girl's shoulder and took her round to the back of the hut. She had put up a small shelter there so she could wash in private.

Later that afternoon Yishaereg's older brother Ali and Temima's son Mohamed Abdu came to fetch Ashebir and take him to the river. They were going to wash and swim. Zewdie gave him that tiny pebble of soap to put in his pocket. She watched him walk down the path with the boys, down the path away from his own gojo-bate, where his own mother lived. He was home and life could begin again.

---

[35] My beautiful.

4

The bridge over the river Ataye became one of Ashebir's favourite places. He loved to watch the clear water rushing over the pebbles and up against the large white and grey stones. The river passed through places they had never been to, and on to places they were not allowed to go. Places far away where, he had heard, the water bubbled hot out of the earth, and steam rose high into the sky.

"I want to go and see where the water bubbles out of the earth," Ashebir would say to his mother.

"No Ashebir." Her voice was always quiet and firm. "It is too dangerous for a small boy. The Afar go there."

He saw the Afar passing along the road to market, walking at the same graceful pace as their camels. Tall beautiful men with their daggers, long red gildim cloths wrapped around their waists like Mohamed Abdu's, and thick black hair carefully kept and well buttered. Ashebir would watch them from the safety of the bushes.

"Why can't I wear a gildim like Mohamed Abdu?" Ashebir asked his mother one day, looking down at his shorts which fell widely round his skinny legs.

"It is not our custom to wear gildim, Ashebir. You have to be a Muslim to wear one."

"And the Afar wear them, Zewdie," Ashebir reminded her.

"They are also Muslim. You be careful of the Afar, Ashebir. They are warriors. They are strong people and have all sorts of customs which can be dangerous for people like us."

"I like the way they look, Zewdie. I want to be tall and strong like them one day." His face made a strong grimace. He stood as tall as he could with his legs apart and pulled an imaginary dagger from his waist holding it high in the air. He liked to make her laugh.

"You will never be an Afar, my boy." Zewdie said, laughing, her one

76

gold tooth glinting in the sun. "You know how to become a real Afar warrior?"

"How?" Ashebir laughed too, thinking she was still joking. "I can do it. Tell me."

She paused, her face looking more serious, making him wonder what she was thinking.

"What would I have to do, Zewdie? What?"

He was impatient that she seemed reluctant to tell him. "What?"

She crouched down level with him. Her eyes looked into his, very serious. She said in a quiet voice, "You would have to do many brave and dangerous things to prove you can be a fearless warrior."

"Really?" he whispered back.

"It's not safe for small boys. That's why I am always telling you not to wander too far up the river. The Afar go there to rest and wash." Getting up again she said, "Enough of this. Help me get some wood on the fire so I can cook our supper."

"Ishi, Zewdie," he said in a low voice. She had stolen some magic from his dreaming by the river. He went off round the side of their house where they kept the firewood, his mind still puzzling over what he had just heard. What dangerous things?

He brought the firewood inside and then went out again with his slingshot. His mother's friend, Mohamed Bilal from Albuko, had told him he could guard his crops if he practiced with the wenchef.[36] Mohamed Bilal had told him he would let him sit in the tall look-out; that he could fling small stones at the birds to chase them away, but he had to practice first.

Ashebir walked up the path to fetch his friend Mohamed Abdu. They went together further down the hillside to a spot where they could practice shooting stones without hurting anyone. They found a clearing in the woods on the hillside.

Mohamed Abdu was a little taller than him and knew so much. Ashebir looked up to his friend and wanted to learn everything Mohamed Abdu knew. He wanted to know where to take the animals, when, how to feed them. Which berries the boys could eat and which ones were poisonous. How to throw a sling and hit a bird in flight. Mohamed Abdu had shown him how to make a slingshot from long strips of dried sisal with a woven pouch to hold the stone.

He felt proud the day when his mother gave him his own sickle and

---

[36] Slingshot.

stick to go with Mohamed Abdu and the boys into the mountains with the animals.

"Stay near Mohamed Abdu," his mother had said. "He knows a lot about living here in the mountains. He is a clever boy."

"I want to be like Mohamed Abdu, Zewdie."

"You will be, Ashebir. And one day soon, maybe we will have our own goats," Zewdie had said.

"Look Ashebir," Mohamed Abdu was saying. "Just swing the wenchef round and round like this."

Ashebir watched from a little further up the hill as the long rope made a wide circle above Mohamed Abdu's head, his body moving round and round with the motion.

Ashebir thought it looked good. Looking down at the wenchef in his hands, he wondered if he could do the same.

Suddenly Mohamed Abdu flicked the rope behind him, flung it forwards and the stone shot sharply out of the pouch. Ashebir ran down to join him and they watched it fly through the air.

"That went so far," Ashebir cried out. "I want to try."

They practiced for some time, taking turns until the sun went down behind the mountain on the other side of the valley.

"Let's go," Ashebir said. His mind was on the Afar, whom he now feared as much as the hyenas that prowled the bush around the village at night, with that haunting woo-oop sound. They sometimes heard stories of a baby or young child being attacked by hyenas, bitten in the face and even dragged away. But now he saw the Afar, behind every tree that threw its shade to the ground in the evening dusk. He heard them in every crackle of a twig in the undergrowth. His heart beating fast, he took in a deep breath and said: "Mohamed Abdu?"

Mohamed Abdu was winding up the long string of his wenchef.

"Zewdie was telling me about the Afar."

"What did she say?" Mohamed Abdu asked, picking up his stick. "We should go, it will be dark soon."

Ashebir drew strange comfort from Mohamed Abdu's apparent unease.

"That we have to stay away from them. She says they are dangerous," he said, as they walked up the hill towards home.

Ashebir climbed up and down every rock that lay in his path and Mohamed Abdu swished his stick back and forth against the tops of the bushes.

"There are stories people tell," Mohamed Abdu said. "Temima also tells me to stay away from them."

"What stories, Mohamed Abdu?" Ashebir stopped on the path in front of his friend.

"Let's just get home," Mohamed Abdu said.

Without another word, they ran. Ashebir felt the dusk falling on his shoulders like a prickly woollen shawl. He did not stop until they reached his hut. He waved from his doorway at Mohamed Abdu, who disappeared up the hill without stopping.

He was panting and out of breath as he came in the door.

Zewdie was inside talking with her friend Mohamed Bilal from Albuko.

"Where are you coming from in such a rush?" the man laughed.

"Mohamed Abdu and I have been practicing with the wenchef," Ashebir said, showing them his sling.

Ashebir put out his hand to greet Mohamed Bilal, bowing his head and allowing himself to be drawn into the man's embrace for a kiss on each cheek and then once more.

"Good boy," Mohamed Bilal said. He looked at Zewdie, approvingly. "Your child is looking better these days."

"Allah be praised," Zewdie said.

Ashebir stood next to the man looking quietly at the floor, his breathing slowing down.

"Ashebir," Zewdie said, "Mohamed Bilal wants to give us a loan so we can buy two goats."

"Really?" Ashebir said, wondering what a loan was. "I can look after them, Zewdie. I can take them to the mountains with Mohamed Abdu," Ashebir said. They were to have their own goats again. He remembered Emet Hawa's ram. How he used to butt his grandmother playfully.

"I hear you are a good herd boy, Ashebir," Mohamed Bilal said. "Your mother is lucky to have you."

Ashebir smiled at the man and his mother. It was good to hear these words.

"Go and bring some water to wash hands, Ashebir, and we will eat." She looked at Mohamed Bilal. "Eat with us Mohamed Bilal, please. We are having sherro wot."

Ashebir went to fill the plastic bowl with water from the insera. The news made him happy. If they got a nanny and a ram, there would be milk and there would be kids.

"Thank you Zewdie, but I must get home," Mohamed Bilal was saying. "Thank you." He got up bowing his head, holding his hat to his chest. He turned to Ashebir. "You know the saying, don't you? Kas be kas, enkolal be igir yihedal – Little by little the egg will walk?' First the goats and then the ox. Insha'Allah." The man chuckled in a nice way and patted Ashebir on the back.

Like a father might, Ashebir thought and smiled shyly. He liked Mohamed Bilal from Albuko. He did not frighten him like his uncle Mohamed Shinkurt. It was not just the stern face that bothered him. The fear that his uncle might send him away again always lurked in the back of his mind. The idea scared him.

"Zewdie, will we get a ram, like Emet Hawa's?" Ashebir said when Mohamed Bilal had left. "What is a loan? Will we get the goats tomorrow?

Zewdie laughed. "So many questions. Let's wash hands and eat. I will tell you as much as I can."

They sat to eat. The light of the kerosene lamp gave a comforting glow. He tried to ignore the dark corners of the hut. They had injera from the same plate, scooping up small amounts of the flat bread, rolling it in their fingers and dipping it into the spicy sherro sauce. Ashebir told Zewdie about practicing with the catapult and how he had managed to fling a small rock far into the valley.

And Zewdie told Ashebir about the loan and how they would pay Mohamed Bilal from Albuko back, little by little.

When they had finished, Zewdie told him that tomorrow she wanted to weed the garden. "We have to look after our few stands of corn and the onions and cabbages," she said.

"I can help you, Zewdie." Ashebir said, remembering Mohamed Bilal's words, that Zewdie was lucky to have him.

"Egziyabher yimesgen, thanks to God. You are a good boy," she said. She bent towards him and kissed him on the cheek.

He leaned against her warm body, watching the embers in the fire, red, orange and blue, changing shape and crackling gently. He was happy now, near his mother every day. But what about Lakew, he thought. Where was he, and when would they see him again?

"Zewdie, when will my father come? We have not seen him since we came from Alem Tena."

"I forgot to tell you," Zewdie said. "You missed him. He came when Emet Hawa passed away. You were still in Albuko."

"Will he come again?"

"He wanted to find work down south. He will come when he can, don't worry, Ashebir."

"I miss him."

"I know you do. But that is our life. We have to manage on our own. We have to be happy that we have a friend in Mohamed Bilal. He will help us as much as he can."

"I like him too, Zewdie."

"We grew up together, you know. Emet Hawa was like a mother to him after his own mother died," Zewdie said. "And Ashebir, he thinks about you and wants you to be alright. He thinks you should start Qur'an classes. Since most people around here are Muslim, he says it would be good for you to go."

"If you want me to," he said hesitating. He swallowed, feeling his stomach tighten. "But Zewdie, only if it is nearby."

"Dear God, of course, Ashebir."

He tried to smile, but his eyes were full of tears. "I thought maybe I have to go away."

"Yeney konjo," Zewdie said, putting her arm around him. "The classes are here in the village. You would go to the Mosque, maybe two times a week, in the early morning or evening."

He sniffed into a corner of his t-shirt. "Do Mohamed Abdu and his little sister Aminat go?"

"Mohamed Abdu goes, but not Aminat," she paused. "Girls are not allowed."

"Why not? Don't girls have to learn too?"

"The Imam only allows boys to come and learn the Qur'an. But when you are all a little older you can go into Ataye to evening classes together. You can all learn to read and write."

"Aminat too?"

"Aminat too." She patted him on the back. "Come now, let's clean up and then sleep. We must be up before that nuisance cockerel next door starts crowing." She rolled her eyes then smiled, making him laugh.

As he lay looking into the darkness of the rafters, he could hear the sounds of his mother's whisperings. She was saying her prayers.

"Egziyabher…this –" she whispered. "Egziyabher …that –"

He knew she was thanking God for this, and asking God for that, in his mercy, and hoping for His forgiveness for sins he could not imagine and did not know about. To him his mother was perfect. She always told him in a quiet firm voice how to behave. She never beat him. She reminded him that they were poor and that he should be humble.

"What is humble?" he had asked.

"Do not think you are bigger than you are. Just put your head down and work hard. This is your life. That is all it means," she had told him, adding, "You are a good boy. You will be alright."

He knew his mother was kind. There were no beatings and shouting like they heard in other homes from time to time. She did everything she could to teach him and to look after him. And most of all she made him laugh. He closed his eyes and thanked God for Zewdie, for his home and his friends, and prayed for Lakew to come and see them one day soon.

**

The next morning, they were up and working in the small vegetable garden behind their gojo-bate. Zewdie said they should make mud so they could build a small enclosure for the animals at the back of the house.

"I will buy the goats next week. By then we must have a safe home for them," she told him.

They worked hard all morning. When the sun reached its highest point Zewdie went inside to take rest. Ashebir wandered off, hearing the neighbours' children playing outside their house. A shower of bright yellow white-eyes, tiny birds, flew suddenly from the fence into a nearby tree as he passed. They whirred and twitched at him from the safety of the branches, as if they were telling him stories.

He reached the compound and stood nearby, watching the children.

"Come, Ashebir," Yishaereg called. "Come and play. You can be the boys' Ababa."

"Their Ababa?" he laughed nervously.

"Please come and play. I am the mother, you are the father," she urged him.

"What about your brother? Where is Ali?" he said.

"He has taken our neighbour's animals to the river with Mohamed Abdu," she said.

Yishaereg's mother did not have any animals. They were too poor.

"Come," she said again. "We are making mud plates and when they are ready we will make injera. You can help us."

He sat next to her on the ground. Her two little brothers and another small girl were with her. He saw the mound of mud they had made. It was a black grey colour. Yishaereg had a plastic jug of water which she was using to mix into the soil and make the clay.

"We are potters," she said. "Look, the clay is nearly ready."

Her two brothers were mulching the soil and water together with their tiny fingers. Ashebir put his hands in to help mix. It felt nice. Warm, wet and smooth. It stuck to his fingers.

"It's too wet," he said to her.

"You're right Ababa," Yishaereg's friend said in a quiet, high pitched voice. She spoke in a whisper.

"Am I your Ababa too?" he asked her.

"I'm being the little boys' big sister," she replied.

The two boys had lost interest and were throwing pebbles at a cooking pot that clanged every time they hit it and made them giggle.

Ashebir felt strange being called Ababa, but also good. "If I am their father," he said, nodding his head towards the two boys, and trying to keep a serious look on his face, "then maybe I have to beat them if they don't come and work?"

The two little boys jumped up shrieking and laughing in mock fear. He wanted to chase after them. But he wanted to make the clay even more, so he stayed where he was and carried on working the soil with his fingers.

"It is too wet," he said again.

"Let's put more soil in," Yishaereg said.

Yishaereg's friend got up and went to collect the soil in the front of her long skirt. She came back holding her skirt up with two hands and tipped the dirt on top of the mound of wet mud. Ashebir, Yishaereg and her friend got to work, mixing the dry grey soil in. They worked quietly for a while.

Yishaereg's mother's chickens were scratching around the compound pecking at the compact earth and making rolling coo-ing sounds inside their throats.

Ashebir imitated them and the girls laughed. The air was dry and hot. It was different being with girls. They played different games from the boys.

"Does your father beat you?" The little girl interrupted his thoughts with her high whispering voice.

"What should I know," Ashebir replied, his hands working at the soil and water. It was becoming stiffer under his fingers.

"You don't know?" she asked, her voice even higher.

"I haven't seen him in a long time."

"Where is he?" Yishaereg asked him.

"I don't know," he said. "Zewdie says he has gone south to work. He will come soon."

"My father will come any day," Yishaereg said. "My mother says so."

"Where is he?" Ashebir said.

"Didn't you know?" Yishaereg's little friend said. "He's a hero. He's in the army."

Ashebir looked at Yishaereg, who was busy with the clay. "Has he got a gun?" he said, keeping his voice low.

"He has to have a gun," Yishaereg said, looking up at him. "He's fighting the people in the north. How could he do that without a gun?"

The two little boys started running about shouting, "Piyaw! Piyaw!" shooting each other and their sister, over and over.

"That's enough," Yishaereg said. "Enough."

"Did you see the trucks on the road?" he asked her.

"Yes, they pass all the time."

"Did he go in one of those trucks?"

"I think so. I didn't see. We were not allowed."

"Did you see his uniform?" Ashebir said. He almost wished he could say that Lakew was in the army too.

"Look, the clay is ready." Yishaereg had rolled some clay into a ball between her palms and was flattening it out and shaping it into a ball. Her fingers were small and delicate he noticed, waving as they worked the clay, like grasses under the water in the river. He watched fascinated until she produced the finished plate on the flat palm of her hand, outstretched for all to see.

"It's beautiful," he said. "I want to make one." He took a small clump of clay and started working it as she had done. He would not ask about her father anymore, he thought.

They made tiny plates and small pots, placing them on the ground in neat rows when they were done.

"I'll make some coffee cups," Ashebir suggested. "Then we can have coffee later, Emayey," he added, looking shyly at Yishaereg.

"We grown-ups can have coffee, not the children, Ababa," she replied seriously.

One of Yishaereg's little brothers had come to sit near Ashebir. He was, as usual crouched on his haunches with his hands on his knees. His belly round. He was so close, Ashebir could feel the small boy's body against his. He noticed the little boy's fingernails. Zewdie said how dirty they were. No wonder, if he's always playing in the mud.

The boy looked up at him. "I want to help you, Ababa," he said, smiling appealingly. "Can I?"

Ashebir gave the child a small clump of clay and showed him how to roll it into a ball between his palms. It felt good showing someone else how to do something for a change.

"Here," he said, "now you can start flattening it with your fingers. Look," Ashebir showed the boy how he'd made his plate, "like this."

By the end of the afternoon, they had made so many plates, pots and cups it looked like a stall in the market. They lined them up in rows in the sunshine to dry out.

"They will be ready to use tomorrow or the next day," Yishaereg said. "You can come then and we can play again. Will you?"

"Yes. I'll come. We can eat injera and have coffee, Emayey." Ashebir stood up feeling happy after an afternoon playing. "I have to go and see my mother now," he said, already walking away brushing his hands against his shorts. They were covered in a thin layer of dry, cracked mud.

**

That night Ashebir woke to hear the rain beating down on the roof. He prayed it would rain enough, not too little and not too much. He drifted off to sleep again. In the morning the sky was clear, a deep blue, and the ground wet and muddy under his feet. He curled his feet into the mud and watched as it rose in between his toes. Then suddenly he remembered the pots.

"I am going to Yishaereg's house," he called in through the door to Zewdie. It was dark inside and full of smoke from the fire. She was making injera to sell in the market.

"Why is it so smoky today, Zewdie?" he asked, coughing and rubbing his eyes.

"The wood was still a bit wet," she turned round to tell him. "Did you see? It rained in the night. It's good we looked after our plants yesterday."

"I am just going," he said again and ran over to Yishaereg's.

"What about our plates and cups?" he said.

Yishaereg was helping her mother grind the grains. Her mother was bent over, moving back and forth, back and forth, crushing the grains between a large wide smooth stone which sloped to the ground and a smaller stone which she held in both hands. It was hard work. Ashebir sometimes helped Zewdie, but he was not strong enough yet to do a good job, neither was Yishaereg. She was collecting the flour at the bottom and putting it into a sack.

"Tadias[37] Ashebir, Al-hamdulillah, Praise Allah. How are you today?" Yishaereg's mother looked up from her work.

He had forgotten to greet them properly. "Al-hamdulillah, Praise Allah," he said. "I am fine. How are you today?"

"We are fine Ashebir, praise Allah. And how is your mother?"

"She is fine too," he replied and waited.

Yishaereg was filling a bag with the yellow-white powdery flour.

"Hello Yishaereg, how are you?" he tried to get her attention.

"Hello Ashebir," Yishaereg looked up. "The pots are alright. I brought them inside last night. My mother said she thought it might rain."

"Where are they?" he asked.

"I put them out in the sun this morning. Over there," she pointed. "They should be ready tomorrow."

He looked and could see them neatly laid out on a metal tray in the sun. He was relieved. He stood squelching the mud under his feet. It gave him a nice warm feeling as it oozed up between his toes. He could smell the smoke trailing on the wind from his mother's fire.

"Zewdie is making injera to take to the market," he said, still looking at his toes.

"U-huh," Yishaereg's mother replied, already back to her grinding, making a scratch, scrape, scratch noise interspersed by her occasional grunts.

The air smelt sweet after the rain. He noticed the bright yellow flowers on Yishaereg's fence. They had appeared as if by magic. They reminded him of the little birds he had seen the day before and wondered where they had gone with their song and their stories. God did wonderful things with the rain. He was tempted to pick a flower for Zewdie on the way home. He would see if some were growing on the other side. Everything looked so bright and clean, the colours in the bushes and the trees, the sky more blue than ever. He squelched his toes some more.

"Maybe we can play tomorrow, Ashebir?" Yishaereg said, holding the half-filled bag by her feet.

"Maybe," he said. "I have to go home now," he said, not knowing what else to do.

He went through the gap in the fence and looked to see if there were

---

[37] Hello there.

any yellow flowers on the other side. He picked one and walked the short distance to his house curling his toes into the mud with every step.

"Zewdie, look what I bought for you," he said holding the small flower out to her.

"Egziyabheresteling," she said. "Thanks to God, I have a good boy. You have brought some light into our little home." She smiled, taking the flower and smelling it.

Her eyes were red from working over the fire. The room full of smoke.

She got up and put the flower in a small dish of water. "That way it will last longer," she said, and went back to sit on her wooden stool at the edge of the fire. She turned the large round injera over to cook on the other side.

**

A week or so later Mohamed Bilal from Albuko came with two goats for Zewdie. He brought them on a rope, trotting on their hard thin legs. They were bleating loudly with their tongues out, straining necks here and there to find something to eat.

Ashebir thought they were the most beautiful goats he had ever seen.

"A mama goat and a papa goat," Zewdie said, smiling proudly. "They will have lots of babies, and the babies will have babies. Then we will have a real herd, Egzhabir si feked."

Ashebir stroked their noses and brought hay and water for them. They kept them behind the house for the first few days in the beret enclosure they had built for them, so they would get used to their new home, Zewdie told him. He loved the strong smell of the animals in their compound and the life they brought.

**

The morning came for his first outing with the new goats. Zewdie had also given him the task of fetching fresh drinking water in their small yellow jerry can. He was by the river with Mohamed Abdu, Ali, Aminat, Yishaereg and her two small brothers. The girls were with the women and older girls, scrubbing clothes with soap against the rocks with small jerky movements, and rinsing them out again. He could hear the swoosh of water as they lifted the clothes out of the stream, and the slap as they tossed them back in again. The two small boys were splashing in the water. They ran after each other along the bank, not too far, then returning to their places in the shallows. All they seemed to do was play. Ashebir was upstream from the girls, digging for water in the sand with Ali, Yishaereg's older brother.

"Stop looking round and dig a bit deeper, Ashebir," Ali was saying.

"I need to check on my goats, Ali," Ashebir said. Seeing them nearby, he turned back to his digging. "There, it's coming now," he said. "I'll just dig a little more." His tongue was sticking out with concentration. He made little grunts as he dug. Hearing a little grunt by his side each time he grunted he glanced up.

Ali was crouched next to him, grunting, his tongue sticking out.

Ashebir giggled and pushed Ali playfully on the shoulder.

Ali fell over backwards, his legs scrambling in the air like a beetle on its back.

"Come on, Ali. We'll never be done," Ashebir said, pulling his friend up again, both laughing. They took a deep breath and started digging again.

As they dug deeper, a pool of fresh water gradually appeared. Ashebir pulled the jerry can closer. He scooped the water up with the cup Zewdie had given him, careful not to collect too much sand. He poured the water into the can, one scoop after the next until the pool was empty. They dug in the sand once again, until there was another pool of fresh water. Ashebir and Ali took turns scooping and digging until the jerry can was full. When they were done, Ashebir got a handful of dry grass, twisted it and stuck it in the top of the jerry can. His mother had shown him how to do that. "To stop dirt from dropping in, Ashebir," she told him. He was proud to remember it even if she wasn't there.

Zewdie had gone to Tulu Market early that morning with Temima and Ali and Yishaereg's mother to sell potatoes and onions. Each carried a heavy load in large baskets strapped to their backs, each with an umbrella to open out against the burning sun. It was a long walk.

"Look at the cows and oxen peeing in the water up there," Ali said, pointing behind them. "I don't like drinking that." He pulled a face.

"This water is much better," Ashebir said.

Though they all knew not to drink the water straight from the river they all did. Sometimes when he felt too lazy to dig in the sand and he was thirsty, Ashebir dipped his t-shirt into the river, filled it with water and sieved it through into his cupped hand underneath to drink. But if he was taking water home for Zewdie he had to make sure it was clean. Sometimes they did just hold the insera or jerry can in the flow of the current and let the river fill the container. It was faster.

Ashebir looked around for his goats. He spotted them with Mohamed Abdu's. They were scrambling along the riverbank, reaching into trees and bushes with their front legs, their necks straining to eat anything, leaves, dried grass, pods, anything.

Mohamed Abdu was perched on a rock further up the river. He was watching the cows taking a long drink and dropping twigs in the water that flowed downstream. Every now and then, Mohamed Abdu shouted over to them, "Look out there's another one coming."

"We're finished," Ashebir called and ran with Ali to join him. They rounded up the goats on the way and drove them towards the river.

"They can do with a drink too," Ashebir said, feeling proud.

When Zewdie was not there he thought of them as his goats. He was happy that he could now bring his own animals to the river, and take his own animals up into the mountains with the boys. Zewdie had said she would soon be able to pay off her, 'little by little' loan for the goats, and then she would start saving for an ox.

They took off their clothes, leaving a pile on the bank, and jumped into the water. It was fresh and deep enough to duck under and kick legs. Ashebir loved being in the water. He walked on his hands over the pebbles kicking his feet out behind him. He ducked his face under, opening his eyes to see if he could spot any fish. He saw Mohamed Abdu's foot and grabbed it.

Mohamed Abdu made a loud noise and jumped in the air with his arms up, splashing down on top of Ashebir again.

"We are flying fish," Ashebir shouted, leaping up. All three flew in and out of the water, their arms spread wide as they surfaced, jumping up as high as they could, before diving and splashing down into the cool clear water again.

Finally, exhausted and out of breath, one by one they crawled out of the water and lay on the shore to dry. Ashebir shuffled himself into the pebbles and sand, lying with his arms outstretched wanting to feel the heat of the sun all over his body. With his eyes closed, he could hear the river running by and the distant voices of the girls further downstream, and the deeper voices of the women. There were several people there by now, washing. He could hear the hard slap-slap of clothes against the rocks. He tried to see what he could see with his eyes shut. It was black and maybe a bit red. Was that his blood running through his head he wondered?

"You know what?" Mohamed Abdu was saying, "My Qur'an teacher is really mean."

Ashebir opened an eye and looked at his friend. He rolled over onto his belly. "Why? What does he do?"

"He hits us with a stick if we talk," Mohamed Abdu said. "Or if we get something wrong."

"Does he hit you on your buttocks?" Ali said, giggling. Ali was always finding something to giggle about.

"No, crazy Ali. But he would hit you on your buttocks – if he could find one," Mohamed Abdu said.

"I've got two buttocks," Ali shouted, laughing. He jumped up, turning his back on his friends. "See. I've got two buttocks." Then he ran off up the bank.

Ashebir watched him, laughing. Ali could never keep still.

"Look at him. Skinny buttocks," Mohamed Abdu laughed. He got up and chased after Ali. "Where are your buttocks?"

Ashebir jumped up to join in the chase, laughing in an excitement that was more theirs than his. In the back of his mind, he wondered where the Qur'an teacher hit Mohamed Abdu, and if he would hit him there too.

They tumbled and ran along the bank for a while and finally went back to their clothes.

"Let's see what the girls are doing?" Ashebir suggested.

They pulled on their clothes and checked on the animals. Rounding them up, they drew them in closer, and returned to where the girls were now busy playing.

"They are making a village," Ali cried out.

"Shall we go and help them?" Ashebir said, already running up to the girls.

"Mohamed Abdu, are you coming?" Ali called out.

Ashebir and Ali stood nearby, watching for a while. Mohamed Abdu came up behind them out of breath.

Yishaereg looked up, shading her eyes against the sun. "Come and make your houses near ours," she said.

"Yes come," Aminat said, jumping up and walking around the two gojo-bate she and Yishaereg had already made, clapping her hands to dust off the soil.

Ashebir liked Mohamed Abdu's younger sister, Aminat. She had lively eyes and a round friendly face, and strong arms, like Mohamed Abdu. So he sat near her. He dug his foot into the soft grey sand, moving it back and forth into position. Then he piled the sand up over his foot in a mound. Ali sat with his back to Ashebir and did the same.

"I'll make my house here," Mohamed Abdu said, sitting a little further away.

"We three will be neighbours," Ashebir said chuckling, not taking his eyes off what he was doing. He patted the mound of sand flat and hard all round his foot. He drew it up into a cone shape just like his own gojo-bate, patting it on all sides with the flats of his hands. Then slowly, concentrating hard so it would not collapse, he withdrew his foot leaving a dark rounded hole where his foot had been. It was the entrance to his little house. "Look, mine's done." He turned round to see how Ali and Mohamed were doing.

They were still piling on the sand, patting it into shape. Then just like Ashebir they slowly pulled their feet out from under the sand, each leaving a gojo-bate shaped dwelling with a dark entrance.

Ashebir carried on, carefully patting the outside of his house with the flat of his hand and shaping the front door with his fingers. He looked up. Aminat was standing behind him, watching.

"Do you want grass for the roof?" she asked

"Yes, get some for all of us, Aminat," Mohamed Abdu said. "We have to make our beret for the animals now."

"Where are my goats?" Ashebir looked up, with a shot of fear in his belly, his eyes searching the banks of the river and the path beyond.

"They are over there with the others," Mohamed Abdu pointed. "See?"

"Oh yes," he said, his head dropped onto his chest. He let out an involuntary sigh. He looked around at the others. He felt silly. But they were busy with their house building and Aminat had gone to look for grasses to thatch their roofs. "Ishi, let me see," he said, to distract himself from his naivety. He built a small fence around his gojo-bate, making it into a real compound.

"Yours is the house of a real habtam,[38] Ashebir." Ali said, looking over at Ashebir's work. "We are not as rich as you. Look at my small compound."

"I am Mohamed Bilal from Albuko," Ashebir said proudly in a deep voice. "I have so many cows and a lot of land, so my compound has to be big."

The others pushed him, laughing.

"Watch it!" Ashebir shrieked. "I nearly fell into my house."

Aminat came back with a bundle of dried grasses in her arms.

"That's too much, Aminat." Mohamed Abdu said.

---

[38] Rich person.

"No, it's good," Ali chided him. "Aminat we can use it for our animal feed."

"Ishi," she said, frowning at her brother. She laid the pile between the boys' houses and wiped her hands down her long skirt.

Ashebir took strands of Aminat's grass and broke off tiny, tiny pieces. He had made a small raised square of sand in the back of his compound for a vegetable patch. He stuck the tiny pieces of grass into the sand in neat rows.

"Look at my bokolo," he said, nudging his friend. "Ali, look at my maize stands."

"Is that maize you are growing?" Ali laughed. "Mohamed Abdu, we will have to eat at Mohamed Bilal's house from now on."

Ashebir worked the sand between his fingers to make an enclosure inside his compound for his animals.

"My house is finished," Ali announced.

"Mine is done too. Let's play now," Mohamed Abdu said.

"We need animals," Ashebir said. He went to where the trees hung over the shore and he knew he could find pods and leaves. He collected handfuls of them and brought them back to his friends. They divided them up between them.

Ashebir placed six pods inside his animal enclosure and broke off pieces of Aminat's grass to lay inside the enclosure for his cows to eat.

"I am taking my cows out to the pasture," Mohamed Abdu said in a singing voice. "Is anyone coming?" He had a pod in between his fingers and hopped it out of the entrance to his compound. He walked his fingers back and got another cow and another.

"I'm coming," Ashebir called out.

"So am I," said Ali.

They played with their animals, taking them to the pastures and back to their enclosures. Ashebir felt it was all so real, that he really was the rich Mohamed Bilal from Albuko.

Ali got up and looked over at the girls. "What are you doing?" he asked them.

"We are having supper. Do you want to join us?" Yishaereg said, waving her fingers to come.

"You've got the plates and cups we made?" Ashebir said, getting up. He left his cows unattended and went over to the girls.

Mohamed Abdu and Ali followed.

"Can we eat with you?" Ashebir asked. He had forgotten about food. Now he felt very hungry, but he had nothing to eat with him that day.

Zewdie had said they would eat injera and sherro wot in the evening. This was play eating but maybe his stomach would think it had had something and stop biting him inside. He looked up and checked around for the animals again. They were all in a stretch of pasture not far from the river.

"I will just go and round them up, so they don't stray too far," Mohamed Abdu said.

"I'll come too," Ashebir said, running alongside his friend.

"When you have finished come and eat," he could hear Yishaereg calling out behind them.

Ashebir saw his two goats. They seemed to stay close to each other. He ran over to them shooing them closer to Mohamed Abdu's sheep and goats.

"That will be alright. We will come again after a while," Mohamed Abdu said.

"Ishi," Ashebir said. "Let's go back to the others and play."

Yishaereg was setting out the small clay plates. Aminat put a leaf onto each one. Yishaereg had made a pile of tiny twigs to look like a fire and was mixing some sand and water together in a tin pot using another twig to stir.

"The wot[39] will be ready in a minute," she said.

"Mmmm, your sherro wot smells good Emayey," Ali said, giggling and nudging Ashebir. They were sitting on their haunches together, near Yishaereg.

"Make sure you wash hands children," she said. "Then we can eat."

Aminat and the boys pretended to wash hands nearby and came back wiping them dry on their clothes.

"Ababa, you can eat first," Yishaereg said, looking at Ashebir, "and then the boys, and then you and I will eat, Aminat."

He felt shy suddenly in front of his friends. It was alright the other day when they had not been there.

"You the Ababa?" Ali laughed, knocking Ashebir over.

"You behave," Yishaereg said in a stern voice, looking directly at Ali.

"Yes, Emayey, sorry Emayey," Ali said, trying to hide his giggles behind his hand.

But Yishaereg had been so serious that even Ashebir felt afraid of her.

"So, eat Ababa, you have been working hard all day," Yishaereg continued, putting a little bit of the water and sand sherro wot on his

---

[39] Hot spicy sauce to eat with injera.

plate. "Eat children," she said, putting some on Ali and Mohamed Abdu's plates.

The boys bowed their heads and said, "Bismillah, in the name of Allah," and started eating.

Ashebir took the leaf and, pretending to put food in his mouth, made munching noises and said how good the food tasted. His stomach was even hungrier now.

"The animals," Mohamed Abdu suddenly jumped up. He looked over to the pasture beside the river. The goats and sheep were gone.

Ashebir jumped up, looking everywhere. Fear in his belly. "Where are they?" he said. "Mohamed Abdu, they're gone."

"Maybe they've run into the field on the other side of the path," Mohamed Abdu shouted. He was already running across the pebbled riverbank and onto the pathway. Ashebir ran after him, hoping they had not gone far.

The animals were not on the pathway, or in the pasture beyond it.

Ashebir ran after Mohamed Abdu up to the brow of the hill where the path met the bridge and the road. The road stretched quiet and empty. It was so still he could hear the river bubbling under the bridge and across the stones to the fields on the other side. The river water ran narrow and the banks wide. He hoped it would rain again soon to fill the river so they could jump off the higher rocks. It was still too shallow for that.

They heard the sound of goats bleating. The garbled coughing noise which Ali could imitate so well.

"It that Ali or the goats?" Ashebir called over to Mohamed Abdu.

"It's the goats. I can see them. They're over here," Mohamed Abdu called back. He was on the other side of the road.

Ashebir ran across to help round them up. They each had a stick in hand and every now and then bent to pick a pebble to throw at their rumps. That always made the goat's hide shiver in a funny way.

They ran with the goats back across the road.

"We should start going home now, don't you think?" Mohamed Abdu said.

When they got back down to the riverbank, the girls were helping the women collect up the dry clothes, folding them into small plastic bowls. Ashebir fetched his yellow jerry can.

"Hey!" he shouted over to Yishaereg's little brothers. "That's our village you are destroying." The two boys were jumping up and down all over the little houses which had looked like a tiny village on a hill of grey sand. They were giggling and having such a good time. Ashebir was surprised they were not tired and hungry like he was, especially the smaller one with his round swollen belly. Zewdie always said it was worms or hunger that made it swell. He lifted the yellow jerry can onto his head holding it in place with one hand, his stick in the other.

"Let's go," he called out to his friends. He was anxious to get home and eat.

They were rounding up the animals, driving them onto the path.

Yishaereg and Aminat were calling the little boys, telling them they were leaving and they better be quick or they would be left behind to the hyenas. Ashebir watched as the girls lifted the plastic bowls full of clothes onto their heads. He headed towards them and onto the path checking that his two goats were there amongst the others.

This was a good time of day. Ashebir enjoyed belonging and hearing the swishing movement and snuffling of the animals as they were driven slowly up the path homewards.

5

She was on her way to join Moe in a country she knew surprisingly little about. Her grandmother had asked, "What on earth is Izzie going to Abyssinia for?"

She had spent four hours in the departure lounge in Moscow, when finally the announcement came for her flight to Addis Ababa. Boarding the plane, she was directed by the air hostess to an empty seat between two large men. The passenger in the seat behind hers looked uncomfortable, his seat far too small for his bulk. Izzie normally preferred the aisle seat, but there was no discussing with the stewardess, so she did what she was told.

She wedged herself in between two large Russians, her feet resting on her hand luggage. They greeted her warmly, trying out barely recognisable words of English, offering shots of vodka and unfiltered cigarettes. They were flying out to join their ship in Aden, they said. Coughing heavily when they chuckled, they reminded her of Great Uncle Sid, who always had a Players hanging off his bottom lip. Izzie was captivated by their simplicity. So this was the enemy from behind the Iron Curtain, the 'reds under the beds'. They seemed harmless enough to her.

She was so hungry that she ate the in-flight meal; sourdough bread, a slab of meat and pickled apples. It was only then that she understood how essential the vodka and thick black coffee were to get the food down.

No sooner were the trays cleared than the lights were dimmed. The stewardess, her hair thin and greying, her face pinched into a look of permanent contempt, prowled up and down the aisle like a school matron at lights-out. She was a far cry from the youthful BOAC hostesses, offering kind words, smiles and baskets of brightly coloured boiled sweets at take-off.

One by one, the men around Izzie fell asleep. The broad knees of the sailor behind her dug into her back through the cloth. She looked around. He had squeezed his huge frame into the tight space available to him. They exchanged apologetic smiles and she resigned herself to an uncomfortable night.

It was not such a big price to pay. She was finally on her way to Moe and Africa, and too excited to sleep anyway. She'd met Moe four years ago; that Christmas when she and Sam had travelled from Lilongwe northwards through Malawi, visiting volunteers. Moe's post had been further north, near the lake. She closed her eyes.

The fisheries office in Nkotakota where he worked was a typical, one-storey, colonial bungalow. The doors opened onto a long, covered veranda, with bougainvillea dripping from the corrugated iron roof in showers of burgundy, pink and orange.

Sam had pulled the Land Rover to a halt on the dirt road outside and switched the rumbling engine off. The sound of a panga, slicing through grass, resonated in the stillness of the heat. Izzie and Sam had climbed down from the vehicle into the hot sun; their clothes, hair and nostrils sticky with dust and sweat. Two chubby mkwanga trees stood like sentinels at the top of the dirt path leading to the offices.

Moe had come round the desk, a broad grin on his sun-tanned face and shaken her hand. His sandy-coloured hair was an unruly mess for someone living in a country whose laws stipulated the length of men's hair and women's skirts; behind the ear and below the knee, respectively. He wore the post-colonial garb; short-sleeved starch-pressed white shirt, khaki shorts and desert boots. There was a sparkle of mischief in his blue eyes and Izzie had greeted him more eagerly than perhaps she should have.

Meeting his eyes had caused an unexpected inner flurry and confusion. She had distracted herself by looking round his office until her eyes landed on the obligatory photo of The Ngwasi Dr Hastings Kamuzu Banda. It hung on the wall behind Moe's desk. She focussed on the white handkerchief sticking out of the top pocket of his three-piece suit. It also looked as if it had been starch-pressed. The President's eyes stared down at her, benevolently it seemed.

Moe had given Sam a bear hug. "How are you, buddy?" he'd said, laughing. "Good to see you."

There was a loud crack a few seats down from hers in the dim cabin. Izzie looked up and watched incredulous as one particularly large fellow's seat collapsed beneath him onto the knees of the sailor behind. Neither woke up. The air hostess looked at them for a moment, before continuing up the aisle and disappearing behind a thick grey cloth curtain. The two men spent the rest of the flight like that, oblivious.

Izzie managed to catch the woman's attention for a glass of water. She sat sipping it, convinced it was laced with vodka. She wriggled to get as comfortable as she could, leant her head back against the seat and closed her eyes again.

That evening Moe had taken them to a roadside bar. A small shack with a low ceiling and dirt floor, in a row of others. They'd sat outside on low stools, drinking bottled beer, Greens. Two Dutch dentists, working at the local hospital instead of doing military service back home, and two of Moe's Malawian friends, had joined them; one a jovial truck driver, the other a local police constable.

She had felt unusually happy and Sam had been relaxed. It was a warm, balmy evening, the sky a deep dark red as the sun went down. She remembered the crickets singing over and over in the dry scrub, an evocative sound, reminiscent of summer cookouts in New Jersey. A line of women and children walked up the dirt road. They were carrying bundles, water pots, or a hoe balanced on their heads, babies on their backs. The men urged their cattle and goats homewards, with low guttural noises, and an occasional crack of switch against hide. An idyllic scene to the foreigner's eye, with surely another reality to tell in those bare-footed, cracked soles. What if I were to walk some way with you, she'd wondered.

The sailor on her right fidgeted in his sleep. When he settled, he was even closer to her than before, breathing out a pungent smell of sleep, vodka and dark tobacco. It was foul. Izzie used her shoulder to carefully manoeuvre him away, not wanting to touch or wake him. To her surprise he turned like a child, his head flopping to rest against the wall of the cabin between the windows.

The smell of stale alcohol which hung in the cabin air reminded her of the strong, pervasive smell of Chibuku. A group of men had been sitting on wooden crates outside the bar drinking the local brew made from fermented maize. It seemed to hang in the sweat of the men who drank it, like the vodka in this sailor's shirt.

Someone in the bar had put on soukous music. A single yellow bulb had come on, attracting an assortment of winged creatures which fluttered aimlessly around it, producing a flickering, eerie light. The home-goers had become shadows on the road, soft voices with shuffling feet and hooves clicking against stones in the dirt. That night the sky had been perfect, an infinite blue-black canopy, ablaze with stars.

Izzie bent down to feel around in her bag for her Walkman. It was difficult to see in the half dark of the cabin and the overhead light didn't work. Finally, she found it and her Malawian soukous cassette. The rhythm always got under her skin. It was impossible to sit still. She moved to the music in her seat, almost imperceptibly, not wanting any of her neighbours to wake.

There had been a bar girl dancing with an older man that night, gyrating her hips and brushing up against him. She was wearing a long green chitenji wrap around her waist. It was covered in black and white photos of the president, Kamuzu Banda. Izzie remembered thinking the girl had surely adjusted the cloth to wear his face across her backside on purpose.

Izzie had wanted to dance too.

"I don't feel like dancing," Sam had said, sitting back and pulling on a joint one of the Dutch guys had just passed him. He was engrossed in the dentists' stories. "Hope we don't get toothache while we're here, darling," he had said, laughing.

He was a loveable fellow. She had known him for years, but she had never got used to him calling her 'darling'. It had started after they got married. It made them sound middle-aged when she still felt like a student.

"Sam Brown," she had said. "I wish you would dance with me even once in a blue moon." She had leant over and kissed him, "and just look at that sky. It's the perfect moment." She had looked up. It was absolutely magical.

"Come on then," Moe had said. As he got up, he put a hand on her shoulder. "Let's go dance."

His touch sent a shiver through her. She knew then that she had to be careful.

"I'll have a beer waiting for you when you get back, darling," Sam had said. "Have fun."

He had been so damn innocent, she thought, lighting a cigarette. She breathed in and blew a stream of smoke softly towards the broken overhead light. She took the earplugs out and listened to the low drone of the airplane engines while she smoked. Flying could be interminable. She stubbed out her cigarette into the small ashtray in the armrest. At least on other airlines, there would have been a film. She closed her eyes again.

She had followed Moe into the bar. It was packed with people dancing, rhythmic, sensual, exuberant. Malawians, young and old, had music in their souls, and especially in their buttocks. She had never seen people dance like that before. Impressive, she thought. Moe was not a bad dancer either. They had laughed into each other's eyes and danced until she felt the sweat trickle down her back. The music filled her belly and vibrated through her body, feeling the rhythm in sync with others around her. The smell of beer, hot breath and cigarette smoke filled the air. There was laughter, appreciation, encouragement and a rawness in the intimate space. Finally, she'd motioned to him to go outside, her throat dry. As they went through the narrow door, he'd brushed his hand against hers for a moment too long. She did not dare look at him as they walked back to the others, sitting under the open sky.

She'd gone to sit with Sam, nudging him softly. She had taken a long drink of the cold beer he passed her.

"You look good," Sam had said, putting an arm around her. "Real good."

"I love the music and the way you guys dance," she had said, nodding at the truck driver, who was boogying to the music in his seat. He had chuckled and raised his bottle towards her. "I saw you," he'd said. "You dance too fine, zikomo kwambiri.[40]"

Izzie heard the click of hooves against stones, loud cracking whips, the guttural noises of the men following their cattle home, and the chinking of beer bottles. Her mouth was dry and she was stiff from the journey. It had been a long drive. She wondered where they had left the Land Rover and where they would sleep that night. Sam was nowhere to be seen.

She opened her eyes. She must have fallen asleep after all, Izzie thought, her ears popping uncomfortably. The air hostess was scolding the passengers into upright positions and collecting empty vodka bottles, giving orders left and right as she went. She ignored the two sailors, who still lay one seat on top of the other, snoring heavily.

They were beginning the descent into Addis Ababa. She leant across her neighbour to take a look out of the window, smiling at him apologetically and holding her breath against the muggy smell that hung about him. She caught a glimpse of the city below, glinting in the sun, surrounded by mountains under blue sky. She started to collect her things together. She wanted to be down in that city with Moe. She would be ready to get off as soon as the air hostess gave the signal.

**

---

[40] Thank you very much (Chichewa).

The arrivals hall was functional in shades of grey, magnolia and pale green. A curious odour of moth balls and spices hung in the air. A man in overalls pushed a wide brush across the floor, a dirty grey cloth wrapped round its bristles, his large pail of water stood in the middle of the concourse.

The luggage belt, worn through in places, lay still; porters sat round the edge, chatting. Above them a banner read: Workers of the World Unite!

Moe would be waiting on the other side. She could not wait to be in his arms and felt a rush of excitement. Stuffing her passport and vaccination certificate back into her handbag, Izzie moved to where she could see her case when it came. A high-pitched whine burst from a tannoy bolted onto the wall, followed by a garbled announcement. No one seemed to take any notice. Izzie looked on in anticipation as the luggage carrier cranked up, clunking and rattling. A thick black rubber flap slapped loudly back in place each time a piece of baggage came in from outside. Izzie stared at it, willing her green case to appear. Vodka boxes tied with string, suitcases and battered zip-ups went past. She watched a square-headed man move forward. He wore a dull suit and looked just like the official checking passports from inside the glass box at Moscow airport. He had stared at her so long that she'd doubted her own identity. The man's porter lifted two large cases off the belt and put them on a trolley under his instruction. She watched him walk straight through customs and wondered if he was KGB. The porter struggled behind, the trolley's wheels rotating in different directions.

A handful of Europeans, dishevelled after the flight, faces weathered red by the sun, stood around waiting. Some wore the trademark safari jacket, with countless button-down pockets for wallets, sunglasses, pens, notepads and insect repellent. They must be working for NGOs, she thought. Diplomats and UN staff would never fly Aeroflot. Izzie tried not to catch their eyes, wanting to hold on to the anonymity of the arrival hall a little longer. She did not want to get drawn into conversation with anyone. Departures and Arrivals were sanctuaries from the demands of others. They provided a space between worlds where she was nameless and answerable to no one. She could not be contacted, corrected, or apprehended. The first person to break the spell would be Moe.

Her body ached from sitting so long. She rummaged in her bag for a cigarette and lit it. She had been counting the weeks, the days, to get there. And now here she was, within minutes of seeing him, and the wait felt like an eternity. She hoped she had made the right decision, that he really did want her to come. The few letters he'd written had been sweet and loving, if a little distant. He missed her, the flat was wonderful with beautiful views over the city; she would love the birds in the acacia trees by a lake somewhere south of Addis Ababa. She could not remember the name. He had not said much about the country, his job, or friends.

There were no more cases coming through from outside. Maybe they had gone to off-load more from the plane. There was a small window with a Foreign Exchange sign above it. A poster of a country boy with long locks of hair and a grin on his face hung on the wall. 'Thirteen Months of Sunshine,' it said across the bottom. She walked over to change some money, wondering where the extra month came from.

A woman with dark, oval eyes smiled at her from behind the glass. "How much do you want to change?" she said, pulling a pad towards her and slipping a sheet of dark blue carbon paper under the top page.

"Fifty dollars, please."

Izzie watched the woman's fingers, her long nails a deep red, as she wrote the amount, the exchange rate, tapped numbers on a large calculator and filled a box with more numbers. She made form-filling look like an art.

"Your passport, please," she said, barely looking up. She took the passport and wrote down Izzie's place and date of birth, passport number and full name, "Izzie Brown," she said. "You were born in London? My brother is there."

"Really?" Izzie said. "What is he doing there?"

The woman looked down at the papers, giving an almost imperceptible shrug. She stamped the form, tore the top layer off, counted a bundle of Ethiopian Birr with impressive speed and pushed the form and the wad of notes through the hole under the glass window. "Enjoy our country," she said. She lay one hand on top of the other, looked at Izzie and smiled.

"Thank you," Izzie said, thinking the woman looked resigned. "I hope so."

By now most people were in the customs queue. A few women pushed bulging bags and cheap suitcases along the floor with their feet. They must be traders. What on earth had they found to bring back from Moscow? She could only imagine what Russia had to offer: desolation; women, wrapped in dark shawls against the cold, standing in line for bread; frostbite and the misery of the labour camps Solzhenitsyn described in his books?

At the front of each customs queue, Ethiopian officials stood over bags and suitcases, searching. Izzie looked at the hold-all between her feet. She did not think there was anything they would be looking for in there or in her handbag, no banned authors. When it was her turn, she decided, she would get in the queue with the woman official. It was better than having a man go through her things.

The same bag and two boxes had been going round for a while. A dark-haired woman in uniform sat behind a desk under an Aeroflot sign. She had the pale, flaccid look Izzie had begun to associate with Russian officialdom. A large photograph of an African in army uniform hung on the wall behind her. His round face did not look unpleasant, though there was something disturbing in his staring eyes. It must be Mengistu. Izzie was not sure if he called himself Prime Minister or President. She went over to the Aeroflot desk. "Is there any more luggage?"

The woman looked up at Izzie, frowning. "No more," she said. "Put name here." She pushed a pad across the desk.

"That's not possible," Izzie said in disbelief. Everything was in it. Her clothes, jewellery, her books, photographs, the lovely one of her and Kate in Edinburgh. She had carefully picked the things she wanted to take and packed every square inch of the suitcase neat and tight. Years of school trunk practice. And now it was all gone, and this woman was clueless. Izzie turned away and blew her nose. The hanky still smelt of Yves Saint Laurent.

"Treat yourself in Duty Free," her mother had said at Heathrow, her lower lip wobbling. She wouldn't cry. Not until later. "Something special from me."

Izzie had liked the look of the tall, sky-blue canister with its black and silver stripes. She had sprayed a little onto her hanky to try it out. Rive Gauche, a rich, sensual smell. So she bought it.

"What have you done with my case?" she said, turning back to the woman.

"I not know," the woman said. "Maybe Moscow, maybe somewhere. Another place."

"Can't you go and check? Ask someone?" Izzie said, feeling the anger and panic in her stomach. She stuffed the hanky back in her pocket.

"Fill form," the woman said, pushing the pad at Izzie again.

Izzie looked at it, English and Russian. "Did you leave it behind in Moscow? I knew I should have checked." She took the pen and started writing.

"You come office. Tomorrow," the woman said. "You keep." She handed Izzie a pink copy, the bottom one with the faintest writing. "Tree-plicat," the woman said, as if the bureaucracy somehow satisfied her.

Izzie lifted her hold-all over one shoulder and her handbag, always too full and heavy, over the other, an empty feeling inside. She wanted to get out of the baggage hall, find Moe. She walked towards the large 'Customs' sign, looking down at her blue and white striped trousers and maroon Converse boots. She was glad that at least she had put one change of clothing in her hand luggage.

**

Izzie saw him. He was tanned and wearing jeans, his worn-old desert boots, and a crisp, white, freshly-ironed shirt, rolled up at the sleeves. He had obviously found himself a maid. There was something raw and irritatingly attractive about him. Young and white in Africa. They had it so good.

"Moe," she called out.

He was talking to a tall, spindly, dark-haired man, who looked vaguely familiar.

Shit, she thought. But she could have guessed. In Africa, the airport was like the local train station. Bumping into someone you knew was almost inevitable. "Moe!" she called again.

He looked up and came towards her, smiling. She dropped the hold-all and bowled into him, burying her face in his chest, loving the feel of his arms around her, breathing him in. Knickerbocker Glory on a sunny day.

He pushed her gently back. "Hey, let me look at you," he said, laughing.

"I look a wreck." She hoped she did not reek of vodka, pickled apples and the damp Aeroflot seats, the sweaty Russian-sailor smell.

"You look great," he said, "just need a bit of sunshine that's all. And there's plenty of that here." He picked her hold-all off the ground. "Is this all you brought, honey?"

"They've lost my case," she said.

"I wondered what kept you," he said. "Not surprising though. There are thousands of bags in Moscow."

"Really? You could have warned me."

"I thought you'd know."

"You think I'll get it back?" she said, her voice choking. She took a deep breath. "I packed all my precious things in it."

"Maybe you'll be lucky, maybe." He squeezed her hand and turned to the man behind them. "Izzie, this is Booker Keyes."

"Hello Izzie," Booker said.

She didn't like the way he looked her over. "Hello," she said, running her fingers through her hair and trying to remember where she had seen him. His grey eyes were edged with sunshine wrinkles giving him a look of permanent amusement. She took his hand. It was reassuringly firm.

"Another Aeroflot victim?" he said, grinning.

"Looks that way," she said. "I didn't know they were infamous for stealing people's luggage."

"Not stolen, 'redistributed'," Booker said, using his long fingers to emphasise the word. Everything clearly vanished into thin air, like so many birds flying away. "Welcome to Marxist theory in practice."

"Booker thinks you've met," Moe said. "He was in Lilongwe for a couple of years."

"At some cocktail do or other, probably," Booker said. "Or at the Club?"

She smiled, remembering how she had refused to return to the 'Golf Club' in Lilongwe after the first visit. It was whites only. And those 'do's', she had either avoided going, or turned up stoned ending the evening laughing hysterically or passing out. She had only known a few people in the ex-pat community well. "Maybe," she said, not keen to chat for longer than necessary. She wanted to get out of the airport. Be with Moe.

"Booker and I work in the same building. He's also with the Agric and Food Institute," Moe said.

Izzie nodded, trying to look impressed.

"You'll want to get going," Booker said. "See you tonight at the rehearsal, Moe." He walked away with a wave. "Good to have you here, Izzie. Welcome."

Moe hitched her hold-all onto his shoulder.

"What was that about a rehearsal?" Izzie said.

"All in good time," Moe took her hand. "Let's get out of here."

"That's a good idea," Izzie said, happy to be swept away.

Glass doors stood between them and the blue sky. The sun was warming up the early morning air, a welcome change from the endless damp chill and dark evenings in London. Dazzling pools of light reflected off car windows. She raised her face to the sun and closed her eyes, breathing in deeply. She'd made it. She put her sunglasses on.

"Here we are," he said, pointing to a pale blue Citroen 2CV.

"Wow. Is it yours?" She had hitched a ride in a 2CV once, somewhere between Toulouse and Perpignan one student-days summer. She loved their large headlamps, and the tarpaulin roof that rolled back like the lid of a sardine tin with its metal key.

"Ours," he said.

She gave him a kiss. "Let's get home," she whispered in his ear.

He ran a hand over his sandy hair and pulled a long face. "I have to be in the office by 10.30."

"You're joking, Moe."

"I have to finish a food aid report. I already nearly missed the deadline," he said, putting her bag in the boot. "There's time for a coffee though, OK?"

"OK, OK," she said, climbing in and shutting the door with a hollow clunk.

He got in behind the wheel. "I'm really sorry, honey," he said. "I'll work real fast, there is not much more to do on it." He kissed her gently.

"Coffee is a good idea," she said, glad she had her sunglasses on, to hide her disappointment. She had imagined them having breakfast in the flat with the panoramic views, making love, chilling out the whole day and into the night. "Food aid report. I can't compete with that."

Moe ruffled her hair and turned the key. The engine started up, a low rumble, like the tumble dryers in Mrs. Shah's Laundrette on Dalston Lane.

Moe pushed a cassette into the player, Bob Marley, and drew slowly out of the parking lot, following a line of blue and white taxis.

"I can't believe my suitcase is probably on its way to a Russian warship. They'll eat all the chocolate I brought you."

He laughed. "Shuffle over, don't sit so far away."

She leant against him, kissing his shoulder. "You sure you have to go to work?

Of course you do," she said all in one breath.

"I'm sure. Not happy about it, but sure, honey."

"I'll keep myself busy," she said. The idea of being alone in the flat, without even a suitcase to unpack, was not appealing. "Oh shit. My batiks were in the case."

"Sorry, sorry, sorry," Moe said. "What a bugger."

She needed some air and undid the catch on the window.

"Just flip it to the outside," he said.

She flicked the window up and it clicked in place. She turned the music up. "I can't believe Bob Marley died. It's nearly a year."

"He's really popular here," Moe said. "Haile Selassie's name was Ras Tafari before he became Emperor, you know? He gave the Rastas some land in a place called Shashamene. It's supposed to be beautiful. We'll go. It's south of Addis."

"I'd love to go." She kissed his cheek and ran her fingers over his shaggy blonde locks. She looked at him. It was good to see him.

They drove along a wide road fringed with three-storey flats, interspersed with shacks, like rotten teeth. Some were set back a little, a stack of tyres out front, men in overalls working on cars parked at odd angles, their bonnets open like crocodiles basking in the sun. Small kiosks displayed colourful piles of fruit and vegetables under blue plastic awnings. They reminded her of the roadside stalls in Lilongwe's old town. Avocados, papaya and pineapple stacked high, luxuries at home.

"Is there water at the flat? You said it was on and off."

"It's not that bad. You can have a shower, I switched the boiler on."

"I've only got one change of clothing," she said.

Moe squeezed her knee. "You can borrow from me," he smiled. "You were never one to worry too much about clothes."

"Ha, ha," she said, winding her fingers into his. "I do care a bit how I look."

"You look gorgeous whatever you wear," he said, lifting her hand to his lips before taking hold of the wheel again. "Maybe Booker's girlfriend could take you to the market. Buy some clothes until you get your case?"

"Booker's girlfriend?" she said. She wanted to linger between worlds a while longer, with Moe. All too soon people Moe knew would complicate things with their life stories, their ways of dealing with life in Ethiopia, their advice. She moved to tuck her leg up under herself.

"You'll like her. She's lovely," he said. "Her name is Leila. She's Syrian, grew up in Paris."

"What does she do?"

"She's a researcher. Works at the Livestock Research Institute."

"I just don't feel ready to hear all that stuff about soaking salad leaves in Milton, how much not to pay the servants and where to buy PG Tips and Cornflakes." She had heard it all before, the concerns which preoccupied some, often frightening, ex-pat wives. While their husbands got on with their jobs and cheerfully popped open another beer, the women were landed with the task of making a home from home in Africa. It was as if they were possessed of a war-time spirit, tracking down the most unlikely ingredients against all odds. They were consumed with a determination to overcome and avoid. Cockroaches, flying insects and large spiders – if in doubt fumigate – dirt, walking in crowded places, communicable diseases, local food and above all, being taken for a ride. Those women expected every other woman to be similarly fanatical.

"Hey, slow down," he said. "Leila's the last one to even think about Milton and Cornflakes."

She lit a Marlborough and blew a long stream of smoke out of the window. "Coffee's a good idea," she said, smiling at him and patting his leg.

"You're impossible," he shook his head, smiling.

Marxism Leninism is our Guideline! Huge white banners were strung from one side of the road to the other over the traffic.

"Down with American Imperialists!" she read out loud.

"The Americans backed Somalia in the last war against Ethiopia," Moe said.

"I thought the Russians were in Somalia. It's very confusing. Why don't they make up their minds?"

"The Russians and the Cubans wanted to bring everyone together. Ethiopia, Somalia, Yemen. You know, International Socialism. It didn't work. Too much bad blood between Ethiopia and Somalia. So with the Americans in Somalia, they ended up backing Ethiopia."

They stopped at a set of traffic lights, which gave onto a wide crossing. The lights were red.

"This is Abiot, Revolution Square." Moe bent his head to peer out.

She ran her fingers through his hair again.

"It's too long. I was hoping you might cut it."

"No way," she said. "You look cute with it long."

"Just tidy it up a little?"

"Your hair will never be tidy," she said. In the wing mirror she saw a man hobbling down the road towards them, a crutch hooked under one arm, an intense look on his face. His matted hair, bare chest, face and arms were engrained with dirt. She wondered how long it took to get that filthy. "The lights have changed," she said. She glanced in the wing mirror again. The man stood, leaning on his stick, staring after them as they drove on into the expansive square. How awful to end up like that. It reminded her of the old winos at Waterloo Station.

"They use this as a parade ground," Moe said. "Massive political gatherings. Mengistu once smashed three bottles of blood-red liquid here, shouting, "Death to counter revolutionaries." I don't know, some people said it was real blood."

"You're kidding."

"It was the beginning of the Red Terror."

Three huge billboards, portraits painted in stark communist pop-art colours were lined up in a row.

"Marx, Lenin," she said. "Who's the other one?"

"Engels."

A red bus in front of them spewed out a cloud of thick black smoke. She unclipped the window and it shut with a slam. "Where did you get the car? I love it."

"From this garage halfway up Entoto, near the French Embassy. A father and son team build new 2CV's out of scrapped ones. The high suspension is perfect for dirt roads. It just bounces along." He smiled at her and winked, his eyes that blue, making her heart miss.

"Have you driven it to the lakes you wrote about?" she said. "It sounds amazing there."

"Abiata and Langano? Yes. Maybe we'll go in a week or two with some friends."

"Sounds good," she said, looking out of the window.

"You'll like them," he said.

"Maybe I just want a bit of the-two-of-us time, Moe," she said.

"There'll be plenty of us time, don't worry. Anyway, it's all open."

They passed a long covered walkway with what looked like craft shops tucked inside.

"There's the poster I saw in the airport," she said. "Is this far from the flat?"

"No, maybe ten minutes, and look, there's the Aeroflot office on the other side of the road," Moe said. "It's called National Theatre round here."

She would come tomorrow, find out about her case, buy a poster. "Do foreigners use the taxis?" she said. "Those must be taxis? The blue and white ones?"

"Yes, and there's lots circling around the town. Most ex-pats have their own cars," he said. "But the taxis are cheap and easy to use. You just wave one down, if they're going your way they'll take you. They take four people at a time."

The engine strained beneath them. They were driving up a hill. It was a long climb. A billboard behind a high wall read: Lycee Franco Ethiopien. Students were walking in through the tall wrought iron gates.

"Is there an English school?" she said.

"Yes, there is. Some of my friends teach there. Crazy bunch," he said.

"What kind of crazy?" She wondered if they smoked, drank too much.

"Fun crazy," he said. "You'll like them. Especially Tom. He's from Notting Hill. Knows Norfolk; used to go on the Broads sailing when he was a kid. We do loads of stuff together. Run the Hash, theatre club, most often we're at the British Embassy Club for the Saturday barbecue."

"Run the hash? Are you smoking again, Mr Bellamy? I thought we'd agreed not to."

"No way, honey. Hash House Harriers. It's like a paper chase. The Hare lays the trail with loops and false trails and the harriers run. All end up in one spot for a down-down."

"Moe? What are you on about?" She turned to look at him full on.

Moe ducked his head into his shoulders and pulled a face. "Have to survive, Izzie. I'm having a good time. You will too, really."

"You know I'm not keen on all this ex-pat stuff. I don't feel comfortable with it, Moe."

They were passing a line of corrugated iron shacks. Garlands of flowers leant against the open doors. Coffins jutted onto the sidewalk, stacked like Russian dolls, the largest on the bottom, the smallest, child-size, on top, waiting for their inevitable occupants. In the dark interiors she could make out men at work producing more. It would have looked grim were it not for the beautifully arranged flowers and the polished sheen of the wood. People filled the wide pavement, rush-hour on foot, most in dark office clothes, the women with white shawls over their heads and shoulders, children in blue school shirts.

Lilongwe had been more colourful, she thought. Even though it was the capital, it was relatively new and still more of a country town. Tall bushes of pink and scarlet poinsettia and yellow elder shrubs grew along the grass verges. The women walked with a slow rhythm, a bundle balanced on their heads. They wore brightly coloured chitenji wraps, and often had a baby strapped to their backs. In Lilongwe old town, tall jacaranda trees lined the dusty roadside, the ground beneath a carpet of purple blossom. Izzie missed Malawi and suddenly realised Addis was going to be very different.

"Watch out!" Izzie put a hand up against the windscreen.

Moe turned the wheel sharply, swerving to avoid the farmer.

Two donkeys, tall straw bales bobbing on their backs, trotted away across the wide roundabout, unaware of the traffic. The man was trying to keep up, wielding a stick, his legs skinny inside oversize wellies.

"Poor man," Moe shook his head. "He must have got a fright."

Izzie had her hand on her heart. "I certainly did."

The indicator click-clacked and Moe turned up a steep, narrow road. "You can drive as soon as we get you an Ethiopian licence," he said. "It's a bit hair-raising but it's all so slow nothing much can happen."

"I can see that." They were not going much faster than the pedestrians. A man wearing a flat, earth-brown hat, was walking up the road beside them with the help of a wooden staff. It had an ornate silver handle. His yellow gown billowed around him.

"This area is called Piazza," Moe said. "We're not far from the flat now. And look," he pointed across her. "That's the Lion Pharmacy. It's a good one."

"Have you been sick?"

"Food poisoning, once. Hilton Hotel."

"There's a Hilton?"

"The manager is a large Scot." Moe chuckled.

"He 'runs the hash' too, does he?"

"He's a sociable fellow, everyone knows him."

Everyone except the donkey-man, the beggar leaning on his stick at the traffic lights, the women on the way to work in their shawls, and him, she thought, bet he doesn't know the Hilton manager. She turned to look back at the man. A large wooden cross hung round his neck on a string of black beads.

"There's a great pool at the Hilton. Natural hot springs."

"Could be a character in the Arabian Nights," she said.

"Who?"

"That man we just passed."

"He's a Coptic priest, or maybe a monk. Some of them wander from one church to the next across the country, collecting alms, eating in people's homes."

"Like medieval times," she said.

A green lorry loomed up beside them, blasting its horn and overtook. Moe waved a hand out of the window and called out, laughing. "Cuban soldiers," he said. "Everyone prefers them to the Soviets. They're mad."

Cubans, Soviets, wandering monks. "You didn't write me about all this," she said.

"I told you, letters are censored and anyway, I'm not much good at writing." Moe stopped the car nose first into the pavement. "Here we are. Enrico's coffee shop."

"What was that Booker said about a rehearsal tonight?" she said, getting out of the car.

"It's the dress rehearsal for The Boyfriend at the English School tonight," Moe said, locking the doors and checking the boot.

"You're in it?" She couldn't imagine Moe acting.

An elderly man hobbled up, his hand raised, calling out. His feet were wrapped in filthy rags and stuffed inside rubber sandals. Strips of old tyre. They used to make sandals like that in Lilongwe market.

"He wants to guard the car while we're in Enrico's," Moe said.

The old man smiled and bowed, lifting his hands to his head, muttering something over and over. His fingers were gnarled, twisted into his palms. Leprosy. She had seen them at Likuni Mission. They used to come for a weekly clinic run by Lepra. If Lepra had an office in Ethiopia, maybe she could get a job with them.

"Win-iston?" a boy at her elbow said. A box of neatly arranged packets of cigarettes, chewing gum and sweets, hung round his neck on a piece of string. He looked up at her with large eyes.

"I have some already, thanks," she said, smiling at him, glad to see he had Marlborough for when her duty free ran out. "Next time, OK?"

"Caramella?" he said.

"No thanks," she said, thinking she really ought to buy something from him.

The boy smiled and shrugged his shoulders, skinny under his threadbare t-shirt. "Nek-est time," he said, and went back to his spot against the stone wall. A man bought one cigarette from him and lit it with the lighter which hung by a string from the boy's box.

Moe took her hand and they walked towards the coffee shop. A fresh bakery smell and the bitter-sweet aroma of ground coffee hovered in the air as they passed through the open door. Inside, trays of cakes were displayed inside a long glass counter.

"This is great," she said, following him.

Enrico's was bustling, people sat around metal tables and stood along the counter. Most wore rather conservative-looking office clothes. Izzie felt slightly incongruous in her blue and white stiped cotton pants and maroon Converse boots. But no one took any notice of her. The place hummed with talk. She sat at one of the tables, watching while Moe went to get their order. People came and went, greeting each other politely with handshakes, small bows, cheeks touching alternate cheeks. She wondered if she would ever become a part of it. Sunshine poured in through the open door, next to which an elderly-looking woman in black sat behind the till, perched like a crow on a high stool, taking the money.

"Italian," Moe said, coming to sit beside Izzie. "Her father was the original Enrico. He stayed after the Italians were kicked out in forty-one."

"Tekur macchiato," the waiter said as he put a small glass of coffee in front of each of them. He then placed a plate of cakes on the table, with two thin white paper napkins, neatly folded into triangles, on top.

"Egziersteling," Moe said, smiling at the waiter and nodding his head.

The man made a small bow. He did not smile. He did not seem to smile at anyone.

"Thank you?" she said.

Moe pinched her nose gently. "It won't be long before you have Amharic rolling off your tongue."

"We'll see," she said, warmed by his compliment. She took a sip. "Delicious. The best coffee." A layer of sandy sugar lay at the bottom of the glass.

"I got your favourite, Mille Feuille, see?"

"Mmm," she said to gratify him, biting into one. "Thank you. This is just perfect. I love it. I love you, Moe."

"Me too, you," he said, grinning.

"I want to kiss you but it doesn't look like it's the right place."

He wriggled his nose. "Bit conservative, you could say," he said, and took a cigarette from her pack. He lit it and blew a perfect circle of smoke into the air between them. It floated up, lost its shape and faded. They sat without talking, the hum of voices and laughter around them. Sunshine warmth, coffee, sweet cakes. Moe seemed preoccupied, twisting the ash off the end of his cigarette into the ashtray.

"Is everything alright?" she said.

"It's the rehearsal tonight. You won't like it, but I have to go," he said.

"Maybe I'll come along," she said.

"You want to?"

"Why not? Might as well." Izzie took another sip. "What did the waiter call the coffee?"

"Tekur macchiato. Espresso with a dash of hot milk."

"It's delicious," she said. "You know, I would like to learn Amharic."

"There's an Ethiopian who works at the Goethe Institute. Leila says he's a really good teacher."

"She's having lessons?"

"I could ask her if we could join them."

"I wonder if it's hard to learn."

"No more difficult for you than Chichewa, I bet." He looked at her with a bright, fond look in his eyes. "How are your folks?"

"They're fine," she said. "Kate and Helen send their love."

"And your Mum and Dad? Did they come around to you joining me?"

"They didn't have a lot of choice, did they?" She shrugged her shoulders almost as if on their behalf. "Anyway, it's not you specifically, Moe, it's me divorcing that is hard for them to stomach," she said. "They worry about what other people will say, what people think. "They gave me a great send off, though. Mum made a delicious Sunday roast with Yorkshire pudding. Dad got out a good bottle of red, even decanted it the night before."

"But they blame me," he said.

"They don't approve. How can they? But they came to the airport. I appreciated that." She remembered the slightly pained look in Dad's eyes as he smiled at her. He had given her one last reminding tap, tap, tap, of his ring on her head, "Noddlebox," he'd said.

She tried not to feel guilty. "I managed to call your Dad," Izzie said, wanting to move on from the uncomfortable, anxious, feeling in her belly. "He said to say 'Hello' and that he is looking forward to having a pint of Greene King with you when you get home. I think he's real proud of you, Moe." She put her hand over his and squeezed it.

They were very close, Moe and his Dad. Loved doing things together, sailing, fishing, listening out for their barn owl at night. Moe's father was an Economics lecturer at East Anglia; a friendly man in a tweed jacket. His mother had left them when Moe was small. She had gone back to live in Holland. She hadn't been happy in England. Moe didn't talk about her much. But he had been drawn to the Dutch dentists in Nkotakota, exchanged the odd Dutch phrase with them. There must have been some connection with his mother there. But Moe's Dad was cautious about Izzie. He doubted her intentions towards his son. She just had to give it time.

"I miss him," Moe said. "Can't really phone that often from here."

"You still don't have a phone at the flat?"

"No. It's a bummer. I registered with Telecom two months ago. Our fixer in the office says it can take up to six months to get connected."

"The flat sounds amazing," she said. "You're on the top floor?"

"With incredible views over the city."

"Do you know other people in the building?"

"There's an East German couple below me. She looks like a proper old washer woman. Pasty. Opens the door with a mop in her hand to wipe the step and vanishes as soon as she hears you coming."

"East Germans?"

"They're training the secret police," he said, lowering his voice.

"Gestapo?" she whispered.

"No, you ninny, that was the Nazis. The East German secret police call themselves 'Stasi'. They have a tough reputation; listen in on everything, record everything. The worst is that they get people to spy on each other, even between friends, family members."

"You're making me go cold all over," she said.

"On a lighter note, there's a friendly Italian family on my floor," Moe said. "They run the gift shop at street level."

"I thought you were going to say, they run a great Italian restaurant."

"There is one not far from here, Castelli's. It's expensive. Special occasions only." Moe looked at his watch. "We'd better get going, honey. I'll be late." He got up, his metal chair scraping across the floor. Izzie finished her coffee, leaving the sandy layer at the bottom of the glass. She didn't take sugar.

6

By the time she reached the second floor, Izzie could hardly breathe. There was no lift, and the flat was four floors up. There was a distinctive smell of Ajax on the mottled marble stairs. They must have scrubbed them that morning. She looked up the stairwell. A window with a deep ledge on a half landing had been left standing ajar, letting in a breeze and muffled sounds of traffic. She held onto the wooden banister, worn soft by years of sliding hands, trying to catch her breath.

Moe was already halfway up the next flight. It was mildly embarrassing. He was fit.

"It's the altitude," Moe said, walking back down. "Two and a half thousand metres. Takes everyone a while to adjust." He put his hand out. "Only two more floors to go, honey."

"Give me a second," she said.

On the level above her, a large door stood ajar. She wondered if that was the East Germans. It was kind of weird, living so close to people from behind the Iron Curtain.

"OK. Let's go," she said, taking his hand. "I'm ready." She could hear voices echoing from below.

When they reached the top, he said, "This is it." He turned the key in a large darkly polished hard-wood door.

Izzie leant against the wall, trying to get her breath back.

"The Italians live over there." He nodded over to other side of the landing as he pushed the door open.

"Wow," she said, going inside. "This is amazing."

Light flooded in through tall picture windows. It was a large, barely furnished, room. A dining table and chairs stood at one end, and a sofa, two armchairs and a coffee table with a glass top at the other. She put her handbag on the dining table and sat down for a moment.

"Where does that go?" she said, pointing to a pane glass door.

"Come and have a look," he said, unlocking the door.

It was the largest terrace she had ever seen. The sunlight reflected off the bare concrete walls, crumbling in patches like dry bread.

"I know, I need to plant something out here," he said.

Brown kites, their wings outstretched, floated in the blue above, letting out mournful cries. She shaded her eyes to watch them. They were so close, she imagined she could see their beaks. Vague smells of stale wood smoke, decomposing rubbish and car fumes wafted up from down below with the light warm breeze.

"Bit of a pong," she said, "but it's amazing." She went to look over the concrete wall. It was a long way down. A jungle of corrugated iron roofs covered the hillside opposite. Greys, browns and rusty reds jammed into each other. The road wound on into the distance, small stores lined either side, painted in pale shades of pink, green and marine blue.

"Piazza," he said, kissing her ear and wrapping his arms around her. "Addis Ababa's Oxford Street."

She leant back into him, closing her eyes to the sun.

Strains of Bob Marley came out of an entrance covered in ivy on the other side of the road. The sign above it read, 'The Blue Nile Bar'.

"Have you been in there?"

"I mostly go when I need a phone. The owner's a good guy. He's got a Telecom payphone."

"It's very different from Lilongwe, and even more from Nkotakota, isn't it?"

"Totally. Takes a while to get used to," he said. "Look, see those boys down there, leaning against the cars? That's Hailu and his gang. He's the youngest of three brothers. He's got a cute little sister as well. They can't wait to meet you."

"Do they go to school?"

"I'm not sure. They look after people's cars and run errands to earn money."

She turned to slip her arms round his waist and looked up at him. "You are glad I came, aren't you?"

"Of course, honey. What makes you say that?"

"I could have gone to Lesotho. They offered me a job."

"I know, but you wanted to come, didn't you?" he said.

"I'm kind of feeling like this is your place, your life."

"I don't want you to feel that way." He pulled her in, kissing her.

"I'd almost forgotten," she said.

"I hadn't," he said, smiling down at her. "Come, let me give you a quick tour." He took her hand and they went back inside, the sounds of the city becoming muffled.

She followed him into a small, dark kitchen. It had a metallic damp smell. A gas cooker stood against the wall, a pillar-box-red gas canister beside it. The window, covered in black mesh, did not let much light in. There was a large fan in the ceiling and a bulb hanging from the end of a wire.

"There's some food in the fridge in case you get hungry before I'm back. I asked Negisst to get some things yesterday. She's not coming today. I thought you'd like the place to yourself."

"Negisst? Your maid?"

"You'll like her a lot. She's lovely." Moe opened a cupboard. "Bulgarian jam, freshly ground coffee, cups and plates." He shut the cupboard again. "Tomatoes and cheese in the fridge," he said, opening it. The fridge hummed, a light flickered briefly and went off. Three tiny white eggs sat in their cradles in the door, below them a row of green bottles. "Cold beer, and some fresh local bread in that plastic."

"You're developing your cooking skills, I see," she said.

"Ha-ha very funny." He gave her a dig in the ribs. "Negisst cooks sometimes and I eat out with friends. There's a Chinese and The Cottage, where they make a really good pepper steak and Irish Coffee."

"You're making my mouth water."

"We'll go, don't worry."

There was a small corridor off the front entrance. He opened a door and flicked the light on. "Bathroom," he said and switched the light off again. They went into another room. "Spare room and study."

A double bed stood against the wall, the pale blue mattress was still in its plastic cover. There was a desk with papers scattered on it, a grey foolscap file lay open on the floor. A small bookshelf stood beside the desk with a lamp, an ebony elephant the only ornament. She ran her hand over the smooth curve of its polished back.

"Kasungu National Park," he said. "You remember that female, right in the middle of the track, her ears open wide like bat wings?"

"I thought she was going to charge," Izzie said. "She was furious. I can still see her standing there, as tall as the trees, her trunk up in the air."

"You had to slam us into reverse."

"Moments like that, you realise how far away we are from the raw dangers of nature, in England."

"In London," he said. "We have pretty amazing stuff in Norfolk too, you know."

"I know, bitterns, badgers and barn owls," she said.

"Good, you haven't forgotten," he said, going into the next room. "This is our bedroom."

There were more panoramic windows, the length of the room, letting in sunlight. She slid one back and looked over the corrugated roof tops on the other side of the road. The noise from the street filled the room. She shut it again. No curtains. Large bare rooms full of light. There was a hard-wood cupboard against one wall and a long dresser, with shelves underneath, against the other.

It was a large double bed with a plain wooden headboard. A roughly fringed cream-white bedspread with dark green, yellow and blue embroidery, lay neat on one side, thrown back on the other, unmade, where, Izzie imagined, he must have climbed out that morning before coming to the airport.

"Is it loud at night?" she said, suddenly feeling awkward.

"It's really quiet, except for the dogs and the odd army truck. There's a curfew from midnight until five in the morning."

"A curfew? You're kidding."

"They've had it since the Red Terror."

"The Red Terror?"

"It happened after the revolution. A bloodbath. '77 to '79. I don't know why they don't report these things at home," Moe said.

"We were in Malawi." She looked at him, feeling shy, like on a first date. She wanted him to take her in his arms again.

"Come here," he said. He sat on the bed, putting his hands out to her. "You're exhausted and there's me going on about blood baths, curfews, Stasi neighbours."

They lay together, curling themselves around each other. She was aware of the dimmed noise outside, their breathing, and her heart. She wondered if he could feel it beating.

"Maybe I'll hold you a while," he said. He touched her face, gently tracing a line over her cheek bones, down her nose, over her lips.

"Sounds like the beginning of a song," she whispered. "Make love to me, why don't you?"

**

She had that post-flight tiredness, too awake to sleep and too exhausted to do much. She pulled on her striped trousers and looked for a floppy t-shirt in the cupboard. It was half empty and smelt musty, and of his aftershave. Moe's pressed shirts hung on wooden hangers, his khaki shorts and a neat pile of t-shirts lay on a shelf. She slipped on a dark blue one and closed the cupboard. She stuck her tongue out at herself in the mirror and went through to the spare room. He hadn't put any posters on the wall, so unlike him. She wondered if he was as happy as they had been in Malawi.

It had been the 'Warm Heart of Africa', sunshine, dusty roads, fields of green maize stalks, the Malawian friends, the music and dancing and Malawi grass that did it. She had only fully realised after leaving, that for some it was not such a dream. Kamuzu Banda's Young Pioneers were a force of oppression and the country was one of the poorest in Africa. She realised she had been naive.

Her eyes briefly scanned his bookshelf, Economic Development in the Third World, North South, On Economic Inequality by Amartya Sen, and other familiar books from his studies. They were neatly stacked, along with Hemingway and Evelyn Waugh.

Moe's old music centre was on a low shelf against the wall in the sitting room. She sat cross-legged in front of it with her canvas hold-all, pulling out books, a t-shirt, pants, a string of beads made from seeds, her elephant hair bracelets, a jumper, until she found the cassette, The Pretenders, Chrissie Hynde.

It came on, the song she had listened to in London, lying in the dark, thinking of him. She sat, hugging her knees to her chest, listening. She loved him more than anything; his laughter, his smile, his body, his impulsiveness, the way his eyes shone an even darker blue when he discussed anything he felt deeply about. She loved dancing with him, sharing a glass of wine, sitting on either end of the sofa with their legs entwined, reading, or just looking at each other, listening to music. She couldn't believe she was finally here in Addis Ababa, with him.

She heard a crow cawing, nagging and insistent, on the wide terrace. It flew off when she opened the door, flapping loudly, still reprimanding her.

Izzie went back to sit in the circle of her things and spotted the present Kate had given her at Heathrow. It was wrapped in bright pink paper, coloured stars stuck all over it. The sort you collected as a child for being on time, polite or eating up.

"Open it when you get there, OK?" Kate had said, her eyes smiling and tearful.

"Granny keeps asking, 'Why is Izzie going to Abyssinia?'" her mother had interrupted, before taking a sip of coffee, leaving a kiss of red lipstick on the rim of the white cup. She had dressed up for the airport. When they were small, her mother wore a hat and gloves to fly BOAC, elegant in a calf-length suit, high heels clacking on the tarmac.

"I did try and explain to her that I'm going to Ethiopia to be with Moe and look for work."

"Don't stay away so long this time, darling."

"My visa's for six months, Mum, and it depends if I get a job. Maybe I'll be back sooner than we think, driving you all bonkers again."

Izzie picked up Kate's gift. She pulled the red ribbon, carefully unpicked the scotch tape and drew the soft paper back.

"Bless you, Kate," she whispered. It was the most beautiful white, Indian-cotton shift, tiny mirrors and white embroidery on the front and sleeves. Five mother of pearl buttons were done up to the neck. It made her think of Sam. She didn't really know whether he had already set off to live in the Ashram south of Bombay, to 'find himself'. She imagined him sitting cross-legged under a banyan tree and smiled. They had been good friends, too young to marry. He was like the big brother she never had. She lifted the tunic to her face and could smell a trace of sandalwood from the shop. She would put it on after her shower. Perfect.

A loud buzz made her jump. She got up, ran her fingers through her hair and went to the door. She could see two small boys through the spy-hole, shuffling their bare feet and whispering to each other. Must be the street boys Moe had talked about. She opened the door.

They looked up, startled. Then their faces broke into wide smiles; their eyes darting from her to the top of the door frame, to each other, to the floor. They giggled, covering their mouths.

"Hello," she said, thinking what sweet little scamps.

"Hello," one said, clearing his throat and scratching his head. Two Coca Cola bottles stood at his feet. He grinned at her, showing the gap between his two front teeth. "My name Hailu," he said, reaching a hand with dirty fingernails towards her and making a slight bow.

His hand felt small in hers, but strong. "Hello Hailu," she said, smiling. Then she turned to the other boy. "And you?"

The other looked at her shyly. With his chin jutting out and head cocked to one side, he looked like a bird, wondering whether to take off or not. He was a little taller than Hailu and wore a threadbare jumper which hung from his neck in tatters over brown shorts. He had a large dry scab on his knee.

Izzie put out her hand.

"My name Mekonnen," the boy said with a raspy voice, like he was about to lose it. He shook her hand and nodded.

"Means Col-on-nelle," Hailu said, pulling Mekonnen's jumper. "He is soldier."

Mekonnen pushed Hailu and they both laughed.

"Joking," Hailu said. "You Mr. Moe friend."

"That's right. I'm Mr. Moe's friend. My name is Izzie."

"Izzie," Hailu nodded at Mekonnen as if approving the name. "You come Soviet plane?"

"Yes, I came with the Soviets."

"Mr. Moe, he tell us, you get Koka," Hailu said.

"Koka?"

Mekonnen pointed at the two bottles of Coca Cola on the floor, and scratched the back of his head.

Lice, Izzie thought. These two were just like the boys in Lilongwe old town. Bright as buttons, rags and joking. Forever on the look-out for a coin, a handful of groundnuts, a sweet. Itching all over. It was the lice, scabies, boundless energy, always on the alert to – run for it.

Hailu picked the bottles up and held them out to her, beaming as if he was giving her the best present in the world.

She took the bottles from him. They were already chilled. "I could do with a Coke. Thank you very much."

The boys smiled at each other then stood looking at her, jiggling from one foot to the other. Mekonnen picked at the door frame. Hailu leant with a hand on the wall, his arm outstretched and then pushed himself upright again. He carried on, pushing himself back and forth like a pendulum, all the time looking at her and then at Mekonnen.

"Mr Moe gave you money for the Coke?"

"Yes, Mr Moe give fifty cents," Hailu said.

Izzie could not help smiling. "How old are you Hailu?"

"Six. Mekonnen, seven," he said, putting his hand on Mekonnen's shoulder.

"Your English is good. Where do you learn?"

"Es-kul," Mekonnen said in his low voice. "We go es-kul."

"And farenj, like Mr. Moe, giving work, we speaking," Hailu explained using his hands, looking serious, as if she was the one who was learning.

"Just a minute," Izzie said. She put the bottles in the fridge and went to hunt in her handbag for a bar of Cadbury's Dairy Milk. She was sure there was one left. She went back to the door. "Here you are," she said.

"Choclit?"

"Chocolate."

Hailu took the bar with both hands, bowing his head and muttering something.

The two boys looked at each other. "Tank yoo!" they sang out.

"Make sure you share it, OK?"

"Share it," Hailu said, looking at Mekonnen.

Mekonnen shrugged his shoulders at Hailu.

"Ciao!" They said and headed for the stairs.

She could hear them, giggling and chatting, until their voices faded to an echo. She closed the door quietly and smiled. She always said she would never have children. Maybe that was why they kept finding their way into her life. Like Ibrahim's children, always running in and out of the house in Lilongwe.

She went to the bedroom and stood in front of the mirror. Leaning slightly forward, she looked into her eyes, blue-grey like her father's. The eyeliner had smudged under her eyes, making her look doleful. She pulled a face. Her hair needed a wash. She would take a shower, eat something then go down onto the street. She would ask the boys to show her Piazza, teach her how to say, 'How are you?' in Amharic.

7

Izzie found herself sitting on the steps at the back of the English School smoking a cigarette, snuggled inside one of Moe's jumpers against the evening chill. It was much cooler than the afternoon. Moe had disappeared to get into his costume as soon as they arrived. She felt exhilarated, resigned and impatient, all at once, like a badly mixed cocktail.

The half-moon gave the evening a soft glow and the sky was full of stars. The infinite. A galaxy. A slice of light cut across the school yard as far as a gnarled old acacia tree. It stood in the middle of the yard, leaning in obeyance, as the wind had blown it, trapped inside a low circular wall. Somewhere in the darkness, crickets sang out. Their repetitive song reminded her of sitting on the veranda in Lilongwe at dusk, of the tall dry grasses on the lakeside road in Nkotakota and the eerie silhouettes of baobab trees by the water.

Moe was coming towards her with, she assumed, his great friend Tom. They were messing around with an intimacy unfamiliar to her. They looked incongruous, dressed up in Bugsy Malone suits and trilby hats, in Africa.

'In Africa'. After her walk around Piazza with Hailu and Mekonnen in the afternoon, Izzie was coming to realise 'Africa' was not one place.

Moe was still laughing when they reached her, his eyes mischievous. He put his hat on her head and drew her up towards him, putting an arm around her in a way which made her smile.

She stood on tip-toe and whispered in his ear, "You look sexy, Mr. Bellamy." She could tell he knew it, and that he enjoyed her saying so.

"Meet Tom," Moe said.

"Great to meet you," Tom said, lifting his hat and bowing slightly. "We've been counting the days, haven't we Moe?" He kissed her on both cheeks as if they were old friends.

Either he'd picked up the Ethiopian custom, or he had, like many expats, assumed an immediate bond with fellow English in a foreign place, thus allowing for the intimacy of a kiss on first encounter. It was a minority community that clung together, after all.

"Did I say the right thing?" Tom said, looking up at Moe and then at her, eyebrows raised. He was a head shorter than Moe.

"Hi Tom," she said, letting out a small sigh, and smiling at him. She wondered how much he knew about her.

"Fancy him dragging you out to a dress rehearsal on your first night," Tom said. He pulled a face of exaggerated agony. He was rather engaging, scruffy blonde hair and a posh London accent. He reminded her of a Labrador puppy.

"I'm fine actually," she said. "It's great to be here."

Laughter came from an open door. Two boys ran out and past them, dashing back in again through another door.

"That's the school hall and theatre," Moe said. "We'll be on in a minute."

A young woman with a head of thick black hair came over to them, swinging a string of beads. She wore a twenties dress which fitted her well, swinging round her slim calves as she walked. "Cheri," she said, pouting. "You making your lover jealous?"

"Izzie, this is Leila," Moe said. "Booker's girlfriend."

"Lovely to meet you," Leila said, kissing Izzie on the cheek. She had an engaging smile.

"Hi there," Izzie said, liking Leila immediately.

"I'm not sure I want that to be my only claim to fame, Moe. 'Booker's girlfriend'?"

Izzie smiled and felt the fatigue of the past few days in her face. "Is Booker here too?" she said, more for something to say than really wanting to know.

"He's inside. Intimate with his beer no doubt, or with one of the girls, knowing him," Leila laughed.

Izzie was a little envious of Leila's effortless energy.

"These two are lovers in the play." Tom indicated Moe and Leila with his eyes and slid a hand round Leila's waist. "Let me know when you've had enough of Booker, eh?" he said.

Leila looked Tom up and down. "In your dreams, boy," she said, giving him a slight shove.

A bell rang out. Like a silver afternoon tea bell.

"Hey, we're on next, mon amour," Leila said. She winked at Izzie and lay a hand on Moe's arm. "Allez, let's go or that dragon will be after us."

Moe gave Izzie a kiss and plucked the trilby off her head. "Tom, can you see that Izzie gets a beer?"

"No worries. I'll look after her," Tom said, leaving Leila's side and moving closer to Izzie.

"Who's the dragon?" Izzie said, stepping away as inconspicuously as possible, in case Tom thought he might slip his arm around her now that Leila was gone.

"Our director," Tom said. "She's not that bad."

"Come and watch me making an utter fool of myself," Moe called over his shoulder, walking away with Leila's hand in the crook of his arm. They made a handsome pair in their costumes.

"OK," Izzie said and smiled after him, wondering if she should feel jealous, but of what she was not sure.

She was never quite comfortable with clubs and societies, or the ex-pat 'in-crowd', their flirting, intimate jokes, hinting at something improper. The ex-pat community did provide quick access to much needed social life away from home. They did great things. Some people discovered theatrical and musical talents they never knew they had. But she wanted to know more about where she was, to work with and meet local people. It was always an uphill climb. She hadn't returned to the Club in Lilongwe after the first invitation. Thirteen years after independence it had still been 'Whites Only'. She could not understand why that was allowed. Some people had told her that by not joining in, she was cutting off her nose to spite her face. So be it.

"There's an icebox in the changing rooms," Tom said.

"I'd love a beer," she said, thinking, I'm probably the icebox around here. Rolling her eyes, exasperated at herself, she followed him into what looked like an office. It smelt of B.O. and mothballs. Costumes and clothes lay in piles on a long table, more hung on railings along the wall.

"Hello there darling, I'm Shirley. You must be Izzie." Shirley had a husky gin and tonic voice. She wore pale pink on her lips, a purple top and strings of bright coloured beads round her neck. She was busy zipping a dress on a girl with long auburn hair. "In heaven's name, child, stay still," she said.

"Shirley is our wardrobe mistress," Tom said, opening a large ice box. "She rules the roost. Been in Ethiopia since the Emperor's time, haven't you?"

"You make me sound ancient," Shirley said, laughing and coughing at the same time. "We've been here ten years. 1972 we arrived. Two years before the poor man was dethroned."

Three girls in 1920's party dresses, glanced at Izzie, giggled and carried on talking. One of them took a long drag on a shiny black cigarette holder.

Izzie felt at a disadvantage. She had the distinct impression that they all knew about her already. But she wasn't sure what they knew.

Tom popped open two bottles and gave one to Izzie. "They are the 'Perfect Young Ladies' in Madame Dubonnet's Finishing School, aren't you, girls?"

As if on cue, they sucked in their cheeks, raised an eyebrow and wriggled suggestively. They had slipped on a new persona with their outfits and were obviously enjoying every minute of it.

Where on earth had she landed up? Izzie took a sip of the cold beer. It was refreshing. She needed another cigarette.

"Stand still girl, or swear to God I'll get my cook to set the buda on you," Shirley said.

"What's that?" the girl said.

"The evil eye," Shirley said. "The evil eye."

"Tom," someone called out. "Where are you? You're on. Five minutes ago."

Izzie followed Tom outside and into the school hall, relieved to get away. She was hit by the timeless smell of all school halls; sweaty socks and sweet floor-polish. There was a full-size stage with clunky black footlights. Rows of chairs disappeared into the darkness at the back. She could make out the shapes of people sitting dotted about in the gloom, whispering.

A woman stood on the far side of the stage, holding a wad of papers. She wore half-moon glasses and peered over the top at the actors. She must be the dragon.

"Move more centre stage Leila, then Moe can come in from the right and there's room for the others behind you both," she instructed. She was obviously a teacher.

An older man with greying hair and a bulbous nose was distorting his face trying to insert a monocle. Two 'Perfect Young Ladies' were giggling at him. He was obviously egging them on and enjoying the attention.

"Can we keep it quiet, please, Brian?" the director said without looking at him.

Moe was standing with Leila, their bodies almost touching, listening to the director-dragon.

Izzie looked for a seat where she could watch unnoticed and saw Booker a couple of rows behind. Her heart sank when he spotted her.

'Come and sit here,' he motioned, pointing at an empty chair next to him.

She smiled and shook her head, raising her beer bottle to show she was looked after.

Suddenly it came back to her where she had seen him. It was at an amateur dramatics production in Lilongwe. She remembered thinking how incongruous he had looked, dressed in period costume, singing a love song. If she remembered rightly, he actually had a good voice.

"I could be happy, if you could be too." It was Moe and Leila, singing.

Izzie got up and went outside. She was overwhelmed with an urge to sob. It happened when she was over-tired. Overwhelmed by the first days in a new place. And, Moe, singing?

A lighter clicked open, lighting up the wardrobe mistress's face, showing her age. She threw her head back and blew out a long train of smoke. "Cigarette?" she said.

"Thanks," Izzie said, taking a light and breathing in deeply.

"Did you see Brian in there?" Shirley asked. "My husband, the one with the monocle? Is he behaving himself?"

"I guess so," Izzie shrugged. "Depends what you call 'behaving', I suppose."

They looked at each other and laughed.

"They're all having a bit of fun, that's all," Shirley said. "Everyone's excited. Dress rehearsal nerves, you know."

"Maybe I'll have another beer. Is that OK?"

"Help yourself, sweetheart," Shirley said. "I'll have one too."

Izzie spent the rest of the evening with Shirley between a cigarette sitting on the wall round the acacia tree, the cool box and the bottle of scotch Brian had left under one of the desks, with two glasses; one for him and one for Shirley.

"He always brings a bottle for the odd tipple between scenes," Shirley said.

It was then that Izzie noticed the slight tinge of Scottish in Shirley's voice. "You remind me of my eldest, you know," she said. Her three children were in Scotland, one in the last year of school and the other two already in university. She missed them, "But this is home now, I can't see myself going back."

Izzie wondered what was so compelling about the place.

**

By the time the rehearsal was over, and Moe was ready to go, Izzie felt decidedly light-headed. She followed him to the car, holding onto him, desperately hoping not to make a fool of herself on her first night.

"You all fff-flirt around a lot," she said, sitting heavily in the car. She watched as the large headlamps lit up the ivy overgrowing the school wall.

"It's harmless," Moe said.

"Some of them are jus' ssschool girlshs," she said. She giggled.

"You're pissed."

"Brian's whisky."

"You never drink whisky, honey," he said, putting a hand on her knee.

"I know."

"The altitude won't help. It'll make you woozy for a bit."

"I like Shshsh-shirley," she said. "We agreed to go to the China Pub one evening."

"China Bar," Moe said.

"Oh, I thought she said, Pub," Izzie said, turning to stare out of the window, glad of the night air on her face. She concentrated on the circles of light coming at odd intervals along the road. She realised it was streetlamps, most of them broken.

Eventually Moe turned down a narrow alley, the car's head lamps providing the only light.

She recognised Girma's hole-in-the-wall shop. The shutter was down, secured with a heavy padlock. Hailu had introduced her to Girma that afternoon. She'd bought a bar of Fairy Soap, six white candles and a box of matches. It seemed that a small transaction was expected, a sort of rite of passage.

"Dembenya,"[41] Hailu had said, looking up at her, grinning broadly. "You dembenya now."

Moe stopped in front of the tall gate to the car park at the back of their building.

The night was chilly. Izzie shivered. She felt nauseous.

Moe looked at his watch. "Nearly midnight," he said. "Where's that zabanya?"[42] He beeped the horn. "Always sleeping."

"Can't blame him," Izzie said.

The sound of a dustbin lid clattering came from further down the dark alley.

"Rats," Moe said.

The tall wrought iron gate opened, scraping the ground. The night

---

[41] Regular customer.
[42] Guard, watchman.

guard came out wrapped head to toe in a thick white blanket.

Moe drove through. "Thank you," he called out softly, waving.

The zabanya bowed.

**

Izzie woke up, light streaming into the large room. The sky a deep, endless blue, and still. One window had been pulled back a little, letting in the sound of traffic from the street below. Her head ached and her mouth was dry.

A large bluebottle flew around the room and struck the window. There was nothing quite like a solitary fly, buzzing against glass, to make a place feel empty. She spotted the note propped up on the dresser. Pulling her kaftan over her head, she got up to have a look. The floor felt cool under her feet.

> *Hello honey,*
>
> > *hope you slept well and feel better this morning. I should have warned you about Shirley and Brian – they can put a few drinks away. Great to wake up and see you there next to me. Didn't want to disturb you. Just want you to know that Negisst will be here today, and that I love you.*
>
> > > > > > *See you later, Moe.*

It was signed off with his usual flourish, a few lines depicting a sailing boat against the winds.

His heart and soul, truth be told, was in the Norfolk Broads. He loved taking his mother's large old binoculars with him on his boat, zooming in on secretive bitterns in the rushes along the banks, and laughing at the loud lapwings shrieking at him to keep away from their nesting grounds. His was a distinct almost artistic handwriting, not a boyish scribble. The motif told her he was still in there somewhere; the Moe having a beer with friends outside a bar in Malawi, the birdwatching, sailing Moe. She wondered whether she would fit in with his theatre crowd. The same lot were probably running the Hash.

Izzie was standing in a warm patch of sunlight. It felt lovely. The fly had crawled halfway up the pane and was taking a rest against the blue of the sky. The bedroom door was shut. She couldn't hear Negisst. Part of her hoped that she had not come yet. She went closer to the window and looked down. She had so wanted to come back to Africa. What was

'Africa'? This was so different. She missed her friends at Likuni hospital, Ibrahim's children – little Victor especially, the warmth and laughter. They had laughed a lot. Back in London, she had missed the out-of-the-ordinary; following the village chief through the maize fields to the woods where the Nyau dancers were getting ready for a full-moon ritual; buying goats in a village to keep the grass down; shopping for groundnuts, kidney beans and papaya in Lilongwe market.

Down below her, Addis was awake and busy. The jagged strips of corrugated iron roofing on the houses opposite seemed to heave. Thin plumes of smoke escaped through the cracks, creating a haze. Blue and white fiat taxis hooted, trawling the curb for passengers, and she could see Hailu with a small crowd of boys outside the Blue Nile bar.

Addis was a real city, with its old Italian buildings, pock-marked roads and cracked pavements. It had traffic, not just the occasional car on a quiet, dusty, road. It had an air of the ancient and mystical with its wandering monks. And then there were the stark billboards carrying communist slogans. Shirley had told her about night-time arrests and the rallies in Revolution Square. Izzie imagined stories and secrets whispering through the warren of alleyways below.

She moved away from the window and looked at her watch on the bedside table. It was eleven thirty. She opened the bedroom door. There was a noise from the kitchen. She looked at herself in the long mirror. The faded blue kaftan hung loosely to her ankles. She liked the white, hand-stitched knobbly buttons which ran down the front. She ran her fingers through her dark blonde hair, kept short and shaggy with scissors and comb in front of a bathroom mirror. She looked pale with slight rings under her eyes. Maybe a trip to the lakes was just what she needed.

**

"Hello," Izzie said, tapping on the kitchen door not to give the woman a fright. "You must be Negisst."

The woman turned; her round face a warm mellow brown, her eyes smiling. She was chopping vegetables with a large kitchen knife. For such a hot day she wore the odd combination of black leggings and a calf-length skirt.

"Good morning, Madam," she said, wiping her hands on her apron. Wisps of hair escaping from under the thin black scarf, which she had wound round her head, her small ears popping out at the sides.

"I'm Izzie."

"My name is Negisst," the woman said, bowing her head and holding a hand out towards Izzie.

It was a strong, firm, hand that Izzie imagined knew how to hold and comfort, that washed clothes, held babies, hugged sadness away, wrung out cloths and wiped surfaces thoroughly.

"How are you, Madam?" Negisst said, smiling. She was shorter than Izzie and a little plump.

"I am fine," Izzie said.

"Breakfast?"

"I'll help myself." Izzie did not want Negisst to serve her.

"Madam rest today, Mr Moe says," Negisst said, turning to fill a kettle from a tiny tap at the base of a tall water filter. "Coffee, good?"

Izzie heard a shuffling noise under the chopping table and bent down to look. A chicken was moving about in the shadows, its legs trussed loosely together.

"Roast chicken and vegetables tonight, Mr Moe says. Good food for you."

"Oh," Izzie said. The chicken's jet black eyes seemed to glare at her accusingly. It jabbed its head about, looking for non-existent scraps.

Moe had kept chickens in Malawi, mostly for their eggs. Gertrude, a copper coloured bantam, had been his pride and joy. She was quite a character and followed him around if he made the right clucking noises. Once he had asked his cook to roast a chicken for supper. "But not Gertrude," he had said. "Don't cook Gertrude."

Sitting on the veranda having a beer the next evening, Moe said he had noticed that Gertrude was missing.

"Gertrude, Mr Moe, Sir?" the cook had said, pointing at a large black hen. "There's Gertrude."

Moe was convinced the man had done it on purpose.

"Negisst?" Izzie said. "Are you going to kill it in here?"

"Yes, Madam," Negisst said, absently pushing the chicken back under the table with her foot. "I make coffee?"

"Coffee sounds lovely," Izzie said and opened the fridge. She wondered where she could go to avoid the slaughter. Hens made an awful noise, whichever way you did it. She took out a dish of freshly cut pineapple, her mouth watering.

"You eat ambasha and honey?"

"What's ambasha?" Izzie said.

"Bread," Negisst said. "I make it at my house, today morning."

"Thank you," Izzie said, touched.

Negisst had put the kettle on the stove and was getting things out of the cupboard, an archetypal mother. She really seemed to want Izzie to feel welcome.

"Will you have a coffee with me, Negisst?"

Negisst covered her mouth, her eyes shining, looking at once pleased and shy.

"No Madam. I work."

"You drink one coffee. We chat," Izzie said, realising she was already talking like Negisst. People often asked her where she was from. She couldn't help herself. Two minutes listening to someone with an accent and she'd picked it up. "Not good to eat alone."

"Ishi," Negisst said.

"Ishi?"

"Ishi, OK by Amharinya."

"You teach me? Your language?"

"You English to me. I teach Amharinya to you, ishi?"

"Ishi," Izzie said, going through to the dining room. Amharinya, lovely word. She was starting to feel better. Moe was right, she was going to like Negisst. Negisst came with a tray and placed the bread, butter and honey on the table and the plate of freshly cut pineapple. She pulled a straw mat from somewhere and put the coffee pot on it and two cups.

"Come, sit down, Negisst," Izzie said, patting the chair next to her.

"Ishi, Madam," Negisst said, perching on the very edge of her chair, her hands folded on her lap.

Izzie realised Negisst was out of her comfort zone. But she needed to have a relationship with Negisst beyond the classic 'Madam'- 'Maid' one. She poured them both a coffee, wondering what to say to make the woman feel comfortable.

Negisst bowed her head, muttered something and made a sign of the cross, "Amen," she said.

"Amen," Izzie said, pushing the sugar bowl towards Negisst. "You can call me Izzie, by the way."

"Yes, Madam," Negisst said and put one spoon of sugar into her cup after the next.

"How many spoons?"

"Arat," Negisst said, "four."

"Eat, Madam." Negisst picked up the breadbasket and put a hunk on Izzie's plate. There were tiny black cardamom seeds in the bread. She passed Izzie the butter. "Eat," she said again.

It looked as though Negisst would butter it and put it in Izzie's mouth, given half the chance. "How did you meet Moe, Negisst?"

"My friend, working Mr Booker house."

"Aha, Booker Keyes." The man seemed to be everywhere.

"Before, my madam schoolteacher. They go London." She made a motion with her hand; the plane taking off into the skies. She shrugged her shoulders and took a sip of coffee.

"And you lost your job," Izzie said. "Not easy."

"Egziyabher yawkal," Negisst said, rolling her eyes to the ceiling. "God knows best."

Izzie spread some butter on the bread.

"Madam?" Negisst shuffled in her seat and adjusted her apron. "You, how many years Addis Ababa?"

"I don't know. I have to find work."

"Turu neow, very good. You get work and stay long time."

Izzie could not imagine finding a job in Addis. It all seemed complicated and overwhelming. "Where do you live, Negisst?" Izzie said, immediately realising how pointless it was to ask. She had no idea where she was herself.

"National Bank," Negisst said.

Izzie shrugged.

"Come," Negisst said, going to the window. "Look." She pointed down the hill, somewhere amongst the trees and buildings. "Ten minutes bus."

"I know we are in Piazza, but I don't know where Piazza is. Are we north, south?"

"I do not know, Madam."

Izzie wondered what sort of a place Negisst had. Moe's flat seemed palatial.

"Your bread is very good," Izzie said, sitting down again, tucking one leg underneath.

"Thank you, Madam." Negisst bowed her head slightly.

"Are you married, Negisst? Do you mind if I ask?"

"I have one husband and four children." Negisst tucked her thumb in and showed four fingers. "Three girls, one boy." She lowered her head and looked at Izzie, her eyes playful and shy; as if admitting to having children was tantamount to talking about sex.

"That's great, Negisst."

"Too many children," Negisst said. "Farenj only one or two."

"Not all farenj, Negisst. Some people have three or four."

Negisst finished her coffee with a loud slurp.

"Does your husband work?"

"He is driver, Madam."

"That's a good job, isn't it?"

"Betam turu neow, Madam. It is very good." Negisst took her cup and headed towards the kitchen.

"Negisst?"

"Yes, Madam?"

"Tell me before you kill the chicken? I don't want to be here."

Negisst covered her mouth and laughed. "Ishi, Madam."

"Izzie, Negisst. It's Izzie."

8

Everyone was talking about the rains, the harvest, the price of food. Children and old people in the village were ill and lying on their cots in the darkness of their gojo-bate. He hated it when he heard the wailing noise which would start up if someone died. Zewdie would pull on her black shawl and walk up the path to Temima's house. They always went together to the lekeso, to whichever homestead was in mourning, wailing their loss.

Ashebir knew that he and Zewdie were only alright because Mohamed Bilal from Albuko, his mother's childhood friend, was helping them. Her brother, Mohamed Shinkurt, sometimes came with a large bag of onions for Zewdie to sell. She would use the money to buy grains to make tella beer, or grind them to make ki'ta bread for them to eat. The harvest in November had been poor and the small rains had only given just enough rain.

He had had his breakfast of hot tea and a piece of ki'ta bread.

"We'll eat when you come this evening," Zewdie said. "Take some 'kollo with you for when you feel hungry."

He took the roasted grains thanking her. "Zewdie don't worry, ishi? Mohamed Abdu and I know where to find berries on the bushes along the river. And," he added smiling, "we are going to try and catch fish to cook over a fire today."

"Sometimes I think you are older than your years, yeney lij," she said. "Look at you, trying to comfort your mother who cannot pack a picnic lunch anymore."

"It will be alright, Zewdie," he said.

"Egziyabher yawkal. But it is not as bad for us as for families further north, especially where they are fighting," she said shaking her head sadly.

"I'm going now, Zewdie," Ashebir said, not knowing what else to say.

He took his bag, his sickle and stick and went round the back of the house to the beret where they kept the animals at night. Their goats, the cow and one ox. He shooed them all out. The goats were especially eager to get going and bleated at him loudly. He tapped his favourite on her nose as she passed him. The ox and cow came along more slowly. Their rumps were starting to look thinner. He called out "have a good day," to his mother.

He heard her muffled voice inside the house, "Egziyabher ante gar yihun," and knew she had called, "God be with you."

He went up the path to meet Mohamed Abdu. Ali was not going with them that day. The sky was a deep blue and the earth dry and dusty around his feet. He took in a deep breath. The air was still a little fresh from the night and tinged with wood smoke. He liked the clack of their hooves against the rocks on the path and the heavy tread of the ox, walking with a slow sway, its tail swishing against the bushes. He gave it a light tap with his stick, as if to say 'hello'.

He and Mohamed Abdu took the path down to the river. They agreed to take the animals to the wide pasture near the river before taking them for a drink. Then they could play and fish. They did not speak much on the way. Ashebir thought Mohamed Abdu looked worried. After some time, he said, "Are you alright?"

"I am fine," his friend said. "My little sister is not well."

"Aminat?"

"No, the smallest one, Konjit."

"Sorry," Ashebir said, hoping it was not serious. The little girl was very sweet and always giggled behind her hand at him. He liked tickling her to make her laugh out loud. Then she would run to her mother's long skirts and bury her face.

They spent the morning walking amongst the animals, playing a little with some boys from the villages beyond Muletta. The sun rose in the sky and they could feel the heat on their heads. They went in search of shade under the acacia tree, where they liked to sit on the large round boulder to talk, play or sleep.

"It's getting really hot, Ashebir. Let's go down to the river?" Mohamed Abdu said after some time.

Ashebir jumped up. "Yes. Let's go," he said. "I'm getting thirsty."

They rounded up their animals, whistling, tapping their rumps with their sticks and shouting, "To the river! To the river!"

The animals understood. The goats and sheep took off, trotting straight for the bridge on the other side of the pathway. The cows and oxen lumbered along at their slow pace behind.

"They want to swim too, Mohamed Abdu," Ashebir laughed.

When they reached the river, they made sure the animals had a good drink. Then they took off their clothes and, leaving them in a pile on the shore, ran and jumped into the water. The cows and oxen stood in the shallows cooling off, turning their heads with those heavy horns slowly one way to look and then the other. The goats and sheep wandered to the banks in search of food and shade.

Finally, Ashebir thought. He had been waiting for this moment. He loved to play around the rocks just below the bridge and look for small fish to catch in his fingers.

"Ashebir look," Mohamed Abdu called out, pointing further upstream.

Ashebir looked up and saw the fish coming up to the surface and disappearing again.

"Degenya! Degenya!" they shouted out together, laughing. Ashebir slipped off his rock in excitement, splashing in the water to regain his balance. He felt a thrill in his stomach. Somewhere up ahead of them the Degenya were at work.

Zewdie had told him about them. They were Amharas from somewhere called Gidim in the highlands. It was not far from Tulu Market where she went to sell potatoes and onions. She said they were Christians, peaceful people and very poor, like her friend, Wozeiro Etalem, who sat under the same tree with her in Ataye market. Zewdie never tired of telling him how Wozeiro Etalem had two sons who had joined Mengistu's army.

"They've gone to the front and never been seen again," she'd say, then mutter "God be with them" and shake her head sadly. "Don't you ever go to the front, Ashebir," she would say. And he would promise that he never would, shaking his head seriously, wondering what it was like to be a soldier in uniform, and fight.

"The Degenya must be catching fish with their poison," Mohamed Abdu called out to Ashebir.

Ashebir made his way towards his friend, pushing his legs through the current.

"What is that poison Mohamed Abdu?"

"It's called birbira. It's a plant with something strong in its juices. They crush it." Mohamed Abdu started crushing some river grasses between a small stone and a boulder. "Like this, you see."

Ashebir watched feeling the river water flowing softly round his legs.

"Then what?" Ashebir asked, picking up some of the grass and absently rubbing it between his fingers, breathing in the sweet smell.

"Smell this Mohamed Abdu," he said lifting the grass to his friend's nose, "it smells like lemons."

"Mmmm," Mohamed Abdu inhaled deeply. "Emet Fahte Ibrahim uses this to make tea."

"So then what?" Ashebir asked again.

"Then they tie the crushed leaves into a cloth bundle which they drop into the river."

"What does that do to the fish?"

"The fish go all funny. They swim deep down into the water," Mohamed Abdu plunged his hand into the water bending his knees to show Ashebir, "and come up again to the surface."

Ashebir copied him, diving his hand down deep then shooting it out and up to the sky with an exploding splash and laughing as Mohamed Abdu fell backwards. They both tumbled into the water splashing each other.

"They don't jump so high, Ashebir," Mohamed Abdu shrieked as he surfaced, wiping the water out of his eyes. "The birbira makes the fish sleepy so they are easy to catch, even with bare hands."

"Let's go up river and see if we can catch any." Ashebir said, getting more excited.

Mohamed Abdu called over to his sister, "Aminat. Aminat."

She was playing with Yishaereg and the boys. "Look out for the animals. We're just going up river to try and catch some fish."

"Ishi, but don't be too long," she called back.

"Look out for Zewdie's goats and the ox too, Aminat, please," Ashebir called to her.

He could see her nodding in reply.

"Thank you," he shouted.

"Look, look, Ashebir," Mohamed Abdu called in an urgent whisper. "Look. The fish, see them coming up to the surface? The Degenya must have missed these."

Ashebir followed Mohamed Abdu taking wide strides working his legs against the current and stumbling over the stones beneath his feet.

They found a good spot and stood opposite each other, legs apart and waited. A fish surfaced in front of Ashebir. He grabbed at it with two hands and it slipped through. He laughed in excitement. Mohamed Abdu tried to get the next one. It became a game, catching one and dropping it when they saw larger ones up ahead.

"Let's go further up river, Ashebir."

Ashebir followed Mohamed Abdu. They climbed out and scrambled along the bank to where they had left their clothes. He pulled on his shorts and Mohamed Abdu wrapped his gildim cloth, and secured the knife he always carried, around his waist.

Ashebir wished he had a gildim and a knife like his friend. When Zewdie decided to follow Mohamed Bilal from Albuko's advice, and sent him to Qur'an classes, he had asked her if he could now wear a gildim. "Please, Zewdie." She had said no, no gildim. It was then that he discovered that the teacher hit the boys over their outstretched hands with a stick, not on their buttocks, as he had feared.

"Which hand do you write with?" the teacher demanded of the boy getting punished. "Put out the other one," he would say. Thwack, the stick would come down with a sharp sting that grew into a deeper pain as the morning wore on.

Ashebir knew. The teacher had dealt him a blow on his second day.

"Just to make sure you know what is coming if you misbehave," the teacher had said.

Ashebir's eyes had filled with tears. He thought it was very unfair.

Mohamed Abdu told him the teacher did the same to every new pupil.

Ashebir hooked the small sickle Zewdie had given him over his shoulder, and set off with Mohamed Abdu along the shore, his eyes scouring the water for fish. He caught four and had to throw them back each time.

"Wait until we catch a big one," Mohamed Abdu kept saying. "Then we'll make a fire and cook it."

Ashebir's mouth watered at the thought.

"Look Ashebir," Mohamed Abdu called out after some time. "Here comes a really big one. Can you see it flopping along?"

They jumped into the river and made ready to pounce. Mohamed Abdu caught it, grasping it tightly as it flapped about. Ashebir grabbed its tail in case it slipped out of his friend's hands. It felt oily in his fingers, the scales rough. They moved together holding on to the slippery fish all the time and climbed onto the riverbank. Ashebir let go and Mohamed Abdu slapped the fish's head against a rock.

While his friend cut the fish open with his knife and gutted it, Ashebir collected dry twigs and made a small fire. They roasted it and ate, first picking the soft white fleshy pieces and then devouring the crispy skin. It was the most delicious and juicy thing Ashebir had eaten in a long time. His heart sang with joy and excitement as he ate, and all the while a tinge of guilt that Zewdie would not get a mouthful too.

"Eat slowly, Ashebir, or your stomach will be full of sharp pains," Mohamed Abdu said.

After they had eaten and licked their fingers, they carefully put the fire out and covered it with dirt.

"Let's go on, shall we?" Ashebir said. "That tasted so good. I want to eat another one."

"Yes, me too, I'm hungry now," Mohamed Abdu said. They continued on up the river, stopping now and then to skim thin flat pebbles across the surface, or to dig in the sand for fresh water to drink.

"The Degenya are clever. They have not left many for us." Ashebir said.

"They only fish out the big ones to sell in the market," Mohamed Abdu explained.

After some time, Ashebir noticed the shadows. The light was changing. He stopped and looked around, then at his friend. "Where are we, Mohamed Abdu?" he said, butterflies of fear quivering in his belly.

A dark mountain rose to the left of them, a huge shadow bearing over him. The soil and rocks were dark, almost black, and there was hardly any grass.

"Maybe this is Hawaitu," Mohamed Abdu said. His friend was also looking anxious. "I think we've come too far, Ashebir."

"Hawaitu? Isn't that near Senbatey?" Ashebir's voice was almost a whisper. "Mohamed Abdu? Isn't this where the Afar come?"

They stood looking at each other. He could hear the river running past them over the rocks and back towards the Ataye bridge. They had come far and it was late in the day. There was a deeper, rumbling sound ahead of them.

"What's that?" Ashebir strained to listen more carefully, trying to block out the sound of his heart and the river.

He crouched down with Mohamed Abdu, holding onto his friend's arm. They listened, their heads close together.

"It must be the hot springs," Mohamed Abdu said in a low voice. He picked up a twig and started drawing in the sand. "Look, the river comes from Ataye up here and meets the one from Senbatey in the south. Where they meet it makes a shape like this," he drew a V. "In here," his stick pointed to the place inside the V. "That's where the hot springs are."

"And that's where Zewdie said the Afar come to make their coffee and take a wash," Ashebir whispered. He paused. "How do you know all that? You said you had never been here."

"You remember you asked me about the Afar that time?" Mohamed Abdu whispered back, frowning slightly. Ashebir nodded. "Well, I asked my father, Mohamed Ahmed, about the hot springs and he drew this to show me."

Ashebir stared at the V. That's what it must be like to have a father at home. You can ask him anything. And you get an answer like that, with a drawing. No wonder Mohamed Abdu knew so much. He looked at his friend again. "So what shall we do now?" he asked.

"What do you think?" Mohamed Abdu whispered. "I want to have a look. What about you?"

"I don't know," Ashebir replied. "I want to look too, but I am too frightened."

"Let's just go a bit closer? Stay down low. Follow me. OK?"

"Ishi. No, wait," Ashebir grabbed his friend's arm. "Just a minute." Ashebir crept back and went to a bush to relieve himself. He looked round and saw Mohamed Abdu watching him, holding onto his mouth to stop the giggles coming out. Ashebir couldn't help smiling and felt laughter rising up. He stayed crouched down, too afraid to stand, his shoulders shaking from the laughter he dared not let out. He could not stop peeing. He was terrified and laughing and peeing all at once.

"Come on, Ashebir," he could hear the giggles in Mohamed Abdu's loud whisper.

"I'm nearly done," he said over his shoulder. Finally, the peeing stopped. Must be all that river water, he thought. He felt relieved, and now, for some reason, braver. He took a deep breath.

"Let's go," he whispered. "But slowly, ishi?"

"OK," Mohamed Abdu nodded.

He moved quietly like a cat in the undergrowth, keeping low behind Mohamed Abdu. They did not have to go far. The rumbling noise got louder and louder. Soon they were crawling through the bushes towards the edge of a flat, dry, wide open space, with tall piles of rocks, and the hot springs. It was a magical place. The grasses growing in clumps here and there looked strangely dry and red. A small herd of camels stood and sat, tied together near the water's edge, where the river curved out of sight. Steam rose from amongst groups of people gathered round the springs which burst up into the air out of the large black rocks.

"The place where the water bubbles hot out of the earth, Mohamed Abdu," Ashebir whispered in his friend's ear.

Mohamed Abdu nodded back at him, his eyes shining with excitement.

Tall young Afar men, their hair hanging in thick ringlets to their shoulders were standing naked by the springs, washing themselves, laughing and chatting. Their strong bodies glistened in the sun. Women were sitting separately, in small groups, talking, washing clothes, preparing food. Ashebir had never seen anything like it. His heart pounded loudly in his chest and around his ears. The steady beat of his mother pounding grain. A strong thick smell drifted their way and hung in the air; animal hide, steaming coffee, and the thick ghee in the Afar's hair. He was hot and sweating, nausea rising in his belly.

He and Mohamed Abdu sat down slowly and quietly to watch from the safety of the bushes. The undergrowth was dry and crackled softly. He tried to keep his whole body still, hardly breathing. He was watching another small group of Afar men. They wore green and red gildim cloths round their waists, and grey-white abujedi cloth around their shoulders. They had long hair, curly and oiled. He could see the fat shining from where he sat, peering through the bushes. Two of them were leaning on heavy sticks; the other three each had a machine gun slung loosely over their shoulders. They looked relaxed, talking.

The group slowly moved towards a hot spring and put their weapons down to sit on the rocks, where a group of young women were brewing something.

"They're having coffee," Mohamed Abdu whispered directly into Ashebir's ear so it felt loud and tickled. He rubbed his ear.

Ashebir put his mouth to Mohamed Abdu's ear and whispered, "Look at their guns."

"Kalashnikovs," Mohamed Abdu whispered back. "And their knives, look how long they are," he added, pulling a face. He looked down and pointed out his own small knife to Ashebir. "I want a long knife and leather sheath like theirs," he whispered.

"They're chewing khat," Ashebir motioned his head in the direction of some older men who were sitting together; a small pile of thin branches covered in green leaves lay on the ground between them. They were picking off the young shoots and chewing, their mouths green. They talked, taking sips of tea and refilling their cups from an old kettle.

Ashebir motioned to stay quiet. They were getting too loud. He took a deep breath to try and quiet his nerves. After a while he leaned towards Mohamed Abdu and whispered in his ear, "Do you believe the stories about the Afar warriors?"

Mohamed Abdu shook his head. "They say that to make us afraid at night," he whispered back.

Ashebir looked up again. One of the young Afar men was looking in their direction. He grabbed Mohamed Abdu's arm tightly. The young Afar turned to say something to his friends. They all looked towards the bushes where they were hiding. One of the Afar was pointing and talking as he stood up. He did not look pleased. He slung his rifle over his shoulder and moved towards their hiding place.

Ashebir froze. He could not think, speak, move. His heart was pounding in his ears. He could feel Mohamed Abdu move closer to him as they inched their bodies lower behind the bushes, trying to disappear into the undergrowth. The Afar was coming closer, shouting at them.

"He wants us to get up," Mohamed Abdu said, panic in his voice.

The young Afar burst through the bush and was on them. He grabbed them both by their upper arms, roughly pulling them to their feet. It hurt. Ashebir felt like a hunted jigra,[43] hanging there as the man dragged them out into the open. He cried out. The young Afar was shouting all the time, gesticulating with his head towards his companions. Ashebir could not understand a word. He could smell the young man's thick sweat and the ghee in his hair.

The young Afar pushed them in front of his friends. He was still gesticulating and shouting. Ashebir could not understand. Why was he so angry? He stood as close to Mohamed Abdu as he could.

People turned heads, men and children gathered around. The women stood on the outer edges, muttering quietly to each other, obviously wondering what would happen next.

Ashebir felt as if he was in a strange land, in a dream, like a trapped animal. There were so many eyes staring at them, none friendly. His eyes filled with tears, making everything hazy. He blinked hard to try and clear them, not daring or able to lift his hand to wipe them away. His arms were heavy and limp by his sides.

The young Afar were getting louder, more and more animated. One of them pushed Ashebir's shoulder roughly, knocking the small scythe Zewdie had given him to the ground. He spoke angrily.

While Ashebir could barely understand a word, it was clear they were more interested in him than in Mohamed Abdu. He was not a Muslim. He did not understand why not, but that's what Zewdie said. He looked down at his shorts and then at Mohamed Abdu's gildim. It was him they wanted. He thought his knees would give way. He concentrated on his feet, digging his toes into the earth to hold his body up. He slowly

---

[43] Guineafowl

squeezed his hands into fists and could feel his jaw tighten.

One of the young Afar grabbed his arm once again and shook him roughly. He bent down, looking Ashebir straight in the face, talking angrily all the time. The youth's eyes were black, his dusty skin drawn tightly over his strong bones. Ashebir could smell his hot breath and the heavy fat in his hair.

Mohamed Abdu objected loudly with a few brief words in Orominya.

The young man shoved Mohamed Abdu away with his other hand and pulled Ashebir towards him. He headed in the direction of a sorghum field.

Ashebir struggled, wriggling and pulling away. He heard himself shouting, "Mohamed Abdu! Mohamed Abdu!" The pull on his arm sent sharp pains into his shoulder. "Help me! No. No. Stop it." He cried loudly. The sobs racking his chest.

An elderly woman, dressed in black from head to toe, suddenly appeared, limping fast towards them. She was shouting, her arms spread wide, as if to include everyone in her tirade. It was Emet Zeineba, an elderly woman from their village.

To Ashebir's amazement, she stood solidly between the Afar youth dragging him away, and the field he was heading for.

"I know this boy," she cried. "He is my neighbour's son." She panted the words out placing one hand flat on her chest which was heaving up and down. She looked very upset. "His mother's a Muslim. Leave him alone. Let him go home in peace."

The young Afar's hand loosened its grip on Ashebir's arm, while he argued fiercely with Emet Zeineba. Ashebir stumbled backwards and towards Mohamed Abdu, rubbing his arm. He could not stop the waves of sobbing, barely able to catch his breath. He wiped his eyes and nose with the back of his hand. He looked around. He could not run. They were surrounded by Afar. He looked up at the old woman. She was so brave. But the young man did not show any respect.

Zeineba moved next to Ashebir. Taking hold of his arm, she pushed him slightly behind her. She held him firmly there. To protect him. He could not stop crying and wiping his face. She was obviously begging the young men to leave him alone.

Another young Afar made a quick move. He lunged at Ashebir, grabbed him and pulled hard. He dragged him away from Zeineba. Another came forward as quickly. He wrenched her hand off Ashebir. The two lifted him off his feet between them and made for the sorghum field.

Ashebir screamed, his mouth wide open, looking back at Emet Zeineba and Mohamed Abdu all the time. He was a goat being taken to slaughter, the urine running down his legs.

Emet Zeineba and Mohamed Abdu ran behind, the old woman hobbling to keep up. She had to make it. She called over her shoulder to others behind them as she hurried after Ashebir and the Afar youth. Those who had gathered stayed where they were, staring, talking amongst themselves. Not moving. Were they afraid?

In between the tall stalks of sorghum was a narrow path. They dragged him along the path. He had fallen silent, except for his panting breath. He could feel sharp knives of pain running up his chest. What did they want with him? Dread and fear ran through his body. Where was Emet Zeineba? He could hear her. She was crying and shouting. He could not understand her words, but her voice was begging for his life.

The Afar stopped with him on the path, not letting their tight grip loose. Emet Zeineba ran up to them, limping, shouting, begging.

Mohamed Abdu was running up the path behind Emet Zeineba, his eyes large and terrified. Ashebir began whimpering again, it sounded oddly shrill in his ears. He was trapped. The sorghum stood tall around them. They were hidden from view. The two young Afar kept their firm, painful, grip on him. He hung limply between them, not daring to struggle or even move. His nose and eyes were streaming and his shorts wet.

The hot argument and shouting went on between the old woman and the two Afar.

Mohamed Abdu was crying and begging in the name of Allah.

Finally, with a disdainful flick of their hands, they let him go. They pushed him roughly to the ground. He fell forward, barely managing to break his fall with his hands. His knees and then his chin hit the ground. He looked up to see their tall, proud figures, their long knives hanging in colourful sheaths by their sides, walking slowly back through the sorghum towards the hot springs. The old woman fell to her knees by his side. He felt her arms around him. Mohamed Abdu knelt beside him, a hand on his back. Ashebir dropped his head and sobbed. It was quiet except for his weeping and their breathing.

"Hush now," she said to him. "Hush. They have gone."

She put a hand on each of their shoulders and muttered "Allahu Akbar, Allah is the greatest. Allah is our guardian," several times over.

The words calmed him. They reminded him of his grandmother, Emet Hawa. She said those words when she made coffee. He sat up, looking at

Emet Zeineba and Mohamed Abdu.

"Are you alright?" Emet Zeineba said.

He nodded, taking a quick look over his shoulder to see if they had really gone.

"Aysoh, they've gone," she said.

He bit his lip but could not help from whining again, the tears running in streams down his cheeks.

"Emet Zeineba," Mohamed Abdu said, "It will be dark soon."

"Hush now, hush," she said quietly. "We have to move quickly out of here. Come on. Let's go."

"Our animals," Ashebir whispered and began crying again. What would Zewdie say?

"You boys will be in big trouble," Emet Zeineba said, sucking her teeth. "We have to get home."

They all got to their feet. Mohamed Abdu helped the old woman.

"Follow close behind me," she said. "I will take us another way. They won't see us, Insha'Allah."

She walked slowly. Ashebir could see she was in pain.

"Are you alright, Emet Zeineba?" he asked, surprised how small his voice sounded.

"I will be fine when we get you home safely," she said. "Now let's stay quiet until we get near our village."

She shepherded them all the way. Sometimes making them go on the path ahead of her, "So I can see you." Sometimes making them follow her, "Stay close behind."

She reminded him of a worried hen with her chicks. She kept them moving, always near her. His legs ached. He touched his friend every now and then, and felt Mohamed Abdu's hand on his shoulder from time to time. They kept close together on the path.

Finally, they reached the village. He looked up at the sky full of stars. They left Mohamed Abdu at his home. Emet Zeineba did not let them stay long. She said she had to get Ashebir home to Zewdie.

"Yes, get him home," Temima said. "We have all been worried. As if we don't have enough with your sister ill, Mohamed Abdu. You wait until your father sees you. And leaving the animals with Aminat like that. It's not like you." Then she looked at Ashebir. "And you, my boy," she went on. "Zewdie has been walking all over the hillside, asking people, 'Has anyone seen my boy?' she kept on asking. 'My only child, Ashebir.' She cried for you."

Ashebir sank his head into his chest.

"I am sorry mother," Mohamed Abdu said.

Ashebir never meant to upset Zewdie. He felt both ashamed and sorry for himself. His whole body ached. Even though it was a short way to their home, it would take all his strength to get there.

"The boys have had enough," Emet Zeineba said, looking at Temima. "They will never do that again." She let out a strange chuckle and sucked her teeth.

Ashebir thought the woman must be completely exhausted. Once they were close enough to their village to relax a little, she'd told them that she had gone to the hot springs to cure the pains in her legs.

"No sooner was I sitting with my legs in the hot water, than I heard all that commotion," she said. "The shouting and crying when the Afar grabbed you, Ashebir."

"Thanks to God you came," Ashebir muttered.

"How often do we have to tell you children not to go there?" she had said, shaking her head.

Zewdie was sitting by the hearth. He could hear her praying. She turned round immediately when she heard them at the door, fear and worry in her face. He stood looking at her, with Emet Zeineba behind him.

Zewdie jumped to her feet a hand raised. "Where have you been?" she shouted.

He cowered back, he had never seen her so angry.

"What about the animals? Aminat brought them, you thoughtless boy."

The old woman's hand was on his shoulder.

Zewdie lowered her hand. She had never hit him. Would she have hit him if Emet Zeineba had not been there?

"Emet Zeineba. Praise Allah, how are you? What are you doing here?" Zewdie said.

Ashebir looked up at his mother.

"Why do you make me worry like this?" Zewdie said. She knelt down, took him in her arms and held him tight.

He was so relieved to smell the warmth of his mother's body and sink his face into her soft gabi, that he started sobbing all over again.

Zewdie tried to calm him and looked up at Emet Zeineba.

"What happened?" Zewdie said, getting to her feet and drawing them both inside and near to the fire.

They sat and Emet Zeineba explained everything while Zewdie listened in silence.

Ashebir could see the horror on her face. She drew him closer to her and started crying. She kissed him many times and then got up and went over to Emet Zeineba and kissed her many times.

"Thank you dear friend, you saved my boy's life," she wiped her nose on the corner of her gabi.

"They could have killed you, Ashebir," she said and started weeping all over again. "Thank you Zeineba. Allah will reward you. Thank you."

Zeineba made that funny chuckle sound again. "You will not be going up the river again for a while, will you?" she said, looking at Ashebir.

"No, Emet Zeineba," he said. She was a brave woman, he thought, a strong woman, even if her body had become old and painful.

"How many times do we have to tell you children to stay away from the hot springs?" Zewdie chided him.

"We didn't mean to go there. We were fishing," Ashebir began to explain but was caught by a wide yawn. "I'm sorry Zewdie," he said and leaned his head on her shoulder.

"Let the boy go to bed, Zewdie," the old woman said. "I will go home now. Try and rest both of you and talk in the morning."

"Zeineba?" Zewdie said.

"Yes, Zewdie," the old woman looked up.

"It's a miracle. It was your birrd, your aches and pains, which saved my boy's life."

The woman chuckled again letting out a grunt as she got up to leave.

"It was her courage, Zewdie, that saved me," Ashebir whispered and was surprised to hear the two women laughing quietly.

9

Two black kites were circling high in the thin morning air, meeting in brief mock battles, separating to glide under the sun, their wings spread wide against the blue. The terrace door was open. John Martyn crooned softly, interrupted by the hollow clatter of water filling an empty pail at the standpipe in the alley below.

"Fasika and Mulu told me about this woman," Izzie said. "They think she might have a job for me. I'm going to call her this morning."

"Hey, honey. Why didn't you say before?"

"I don't know. You worked late last night and I wanted to hear what had happened. The food shortage situation is terrible. I thought it could wait."

"Tell me now, then. This is great, honey." He ruffled her hair, looking genuinely pleased. He took a piece of Negisst's ambasha bread and buttered it.

"She's a farenj, lived here for years, was married to an Ethiopian. Fasika says she's a real character, a heart of gold and slightly ibd."

"Ibd?"

"'Mad', crazy. Weren't you listening in class?"

"I take it, slightly eccentric?" he laughed. "You'll get on with her a treat then."

"I like eccentric," Izzie said, pushing his shoulder gently. "Pass me the tomatoes?"

"Could enter those for a warped vegetables competition," Moe said, picking one that looked like it had two legs and put it on her plate.

"Hmmm, thanks," she said. "It's a government project, funded by an international organisation. They want to open a factory for the disabled in Nazareth."

"Nazareth? Honey, that's a good hundred K south of Addis."

Izzie leant over and kissed him.

"You're not moving to Nazareth," he said.

"The main office is here in Addis. It's a government office. I'll find out more when I speak to Uschi."

"She's German?" Moe said.

"You sound surprised. She's from West Berlin. She met her husband in London in the sixties. They were both artists. Now she does clothing and textile design and trains disabled in sewing. Fasika was related to Uschi's husband. She said he died a few years ago."

"In the Red Terror?"

"I don't know, she didn't say."

"OK. So, more about the job?"

"They want to train disabled, who are begging on the streets, to make children's clothes from locally made materials. High fashion. Top Shop stuff." She laughed. "I'm obviously exactly the right person for the job."

"You are of course the fashion guru of the British community," he said.

She stuck her tongue out at him.

"By the way, everyone's asking when you're going to join us on a Hash?"

"They just want to see me drunk. All that running and ra-ra. Take me bopping on the Debre Zeit road any day, Moe."

"Leila is coming on the Hash this weekend."

"What happened between Leila and Booker? Did he say anything to you?"

"I don't know." Moe said.

"Shame they're splitting up," Izzie said. "I like her. She's good for him."

There was a noise at the front door.

"That'll be Negisst," she said.

"Is that the time already?" Moe said, looking at his watch. "I have to go. Good luck with the German dressmaker, honey. She'll love you. I'll keep my fingers crossed you get the job."

"Thanks," she said, lifting her face.

He kissed her, "See you later, honey."

"Later, later," she said and heard him laughing with Negisst in the corridor as he went out.

"Morning Negisst," Izzie called out. "Tenasteling."

Negisst came in and stood in the doorway, smiling shyly as if Moe had said something quite cheeky. She bowed a little and took off the white shema, so it hung loosely round her shoulders, revealing her head tightly wrapped in a black scarf. Almost all middle-aged women wore black headscarves. So many deaths, Negisst had told her. Disease. Political. Diarrhoea. Hunger. Birrd – the word used to describe cold to the bone and, it seemed, every other ailment which did not have a specific name.

Izzie felt like giving Negisst a hug; she looked so warm and motherly.

"How are you today, Izzie?" Negisst said.

"I am fine, Egziyabher yimesgen," Izzie turned her eyes skywards. 'Thanks to God.' She was not sure she believed. If there was a God, he had been indelibly etched on her mind as an old white man with a beard, looming out of the clouds in her children's bible. She wondered if Negisst's Egziyabher was black.

"How are you, Negisst? And the family?"

Negisst smiled, lifting a corner of her thin white cotton shema to cover her mouth.

Izzie's Amharic amused Negisst.

"We are fine, Egziyabher yimesgen," Negisst said, turning her eyes to the ceiling.

"The children in school?"

"Yes, everyone's in school. Only the small one's at home, sick."

"Oh Negisst. She at home alone, is she?" Izzie said, hoping she wasn't.

"A girl is there. From the village."

"You have someone working for you, Negisst?"

"I am working here, Madam," Negisst smiled, her head on one side. "A girl is working in my house."

It had not occurred to Izzie. How stupid. "How old is she?"

"I don't know, Madam. Maybe twelve. She was born in the Emperor's time. Before the revolution, before the drought," Negisst said.

"The girl is going school after work?"

"Night school, Madam."

Hundreds of people went to night school. Izzie had seen them streaming into the University at Arat Kilo in the early evening.

"Mengistu says all people must read and write. Girls too," Negisst said.

It was incredible that when the Emperor was deposed, not more than ten percent of the population could read and write. "And you? What about you, Negisst?" Negisst was putting all her children through school and couldn't read herself.

Negisst sucked her teeth and smiled. "I am too old."

"No you're not."

Negisst shook her head and Izzie decided not to persist. With a job, a husband and four children, cooking, baking ambasha, Negisst had enough on her hands.

"Did you take the little one to the doctor?" Izzie said.

"No. Doctor too much money. I made tea. My medicine is good. Egziyabher sifeked, she will be better tomorrow. If God allows."

"Will you give me your medicine too?" Izzie said. "If I get sick?"

"I am making you good tea," Negisst said, giggling. The idea of giving Izzie her medicine seemed to delight her. "But you not getting sick, Madam. You're strong farenj."

Izzie left the breakfast table, picking up her cup and plate. She had to go to the Blue Nile Bar across the road to call Uschi. If Negisst's Egziyabher allowed, she was going to get that job.

"No, Madam. I am doing that," Negisst said.

"Let me do it, Negisst. I don't want to forget how to clear the table," she said, laughing and going into the kitchen. "You can take Moe's things. He's a lazy sod sometimes."

"Sod?" Negisst said.

"Lump of earth."

Negisst obviously loved that. "All men sod," she said.

**

Izzie greeted the old zabanya at the main entrance. "Salaam," she said. "How are you?"

He waved his stick at her. The one he was not averse to using on the backs of the boys' legs, if they tried to dodge past him into the building. The children would dart away, shrieking and giggling. If he caught one, there were tears. He walked with a slight limp and she wondered if he'd fought for the Emperor against the Italians, been wounded at the front against the Somalis.

Piazza was already on the move. Izzie stood on the kerb and looked left and right. It was like waiting to jump in under a skipping rope. Each time there was a gap another car came and she hesitated. Hearing the turquoise woman's voice, she turned around. Izzie had seen her before, pacing Piazza, back and forth, like a lioness trapped in a cage. There she was again. The way she dressed at odds with the rest of the women on Piazza. Her black stretch pants showed too much bottom. Her thick legs rubbed against each other as she walked. She wore a frayed turquoise-blue sweater pulled down tightly over her ample papaya-shaped breasts.

She shouted now and then, at no one in particular.

Perhaps there was something enviable about being crazy in this city, with its lid on untold stories. Negisst's brother had been a soldier but when Izzie tried to find out more, Negisst got busy with her dusting. Moe said he thought he was in prison, like so many others. The Red Terror had cost many lives. Not more than five years back. Students had been shot, left dying on the streets, hanging from lampposts, Shirley had told her. She and Brian had been in Ethiopia at the time. It was horrendous, she'd said.

But her Ethiopian friends didn't talk about that time. Izzie realised how little she knew about what they and their families had been through. There was a heavy silence. The turquoise woman was lucky; she could shout her thoughts aloud, without fear of arrest.

A few people on the pavement turned and laughed at her rantings, making fun of her. Others walked past, taking no notice. Piazza regulars were used to the woman.

Izzie caught the woman's eye by mistake. They were bloodshot and disturbed. Izzie looked away, determined to cross the road before the woman came any nearer. She jiggled the coins in her pocket, hoping Awgucho was in the bar and that the phone was connected. The job sounded good and her savings were running out. Aeroflot's compensation for the lost suitcase had barely bought a pair of shoes.

Izzie suddenly felt a tight grip on her arm and found herself face to face with the turquoise woman. She must have lunged when Izzie looked away.

"Let go," Izzie said, trying to shake her off. It was unpleasant and she did not like drawing attention herself, being one of the few farenj in Piazza.

The woman pulled her closer, smiling, her hold uncomfortably strong "Izzie, Izzie, Egziyabher yawkal," the woman chanted. "Izzie, Izzie, Egziyabher yawkal." Her breath smelt foul, early morning stomach odours, tobacco and garlic. Her teeth were stained green from chewing khat.

A small crowd gathered. Women called out in high-pitched voices.

Izzie struggled to free herself, trying not to panic. What was the woman on about? 'Izzie, Izzie, God only knows?' And how did she know her name? "Help me," she shouted towards the zabanya.

He was there, behind the woman, his stick raised.

"Don't hit her," Izzie shouted.

Hands pulled and tugged to get the woman off her. Finally, she was free. The zabanya and another man held the distraught woman between them. She was crying, her arms flailing like someone drowning. She looked at Izzie with no sign of recognition.

Izzie felt dirty. She rubbed her sore arms. The woman must have a demon inside.

"Lock the crazy up," one woman said. She lived down the alley behind Girma's suk.

"No, they should take her to church," another said, her hand on Izzie's arm.

Did they exorcise devils? Anything was possible. Despite the communist propaganda, religion ran in their veins, it was in their language. Without God's name, Amharic would fall apart. Izzie took a deep breath.

"Are you alright?" It was the woman with the blue cross on her forehead. Izzie had seen her a few times at Girma's suk.

She was touched by their concern.

"I am fine, Egziyabher yimesgen," Izzie said. Her voice came out quiet and strained.

Someone laughed, "The farenj speaks Amharic."

"She's our neighbour," the woman with the blue cross said.

The turquoise woman was being led away.

Izzie was about to go back to the flat, abandon her intention to make that phone call, when she saw Hailu running into the middle of the road. He was dodging the passing cars. He stopped in the middle, on tip-toes, one hand held high in the air. He brought the traffic to a stand-still. "Come, Izzie, quickly," he said, motioning frantically at her to cross.

"Ishi, coming," she said, wiping her eyes. "Thank you," she said to the women around her. She put her hand on Hailu's head when she reached him and they crossed together.

"She crazy woman," Hailu said. "She go Kebele prison."

Biniam, Hailu's oldest brother, stood nearby. He had one foot propped against the wall behind him and his arms folded across his chest. He was chatting with the bigger boys. They all had wooden shoe-shine boxes at their feet. Mekonnen was leaning against a parked car waiting for a customer.

"Prison?" Izzie said.

"She sleep little then go home," Hailu said, smiling up at her.

"God," Izzie said. "Poor woman." She felt in her pocket for her cigarettes. What was 'home' for a woman like that? she wondered. The cigarettes were gone. Someone must have nicked them in the scuffle. "Damn."

Mekonnen came up to her tapping his head with his finger. "She bad, very bad," he said.

"She's just not well," Izzie said.

The boys gathered around her, taking turns to shake her hand.

"How are you all? How is your mother, boys?"

"She is sick, birrd," Biniam said. "You come home, see our mother."

Their mother made a living by selling small piles of onions, tomatoes and chilli peppers by the roadside and seemed to regularly suffer from birrd. "I have something to do and then I'll come, ishi?" Izzie said, a little surprised by Biniam's insistence. She had never been to their house.

"Bira, Ambuha water today buying, Izzie?" Biniam said. He wore a tiny wooden cross on a black thread round his neck.

Izzie touched it. "What is this in Amharic, Biniam?"

"Meskel."

"Meskel," Izzie said. The jewellery shops along Piazza were full of them. A lot of gold. The silver ones were delicate filigree. She preferred the old worn soft silver ones.

"Silver very expensive," Hailu said, shaking his head knowingly.

"But they are beautiful," she said. He was right, they cost a lot.

"Has anyone got cigarettes?" She looked around the boys.

"What you want, Izzie? Benson Gold, Win-iston, Mar-le-boro Red?" Hailu said.

"Winston," she said, giving him some money. He darted across the road to Girma's suk. One day one of them would get run over.

"Where you going, Izzie?" Mekonnen said.

Izzie liked the shy Mekonnen with his raspy voice. Though he and Hailu were brothers there was little resemblance. She half suspected they had different fathers.

"To the Blue Nile," she said, nodding her head towards the bar.

"No drinking bira," Biniam laughed.

"No bira. I make telephone call," Izzie said. She put her thumb to her ear and small finger to her mouth as if to make a call.

Hailu was back at her elbow with the cigarettes and change. She gave him a few centimes.

"Thank you Hailu," she said, "Ciao, ciao." She walked towards the bar.

"You coming our house after?" Biniam called after her.

"I'm coming your house after, Biniam."

**

A tree had squeezed its way between the Blue Nile Bar and Addis Sports next door, spreading shade over the inner courtyard and cracks through the walls. The pale blue paintwork was peeling under the ivy, exposing crumbling mud brickwork. A short flight of steps took her up to the entrance. The bar was empty. Later in the day it would pick up. Awgucho stayed open until an hour or so before curfew, and most evenings she could hear the faint rhythms of Tilahun, Aster Bekele or Bob Marley floating up through the open windows of their flat.

The dark interior was a stark contrast to the bright morning outside. A boy was sloshing water from a bucket onto the floor with a mop, leaving odd-shaped patches of damp in the concrete. There was a pungent smell of stale beer and Dettol. In the evenings the place was more inviting with its warm bodies, cigarette smoke and cheap perfume. The tables and chairs were the uniform hollow aluminium and grated against the floor as the boy moved them around.

Awgucho came out from behind the bar where he was bottling up. "Hello Izzie, how are you? Bit early for a beer," he said, smiling and holding a hand out. He had a lazy right eye which made him look sceptical until he smiled. He always wore his shirt rolled up at the sleeves and a pin-striped waistcoat which Izzie fancied might once have belonged to a city gent's three-piece. She imagined it emerging from the Waterloo and City Line at Bank on its way to Lloyds in a former life.

"Morning, Awgucho," she said, shaking his hand. She got out a cigarette, offering him one. "Have you got a coffee for me?" she said, lighting up. She still felt a bit shaken.

"I do," he said, disappearing behind the bar. He came back with two small glasses of steaming black coffee. "Sugar?"

"No thanks," she said, taking a sip. The sharp, bitter taste had the same effect as a shot of whiskey. "I needed that. Is the phone working today?"

The phone booth gobbled up coins, no refund and the money was collected by Telecommunications. Awgucho was always apologetic but said he wasn't allowed to stick an 'out of order' notice on it. Most of the time he was waiting for someone to come and repair it.

"Egziyabher alle, Izzie. If God is with us, the phone will work. Hurry up, before Telecomm finds out and shuts it down," he said with a laugh.

She finished her coffee and went to the booth.

"Hello? Hello?" Izzie said. The line was working but she could barely hear a thing for the crackling. "Hello. This is Izzie Brown speaking... Is that Uschi? Hello? ...This is Izzie. Yes, I've been in Addis a couple of months and am looking for work. ...Fasika gave me your number... Yes, she said you need someone with a business background...That's right. ...That would be great. I'd love to. ...Yes, I know Enrico's. ...It's near the office? ...What time did you say? ...Eight-thirty tomorrow morning? ...Yes Uschi, me too. Look forward to seeing you then, bye." Izzie hooked the phone back on the wall. Uschi sounded uncomplicated and spoke with a charming European-Ethiopian accent. If the office was near Enrico's, Izzie thought, she could walk to work.

Izzie waved thanks to Awgucho and went down the steps into the sunshine. She was immediately surrounded by the boys.

"You come my house now?" Biniam said.

"OK, Biniam. You sure your mother won't mind."

"Our mother sick," Mekonnen said. "You come, Izzie."

They took her up the narrow street opposite their flat. Halfway up the hill was a tall metal gate, its yellow paint peeling off to reveal rust beneath. Hailu banged on the door with the palm of his hand, making it rattle loudly.

"Abate, abate?" a woman's voice called from inside.

"It's us," Negussay said. "We have a visitor. Let us in."

A woman wearing a smock over her long skirt and a colourful scarf round her head opened the gate. "You bad boys what are you up to?" she said and laughed.

"She always saying we bad boys but we good. Every time good," Hailu said.

Izzie bowed her head and shook the woman's hand.

"She Greek man's maid," Mekonnen said.

"Who is the Greek man?" Izzie said, following the boys over the cobblestone courtyard. The villa had a shabby front porch and damp stains seeping up the walls. A donkey with large sad eyes stood tied to a post in the compound, a bundle of firewood strapped to its back.

"This Greek man house," Hailu said. "Business man," he added, a proud smile on his face.

They took her down the side of the house, under the eaves of the corrugated iron roof. The small inner garden was overgrown with weeds. A row of rusting tins stood against the fence, an assortment of plants at various stages of life and death growing over their rims. The

Greek man's maid went back to her washing line, hung with wide trousers, billowing Y-fronts, socks and white shema. She pulled a cloth out of a large plastic washing up basin and shook it out with a snap. The smell of frying onions and spices came from an open door, making Izzie's mouth water. She could see nothing through the windows, siesta-dark inside. The wooden shutters, the palest turquoise washed paintwork cracked and flaking, gave the place a Mediterranean air.

"Here, Izzie, come in," Negussay said.

They had reached the rear of the house. Izzie bent her head to get inside. It was pitch black. She could not see a thing. "Hello?" she said into the darkness, touching a damp wall to feel her way.

"Mama, its Izzie," Hailu said.

"Izzie, it's you, Egziyabher yimesgen. Come in."

10

It was a roomy office, modern and comfortable with a carpet. It had a picture window looking out onto a small park with an enormous statue of Lenin in the middle. He was facing the Bole Road and looked as if he was on his way to the airport. She didn't think much of this communism. Her suitcase had doubtless been shared out equally between Aeroflot staff in Moscow; and boys like Hailu and Mekonnen didn't get such a good deal out of it either.

"Izzie. How lovely to see you," Fasika said, as Izzie walked in. Fasika made Izzie feel special. "How are you?"

They shook hands and kissed each other on alternate cheeks. Izzie took a chair opposite Fasika's desk.

"I've just come from Hailu and Mekonnen's house."

"What on earth were you doing there farenj?" Fasika laughed. "Ibd nesh enday, you're completely crazy.

"They live in the coal shed at the back of the Greek man's bungalow. The three boys and the little girl live there with their mother, Abebech, and the grandmother. It's awful. There's no water, no light. I don't know how anyone can survive like that."

"So many people in Addis do, Izzie."

"It's desperate. And the boys are on Piazza every day, working, playing, laughing. I don't know how they do it."

"It is all they know, Izzie. And what to do but laugh, if you have nothing?" Fasika said.

"Abebech is sick. Birrd they said."

"It's no wonder, poor woman. There's not a lot you can do."

"I took her to the flat."

"Enday?" Fasika said. "You're joking."

"How is she going to get well in that place?" Izzie said.

"Izzie, you can't do that."

"I just told Negisst to run a hot bath for her, feed her and let her rest there for today," Izzie said. "Negisst knows how to make medicine teas. She said she would concoct something to make Abebech feel better."

"You'll end up with the whole of Piazza in your bathroom," Fasika said, looking over her typewriter at Izzie and smiling. Her dark red lips reminded Izzie of the lipstick her mother wore. "Anyway, Izzie, where did you disappear to? Mulu and I were wondering about you."

"I was here only two days ago," Izzie said, laughing. "I can't keep disturbing you."

"Did you want to see Moe?" Fasika said. "Tell him about the new house guest?"

"He won't mind," Izzie said. "Is he around?"

"He went for a meeting at the Ministry of Agriculture."

"Actually, I came to see you and Mulu."

The phone rang. "Hello Mr Riley," Fasika said. "Yes, I'll get it ready as soon as we hear from Rome. …Yes. …OK, bye." Fasika put the phone down.

"Is there any mail for us?" Izzie got up and went to the pigeonholes. There was one for each of the Agriculture and Food Institute staff. She shared Moe's compartment. It was empty. She had half hoped for a letter from home.

"Hello there, Izzie," Mulu said, coming into the room. "How are you?" Mulu wore a plain grey suit, her skirt just below the knee. Her hair was a mass of tight afro-curls kept short and funky; not straightened, long and shiny like Fasika's.

"I'm fine," Izzie said. She exchanged kisses and cheeks, noticing Mulu's light perfume.

"How did your meeting with Mr Riley go, Mulu?" Fasika said.

"We discussed the delegation from Rome," Mulu said, going to her desk by the window and opening a brown foolscap folder. She took out a wad of papers.

"The food situation is not good," Fasika said, looking at Izzie.

"Moe was telling me," Izzie said.

"Maybe another disaster," Mulu said.

"What did he say about those figures?" Fasika said.

"The Relief Council figures? He said they are exaggerated. Wondwossen will be furious," Mulu said.

The telex machine pinged and started rattling a message out in the corner.

"Must be Head Office," Fasika said, going over to have a look.

She had a lovely pastel-coloured, calf length dress on, a fitted dark blue jacket on top. She walked on her heels with the swaying hips of a confident woman. Some people just had the knack, and the body, Izzie thought. She had never had a sophisticated, beautiful, friend like Fasika before. Hers usually wore tatty flared jeans and tight t-shirts.

"I don't know why they bother hiring people in from Rome, you two could run this office single handed," Izzie said.

Fasika raised an eyebrow and looked at Izzie in a way that said, You might have a point, but nothing's going to change around here.

"The Relief Counsel?" Izzie said.

"They manage food supplies, monitor shortages and liaise with donors when the country needs food aid," Mulu said. "Wondwossen is their Director of Operations. He's a relative of Fasika's."

"Why will he be so mad?"

"The RC is predicting a massive food deficit. If we don't agree with Wondwossen's figures, other donors won't either, and Ethiopia won't get the grain he's asking for," Mulu said.

Fasika came back with the telex.

"Who is right?" Izzie said.

"We'll definitely have a food shortage if the main rains don't come soon, June-July," Mulu said. "The question is how big a shortage."

"Coffee, Izzie?" Fasika said, pushing a button on the wall behind her desk. "Mulu? You too?"

Mulu put a finger up and nodded.

"I'd love one," Izzie said. "I came to tell you I called Uschi this morning. I'm going to meet her tomorrow."

"That's great," Mulu said. "Good for you."

"You'll take the job if she offers, won't you?" Fasika said, reading the telex. "There's five of them coming, Mulu."

Mulu shook her head and sucked her teeth. "You better make a reservation at the Hilton."

"I'll definitely take it," Izzie said. "I can't just sit around reading Doris Lessing and learning Amharic forever."

A girl came in with a metal tray. Her thin ankles poked out under her long skirt and she wore black plastic shoes, like the ones Girma sold in his suk.

"Three macchiato please, Kidist," Fasika said.

"Ishi," the girl whispered.

"Without sugar, Egziyabher yimesgen," Izzie said.

Kidist smiled shyly at Izzie and left the room.

"People love your Amharic, Izzie," Fasika said. "But maybe not the zabanya jacket." Fasika looked at Mulu and they both laughed.

"Fasika!" Izzie said. "Don't be so rude about my jacket. I love it. Khaki is all the rage at home. And it's so practical with all the pockets."

"Not here, sweet Izzie," Mulu said, smiling at her. She had broad cheek bones and a soft gentle face.

"No one would be seen dead in khaki here," Fasika said. "We have to smarten you up a little, Izzie."

"I'm no good with dresses."

"Turn round, let's see," Fasika said.

Izzie stood up and turned round.

"No, you're right," Fasika said. "Kit yelleshim."

"What's that supposed to mean?"

"No arse," Mulu said. "You need an arse to wear dresses. Look at hers."

"I obviously need to work harder on my Amharic," Izzie said.

"And on your arse," Fasika said, laughing. "We need to feed you up on injera."

Izzie pulled a face at Fasika and drew her chair up to the desk. "I thought Hailu and his little gang were my best teachers. But I obviously need to learn more from you, Fasika. I didn't know you could be so rude."

"You haven't heard anything," Mulu said, chuckling and sucked her teeth.

Kidist came in with a tray of coffee and placed one in front of each of them. She moved round the room like a shadow.

They bowed their heads in turn and said, Egziyabher yimesgen.

Kidist smiled and left the room without a word.

"Moe might go to Massawa next week. Did he tell you?" Mulu said.

"He did mention something about going away, but he wasn't sure," she said. "He said Mr Riley wants to know the capacity at the port for importing grains."

"Massawa's only a small port," Mulu said. "If there's an emergency, we need to know how much can pass through before we start ordering and shipping stocks."

"Isn't it dangerous for him to drive through Tigray?"

"Not for a UN vehicle. The TPLF ambush trucks carrying food supplies and ammunition," Mulu said.

"What's that again?"

"Tigray People's Liberation Front," Fasika said.

Izzie took a sip of her coffee. Daytime Addis seemed so calm and yet there was hunger looming and the whole country was at war. It was hard to grasp the reality of it.

Amari, one of the drivers, came in with a waft of sweaty heat from outside. He greeted Izzie, taking her hand in two of his, he shook it enthusiastically. He had a round belly and a smile to go with it. He gave Fasika a paper to sign and picked up some keys from her desk. "I'm taking Mr Riley to a lunch meeting. Not sure where yet."

"The Ghion Hotel," Fasika said. "I'll tell him you're waiting downstairs."

He raised his hand and left. "I'll see if Kidist has a coffee for me too," he said as he went out of the door.

"You know with the war and all that," Izzie said. "Is it true the air force bombed a market in Tigray with napalm a week ago? Is that possible?"

"Anything's possible, Izzie," Mulu said.

"I was convinced that would never happen again after Viet Nam," Izzie said. "How could they?"

"This government, with the Soviets behind them, is capable of anything," Fasika said.

"And it's the countryside that suffers," Mulu said. "The people come down from their villages in the mountains, go to market to sell their produce, and then – God, it's not worth thinking about – "

"They are fighting everywhere," Fasika said. "I don't know when it's going to stop. The Eritreans want independence, Tigray doesn't accept Mengistu, the Somalis want the Ogaden back."

"And now we've got the real possibility of a famine," Mulu said.

"Wondwossen is convinced," Fasika said. "I saw him a few nights ago. He's at his wit's end. Seems like neither the government nor the international community will listen."

"Can't you persuade Mr Riley?" Izzie said.

"You think I haven't tried?" Mulu said. "He thinks we are influenced by Fasika's connection."

"What about Booker and Moe, then?" Izzie said, knowing she was out of her depth and pulling at straws.

"Your Moe is young and inexperienced. They won't listen to him here or in Rome," Mulu said. "Anyway, Izzie, if they won't listen to us, why do you think they would listen to those two?"

"Sorry. You're right," Izzie said, knowing her wrist had been slapped.

She was starting to learn that Ethiopians didn't mince their words.

"It's also because we have a Soviet-backed government," Fasika said. "Western governments don't trust Mengistu and his Derg.[44] They think the Soviet bloc should deal with Ethiopia's problems."

"What about Eritrea?" Izzie said.

"What of it?" Mulu said.

"Don't you think it should be independent?" Izzie said. "It would be one less war to fight. It's costing lives and money. It is different, isn't it? It was separate for some time."

"To be honest, all I want is peace," Fasika said. "So many people have died, one way or another. It's enough."

Izzie looked up to see tears in Fasika's eyes. She glanced at Mulu.

Mulu shook her head and frowned. She tapped her teeth with the end of her pencil and looked down at her papers again.

Fasika blew her nose and looked down to read the telex.

Izzie took small sips of coffee. She had never talked about so much with them before. She hoped she had not overstepped a line. Shirley and Brian talked about the war, executions, arrests at night, people disappearing after curfew. And though she found the empty streets after midnight slightly menacing, she could not quite believe what they said. She could not take it in. "Fasika?" she said, half standing.

Fasika wiped her nose and smiled. "I'm fine, Izzie," she said. She picked up two white sheets of paper and slid a dark blue carbon in between. She tapped them on the desk and fed them into her typewriter. "It was my older brother," she said. She wound the paper on and snapped the bar in place to hold the paper down. She looked at Izzie. "My brother was a junior minister under Haile Selassie. At the time of the revolution, he agreed like everyone that things needed to change, but not to overthrow the Emperor, not to kill him."

"I thought Haile Selassie died of natural causes?"

"They suffocated him and pretended he'd passed away. He was an old man, so everyone believed them," Mulu said.

"My brother told us he was murdered." Fasika blew her nose again, leaving red blotches of lipstick on the white tissue.

"The Derg had several high-ranking officers executed in November 1974," Mulu said. "Others have gone the same way since. They said Fasika's brother was a counter revolutionary. It's this socialism. You're either with them, or you're against them. That's how they think. And

---

[44] The Provisional Military Administrative Council, ruled Ethiopia from 1974 to 1987.

once they've decided you're against them, you've had it."

The door opened and Robert Riley Jr. walked in, a perfect crease in the trousers of his light grey suit, the white collar of his pressed shirt showing off his pool-side tan. "Hello Izzie, how are you doing?" he said with a broad grin. He was middle- aged, American and the Resident Representative.

"Fine thanks, Mr Riley. Fine. Still job hunting but nearly there, hopefully."

Fasika was already tapping on her typewriter. The keys clicking furiously.

"You have that travel application ready, Fasika?" he said. "The delegation will need permits from the Ministry of Information to go up north."

"It's nearly done, Mr Riley," she said, looking up at him briefly. "We just got the confirmation of names from Rome. I'll book them into the Hilton."

Izzie looked at Fasika. No one could possibly tell she had just broken down. She was as composed and beautiful as ever.

"Brilliant," Mr Riley said.

"Amari is waiting with the car outside, Mr Riley. You're going to the Ghion Hotel for lunch?"

"Really," Mr Riley said. "I don't know what I would do without you girls." He left the office smiling and shaking his head.

Fasika and Mulu looked at each other.

"'Girls,'" Izzie said when he'd gone. "It must be time for a revolution."

11

April 1982, Addis Ababa

Izzie got to Enrico's in good time. She liked going there, its bitter-sweet smell of coffee, the freshly baked pastries covered in powder sugar. It was always busy, and no one took any notice of her. She sometimes walked down from Piazza to sit with the Guardian Weekly and a macchiato.

A glint of sunlight caught in the woman's silver-fair hair as she came through the doorway. It must be Uschi. She looked around with a confidence unusual to ex-pat women. Izzie was more nervous about the interview than she had expected.

"Just be yourself," Moe had said in the morning, giving her one of his big hugs.

Uschi spotted her, waved and made her way over, excusing herself between the occupied tables.

Izzie raised a hand in acknowledgement. She crossed her fingers under the table and made a silent wish that by the time she met Moe for lunch, she would have a job.

Uschi wore a summer dress under a pale yellow jacket rolled up at the sleeves and was clutching a wad of buff-coloured folders to her chest. A bulging handbag hung from the crook of her arm. She was a little plump and walked with the short busy steps of someone wearing heels. She had that touch of sophistication middle-aged continental women had over their British counterparts. Izzie looked down at her Converse boots. She hadn't found a pair of shoes she liked since her arrival.

Uschi stopped to greet an Ethiopian woman in a dark suit. They must know each other well, the better you know someone the more kisses. Uschi nodded in Izzie's direction. The woman looked over and smiled. Izzie tried to look friendly, her heart in her mouth.

"There you are," Uschi said, when she finally reached the table. She let out a little chirping laugh. "I'm late." She had the joined-up freckles on her face and arms of an old-timer in Africa.

"That's alright," Izzie said, just managing to whisk her coffee out of the way as Uschi leant forward, spilling folders across the table.

Uschi sat down, dumped her bag on the empty chair next to her and put a hand on her chest, out of breath. She wore a large beaded ring and bracelets which jingled against each other. "High blood pressure," she said. "They say the altitude's no good for me."

"I'll get a waiter," Izzie said. She'd seen Ethiopians clap for waiters, but couldn't bring herself to. She waved. They were all occupied. "Poor you," she said, not sure what high blood pressure did, but it didn't sound good.

Uschi shot Izzie a mischievous look, laughter wrinkles round her blue eyes. "I'm fine now. Just takes me a few minutes. So," she said, wriggling in her seat and putting a hand out. "I'm Uschi and you are Izzie. We have found each other."

Her hand was firm and friendly.

"Must have been tough trying to work out which one I was," Izzie said. "I was tempted to call out farenj, farenj when I saw you walking in."

Uschi laughed, shaking her head and running her fingers through her hair. She reached into her bag and pulled a thick, well-thumbed, magazine out. "This is Burda, my Bible. The latest in children's clothing design." She passed the magazine to Izzie.

"Fasika said you're working with the disabled."

"That's right. We want to give them an alternative to begging. The idea is to assemble them, give them a medical – Some will need callipers, you know, prosthesis, wheelchairs and so on. And train them to stitch beautiful things."

Izzie flipped through the Burda. "How many people do you plan to employ in the factory?"

"We have machines for sixty men and women."

"Enday, be Egziyabher, that's a lot. I helped a woman set up a tie and dye workshop for the handicapped in Lilongwe. But that was for about ten people."

Uschi laughed. "Fasika said you'd be the right person. She told me you're learning Amharic and have a business degree. She says you love it here."

Izzie was slightly taken aback. She had not thought of herself as, 'loving it' in Addis. The place intrigued her. She was charmed by the Ethiopians she'd met, the Piazza boys and their mother;

Negisst, Fasika and Mulu. "I would love to give it a go," she said.

"You sew?"

"A bit. Aeroflot shared the contents of my suitcase amongst their comrades in Moscow. I can't afford the clothes in Mercato. So I borrowed a machine and have been making a few things."

"Ha." Uschi banged the table, her bracelets jangling. "Another victim."

Izzie shrugged, smiling. "There you go." She was over it.

"Here, let me show you," Uschi took the Burda back from Izzie.

Izzie checked her bag was still hanging on her chair and put it down between her feet. It was not really necessary to worry in Enrico's. One advantage of living under a socialist dictatorship she'd noticed, was order and control. There were petty pickpockets but few thieves. The streets were relatively safe day and night. It was just not safe to speak.

Uschi opened the pages where the corners had been turned down. "Look, these are the designs I'm adapting." She pointed out little jumpsuits; pretty dresses with buttons up the front; boys' trousers and jackets.

"They look cute. Grown-up fashion for kids. I love the dungarees. For girls too."

"We'll use local cloth. We'll have to be creative. And we have to keep the prices down. We're competing with cheap imports." Uschi rummaged in her voluminous bag and pulled a dress out. "This is one of our samples; for a four-year- old." It was made in white cotton with colourful pockets.

"It's very pretty," Izzie said. It was sweet and beautifully made, but it was not really the clothes that grabbed her. It was the challenge of setting up the factory, giving the people who begged on street corners a job.

Uschi shuffled in her chair, looking round behind her. "Where is that man? I could do with a chai." She clapped her hands. "So," she went on. "We have a building, sixty sewing machines and clothing samples. You'll meet Genet. She works in my office making the samples. She'll be the assistant trainer and supervisor."

"Where is your office?"

"Two minutes up the road."

"And the factory's in Nazareth?" Izzie had checked it out on the map. It was near a place called Mojo, the junction where the road went south, lined with blue blobs denoting the Rift Valley Lakes: Koka, Zwai, Langano and Abiata, and more further south.

"That's right but there's a lot to plan and organise first. We do everything from the head office in Addis. It's called the Agency for Disabled, Children and Destitute. ADCD for short. Our Director is away on political training in East Germany at the moment." Uschi chuckled. "I gave him a list of useful words in German before he left; the masses, commune, workers of the world unite." She let out a short chirrup laugh. "He was grateful and said I was a true comrade."

The waiter appeared.

"Ah, there you are," Uschi said in Amharic, smiling up at him. "How are you?"

He reminded Izzie of a butler. He was always courteous and never smiled.

"I'll have a chai, please," Uschi said.

The waiter nodded and turned to Izzie.

Will you have another one, Izzie?"

"Thank you. I'll have a tekur macchiato, no sugar." Izzie looked at the waiter. "The coffee here is good."

He nodded and left them, his round metal tray dangling from his hand.

"Ethiopia loves her coffee," Uschi said. "You know what they call it?"

Izzie shook her head.

"Arangwadey werk, Green Gold. It's the main export. Have you been to a coffee ceremony? Seen them roasting the green beans?"

"My maid, Negisst, invited me to her house. I love the smell of the incense and the way the room fills with smoke."

"Itan," Uschi said. "You can buy it in Mercato."

"Fasika said you're fluent in Amharic."

"Kitchen Amharic. I learnt it cooking hot spicey wot with my mother-in-law," Uschi said.

"I'm going for lessons at the Goethe Institute."

"The Amharic will be useful for our work. Who's teaching you?"

"A guy called Solomon," Izzie said. She pulled her chair closer to let someone pass behind her.

A young couple sat at the next table.

"Ha. Young Solomon."

"You know him?"

"I occasionally go to the Goethe Institute for films, cultural events. Keep my hand in," Uschi chuckled. "My compatriots all think I'm quite mad. Solomon is good, is he?"

"Very good. We have three lessons a week. Then I practice on the street kids in Piazza and with our zabanyas. Fasika calls my Amharic: "ye Piazza Amharinya."

"You've picked up a good accent," Uschi said, looking impressed.

"Uschi, what do you need me to do?" Izzie said, getting her CV out of her bag and holding it out for Uschi to take. She didn't dare assume she had the job, though Uschi was talking as if she'd already decided.

Uschi glanced at the CV and put it in one of her folders. "Fasika told me about you. It's enough for me. What do we need you for? Well, we need job descriptions for a factory manager and store keeper, we need threads and material. ADCD has to cover those. We need to do the costing and sales prices, make budgets, set up the accounts, production plan, stock keeping system, marketing; I don't know what. Gezahegn knows I can't do it. I can design clothes, make patterns and train people to sew. But all the rest, I am hopeless at it." Uschi shuffled in her seat.

"Who's Gezahegn?" Izzie said.

"My Ethiopian boss. I have a boss at International too."

"What's he like, Gezahegn?"

"Tall, handsome, dark. He's a Gurage. They are good businessmen and love dancing," Uschi chuckled. "He's very polite, very serious about the work. That's why he's still head of department."

"How do you mean?"

"They normally put a party member in that position."

"Does he know about me?"

Uschi was rummaging in her folders and papers. Her bangles clinking. "Ah, look, here we are," Uschi said. She extracted some papers and gave them to Izzie. "Gezahegn wants a project document, a business plan, before he'll allocate funds. That's what we need you for."

Izzie flicked through the pages of randomly typed paragraphs, figures, calculations, drawings of samples, pencil notes scribbled in the margins. "What is this?" she said.

"The beginnings of a project document?"

"I see," Izzie said. She couldn't help smiling. "It needs some work doing on it."

"You think you can help me?"

"I would love to, Uschi," Izzie said, "it would be great."

The waiter appeared with their drinks. He bowed his head almost indiscernibly.

"I'll get it," Izzie said.

"No, no." Uschi lent over to dig in her bag. "Absolutely not." She pulled out a black leather purse held together with an elastic band. She gave the waiter a one Birr note. "Egzierstelin," she said, her eyes shining.

He smiled at her.

"He smiled at you," Izzie said, watching the waiter walk away. "Look at him, he never smiles at anyone."

"He and I have known each other – for – ever," Uschi said with a dramatic flourish of her hand.

"You mind if I have a cigarette?"

"Go ahead. I used to smoke. Given up. My heart."

"How long have you been here?"

Uschi shook her head. "Oh, goodness me, seventeen years?"

"You must like it," Izzie said. Seventeen years ago she was buying gobstoppers and sherbet with her thruppence ha'penny weekly pocket money.

"I love it. I love living in a city surrounded by mountains, the smoky atmosphere, the sea of white shawls outside the churches. And the people. You make a friend here, and you have a friend for life. But you have to watch your back."

"How do you mean?"

"There's a word in Amharic, tenkulenya. Means bendy-bendy." Uschi made a snake-like motion with her hand across the table, her bracelets chinking against each other. "It's the word they use to describe people who climb over others to get on, to get what they want. And, politically, this can be very dangerous."

Izzie was not sure what to say. She and Moe had talked. Should they stay in a place like this? The politics was complicated. A socialist state that ruled from palaces. Moe said he was not leaving. He was getting good experience and he earned more than he would get at home. She'd agreed to give it a go, if Uschi offered her a job. She did not want to work in an air-conditioned office, she'd rather work right in the thick of it. A job in a government office would be perfect.

"I'm just telling you how it is," Uschi said, quietly. "If you want to live and work here, you have to know who is in the party and who is trying to get by. Party members head departments, they are the Committee Chairmen and women in the Kebeles, they get priority for school places, jobs, the majority of university places overseas. They report on each other, just like the Stasi." Uschi took a sip of tea. "What can I say? We've trained them, at least my brothers and sisters in East Germany have."

"You must have been here during the Red Terror."

"It was dreadful. Dreadful," Uschi said, leaning across the table towards Izzie. "We tried to stay at home as much as possible. Let's just leave it at that."

Izzie looked at the pile of folders, at the open door onto the pavement and the shadows of people walking in the sunshine outside. Uschi's fingers were busy turning and folding one of the paper napkins.

"There," Uschi said, holding up a white bird.

"How did you do that? It's amazing."

"Beautiful things are everywhere around us," Uschi chirped, turning the paper bird around in her fingers.

"People like you make things beautiful," Izzie said.

"How long are you planning to stay, Izzie?"

"In Ethiopia? I don't know." Izzie realised Uschi had not asked about her boyfriend, what he was doing. She was the first person not to connect her decisions with him. "I think I'm happy to stay as long as I can work. At the moment I have a tourist visa which expires in three months."

"You'll need a work permit."

Izzie's heart sank. She had been told it was impossible to transfer a tourist visa into a work permit.

"You'll need an entry visa in your passport."

"Everyone's told me it's impossible once you've entered the country."

"Leave it to me," Uschi said. "I can organise it."

"You can?"

Uschi tapped the side of her nose. She took the papers back from Izzie, shoving them into their folder again. "I have good connections."

"It's a real pea soup," Izzie said. "Were things better in the Emperor's time? Some people say it was."

"People always say it was better in the past. But he should have modernised the state. It was feudal. He did open up schools, but not enough and not fast enough. His rule only benefitted a few. Izzie, I grow flowers in my garden and design beautiful clothes for children. I want to see colour and pretty things."

"You have a garden?"

"When we came to Ethiopia, my husband and I were given a beautiful little villa in a walled garden. I have a kitchen where we bake cookies all year round and Stollen at Christmas. My paradise."

"Did you ever see the Emperor in his car? I heard that people got down on their knees when he drove past."

"I met his granddaughters."

"The princesses?" Izzie said, lowering her voice automatically. "They're in prison, aren't they?"

"With their mother, Princess Tenagneworq," Uschi sucked her teeth. "I don't know why they don't just let them go."

"They must get special treatment though, don't they?"

"Ha. You must be joking," Uschi said, raising an eyebrow. "They went to Clarendon. You know it? A very good girls' school in England. Cucumber sandwiches, tea at four and all that."

"I guess they are punishing them for that now." Izzie wanted to hear more but could tell it was not the place.

"They are not well, you could say." Uschi coughed.

The waiter was serving the young couple at the next table. They looked up at him, then consulted each other, ordering coffee and cakes as if they were planning a wedding feast. The girl laid her hand on the young man's.

"Sweethearts," Uschi said. "Ha. They have to be so careful."

"Do they have arranged marriages here?"

"In the countryside, definitely they do. That's where many of the bar-girls come from. They're runaways from marriages to older men."

"I wondered," Izzie said.

"But in Addis, things are changing," Uschi said. "Youngsters want to choose for themselves. Their parents don't always agree."

Izzie noticed the soft aging under Uschi's chin, the silver Ethiopian cross against her sunburnt skin. It hung on a thick black thread round her neck in the traditional way.

Uschi touched the cross where Izzie's eyes had settled.

"It's a lovely cross," Izzie said.

"It's a Lalibela cross. A woman sold it to me in Senbatey Market. She needed to buy food for her children. I wear it and think of that." She rubbed the cross between her fingers. "Makes me feel a bit guilty." She packed her files back into her bag. "I think you and I are going to have fun," Uschi said. She smiled cheerfully and got up. "Let's go and meet Gezahegn, shall we?"

"I'd love to," Izzie said. She got her bag from under her chair and stood up. I've got myself a job, she thought. I've damn well got myself a job.

As Uschi passed the young couple, she put the paper bird down on the table between them and said something that made them look at each other and laugh.

Izzie smiled at them, wishing she could say something fitting in Amharic. She followed Uschi out into the sunshine, past the cashier perched on her stool, dressed in black.

**

They drove round the back of an uninspiring breeze-block building. Uschi waved at the zabanya, who stood to attention, saluting. Izzie could not make out if he was joking or for real. A tall flagstaff, bordered by dusty plants and white-painted stones, stood in the middle of the car park. The national flag looked sadly deflated, strapped to the mast, waiting for a ceremony.

Uschi drew up between a pale blue VW beetle and an old Ford. Not many came to work by car. She pointed to a row of single story buildings at the end of a dirt path beyond the car park. It had a corrugated iron roof and doors that opened onto a wide veranda. People were sitting against the wall, waiting. They looked like beggars, wrapped in the traditional gabis, their clothes a grey-brown colour.

"That's social services and admin," she said, getting out of the car. "They look after the elderly and orphans. And duriyey."

"Duriyey?" Then Izzie remembered, that was what Hailu had called the big boys in Georgis.

"Vagabonds," Uschi said. "Another good word for you."

"I thought ADCD was for the disabled," Izzie said.

"ADCD runs shelters for children, old people and the destitute and manages handicraft workshops for the handicapped." Uschi hooked her overflowing handbag into the crook of her arm and locked the car. "The accounts department is over there too. Ha. We need a good project document Izzie, so they release our money." She turned towards the five-storey building. "Our office is this way."

Inside was like the sanatorium at school. Green walls, concrete floors and an echo. It was cooler inside than out and there was a vague smell of dirty socks and washed concrete.

"Ato Gezahegn's office is on the second floor," Uschi said, going up the stairs, pausing now and then to catch her breath. "This will be the death of me."

Izzie followed. A man on crutches leant back into the corner of the half-landing to let them pass. His right leg was withered, his foot pointing to the floor, flaccid and twisted.

"Egziersteling," Uschi said as she passed him.

Izzie smiled, trying not to show any signs of pity.

"Polio," Uschi said when she reached the first floor. "He works with the cashier."

Take two, Izzie Brown, Izzie said to herself, caught out by her own prejudice. She had assumed he was there to ask for help.

They reached the sound of voices and clacking typewriters on the next floor, a long dim corridor with doors off to the left and right. A short man in a leather jacket walked past and nodded at them. Two women stood chatting. They greeted Uschi and Izzie, bowing heads and shaking hands.

"Izzie's coming to work with me," Uschi said.

Izzie felt a little awkward, like the new-girl.

"Very good," the one with dark rings under her eyes and tiny gold earrings said. A bright smile transformed her face. "Welcome to ADCD, Izzie," she said.

"We are going to meet Ato Gezahegn," Uschi said.

"Good," the other woman said. Her face gave nothing away. No promise of friendship, no disapproval.

Izzie had a feeling she would get closer to reality inside these walls. She followed Uschi until they reached the end of the corridor.

"Here we are," Uschi said.

"I don't know why, but I feel stupidly nervous," Izzie said, her throat dry.

"Deep breath," Uschi said and knocked on a door

"Abate?" a man's voice called from inside.

"Good morning, Ato Gezahegn." Uschi walked in like an ocean liner with Izzie, a small tug boat, hesitating in her wake.

The room was bright with large square windows; one was open, letting in the sound of the street below. There were two desks and a scattering of chairs. Three grey filing cabinets stood, backs against the wall, like soldiers to attention. A sisal plant sat on top of one of them, its tendrils climbing out of the pot like a spider. Izzie had planted some on their balcony. They didn't need much water.

Ato Gezahegn looked up, stubbing out a cigarette. He was wearing a jacket and tie. Uschi was right, a handsome man with classic features.

A standard issue photograph of Mengistu hung on the wall behind him. Izzie was struck by the contrast between the military dictator, with his soft rounded face, and the chiselled features of the sophisticated-looking administrator.

"You must be Izzie," Ato Gezahegn said, leaning across his desk to shake hands. "How are you, Uschi?" He didn't bow his head like others. "Come, pull that chair over. Has Uschi shown you her office yet?"

"No," Izzie said, glancing at Uschi. "We came straight here."

A stack of buff coloured folders occupied one corner of his desk, an in-tray of typed papers the other. The ashtray already had four stubs in it. Izzie could do with a cigarette. She clasped her hands together on her lap and took a deep breath, willing the tightness in her chest to ease off.

"Well, this is the Production Projects Department," he said. "The workshops we manage were set up by noble philanthropists in the past to provide employment for the handicapped. Their contribution to society, you might say."

"The government took over the workshops after the revolution," Uschi said.

"What do you produce?"

"Hand-knotted carpets, embroidered items, national dress," he said. "We also have a weaving section where we make cloth."

"Is it possible to visit the workshops?" Izzie said.

"I'm sure we can arrange it," Ato Gezahegn said.

"Don't go stealing her from me, now," Uschi said, wagging a finger at Ato Gezahegn.

He shook his head and patted the desk. "I am exploring, Uschi. It is not for you to worry."

"I know you," she said, adjusting her hair, her bangles clinking.

"We market the products as well," he said, looking at Izzie. "We have two shops in Addis, one on Piazza and the other near National Theatre."

"Prime spots," Izzie said.

"That's where we'll sell the children's clothing too," Uschi said.

"I think I've seen the one on Piazza, near the fruit and vegetable stalls?" Izzie had looked in the window. It was run down and dusty. The products looked sad and unappealing. She couldn't imagine anyone going in to buy children's clothes there.

"We have to do something about the shops, Ato Gezahegn," Uschi said.

"We will, we will," he nodded at Uschi.

Uschi smiled and crossed her legs, pulling her skirt down over her elegantly plump knees. She brushed non-existent crumbs away, her bracelets clinking.

"And there's a farm in Arussi," he went on. "A fruit farm. We have over a thousand lepers and their families living and working there."

"We had a weekly clinic for lepers at the hospital I worked at in Malawi," Izzie said, wanting to use every ounce of her experience to impress the man.

Ato Gezahegn looked at Izzie again. "Do you read Amharic?" He passed her the document lying on front of him on the desk. It had a large blue official-looking stamp on the bottom right hand corner. A seal with a worn wooden handle stood in its ink pad next to a stapler in front of him.

She looked at Uschi and then at Ato Gezahegn. "Is it necessary for the job?" she said.

"I think Ato Gezahegn is testing you," Uschi said, with a wink. "Go on, try."

"Di Ri Ji T ye Do Ku Ma N en na Li Jo Ch," Izzie read out, feeling like a five-year-old. "I can't read very well, as you can see."

"On the contrary," Ato Gezahegn said, taking the document back, smiling at her for the first time. "You know what it means?"

"No, unfortunately, I don't," Izzie said. "Well, actually, lijjoch. That's 'children' isn't it?" She glanced at Uschi triumphantly. She suddenly realised she wanted the job, wanted to impress this man. There was something elusive and striking about him. She couldn't put a finger on it.

"Not many farenj make the effort to learn our language," he said. "Not even the Soviets. They depend on Ethiopians who have returned from studying in the Soviet Union."

"It's a disgrace," Uschi said, tutting and brushing off her skirt again. "There are qualified engineers and doctors assigned as translators for the Russians."

Ato Gezahegn cleared his throat, and leant back in his chair. "So you are a business woman."

Izzie would not describe herself in that way. She had not enjoyed her studies particularly. "Not quite a business woman," she said. "Though I do have a degree in Business Studies, Marketing." Her eyes wandered to the photo of Mengistu on the wall behind Ato Gezahegn.

"Marketing," he said. "There you are Uschi, Izzie can help us out with the shops too." He turned to Izzie. "Uschi will tell you, we have good business women in Ethiopia. They are traders; selling wool, grains, spices, khat. You've seen them with firewood on their backs, bent double like donkeys?"

"I've seen them," Izzie said, wondering where this was leading.

"Well they didn't learn business. They just do it. They didn't go to school. They can't read and write. So until the next generation have been to school and college, we need people like you to work with us."

Izzie felt slightly uncomfortable. "I really want to work here," she said. "Do something useful."

"I can see that."

Uschi leant forward, passing him Izzie's CV.

"Ah," he said, leaning back and turning the pages. "Have you got references from," he looked over the page, "Likuni Hospital?"

"I have one from Sister Monique." Izzie got Monique's letter out of her bag and passed it to him. "She was the matron in charge. And there's one from Dr. David Goffe attached to it. He was my law lecturer at the Business School in London."

"White Sisters of Africa?" Ato Gezahegn said, reading, his eyebrows slightly raised.

"I guess in colonial times they were all white, but now there are Kenyan and Malawian sisters in their community."

"So it worked," Ato Gezahegn said, clearing his throat.

"What?"

"Converting African heathens to Christianity."

Izzie shifted in her chair. "I suppose," she said. "Though I am not necessarily convinced it is a good thing." She thought of the Nyau dancers swirling in their elaborate costumes under the full moon, raising dust clouds. They had not been influenced by the missionaries.

"Mother Teresa's Missionaries of Charity work here," he said. "You should go and see. They take care of people no one else will go near. They wash them, feed them, look after them until they die."

There was a knock at the door. A young woman wearing trousers and a loose black jacket came in. She was slim and had a short afro. "You wanted to see me, Gezahegn?" She looked at Uschi and Izzie. "Hello Uschi," she said, shaking her hand.

"This is Izzie," Ato Gezahegn said. "She's going to work with us."

"Hello. I'm Simaynesh," the woman said.

Izzie could tell this woman was not particularly fond of farenj. Her handshake was brief and firm. She seemed impatient, like she had other things to do.

"Izzie has a background in business and marketing. She's going to work with Uschi on the Nazareth project. But I want you to take her to the Ethio-Craft and Medhan Alem workshops."

"You want her to work on the evaluation?"

"Let's see. It might be useful," he said, leaning back in his chair.

"We've already set down the parameters," Simaynesh said. She did not sit down. "But it might be helpful to have another pair of eyes."

"Gezahegn, could we have Izzie work on the Nazareth document first?" Uschi said. "We need Accounts to release the funds for us to get going." She turned to Izzie with one of her bird-like chuckles. "He's going to steal you from under my very own eyes."

179

"Was there anything else, Gezahegn?" Simaynesh said. "I have to get on. Let me know what you decide." She was heading for the door. "Nice to meet you Izzie. See you later Uschi."

"Simaynesh is our resident hardliner. Our in-house feminist," Ato Gezahegn said, once the door shut. He reached for his cigarettes and lit one. "Cigarette?"

"I'd love one," Izzie said, relieved.

"She's good. MA in Social Sciences from Addis Ababa University."

"I think you say, 'Her bark is worse than her bite?' No?" Uschi said, looking at Izzie.

"She needs a husband," Ato Gezahegn said almost to himself. He cleared his throat. "Good," he looked up at Izzie. "When do you start?"

"Immediately," Uschi said.

This was going faster than Izzie had anticipated. "I need to sort out my papers," she said. "I have to get my tourist visa changed into an entry visa before they'll give me a work permit."

"You'll talk to Comrade Aklilu?" Ato Gezahegn said to Uschi.

"Of course," Uschi laughed and shuffled in her chair, obviously delighted. She reached for her bag and stood up ready to leave.

"I hate to ask. But I need some sort of remuneration?" Izzie said. "Is it possible?"

Uschi looked at Ato Gezahegn.

He tapped his cigarette against the ashtray and took another drag. "I think we can organise something. Once you have the work permit we'll put you on our payroll. The minimum wage is fifty Birr a week."

"Thank you," she said. Fifty Birr was better than nothing and made her a recognised member of staff. She couldn't wait to tell Moe. An Ethiopian government employee?

"We are on the way. Bring your passport tomorrow and I'll speak to Comrade Aklilu," Uschi said.

"Who is Comrade Aklilu?" Izzie asked, once they'd left Gezahegn's office.

"The Minister," Uschi said. "An old friend."

12

June 1982, Ataye

Yishaereg and Ali's youngest brother was ill. Ashebir went to ask after him now and then.

"His stomach has swollen up," Yishaereg said, twisting a piece of string in her fingers. "He's shaking as if the devil is inside him."

"It's not the devil," Ashebir said, "It's 'swollen belly.' That's what Zewdie told me."

"Mother says there's nothing Emet Fahte can do," Yishaereg said. Tears ran down her face leaving a line running down each cheek.

"He won't die, Yishiyey," Ashebir said. "He won't die."

"He is just lying on his cot. Mother says we can't do anything but wait for Allah to take him."

The little boy died that night when the hyenas were cackling and woo-oooping in the valley below.

In the morning, hearing the crying and wailing, Ashebir and Zewdie ran up the hill from their house.

"It must be the little boy," Zewdie said. She started wailing as soon as they were in Yishaereg's compound. Ashebir did not like his mother's pain. He burst into tears at the sound of it. He stayed near her as she wailed with the other neighbours.

Under the eaves, he spotted Yishaereg, holding her other small brother close. They both stood staring. He wanted to go to her but his legs would not move. To his relief, Zewdie sent him to take the animals out, while she stayed at the lekeso. He turned and walked slowly out of the compound. More people from the village were coming to the lekeso. As soon as he was past the hedge, he ran down the path to the beret behind their house. He climbed into the enclosure and nuzzled his face against the neck of his favourite goat and wept. He felt the sobs all over his body and his own hunger pain in his belly. She bleated and nudged him. The animals wanted to get out onto the pastures.

He and his friends could not laugh and play that day.

"Let's not go to the river today," Ali said. "It will remind me of my baby brother." Yishaereg's mother had sent him with the neighbour's animals. He would get a little food for the day's work.

"You remember how he giggled while he stamped all over the gojobate we built?" Ashebir said, remembering sweet things about the little boy.

"He used to play with my little sister, Konjit," Mohamed Abdu said. "We are lucky, she got better." He raised his eyes to the sky like his mother Temima did, and said, "Allah be praised."

"Let's go to Muletta," Ali said and they all agreed.

**

Some days later, Zewdie said she would sell firewood in the market. "If I get a good price in the market, I hope to come home with a small bag of millet, God willing."

They had tea and bread before Ashebir left with their animals, a handful of roasted 'kollo in his pocket.

"You are growing, yeney lij, and you need to eat," she said.

He knew his mother worried that he was not getting enough to eat. There was worry-talk all over the village. He felt better with his friends. They played, despite the bad news in the air.

He walked the narrow paths with his friends, driving the animals ahead, until they reached the slopes and wide pastures.

Ashebir found a rock to sit on and cupped his hands round his mouth. He blew a tune using his fingers to change the notes. Today his fingers were playing well. Sounds of an owl on a quiet night: 'leyliti googooti, leyliti googooti,' drifted across the rocky mountainside, the notes floating in the hot air.

"Ashebir is playing music for the goats," he heard Ali shout.

Ashebir stopped playing and looked around. Ali's voice had a distance to it. He guessed his friend must be up a tree but could not spot him. Ali was better than anyone at hiding.

"Where are you Ali?" he called out, standing up and shading his eyes to look around.

"Up here," Ali called back. "With the birds."

Ashebir looked further up the slope. Ali was standing up among the top branches of a prickly acacia, waving his arms.

Ashebir laughed. "You are a bird, Ali. Are you an eagle or a raven?"

"I am an eagle," Ali shouted back. "Not a dirty raven."

"Listen, I will play for you, Ali eagle." Ashebir sat down on his rock and carried on playing.

"Al-hamdulillah," Ali called out, bowing from his tree top. "Praise Allah for all that is good. Thank you for your song."

Ashebir played on, his tune echoing in the still heat of the dry season. Waiting for the rain, waiting for the rain. He tried lifting the tones to imitate the eagle's shrill cry, but they still sounded like an owl.

"You are the bird, Ashebir, not me," Ali shouted. "You are the one singing, the one with a bald head like a vulture."

Ashebir wiped a hand over his smooth head and growled in protest. He was not a vulture. He would not be hungry all the time if he was, he thought, turning his mouth down. But he knew Ali. He was full of joking, laughing too loud, and running too fast. He was skinny with strong tight muscles in his legs and arms. Everything about Ali was energy, like the wind. And he ran past his little brother's death as if in so doing he could pretend it never happened.

Ashebir heard the sound of animals, coming from further down the hill, and could smell their hides and pungent breath before he could see them. He looked round and raised a hand, "Greetings, Mohamed Abdu, owner of a hundred sheep," he called out, as his friend came running, aiming pebbles at their rumps.

Mohamed Abdu was out of breath, "Greetings, mountain minstrel, singer of a hundred songs." His friend laughed. "Ali is right. Zewdie has turned you into a bird, a bald vulture, with your melata."

Ashebir passed his hand back and forth over his head again.

Mohamed Abdu jumped up and down in front of him, flapping his arms like wings. "Vulture, vulture," his friend sang out.

Ashebir got off his rock and chased after Mohamed Abdu. They were both laughing and shouting, flapping their arms. Ashebir felt clumsy and wished he could fly gracefully like the kites in the sky. He loved the way they floated on the hot air, their wings spread out. He often watched them and had tried drawing them on the walls of his gojo-bate with his chicken feather and red clay dust mixed in a little water.

He held his arms out wide and ran slowly, making swooping movements. He closed his eyes and pretended he was floating with the kites, way up above the mountains.

Mohamed Abdu was just behind him circling with his arms spread out too. They ran up the hill, around the base of Ali's tree, and down again.

Finally, exhausted, Ashebir went back to his rock and slumped over it, breathing heavily. He looked at Mohamed Abdu, who flopped on the ground in front of him panting. They had lost their energy, he thought.

Ashebir passed a hand over his bald head again. "Zewdie rubbed ghee in my head last night," he said, scowling.

"I don't like you rubbing it in while I'm sleeping," he complained that morning when he woke.

"I have to oil it after shaving," she explained. "I'm sorry."

However much he rubbed and wiped his head with a cloth, he could not get rid of the thick smell that followed him everywhere. It reminded him of the young Afar men at the hot springs. His stomach turned in fear every time he got a whiff of it.

Zewdie had left a small tuft of hair growing in the middle of his head.

"Why does she do that?" Mohamed Abdu asked.

"I don't know. She says Christians do it. If God wants His child back, He can get a hold of the tuft of hair, and lift him up to heaven. That's what Zewdie told me."

"Sing, bird, sing," Ali called out again.

When he got his breath back, Ashebir picked up his tune again: 'leyliti googooti, leyliti googooti.'

The animals had spread out, snuffling, swishing tails and cracking branches as they searched for something to nibble on. The air hot and still. The sun burnt down on his head as he played music through his fingers. He stopped to pull his straw hat out of the bag and put it on. Zewdie had bought it for him. It was made from Molu Lake grasses. He had worn the hat so much that it no longer scratched like the first time he put it on. It had become moulded to the shape of his head, flopping softly, giving him shade. He peered out from underneath, looking around him and at the animals. The earth was dry with only a few tufts of grass for feed. Waiting for the rain. Waiting for the rain.

Zewdie could no longer buy sorghum to make injera, or tella beer. The price was too high, she said. She went more often to collect firewood to sell. It was hard work for her. Baking injera or brewing beer had been better, and then they had eaten more every day.

He looked at their ox and the cow. They were thinner. But those clever goats always found something to eat in the hardest places. They stretched and nibbled into nooks and crannies. He laughed a little, watching them. He liked the goats.

"Don't stop singing mountain bird!"

Cupping his fingers round his mouth, he picked up his tune. His eyes closed, he imagined he was wandering in the mountains, playing a masenko.[45] He was Ali the eagle's minstrel. He was playing for the animals, for the rain to come and for the harvest. He imagined his tune floating up to the heavens in a prayer to God, to Allah, asking for the rain to come, for a little more harvest than expected, a little more grazing, a few more wild fruits on the bushes.

Mohamed Abdu got to his feet. "Shall we move on? There's not much for the animals here."

Ashebir sent a piercing whistle in the direction of Ali's tree. "Ali," he cried out. "Innihid! Let's go."

"Innihid!" Mohamed Abdu called out, echoing his words.

Ashebir moved on up the hill alongside Mohamed Abdu. He watched as Ali scrambled half way down his tree, catching his clothes on its thorns and cursing. He jumped, his arms spread out wide, head peering down to the ground below, between his sprawled out legs. When he hit the ground he ran chaotically, arms spinning, propelled by the speed he'd picked up in flight, down the hill towards them. Ashebir and Mohamed Abdu watched him, laughing.

"Whaaa-aaa!" Ali yelled out, his mouth wide open. He reached them out of breath, laughing loudly. Ashebir caught him, stopping his run, and tumbled with him to the ground in a mock fight.

"Come on you two, Innihid!" Mohamed Abdu said.

Ali jumped up and ran on ahead, shooing the animals as he went, setting the goats and sheep off in a chorus of bleating and yammering.

Ashebir walked beside his friend. He would never forget Mohamed Abdu staying by his side, even at the worst moment.

"Mohamed Ahmed is not happy," Mohamed Abdu said. "He says it's going to be a poor harvest again."

Ashebir had heard his mother talking about the bad harvest with the women. He gritted his teeth, pulling his hat down over his eyes.

"Hid!" he shouted at the ox. "Get going." He threw a stone with a sharp flick of his wrist at Zewdie's ox. It was standing with its head in the shade of some trees, flicking its tail, not wanting to move.

"Move on," he shouted again, running towards the stubborn ox, his stick high in the air. The animal moved on slowly, its wide horns suddenly looked too heavy. Ashebir walked back to join his friend.

He glanced at Mohamed Abdu. Talk of a poor harvest reminded him of when they first arrived from Alem Tena. When he and Zewdie talked about that time, she would say: "Mohamed Shinkurt sent you away so

---

[45] Traditional Ethiopian instrument.

you would eat every day until we had a home." Her eyes would fill with tears. He still made her promise never to send him away again.

"You know if things are bad, it will be worse for Zewdie, and for Ali's mother. We are alone. We don't have land," Ashebir said.

"Aysoh, Ashebir, maybe the rain will come," Mohamed Abdu said.

Zewdie said they would get a small share of Mohamed Bilal from Albuko's harvest, for lending their ox for ploughing. And his uncle, Mohamed Shinkurt, would give them what he could. But Ashebir now understood, that it was only children from very poor families that were sent to look after other people's animals for food. Being an erregnya was thought of as shameful. He kicked some pebbles in the dust in front of him. He was not ashamed, he had just been afraid that he would never see his mother again.

"You know I had to work as an erregnya. And it was hard. Too hard. I don't want to be sent away again."

"How was it?" Ali said, looking unusually serious.

"No one in that place looked after me really. You are not their child. So its not the same. I got food but not every day. I prayed at night, whispering in case they heard me, "Please God, take me home to my mother soon." You are with strangers in a strange place."

"Come on, let's go. Innihid," Ali said. "Don't worry any more Ashebir."

His friend Ali did not like talking difficult things.

"Let's see if there are any fruits on the cactus further up the hill," Mohamed Abdu said.

"Yes. We can fight the 'cactus guards', see if we get to the fruits before the baboons," Ali said, already walking up the hill.

"Come. Ashebir," he heard his friends calling. They were waving from a bit further up the mountain. They had herded the animals on ahead of them, including Zewdie's goats, her ox and the cow.

In the early evening, as he came nearer their house, he could see a thin plume of smoke coming out of the coal black chimney on the roof. He felt a shot of excitement in his belly. Zewdie was making ki'ta bread. Things were not so bad.

He walked into their compound, calling out, "Tenasteling," as he drove the animals towards the beret enclosure at the back. As he passed the open door he could smell the wood smoke, the spicy wot sauce and bread. It made his stomach rumble. He closed the animals' gate behind him and ran inside. "Hello Zewdie," he said. "How are you?"

"Look, yeney konjo, my lovely. I sold the firewood and got this bag of millet," she said. She looked tired, even though she was smiling. "I am sure you are hungry."

"I am," he said, taking his place beside her by the fire. "It smells good. I saw the smoke from far away and knew you were cooking."

She smiled. "You are a good boy. God knows, what would I do without you."

"Don't send me away again, Zewdie," Ashebir said.

"Why think of that now? If it's God's will, it will never happen again."

"Ishi," he said, too tired to talk any more.

They bent their heads and gave thanks for their evening meal.

13

It was still dark and cold when Zewdie woke Ashebir. "Come Ashebir, remember? We are going to Gemoj today."

He sat up and rubbed his eyes. Slowly he made out the shapes in the room; the solid pole holding the roof up day and night, the insera, his mother lighting the kerosene lantern. He saw her face in the white and blue light. Like a spirit-face, he thought. The light and shadow changed with her movements. He sat on his cot and watched her sleepily.

"I asked Temima if Mohamed Abdu could take the animals today," she said. She was packing ki'ta bread into a small woven picnic basket bound in goat's skin.

He opened his eyes just enough so he could see what he was doing, climbed down from his cot, and pulled on his clothes. He went outside to relieve himself, and washed his face and hands. He was shivering from the cold when he came in, his eyelashes dripping water. He stood by the insera, in a sleepy daze, watching Zewdie.

"Here put this gabi on," Zewdie said, wrapping an old greying shawl around his shoulders, wiping his face with it as she did so.

He was grateful and pulled it close around himself.

"Your clothes are falling apart," she muttered. "We have to get you new shorts, and a t-shirt. They have used ones quite cheap in the market but I have so little money." She tutted.

"It's alright, Zewdie," he said in a low voice. He really didn't mind. Everyone's clothes were torn and thin.

"Take your tillik'o,[46] we're going to chop wood, and your stick," she said, "in case we have to chase hyenas on the way." She pinched him and laughed.

He was frightened of hyenas. He heard them every night, woop-

---

[46] Panga, sharp long knife with a wooden handle for cutting down firewood.

oooop. They were known to prey on people, especially before dawn. "Can we leave a little later? When they've all gone home?"

"No," Zewdie laughed. "We have to leave right away. It is far where we are going," she said. "It's way behind the Muletta mountain range, south of Ataye. We have to walk down into a deep gorge."

"Let's wait a bit? Zewdie?" He said again as she gently pushed him out of the door and closed the padlock with a loud click.

"We will collect a lot of firewood today, Ashebir. Mohamed Bilal from Albuko is clearing the forest for a new plot of land he wants to plough." Zewdie adjusted the sisal twine which hung over her shoulder. "And it being so dry, it will be easy to cut. He said we should go soon, before more people hear about it."

Ashebir stayed close behind his mother in the dark. They walked deep into the mountains. The sky was full of stars. He was glad of the warm gabi round his shoulders. He listened out for the sound of hyenas, clutching his stick, at the ready. He especially didn't like it when they cackled and laughed, chuckling as if they would get the better of him. He would show them.

He could hear his Uncle Mohamed Shinkurt's voice, "Be careful of the hyenas before dawn and at night Zewdie, they always go for the weakest, women and children." Ashebir looked at his mother. She walked firmly along the path ahead of him, her bag and tillik'o over one shoulder and the rope to tie the firewood over the other. There was no sign of fear in her body. He thought of her strong arms and hands, pounding grains, chopping wood, carrying water, lifting and carrying goods to and from the market. Why did his uncle say women were 'the weakest', he wondered, when he saw every day what his mother and Temima had to do. Yishaereg was weak with her small hands, but she too was getting stronger. One day she would have to do all the things their mothers did. He did not think a hyena would attack his mother. But he was a child with skinny legs and hunger in his belly. He moved a little faster to be as close to Zewdie as possible.

**

At last the sky became lighter. The path was rocky and wound steeply down into the valley. It made the going hard. Suddenly, he froze. Fresh hyena dung in the middle of the path. A loud buzz of flies had settled on it. The strong smell of wild animal hung in the air.

"He must be close, Zewdie," he said. "Maybe he's looking at us."

Ashebir scanned the mountain slopes and valley below him, his eyes screwed up to focus minutely on every bush, every dark shadow as the sky slowly dawned pink in the distance.

"Aysoh, don't worry," Zewdie said. "Come in front of me." They carried on down the path into the valley, with her gently pushing him on.

While her hand on his shoulder was a comfort, her tutting, and whispering prayers made him nervous. He turned and tried complaining some more, his body shivering. "I am really afraid Zewdie. Please. We are all alone. Let's go back."

"Yeney konjo, my sweet boy, what will we eat in the next days if we return with nothing? How will I buy you a new pair of shorts? We have to work, then we can go home."

"What if the hyena comes? There may be more of them together."

"We are strong. You have your stick don't you?" She laughed in a way that betrayed her own fear.

"Zewdie?" he said.

"Come on, come on, keep going, we are nearly there."

Bit by bit they made their way to the bottom of the valley. They had to climb over boulders and down narrow pathways. Sometimes he turned to put out a hand to help his mother. She took it, smiling.

"Look, there is hardly any water in the river," she said.

"When will the rains come?"

"Very soon. Maybe in a month or so," she sucked her teeth. "It's in God's hands, Egziyabher yawkal."

Suddenly there was a thunderous rumbling. Anger filled the sky. He ducked down, terrified. His mother had done the same. They both dropped everything. They huddled together, crouched, hands over their heads. Ashebir peeked up into the vast blue above them, his heart pounding. There was not a rain cloud to be seen, not even a wisp. The noise got louder. Were the mountains around them shaking with God's wrath?

Zewdie shouted something. He could not hear a word.

Then he saw them coming, a row of killer bees striking across the sky. They swooped and vanished leaving a humming-drumming sound behind them.

"Fighter jets," Zewdie said.

Ashebir stood, his legs shaking, and helped his mother up. "They are so loud," he said, rubbing his ears. He took a deep breath down into his stomach and blew it out again long and slow.

"People say they are heading north. That they rain fire down on the people up there. So many die, even in the markets where people like us go, my lovely, yeney konjo."

"Why do they do that?" he asked.

"Egziyabher yawkal," she said, brushing her long skirts down and picking up her things. "People are hungry," she sucked her teeth, and threw a glance up in the sky after the jets, "And they are fighting."

She walked on down the path, whispering and clicking her tongue. She was praying.

Ashebir wished the rains would come. He wished there was enough to eat. He wished the jets would stop coming. They made his heart thump in his belly.

Zewdie pointed to a flat area on their side of the river. "That's where Mohamed Bilal from Albuko has been clearing the forest to grow food. We need food."

"It's big," Ashebir said, wondering how long it would take to collect all that wood. He was still on the alert for signs of hyena. There was a strong smell of wild animals in the air. He was sure they were close by, watching.

Chopped down tree trunks and large branches were piled around the clearing. The sun had risen but still had to climb over the top of the next mountain before it got warmer. Ashebir followed his mother into the clearing.

"It looks so sad, Zewdie. All these trees cut." Ashebir was tired after the long walk and felt hopelessly small surrounded by the broken tree stumps, and huge branches scattered everywhere. Where would he start with his tillik'o, he wondered? It hung limply in his hand. "They look like dead people," he said.

Zewdie headed for a pile of tall trunks covered in branches. "Come, yeney konjo, let's get to work."

Even if she was tired his mother was strong. She set to straight away, chopping long branches off the stumps. The sound of her tillik'o echoed around the valley. He followed her example, he had no choice. All the time he was frowning, complaining under his breath, his lips moving and clicking with his words and the dryness in his mouth.

They pulled the branches from the piles of wood and cut them to size, chopping the smaller branches from the larger ones.

Suddenly Ashebir cried out, "Weyne! Weyne!" He had missed the branch and sliced his leg with a downward chop. Blood poured out. He threw down his tillik'o and clasped his shin, his eyes screwed tight. He knew the pain. This cut joined a row of others down his shins.

Zewdie went to him, "Ayezoh, ayezoh," she said. "Calm down, calm down," she patted his back. "This is our life, Ashebir, Egziyabher yawkal. It's a hard life. But it is our life."

He cried, holding onto his mother's shoulder, as she rubbed sand into the wound.

"This will stop the bleeding," she said. "Ayezoh, ayezoh." She stood up and wiped his face clear of tears with her hands. They felt rough against his skin but he was glad of her attention.

"Come on, back to work," she said. Picking up her tillik'o, she went back to chop branches, laying them in an ever growing pile.

The pain was still there and it began to throb. The sand irritated. Ashebir bit his lip and held his breath, desperate to stop the crying, letting out small grunts. He sniffed hard, picked up his tillik'o and chopped.

By the time they had collected as much as they could carry, the sun had moved past its midday point. Zewdie took her length of rope and bending over, tied the tall pile of branches into a bundle, letting out small grunts as she did so. It was almost as long as she was tall. She made a smaller bundle for him. It was almost as long as he was tall. She stood looking at her handiwork before bending over so that Ashebir could help heave her bundle onto her back. She groaned slightly as the load settled on her. Taking the ends of the rope, she bound them round her shoulders and across the top of her chest. He stood back to watch her. They had taken one break to eat the ki'ta bread Zewdie had packed in the morning. He was aching tired, hungry, and his leg hurt.

She turned with the large bundle of firewood strapped to her back and caught Ashebir's forehead with one of the branches. He cried out in pain. He felt the tears running down his cheeks like rivers.

"Ashebir, ye arba ken idilih neow.[47] Don't worry, just take a deep breath and let's get going."

He knew his mother could not see anything with that huge bundle strapped to her back. She was bent double. He felt the warm blood trickling down his face and wiped it away. He wiped his hand, covered in blood, down his shorts.

"What 'forty days' luck'?" His voice came out a weak high-pitched sound.

"You know. In the Orthodox Church, girls are baptized at eighty days and boys at forty days," Zewdie explained. "Ashebir, rub sand in it. It

---

[47] This is your forty days' luck.

will stop the bleeding." She pointed at the sand and hitched the pile of wood on her back. "It's just a saying," she carried on, while he rubbed the sand into his forehead, listening and trying not to whine. "If you hurt yourself and there's nothing anyone can do, they say, 'it's your forty days luck'. It's a way of comforting."

He did as she said.

"Pick up your wood. We have to reach home before dark." She started walking slowly along the path out of the clearing.

Darkness meant hyenas. He wound a cloth up and put it on his head, still sniffing. He hauled his bundle of firewood onto a stone, about his height, and lifted it from there onto his head. He hooked his tillik'o over his shoulder and picked up his stick. He kept the wood in place with one hand and held his stick firmly in the other.

"Wait for me," he called out and followed her along the path towards the river. He thought he must look like a cow with a white fleck with that wound in the middle of his forehead covered in sand, and his mother, bent over under her pile of firewood, looked just like a donkey.

Ashebir stayed as close behind Zewdie as he could. They started the climb up the escarpment away from the valley. He clutched onto the sharp branches to stop from slipping. Every now and then he looked at his mother and felt sorry. He knew she would be in pain that night. He was alert, scouring the hillside to the left and right for hyenas, peering at his feet not to stumble. The late afternoon sun was hot. He felt the sweat trickle down his face and his back. They walked slowly. He had to keep going one step after the next or Zewdie would leave him behind. He felt his breath coming in, going out, coming in, going out. He walked one step, next step, one step, next step. Up and up. Women and children, he thought, Uncle Mohamed Shinkurt said hyenas go for women and children.

"Zewdie," he called after a while. "Can we stop?"

"Yes let's," she said, to his relief.

Zewdie's load was heavier than usual, he thought, and he needed a drink. They had collected water from the stream to carry with them. He followed Zewdie to the shade of an acacia tree. He took his bundle off his head so he could help her lower hers to the ground.

"There. Now you can sit, Zewdie," he said. He took a drink of water then walked around the tree looking for something to play with, before sitting down beside her. The hum of wild bees in the brush and acacia gently filled the air around them in the otherwise quiet valley.

"Are you alright, Zewdie?" he asked, moving the smooth pebbles he had found, around in his hands, looking at her, worried.

"I am fine, thanks to God," she said quietly.

"Is it far now?"

"It is as far as we came," she said. "It is as far as we came."

"Your bundle is too heavy, Zewdie."

"A burden is only heavy when we think about how heavy it is," she said, smiling at him. "How are your cuts?" she asked, passing a finger lightly over the fleck on his forehead.

He flinched backwards, brushing her hand away. "It's fine. Don't worry," he said.

They sat quietly for a while. It was peaceful.

"Come on, we can't sit here all day," she said.

He helped her lift the firewood onto her back again. Then he lifted his bundle onto his head, shifting it around to make it as comfortable as possible.

"It's the life God chose for us," Zewdie said, letting out a small hummm, like the bees, as she set off up the path ahead of him.

**

It was late evening when they finally reached home. The crickets had finished their song. And once again he had the old gabi wrapped round his shoulders against the chill of the evening mountain air.

He sat beside Zewdie by the still fire and ate a piece of ki'ta bread before climbing onto his cot. He did not even take off his clothes. He drew his ox-skin over himself to keep out the cold and fell into a heavy sleep, dreaming of prickly bushes, steep pathways, dark places in the shadows, and hyenas.

The following morning Zewdie sent Ashebir to Mohamed Bilal from Albuko's house to ask if they could borrow one of his donkeys. I want us to take the firewood to market today," she said.

"I can carry mine, Zewdie, and we can put yours on the donkey," he suggested.

"That is just what I was thinking, yeney lij," she said, smiling. "Now go quickly, while he is still at home."

He reached Mohamed Bilal's compound and knocked on the korkorro corrugated iron gate. It shook making clattering noises. A boy opened up and Ashebir stepped inside. He was relieved to see that Mohamed Bilal from Albuko was still there. He greeted his mother's friend politely, the way she had taught him.

"As-sallamu aleykum, Ato Mohamed Bilal," he said, dipping his head respectfully as he took the man's outstretched hand. It felt strong around his small hand. Maybe his own hand would be like that one day.

"Tadias, Ashebir," Mohamed Bilal from Albuko greeted him warmly, so he felt welcome. "Hello there, my boy."

Ashebir also greeted Mohamed Bilal's wife.

"How is your mother today, Ashebir?" she asked him.

"She is fine, Al-hamdulillah, Praise Allah."

"Good boy, Ashebir." Mohamed Bilal from Albuko patted him on the back. "I can see you are learning something at your Qur'an classes. Did the teacher beat you yet?" The man let out a chuckle.

"Once. He beat me on my second day."

"Oh. What did you do to deserve that?" Mohamed Bilal from Albuko asked him.

"Nothing. He just said it was 'to show me'," Ashebir replied.

Mohamed Bilal from Albuko chuckled. "And he hasn't beaten you since?"

"No. I try to follow his instructions," Ashebir said quietly. "I like the writing."

"Oh yes, and how is that?"

"We have to make ink from the black soot on the bottom of our cooking pots. We mix it with the juices of the geirar tree. It gets all sticky but we have to mix it hard and then leave it."

Mohamed Bilal from Albuko and his wife both listened to him. Two of their children, older than Ashebir, came out of their gojo-bate and greeted him, shaking hands and bowing heads. He started to feel nervous with all the attention and shuffled his feet in the earth. Zewdie would be waiting for the donkey.

"Go on Ashebir. Tell us. How do you write with that stuff?"

"Well," he had to clear his throat. "We leave that sticky stuff for two or three days until it becomes soft. The teacher asks us to bring chicken feathers and we dip the point into the ink and then we write."

"I can collect soot from our pots, Ashebir," Mohamed Bilal's wife said. "You just come now and then, and I will give you."

"Thank you," he smiled. He wanted to make more ink to draw at home.

"They write on wooden slates," Mohamed Bilal told his wife. "Isn't that right Ashebir?"

"Yes, we do," Ashebir nodded his head. "We do. I really like it. I also started to draw pictures to decorate our gojo-bate."

"Your mother told me. I must come by sometime and have a look," the man said, smiling at him kindly. "So Ashebir. I am sure your mother has sent you for something?"

"Please, Ato Mohamed Bilal, my mother sent me to ask if we can use one of your donkeys today?"

"So you went to our fields in Gemoj and collected firewood yesterday, is it?"

"Yes we did. It was very far."

"You are a strong boy to go all that way with your mother, Ashebir," Mohamed Bilal's wife said.

Mohamed Bilal's wife went inside, telling Ashebir she had made breakfast and did he want any? "Come, eat," she said.

"You get inside and eat, while my boy fetches the donkey," Mohamed Bilal said, gesturing for Ashebir to get in the house. "We'll put some meat on those skinny bones," he said and laughed in his friendly way.

"Come in, come in," Mohamed Bilal's wife said. "You can wash your hands in the bowl in the corner."

It was full of smoke inside. Mohamed Bilal's wife had the fire going for making injera. He washed his hands, and then sat on the low stool she had pointed out to him near to the open fire. He looked around their house. It had more space and more things in it than theirs. He looked up into the ceiling and saw how dark it had become from all the wood smoke. Long thick spiders' webs hung down, coated in black and moved softly.

"Here you are, here you are," the woman was saying to him. "Your mother always says you are a bit of a dreamer, eyes wide open and staring into the ceiling. What is there to see?" She said. "What is there to see?"

She gave him a plate with some injera and sauce and a glass of hot tea. He watched her put one sugar in it and was very happy. He bowed his head and muttered, "in the name of Allah," as he took the plate in both hands. She placed the glass of tea on the ground beside him. They had not eaten injera at home for a while. They had ki'ta bread and 'kollo. He ate hungrily, wishing he could take some for Zewdie.

When he was finished, he thanked Mohamed Bilal's wife and went out into the sun. Mohamed Bilal from Albuko said his son would go with him and the donkey, to help Zewdie load it up.

Mohamed Bilal's wife gave him a small packet of food for Zewdie. "Tell her to take it to market for her lunch," the woman said. "And take this bag of millet, your mother can make injera or ki'ta bread."

Ashebir took the food gratefully in two hands. He could not believe his luck. He bowed his head, "Al-hamdulillah, thank you, thank you," he said.

When they reached his home, he could see Zewdie had been sweeping their compound. There were neat circular marks in the dusty ground around their gojo-bate. The broom, made from a few branches, was leaning against their door. The huge pile of firewood was waiting to be loaded up, his smaller pile beside it. Zewdie appeared, looking happy to see them and thanked Mohamed Bilal from Albuko's son many times for bringing the donkey.

Ashebir gave her the bag of millet and the food for her lunch. "Look what Mohamed Bilal's wife has given us, Zewdie. And this packet is for you. I already ate mine at their place." He held the food out to Zewdie.

"I don't know what we would do without your family's help," she said to Mohamed Bilal's son. "Please thank your mother and father for me."

"It is no problem, Wozeiro Zewdie," he replied. He was already busy preparing the donkey. "Let's lift the firewood onto her," he said, taking one end of the large bundle.

"I will hold the donkey, while you both load it." Ashebir said. He held the animal still, stroking her soft nose. The donkey had large brown eyes and stood quietly, shaking her head from time to time and stamping a hoof to get rid of the flies.

"Ishi," Zewdie said.

"Did you hear there will be football in Ataye on Saturday?" Mohamed Bilal's son said, as he helped Zewdie lift the firewood onto the donkey's back.

"No, what is going on?" Zewdie asked.

"It's a competition. People are coming from villages all over the Awraja."[48] Mohamed Bilal's son said.

"Our village has a team," Ashebir told his mother, proud to be able to explain something to her. "Ali, told me. He wants to play when we are bigger." He turned to Mohamed Bilal's son, "Are you playing?" he asked.

"My cousin and I are both in the team. You should come and watch, Ashebir," the boy said. "Maybe one day you and Ali will play for our village too," he laughed and rubbed the top of Ashebir's head.

"When I am taller," Ashebir giggled going up on his tip toes. He looked at his mother.

---

[48] District.

"We'll have to feed you up," she smiled at him with that sad look in her eyes. She secured the firewood with sisal ropes, which hooked under the donkey's tail and went round her belly.

"But can I go and watch, Zewdie?" he asked. "Please?"

"We will buy barley when we've sold the firewood, Insha'Allah," Zewdie said looking up at the blue sky. "I'll roast 'kollo for you to sell at the football on Saturday. Ishi?"

"Very good," Ashebir said, smiling broadly at Mohamed Bilal's son. "I will look out for you and shout for you." He laughed, then looking at his mother he said, "when is Saturday?"

To his dismay, Zewdie and Mohamed Bilal's son looked at each other and burst out laughing. Zewdie's one gold tooth twinkled in the sun. Ashebir stamped his foot playfully and frowned with his mouth pulled down.

"It's not today, not tomorrow, but the next day," Mohamed Bilal's son said. "Saturday is always the day after Friday prayers."

"On the way to market we will learn the days of the week, Ashebir." Zewdie said, as she pulled the ropes tight round the donkey. "Come on, get your bundle of firewood, let's go."

"Have a good day," Mohamed Bilal's son said, "and see you at the football Ashebir. On Saturday. Remember? The day after prayers, ishi?" The boy chuckled to himself as he left their compound.

Ashebir wound the cloth round and placed it on his head. Zewdie helped to lift the firewood up and they walked out of the compound, he with one hand steadying the load on his head, Zewdie and the donkey leading the way.

**

"Seynyo, Makseynyo, Ehood,"[49] Ashebir chanted as they walked up the path towards their house that evening. "Seynyo, Makseynyo, Ehood."

"No. Seynyo, Makseynyo, Erob,"[50] Zewdie said.

"Today is Thursday, Hamus, and tomorrow is Friday and the next day is Saturday football," he said.

"That's right. And we have enough barley here to roast 'kollo for you to sell on Saturday. We'll roast it tomorrow so it is fresh."

---

[49] Monday, Tuesday, Sunday.
[50] Monday, Tuesday, Wednesday.

"We are lucky. Egziyabher alle. We sold all the firewood," he said, following his mother into their compound. He helped her unload the small sacks of grain they had bought. He was tired and saw that his mother was too.

The sky already pink, the crickets loudly dancing their feet in the tall dry grasses and the air laced with evening woodsmoke. Ashebir went round to the beret to check on their animals. Mohamed Abdu had brought them home. "The animals are all here," he called out, climbing in to stroke his favourite goat's nose and give her a handful of straw. Her belly distended, she would be having her little ones soon. He could not wait to see them. The cow let out a long loud moan. "OK. I will give you too," he mumbled, going over to stroke the thick soft skin that hung round her neck, rubbing his nose against her.

He stood amongst them, talking softly for a while, until he heard his mother's voice calling.

"Come here, Ashebir. You have to take the donkey back before it gets dark."

He closed the beret enclosure and went round to the front where Zewdie had already wound up the ropes. The donkey stood waiting, stamping her hoof, free of all burdens.

"She is a gentle donkey, Zewdie," he said. "I wish she were ours."

"Me too, Ashebir, but I don't even know how long we'll be able to keep the other animals. Soon I'll sell two of the goats to buy more millet. I need to make injera to sell."

"Please, not my favourite, Zewdie."

"We will keep her until she has had her kids," Zewdie said. "Now go. Mohamed Bilal will be waiting."

Ashebir led the donkey away up the path and then winding down below Mohamed Abdu's house and around the hillside, full of worry about his goat. The donkey started trotting.

"So you know your way home," he laughed, tapping her rump gently with his stick to see if she would go faster. She kicked up slightly at him, letting out a loud braying noise. "Let's go then," he called after her, running to keep up.

The donkey reached Mohamed Bilal from Albuko's compound first, Ashebir running and out of breath behind. He could see Mohamed Bilal's son, standing in the entrance.

"So, Ashebir. The donkey beat you home. You will have to do more training before you can be a footballer."

Ashebir laughed and bent down to his knees, catching his breath, bending right and left to break the sharp pain in his side.

"I can run faster than a white hyena and fly longer on the wind than a buzzard in the sky," Ashebir boasted, standing up again.

"A white hyena?"

"Yes. I have seen one near our house," Ashebir wanted to impress the bigger boy. There was no such thing as a white hyena.

"Faster than a white hyena, eh?" the older boy laughed.

"Yes."

"So, did you sell all that wood?"

"Yes. And we bought enough barley to roast 'kollo for the football."

"Good boy. So I will see you there."

"I have to get home now," Ashebir said. "Zewdie said thank you for the donkey."

"I will tell my father. Now you run home fast, like the white hyena," the boy said, laughing.

Ashebir waved and ran off down the path. As soon as he was out of sight he ran in the funny sideways lolloping way of the hyena and made low woo-oop woo-oop sounds.

14

June 1982, Addis Ababa

The best place to write letters, when the sun was not too hot, was on the terrace. They had agreed to introduce greenery into their city centre living. Round terracotta pots, spewing out large green leaves, now stood along the wall to the roadside. Moe had even managed to secure a stumpy palm tree, which immediately lent an exotic air. They had bought a small round metal table and four chairs so they could sit outside.

Izzie got a beer from the fridge and a bowl of 'kollo. Writing with a fountain pen was more expressive she thought, as she picked up a few sheets of A4 paper and her cigarettes. She would write to her sisters, send it to one and hope it would be forwarded to the other. It was long since she had heard from home. She missed them. Especially since she and Moe were constantly rubbing each other up the wrong way.

Addis Ababa 6ᵗʰ June 1982
On the Terrace

Dearest Kate and Helen,

How are you? How are Mum and Dad? And the boys, Helen? Hope everyone is OK and maybe enjoying Wimbledon — has it even started? Am so out of touch.

I have news for you. My work permit has come through. Am so excited. I will start getting paid from the end of the month. Arrive in Feb, job in April, work permit and pay in June. Not bad, eh? It is quite difficult as an ex-pat to get work when already in country. So no chance with the usual SCF and Oxfam etc. As it happens it has worked out really well with Uschi. And being a government ministry they could help me sort all the paperwork.

Oh I have to say I miss you all! Do write when you get a moment. I

*wonder if post gets held up and lost at the censors on the way in and out?
A colleague of Moe's is going home so I thought I would give him this to
post from London.*

*Had an incident the other evening. Was visiting a friend in an area
called Stadium – near the football stadium.*

She sat sucking the end of her pen. Looked up at two kites circling in
the blue above. Allowed the noise from the traffic below to disturb her.
Lit a cigarette and dragged in deeply making it crackle at the end. No,
she wouldn't tell them the Stadium was also the scene of horrific
shootings in the Red Terror. She couldn't help thinking of those
prisoners, corralled in there.

*I had Moe's best suit on the passenger seat. (Well he only has one
suit so I assume it's his best – ha-ha!). When I was leaving, a street boy
called me from behind the car. 'Come and look! There's a problem with
your tyre,' he said. Stupid me, I got out of the car and went to have a
look. As I did that, another boy rummaged with the passenger door,
opened it, grabbed Moe's suit and made a run for it. They both did. I
shouted, locked up and ran after them. But was too late. I called out,
begging them to give it back. Another boy came over. His name is Kasu.
I wasn't sure if he was part of the gang. I was shaking! Anyway. Kasu
said he would take me to the city market, Mercato. He said all the
thieves take their stolen goods there to sell. He knew where to go and
said we might find it. I don't know why he wanted to help me but he
did. We agreed to meet the next day. My God. Mercato. I followed him
down narrow, narrow alleyways, men sitting on the floors of dim shacks
chewing on fresh green khat leaves (it's a stimulant), women sitting on
the ground selling little piles of charcoal and stony white incense for the
coffee making ceremony, and herbs which they also put in the coffee. I
don't really like that flavour. It's all quite busy, quite dirty, smelly, a
mass of poor humanity, mixed with city shoppers. You can get
everything there. It's supposed to be the largest market in Africa.*

*I went with an Ethiopian friend once, she took me to where they make
shiny leather saddles and bridles for the horses and mules. Amazing
craftsmanship. And fab, brightly coloured, embroidered cloth to lay over
the horse's back under the saddle. It drapes down both sides. I bought
one to put over the back of our sofa. Looks so cool. The country people
love their colour and pomp. Anyway, of course we didn't find Moe's
suit. Kasu said I should go to the Police. So I did. Funny old business.*

I waited for some time. When it was my turn, the officer behind the counter said I would have to go buy paper and a folder so they could make the report. They had none left, and no money to buy any. Oh, I just left it. Am sure they have better things to do than look for a suit. Poor old Moe. He'll have to get one made. There are good tailors here.

This country is just incredible. Intense. And to be honest, Moe and I are struggling a bit. We need to get out of Addis. We thought we would go to Harar, a beautiful walled city in eastern Ethiopia. But we 'farenj' (foreigners) can't go beyond the borders of Shewa province without permits from the Ministry of the Interior. We tried to get a permit for Harar but it was turned down. Too much going on with uprisings, war and famine. Security is tight. It's funny how you get used it — to soldiers, and security guards from the Kebele (local council), standing on street corners with guns.

Anyway. We decided to go to Ambo instead. It's within Shewa province, so we are allowed to go there. It's a small town about 100 miles to the west of Addis. Moe and I went with a couple of friends. We all went in the 2CV — it just bounces over the dirt roads and potholes! Love it. Negisst made us some of her delish Ambasha dabbo… thick bread… and we took cheese and tomatoes. People told us there are good Italian restaurants there — run by Ethiopians. Pasta and pizza are the best remnants from the short-lived Italian rule. There's an old Italian villa down the road from us, rickety wooden porch, pale blue paint peeling off the walls, a bit run down. They serve the best pizza ever.

So back to Ambo. It was magnificent. We drove through the Menagesha forest, passing a large lake with wonderful bird life. I think it's one of the reservoirs for Addis. A gentle dirt road lined with these tall, tall Juniper trees, like driving through a cathedral. The forest was planted in the 15th Century. Imagine, so old. It's beautiful around Ambo. Really fertile, with open landscapes, mountainous surroundings and forest. Pretty houses built by the Italians falling to ruin and grapevines lining the hillsides. The local red wine — Gouder tastes pretty OK. It might not meet Uncle Sid's standards, but still not bad! We tried to find the Gouder Falls but got lost.

On the way back we stopped at Mariam Church in Addis Alem. The small town was built by Emperor Menelik II. He wanted to make it his capital but his wife the Empress Taitu had other ideas. It was her who founded Addis Ababa. She built a house near the hot springs here. Fasika says we can go there — to Filowha — for a steam bath some time. Sounds appealing. The evenings can get very chilly. Not far from Addis

Alem we stopped at a bungalow set back from the road under juniper and eucalyptus trees. Metal chairs and tables set out on a paved terrace, pots of plants, bush and creepers. Booker (the Brit who works with Moe) recommended it. It used to be an Austrian restaurant, now run by Ethiopians and serving the most delicious apple strudel. So incongruous. It was perfect with hot coffee.

This place is full of contrasts, the Emperor and Empress riding into battle against the Italians, ornately painted churches, priests walking up the main Churchill drag, apple strudel under trees in the countryside, political prisoners, street boys and hawkers, marches and banners. 'Workers of the World Unite!'

I think that's me for now. Send me your news. I hope everyone is OK. Apart from a bout of 'Giardia' (parasites – gives you diarrhoea and awful tummy cramps. The meds you have to take is even worse. Ghastly.) I am doing fine.

She signed off with her usual flourish, loads of kisses circled with hugs and a drawing of a small bunny at the bottom of the page, with a tulip bending over its head.

∗∗

That evening they were meeting Tom in the Nyala Bar because it had a TV set, and they knew the manager, Almaz.

"World Cup, Izzie. Soviet play Brazil," Hailu said, running up behind them with Mekonnen and two other small boys.

"Hi there guys," Moe said.

"How are you today, Mr Moe?" Hailu said, holding out a hand and bowing theatrically. He carried a cloth football tucked under his armpit.

"Here," Moe grabbed it and kicked it up and down on his toe a few times. "Let's have a warm up."

The boys stood back, laughing. Other children came closer to watch, giggling. The man in the sports-shoe shop stood in his doorway watching, picking at his teeth with a stubby tooth stick. A few of the evening strollers along Piazza turned their heads to look, smiling, as they went past.

"You want me to put a hat on the ground?" Izzie said.

"What's with you and a little fun?"

"Sorry," she said, taking his arm. "Ever since that mad turquoise woman grabbed my arm, I just don't want to draw any more attention to myself than I already do." Izzie said. "We're in the minority here." Izzie looked around. Not another white face to be seen.

Moe hooked her arm into his. "OK, sorry," he said. "Just a bit of fun with the kids. That still has to be possible?"

"Izzie, look," Hailu had the ball back and was kicking it from his toe to his head to his shoulder and down to his toe again. "Me good football. Better than Mr Moe." He laughed.

Izzie's heart melted on the spot. She put her hand on Hailu's head. "My little friend," she said. "You know, if it wasn't for Hailu I wouldn't have crossed the road to make that call to Uschi," she said, turning to Moe. "You saved me, little man, didn't you?"

Hailu puffed his chest out and patted it with his hand. "I big friend of you, Izzie." He giggled again.

Mekonnen came to put his hand on Hailu's shoulder. "Me too," he said.

"Let's go," Moe said, pulling her along gently. "We want to get to Almaz's bar before it gets too full.

"Ciao, ciao, lijjoch,[51]" Izzie waved at the children. "Keep away from the big boys in Georgis tonight."

"Ishi, Izzie, ishi," Hailu said, bowing his head and looking serious.

She knew that 'Ishi,' of his and that he would go anywhere a few cents could be made, even to Georgis.

Mekonnen pushed Hailu. "She's right," he said. "Much too danger in Georgis."

Moe squeezed Izzie's arm. "Let's go," he whispered in her ear.

Izzie lifted a cautionary finger towards the boys. "Stay out of trouble," she said.

Izzie and Moe turned and walked into a narrow street, lined with coffee shops and bars. There were more children out than usual. They carried trays of roasted nuts and 'kollo to sell. A small boy brushed past, a box hanging from his neck, stocked with cigarettes, cheap lighters, chewing gum and caramella.

Izzie was not keen on football. But this was different. If the Soviets lost, it would feel like a small victory for many ordinary Ethiopians, who felt oppressed by the Soviet presence. The whole city was itching with the anticipation of a Brazilian victory.

On the other side of the road, three women sat on low stools, turning corn over on the red hot coals, flickering inside their small iron braziers.

---

[51] Children.

The large round wicker baskets beside them were full of fresh cobs in their green husks, sticking out at angles. A small group of people stood watching and waiting. The smell reminded Izzie of the roast-chestnut stall on Dalston Lane.

Mahmoud Ahmed's haunting voice floated out of the Sholla Pastery Shop. Izzie did a little jig to the music as they passed the open door, and breathed in the warm smell of fresh loaves and dark roasted coffee beans. "Hmmmm, delicious, Moe, eh?" she said, smiling her contentment.

He kissed her cheek. It felt like a little reward, a pat on the back. She felt more relaxed now.

Further along, a skinny girl with high cheek bones and large eyes leant against a doorway talking to a man. Her eyes darted from him to the street and back again. Something was being negotiated. The girl giggled and chewed on her fingernail. Suddenly she nodded. It had obviously been decided. Brushing the strings of plastic beading with a dull clatter to one side, she pulled him in behind her.

Izzie looked at Moe, raising her eyebrows.

"Why so surprised?" he said.

"She's too young," she said. "Hope he misses the match."

"Unlikely," Moe said. "He'll be out in two minutes."

"Oh, you should know?" Izzie said and pinched his arm.

"That's not fair, honey. Seriously." The sound of a football crowd came from the next bar. "We better get a move on or we won't get a table at the Nyala."

"Are you off to Massawa next week, Moe?" she said, trying to keep up with his long strides. "Fasika said you might."

"Yes, most likely."

The man with elephantiasis was sitting at the top of the path, his back leaning against a corrugated iron fence. His usual spot was outside the Kebele[52] Store on Piazza. His trousers were rolled up to display his horribly swollen lower legs and feet, like those of some grotesque blown up plastic doll.

Izzie nodded at him and dropped some coins into his rusty tin. It must be the worst disease. His flesh had turned a mottled mix of pink, red and dark brown, the open wounds seeped liquid and yellow pus. He stank; stale urine, thick garlic sweat and rotting flesh.

---

[52] Equivalent of a local council. Political and administrative hub. Everyone had to register where they live. The Kebele Store was where people could go with their registration card and get rations at a cheap price: flour, sugar, rice and some cheap items of clothing.

"Wonder if they can treat it?" she said, lifting her white cotton shema round her mouth after she had walked past. She shivered.

"No idea. It looks gross, that's all I know," Moe said. "Maybe he prefers to stay like that so he can get some money. Maybe you just encourage him by giving, Izzie." He took her hand, pulling her away and they joined other people walking down the narrow hillside path with dwellings on either side.

"Surely not," she said and kissed his cheek to comfort them both, catching a whiff of the after-shave she had bought for him. "Hmmm, you smell good."

He grinned at her.

Discarded items, cigarette butts and plastic bags were scattered along the pathway. Dark piles of decomposing waste filled the ditches between the small houses, and a strong smell of urine wafted intermittently from shady corners.

Thin wafts of smoke, carrying the smell of burning itan incense and freshly roasted coffee beans came from an open door as they passed.

Izzie could hear women's voices inside. "That smells good," she said.

"You want to join them while Tom and I watch the football?" Moe said, giving her a light nudge towards the door.

"No. I'm looking forward to a cold beer, and to seeing Almaz."

Izzie could see the bar half way down the hill, tucked in under an awning of ivy. The doors and windows were open wide, sending shafts of smoke-filled light onto the dusky footpath. They were close enough now to hear the singing fans and hooters in the football stadium, echoing onto the path from inside.

She followed Moe into the neon lit bar. Men sat around metal tables, a beer in one hand, cigarette in the other. Anticipation filled the room. The TV was in its place, bolted to a wooden shelf behind the bar.

"We're lucky," Moe said, pulling out a chair at the last empty table.

A slim girl came tottering over on platforms with a metal tray dangling at her side. "What do you want?" she said. She had sullen dark shadows under her large eyes and wore tight jeans and a thin top. A tiny flat metal cross hung on a black thread round her neck.

Izzie felt hands squeeze her shoulders and turned to see Tom grinning over her head at the girl.

"Mine's a draft, beautiful," Tom said. He looked at Moe with wide eyes. "She's a new one." He glanced down. "Hi there gorgeous."

"Hi there Tom," she said, rolling her eyes. "And two beers for us too, please." She smiled at the girl.

"Enday," the girl said. "You speak Amharic?"

"Just a little," Izzie said. "I'm learning."

"It's surprising, what is your name?"

"Izzie."

"That one is pretty," the bar-girl glanced at Tom. "But yours is better looking." She turned on her heel to go back to the bar, swinging her tray slightly to the minimal rhythm of her hips.

Izzie laughed.

"What did she say?" Tom said, pulling up a chair, hope written all over his face.

"She's out of your league," Moe said.

"Give over," Tom said, cuffing Moe's shoulder. Tom leant over and kissed Izzie on both cheeks. "You're looking lovely as ever."

"And you as randy as ever," she said. "When are you going to get a girlfriend?" She saw Almaz making her way over to them.

Almaz was still young enough for her roundness not to matter. She had a smooth face, her eyes lined with kohl. Her long white cotton dress billowed above and below the wide sash she wore round her waist. The national colours, red, yellow, green and black, were embroidered down the front and round the cuffs. A thin white shema was wrapped round her bushy hair, the colourfully embroidered edge arranged to hang loosely on one side. Izzie wished she could dress with such laid-back flair.

"How are you people?" Almaz said, when she got to their table. She put her hands on the back of Moe's chair.

"Hey, Almaz," Tom said, getting up and reaching over to shake her hand and kiss her. "Who's the new girl?"

"How are you?" Izzie said, offering her cheeks and breathing in Almaz's warmth and cheap perfume. "I love your dress." Farenj never carried off Ethiopian national dress as well.

"Thank you, yeney konjo," Almaz said. "I'm fine. So, you all here for the Soviets then?" she laughed.

"Of course," Moe said.

"How are you, handsome?" Almaz said in a softer voice, putting a hand on his shoulder.

Moe smiled up at her, "Fine," he said. "You're looking well."

"Tonight will be a good night for business," she said.

"You're backing the Brazilians, I bet," Tom said.

Almaz moved to stand between Moe and Izzie, and putting her arms round their shoulders, she leant forward, looking round at them all. "Big trouble if I do," she whispered.

"You think so?" Moe said.

"We have some special guests here tonight," she said, her eyes scanning the room briefly. She laughed. "Don't look so worried. But I don't want any trouble. You people enjoy." She turned to go and then looked at Tom. "You want me to send her over after the match?"

Tom looked a little awkward as he raised his thumb and nodded.

"Not so sure after all, hey Tom?" Izzie said and laughed.

"There must be some Kebele or party members here," Moe said. "Ethiopian Politburo."

"I'm sure she can manage them," Izzie said.

Almaz was warm-hearted and jovial on the surface, but business was business and politics was something to be dealt with in the same way. Almaz had her girls and there were rooms for the purpose out back, as well as one room for those who wanted to chew khat. Izzie was sure Almaz knew how to divert any man's attention. She looked at Moe. She was never quite sure what to believe when Almaz said that she 'kept an eye on him', when he was in the Nyala without her. Apart from anything, it was pretty obvious Almaz fancied him herself.

The slim bar-girl came back with three glasses of draft. Moe reached in his pocket to pay. Tom had his hand on the girl's bottom.

"Tom," Izzie said.

"I'll get the next one," Tom said.

"No, I mean get your hand off her backside. Did she ask you to touch her up?"

Tom looked up at the girl, withdrew his hand and said, "Maybe, if Brazil wins," he said and winked at the girl.

"Not funny," Izzie said.

The girl looked mildly at Tom, thanked Moe for his tip, and smiled at Izzie as she went by to the next table.

"Look at that old geezer in the corner," Tom said, unruffled.

An old man was standing by a table next to the open window that looked onto the path outside. He was scratching his crotch. His baggy grey trousers hung loose, held up by string around his waist. He lit a cigarette, cupping the match in his hands, almost stumbling as he leant forward to draw on the flame.

"He's already drunk," Izzie said.

He flicked the match dead and threw it into the ashtray. Taking one step back, swaying slightly, he puffed on the cigarette until the tip crackled red and a small cloud hovered in front of him. Suddenly he swallowed the burning cigarette.

People turned to watch, holding their laughter.

"What on earth is he up to?" Izzie said.

"I've seen him do this before," Moe said.

"Really?" Izzie said, trying to push away her sense of unease.

The deep wrinkles in the old man's face twisted in agony. His eyes popped out, staring round the bar, not looking at anyone in particular. Everyone laughed. Hopping about, he reached behind his neck and retrieved the burning cigarette from his collar. He put it between his lips and his face became expressionless. He sat down, pulled his chair closer to the table, picked up his beer and downed it in one go.

"Blimey," Izzie said. "How did he do that?"

"No wonder his clothes are full of ciggie burns," Tom said, laughing.

The old man was sitting with his elbows on the table, hugging his ears as if it to shut out the world.

People turned away and carried on talking, a few watched in case he did something else.

"Here," Moe called to a bar-girl, waving a one Birr note. "Get him another beer from us."

Izzie ran her fingers through Moe's hair and thought how handsome he was with his slightly crooked nose. "That's sweet of you," she said.

"Hey, love-birds, the match must be starting soon," Tom said. "What time is it, anyway?"

A small girl wandered past their table with an enamel dish of 'kollo. Tiny brown roasted barley seeds.

"Isn't she cute?" Izzie said. "So small to be out here at night selling 'kollo."

"It's nearly eight. It's supposed to start at eight," Moe said.

The girl wore a faded cotton dress which hung limply around her thin calves. She had the cracked soles of someone who had never worn shoes. She looked around vaguely, nibbling the 'kollo in her tray. She was beckoned over by a young man in a red and white baseball jacket. She made her way through the metal chairs and tables and sold him one small bowl.

Izzie watched as the little girl tipped the contents into his hand. He offered some to his friend before chucking the rest in his mouth. The two young men chewed for a while. The child watched them, perhaps hoping for a second sale. Her customer ignored her. He said something to his friend, pointing his chin towards a bar-girl. The little girl turned away.

"The whistle's gone." Tom turned his chair towards the screen, lifting his beer to his lips.

"What if Brazil wins?" Izzie said, sensing the nervous tightening in her chest.

"I'm sure it will be fine, honey. Let's see," Moe said and kissed the end of her nose.

Almaz turned the volume up. Chairs scraped the floor to face the TV.

Izzie looked around. Everyone was glued to the screen. "Are they so keen on football, or is it just this match?"

"Ethiopia just played the African Cup in Libya," Tom said.

"They were beaten three nil by Nigeria," Moe said.

"Problem is, at least one or two players disappear every time Ethiopia goes overseas to play," Tom said. "They can't keep a decent team together."

"They don't want to come back," Moe said. "It's a pity, but you can't blame them. Football is a way out."

"Watch out," Tom said, leaning forward.

The stadium inside the TV set roared.

The people in the bar stood and sat like a wave, giving out a low groan. The Russians had scored a goal. Player number 12.

A wiry man in a dark, worn jacket was still on his feet. "Etiopia Tikdem!" he shouted amidst the clamour from the TV set. "Ethiopia First!" A few others around him stood up, raising their beers in agreement.

The young man in the red and white baseball jacket looked at them with disdain and muttered something to his friend, who nodded his head.

The ball was in play again.

The Soviet supporter took a long drink of beer and ordered another. It was Tom's bar-girl who put one in front of him, contempt in the raised black pencil line of her eyebrow.

Izzie noticed some anxiously looking from the screen to the Soviet supporters. A man at the table next to them downed his beer and ordered another in one single movement, his eyes not leaving the TV set. It seemed like most people were waiting for Brazil to score a goal.

When it came the room erupted, a raucous cheer drowning the noise from the TV. Even Izzie stood up and cheered.

"So you do like football," Tom said, clinking his glass against hers. "Over here," he called to his bar-girl. "We'll have three more."

"He's looking unhappy," Izzie said, nodding at the Soviet supporter.

His shoulders were hunched up round his ears, pointed like the wings of a vulture in waiting. He looked around the bar, derision on his face. His companions stared at the TV, occasionally looking at him as if to check, nodding. Almaz went to his table with a beer, laid a hand on his shoulder. He looked up and seeing her, smiled and wrapped his arm around her waist.

"I hope he won't cause trouble," Izzie said. "Almaz is obviously trying to butter him up."

"It will be fine," Moe said. "There's only a few of them. And there are no Kebele at the door."

The one-all draw was good for business. The little girl was back with a box of cigarettes and sweets. She must have sold all her 'kollo.

Izzie wondered if it was the child's mother who stocked her up and sent her out.

Another girl came in the door with a large enamel bowl of roasted peanuts.

Moe waved at her to come. "I could do with some of those," he said.

The child came and stood next to Izzie, looking at her with round eyes.

"She's worn out, poor soul," Izzie said, putting her hand on the girl's back.

"Here, give us five cups," Moe said.

"Amisst,[53]" Izzie said.

"Ishi," the girl said, sucking the word in with her breath.

Moe gave the girl two Birr.

She looked at Izzie again. It was too much money.

"Hijee, hijee," Izzie said. "Go, go, it's OK."

The child smiled, her eyes shining, and turned to look for another customer.

"That's exactly how you inflate prices for farenj," Tom said.

"Who cares," Izzie said, picking at the peanuts. "Mmm, they're good. You want to fight over two Birr?"

"Watch the screen," Moe said. "Brazil have the ball."

The ball flew over the goal and into the crowd behind. Once again the people in the bar rose and fell, anticipation followed quickly by disappointment.

"They're openly backing the Brazilians," Izzie said in a low voice.

The Soviet sympathiser stood up and walked slowly to the bar. His bony shoulder blades held up the ample cloth of his jacket. He said something to the slim bar-girl. His face looked harsh.

"What's he saying?" Tom said.

---

[53] Five.

"No idea," Izzie said.

There was a commotion at the door. Three men rushed in, knocking people out of the way. The child with the peanuts ducked low and ran outside clutching her bowl, letting out a frightened squeal.

The men brushed rudely past Izzie. She pulled herself in tight, ducking her head. She felt Moe's arm around her and huddled in close.

"Are they armed?" she said, her teeth gritted as if she was freezing.

The party man was still at the bar. He pointed at the man in the red and white baseball jacket and his friend. His face looked as if it would spit.

The two young men got up, backing away, fear in their eyes. "It's only football," one called out, his arms spread wide. "It's a game be Egziyabher."

"Innihid, Innihid," the men who had rushed in shouted at him.

In moments the two lads were bundled out of the bar.

There was silence except for the TV, the whistling crowds in the stadium. Not a chair scraped the floor. Someone coughed. The old man in the corner held his beer and stared at the screen. The children were gone with their bowls of 'kollo, peanuts and boxes of cigarettes and caramella.

The man in the dark jacket went back to his seat, to his friends. He swaggered slightly. Almaz went to his table and spoke. He looked at her. Neither of them was smiling.

Revulsion filled the room like the stench rising from a rubbish dump, clogging the lungs.

Izzie could barely swallow. "Let's pay and go," she said, not sure if she could stand, her legs like jelly.

"It's done now," Moe said, his voice odd. He cleared his throat.

"Look, Brazil have the ball," Tom said. His voice was croaky too. He tipped some beer down his throat.

Izzie watched his Adam's apple go up and down as he swallowed. She could feel salty tears burning in her eyes and wiped them away quickly.

The Brazilians were closing in on the goal. A pass from right to left. No 11 picked it up and sent it flying. A goal.

The bar stayed quiet. Nobody moved.

The old man tapped his bottle on the table; one, two, three, four, over and over.

"They won," Izzie whispered. "Brilliant, they won." Her eyes filled with tears.

"Two one to the Brazilians," Moe said.

Almaz was standing behind the bar, opening a bottle and pulling glasses off the shelves behind her. She was calling her girls, gathering them around, pouring a small shot of liquid into each of the glasses on their trays.

The slim girl came tottering over on her high platforms and placed a glass in front of each of them. "Innashenefallen," she said in a low voice.

"What did she say?" Tom said.

"Something like, we'll win, we will overcome," Izzie said, her throat feeling tight.

"There's something about these people," Moe said, shaking his head. "That Almaz sure has guts."

"Wonder what they'll do to them," Izzie said. "Two mates out for a beer, watching football." She took a sip of the drink. It burned down her throat. Pure alcohol. It was just what she needed. "They must have had an eye on them. But just about everyone wanted the Soviets to lose. So why them?"

"They pick off one or two and it shuts up the whole room," Moe said. "That's the thing. Spreads fear. See how effective it was?"

"It doesn't matter to them," Tom said. "Could have taken anyone."

"Except us," Izzie said.

The bar-girls were setting down a shot in front of every customer.

The TV screen was blank. Almaz put on music.

The Party man and his friends downed their shots in one, got up, their chairs roughly scraping the concrete floor, and walked out. Everyone watched in silence as they left the bar.

15

Comrade Abebe was there as usual. They could hear his voice through the tannoy on the other side of the market. He had an exaggerated gait, picking up his feet over the uneven ground in his thick barabasso[54] sandals. And with the large horn-like loudspeaker held up to his mouth, he could never quite see where he was going. No one particularly liked him, everyone was happy to find him amusing to temper the darker side of his presence.

There were days when Zewdie and Etalem had to hide their laughing faces behind their shawls. "His sandals are a few sizes too big," Zewdie would chuckle.

"I wonder what he wants today." Etalem said, shading her eyes and looking across the market.

"Look," Zewdie said. "People are getting up and heading for town."

As he came nearer they could hear him: "News of our Heroes from the front," he called out through his white trumpet. "There is a list of names hanging outside the Awraja district office."

Zewdie looked at Etalem. Her friend had two sons in the army.

"Ethiopia Tikdem," he called out. "Ethiopia first."

Some boys ran over to dance around behind the old man throwing their fists in the air and shouting out, "Ethiopia Tikdem."

"Shall I come with you, Etalem?" Zewdie said.

"Would you?"

"If you have husbands, sons and brothers at the front you can get news of them from the Awraja office," Comrade Abebe announced again as he walked past them.

They called a young boy over to look after their produce while they were gone and went together. Like most, Etalem could not read and

---

[54] Sandals made from recycled tyres

Zewdie only a little. Two boys standing by the list were doing their best looking for names as people came forward pushing, some already crying, expecting the worst.

Etalem collapsed right there on the concrete step when one of the boys found her son's name amongst the dead. "Weyne. Weyne. Yeney lij. Weyne. Weyne," she wailed. "Yeney lij." She sat up hitting her chest with both hands, wailing, her eyes rolling up towards the sky. "My son, my son."

"Come, come, Etalem." Zewdie tried to get her up, out of the way of the crowd that had gathered on and around the veranda outside the Awraja office. Distress on every face.

"Weyne. Weyne." Etalem sobbed.

"How can you be sure?" Zewdie shouted to the boy, trying not to be pushed out of the way. "And what of her other son, Ephraim Mengistu?"

The lad was overwhelmed by people shouting out names. He could clearly not hear her. Etalem was not a large woman but Zewdie could not lift her. She had become a dead weight. Zewdie looked around for help. A man she recognised from the market, one of her tella customers, helped to pull Etalem to her feet. Between them they managed to drag her to the shade of a tree not far from the Awraja office. Etalem's body was limp in Zewdie's arms. She obviously couldn't walk alone. She sobbed and wailed, her head falling back. She sank in a heap under the tree when they let go of her. There was wailing all around them.

"Thank you," Zewdie said to the man trying to smile but her eyes were full of tears and she could barely get the words out.

She touched Etalem gently on the shoulder before returning to the veranda to get news of the other son.

She caught the boy's eye. "Ephraim Mengistu," she called out to him.

The boy turned to the list and ran his finger down one page and onto the next. She kept her eyes on him, all the while begging the good Lord to save at least one son. He turned back to find Zewdie's face in the crowd.

"Missing," he said.

"What does that mean, 'missing'?" she shouted over people's heads, as those pushing forwards sent her further to the back again.

"Dead, or taken prisoner," came the reply. She noticed the boy's face was hard and drawn. She wondered how long he had been standing there passing out bad news, and, worse still, how many of those on the lists were known to him. His friends, an uncle maybe, a brother.

"Etalem, Etalem," she called as she ran back. "Ephraim is missing. They say maybe he has been taken prisoner." She did not say: 'or maybe he's dead.' Her friend would have nothing to pray for.

Etalem looked up, still sobbing, with a mixture of hope and despair in her eyes.

They say the Eritreans look after our boys, Zewdie reminded herself, seeing her friend was too distressed to hear anything.

She knelt by her friend to comfort her. "He will find his way home. God is with him." She looked up around her. There were so many people crying. Everyone knew someone who had gone to the front. She did not know how she was going to get Etalem back to her home. She lived near Tulu Market. It was quite far.

"How is she?"

She looked round to the voice behind her. It was the man who had helped them earlier.

"I don't know how to get her home," Zewdie said.

"I live near Wozeiro Etalem's village," the man said.

"You know her well?"

"I knew her husband before he passed on, God be with him," the man said. "I can take her on my mule. She is not fit to walk."

"Thank you sir, thank you." Zewdie bowed her head relieved. "I don't know what I would have done without your help."

"We are all here for each other," the man said, smiling sadly.

She looked up at him again. "You must know her boys?"

He nodded. "Since they were so small," he said, putting out his hand low to the ground.

"I'm sorry," she said.

"Wait here with her and I will come with the mule."

**

Zewdie put ki'ta bread, a bottle of freshly made tella beer, sweet itan incense and a small packet of green coffee beans in a basket, and set off for Etalem's village to the lekeso bate[55]. People would have been visiting Etalem's house over the past few days since they heard the news.

"Do not worry if I am late Ashebir, ishi?" she told him when he left with the animals in the morning. "There is bread in the large basket for when you come."

---

[55] At the home of the person who has died a small shelter is erected to cover visitors from the sun and food is offered. Family, neighbours and friends come to pay respects.

"Ishi, Zewdie," he said.

At Etalem's house things were worse than she expected.

"Please try and get her up again, Wozeiro Zewdie," Etalem's neighbours begged. "Maybe she will listen to you."

"Etalem," she said, as she entered the darkness of the small thatched gojo-bate.

Etalem had shaved off her hair. She lay on her cot shivering and muttering as if the devil was inside her.

"She has wailed and cried without stopping for three days and three nights," one woman said.

"There is hardly a sound left in her voice," another said.

She sat on the edge of Etalem's cot. "It's me, Etalem my friend, it's me, Zewdie."

Etalem's face was covered by a thin black shawl. She turned slowly towards Zewdie's voice.

Zewdie gently drew the shawl back. Her friend's eyes were red and sunk in deep dark circles. No wonder the women thought she was possessed by the devil.

"It's me," she said again, on the verge of tears. She gently stroked her friend's forehead and cheeks. "What are you doing to yourself? We have to get you out of this."

Etalem curled her body towards Zewdie and moaned, her eyes full of despair.

"Maybe it's her son's spirit," one old woman whispered.

"We should get the healer to come," another said.

"Yes, go and fetch her," Zewdie said. "And someone re-kindle the fire, we will make coffee." She passed them the small bag of green beans.

She talked quietly to Etalem for some time, praying with her and entreating her to draw on her old strength for the sake of her other children. She got water and a cloth and gently wiped her friend's face and hands.

"Look, I bought you some of my ki'ta bread," Zewdie said. "Try some, just a mouthful. Here, with a sip of water." Finally, Zewdie managed to get Etalem to eat.

The village healer came and burnt a strong smelling mixture in the dark room. Etalem lay on her cot, Zewdie holding her hand.

The old woman said it would, "Rid the place of any evil." And left tutting and cursing. They heard her spit loudly on the ground outside the door.

Zewdie squeezed her friend's hand.

The women started preparing the coffee. The room slowly filled with smoke from the sweet itan on the hot coals and the strong bitter coffee beans roasting over the fire. They made fendisha, throwing some outside the entrance to keep the spirits happy.

Etalem sat up. She took a sip of the sweet black coffee.

"Come now, that will give you strength," Zewdie said, smiling.

Seeing the brightness fading outside the door, Zewdie turned to her friend. "I must go, Etalem. It will soon be dark, and it is far."

"Ishi, Zewdie," Etalem whispered.

"Promise me you will get up every day," Zewdie told her friend. "You will get stronger, I promise. I will pray for you. I will be waiting for you in the market."

"I will try, Zewdie," Etalem said. "I promise."

**

Zewdie sat under the tree selling her tella beer, her elbows on her knees, looking out across the market, waiting for Etalem. What a terrible time. So much suffering, she thought. Suddenly, she stood, looking closely. There she was. At last. It was Etalem, walking slowly towards her, with a basket of potatoes on her back.

"Etalem, Etalem," she called out, walking quickly over to help take the load off her back.

She greeted her friend with kisses. "Welcome, welcome. I am so glad to see you."

"Thank you, Zewdie. God bless you."

The dark shadows under Etalem's eyes had not faded.

"You became so thin. You must eat and look after yourself," Zewdie chided her. "If you get sick who will look after your children?"

"I wish I could eat them back in, Zewdie," Etalem said, tutting as they laid the potatoes out ready for sale. "God only knows. I will not send another of mine to fight."

"We are all Ethiopians," Zewdie said. "You are right. There is no need for us to fight each other."

"Look at us, Zewdie, my friend. God knows we don't have enough to eat," Etalem said. She looked at her. "Zewdie, what has happened to you? Are you sick?"

"I didn't know it was so obvious," Zewdie said. She drew her shema across her nose and mouth. She closed her eyes and asked Egziyabher, or Allah, she didn't mind which, for strength, and then looked out over the market again.

"What is it Zewdie?"

"I just feel weaker than before. Emet Fahte says it is birrd."

"Have you been to take holy waters?" Etalem asked.

"Not yet. Maybe I should try."

"I went to the priest. He blessed me and gave me holy waters," Etalem said. "He told me to pray for Ephraim and that the boy would come home. Since then I have started to feel better."

"I will go. Maybe I will go," Zewdie said.

Zewdie and Etalem sat under their tree watching and waiting, flicking flies away from their products. Then she spotted the old man.

"Look Etalem, Comrade Abebe from the Kebele, is coming over," Zewdie said. "I wonder what he wants." She did not care for the man. He was only interested in politics and furthering himself. And he had a round belly. "He knows where to find a good meal," she whispered to her friend.

"Tenasteling, Wozeiro Etalem," he said. He leant forward, putting out both hands to shake hers. "How are you?"

"I am fine under the circumstances, thank you," she replied, shaking his hand and bowing her head slightly.

"Good day Wozeiro Zewdie, how are you?" he greeted her in turn.

"I am fine, thanks be to God," she said, shaking his hand with one hand, and shading her eyes from the sun with the other.

" Your son did not die in vain, Wozeiro Etalem," he said. "He is a Hero of the revolution."

Etalem's mouth was shut in a thin line. She stared at the man.

Comrade Abebe cleared his throat, his eyes shifting away in discomfort.

Zewdie kept her eyes on him. "Maybe you would like to buy some potatoes, or have a drink of tella?" she said, feeling her throat tight.

"Thank you, thank you," he said. "I will send my wife for some potatoes." He coughed again. "Have a good day," he bowed briefly and walked away, his loudspeaker dangling by his side.

"What does he know?" Etalem burst out. "His sons are safe at home."

"You did well, Etalem. If you say anything they will accuse you of being against the revolution. The Kebele could arrest you. They believe your Samuel is a Hero, that he died for the Motherland."

"Do you believe we should fight the Eritreans, Zewdie?" Etalem asked in a low voice.

"I don't know, Etalem. I don't know."

Zewdie sat looking over the market. She felt unhappy for her friend. But she did not have any answers.

Etalem's neighbour, who had helped them on the day they heard of Samuel's death, stopped to greet them both.

"It is good to see you back in the market," he said to Etalem, smiling warmly, before turning to greet Zewdie.

"I will buy one pile of potatoes Wozeiro Etalem, and drink a glass of your fine tella, Wozeiro Zewdie."

Zewdie looked at Etalem and they smiled.

Zewdie poured him a glass of the cloudy liquid.

He drank, breathed out satisfied, and smiled. "This is the best tella in Ataye market, Wozeiro Zewdie," he said.

She did not want to charge him, but he insisted. "How will you live if you give all your friends a glass to drink?" He gave her the empty glass back and some coins.

"He is a good man," Zewdie said when he had left them.

Etalem nodded in agreement.

The afternoon brought more customers for Zewdie's tella. Her tin slowly filled with coins.

God is good, she thought. I'll be able to buy an egg for Ashebir today as well as the other things we need.

**

It had been another long hot day. Dry, dry, dry, crackling underfoot. Zewdie had just come from the market and was exhausted. Ashebir was still out with the animals. The small papaya tree Ashebir had planted sent a shadow across the ground. She went in to the house and fetched a jug to water it. He was keen to see fruits growing on it. She had to keep explaining that he would have to wait a few years yet.

She thought about the rumours in the market. The fighting in Tigray and Eritrea was getting worse. And the drought was even more severe further north. People were shaking their heads, saying that families in the north were leaving their homes and walking for miles in search of food. She could not imagine life getting that bad. The big rains had been poor, making the dry season seem long. The Ataye river had become shallow for the time of year, and the harvest had not been good, but they were just managing, day by day.

"Ke ij wadde af, Zewdie," Temima kept saying. "We're surviving from hand to mouth."

And it was true, every coin she earned she spent on food. Now Zewdie needed more grain to brew beer or make injera. She had run out. She did not want to ask Mohamed Bilal from Albuko again and decided she would go to Jebuha with Yishaereg's mother and some of the other women.

She went inside, cleaned around their home before going out to collect firewood to light the fire. While she waited for the flames to die down and the coals to become hot, she rubbed a drop of Emet Fahte's eucalyptus oil between her palms and massaged her legs with deep round movements, drawing the pain out. It made her head dizzy and she wished she had someone to do it for her. Her mother had been good in such things. She sighed. She missed her so much.

When she finished, she stretched her legs out by the warmth of the fire and breathed in the sweet warm smell of the eucalyptus. The pain eased. She started making supper for when Ashebir got home.

"Ashebir," she called, hearing some movement outside. The goats were bleating and she could hear the rustle of the cows' hides against the bushes. "Is that you?"

"Tenasteling Zewdie," he called out. He sounded strong and cheerful.

He put his head through the door, waving both hands playfully. His face was fine; his arms had not one extra ounce of flesh on them. But he seemed happy, and never complained.

"How are you?" he said.

"Fine, fine, thank you," she said, smiling back at him, wondering what kept him going.

"I am just coming. I'll put the animals safely in the beret," he said and went out again.

Through the open door she could see dusk was falling. She got up to have a look. Walking a little way down the path, she stood quietly gazing out across the hillside. The sky did not disappoint her. It was a beautiful soft grey-pink colour. God's beauty.

Why didn't He send us rain in time anymore? she wondered.

When they were sitting by the fire, eating, she said, "Ashebir, do you remember the time we went to Jebuha, at harvest time?"

"No," he said, chewing, his mouth smacking. "Where is Jebuha?" He swallowed and looked up at her, his eyes now sleepy.

"Did you have to go far with the animals today?" she said. It was hard for the boys to find grass for the animals.

222

"We went way beyond Muletta. It is very dry everywhere."

"You look tired."

"I am fine. Don't worry," he said, shaking his head. He smiled quietly at her. "Eat Zewdie," he said.

"Ishi," she said. "I'm eating."

These days he was always saying, "Don't worry". He was still young and yet so grown up. He had been uneasy since she became unwell. She could feel his eyes following her around the room and watching her while she cooked or ate. He helped her carrying things and fetched water from the river so she would not have to go so often. She knew he was afraid, that if things got worse, if she got sick, if they had to sell all the animals, she would have to send him to work as an erregnya again.

"Jebuha is a small village in the countryside outside Robit," she said. "We have to go past Senbatey camel market to get there. We have been before."

"Why do you want to go?" he asked. "It is so far."

"We can get a share of their harvest," she said, suddenly feeling the shame of it. Only the poorest families did it. Sitting and waiting round the edge of the fields for a share. It was begging.

He looked at her.

"The people of Jebuha are Muslims, like our friends and family here, and known for their generosity," she said. "They believe they will be blessed in their next life, if they help the poor in this one."

"We are poor, Zewdie," Ashebir said.

"Yes, we are, yeney lij," she said. "It is not our fault. It is God's will."

"Is it alright to do that, Zewdie?" Ashebir looked doubtful.

Zewdie thought for a minute. She had taught him to work hard for everything. Now she was going to teach him to beg.

"It's called bwagetta, Ashebir," she said. "It is like begging. But we have no choice. I need the grain to make beer. We cannot live on dry ki'ta bread forever."

"Ishi," he said, taking another mouthful.

"We will leave the day after tomorrow, early in the morning. You can ask Mohamed Abdu or Ali to take our animals."

"Seynyo, Makseynyo, Erob. Erob then, Wednesday," Ashebir said smiling at her.

How was it that he always found something funny to say? "Well remembered," she laughed. "You are right, we'll go this Erob."

"I will have to miss my Qur'an class again."

"Comrade Abebe made an announcement in the market that the

Kebele have started literacy classes," she said. "It is no good to go through life illiterate."

"But I am learning to read and write in my Qur'an classes."

"Yes, that's right. But that is Arabic. They will teach you to read and write Amharic."

"Ishi, Zewdie, if you want," he said, chewing on his food and staring into the fire.

"Finish your bread and go sleep," she said.

"Ishi," he said again. He took another mouthful.

When he finished she pulled him towards her and kissed his cheek. "Sleep well," she said. She watched him as he went outside. To relieve himself, she was sure, and to stroke his favourite goat. She pulled her gabi around her, picked up the dish they had been eating from and went to wash it outside.

16

Two days later, Zewdie woke Ashebir for the walk to Jebuha. It was still dark. They went up the path to join Yishaereg's mother and two other women from the village who had gathered quietly. They too had no husband at home, no land, and were too poor to buy food. They greeted each other in soft voices before setting off.

"Wrap your gabi tight round you, Ashebir" she said quietly. He was walking close by her side with his stick over his shoulder, carrying a bag to fill with grain, Egziyabher sifeked, God willing. She put a hand on his shoulder to guide him.

They reached Jebuha in the late morning and sat in a small group on the edge of the wide open field where the newly harvested millet was being threshed. Ashebir sat quietly near her on a boulder. She turned to look at him. He was watching the oxen being driven round and round to separate the grain from the chaff. Clouds of dust billowed in the air. She could see him scratching his nose. She waited for the sneeze.

"Egziyabher yibarkih," she said. "Bless you."

He nodded and carried on watching the threshing.

Zewdie turned to watch too. She noticed the ribs on the oxen were beginning to show. It was a bad sign. She wondered about the price of livestock. On the way, they had seen people herding goats, sheep and cattle towards Senbatey market. The animals were known to lose weight on the long trek down from the highlands. So they would not get as good a price. And with so many people selling, the price was sure to fall further. She had to talk to Mohamed Bilal from Albuko. Maybe she should sell her goats before the price fell even more.

Ashebir sat with his chin on his knees, his arms wrapped round his ankles, as if he was holding himself together. He always sat like that when he wanted to stop the pains in his stomach.

"Ashebir," she said. "Have some 'kollo." She passed him the small bag.

"Thank you," he said.

"Just a handful for now," she said. "It has to last us the day."

"Ishi," he said.

"Do you remember this place now?"

"Yes, I know it," he said. "I like watching the oxen going round and round." He shuffled himself around on his rock and looked happier now that he was chewing.

"Look at you with your deep brown eyes, yeney lij," Zewdie tried to laugh. She wanted to keep his spirits up.

She did not like sitting and waiting like a beggar. She had always worked.

"By the end of today we will have some grain, Ashebir," she said. "You can help me grinding and then I can brew tella."

"Maybe when you have sold the beer you can make sherro wot for us, Zewdie?"

"Yes, maybe I can, God willing," she said, smiling at him. "Insha'Allah."

The sun felt hot on her head. There was not much shade nearby. They would think her lazy if she sat under the trees. They might not give her anything, she thought, putting up her umbrella.

She heard his quiet voice: "Zewdiye, go over there and sit in the shade for a while."

She looked to where he was pointing. There were patches of shade on the ground under some short, twisted, acacia trees just behind them.

"I will wait in our spot. Ibakish, please, go, just for a while."

"Ishi, ishi, yeney lij," she said softly. "Alright, my child. I'll go."

She went to sit in the shade of the acacia. The aching in her feet rose to her knees. She massaged them gently. She suddenly felt miserable. What if she didn't manage? "Be Egzyhaber, give us some grain today, enough for me to work with. Guide us safely home tonight," she whispered. "Thank you for my boy and all our blessings."

She sat with her eyes closed. A whip cracked every now and then, loud in the still air. She could hear the farmers calling out instructions to their animals. It all seemed to fade to some place far away.

She woke to hear Ashebir calling her name. People were running from the edge of the field towards the place where they had been threshing. Ashebir was standing near the front of the queue. He's a fast runner, she thought. Even if he was tired and hungry, his legs still raced across the pastures.

She walked over to him. "Good boy, Ashebir," she whispered into his ear.

He looked at her with a broad smile. "I was almost first, Zewdie."

"Well done. The first ones in the line usually get the most."

"Open up the bag, Ashebir. It's our turn now. Look." She bowed her head to greet the farmer. "Peace be with you," she said. "May Allah reward you. Thank you, thank you." She felt tears well up in her eyes. She was so grateful to the man, and so ashamed.

The man bowed his head and smiled. "Peace be with you, sister," he said. She could see he felt sorry.

"We cannot give you very much," he said. "The harvest around here is not as good as we hoped for."

"It is worse in our area," she told him, "and we hear it is even worse further north."

The man shook his head sadly, "Look how many people have come."

She stood back while Ashebir held their bag open and the man poured millet into it. The man was generous. Ashebir put the bag on the ground, wound the cloth into a knot, and then started to lift it.

"Come, let me help you," she said, lifting it with him onto his shoulders. She held the bundle while he slid his stick under it to take the weight. "Is it too heavy?" she asked, thinking it looked almost as heavy as the boy himself.

"No, it's fine." Ashebir replied. He walked away towards the path they had arrived on earlier in the day.

Zewdie said goodbye to the man and followed.

"Ashebir, let's wait here for the others. We will walk home together."

One by one, the three women from their village gathered, each with a bundle of grain.

"We should hire a donkey to get us as far as Senbatey," Yishaereg's mother said.

The others agreed. Zewdie was relieved that Ashebir would not have to carry their bundle all the way. He would not let her take it.

The sun was already sending long shadows across the fields. It would soon be dusk. They would be walking in the dark. There was no choice. Zewdie gave Yishaereg's mother fifty cents as a contribution and together they hired a donkey. The young man strapped their bundles to the donkey's back and set off. His face was hard, his lips a thin line. Zewdie hoped he was honest and would not run off with their precious grain. She and the other women would certainly not catch him and Ashebir was not strong enough to overcome him. She walked alongside him and the donkey, as fast as the dull ache in her legs would allow, motioning to the other women to keep up.

Finally, one of the women said, "Yeney lij, we are exhausted. In Allah's name, can't you go a little slower?"

"Happily, Emmebate," he said. "But you are all going so fast, I thought you are in a hurry to get home because of the hour."

The women laughed. "We were trying to keep up with you," they cried.

The boy turned and smiled at them, such a beautiful smile.

Zewdie felt bad for mistrusting him so. "You are a good boy," she said. "Let's go. Not too fast and not too slow."

She picked her way along the narrow paths. They went over rocks and among the trees. She had her eye on Ashebir, and the boy in front with the donkey. She thanked God for the grain. She would grind it into flour to make tella and injera. For the next two weeks, she and Ashebir would eat. At least that, at least.

They reached Senbatey market and bade farewell to the boy. Ashebir took the sack of grain on his shoulder once more. It was already so dark, she could hardly make out his small face.

"Are you alright?" she asked him.

"I am fine, Zewdie. Don't worry," he said, making the tutting sound he had learnt from the adults, and sucking his teeth.

It made her smile.

"Tell me when you are tired and I will take my turn. I am still strong as an ox you know," she said.

"But I am as strong as a donkey. Donkeys are more used to carrying than an ox."

She laughed. "How right you are."

"Let's go," Yishaereg's mother said. "It is getting late and it will take time to reach home from here."

"Ishi, ishi, let's go," another woman said.

Zewdie put a hand on Ashebir's shoulder and they set off.

"It is good that we come and go in the dark," one woman said. "No one will know where we have been."

"Except they will wonder when we're busy grinding grain in our compounds tomorrow," another woman laughed.

"Praise Allah for this gift," another said.

"Praise Allah," Zewdie agreed and squeezed Ashebir's shoulder to encourage him. She looked up into the night sky as they walked across the dry open plains. The moon rose amongst the bright stars. Nearly a full moon, she thought. That is good. It will light our way. They walked, talking quietly amongst each other. They walked in their own thoughts, silently. Sometimes one of the women would start to hum a song and another would join her singing softly.

"Are you alright?" Zewdie asked after some time.

"Yes mother, I am fine," he replied. His voice was quiet and husky as if coming from a deep sleep.

"Let me carry the bundle now," Zewdie said, trying to sound firm.

"No. You are not well. I can carry it," he said.

"Let me carry it a little way, for a short while," she said. "Then you take it back."

He was quiet. "Ishi," he said, after a while.

She lifted it from his shoulders onto hers.

"There," she said.

"Can I sit for a moment?" he asked.

"No. Better to keep walking," Yishaereg's mother said. "If you sit, the cold night will creep into your bones. You will not be able to move. When the hyenas come, you will make a good supper for them."

"Hush now," Zewdie said, "Don't frighten the boy."

"Let's keep walking, Zewdie," Ashebir said, looking up at her. "If I sit, I will fall asleep."

"It is good if we keep going. We will reach home, then you can sleep in your cot. Ishi?"

They carried on walking. Zewdie could feel Ashebir clutching her long skirt. Theirs was a hard life, she thought. Only God knew how hard. They seemed to work and work and get less and less. She wondered if it was possible for anything to change it.

By now the women had fallen silent. Everyone was walking one step after the next, one step after the next, across the barren country, lit by the moon. She could hear the hyenas' cackling laughter and eerie woo-ooooping noises coming from somewhere in the mountains. As they passed a village, dogs came running out. They stopped in a row not far from them, barking, their necks stretched out. Every now and then one would lie down to scratch itself violently, bighting at flees on its back before getting up and joining the chorus again. Dogs are dirty animals, she thought, no wonder the Wollo Muslims didn't like to have any in their villages.

She felt Ashebir's hand pulling on her skirt.

"Ayezoh, Ayezoh," she whispered to him. "They won't come near. They are afraid of us."

They continued walking as the moon rose high in the sky. She thanked the Lord for his light and prayed they would reach home safely.

"This is our life," she said, looking down at him. "It is a hard life, but never give up. You have to keep going."

She dared not comfort him. If he stopped, she would not get him home that night. It was too dangerous for the two of them to stay out there alone. She kept walking, feeling the tug of his fist clinging to her skirt, never slowing her pace, but still not going too fast. Her own body was crying out for rest, her legs aching. Tomorrow she would rub eucalyptus oil in them and rest in the shade of their house.

They walked along narrow paths up and up, winding into the mountains towards Ataye and their village. Zewdie kept close behind Yishaereg's mother. She could hear the woman's heavy breathing. She was not well either and had been to see Emet Fahte Ibrahim only the week before.

She felt a light tugging on her skirt and turned round.

"Zewdie, look," she heard Ashebir's small voice. "I can see the warka tree near our house on the hillside," he said.

"Yes, we are nearly there," Zewdie smiled. She stroked his head. The women began to say 'good night' to each other. They shook hands, bowing heads and praising Allah for their safe return and the gift of grain. One after the next they broke off, taking different paths. Zewdie and Ashebir took the same path with Yishaereg's mother.

"Good night, Zewdie," the woman said when they reached Zewdie's home. "Good night, Ashebir. You are a good boy."

"Ishi," Zewdie heard the boy whisper.

"He is too tired to speak," Zewdie said, laughing a little. "Good night, good night," she called softly as Yishaereg's mother carried on up the hill.

17

The door to the terrace was open; the only sign that someone was in. Izzie walked through to the sitting room and put her bag on the dining table. She felt elated, nervous and hungry all at once and was not sure which to deal with first. The light outside the picture windows had faded into darkness, transforming the furniture into gloomy shapes. A figure was stretched out on the sofa at the other end of the room.

"You're back," she said quietly, and walked over.

Moe was asleep. One arm cradled around his head. His other hand lay across his broad chest, fingers splayed as if protesting undying love in a Shakespearian drama. His face, devoid of the indifference his moods sometimes gave it, was soft with the quiet innocence of sleep. As he lay there, she was reminded of the gentle strength in his body, which had drawn her to him in the first place. She crouched beside him and traced a finger across his eyebrows and down his oddly crooked nose, not touching. She moved away slowly, afraid to wake him.

He frowned and rubbed his eyes.

"Hi," she said and bent to kiss his lips. "I didn't mean to disturb you. I couldn't help myself."

He cupped his hand round the back of her head, holding her for a moment.

"Hello," he said. His voice sounded tender. "You just in? It's almost dark."

"Had a meeting with an international NGO," she said, sitting down on the floor beside him.

He stretched and gave his head a scratch.

"Picked up fleas?" She ruffled his hair. "How was the trip?"

"As ever, mixed. And I feel knackered," he said. He cleared his throat. "You look pleased with yourself, how did it go?"

"Very well," she said. "They might give us some funds for the

Nazareth factory, running costs."

"Well done, honey. They like your proposal then."

"And, best of all, they might fund my salary and Genet's, as long as ADCD keeps paying their share. It was a bit cheeky to ask, but, 'Ha!', as Uschi would say, it worked."

Moe pinched her nose. "Good for you."

"The guy said they had no projects in the disabled sector. He thought I could be a useful link for them. He wants me to write them more project proposals. Gezahegn has all sorts of ideas, like a grinding mill for Tibila Farm. But that will have to wait. We have a lot on with the carpet workshops and trying to get the Nazareth factory off the ground."

"What were they like? Worn cords and desert-boots?"

"It's a one-man-band. He's got a small office in Casanches. He was nice. He met his wife in Indonesia. They've got a little girl they adopted there. I thought that was pretty cool."

"Well that's you sorted then, isn't it?"

"I said, 'they might fund my salary'," she said. "But it would be great, Moe. You know how I hate having to depend on you."

"Reached my sell-by date, have I?" He pulled himself up, leaning on one elbow.

"Don't make me sound so mercenary." She gave him a kiss. "You know that's not what I mean." She got up to switch the lamp on in the corner of the room. The taut ox-skin shade, with a hand-painted man and donkey on it, gave out a square of warm, yellowish light, making the rest of the room even darker. "I'm really thirsty," she said.

"Me too," he said, coughing again. "Parched."

"Cold beer?"

"Love one."

She came back with two beers and a bowl of mixed 'kollo and peanuts. Negisst bought it by the kilo from Mercato, and they shared it between them. "I'm going to write to Uschi about the NGO money. She'll be thrilled."

"And some," he said. "How long is it since she left for Rwanda?" He sat up, stretching his long legs under the coffee table, and reached for the short stubby bottle of Meta. He drank almost half down in one go.

Izzie closed the window behind them, shutting out the strains of music coming from the Blue Nile Bar. "I guess it's about four or five months since Uschi left. It's taking so long to get this project off the ground." She curled up on the end of the sofa and lit a cigarette. "Didn't help, her organisation pulling out like that, transferring Uschi."

Moe finished his beer. "At least Gezahegn wanted to keep you on, even without Uschi there." He rubbed his hands together, wedging them between his legs.

"Are you cold? Here take the gabi." She passed him the large soft shawl. "There's so much work to do. All ADCD's projects either need money or an evaluation. It was a stroke of luck meeting Uschi. Who else would have cut through the red tape and got me a work permit? Ha!" Izzie was glad for the diversion. Talking work was better than touching the raw edges of the bitter arguments they'd had on the eve of his departure. Any mention of it might send them spinning into that place where every word seemed to trigger yet more misunderstandings.

"I could eat," he said, taking a handful of 'kollo.

"You too tired to go to the China Bar? I can't be bothered to cook, can you?"

"Let's see if Tom wants to join us. Or maybe Shirley and Brian. They said something about going to Langano over Ethiopian Christmas. I'd quite like to join them."

"OK," she said, disappointed. "If you like." Why always with other people? Why not just the two of them? She bit her lip to stop the words coming out. She was fond of Tom, but not all the time. He drank too much and his incessant awkward womanising got old quickly. Shirley and Brian were different. Brian always had something interesting to tell and Shirley was lovely and fun to be with.

Moe got up and went to the phone. "Shall we say seven thirty?"

"I suppose that's alright," she said, looking at her watch. "Just enough time for a shower." She wished she could be self-assured in these moments, that she could say, "Let's just go out the two of us," in a firm, friendly, uncomplicated way. But she couldn't.

"Hey Tom," Moe's voice came alive. He stood tall, relaxed in his bare feet, his jeans dirty from the road. He laughed. "Tell me about it…yeah…" He winked at Izzie, his eyes shining.

She smiled back, slightly irritated that she felt the need to compete for Moe's attention. With Tom of all people. She drank her beer down and went to get another, giving Moe a peck on the cheek as she passed him. What was it about Tom that made Moe spark up? But it wasn't just Tom, Moe always lit up when he was with other people.

Moe put the phone down. "Seven thirty at the China Bar. He'll call Shirley and Brian."

She put a beer on the table for him and sat back on the sofa with hers. "I was kind of hoping for an evening just the two of us," she said and immediately regretted it.

"Now you say it," he said, holding out his hands and shrugging. "Bit late."

"If I'd said anything, we'd have started bickering again."

"I don't know why you seem to need constant reassurance?" he said, running his fingers through his hair, looking dismayed. "I love you. What more do you want?"

Izzie hugged her knees into her chest. "We had that row, and then you had to go on your field trip. It's been more than a week, incommunicado."

"I can't even remember what we fought about." He sighed. "It's gone. Forgotten about, as far as I'm concerned."

She went cold inside and took a deep breath. "Maybe that's the difference between us. I've been mulling it over. Now you're here and you're kind of tender but also a bit cold. I don't know where we stand. I miss how we were together, Moe," she said. "I feel starved," she began and stopped. "Don't say anything. I know. I know."

"Don't talk about starving," Moe said. He put his hands deep in his pockets and hunched his shoulders up. "All the indicators show that people in the countryside wake up and go to sleep hungry. But that doesn't seem to count. Only when they start dying in large numbers are they 'starving', apparently. Only then is it a famine."

"I knew it as soon as I said it," she said. "Forget it. There's too much going on out there for me to feel sorry for myself. I know that."

"The data we've collected on the last few trips look horribly ominous. You know, people are surviving on a plain piece of bread made from sorghum or millet. Some on a handful or two of 'kollo a day. No eggs, no veg, and forget about meat. Now is the time to do something. Now is the time but everyone is stalling. It's all bloody politics."

"I know. I'm sorry. It's dreadful."

"I can do without your drama Izzie. 'What about us, what about us.'" He ran his hand through his hair again and looked away. "There's stuff going on out there that I'm trying to get my head round. Trying to translate it into convincing stats so that these idiots, all of them, both the government and the international community, do something." He stood there, suddenly looking helpless. He was like an enormous teddy bear, his sandy hair standing up in all directions.

She wanted to go and hug him but knew he wouldn't let her. It was the first time she'd heard such a heartfelt outburst. He kept it all inside. He was a number-cruncher, that's how she saw him. But the numbers had obviously got to him.

"It gets me down too, Moe, seeing so many poor people on the streets, even here in Addis. They are hungry here too."

"Music," he said and sat on the floor, legs crossed. He rattled through their cassettes, looking.

"People at home don't have to feel guilty about being 'hungry for love', or about eating out in a restaurant. But it's all happening under the same heaven, the same stars, we're all in the same world. We are all responsible in the end." She said, not sure if she was talking to him or to herself.

He pushed a cassette in the player. "Elton John alright?"

"Come here. Let me give you a hug, will you?" she said.

"Sometimes you're hard to follow," he said.

She was relieved to see him smile.

He got up and in a few strides walked straight onto the sofa. He sat down at the end, his knees up round his ears and pulled her towards him, putting his arms around her. "Just relax, let's try and take it easy," he whispered.

She closed her eyes. His closeness and warmth and Elton John's song lifted her spirits. Maybe they could make it?

Moe leant over for his beer and drank it down. He kissed the top of her head. "I'm going to shower," he said. "I stink."

"You don't stink, you smell lovely," she said. "You smell of the highlands; eucalyptus leaves, prickly cactus, cow dung, dust."

Moe laughed. "You must be the only farenj that thinks cow dung smells good." He untangled himself from her and stood by the sofa in the square of yellow light, holding his empty bottle.

"Maybe we should get out of town, like you said," Izzie said, thinking how tired he looked. "Let's ask Brian and Shirley about Langano, shall we? It would be lovely. Have a swim in the lake, sunbathe."

"Tom said Brian and Sheila have got a windsurfer now," he said. "I can't imagine they use it though!"

"Maybe they got it to entice the likes of us to join them?" she shrugged.

"I daresay."

"You miss sailing, don't you?"

"To be honest, yes, I miss sailing with Dad. We used to talk a lot." His large blue eyes had a vulnerable, pained look. "Let's try and be more relaxed, OK?"

"OK," she said. "I'll try."

"Me too." He turned and disappeared into the darkness.

She sat back with her beer, half hearing the sound of traffic passing below, half listening to Elton John singing, 'Daniel'. Maybe she expected too much. Maybe there could be a comfortable relationship, beyond the first infatuation, if she would just let it happen. But there was something else. There was something distant about Moe. She had felt it since she first arrived but couldn't put a finger on it. She couldn't bear the idea of losing him. She reached for a cigarette and lit it, blinking away the tears smarting in her eyes. Only one left in the pack.

**

The old man, swathed in a thick white gabi, came rushing towards the car. Rushing in the sense of propelling himself forward with urgency rather than speed. "Hello madam," he said. His eyes were set close together above a nose that seemed to have melted into his face, an immediately distinguishing feature.

"How are you, be Egziyabher?" he said and bowed slightly a couple of times.

"I am fine, Egziyabher yimesgen," she said, taking his outstretched hand, like soft gnarled wood, in hers.

"Eney negn, I am the one," the man said, still bowing. "I will be zabanya for your car."

Moe had parked the car under one of the tall ash trees which grew out of the wide pavement near The China Bar. He was locking up.

"Ishi," Izzie said. "Thank you."

Izzie slipped her hand in Moe's. They walked towards the ivy-covered entrance to The China Bar, above which hovered a large red dragon with green wings, eyes glaring.

"How can you be sure you're not going to catch leprosy?" Moe said.

"Because Gezahegn says we won't."

Since Uschi left, Gezahegn had assigned her to work with Simaynesh on an evaluation of two of the largest carpet-knotting workshops in the capital. One of them employed two hundred and fifty leprosy patients. "They are all getting treatment. Can't pass it on any more."

"I hope he's right," Moe said.

"By the way, Gezahegn's ordered a turkey from Tibila Farm for us."

"A full-on turkey dinner for Christmas?" Moe put his arm around her. "Are you up to that?"

"Totally," she said, snuggling into him, smiling. What was it they said about food and a man's heart? "You'll have to help. We'll have it on the terrace, invite our hundred closest friends."

"Including Negisst and family, Mekonnen, Hailu, their mother and twenty nearest cousins, aunts and uncles, our zabanya, and him too, I suppose." Moe nodded and smiled at the waiter who was holding the door open for them.

"That's right," Izzie said, poking him.

"Do we get mince pies?"

"Maybe. Booker said he would see if the Victory Store has got mincemeat next time he goes."

She didn't have a card for the ex-pat store. She was not with an international organisation nor was she a diplomat. They sold English marmalade, Corn Flakes, American peanut butter and imported wines. She and Moe had agreed it was too expensive. They found most things they needed in the vegetable stalls on Piazza and at Solomon's grocery opposite the National Theatre.

A short waiter, his white jacket buttoned up over an unusually round belly, stood on the red carpet amongst the tables. He had his hand outstretched like a traffic cop, indicating their table. It was laid for six and empty. A red lampshade hung above it, colourful trinkets dangling from around the edges.

"How are you this evening?" the waiter said, pulling her chair out for her.

"Very well, Egziyabher yimesgen. Very well. How are you?"

He smiled. "I am fine, Egziyabher yimesgen," he said.

"We'll have a bottle of Gouder to get started," Moe said.

"And some of your lovely spring rolls while we wait for the others," Izzie said. She sat down and laid the starched white napkin across her lap with a little flourish like a matador in front of a bull. "I'm starving." She looked at Moe. "Well I am. Hungry. All I had was a samosa for lunch."

**

Brian chomped when he ate, spoke with his mouth full, and washed his food down with large gulps of red wine. His face was burnt a deep red and his nose carried the tell-tale signs of one too many sundowners. Brian, like Leila, was with the Livestock Research Institute and spent a lot of time outside the capital.

"We were in the Awash valley. Just got back. Bloody hot," he said.

"Hell on earth," Shirley said, her deep blue eyes sparkling over the rim of her wine glass. She had wavy greying-blonde hair and sun-aged skin.

"The Danakil is hell on earth, sweetheart," Brian said. "Not the Awash."

"Ohhh, I am enjoying this. How lovely of you to ask us. Just what I needed," Shirley said, ignoring him. Everyone who knew her said Shirley had 'a heart of gold', always laughing, a scotch in one hand and a cigarette in the other. Izzie loved Shirley's energy, and how she and Brian straddled Ethiopian and ex-pat circles with ease.

"How's the project going, Shirley?" Izzie said.

"Oh it's very exciting. We now have ten groups. I don't know, about eighty girls. And we've started making tomato chutney as well as the jams."

"Absolutely delicious on ambasha bread with a hunk of Sholla cheese," Brian said, smacking his lips.

"The girls?" Tom said, perking up. He snorted into his napkin.

"Heavens above, Tom," Izzie said, meaning it.

Tom shrugged, "What?"

Izzie turned to Shirley, "It's amazing what you've done, really."

"Well, when you think we started off with five girls, making jam in Tsehainesh's kitchen."

"And now there's eighty girls earning an income and not going into prostitution," Brian said. He was clearly proud of Shirley. "Great success."

"Where can we buy it?" Leila said.

Despite the stress over Booker she looked fine. It was good Brian and Shirley had brought her with them.

"Solomon's and the Stadium grocery have agreed to stock it," Shirley said, making a thumbs up. "Tsehainesh and I had to chat them up like mad. But it's a local product and it tastes good."

"ADCD is setting up a project to rehabilitate prostitutes," Izzie said.

"Tell us where," Tom said. He looked suggestively at Moe.

"Don't draw me into this, Tom," Moe said, waving his chopsticks and shaking his head. "You'll get me in trouble, man." Moe looked at Izzie, "Right?"

"Tom, for God's sake pull yourself together," Izzie said. "It's serious. We are talking about young girls who have run away from marriages they didn't choose, often to much older men. They end up in the bars we go to. Even." She knew she was sounding preachy.

"We have to get a woman for Tom," Leila said. "Mais franchement, honestly, this is getting beyond a joke." She did not look pleased.

"I missed you, Leila," Izzie said. "Especially with that one away too." She lifted her chin towards Moe."

Moe was sitting with Leila on one side, Shirley on the other. He was tucking into the food as if he hadn't eaten for a month. "Pass me the rice, Leila," he said, "And the veg, thanks."

"How was it in Debre Berhan?" Brian said. "How's the research going?"

"Very good, thanks," Leila said. "We are still doing the household interviews." She had been at the LRI research station, about two hundred and fifty kilometres north of Addis for the past ten days. Izzie wanted to go with Leila to see the place but they had not yet managed to find the time, or to get the travel permit.

"How's things otherwise, Leila?" Moe said.

Izzie noticed his fond look and felt a slight pang. He shared her admiration for Leila. She was lively, confident and very attractive. Most people knew Booker wasn't always faithful when Leila was in Debre Berhan. It was a mystery to everyone.

"You mean how is my Booker-life?" Leila sipped her wine and smiled. "I haven't seen Booker for a while, to be honest."

"Those Afar are incredible, you know," Brian said, turning to Izzie. As soon as it turned to affairs of the heart Brian lost interest. He loved nothing better than to talk about the Afar and the Borana. "Jolly resilient. But they're starting to feel it. Not enough grazing for their livestock. The camels and goats can manage – they nibble away at anything – but it's the cattle. Getting mighty thin." He sucked his teeth.

"I thought they have a huge area to roam over," Izzie said. "Doesn't it stretch from the Awash all the way up into the Danakil desert?"

Izzie heard Shirley's husky voice, "Booker doesn't deserve you, sweetheart." Part of her wanted to join their conversation, but she tried to concentrate on Brian, not wanting to offend him.

"That's right, darling, they do," Brian said, parking a small lump of food in his cheek like a hamster while he talked. "But there's not enough grazing. That's the problem. The Derg is trying to settle them. Fat lot of good that will do."

"He's crazy," she heard Tom saying. He had his arm around Leila. "I would go to the ends of the earth for you."

Leila laughed. "Don't worry about me, I am fine. It's my decision."

"You can't settle pastoralists unless they want to settle," Brian was saying.

"That's right," Leila said. "They inhabit a world beyond political slogans."

"We saw a small group of them near the hot springs when we went to the Awash National Park, didn't we Moe?" Izzie said. "They're stunning. So upright and proud, both the men and the women. So distinctive. And that incredible hair."

"That's something quite particular to Ethiopia, hairstyles," Shirley said. "You can pretty much tell which part of the country people come from, from the hairstyle."

"Punks and skinheads differentiate themselves by their hair, or lack of it, Shirley," Tom said, laughing.

"True," Shirley said. She plucked a ball of sweet and sour chicken from the bowl with her chopsticks. "Anyway, the Afar are terrifying, if you ask me. You have to keep a respectful distance, like with the Masai in Tanzania."

Brian took another large mouthful of wine and turned to Izzie. "Did I tell you about the Borana, Izzie?"

"That's somewhere else I'd like to go," Izzie said. "You told us about the very deep, ancient wells and how the cattle drink massive amounts of water to last several days."

"Up to sixty litres," Brian said. "You'll have to come and visit with us next time we are in Yabello."

"Brian loves it there," Shirley said. "It's very simple accommodation under the acacia trees. There's a bucket shower." She rolled her eyes to the ceiling. "And Werkenesh cooks the most amazing food."

"Beautiful birds, peace and quiet," Brian said. "You have to admit, you love it too, Shirley darling."

"It's so frustrating having to get travel permits," Moe said. "But we should make an effort, Izzie. Plan a trip."

"In Haile Selassie's time you could go anywhere," Shirley said. "We used to take the train to Dire Dawa and stay a few days before going on to Harar. I love Harar. It's a charming, walled city with narrow pathways between the houses, gorgeous jewellery. The women wear an immense amount of gold at weddings. Quite extraordinary."

"The women are beautiful," Brian said, looking at Tom and Moe. "You must go."

"You always say that, Brian," Izzie said. "What about the men? Is there anything to entice Leila and me to go there?" She winked at Leila.

Shirley rested her hand on Moe's arm, "You need go no further, Izzie. This one's totally irresistible, sweetheart. Lucky for you I'm not twenty-five years younger."

"I don't know Shirley, you're looking pretty good," Izzie said. "I do keep an eye on you, you know."

"Wise woman," Shirley said, helping herself to the dish of vegetables, bright reds and greens.

"I hasten to add. I've got the prettiest of them all," Brian grinned, raised his glass towards Shirley and took another healthy gulp of the red wine.

"Darling," she said.

"How do you say 'lovers' in Amharic?" Leila said. "Are you two still going to classes? I might start up again."

"I'm not, she is," Moe said, nodding his head in Izzie's direction.

"Fikreunya," Izzie said. "Lovers. It's a pity you two have stopped coming. Come when you can Leila. It would be lovely."

"There's so much on at work, honey," Moe said. "I know excuses, excuses. But we've got rehearsals for As You Like It coming up as well."

"I'll have to dig deep into the cupboards for costumes for that one," Shirley said. "Silk shirts and velvet gowns – lovely, can't wait."

"I don't know why you've taken such a big part, Moe," Izzie said, sounding more petulant than she meant to. To distract herself, she topped up her bowl of rice with sweet and sour chicken and popped a round ball of it into her mouth with a chunk of pineapple. It did not disappoint.

"Calm down, sweetheart. We need him. He's good," Tom said. "After you with the beef, Moe, looks like we could order some more?"

"Never really works, Tom, telling a woman to calm down," Izzie said.

"You're playing Orlando, aren't you?" Shirley said. "Who's your Rosalind?"

"Undecided," Moe said, passing the bowl to Tom.

"Why don't you play it, Izzie?" Leila smiled, putting her head to one side like a bird.

"Good idea, Leila. Good idea," Izzie said, taking a sip of wine. Leila loved teasing. "So who will go bopping on the Debre Zeit road with you, when I'm learning my lines, huh Leila?"

"Kidding," Leila said. She turned to Brian. "Of course you're in it, aren't you? Is this the play with the crazy donkey-man in it? Good part for a livestock expert."

"That's A Midsummer Night's Dream, darling," Brian said. "I'll probably be one of the old uncles. Seems to be my speciality."

"Deborah is incredible," Shirley said. "She has put on a performance of Shakespeare in every posting."

"I think she wants to make this an open air one," Brian said, "In the Embassy grounds."

"She'll need a forest," Moe said. "She's quite strict, isn't she. I mean, on the verge of intimidating. I guess, being the Ambassador's wife -"

"She's got a soft centre when you get to know her," Shirley said. "A sweet person, I think. And she buys my jams."

"I thought someone said she would put it on in that patch of ground, amongst the rhododendrons, near the Club?" Izzie said.

"Whatever she does, you'll see, it will be amazing," Shirley said.

**

She had gone with Moe to the British Embassy for the auditions, mostly because she was curious to see inside The Residence. They had driven past the thatched Club House, where they sometimes went for a barbecue on a Sunday, up a narrow road lined with tall eucalyptus, towards an imposing colonial style villa overlooking a golf course. Expansive whitewashed steps, a potted plant on each end, spilled down to the drive from under a wide canopy held up by large white pillars and covered in wisteria. At the top of the steps, an old zabanya in uniform indicated for them to pass through the polished cedar-wood doors. Izzie had felt like a child sneaking into the Forbidden Palace. They passed an office with a telex machine and a photograph of Prince Charles on the wall next to one of the Queen and Prince Philip.

The drawing room was all creams and pale greens. Punch and Judy stage curtains hung in cream-coloured and burgundy stripes with tassels, from ceiling to floor; polished coffee tables; plush floor rugs. Not a single Ethiopian hand-knotted carpet in sight. Everyone had a drink in hand. Auditions had already started. They were late.

The Ambassador's wife, Deborah, small and neat, her greying hair in a bun, a touch of pink on her lips, had given them the barest of nods and rung a silver bell.

Izzie, feeling like a small girl on her first day back at school, had pulled on Moe's shirt-sleeve. "Don't leave me alone," she whispered at his back. She half-wished she had stayed at home. They sat on the remaining armchair, she in it, he perched on the arm. She noticed the two shiny black hookahs, inset with mother of pearl, on the mantelpiece. Exquisite.

A door on one side of the fireplace opened, ushering in an elegant Ethiopian. He was dressed in a glistening white tunic over starched trousers, large gold buttons up the front and cuff-links to match. A broad pillar-box-red sash, wound round his slim waist, seemed to hold him and his uniform together. He entered quietly, proud, balancing a silver tray on his hand, and took their orders for drinks.

She had whispered, "Gin and tonic, please," wondering how he felt in this room full of ex-pats. It was his job. A good job, presumably.

Once he'd left, Izzie heard a quiet voice somewhere in the room say, "He's a dear, but there's only bone between the ears, I fear." The words shattered Izzie, like glass breaking inside her. She had wanted to walk out but could not move.

**

"The British Embassy compound is massive," she heard Leila saying. "You've got stables and a golf course. You must have a forest in there somewhere." Leila took a sip of wine. "Why did you guys get such a lot of land anyway?"

"We fought Theodros, made friends with Menelik and got ninety acres of untouched Ethiopian hillside," Brian said. "The true beginnings of our diplomatic ties with Ethiopia go back to 1896, same year as the battle of Adowa, when Menelik slaughtered the Italians." As he spoke, some rice flew from his mouth onto the white tablecloth.

"Theodros was a maniac. Totally irrational and violent," Moe said. "Maybe caused by VD? He had several mistresses."

Moe sometimes surprised Izzie with his odd bits of knowledge.

He was pouring wine into everyone's glasses and caught her eye for a moment. His had lost that pained look and were shining again.

She smiled back. She too felt better, now they'd met with friends. She even felt closer to him in a funny way.

"Shall we get another bottle?" Shirley said, holding up a hand for the waiter, her bracelets chinking. She reminded Izzie of Uschi.

"And some more of the beef," Tom said.

"Langano," Moe said. "That's what we wanted to ask you."

"We're going straight after Christmas," Shirley said. "Oh do come. It's so boring just the two of us. We want to have barbecues on the beach, read, relax."

"Drink beer with my feet in the water," Brian said.

"You know, Shirley," Izzie said, horrified to feel tears welling in her eyes. "We really could do with a break. It would be amazing."

"For God's sake come, sweetheart," Shirley said.

"You alright, Izzie?" Leila said, almost getting up.

"I'm fine. Really. Just a bit tired," Izzie said. She dabbed her eyes with the stiff white napkin. She felt Brian's solid hand around her shoulder.

"Come with us to the cottage. Bring a tent. It will do us all a world of good, darling," he said. "You come too Leila. And you Tom. You can bring Meheret with you if you like." He laughed with a chortle, like water going down the plug.

Izzie couldn't help smiling. Who was Meheret? Brian was a funny fellow.

"Honey?"

"I'm fine now," Izzie said. "Anyone got a cigarette? I've run out."

18

Every lamppost, every building, fluttered with national flags. Solid bright green, yellow and red stripes the length of Piazza. They had appeared almost overnight, to demonstrate just how important the second Congress of COPWE[56] was to the nation. It was taking place just before Ethiopian Christmas. It was clearly possible to organise anything, if it was a priority. Izzie wondered whether the flags reached into the countryside. Whether they were tied to stubby acacia trees on the slopes of the Bale mountains, or perhaps to a long stick in the ground by the hot springs in the Awash valley, where the Afar bathed.

She was heading for the fruit and vegetable stalls, some twenty yards from the bridge, at the end of Piazza. Each had the uniform blue plastic awning, held up by wooden poles, giving shade to their fruits and vegetables. Just beyond the fruit stalls an almost stagnant stream moved slowly under a bridge in dark green swirls, its banks strewn with rubbish and overgrown with unhealthy looking greenery. It was a murky place and had the stale smell of things disintegrating. She couldn't help but imagine bodies.

To her the bridge represented a boundary between familiarity and the unknown. Piazza, with its familiar shops and cafés, street children and beggars she knew on this side, and the long road which passed Police Station Number Two and ended up at the Arat Kilo roundabout and the University gates, on the other. There, once again, familiar cafés bustled with life; students filling seats and tables, chattering like flocks of starling over glasses of hot sweet tea and coffee. The number of students, young and old, heading for night school every evening, never ceased to amaze. Education gave a glimmer of hope, a faint vision of better paid jobs, of a different future.

---

[56] Commission to Organise the Party of the Workers of Ethiopia.

She could never digest the fact that just a few short years back, the University, and the campus up the hill at Amist Kilo, had been the central stage for the makings of a dark history. So many students detained and killed. Night-time raids, loud banging, doors kicked in by young adrenalin-charged armed soldiers. There were prisons and detention centres all over town. Just six years ago. Streams and roadsides became open burial grounds. No one was allowed to collect the bodies. Students, fathers, mothers, even children, lay brutalised, exposing the example the Derg was intent on making of them. The thought appalled and confused her. Such a contrast to the wonderful posters advertising 'Thirteen Months of Sunshine', and the warm smiles, greetings, laughter and friendship she found around her. The prisons were still full of so-called counter-revolutionaries, political prisoners. Everyone had to tread with care, watch what they said and who was listening.

It was still early. Fresh produce was already on display: knobbly tomatoes, red peppers, sucked in like a toothless old man's face, a papaya sliced open on top of the pile, to show off the orange-pink flesh and shiny black pips, bunches of bananas hung from hooks.

"Tenasteling," she said, seeing the vendor inside. "How are you?"

"I am fine, Egziyabher yimesgen," he said, bending slightly as he emerged from the dark interior into the sun. "How are you?" He wore a green three-quarter length coat over his clothes and was rubbing his hands together, a grin on his face. He stood next to her, looking understandably satisfied with his display.

"I am well, Egziyabher yimesgen," she said. "Are you ready for Ethiopian Christmas?"

"We are all still fasting. My wife spends day and night in Mariam, singing and praying." He nodded his head towards the church up the road beyond the bridge.

Izzie nodded. Of course. They had had their farenj Christmas. Food and more food on the terrace. At least ten visitors to eat Gezahegn's turkey from Tibila Farm. A party with the Piazza boys in the evening. She had not gone to church, unlike Negisst, the fruit and veg vendor's wife, and many others. They were all fasting, filling churches around the city, praying all night, sending humming-song into the dark of curfew and star studded skies. Izzie sometimes felt like joining them. Theirs, she knew, was a deep strong belief but it also felt like a political statement against the Derg, its military dictatorship, and their Soviet friends.

She and Moe were going to Langano to join Shirley and Brian in their lakeside cottage for a few days over Ethiopian Christmas. She was bringing the fruits and veg, Brian had said they would bring meat and crates of cold beer for the barbecue, and of course there would be fresh fish.

"What do you want to buy today? Papaya? Cabbage?" He dipped his hand in a tin can and sprinkled water over a pile of green leaves.

"The papaya is good," she said. "I buy two and one large cauliflower." She practiced her Amharic on him, to his amusement, and could nearly name all the fruits and vegetables.

She sniffed the bottom of a pineapple, her mouth watered. "This one, please," she said, giving it to him.

"Potatoes?" he said.

She had to carry it all home again. "Two kilos, small ones, and two kilos tomatoes," she said, and went to stand in the sun as he weighed them on his old-fashioned scales. A sack of avocados leant against the doorway. Moe had said he would make a dip. "Five avocados, please," she said.

"To eat today or tomorrow?"

"Tomorrow, the day after," she said, "and the tomatoes, not too ripe."

A small boy appeared, a miniature version of his father. The left clasp was missing on his worn out dungarees, leaving one side of the bib hanging.

Izzie smiled, looking at the two together. "Tenasteling," she said. "How are you?"

"I am fine," the boy said, shaking her hand.

"Solomon wants to be a taxi driver, isn't it?" The vendor laughed and ruffled his boy's hair. "I tell him he will work in the shop when my wife and I are old."

"How many children you have?"

"Seven," he said, "and Solomon is the last."

Izzie wondered how the man and his wife could feed, clothe and school seven children from this one small business.

A loud voice suddenly broke the peace. A white pick-up moved slowly down the road, a tannoy fixed to its roof. The man next to the driver was shouting into a microphone. Some women pulled their white shema over their heads and carried on walking. Three boys stood on the edge of the pavement, watching.

There would be a massive rally in Revolution Square at the weekend. Mulu had told her how the Soviets wanted Mengistu to get on with establishing the communist party in Ethiopia. COPWE, the Commission to Organise the Party of the Workers of Ethiopia was the path to achieving that. It had procrastination written in its title. Not even the Soviets could tell Ethiopians what to do.

"What are they saying?" Izzie asked. The Kebele pick-up trucks unnerved her. Their barking tone a reminder of the totalitarian state, the military regime.

"They are calling us to the meeting on Saturday," the vendor said, muttering something she did not understand.

"Do you have to go?"

"The Kebele cut our rations if we are not there," the vendor from the next stall said. He stood on the pavement, watching the pick-up disappear up the road, hands on his hips as if he were seeing a rogue off his premises. He turned and stretched out a hand towards his goods, bowing a little, like an actor on stage. "Look at my vegetables. You have to buy from me too."

How adept Ethiopians are. Too often they smiled outwardly while growling in the depths of their belly. "I'll buy your oranges," she said. "How much one kilo?"

"How many kilos oranges?" small Solomon piped up at her elbow, his large eyes alert.

His father laughed as he put the avocados into her basket. "Good boy," he said.

"See, Wozeiro Izzie, you are our dembenya[57] today."

She liked the way they called her 'dembenya'. It had an endearing quality, like London bus conductors saying, 'love'. 'That'll be two-and-six, love'.

"Can you count out twelve?" Izzie said.

The boy nodded.

"Give me twelve oranges then," she said.

After Izzie had paid, the vendor threw two small papaya into her basket. "Goursha," he said. An extra mouthful for free.

"You come to me next time, ishi?" the vendor next door called out as she left. "I will be hungry after Christmas."

"Ishi," she said, smiling. "Next time."

The two vendors laughed.

She walked home enjoying the warmth of the sun, the movement of people around her. There was enough space to walk freely, not too crowded and not too empty to feel alone. She thought of her mother, 'People with their eyes on the pavement miss the best things in life, like

---

[57] Regular (cherished) customer.

baskets of geraniums in window-boxes, turrets and gargoyles,' she always said. Izzie looked up at the old Italian buildings along Piazza, with their first floor balconies and wooden rafters. They looked like a stage set for Romeo and Juliet, a curious contrast to the newer buildings with their plain glass windows and flat concrete walls. She wished her parents could see it, see her in it.

She looked in the shop window selling electrical goods. A man stood in the entrance, smoking a cigarette.

"Come inside, farenj," he said. "Fridges made in the GDR. Good quality. Hairdryers, kettles, hot plates from the Soviet Union."

She wondered briefly about getting a kettle. "No thanks," she said and carried on before he tried to convince her. It would be too expensive.

As she came nearer her building, she wondered where Hailu's little gang was. They usually appeared out of the blue to relieve her of her bags, talking and joking. They would get a few centimes for lugging her groceries up the four flights.

Then she spotted them. They were sitting on the pavement, feet in the road, heads together. The road was like their sitting room. Cars passed by. Taxis stopped to offload passengers and suck more in. Mekonnen had his head in his hands; Hailu his arm around his brother's shoulders. As she got nearer, she could hear Mekonnen crying. Hailu was saying something to the small crowd which had gathered. When something happened, people stopped and asked questions, or stood nearby, watching. There were always witnesses, an audience.

"What's happened?" Izzie said.

"Fighting," the woman with the blue cross on her forehead said. A small girl was holding her hand, barefoot, a slug-like blob of snot hung between her nose and upper lip.

"Where is Abebech?"

"Their mother is marketing," the woman said.

There was blood on Mekonnen's t-shirt. He held his face in his hands.

"Take them to your house," she went on.

"Me? Is it good?"

"They have no water or light at home," the woman said.

"Hailu," Izzie said, touching the boy's shoulder. "You come my house?"

Hailu whispered something in Mekonnen's ear. The two boys looked at each other and got up, Mekonnen holding one hand firmly over his right eye.

Izzie suddenly realised how vulnerable they were. "Negisst is at home," she said, offering herself and the boys reassurance. Negisst would know what to do.

The zabanya, who often barred the boys' entry to the building, needed no persuading this time. He nodded and let them pass. Izzie was touched.

**

Izzie put her shopping down and unlocked the door, arms aching. She stood for a moment to catch her breath. Mekonnen was whining on the half landing, Hailu whispering. She looked over the banister. "Come on, Hailu, get him up here," she said, anxious to see how bad the wound was, imagining dark red drops of blood on the white marble steps. "Negisst," she called, going into the kitchen with her baskets. Sharp pineapple leaves stuck out of the top of one. She should have bought two.

"Madam?" Negisst appeared, wiping her hands on her apron.

"It's Mekonnen, he's hurt."

Mekonnen's wails and whimpering, sounds of a trapped animal, echoed against the walls in the corridor. Hailu put his head round the kitchen door.

"Have we got ice?" Izzie said, picking up a clean tea towel. She took Mekonnen by the shoulders and steered him gently into the bathroom.

She pointed to the toilet seat, "Sit, yeney konjo."

His hand was still clasped over his right eye, his fingers stained with blood, his little fingernails lined with dirt. His other eye looked around, a mixture of pain and fear, his breathing shaky from the crying.

"Aysoh, Mekonnen," Izzie said, trying to soothe him. "Sit down. Aysoh, take it easy." She held the cloth under the cold tap and wrung it out, seeing herself in the mirror as she looked up. Her eyes were her Dad's deep green-blue. She cut her hair shaggy to her shoulders. Her face looked tanned against Moe's white t-shirt. "Washing is good," she said, turning to him.

Mekonnen was still standing, his good eye looking from the cloth to her face, as if assessing the risk.

Hailu sat half perched on the edge of the bath tub. He could never stay still for long, a bird ready to fly.

Negisst came in with her warmth and reassurance. She spoke to the boys. It sounded half kind, half telling off.

Izzie could hear a lot of, "Egziyabher". What would Negisst do without her Egziyabher?

Under Negisst's instruction, Mekonnen sat down on the closed toilet lid and slowly moved his hand away from his face.

"Oh God," Izzie said, exchanging looks with Negisst.

His eye was the size of a small egg.

Negisst sucked her teeth. "Egziyabher yibarkih," she said.

"I'll hold the ice on it?" Izzie said.

"Ishi, very good."

Reassured, Izzie squatted beside the boy, tipped some of the crushed ice into the cloth and held it gently against his eye.

Mekonnen winced.

Izzie expected him to start wailing again, but he didn't. He sat still.

Hailu was talking to Negisst, explaining with his hands, his face surprised then indignant. He flung something invisible, jumping in the air.

Negisst listened, sucking her teeth and shaking her head. "Whey guud,[58]" she said.

"What's he saying, Negisst?"

"One thing is, it is not good they go to Georgis. Their area is Piazza," Negisst said. "But all boys want money now. It is Gena."

"We want to buy chicken for Abebech," Hailu said. "We want her to cook doro wot[59] for Christi-mas."

Izzie thought of all the food they had bought and consumed for their Christmas. How many sweets and cigarettes would the boys have to sell to buy one chicken? "But what happened to Mekonnen's eye?"

"They were selling cigarettes in Georgis," Negisst said, pointing at the two boys. "Not good. Big boys they come."

"Hailu, he call them duriyey," Mekonnen said under his breath, nodding at Hailu and frowning. He sucked air in between his clenched teeth and winced, "Wey."

"Duriyey?" Izzie said.

"Dirty beggars," Negisst said, a smile escaping. She covered her mouth. "Very bad word. Very bad. The big boys throw stones."

"Me very fast running," Hailu said, moving his arms like a sprinter, his head tilted up and back. "Like Wodajo Bulti." He giggled, covering his mouth and shrugging his shoulders up to his ears. He looked around awkwardly. He must have felt bad about leaving his brother behind.

"Wodajo Bulti?" Izzie said.

---

[58] An expression like 'My goodness'.
[59] Chicken cooked in hot spicey sauce with hard boiled eggs. A dish prepared for special occasions.

"He winning big farenj races. Very fast Ethiopian runner," Hailu said, nodding enthusiastically.

Izzie took the ice-cloth away. "Let me see." The swelling came from the upper lid. The eye itself did not look damaged. She held the ice against it again, her hand on the boy's shoulder. He was even skinnier than she thought.

"Boys, you eat breakfast today?" she said.

Hailu shook his head.

"Negisst, can you make them some eggs and bread?"

"Ishi, very good," Negisst said and left the room.

"Boys, you like pineapple?"

Mekonnen's good eye smiled a little.

"If his eye no good after the weekend, after Christmas, we go doctor," Izzie said. She had found some gauze and was making an eye patch.

"Where?" Hailu asked.

"The big hospital opposite the Posta Bate. The Black Lion?"

"People go hospital, they die." Hailu clutched his throat, rolled his eyes to the back of his head and flopped it to one side, his tongue hanging out.

"Hailu," she said, putting a hand on his shoulder and laughing. "People die if they go to the hospital when it's too late. Understand? When they come too late. Now you two go and eat. On Monday we'll see how Mekonnen is." She went to find Negisst in the kitchen. "Can you cut some pineapple for them too?"

"You are a good neighbour," Negisst said.

"And I am glad I have you, Negisst," Izzie said.

"Tonight I will be in church, praying. Until dawn. It's the night our Lord was born."

"Pray for us too, Negisst, will you?" Izzie put a hand on the woman's arm, "And take care."

"I pray for you every time, Izzie yeney konjo," Negisst said.

**

They had decided to have a night out before leaving for Langano in the morning. Moe was driving. They passed through the shanty town on either side of the Debre Zeit road, a jumble of shacks crouching behind corrugated iron fencing and bush, squat office buildings, dusty trees and stray dogs. Evening pedestrians emerged from stony dirt pathways, a thick white gabi thrown over their head and shoulders, to walk along the roadside. Suks, some with colourful fairy lights strung up for Christmas, displayed their fruits and vegetables tumbling onto the sidewalk. Crates of coca cola, Fanta, sprite and beer stacked by the entrance.

Peering out of the window for signs, Izzie had a sinking feeling she had missed it. "I'm sure it was on the left of the road, wasn't it?" she said.

"It's always further down than we think," Moe said.

They passed one bar after the next, their doors open and shutters drawn back, squares of orange light, shadows of customers gathering at the counter for a drink.

Further along, butchers' kiosks stood like upright open coffins in a row, white-washed and lit by single bare bulbs. Deep red, bony carcasses hung from large meat hooks inside. The butchers, in white coats, sliced raw meat to serve to waiting customers with a pinch of hot spicey berberri powder.

On her trips to Nazareth, Izzie always sat in the car while the team stopped for breakfast at Dukam, a small town outside Addis Ababa. Dukam was famous for its butchers. "Genet and the others enjoy having a go at me for not eating kitfo,[60]" she said. "It's almost as if eating it, is like passing a test."

"It's not that bad." Moe ran a hand through his hair and peered through the window. "Where is this place?"

"You shouldn't eat it, Moe. You'll get tape worms."

"It's no different from steak tartare," Moe said.

"I don't eat steak tartare either," she said.

"You know how long a tapeworm can grow?"

"I don't know, five feet?"

"Thirty feet, more."

"What? You are kidding."

"One of the admin guys in the office had one."

"Don't say another word. How they got it out, all that. I don't want to know." Izzie pointed, with a mixture of relief and excitement. "There it is." A single bulb hung in front of the open doors, lighting up the letters KOKEB BAR. Sheets of corrugated iron roofing extended over the wide veranda at the entrance of the former bungalow.

Moe slowed down, drove over the uneven verge and down into the dirt and stone drive in front of the bar. He switched off the engine. "Well spotted, honey," he said and kissed her.

Izzie smiled and shook her head. "You're in good spirits tonight."

---

[60] Slices of raw beef.

"It's Ethiopian Christmas eve. We're on holiday. Come on, let's go. I hope it's the same band as last time."

She climbed out of the car, checking her pocket for cigarettes. "Sounds like it, listen." She could already feel the music throbbing in her belly.

Moe stood waiting, hands in pockets, bouncing on his heels.

She pulled one of his hands out of his pocket and looped his arm round her shoulders; slipping under, she put her arm round his waist. "Remember dancing in Lilongwe Old Town?"

"Kwassa, kwassa," he said, drawing her in close. "The record players were so scratchy. You can't beat live music."

A couple sat on the steps to the entrance, talking intimately, each with a beer in hand. Izzie wondered if the man was the girl's boyfriend or a punter, negotiating a price. The girl laughed, throwing her head back. The two stood up, the man holding her close. It looked almost too close for her liking.

"Kwassa, kwassa. It is amazing music," Izzie said, looking up into the endless wide sky, ablaze with stars. "I'd love to hear it live."

"Miss Boogie-all-night," Moe kissed the top of her head.

"There was no curfew in Lilongwe."

Coloured lights flashed intermittently, lighting up dancing silhouettes, like black cardboard cut-outs. Two men came out and disappeared down the side of the building; another returned, fingers still on his zip. The faded pale blue walls around the door were pock-marked with incident; odd-shaped patches of grime, chips and holes exposed dirty white plaster underneath. Inside, it rocked.

Izzie, moving to the warm pulsing rhythm, drum beat and bass guitar. She followed Moe into the wave of sound, into the midst of the dancing, bumping against bodies, the air thick with the smell of spice-infused sweat, alcohol and cigarette smoke. The dark corners of the room occasionally lit up with the gaudy red, white and green disco light twirling from an overhead beam. Each time she glanced up, Izzie caught smiles from men dancing nearby; a raised eyebrow saying, 'come on'; eyes hinting, 'I like it.' She wrapped her arms around Moe from behind and breathed in his familiar warmth.

Izzie imagined Negisst, Simaynesh, and Mulu from Moe's office, swathed in white cotton gabis, humming prayers in one of the many churches and cathedrals in the city, Selassie Bate-ey-Christian, Mariam, Georgis; the chanting priests chinking silver rattles and wafting incense in the air around them. And there she was, in a run-down bar on the Debre Zeit road, dancing herself into a sweat, giddy with the extremes this city threw at her: the Communist banners and flags, the ever present Egziyabher, the praying, the begging, the humming, the thudding drums and the draining struggle with Moe, their bewildering love affair on and off like the smile of a clown. Happy, sad. Happy, sad. Blinking lights. On, off. On, off. There was no air in the place, just live, moving rhythm and Moe's body against hers.

The band, four guys with thick afros, in jeans and traditional white cotton smocks, played a fusion of Eskista and funk. One played the saxophone, lifting it and the whole place to the tin roof rafters.

"They're brilliant," she mouthed when the piece came to an end.

Moe pulled her closer, soothing her back with his hand. "And there's nothing I love more than dancing with you," he whispered in her ear.

Dancing, getting out into the country, that's what they should do more often. It always brought them closer. But they were wrapped up in their work, came home tired. The small victories and enormous frustrations were taking their toll. It was taking time to grasp the reality. They were less able to influence as much as they had perhaps hoped. She looked up at him and saw him smiling at her.

He motioned his head towards the bar. "Look, Tom's already here."

"Beer?" Tom mouthed and pointed to his raised bottle.

"I could do with a drink, what about you, honey?"

"Me too."

Moe had already taken her hand. They moved, pushing a path gently through the dancers. Young men in jeans, some wearing dark glasses, handsome and cool, a cigarette hanging on a lip. Shabbier specimens in thin woollen jackets, older with blood-shot eyes and thick alcohol breath. Plump women, a t-shirt stretched across large breasts, a bit of bra showing, skinny ones on platform heels, tight tops and jeans, black kohl highlighting their oval eyes, and dark red lipstick their lips. Cheap jewellery swung from their ears and chinked round their wrists. Izzie was never sure if they were on the game or not. The bar-girls who worked in this place certainly were, and divided their time between serving drinks and going round the back with one of the customers. The dark rings under their eyes told their story, their faces alternately bright and sullen.

The way some of the men gestured at women, any woman, including her, with their bragging and self-assured sense of ownership, was irritating. Doubtless, their wives and girlfriends were at home, chopping onions, garlic and tomatoes for the doro wot they would eat the next day. None of these guys would marry a girl who worked in the bars.

Prostitution was one of the few alternatives for women with little or no education in a city with hardly any jobs. And men needed women for entertainment, to forget. There was a lot to forget. They did not see the women as allies, co-conspirators. They believed them to be inferior for what they did. They satisfied themselves, played and danced for a while, then left, often treating their source of relief with disdain. Having said that, there was a lively atmosphere in the bar. A lot of smiling, innuendo, teasing and laughter. Beer, whiskey and the music helping to forget.

Simaynesh said prostitutes were among the poorest in the city. They brought their children up alone. It was not possible to buy contraceptives, there was no family planning, and men preferred it without anyway. It made Simaynesh furious. The revolutionary government had to do something about it, she said. After all, prostitution was illegal in the Soviet Union, wasn't it?

Izzie looked up at Moe, his face and eyes were bright, his arm around her. She felt like she had got him back again, even if just for this moment. Sometimes he made her mad, when he couldn't take his eyes off another woman. 'Hey!' She would nudge him, trying to make it funny. 'Over here buddy.' There was something charming and unattainable about him and women seemed to like that. He had told her he was not thinking about the future. She was trying to work that out, what that meant for her.

Tom stood with one arm on the bar, holding his beer, the other round the shoulders of a slim girl, a hand dangling above the barely visible swelling of her breast. His shirt sleeves were rolled up, exposing brown arms covered in fine, sun-bleached hair. He had the confidence of a few drinks. "Meet," Tom turned to the girl, "What was your name again?"

Izzie looked at his thick fair hair and the cut of his face. He was not as tall and solid as Moe but to anyone who thought all farenj looked the same, the two could be brothers.

It was packed. People around them struggled and shoved to get closer to the bar, waving a Birr note and calling out, 'Hullet Bira!'. Two beers! 'Whiskey! Whiskey!'

"Let's move away from here," Moe said, taking his beer and passing one to Izzie.

Tom's girl smiled, her teeth biting the rim of her coke bottle. She wore a cheap nickel ring on her pointing finger and her nails, bitten to the quick, had nearly worn off dabs of red polish on them.

"My name Mariam," she said, with some effort.

She wore a low cut, pale blue chiffon top and a metal cross on a black thread round her neck. She was pretty.

"Mariam," Tom laughed, keeping his arm around her, as they moved away from the crowded bar.

Izzie headed for the space by the window, trying to shut out the critical voice in her head. She wanted to enjoy the night with Moe, not get in a row with Tom. Seeing farenj men with these girls bothered her. As far as these bar girls were concerned, all farenj were rich. They symbolised opportunity. Escape. She wished Tom would cut it out. It felt like a tabby cat playing with a tiny fieldmouse. It was not an even playing field.

The window, lined with metal bars, was open. It looked out onto the car park. A couple were leaning against the 2CV, talking. People up on the road walked past under the night sky, carrying bundles she imagined contained a live chicken, eggs, onions, peppers and tomatoes. The other side of the road was lined with bars, lit pink, pale blue and red; and a bakery next to a tiny suk like Girma's hole-in-the-wall. A small group of people hovered around the shop, dark shadows, like moths round a bulb. Life, Izzie thought, slipping her arm around Moe.

"I'm with Mariam on Christmas eve," Tom said. "Well I'm darned."

"Tenasteling, Mariam," Izzie said, putting a hand out. "My name is Izzie."

"Wey. You speak Amharic?" the girl said, kissing Izzie on both cheeks.

"Yes, a little." The girl was sweet, she thought. Very young.

Tom gave Izzie one of his, 'Don't spoil my fun,' looks.

Izzie raised her eyebrows at him as if to say, Who, me?

"Hi Mariam," Moe said, shaking her hand.

Izzie lit a cigarette for Moe and another for herself. She offered one to the girl.

"Hey," Moe said looking over her shoulder, blowing a stream of smoke towards
the ceiling.

She looked round to see Tom's flatmate, emerging from the dance floor. He was a short, middle-aged American with jet black hair and doey-brown eyes. He was there working on a road-building project. He'd left his family behind in Louisiana. He missed them and often got drunk.

"Hi there, Matt," she said, a part of her feeling sorry for him, but then there was always the other side.

Matt had a look of pure delight on his face. A pretty young girl, her arm hooked through his, was whispering in his ear. He shrugged his shoulders. "Don't understand a dang thing she's sayin', but whatever it is, she's blowin' ma mind away."

The band was good.

"Shame Leila couldn't come. She loves this music," Izzie said, raising her voice as the band got into the next set. "Hey, Let's dance, Mr Moe?" she gave him a little tug.

"I'll come in a minute, honey," he said, squeezing her hand. "Just want to finish this beer."

"Promise? I might get eaten alive in there." Izzie looked at the girls and motioned towards the dancing. "Let's go." she said.

"Ishi." Mariam took the younger girl's hand and pulled her along.

The girl looked apologetically at Matt and followed Mariam.

They were quickly surrounded by men, like the tide around a sandbank.

"Hey, farenj," they said, sucking their teeth and showing off their dance moves. "Dance with me." A short man wearing a trilby hat raised his arms above his head and gyrated his hips at her.

The girls laughed. He was good.

"We're together," Mariam said. "Leave us in peace."

"We're sisters," Izzie said, pulling the girls in around her.

"But you are beautiful." He looked at Izzie.

She knew the routine; her eyes, her hair...

"I love you."

"You don't know me."

He moved closer. She could smell the alcohol on his breath, the nicotine and days of sweat in his shirt.

"My boyfriend is over there." Izzie pointed towards the corner where Moe stood drinking and laughing with Tom and Matt. She felt a twinge of guilt for invoking the 'my boyfriend' line, instead of standing up for herself. It was a cop out. She turned to the girls and they moved in, dancing closer together.

The man grinned, tipped his hat and carried on gyrating, puckering his lips and sucking his teeth.

Izzie laughed.

Tom joined them, clasping a bottle of beer and dancing with short jerks and hops.

"You laughing at me, Izzie, darling?" Tom shouted over the music. He staggered into other dancers, who elbowed him back in place.

"No, Tom, you're a real mover." Izzie gave him an encouraging pat, like she would a good dog. "What about the others?"

"They've started on the whiskey."

Behind the girls she saw Moe making his way towards her. He circled behind and around her, softly bumping her hip, her thigh. When the set came to an end they were both dripping. She wiped her face.

"You're working up a good sweat there," he said, his eyes looking her over.

She took his hand. "Don't you disappear for the next one."

The sax player started up, raising anticipation, expectation, holding a long note before the band came in, full on with the drums beating. A warm night under Ethiopian stars, Moe with her, Eskista funk throbbing through her belly, through her bones. Bliss.

**

"The Oppressed Masses will be Victorious," Izzie shouted into the black starlit sky, her arms open wide. The night air was fresh, welcome after the closeness and heat of the bar, like a cool shower after a sauna.

"What's that?"

Izzie heard Matt's voice behind her. She was amazed that he was capable of listening, let alone responding.

"It's written on a banner across the entrance to my office." Izzie got out her cigarettes and lit one. "Want a drag, Moe?"

Sounds were fading around them, going-home, shutting-down sounds. The musicians were packing up to the sounds of Tilahun Gessesse on the turntable. Dancers, drinkers, couples, were spilling out under the KOKEB BAR sign and down the steps. The disco lights still turning and flashing behind them.

Izzie jingled the keys and went to open the car doors. "Blessed are the poor, for they shall inherit the earth," she muttered. "Ha. Communists and Christians are all the same."

"What's the deal after Christmas, anyways?" Matt said. "This political rally. Sounds like, you know, copulate." He tripped forwards, laughing.

"It's the second Congress of the COPWE, Matt." He was getting on Izzie's nerves. "The Commission to Organise the Party of the Workers of Ethiopia."

It was pointless. Even sober Matt wouldn't be listening or interested. In her office, work had been interrupted by political meetings and the hanging of flags. The flowerbed around the flagpole in the car park had been replanted and the stones bordering the pathway up to Social Services given a fresh coat of whitewash. It must have been the same at his office. Didn't he talk to anyone? See anything?

"Come on let's go." Moe looked at his watch, the one with the thick black leather strap, a treasured present from his Dad. "We've got forty-five minutes to curfew. I'd prefer to be home. The Kebele are serious these days. COPWE, Christmas eve -"

"What shall we do with these two?" Tom was swaying from side to side and holding onto Mariam. "Matt?"

Mariam's giggle had become strained.

"Take them on home, buddy, that's for sure," Matt had the younger girl's hand in his and was taking concentrated steps towards the car. "I ain't hadda good bonk since —"

"You're joking," Izzie said. "She's too young for you Matt."

The girl tripped along beside him on her high platforms.

She must be tiny with them off, Izzie thought and turned to Mariam. "Are you two sisters?"

"No. She's my little cousin," Mariam leant across Tom, a hand on his chest and smiled at the younger girl. "Aren't you, yeney konjo?"

"Leave them to decide, honey?" Moe said.

"How can they decide?" Izzie said. "They hardly speak a word of English."

Moe opened the back door, with an arm outstretched, to usher the others in.

"There's not enough room in the car," Izzie stood beside Moe, watching Tom and Matt. "The police will stop us."

"How about we stuff them in the boot, Matt?" Tom said.

Matt's high pitched giggle ended with a hiccup. "Oh Gawd, I gone drunk too much, there."

"Get rid of it." Moe pointed to a ditch nearby. "No throwing up in our car."

Matt raised a hand. "I'm cool. I'm cool."

Izzie got in behind the wheel, leaving her door open. "Matt, you can be good company, but right now — " He was amazing on the guitar. He sang Bob Dylan. He clearly loved his kids and proudly showed off pictures of his wife.

"In you get," she could hear Moe's voice. "We haven't got time for this."

Izzie put the keys in the ignition and turned to watch the clambering bodies on the back seat. There was a strong smell of whiskey, male sweat, rancid butter and sweet perfume. "Come on, guys, sort yourselves out," she said.

There was a scramble in the nearby bushes, a dog yelped followed by a volley of barking. A woman's voice, shrill and full of invective, came from behind a corrugated iron fence. A deeper man's voice responded and then there was silence. Izzie waited for the woman to carry on, waited for her to get the upper hand.

"Yours darn well got bigger boobs than mine," Matt said, his voice an octave higher than usual.

"Want me to check?" Tom's voice was a slur.

"Guys," she heard Moe say. She could tell he was anxious to leave but at the same time trying not to find it funny.

Izzie checked the time. Thirty-five minutes to curfew.

Mariam said something to the younger girl who responded with, "Ishi, ishi."

They were all finally packed in. The back door slammed with a clunk and Moe got in beside her, shutting his door. "Let's get going, honey," he said.

"The girls are not going back to Piazza with those two, Moe," she said.

"It's not our problem, honey," he put an arm around her shoulders.

Mariam's laugh sounded more like she was anxious, than having fun.

Izzie pulled her door shut and turned the key in the ignition. The car's engine rumbled into action and they were off, bumping over the gravel and onto the Debre Zeit Road.

"Mine's got a bony bum," she could hear Tom in the back.

"Maybe neither of them gets to eat as much as you do." Izzie glared at Tom in the rear view mirror and glanced at Moe. The price of teff was going through the roof. Everyone was complaining.

"They're just having a bit of fun," Moe moved closer and stroked the back of her neck. "Try not to take everything so serious."

It felt more patronising than comforting. She could tell he was torn between her and being one of the boys.

"Wandering eyes," Uschi always said with a chuckle. She liked Moe. 'But, Ha!" she said. "You'll have to watch that one, Izzie."

She caught Mariam's eyes in the rear view mirror. "They wanted to put you in the boot," she said, returning her eyes to the road ahead.

"Endaye?" Mariam said. "Your friends?"

Izzie shrugged and nodded her head in despair. Yes, her friends.

"What are you telling her?" Tom's voice had sobered up.

"I just told Mariam that you're a rotten scoundrel," Izzie said.

"And who says youse knowin' the word for that, huh?" Matt said.

"Duriyey. I learnt it today," she said. "I didn't tell you about Mekonnen, did I Moe? He's got an eye like a golf ball."

Mariam leant forward over the front seat. "Take us home," she said in Izzie's ear.

Izzie could smell the butter in the girl's hair and the remains of her perfume.

"Ishi, at-hassebee,[61]" Izzie nodded. "They want to go home, lads," she said, loud enough for them to hear in the back seat, feeling slightly triumphant.

"What happened?" Moe said. "Poor old Mekonnen."

"Some big boys threw stones at him. They were selling cigarettes near Georgis," Izzie said. "Hailu ran like the wind and got away of course."

"Ezi neow,[62]" the younger girl said in a thin high voice. "Yinya bate ezi neow."

Izzie slowed down and stopped the car on the dirt verge near a wide stony pathway. "Your house is here?"

Mariam leant forward and kissed Izzie's cheek. "Egziyabheresteling," she said. She shook Moe's hand, giving him a smile.

"Goodnight," Moe said. "Happy Christmas."

Izzie reversed a little, to light their path with the head lamps. So they lived just up the road from the bar. Pitiful that their families needed them to do it. The younger one was obviously new to the game.

Izzie shut down the engine. Silence, for a moment. She looked out of the window and up into the heavily starlit sky. A car went past, followed by an army lorry, its tarpaulin thrown back. It was empty. A little further on, a man stood by a gulley with his back to them, legs apart, concentrating. She turned to watch the girls clambering out of the back.

"Ciao," Tom lifted a hand. He looked a little worse for wear. He wouldn't regret not waking with Mariam next to him in the morning.

There was a faint smell of woodsmoke, berberri and onions in the air. "Everyone's cooking doro wot for tomorrow." Izzie put a hand on Moe's knee.

"And we'll be on our way to Langano."

"I thought we'd get up crack of dawn," he said.

"Me too. Breakfast on the way. The juice-bate in Debre Zeit."

---

[61] OK, don't worry.

[62] Here it is, our house is here.

"Trust Hailu to get away," Moe chuckled. "Is Mekonnen alright?"

"We'll have to check on him when we get back after the week-end." Izzie watched the girls walk slowly, arms linked, wobbling on their high shoes over the dirt pathway in the light of the headlamps. Finally, they stopped at a corrugated iron fence and disappeared inside. They did not look back once.

"There goes my bonk," Matt said.

19

March/April 1983, Addis Ababa

As she came out of the entrance to their building, she could see Mekonnen's head bobbing in and out through the morning traffic. "Izzie, Izzie. How are you? Where are you going?"

"Tenasteling, Mekonnen," she said, looking at him carefully, now he was standing right in front of her. His eyes shone expectantly. He had been especially attentive since the incident with the duriyey in Georgis. As for his eye there was nothing to see, not a scar, not even a scratch. "I am going to my office," she said. "Walking."

"I coming," he said. "I take that."

She was carrying her typewriter.

He took it out of her hand. "We go this way," he said, as if she had never gone that way before. He guided her along Piazza and down a small road, to avoid going past the Cinema, where, he said, all the duriyey hung out.

They came up to the Russian Library, behind the Ministry for Information. A poster advertising a photographic exhibition, 'Sixty-five years of the Russian Army', was plastered to the wall. Izzie wondered who would want to go to that?

The old man who used to sit there stitching ever more patches onto his worn trousers had gone. He had died they said. His little granddaughter was sitting there. Her long matted hair had been shaved off, making her eyes look even larger.

"Her mother – too much drinking," Mekonnen said. "Living Tekle Himanot, in Mercato."

When they asked how she was, the child started crying. Her mother was in trouble. She had been sent out to get money.

Izzie gave her a one Birr note. "For dabbo, ishi? Buy yourself a bread?"

"Ishi," the girl smiled.

Izzie sighed. She would ask Gezahegn again, or maybe even better, she would go to Wozeiro Meheret from Social Services. See if they could find the girl a place in one of the children's homes. Fasika and Mulu would laugh. 'You can't take them all home,' they kept telling her.

**

There was a weird silence in the building. It was Friday. Everyone had gone to the political meeting. The office Izzie shared with Simaynesh and Genet felt the emptiness, the absence of chat and laughter which usually accompanied the clack and ping! of her typewriter. The two extra chairs they had managed to wangle out of Office Provisions, stood empty. They were normally occupied at this time of the morning by Elsabet, her cheeks flushed with gossip and hair coiffured, Wozeiro Meheret, with her gentle voice and shy smile, or Ato Embaye, who did the payroll. He always had news and stories from the night-time vigil by his radio. A regular flow of colleagues, including their boss, Gezahegn, sought out their office like a refuge. It was one of the few places in the ADCD where they could talk freely. Even Ato Solomon, Head of Planning, sometimes joined them, his eyes still blood-shot from the previous night's whiskey. His solace since the death of his wife. No one blamed him.

Everyone was at the obligatory weekly political meeting. Today they would vote for the Chairman of the ADCD's People's Control Committee; a recently added construct of the revolution. The purpose of the Committee was to review all government employees' job descriptions, and monitor and control their activities. Izzie had never been to a political meeting and wished she could be a fly on the wall for this one.

She wondered if they would vote Comrade Adugna as Chair, a jolly man with a round belly, whom everyone greeted like an old friend but no one trusted. He was a party cadre with an eye on Gezahegn's position. Rumour had it he would soon be going to East Germany for political training. He would be away for three to four months before returning to get his promotion.

Izzie could feel Mengistu's eyes on the back of her head. His photograph hung on the wall behind her. She got up and walked over to the window, which took the width of their office and overlooked the car park. A row of bedraggled women and men, their traditional white cotton clothes resigned to the colour of dry grey soil, sat queuing on the veranda outside Social Services. Proud, patient people, the poor of

Ethiopia, she thought, always waiting for something; rations, bread, to leave food for a family member in prison, rain. They were all waiting for the rain. The small rains were due. But for now it was hot. Dry. The heat seemed to make things echo, even the silence seemed to shimmer with the sound of hot air.

Sandrine had come over to the apartment for her English class the evening before. Izzie had started giving English lessons to supplement her income. She liked Sandrine. A petite French woman in her early forties. Izzie hoped she could help her talk as fast and passionately in English as she did in French. Sandrine was worried about her colleague Jean-Thierry. He was up in Mekele, Tigray province. Right in the middle of the war zone.

It was not possible to move outside the city, she said. It was surrounded by guerrilla activity. He was trying to assess the situation and how to get supplies to the hungry, who had made their way from the countryside into the city.

She and Jean-Thierry were doctors with the International Red Cross. She had rattled her fears and excitement off in French, as she walked in through the door Izzie held open for her.

"Beer?" Izzie had said. "Or something stronger?"

Sandrine had made her way in small quick steps across the sitting room, sat on the sofa, knees together and bent to one side, plonked her handbag on the glass table, and looked up at Izzie with pursed lips, as if expecting solace and immediate answers. To everything.

"Sandrine," Izzie had said. "Slowly and in English, OK?"

"OK," she had said. "Bien sur, of course."

Izzie had heard about the situation in Tigray. Booker had said that agricultural development agents working in the area around Mekele were being trained to use guns before going out into the field. The Tigray Liberation Front was active and gaining ground in the whole province. At the same time drought had taken its toll on consecutive harvests. It was dire. Save the Children had already opened a feeding centre for children in Korem. So many were in a critical way. Rumour had it, that they were having to select who was 'bad enough' to let in. Unimaginable. Izzie thought of their excesses; beer in the fridge, the bottles of Drambuie, gin and whiskey on their shelves, nights out eating at the China Bar, in The Cottage, and felt guilty. But not guilty enough to stop doing it all.

Setting up a factory for making children's clothes and assessing carpet knotting workshops suddenly lost their significance compared to what

Sandrine and Jean-Thierry were doing, along with others at SCF and Oxfam. Oxfam had set up a programme in Gondar, and Fasika had said that the Ministry of Health was setting up mobile clinics in Gondar, Wollo and Tigray. Ethiopian nurses were volunteering to go, despite the guerrilla warfare.

She turned and looked at the photo of Mengistu. "What are you going to do about it, huh?" she said. He wasn't really going to ignore it, make the same mistakes as the Emperor, was he?

She rolled up the sleeves of her t-shirt, the dark red one Moe had bought her. She wore it every Friday on political meeting days. She wondered how Moe was doing on his field trip and realised that she did not miss him as much this time. She had a full life herself with her colleagues at work, Negisst at the flat, Fasika and Mulu in Moe's office, and the boys on Piazza. They all made her feel at home.

She lit a cigarette and inhaled deeply. Still she felt uneasy with the situation and there was still a creeping distance between her and Moe. Let alone the stories of hunger filtering through; the daily grind of poverty around them was getting to her. Every day on the way to work, or walking up Piazza to get their veg, or down at National Theatre, at the bottom of the long sweeping hill that was Churchill, where they shopped at Solomon Hailu's; the chant followed her constantly, "Farenj, farenj, five centimes, give me money."

"Give me money."

"Give me money."

The boy with the cigarettes and chewing gum touching her arm, urgently pulling on her sleeve, "Farenj. Buy caramella. Buy caramella."

The stares.

The lump of rags on the pavement she couldn't help looking at longer than necessary, until it moved. The leftovers of a body, wracked with disease, amputated legs, leaning on a wall, against a lamppost – hands out, begging. The bigger boys beating up the smaller ones, who ran away, pants in shreds, held up by string, holes large enough to show their small backsides. A blind woman in rags, empty eye sockets, walking slowly along the pavement, one hand on a child's shoulder, the other out begging. The smells, the urine, the putrid rubbish in gutters down alleyways. The child shitting yellow shit on the roadside.

And she was walking by, walking by, seeing it, wanting to do something about it. But just walking by, sometimes numb, sometimes eyes burning with tears. So now and then, on days off, she stayed in the flat. Just to hide. Not to have to look. To see.

She took another drag on her cigarette, pulled up her chair and continued typing. She made a note on her pad to call and make sure Physio-Bert, as they called him, was still coming with them to Nazareth. He would do physical examinations of the disabled as they were selected. Bert, the Dutch volunteer with a broad smile and healing hands. Nice guy. But not really my type, she thought. Ha! It occurred to her that her mind had not wandered to other men for a long time.

When Bert came to the office, he filled the door and the space between the walls with his voice and laughter. Everyone loved him. His boss in the prosthesis workshop at St Paul's Hospital had promised to assign him to the Nazareth garment factory project for the selection process. Izzie and Genet were looking forward to working with him again. It was through Bert that she had met Sandrine and Jean-Thierry. The International Red Cross also provided prosthesis, often to war disabled, and in part funded the workshop at St Paul's. It was great to discover all the different work that was going on in Ethiopia. People, largely Ethiopians, making a real effort.

Genet. Her small desk and treadle-machine stood silently in the corner next to the cupboard full of colourful threads, cloth and samples of children's clothing. Genet was quiet, got on with her work and was full of creative ideas and enthusiasm when asked. She had stepped up to fill Doris's shoes. She was a good seamstress and with the help of Uschi's Burda magazine, donated with a flourish to the project, came up with a range of simple but beautiful children's clothes.

A thought struck Izzie. She wound the sheet of paper back and looked at the title on the top of the page: The Nazareth Small Scale Industries Garment Factory Project: Selection of Disabled. She tippexed out: 'Disabled' and typed: 'Workers'.

She and Genet had wanted to call the factory, Jacaranda and have pretty labels of purple-flowering trees sewn into the clothes. Comrade Adugna had said it didn't, 'sound revolutionary enough'.

Izzie squirmed as she remembered how she had said, "Enday?" before suggesting he might prefer a label with a hammer and sickle on it. He had laughed, though she could see in his eyes he was not pleased. So far she got away with it. Maybe that would change when he came back from his political training. For now her mix of English and newly learnt Amharic seemed to amuse him as much as it did everyone else.

Moe had told her to watch it. "They'll kick you out, Izzie," he'd say. It was a privileged position, being a farenj. She would get off lightly. She thought he was exaggerating.

She could do with a coffee. The shy, slip of a soul, Desta, who came round with tea and coffee, had not been spared the obligation to vote. This was Communism. Everyone had to take part. The big people and the small people. But as ever, the big people had a voice, large villas and cars, and were mostly men. The small people had their bare feet in plastic shoes, if they were lucky, and lived hand to mouth. And everyone, big and small, was extra careful about what they said to whom. She carried on with her proposed plan for the next phase of the project, ordering it with neat numbered headings. Keep it short. To the point.

**

She looked up as Gezahegn came in. "Tenasteling, Geytey," she said, pleased to see someone at last.

He grunted as he sat down opposite her desk. Crossing one leg over the other, he took a pack of cigarettes out of his jacket pocket and offered it towards her.

"Just put one out, thanks," she said, wondering why he seemed older than he normally looked. She carried on typing, knowing he would talk when he was ready.

He lit up, cupping his hand round the match as he drew on the cigarette. There was the odd distinguished fleck of grey in his hair, his cheeks clean shaven. He had high cheekbones and a strong jaw. Izzie noticed the line of dust round the hem of his dark trousers. Ninety percent of homes in Addis were tucked behind corrugated iron fencing, down narrow, dirt and stone pathways. But his shoes shone. Gezahegn stopped by the shoe-shine boys outside Georgis every morning for a ten centime polish.

"Wearing your revolutionary t-shirt?" he said with his wry chuckle.

Izzie could tell he was agitated. "Etiopia Tikdem," she said. "Been having my own private Party meeting in here." She knew Gezahegn didn't like the political meetings. She guessed he had been happier being a civil servant in the Emperor's time. She imagined the etiquette, old traditions and clearly defined class structures probably suited him better.

He blew out a train of smoke and looked more relaxed.

"How was it?" she said. "Anyone vote for you?" She couldn't resist teasing him.

"One thing is: your job description is still to do what I say. That has not changed."

"You're the boss."

"Until I get 'promoted' out of the way, of course."

"I would resign. Be Egziyabher, I'm not working for anyone else."

He shook his head and smiled, "Anchee.[63]"

"If they had let me into the meeting, I would have voted for you, Comrade," she said.

"It won't be long before all heads of department have to be cadres."

"Comrade Adugna is set to take up his place then," she said.

Simaynesh came in with her pent up energy and shut the door behind her. She was smart, never wore make-up and had beautiful clear skin. Izzie admired her intensity and was proud to be counted among Simaynesh and Gezahegn's friends.

Simaynesh looked at Gezahegn, her eyes shining. "Who did you vote for?"

Izzie could not make out if she was angry or excited.

"Did you see that?" Simaynesh said. "Only one woman on the whole committee."

"I thought under Communism – " Izzie said. "Women's equality and all that? Am I being stupid?"

"Forget it," Gezahegn said. "Our women are too busy carrying firewood down from the mountains like donkeys."

"There are plenty of educated women in our offices," Simaynesh said. "We're just too intelligent to join the Party, that's all." She looked compact and smart in her dark jacket and skirt. The few clothes she had were well looked after.

"There's your answer then," Gezahegn said. "Join the Party."

"Sure." Simaynesh turned up her nose. "See where that got me."

Izzie looked at Simaynesh to see if she would say more, then at Gezahegn, who frowned briefly and shook his head.

"Anyway, I'm hungry. Push the buzzer, Izzie, yeney konjo?"

Izzie put Simaynesh's hunger down to her busy mind. She was always hungry. Izzie leant back to push the button on the wall.

"I voted for our friend, Comrade Yared," Gezahegn said.

"Yared?" Izzie said. "He's a Party member?" She scrabbled through her mind, trying to remember if she had said anything to him she shouldn't have. "He's a nice guy."

"Chairman of his Kebele, that one," Simaynesh said. "A real bendy-bendy tenquolenya." She made a snake-like movement with her arm and followed it across the room to her desk beside the window. "You're

---

[63] You – used in a friendly endearing way.

right. He's not bad. He's a good man. But it takes a lot of guts to balance along the fence like he does."

The sky outside remained its relentless blue.

"No rain," Izzie said.

Desta came in with an empty metal tray and looked at them, eyebrows raised.

"Three macchiato, please, Desta," Gezahegn said, glancing at Izzie and Simaynesh.

"And three samosa," Simaynesh said, holding out a one Birr note. "Can you get them for us from the restaurant downstairs, please, yeney konjo?"

"Egziersteling," Izzie said. "I've been dying for a coffee, Desta."

Desta smiled, made a small bow and backed out of the room closing the door behind her, not having spoken a word.

20

May/June 1983, Ataye

Ashebir woke up, climbed down from his cot and went outside to relieve himself. He went back in to fill the small plastic jug with water from the insera, making sure not to take too much, and went out again to wash his face and hands. As he ran the water over his bare arms he saw the red swelling. He touched it gently with a finger. It hurt. It wasn't a mosquito bite. He heard Zewdie's morning coughing.

"Zewdie look," he said, holding out his arm.

She came to the door to inspect it in the sunlight.

"It's a blister," she said, turning away to cough into her shawl.

"What's a 'blister'?"

"You get a blister from a burn," she said. "If you burst it, water will come out."

He looked more closely at the 'blister', and then at his mother, wondering how it got there. "I didn't burn myself."

"I think one of those little red and black spiders has bitten you in the night," she said. "They usually come when people are sleeping. They leave a trail of poison and that's how the blister comes."

"Will I die?" He knew poison was dangerous. People died from snake-bite poison, maybe he could die from spider poison.

Zewdie laughed. "No," she said. "It will dry in the sun. It will be gone in a few days."

"Zewdie, is it true that cockroaches can crawl into your ear when you are sleeping?"

She laughed again. "Where did you hear that?"

"Ali said it happened to his grandfather. He had to go to that healer in Somali Sefer."

"Did he get it out?" Zewdie asked, looking at him.

"The old man said the cockroach would not be able to turn round and get out. It would die in his ear."

"It happens. We have to keep our gojo-bate clean so the cockroaches don't come. They are looking for food, like all of us." She sucked her teeth.

"We don't have much food, but they still come and look," Ashebir said. "I hope they don't look for ki'ta bread in my ear."

"Egziyabher yawkal," Zewdie said, smiling at him. "I am sure they won't, don't worry." She rubbed his head gently with her hand.

He smiled up at her. They looked at each other. Her face was changing every day. He did not like the dark rings under her eyes.

The goats started bleating.

"They're getting restless," Zewdie said. "Off you go."

He went inside, put a handful of 'kollo in his pocket, his elephant grass hat in his bag, picked up his stick and sickle and went round the back to chase the goats out. He gave his favourite a rub on her head.

"She's going to have another baby, Zewdie" he called out as he left. "It's good we kept her."

"Yes, she keeps giving us kids to sell," Zewdie said. "Take care yeney lij. Egziyabher ante gar yihun."

When he got to the river he waded in, stepping over the rocks, to have a good wash, leaving his clothes on the bank. He rubbed himself all over and then looked at his arm again. The 'blister' had burst. He climbed up the bank to lie in the sun with his friends.

They lay chatting, throwing pebbles in the water. When he was dry he saw red marks and more blisters had spread down his arm. He showed Mohamed Abdu and Ali.

"Does it hurt?" Ali asked.

"A bit," Ashebir said. "Zewdie says it's spider poison."

"The sun will cure it," Mohamed Abdu said. "That's what Temima always says."

"My mother too," Ali said. "She thinks the sun makes everything better."

"It doesn't heal our hungry bellies," Ashebir said.

Ali stretched his hands out towards the sun, pretending to grab handfuls of it to fill his mouth. Ashebir and Mohamed Abdu laughed and copied him. They chewed with their cheeks puffed out and rubbed their bellies.

Ashebir looked at his arm again. "Look, where the water comes out of the blister my skin turns red like a burn," he said.

"Just lie with it in the sun," Ali said.

So he lay on the bank, his wound facing the sun, hoping it would get better.

**

273

Ashebir was already home when Zewdie came back from the market. He had put the goats in the beret and was sitting in the shadow of the house, his arm stretched out, absorbed in examining it.

"Tadias," he heard her say, as she came into the compound. "What are you doing?"

"I am waiting for you."

"What is it? Are you alright?"

"I am fine, Egziyabher yimesgen." He looked up at her. "It's just my arm."

"Let me have a look," she said.

"It hurts." He held it further out, so she could see how much it hurt. He pointed out the large, red swollen patch full of yellow pus, and looked in her face to see what she thought. "It is getting bigger and bigger. It might spread over my whole body," he said. "I have washed it in the river and dried it in the sun every day but it has spread even more."

"I have to take you to Emet Fahte Ibrahim," she said. "She will know what to do with your megil.[64]"

"What did you get in the market?" he asked hopefully. He was hungry all the time.

"I sold the firewood and bought enough sorghum to make ki'ta bread for two days." she said. She held up a small bag. "The prices have gone up again. I think we have to sell two of the goats."

"We've already sold the cow and the ox," he said, frowning.

It had been another long trek to Senbatey market and back. They had got disappointingly little money for them. Their ribs had been clear to see. Their once shining hides had become rough and dull. Mohamed Abdu said the animals had worms.

They had seen so many dead animals on the way. Lying on their sides, crows and vultures hopping around them, picking bits of dried meat from the bones, a buzz of flies around each carcass. They had walked on in silence with their own skinny ox and cow. Their shema pulled tightly round their noses and mouths. The stench was bad.

"We will have to sell them if we want to eat," Zewdie said, coming out of the gojo-bate again. And we have to have something to give Emet Fahte for looking at your spider bite."

He followed her out of the compound and up the hillside behind their house. "Are you sure she knows how to make spider bites better?"

"Spider bites, snake bites, fever, aches and pains, birrd," she said. "She

---

[64] Pus from the infection which occurs after a spider bite.

knows it all. Maybe she can even take cockroaches out of your ears," she added with a smile.

He rubbed his ears and shook his head.

They walked up past the large warka tree, where he sometimes played with Mohamed Abdu, Aminat, Yishaereg and Ali, to the top of the hill. Emet Fahte's house was on the other side of the hill down a narrow path, overlooking the valley. All the way, he held his sore arm out in front of him.

He was afraid of Emet Fahte. She had painful ways of curing things. A few days after they had been in Jebuha that time, Yishaereg's mother became seriously ill. Everyone said it was mogne bagegne.[65]

"Will we get that illness too, Zewdie?" Ashebir had asked his mother. It was not the disease that worried him as much as Emet Fahte's cure for it.

Zewdie told him she would try and make sure they got enough to eat. But he knew they were both hungry. Sometimes when he ate, it all came out fast the other end again, like sherro wot.

There was talk that Emet Fahte had saved Yishaereg's mother by cutting her and letting the blood out.

Yishaereg had told him the blood was almost black.

"Were you there?" he had asked Yishaereg.

"I had to hold her hand," Yishaereg said. "Who else could be with her?"

"Where did Emet Fahte cut her?" Ashebir asked.

"Just above her elbow," Yishaereg said. She rolled up her sleeve to show Ashebir where the spot was.

"Did she use a knife?" he asked.

"No, a razor blade," Yishaereg said, frowning a little. "She always uses a razor blade."

Ashebir had looked away. He remembered Yishaereg had been there that time of the screaming. There had been a celebration for the girls. They were taken to Emet Fahte's house by their mothers. He and his friends were told to stay away. But they hid in the bushes nearby, their hearts beating in their mouths from excitement and fear. After some time the girls began screaming one after the next, in a terrible way, which made him tremble. Afterwards, there had been crying and singing. The mothers seemed to be happy. He did not see the girls for a while. Ali said they were in a hut somewhere on the other side of the hill. He said they

---

[65] An illness from eating rotten corn.

were lying on the ground, their legs tied up at the feet, like chickens.

The sound of their pain had reminded him of the time when the old man came to their house when they lived somewhere on the other side of Addis. It seemed a long time ago. It was when Emet Hawa was still alive. He must have been about five. Some visitors had been drinking coffee with Emet Hawa and Zewdie. He was playing outside with his friend, Boleke, when his mother called.

Zewdie was standing by the large smooth stone near the entrance to their house. She sat down on it and drew him towards her. She told him the village healer was there, and that since the time of Abraham, all Ethiopian boys had been cut, and now it was his turn.

He could tell from the way she spoke, from the way her eyes looked away from him nervously that this was not going to be a good thing. He remembered wanting to hide amongst the prickliest bushes so the grownups couldn't get him. He could hear his friends' laughter, calling him to come and play.

Zewdie had taken his hand firmly in hers.

He had pulled away from her to no avail. "I don't want to Zewdie, please. I don't want to."

"It should have been done a long time ago," she said, and pulled him towards the dark opening of their door, away from the sunshine. "He is good at his work. It will be over fast."

It had been bright outside. He remembered a rush of small yellow birds flying from their hedge up into the neighbour's tree. Inside, the air was thick with wood smoke. There was the strong smell of the men, and of coffee and burning itan.[66] After the bright sun, it took him a while to make out the shapes of the men sitting on low wooden stools around Emet Hawa's coffee pot. The men were wrapped in gabis, throwing fendisha into their mouths. He usually loved fendisha but his stomach felt tight. All those familiar things smelt bitter. He began to wail uselessly.

The old healer had turned in his stool to look at him. He felt the man's large hand take hold of his arm and he stopped his outburst immediately.

"Ayezoh, calm yourself boy," the old man said, pulling him nearer.

Ashebir stood face to face with the healer. He had small bright eyes and deep lines in his cheeks, like bark on a tree.

He saw a fresh cloth on his mother's cot in the corner. He started to cry again.

---

[66] Incense made from tree resin.

The man stood up and drew him towards the cot. "Your mother can take your clothes off for you."

Ashebir turned and saw her standing in the light of the door, holding a corner of her white cotton shema across her mouth. Something she always did when she was upset.

"Come, yeney lij," she said, and started pulling his shorts down. He struggled again, hitting out with his elbows, trying to rid himself of Zewdie, and the old man's hold.

"No. Please, Zewdie," he cried out. "No."

The men moved around him, their soft gabis brushing against his skin. They lifted him onto the cot. He could hear their low voices mumbling and Zewdie saying, "Es-ssay, es-ssay. Calm down, my child." He knew then that she was afraid too. "Egziyabher alle, it is His will."

The men stood on each side of him, holding him down by his arms and his ankles. He arched his back. He lifted his head to peer down his body at what they were doing, his mouth drawn back, tears running down his cheeks. The old man pulled the skin forward over his penis and quickly tied a string tightly round it. A hand covered his eyes and pushed his head back onto the cot. At the same time pain ran through his body. One sharp slice, like a knife cutting open an ox's throat. The razor blade.

Everything went black. He heard a loud scream. He called out to his mother. He opened his eyes and saw the blood on the fresh cloth. Everything went black again. He was shaking violently. Sharp pains travelled up and down his body until they gathered in that place, burning and biting.

The old man was washing him, the cool water turning pink. Then he covered the place with a cloth.

Zewdie was trying to soothe him, pulling a gabi over his body to stop the shivering. He heard her voice coming from somewhere out of the old man's muttering. Then all was still, just the pain running in his veins.

"I've brought you sweet papaya." He could hear her voice. "Have a sip of Coca Cola."

He could not lift his head to drink.

As the days passed and the pain left him, he remembered how he felt proud to be like all the other boys. "Now you will grow up to be a man," his grandmother had told him with a smile.

**

Ashebir looked at his mother walking down the path ahead of him, towards Emet Fahte's. His teeth were clenched and his sore arm ached from holding it out all the way. He let it drop by his side.

"Ashebir," he heard Zewdie's voice. "Where are you in your dreaming? We're nearly there."

From the top of the hillside, he could see into Emet Fahte's compound. It was neat with a patch at the back where she used to grow herbs and vegetables. It was bare now, a few dried-out maize stalks drooped in the heat. Everything crackled as they walked along, the soil hard and dry under his feet. The late afternoon sun burned down on his head, his hair grown thick and bushy. He followed Zewdie to Emet Fahte's gate, sweat trickling down his face, his throat dry.

"You remember the time the old healer came to our house, Zewdie?"

"You remember that?" Zewdie turned, looking surprised.

He nodded, wondering what Emet Fahte would do to his arm.

"She's not going to cut you," she said. "Ayezoh, it will be alright." She smiled and patted his head, then turned to the gate.

"Tenasteling, Emet Fahte," she called out.

"Come in, come in," Emet Fahte said in a thick rattling voice. People said she smoked tobacco, but maybe she had the same coughing sickness as his mother.

He followed Zewdie through the gate. There were a few scrawny chickens scratching around her compound making their 'rrr-kuk-kuk-rrrr' noises deep in their throats. Not many people had chickens. He wondered whether Emet Fahte cut their necks with a knife, or twisted them quickly, when she wanted to eat one.

"Tadias, Wozeiro Zewdie. It's you, and your son."

His mother shook hands with the woman, bowing her head and greeting her politely.

"What is your name, boy?"

"Ashebir Lakew," he said, looking up at her and thinking how ugly she was. Her cheeks wrinkled and sucked in, her mouth bereft of teeth.

"You are the one who is sick. Where did that spider bite you?" she asked.

He was shocked. How did she know about the spider? The children in the village said the old medhanit ahwahkey[67] was a magician. Maybe she really was. He looked down at his arm.

"Don't be afraid. It is clear to see on your arm," she said, sounding a

---

[67] Traditional healer.

little cross. "It is a bad bite and now it is full of pus." She chuckled in a strange way, and then coughed, it rattled long and hard in her chest. She went and spat into the thick cactus that made a fence around her compound.

Ashebir looked at his mother. She gave him a smile that made him feel a little better.

The old woman came back and took Ashebir's wrist in her hard and bony hand, and pulled so that his arm was outstretched. He did not like the feel of her. She turned his arm slowly this way and that, more gently than he expected, looking closely at his wound.

"Send the boy back to me tonight after midnight and before dawn," Emet Fahte said, looking over his head at his mother. "I will chew some lentils into a mixture and spit it into the wound directly. It will only work if he comes before dawn, mind you. He has to be here when it's still dark."

"Thank you, Emet Fahte," his mother said. "Praise Allah we have you here in the village to look after our sickness."

"Send him tonight," the old woman replied. "Alone."

"Ishi, but how can I repay you?"

"Send what you can, as you like," she said, "when the wound has healed, not before."

Zewdie bowed her head and said, "Praise Allah, thank you."

He felt Zewdie tapping his shoulder. It was time to go. He followed her back up the narrow path.

"Why do I have to come back alone, Zewdie?" Ashebir said. "And why does she have to spit on my arm?"

"Emet Fahte knows best," Zewdie said. "I would take you to the clinic but it will cost us money we don't have. Now watch the path so you are sure to know your way tonight."

"I know the path well."

"At night it can look different."

"Ishi, I will watch out," he said. He looked at his mother's back. She was walking slowly like she did when her legs pained her. She was coughing into her shawl. "Why didn't you tell her about your coughing? And your legs?"

"Let us heal your arm first. I will be alright. We will make tea when we get home."

"I want to help you make the fire," he said.

She turned and smiled at him. She looked too tired.

∗∗

That night, when everything was still, Ashebir set off along the path. He was looking in every direction for snakes, hyena and Afar warriors. He stopped and turned round to look at his mother who was standing just outside their gate.

"Go, go," she whispered. "Egziyabher is with you. You will be fine."

He gripped his stick firmly. "What if there is a hyena on the path?" he whispered loudly back.

"Go," Zewdie said. To his surprise she turned and disappeared into their house.

He stood looking after her, hesitating, fear in his belly and beating heart. He started walking again, slowly. He was thankful for the full moon that shed light on the path. The neighbouring houses loomed behind their bushy fences. At least it was not completely dark, like the nights when the moon was a toenail in the sky. Everything was still and quiet. With the drought, even the crickets had stopped singing.

He was walking towards the large warka tree, where they sometimes played in the late afternoons, when he saw it. He stopped. A white hyena stood in the light of the moon under their tree. It's not possible. But there it was. It was sniffing around looking for something to eat.

It hasn't seen me.

The hyena looked up and stared. Ashebir's heart rushed into his ears and filled his head, pounding loudly. The hyena's white shining eyes were like those of a mad spirit. Its broad shoulders rose up thick and strong. It bent its back legs as if getting ready to leap.

Ashebir turned and ran as fast as he could. He tripped over a branch and fell, grazing his knees. He looked back, got up again and ran. He reached their home so out of breath that his chest hurt.

"Zewdie," he shouted as he ran through their gate. "There's a white hyena on the path."

"Sshh," Zewdie said as she came out of the house, pulling a gabi around her shoulders. "You'll wake all the neighbours."

He was bent double over his knees, trying to get his breath. He looked up at her breathing hard, "There's a white hyena on the path."

"There is no such thing as a white hyena," Zewdie whispered loudly. "You are imagining things my little dreamer."

"It's under our tree."

"The warka tree? It's not possible," Zewdie said. "Now go to Emet Fahte's house."

"But it's there, under the tree," he said, pointing up the path. "Really." Why didn't she believe him? He had seen it. "It's just next to

Wozeiro Zenabwerk's house."

"Go now, Ashebir. That's enough."

"Please come with me, Emayey." Ashebir whined.

"You have to go alone," Zewdie whispered. "Emet Fahte said."

He made his most pleading face, hoping she would change her mind. Zewdie put her hands on his shoulders and gave him a small push. Tears came to his eyes.

"Just go," she said.

He went back up the path, trying to breathe deeply, his legs weak from fear, his knees hurting from the fall. He had no choice. He turned to look at Zewdie again. She stood at the bottom of the path, her gabi wrapped round her shoulders, watching.

"I'll be here waiting for you," she said quietly.

"Ishi," he whispered, wiping the tears from his cheeks. He walked carefully on up the path not making a sound. He wondered if the white hyena had appeared to him like a spirit, to warn him because he had lied to Mohamed Bilal from Albuko's son that day.

"I can run as fast as a white hyena," he had told him.

"There's no such thing," the older boy had laughed.

"There is," Ashebir had replied. "I've seen one."

He would never lie again, he thought. He was sure the white hyena was waiting to teach him a lesson. But when he reached the tree, the hyena was gone. He looked around. He couldn't see it anywhere. He walked quickly and quietly to the top of the hill. The moon lit everything. There was nothing to see. He continued down the path using his stick to knock the bushes and tap the ground to warn any snakes to keep out of the way. Finally, he reached Emet Fahte's gate. He knocked. It rattled.

She opened the gate, already chewing.

It must be the lentils, he thought, disgusted.

She peered this way and that over his shoulder then waved her hand at him to get inside her compound. He tried not to be afraid of her, but in the moonlight and shadows she looked as if she might cast an evil eye on him. Her face was heavily wrinkled, strands of white hair stuck out of the black cloth she wore wrapped round her head. In the afternoon he had seen that she had holes where other people had teeth.

She did not say anything to him. She just chewed. She waved her hand for him to follow her round the back. She pointed at a low wooden stool under the eaves, still chewing. With her lips pouting and her cheeks sucked in, she looked strange. He understood she wanted him to sit on the stool. He was thankful that this side of the house was lit by the moon. He sat down and looked up into the sky. It was full of stars. She pointed at his arm and he stretched it out towards her.

He forgot about the white hyena. His eyes were now on the old woman. She got down on her knees letting out a grunt. For some moments she carried on chewing the mixture, her head bent over the sore on his arm. He could smell the wood smoke in her clothes, and the ghee in the cloth around her head. He could hear the saliva clicking in her mouth and started to feel sick. She was breathing deeply. He sat rigidly, holding his breath. A porridge-like substance came slowly out of her pursed lips, like a worm, onto the infected spot.

He shrank back against the wall of her house. She stopped and stood up with a groan. She coughed and went to spit the rattling stuff in her chest into a dark corner. She came back to him, held his arm and softly massaged the mixture into the wound, murmuring as she did so.

"Don't touch this and don't wash it for three days," she said, her throat full of the next cough. "Or it won't work and you will have to come back again." She led him back round the house, opened the gate and waved her hand at him to go.

He ran, keeping his arm outstretched, until he reached their home. When he got to the gate, he realised he had left his stick behind. He did not want to go back there ever again.

Zewdie was waiting for him. "Are you alright?"

"I am fine," he said, going past her and straight to his cot.

"You are angry with me?"

"No," he said and pulled his ox-skin over himself, leaving his arm outside. He closed his eyes and fell asleep.

21

It was dawn. Ashebir climbed down from his cot and went outside as usual.

Their small home was filling with smoke, as Zewdie prepared the fire to make ki'ta bread and set a pot of water on the flames to boil.

He came in and sat in his place next to Zewdie, pulling his knees in to his chest to stop the pains in his stomach. He watched as she put a spoon of tea in the boiling water and sprinkle a pinch of spices over the bubbles. As she stirred he enjoyed watching the water change colour and how the sweet smell of cardamom and cloves mixed with the wood smoke. When the tea and bread were nearly ready, he heard a noise outside.

"I have a surprise for you," she said.

"What?"

"Lakew has come." She seemed to laugh but it turned into a cough and she put a hand to her chest.

"I don't believe you," he said, jumping up. Where is he? I don't see him."

She coughed and he could hear the rattle, just like Emet Fahte's.

"Zewdie, you are sick, aren't you?"

"I am fine. It will pass."

He could tell she was lying to comfort him.

"Where is he?"

"He went to see Mohamed Shinkurt," she said. "Maybe that's him coming now. I told him to eat breakfast with us."

"Tenasteling, Tenasteling. Hello. Hello. Is there anybody in?"

Ashebir ran outside and into the man standing in their compound. He put his arms around his father and buried his face in his chest. He could hear the chuckles and looked up. Lakew had a wide smile, just like Zewdie's.

"How are you, my boy, yeney lij?" It was good to feel his father's hand on his head.

"I am fine Ababa, Egziyabher yimesgen, thanks be to God." He felt better now Lakew was home. Everything would be good. Zewdie would get better.

They went inside together, Lakew ducking his head in the doorway.

"Come let's eat," Zewdie said. "Ashebir, fetch some water and the two stools. We can eat outside."

Ashebir filled their plastic bowl with a little water and offered it to Lakew to wash his hands before washing his own. He got the low wooden stools and put them on the rush mat for Lakew and Zewdie to sit on under the eaves. He sat himself on the mat opposite them. They each had a glass of hot tea and helped themselves to bread from a small ochre-red clay plate.

Ashebir ate the bread slowly and slurped his tea loudly like his father.

"The drought is bad," Lakew said after a while. "Many people are leaving their homes. Some even carry the frames of their houses on their backs to sell for firewood."

Ashebir looked at Zewdie. She shook her head slowly. "God help us," she whispered. "The price of grain has gone up so much we can hardly buy it anymore."

Lakew looked at her. "I am worried about you."

"I spoke to Mohamed Bilal from Albuko, and our brother, Mohamed Shinkurt, yesterday. They agree it's time to sell the remaining goats."

"Enday?" Ashebir looked up. "All of them?"

"Hush, yeney konjo," Lakew said gently.

Ashebir picked up his tea and took another slurp, looking from one to the other, listening, anxious.

"I cannot sell enough firewood to buy grain to make beer or injera like before," Zewdie said. "Only the well off in town have money to buy beer anyway. What to do? Egziyabher yawkal. He is our saviour." She put her glass on the ground and rubbed her hands slowly up and down her legs. She did that often these days. She said it eased the pain. "We are eating so little now, Lakew. I am worried."

This kind of worry-talk happened often these days. It took away the possibility of laughter and smiles. After eating a little, Ashebir needed to go round the back. It would all come out in a rush. He got up.

"You've got diarrhoea again," she said. "I will prepare tea with tobacco leaves for you."

He turned up his nose. It was bitter but it stopped the runs.

"Are those your drawings?" Lakew called after him.

"I will show you later."

He made soothing noises as he passed the animals' beret. Seeing him, the goats gathered by the gate, eager to go out. He ran up the path behind the house feeling angry When they were gone it would be quiet and empty. It was dry everywhere. He hated it. He found a spot in the pasture, pulled his shorts down and crouched. He looked at the bare hills while the watery stuff came out. He grunted, the pains cutting his stomach. When he finished, he pulled up his shorts and tied them with a piece of string so they would not fall down. They were the colour of the earth around him. Zewdie wished she could buy him new clothes. He walked back down the path towards the house looking at his t-shirt full of holes. It had once been white. The faces on it had faded, as had the writing, which he could not read. Zewdie said it was farenj writing, and that only a few people in Addis could read and write that language.

He passed the beret again. "Soon," he said. "We'll go soon."

The sun was hot, and the sky its everyday deep blue. He liked seeing his drawings on their gojo-bate. He would show them to Lakew. He'd done them with a chicken feather and the black ink from the Qur'an class and sometimes with red brown soil mixed with water. He was sorry he was too tired to draw when he came home in the afternoons these days. What would he do when the animals were gone? He said a quick prayer that Zewdie would not send him away to look after someone else's animals.

He washed his hands. Zewdie told him to always wash hands after shin-te-bate.

"They expect the harvest to be bad again," Lakew was saying. "It's hard to find work. So many men, and even women, are looking for daily labour."

Ashebir sat in his place again and looked at Lakew. His face was round like Zewdie's, the skin stretched across his cheekbones. He had short thick fingers, the fingernails cracked and worn. His father worked hard.

Ashebir's throat was dry. He took another sip of tea. It was cold.

"Here. Drink this," Zewdie said, pouring hot yellow liquid into his glass.

He slurped the hot tea and turned up his nose. Zewdie had mixed tobacco leaves in it, but no sugar. The price of sugar had also gone up. He took another slurp, only because the bitter liquid would stop his diarrhoea.

Since Zewdie and Lakew were not talking any more, he said, "What have you been doing?" It came out quietly. He coughed, feeling awkward. Children had to wait to speak to adults.

Lakew and Zewdie were looking at him with gentle, troubled faces. A mixture he saw in Zewdie more often these days.

"Where have you been?" He said again, tears welling in his eyes. He sniffed and wiped his nose on his t-shirt.

"I have been digging terraces on the mountainside. Every week they give me a bag of grain. If you look inside the house, you will see the last bag I earned. I bought it here for you and Zewdie."

"Egziyabher yimesgen," Ashebir said, bowing his head and leaning slightly forward towards his father.

"You are welcome."

"Why do you dig terraces?"

"Because sometimes when the rains do come, it floods. All the soil we need for farming gets washed away down the mountain. Then there's no soil left to plant. The terraces stop that happening."

"It is a good job then," Ashebir said.

"It is a good job," Lakew said. "But it's hard work and the pay is poor. I don't get money. I get food."

Ashebir slurped his tea again. It was bitter. "Ababa," he said. "Did you see the trucks and tanks passing on the road?"

"I did, my boy."

Ashebir was surprised to see he was not excited about it. "Yesterday when I was with the goats by the river, the trucks just kept coming." He loved seeing the battered green army trucks and tanks. Their rumbling shook the whole earth and sent ripples through the river as they crossed the bridge. "At first Mohamed Abdu and I thought it was thunder. That there would be rain clouds over Muletta mountain. But there was nothing. Just the blue sky and the loud noise." Ashebir looked at his father again. "They came one after the next. A long, long line. We ran up the banks after the trucks shouting: Wotaderoch! Wotaderoch![68]"

"I saw them too," Zewdie said, sounding tired.

"They are still passing today," Lakew said. "They have been going all night."

"They sometimes pass for two or three days at a time, day and night," Zewdie said.

"Some of them waved, and others just looked at us. Some of them looked sad," Ashebir said. "Why are they sad? It's good to be a soldier, no?"

---

[68] Soldiers!

"They are boys and young men sent to fight," Lakew said. "They don't know if they will ever go home again."

Ashebir looked at Zewdie.

"Sending them to the front. Shame. Shame." She covered her mouth with her white cotton shema, coughing. "Like our nephew Yimam, and Etalem's two sons. They have all gone."

"Yimam went?" Lakew said.

"Yes, and we have no news of him." Zewdie shook her head.

Ashebir leaned forward to tap his father's knee.

"I ran after them with my friends. We were running and running and shouting, "Marxism! Leninism! Memeryachin Neou!" "

Lakew laughed and clapped his hand on Ashebir's shoulder. "Where did you learn that?"

"The Ataye Youth Association shouts that when they practice their marching. I sometimes go to the road near the Kebele offices in Ataye with Ali and Mohamed Abdu to watch them. They have green uniforms. The leader carries the Ethiopian flag and the girl behind him the red one with the yellow hammer and sickle on it." He got up and marched up and down, swinging his arms grandly, lifting his knees high in the air like the young people in the Ataye Youth Association.

Zewdie and Lakew laughed.

"You have to be careful, Ashebir," Lakew said, still smiling.

"Is it bad?" Ashebir said, giggling, and out of breath. He sat down on the mat again.

"It's politics," Lakew said, looking at Zewdie. "You are too young for that, Ashebir."

"I do know about it," Ashebir said. "They get killed at the front." Ali and Yishaereg's father was a soldier. He died at the front. The people from the Peasant Association told their mother he was a Hero. Ali and Yishaereg and their mother were not happy about it. They wanted him home. But now he would never come. "You won't go to the front, Lakew, will you?" he said.

"Not if I can avoid it," Lakew said, putting a hand on Ashebir's head. "I want peace, work and food, and then maybe I can live here with you and your mother."

"Come and see my drawings," Ashebir said, putting out his hand to pull his father up.

They walked together round the gojo-bate to the place where the smooth mud wall was covered in his drawings, some already faded.

"This one is a chicken," he pointed. "This is ripe sorghum, and here are the eucalyptus trees. This is me sitting in Mohamed Bilal's look-out with my sling."

"That's a good one," Lakew said, looking closer. "Did you kill any birds?"

"I can, but I didn't have to," Ashebir said proudly. "We just throw some stones with our slings to stop them from landing on the crops. I don't like killing them."

"And here are the soldiers," Lakew said. "They are a different colour."

"I mixed red clay with water to draw those. I ran out of ink from our Qur'an class. I go to Kebele classes now," he said.

"You are learning to read and write?"

"Zewdie said it is good to know how to read and write."

"She's right." Lakew looked at the drawings. "And here is the road," he said, laughing. "You are good at drawing cars and buses."

"And here's a bicycle," Ashebir said. "I would love to ride a bicycle. We were up on the hills along the Dessie Road. There was a bike race. Mohamed Hussain was in it. I saw him."

"Did he come in first?"

"No. But he did in my drawing. Look." He pointed at the cyclist he had drawn, arms up in the air, passing the finish line.

Lakew was laughing. "You are a great artist, Ashebir."

"Really?"

"Really."

Ashebir turned to look for Zewdie. The two stools stood on the rush mat. The plate and glasses had disappeared. A shower of small yellow white-eye birds flew onto his papaya tree and flew off again as quickly into the neighbour's sisal hedge.

"I have to take the goats out to the pastures now. I will see if I can meet Mohamed Abdu on the path." Ashebir said. Then he turned and looked at his father, "Please let us keep two of the goats."

"I have to take them all to market, Ashebir. Your mother needs the money for food and medicine."

"Let's at least keep my favourite, the one with the black fleck on her nose. She will have kids again soon. My friend Mohamed Abdu thinks she's got two in there."

"Then she'll fetch the highest price," Lakew said. "You know, we used to get five hundred Birr for an ox, Ashebir. Now we only get twenty or thirty. So just imagine how little we are going to get for those goats. If your mother waits any longer she'll get nothing for them."

He liked Lakew explaining things to him, like Mohamed Ahmed did with Mohamed Abdu. It made him feel more grown-up, having a father. He knew his father was right but he didn't want to accept it. He could see in Lakew's face that there was no more arguing to be done. He sucked his teeth, like Zewdie did and turned to go and find his friend.

"I will see you before you go?"

"Of course," Lakew said. "I will stay a few days. We will see each other this evening."

22

The noise of corn popping against a saucepan lid came from the kitchen.

"Chai? Bira?" Simaynesh called out.

Izzie leant against the door to the narrow kitchen. Room for one person at a time. Wire meshing, thick with grime, covered the windows. The welcome smell of popcorn mingled with the stronger smell of berberri and oil.

A crow cawed insistently from a ledge above the window, as if it expected a response, or that someone come sort things out.

"It can smell the popcorn," Izzie said. "I'll have a beer, thanks. Shall I get it?"

Simaynesh was shaking the pot over the blue flame, which hissed from a two ring gas stove on the kitchen top. "Don't worry. Sit down," she said.

"Where's the ashtray?"

"On the windowsill."

The sky outside was a pale evening blue, with streaks of pink and orange. It had been another hot day. Down below, traffic rolled slowly past. The pavements were full of people walking home. Izzie lit her cigarette, blew a train of smoke into the air. She sat on the sofa, tucking her legs underneath. It was a tiny flat at the top of a dark stairwell on the Bole Road. It felt familiar and cosy to her. And she had to admit, she felt slightly proud to be invited into Simaynesh's home. Her private space. Not many people got that far.

Simaynesh brought the beer and a basket full of fluffy white fendisha.

"Egziersteling," Izzie said, taking a handful and smiling up at Simaynesh.

"It's been a long day," Simaynesh said, curling herself into the other end of the sofa, lighting a cigarette.

"I can't believe they made such a big deal of it," Izzie said, shaking her head.

"They have to. Have to show they're doing something for our Heroes. That's the trick. The socialist trick. And we Ethiopians are good at pomp and ceremony, at hiding all the problems, the rubbish and the poor. Like the saying goes, 'swept behind velvet curtains'. Anyway, here's to Nazareth, to our factory workers."

"Workers of the World Unite!" Izzie said, feeling slightly half-hearted, and chinked her bottle against Simaynesh's. She took a long drink. It was lovely and cool.

Simaynesh put her bottle down on the Formica coffee table, the corners chipped and peeling. Books with tobacco brown pages were stacked underneath; some had been covered with newspaper, hiding the titles. Must be left over from student days.

"Uschi would be mortified," Izzie said. "'Ha!' she would have said, 'What about my beautiful Burda designs? All my lovely children's clothes?'"

"Uschi's gone. Long gone. The kids, the Heroes' children, need uniforms."

"Are you really going with them?"

"To Cuba? Yes, of course. There are about fifty of us social workers assigned to fly with them to 'Youth Island'. We'll settle them in and come back. I'm looking forward to it." Simaynesh crooked her head to one side like a bird contemplating, then nodded definitively, as if convinced and took another drink.

"Sounds like something out of a fairy tale: 'Youth Island'."

"There were pirates on the island hundreds of years ago. I think that book, Peter Pan, was based on it." Simaynesh laughed. "Mindin neouw? You look surprised by all this."

"I'm just trying to get my head round it. These kids lose their dads fighting on the front in Eritrea…"

"…and Tigray and the Ogaden." Simaynesh took another sip of beer. "For the Motherland." She raised her bottle.

Izzie clinked her bottle against Simaynesh's. "They get put in a boarding school specially for them. And now they are being sent en masse to school in Cuba. It's so far away."

"That's right. But it's good for them. My youngest brother went to school there. He was the only one, out of seven of us, that got the chance. He went on to university in Havana. He's done really well."

"Is he still there?"

"Of course. Why would he come back? He's got a job. He's a successful engineer. He married an Ethiopian girl who also studied there.

Maybe one day they'll go to the U.S., who knows?"

"And will they have to learn and study in Spanish?"

"As well as," Simaynesh said. "There are Ethiopian teachers there too. So they learn in Spanish and Amharic."

Izzie could not make out if Simaynesh approved of the kids going, or not. So many people had left Ethiopia at the time of the revolution and Red Terror. So many qualified and trained people. She could not imagine Simaynesh, or Gezahegn, leaving. "I can't help feeling sorry for those children though. Do you think they're well looked after? I mean do they still get to eat injera?"

Simaynesh laughed outright. "Why do you always have to feel sorry, Izzie? One thing is, they will have to work hard in school and on the school farms. Of course. But it's good for them. They are the lucky ones. And yes, I am sure they will get to eat injera. I am sure we export teff to Cuba. There are so many Ethiopians there by now. I will tell you when I get back." She patted Izzie on the knee. Still smiling her amusement.

"I suppose." Izzie still bore the impressions and heat of the day. Beginning of October and still no rains. They should have started around May, June time. They had stood in a large military parade ground, under the sun for hours; listening to long speeches, watching the display, the marching children, row upon row of boys and girls dressed in the uniforms stitched at the garment factory in Nazareth. Yellow shirt sleeves, brown skirts and trouser pieces had been fed, treadles clacking, under whirring needles for the past two months. The colours were awful. They reminded her of the old banana-split toffees. Yellow and brown. But she had not been able to do anything about it. The bales of cloth had been delivered, probably from another state factory, or imported from the Soviet Union. Solid durable cloth. She hoped it didn't itch.

A barking Kebele announcement echoed from the street below.

"There they go again," Izzie said. The words were muffled. "What do they want now?"

Simaynesh swiped the air in disgust. "The same. Calling for all men to sign up for the front. Eighteen to thirty-year-olds."

Izzie shook her head and took another handful of popcorn.

"What is it, my friend? We did a good job, enday. You did a good job. Without you the factory wouldn't be there."

It was an unusual complement coming from Simaynesh. But Izzie knew it wasn't just down to her, though she had put all her effort behind it, getting funding and materials to make it happen.

"Well, not just me, to be fair. Gezahegn was always full behind it, and

Genet, especially her, she has worked her socks off. Then there's the guys in Nazareth."

"Let's just say it has been a great team effort. I would never have thought it when I first saw you that day, with Uschi, in Gezahegn's office."

"You know," Izzie said, ignoring Simaynesh's jibe. "It felt like quite something to have been invited to that massive event. The only farenj." There had been literally hundreds and hundreds of school children, all sizes, standing in rows, wearing their new uniforms. Extraordinary. And then the military in their uniforms. Standing to attention while speeches were made.

"It's what the Central Committee like. All that parading. And yes, to invite a farenj. Hmmm." Simaynesh looked sideways at her, smiling. "And not a very high profile one at that…"

"Drop it!" Izzie said, laughing. "Enough. I wanted to say something else. You know Girma, the one with the shrivelled up legs?"

"The one who used to beg outside Meskel coffee shop?"

"That's right," Izzie stretched. Her leg had gone to sleep. "Now he's got a wheelchair and a job. He's renting a small room and sleeps under a roof for the first time in years."

"Good for him," Simaynesh sucked her teeth.

"When he got his first pay packet, he waved down a taxi-gari[69] to take him around town. He had them lift him out of his wheelchair and into the buggy and off he went, laughing like a king."

"Egziyabher sifeked, with God's permission, anything is possible. Let's hope we can keep the factory going." Simaynesh patted Izzie's leg again. Her hands were small with short nails. Everything about her was compact.

"But making uniforms, that was not the point," Izzie said. "We had a beautiful range of children's clothes." She finished her beer. "Genet put so much effort into creating the first designs."

The next Government order was already on the cutting tables, Peasant Association uniforms. Grey khaki. It was depressing. Even Girma and the other workers complained about it.

"Those guys have a job and the factory has orders, that's the main thing. Aydellem enday, farenj? Am I right or am I right?" Her eyes sparkled triumphantly. She looked beautiful when she smiled. Otherwise she could be quite intimidating.

---

[69] A horse-drawn buggy.

Izzie had noticed Simaynesh's eyes when they first met in Gezahegn's office. They had a harshness in them which had put her off. She never imagined they would become friends. "I thought you were incapable of smiling when I first met you," Izzie said, "let alone laughing."

"We Ethiopians are careful making friends. We will smile and chat with you, we'll invite you. But trust you? Trust anyone? Some of us don't even trust our family members."

"You trust me, though, don't you?"

"Of course," Simaynesh said. They looked at each other and laughed. There was that double edge again. They both knew it.

The pick-up truck carrying the voice with the tannoy was outside again. Metallic barking came up from the road below. Like a carrion bird bringing foreboding news of death and destruction, it cawed on and on.

Izzie shivered. The sky had become darker and the air cool. "Can I shut the window?"

"Sure. I'll put a light on." Simaynesh went over to the side board and switched on a wooden carved lamp, lighting up colourful figures of women wearing traditional dresses, making coffee and spinning cotton, painted onto the ox-skin shade. "You know, in Tigray and Eritrea the women are proud to be freedom fighters. They are all equal. Here we don't expect women to join up but I think we should fight, if the men have to."

"I guess so," Izzie said, wondering how enthusiastic Simaynesh really felt about the idea. "I just can't understand why you Ethiopians have to keep on fighting each other and even more so now, with the famine on our doorstep."

"You know, if my little brother were here, he would be in the air force."

"Is that so great? He would have to bomb innocent villagers."

"They are not all innocent, Izzie. Eritrea is part of Ethiopia and we have to protect our interests. Not all Eritreans want independence. There are so many Eritreans here in Addis. They want to stay part of Ethiopia."

"But everyone is terrified of their kids going to the front." Izzie was once again struck by how cold and pragmatic Simaynesh could be. "Did you hear what Genet said in the office the other day? She wished she could eat her boy back inside. He's only fourteen but is as tall as a twenty-year-old. She's afraid they'll see him and take him."

"I know, there are all sorts of stories. Egziyabher yawkal. When my mother's neighbours heard the Kebele were coming house to house, they hid their two boys inside a cupboard; locked them in. When they refused to say where the boys were, the Kebele arrested them. By the time they got home again the children had suffocated."

"You're joking."

"Befitsum. I promise you."

Izzie looked away and found herself staring at two slightly worn black and white photos. They hung on the wall in simple wooden frames above the lamp. A middle aged man in national dress with fine features stared out of one, his face dead-pan serious. Next to him a similarly sombre woman, her face framed by a thin white shawl, beneath which she wore the inevitable black scarf bound tightly round her head. Father and Mother. Similar photos hung on most sitting room walls. The subjects looked as if they knew the gravity of their place, on the wall. And of their time in history, under Haile Selassie. "Do you have a photo of your brother?" Izzie said.

"Over there," Simaynesh pointed at the side board, but she did not go and get it.

"They don't get much training, do they, these conscripts?" Izzie said. "Are they even properly armed?"

"You love Ethiopia, Izzie, but its people do terrible things to each other. For what, you might ask? Egziyabher yawkal. Only God knows."

"If there's a God at all." Izzie lit two cigarettes and passed one to Simaynesh. She drew on it until it crackled. It seemed as if God had forsaken this country and still the flocks of white-shawled women gathered in the church compounds, humming and praying, sucking their teeth. They gathered, wailing and praying around the buses and trucks which took their husbands, sons and brothers off to the front, every morning after curfew broke, at five a.m. Many would not return.

"Tell me about your latest assignment in Ambo."

"It was very different to the trip I made there last year with Moe. I loved the little church in Addis Alem. They didn't like us taking photos though. And it was all locked up."

"Mariam? We should have gone there for the Meskel celebrations. There's too much politics going on. I miss the religious festivals. We used to have a great bonfire in Meskel Square, what's now Revolution Square. Anyway, tell me, how did it go?" Simaynesh cleared her throat imitating Gezahegn, and in a deeper voice, said, "And your job description is to do what I tell you to do."

Izzie laughed. "Well sort of, it was actually Comrade Adugna who asked me to go. He wanted to hear what a great job Ethiopia is doing for the war heroes. It was awful. He won't be very happy when I give him my report."

"What's going on there? I thought they had a good rehabilitation centre there for them?"

"What is it about planners?" Izzie said. "Why do they always come up with sewing for women and disabled? You have two hundred young men, give or take, sitting behind machines in a factory miles from anywhere, with a leg or an arm missing, making underwear. Underwear, Simiye. It's a God-forsaken place for young people. Most of them are boys, young lads. Nothing to do. Young soldiers stitching very badly finished underwear which the project manager says no one wants to buy. It's like something out of a Monty Python sketch."

"Monty Python?"

"A comedy programme at home." Home felt very far away these days. "They want to be mechanics, they want to study, play football, have families but they get no support. No psychological rehabilitation to help them live with their new disabilities. A lot of them are depressed. They want to watch movies. And why not?"

"There is no money for rehab. This is how we are forced to treat our Heroes," Simaynesh said. "They get back from the front and are often too ashamed to go home, or home is too far away and they have no money to get there. They get rounded up and put into centres. That's what we do."

"They said we were the first people who actually asked them what they wanted. How they felt. I was sorry."

"There you go again, farenj. No good feeling sorry. We have to take action with the small resources available to us."

"Resources? They work short shifts because there's not enough cloth, not enough pairs of scissors, no buttons and the button-hole machines don't work. And that apart, they are young. What about a life. They're bored. What about girls, women, the chance to get married, have a home, have kids? Most of our disabled knotting carpets in the Agertebeb workshop, and our workers with leprosy, have families, children. And at least what they produce is beautiful. Really beautiful."

"Fighting and mending. That's what we are doing. You know we have all these prosthetics workshops around the country: in Addis, Mekele, Asmara, Harar. Ibd nen. We are crazy. We must be the biggest producers of limbs in the world. We'll be exporting them next." Simaynesh got up. "Let's talk about something else."

"How about love. Fikrey yelleshim enday, Simiye?"

"If I have a lover?" Simaynesh laughed. "Of course."

"Really?" Izzie could not imagine Simaynesh being romantic. She fought everything around her; men, the system. Gezahegn had said Simaynesh had been politically active as a student at the time of the revolution and had been in prison. That she had been lucky to come out alive. "I thought you said we don't need men?"

"I don't. Not like you need your Moe."

Izzie shrugged, feeling uncomfortable. She wished Moe loved her the way he had when they were first together. But it wasn't the same for her either. When they were together they argued over petty things. It was tiring. "I don't know any more, Simaynesh. Sometimes I wonder if my work is getting more important than him. Anyway. Tell me about your man. Do I know him?"

"Tall as a giraffe, black as a night sky, teeth like a Colgate advertisement, dances like a Guragey." Simaynesh smiled with a hand over her mouth, her eyes shining wickedly.

"Simi," Izzie shrieked. "You are kidding me. Or, wait a minute. Let me guess. Is he one of those tall, tall guys from Senegal? I've seen them at the ECA and sometimes on Piazza. Everyone stares at them. Very handsome."

Simaynesh lit the candle on the table, smiling to herself. She took a handful of popcorn, chucking them in her mouth. "You hungry too?"

"Enday, you don't get off that easy, yeney konjo," Izzie said.

"Be semaam, come on, of course he's not one of them. That would be too obvious, huh."

"Anchee, don't tease. I promise not to say a word. Not a word."

"OK, he's a Nigerian. He works in the OAU and I met him through my cousin. He is not staying long. Maybe another three months. So we are just having a bit of fun. There. Now you have it. That's it."

"Wow," Izzie said, feeling quite the innocent. "So that's how it's done."

"Keep it simple, Izzie. You get too wrapped up, involved. You expect too much. It gets complicated."

"You are right, too right."

"I am still hungry, how about you?" Simaynesh said. "Let's go to The Hong Kong, shall we?"

"Good idea."

"When does Moe get back?"

"In a couple of days. Friday, I think."

"Did he go up north?"

"No he's gone down to Arussi. Wondwossen at the Relief Council wants them to go up north, but they can't get travel permits. He wants the farenj community to see what is going on for themselves. He can't seem to convince them just how bad the famine is. Moe gets it. He's so frustrated."

"So is he the one, Izzie?"

"Marriage?" Izzie had a sneaking feeling he wouldn't commit. "Don't know. Probably not. Oh sod it."

"You're too dependent on Moe." Simaynesh was pulling a light jacket over her shoulders. "Come on, let's go."

Izzie got up and pulled on her old khaki jacket. "We were so passionate. I miss that."

"Then it's over."

"It's not just about sex. We make love but it's the emotion, the loving. The look he used to have in his eyes."

"That's fairy tales, Izzie. Romantic stuff. You need to get tougher."

"I am getting tougher," Izzie said on the defensive. "As I said, I don't think it's just him."

"You love your work. That's good. What's he up to when you're in Nazareth or Ambo?"

"Usual stuff, I suppose. He goes to the British Embassy Club, runs the Hash, out with Tom in some bar on the Debre Zeit road."

"You're becoming a real habesha, Izzie. He needs his farenj."

"I wish I were more like you."

"You're good, Izzie. I wouldn't change you. You just need to toughen up a bit that's all. Let's go eat. We women need our food."

23

Genet had not been in the office or called for a week. Izzie sat behind her typewriter, tapping ash off the end of her cigarette. The pit of her stomach flickered nervously at the thought that Genet might have been arrested. Day-time Addis was relatively peaceful. Albeit an uneasy peace. A sense of security was held in place by Kebele guards, like stitches on a worn out shirt, they held things together with their long sticks and old rifles. They walked between the shacks, in their old coats and jackets, pinched, drawn faces; observing, collecting information, giving orders, updating lists of who lived where. They were men and women who had thrown old neighbourhood friendships to the winds of mistrust. The Kebele were part of the foreground and backdrop. Just like poverty. They pervaded everything, a daily assault on human dignity. And despite all that, neighbours greeted each other, smiled and laughed. The small group of women who chatted outside Girma's small suk in the early morning, youngsters coming out of Mahmoud's music shop at the top of Piazza after school, Hailu and the boys playing outside the Blue Nile Bar.

And then there were the soldiers, who would suddenly be there one morning, or late of an evening, creating a sense of uncertainty. They would appear standing at intervals in doorways, on a street corner, and all the way down Churchill. Their army fatigues tucked into heavy black boots, Kalashnikovs held loosely but always at the ready. "Security's tight", people would say. "Security's tight." But what did that mean? The war was getting closer? Eritrea, Tigray, Gondar, the Ogaden were all far away. A coup was anticipated? But who would dare. The kites circled high in the sky on the winds of hot air, the crows hopped and cawed on korkorro rooftops, an ugly menace. The Kebele guards' and the soldiers' intermittent appearances were a constant reminder of grim possibility, of incidents behind closed doors, of those already languishing in prisons around the city. Experiences that, as an ex-pat, she was exempt from.

Even if the woman was not political, someone in her family might be. Logic, statistical probability and recent history told Izzie that there had to be shadows behind peoples' smiles and laughter; family members and acquaintances still being arrested at night, interrogations. Everyone she met was warm and laughing, so it was easy to push to one side, until something happened. Like Genet not coming to work.

Izzie wished she could just be cross or indignant with the woman for not being there. She needed her. They had just got in the second order for Peasant Association uniforms. That miserable grey khaki. Bolts and bolts of the cloth piled up in the store. They had to check the patterns and get the machines whirring.

The thought of Genet made her stomach turn again. She looked at her watch. She would ask Gezahegn what he thought when he came in. Although Comrade Adugna was now her official head of department, she still considered Gezahegn her boss. He had now been assigned to a new project with Simaynesh under Ato Solomon's Planning Department. They were drawing up plans for an assessment and field trips which would happen when the so-called Experts came from Geneva. Another programme for the disabled in Ethiopia funded by an international organisation. A significant proportion of the funds would be going to ex-pat salaries, their air fares, housing and their children's school fees. It just didn't make sense when the expertise was already there in-country.

Anyway Comrade Adugna was the last person she would want to ask about Genet if something untoward had happened to her. She would rather get Gezahegn's take on it first. She went over to the window to see if his car was there. And there it was, a battered old thing, like a faithful mule. She would go to his office. This couldn't wait. She had to do something to calm her nerves. She went up the two flights of stairs, holding onto the metal rail and getting out of breath.

She knocked on his door and waited for his grunt before going in.

"Ah! Good morning," he said. "Tenasteling. What can I do for you? Coffee?" He lent back to push the buzzer on the wall behind him.

She sat on the chair opposite him catching her breath. "The altitude," she said.

"Not the cigarettes?" He smiled ironically.

She waved her hand in denial. "It's a week since Genet was last in. She hasn't called or anything. We need her in Nazareth tomorrow." She suddenly felt like a child blurting everything out.

"Maybe she's sick. What do you want me to do about it?"

"Help me find a reason. I am worried. She's never sick. She would have called. She knows we have the next order in. What shall I do?"

Desta came in with her metal tray and a quizzical, 'What is it to be, I know already,' look on her face. She looked at Gezahegn, said, "Ishi," quietly and backed out again.

"I thought I would find you here," Simaynesh burst in. "Come to see your Uncle?" Simaynesh looked at Gezahegn. "No, it's OK I saw Desta. She's bringing me a coffee too and three Samosa."

"I just had breakfast," Izzie said.

"I'm starving," Simaynesh said.

"Genet's missing," Gezahegn said, throwing a look in Izzie's direction.

"We can't do without her," Izzie said.

"You're right. Genet seems to have vanished. I thought maybe she was sick. They don't have a phone at home, otherwise I would have called. You're right. It's been a week."

"Do you know where she lives?" Izzie said.

"Genet? Somewhere in Mercato, I think," Simaynesh said.

There was a noise outside the door.

"Ask Ato Embaye, he'll know her address," Gezahegn said, getting up. He opened the door. Desta stood on the other side with a tray full of coffee and samosa. She looked so small next to him. "Egziyabheresteling, thank you, Desta," he said, as she walked across the room to place the tray on his desk. "Why not go and see if she's at home."

"Shall I?" Izzie said.

"Sure," Simaynesh said. "We can go together. Let's eat first and then we'll go. Thanks Desta, yeney konjo."

Desta bowed her head slightly, smiled her shy smile and left the room.

**

Ato Embaye's job was to do the payroll. He carefully folded everyone's pay into small brown envelopes and took their signatures in a large ledger on receipt, at the end of every month. His tweed jacket had worn thin and hung loosely from his shoulders. He was Eritrean and listened to the radio in Tigrinya, Italian, English and Amharic and guessed at French when he tuned into Radio de Djibouti. He kept everyone in Izzie's office up to date on the news and the fighting in Eritrea and ranted on about Mengistu's false propaganda. He said the Eritreans were much stronger than the Derg made out. He pooh-poohed the risk he took, coming to work every day with bright eyes and stories from his night-time vigil by the radio. He said he kept the sound down, in case the neighbours reported him to the Kebele. "Me, a counter-revolutionary? They wouldn't bother arresting a skinny old pauper like me."

He said Maggie Thatcher was 'England's Theodros'. If anyone challenged him that she did not fling her opponents off cliff tops, or chop their hands and feet off, he would remind them that Mrs Thatcher charged police horses at her very own coal miners. "What is the difference?" he would say. "What is the difference?"

He had ten children to feed on the minimum wage of fifty Birr a week. He could remember their names but not their birthdays. His wife wove beautiful round table mats from long strips of dried elephant grass to add to their income.

Izzie found him in his small office in the basement. He was sat tapping a calculator, which regurgitated a ribbon of paper across his square wooden desk.

"Izzie," he said, getting up and wiping his hands down the sides of his jacket. "Dehenaneshwey? How are you doing?"

His hand was strong and bony in hers.

"I'm fine Egziyabheresteling, Ato Embaye. How's work?"

"It's good. It's good,"

" And your wife and the children? How are they?"

"Everyone is fine, Egziyabher yimesgen, Izzie." He shook his head with a wry smile. "Here I sit on a pot of honey. At home there's not a centime left. You know the price of teff has quadrupled?"

"I know. It's terrible," Izzie said. "How do you manage?"

"Kebele rations." Ato Embaye rolled his eyes to the ceiling, "Egziyabher yawkal. God only knows, we are fine."

Izzie wanted to move on to Genet but allowed a moment to pass out of respect, and in deference to the Almighty, in case He was there, listening.

"Ato Embaye," she said. "I'm worried about Genet."

"You think the hyenas have come in the night and dragged her away?" He grinned and winked.

Izzie looked behind her at the open door. "You think?"

"Heaven only knows, yeney konjo," he said, wiping a hand over the fine grey hair that covered his scalp. His soft brown eyes suddenly looked gentle and sad in his finely chiselled, almost skeletal, face.

Izzie lowered her voice. "Do you have her address? Simaynesh and I want to go to her place. See if everything is alright."

"Yes, that's right." Ato Embaye turned to a tall metal filing cabinet and pulled a drawer out. "Genet Teshome," he said. He knew everyone in the building. "Send her my greetings."

**

The maid at Genet's house stood barefoot in the crack of the open door. "They went to Kidane Meheret," she whispered.

Simaynesh sucked her teeth, "What happened? Genet went too? Someone's sick?" she rattled her questions out.

Izzie noticed Simaynesh had stuck her foot in the door so the girl could not shut it even if she wanted to. The nerves Izzie had been controlling on the drive from the office finally surfaced. Tears welled in her eyes. She put a hand on Simaynesh's arm wanting her to be gentler.

"Yes," the girl said in a small high voice. "I don't know," she said and took a step backwards into the darkness behind her. "I don't know." She obviously thought she had said enough.

**

"Where is Kidane Meheret? Is that the church up on Entoto?" Izzie said. "Negisst has been there." She was relieved. At least Genet was not locked up in the darkness of the cell her mind had been conjuring up; had not been picked up by the soldiers in the night, black-booted, khaki uniformed, in their short-wheelbase jeeps.

"Yes, that's right. It's a church on Entoto," Simaynesh said, sucking her teeth loudly. "They must have gone for holy waters. It has to be something serious for them to go there."

"I put some petrol in the tank yesterday," Izzie said. "Let's go see, shall we?" She would risk Moe's wrath for using up too much of their fuel ration. "You know the way, don't you?"

"Sure. Just take a right out of here and we'll head out of town, up Entoto mountain."

Driving the 2CV over dirt roads always felt like riding a horse, clambering over boulders, veering over to one side and then to the other. Izzie slowed down to pass a woman, bowed double under a stack of firewood, and her two laden donkeys. The strong smell of donkey-hide reminded her of pony-treks and Dorset countryside. It wafted in through the window. They stumbled along, hooves clacking. The thick strips of rubber, strapped round their loads and under their tails, stretched and squeaked. Izzie drove slowly, watching carefully in the wing mirrors, hoping she wouldn't scratch the side of the car. Moe would be livid.

So many things made him cross these days. It was bound to be wrapped up with her. Leila always said, "No! Izzie, lovely. It's not you. He has so much going on in his head right now. It's the famine and no one apparently doing anything about it. And like Fasika says, the Relief Council want the international community to take action now. They are just not listening." There was a lot of tension around for sure.

A small boy with a stick across his skinny shoulders stood and stared at the car. Izzie could see him jump to life in the mirror as soon as they had driven past.

"Farenj, Farenj," he shouted, waving his stick.

Simaynesh leant across Izzie, "Habesha, Habesha," she called through the window and laughed for a moment.

Izzie smiled, looking at her friend. She was pretty when she laughed.

They had been circling up and up the track for about twenty minutes. "How much further do you think it is?" Izzie was starting to worry that she would use up all their fuel on this expedition.

"Not far," Simaynesh said.

"Is that a farenj 'not far', or a habesha 'not far'?" The Ethiopian 'not far' could mean anything from twenty metres to another hour in the car. Izzie prayed it was the former.

"Just keep following the road, yeney konjo."

Simaynesh was obviously not sure. Izzie looked up at the sun's rays spotting through the eucalyptus and breathed in the warm smell. "Do you believe the church can heal people?"

"Absolutely. It's surprising what God can do, when you can't afford a doctor, or a traditional healer," Simaynesh said. "It's called faith."

"Negisst's mother is a *wogeysha*,[70]" Izzie said. "She gave me a massage with eucalyptus oil the other day."

"For your stiff shoulder? You're joking. You didn't tell us."

"I thought you would laugh," Izzie felt a little sheepish. "And see, I was right."

"And?"

"It was agony."

"Anchee," Simaynesh put a hand on Izzie's arm.

---

[70] Traditional physio.

"She told me to take a salt bath afterwards. The next day the pain was completely gone. I couldn't believe it."

"You're becoming a real habesha. I keep saying it."

Izzie shook her head and smiled. She didn't know what made her want to be like her Ethiopian friends, to be part of them, but she did.

A rock hit the bottom of the car with a jarring clunk. "Oops," Izzie said, steering up onto a verge sparsely scattered with brush. It was all so dry.

"Here, turn in here," Simaynesh said, pointing up towards the left.

"Aha," Izzie said, "A farenj 'not far'." She turned off and climbed the hill, the engine straining.

A round church with a wooden veranda, its tin roof glinting in the sun, appeared at the end of the road, surrounded by thin stands of eucalyptus. To the left was a row of huts and a wide dirt path lined intermittently with clumps of sisal.

Izzie brought the car to a halt and switched off the engine. That was when she heard the loud guttural noise, like a gagged animal. Two men and a plump woman in a long skirt, a thick white gabi wrapped round her head and shoulders, were half-carrying, half-dragging a young woman between them up the path. They were obviously trying to get her to the church. She was putting up intense resistance, throwing her head back, buckling her knees under and pulling away, her elbows jutting in and out.

"My God," Izzie's knees felt weak. "It can't be."

"Genet," Simaynesh called out, and ran over to the miserable troupe.

Izzie followed, not sure what to do in the commotion but watch in horror. As she and Simaynesh drew near, the struggle stopped. Genet's hair, usually neatly straightened, long and shiny, stood out in a tangled mess around her head and over her shoulders. Her face was filthy. She wore a traditional white cotton dress which had become dirty. Her feet were bare. For a moment she hung limp in her custodians' arms. Her blood-shot eyes stared from dark sunken sockets, without recognition. She held her cheeks sucked in and there were drops of dried blood on her pursed lips. She yelled suddenly, as if something had taken hold of her. She went into a shock of spasms, almost knocking over the sturdy woman holding her.

She should see a doctor. Someone qualified, calm, someone in a knee-length white coat. Somewhere clean. "We should take her to hospital," Izzie said, stepping forward and felt Simaynesh's hand restrain her.

"Weyne, Weyne, be Egziyabher," the woman wailed. "Yeney lij, yeney hod ena samba lij."

"What's she saying?" Izzie said. The woman reminded her of Negisst.

"She must be Genet's mother," Simaynesh said, still holding Izzie's arm. "She's praying to God. She's calling Genet child of her belly and lungs. It's a saying to show just how much she loves her. Like, 'the air that she breathes'."

"Weyne, be Egziyabher. Yeney lij," the woman went on, apparently emboldened by their presence.

"The buda has taken our sister's soul," one of the men said, his brow lined with worry. "Our mother, she -,"

"Come on," the other said, nodding his head towards the church. "They've already started."

"Go, go," Simaynesh said. "We'll follow."

Izzie stood, watching aghast, as the four struggled down the path and up the steps onto the veranda, like ants transporting a morsel of food. "What's the buda?"

"The evil eye," Simaynesh said, quite serious.

Izzie found herself torn between everything she had grown up with and her faith in Simaynesh. She tried to reshape her thoughts around the idea that the buda was possible, that Genet was possessed and that she was in the right place.

The wooden doors to the church stood open. From the dim interior came the deep rhythmical chanting and murmuring of priests. Izzie hoped the sound would give her some solace too.

"Here, Izzie, take your shoes off."

Izzie felt reassured when Simaynesh took her hand. She followed her friend's footsteps into the church. Inside was loud and chaotic. There was a stuffy smell of sweat, unwashed hair and old socks, laced with incense. The thick smell filled Izzie's nose. She wriggled spaces for her feet between the prostrate bodies, legs, hands and feet around her. She stood close to Simaynesh against the wall. People were leaning on wooden prayer sticks, sitting and lying on the ground, praying and weeping, some swaying back and forth, over and over. Izzie looked at Simaynesh. Her eyes were closed, her lips moving. She had let go of Izzie's hand. Izzie wondered if she could catch something in this crowded, muggy place. If so it was too late, she was in there now.

Priests, wearing round maroon velvet hats and voluminous robes, held intricately carved wooden and silver crosses in their hands. They chanted in warm monotonous waves of deep, soothing sound. A small boy, wrapped in a thin white cotton shawl, stood holding a long taper; his wide eyes looked straight ahead. The boy and the priests stood in a semicircle in front of thick curtains and a faded fresco of Georgis on his white horse, lit up by flickering candle-light. Georgis the rescuer, poised above the dragon with his spear lifted high.

Genet sat on the ground nearest the priest, the one leading the liturgy. Izzie followed Genet's staring eyes to the wall and a painting of the crucifixion. Genet's face was more relaxed than before, her lips slightly parted. Genet's mother sat beside her, stroking her hair and muttering. Every now and then she lifted Genet's hand to her lips.

One by one people moved towards the curtains, knelt and kissed the ground. A woman pulled her small boy by his arm, so skinny, and made him kiss the ground too. When they turned, Izzie could see his wide eyes and the trail of tears down his dirty cheeks.

"The sacred tabot is behind the curtains," Simaynesh whispered.

"What's the tabot?"

Simaynesh leant close to Izzie's ear, "It's the ark of the covenant. It holds the ten commandments."

Izzie felt humbled by the fact that she was there, by Simaynesh's humility, her belief. She closed her eyes to allow the chanting, murmuring voices to fill her mind and soul, to send her own message to heaven. "Please God, Egziyabher, make Genet better. Make these people better. Stop their suffering. Look at them, be Egziyabher, they don't deserve it. Make them better, make them better. Please God, if you are there, make Genet better."

The priest moved from one person to the next, murmuring, his tongue clicking, repeating the words, "Be'simeab weld wemenfes Kidus",[71] as he rested his cross on their heads. When he finally came to Genet, he bent over and chanted in a low sing-song voice. The elder of the two brothers held her sitting up, as the priest rubbed the cross slowly over her head and face, her chest and back.

Simaynesh nodded towards the crucifixion, "Yesus," she said. "Yesus will rid her of the buda."

It seemed Genet was the last to receive a blessing. The priest stood up and made a sign of the cross. People started slowly moving towards the square of light in the open doorway and out of the church.

Izzie stood waiting for Simaynesh to give her the cue to leave.

Genet's keepers were trying to get her out of the church.

Once more she put up a fight, this time it seemed she wanted to stay

---

[71] In the name of the Father, the Son and the Holy Ghost.

in the church. When they reached the door she began howling and straining, her hands and feet jammed against the frame of the doorway.

Some women came and spoke to the mother. The family let go of Genet and stood by watching, as she crawled back into the church. A priest bent down and took her hand. She sat on the floor looking up at him as he hit her with short sharp taps round her face and hands until she lay prostrate before the crucifixion.

"My God," Izzie whispered. "Now what?"

"Just wait," Simaynesh said.

The priest nodded to Genet's mother, who moved towards her with the two men. They turned her round to a sitting position and lifted her out of the church. She struggled some more. One of the men took a scarf and tied her wrists together. Finally, they were outside.

Izzie realised her own fists were clenched in her pockets and that she was biting her lip. "Let's get out of here," she said and moved towards the door. She had to get out into the sunshine.

When Simaynesh joined her, Izzie concentrated on getting her shoes on to hide the tears. "We should take her to hospital," she said. It came out low and gruff.

"What is it?" Simaynesh said. "You saw how she calmed down in the church."

"Look Simaynesh," Izzie said, pointing down the path. "They're carrying her away trussed up like a goat and we are standing here, watching?"

"The priest said she's been here seven days and he's seen a huge change. She was like a wild animal."

"And now she's not, or what?" Izzie headed for the car, struggling with her emotions. She suddenly needed to be with Moe, the Moe that used to be. That Moe would have comforted her. She could weep.

Simaynesh got in the car beside her. "What is it yeney konjo? Ayezosh, she will get better."

"I wish I had your faith." Izzie wiped her nose on her sleeve and opened the window beside her.

"Did you not see the kindness in the priest's eyes? He cares for all these people. He is God's messenger. He will cure her."

Izzie started the engine; the familiar tumble dryer. "I hate leaving her here."

"Is she your sister?" Simaynesh laughed, a little harshly Izzie thought. "Don't worry. We will come. If she's not back in a week, we'll come back, ishi?"

Izzie drove back down the mountain path. The sun was dipping down, sending out rays amongst the tree trunks. A soft haze lay above the dry scrub. "It's beautiful here, and so close to the city."

"Gezahegn will wonder where we got to," Simaynesh said, lighting one of Izzie's cigarettes.

"Light one for me will you?" Izzie glanced at her watch. "He'll be at home eating his injera by now."

"Is it so late?"

**

It was dark by the time Izzie drove down the alleyway past Girma's hole-in-the-wall suk. A naked bulb hung from the ceiling on a short wire. She could see the yellow tins of baby-milk powder and blue and white Omo boxes stacked on the shelves behind him. She honked her horn twice. He waved back, smiling. How was it that they were always smiling? Always laughing? She could do with a drink; a long cold beer, a cigarette and someone to talk to.

She nearly tripped over Moe's bag in the hall, its innards spilled onto the floor. What was he doing back so soon? Her stomach turned. There were no lights on and no sound. She crept through to the bedroom. Lights reflected into the room from Piazza below, displaying Negisst's work. The bed tightly made up, smoothed flat.

A piece of paper, torn from a notebook, lay on the dining table beside the stack of neatly woven mats.

Where are you? Have gone for a beer with Tom. Where's the car?
Moe.

She sat, turning the paper round in her fingers, staring at the table. A numbness in her limbs and mind. She would sit there for hours if she didn't do something about it. She lifted her t-shirt to her nose and sniffed. All those people, the disease, the madness clung to the white cotton. The morning suddenly seemed a long time ago. She went and changed. Got her old khaki jacket, put some Birr, cigarettes and matches and the car keys into the pockets, and went out of the door.

Maybe they were in Almaz's bar. If not, maybe she'd have a beer with Almaz. She would know about the buda, about Kidane Meheret. Maybe she could talk to Almaz about Moe. If anyone knew how to get the man back, she would. Izzie put the thought away as soon as it entered her head.

Even though it was not late, and others sharing the narrow path towards the bar took no notice of her. Izzie was slightly unsure about her decision to venture out on her own. She did not like the anxious feeling in her stomach. The anticipation of seeing Moe, if he was there, and the possibility of being in Almaz's bar on her own, if he was not. She walked, hands in pockets, down the pathway. A shaft of light lit up the corrugated iron fencing opposite the bar and she could hear the music. Ethiopian eskista. The sound lifted her spirits and she was smiling as she walked through the door, now looking forward to Almaz's surprise at seeing her and the woman's warm greeting. A few regulars were there, including the old man sitting at his usual table by the window. A young man was dancing up close to the skinny bar girl on platforms, her head hung like a drooped flower and moved slowly, side to side with the rhythm.

Hearing Moe's laughter, Izzie looked sharply across to the other side of the bar. She saw his mop of sandy hair. He had his back to her, with Almaz on his knee, her arm around his shoulders. There was no sign of Tom. A young man in a baseball cap nodded at Moe and then raised his eyes towards Izzie.

She wished she could turn and run but she could hardly breathe, let alone move.

Almaz looked over Moe's shoulder. Her face lit up.

The neon light strip, the metal tables and chairs, the row of whiskey bottles on the shelf behind the bar, Moe's old brown desert boots, all seemed to cascade around her. She put a hand out and caught hold of the back of a chair.

Moe had turned round and was probably looking at her.

Almaz was making her way over between the tables, her arms open wide. "Izzie," she said. "How are you, yeney konjo?"

Cheap perfume and the bitter smell of khat, overwhelmed her as she was enveloped in Almaz's embrace. The woman kissed her on each cheek several times.

Izzie pulled away, wanting to get out.

"Anchee. You disappeared," Almaz said, not letting go of Izzie's arms.

She did not want to be held on to. "I didn't disappear," Izzie said, moving away, anger shooting through her like an electric impulse.

"Izzie," Moe said. He was suddenly standing beside her.

She could sense his strength, his unrelenting self-confidence. "Just let me go?" Izzie turned towards the door and pushed past two men coming in. They had obviously already been drinking elsewhere and were now looking for another beer.

Moe caught up with her on the path. "Hey, honey," he said.

"Don't honey me," she said.

"Where were you?"

"Who cares?" Izzie walked as determinedly as she could back up the path to where she had parked the car. "I got your message, thanks." She wished she could be more grown-up but didn't know who was wrong and who was right in their relationship. "Having a good time are you?"

"For God's sake stop." He grabbed her arm.

"I wanted a beer with a friend," she said, trying not to cry.

"Almaz? Honey, you wanted a beer with Almaz?"

She could not bear the hint of pity and amusement in his voice. "I was looking for you, funnily enough," she said. "And thought I would have a beer with her if you were not there."

"She's not your friend."

"She's yours is she? Well obviously."

"She's a businesswoman. Her business is booze and sex. She's not interested in us, in you."

"Done good business tonight, has she? Paid extra for the madam of the house, did you?"

"Don't even go there, Izzie. If you calm down we can go back in and have a beer."

"Why is it always me? Why are you always telling me to calm down? You come back, leave a cold, unfriendly note, 'Where's the car?'" she was almost shouting. A group had gathered to watch, some giggling. "It's up there. On the road. If you want to know. I'll walk home." She took the keys out of her pocket, threw them up in the air for him to catch, wishing she could be with him instead of shouting at him and walking away.

She walked back up the path at a pace. If he followed and made up, alright, if not she would find a way to comfort herself. Have a drink at home.

She didn't hear his voice, or footsteps on the path behind her, just felt his hand on her shoulder and his arm draw her close.

"Honey," he said quietly. "I'm hungry, how about you?"

"I could eat."

"You fancy a pizza and beer at Oroscopo's?"

Oroscopo's was on a road further down the hill, a small restaurant on the corner just along from Enricho's coffee shop. The manager and waiter was a small lively man with a quick smile and he loved to talk. It was a cosy place. He served good pizzas and Gezahegn's favourite, zilzil tibs, slices of beef lightly tossed in a pan with onions and hot green chilli peppers. They very occasionally went there for lunch.

"OK," she said with a small shrug.

He jingled the keys.

"You drive," she said. "I am really tired. It's been a long day." She took in a slightly shuddering breath. "And please, no arguing, OK?"

"OK," he said, as they walked alongside each other towards the car. "What do you fancy?"

"Veg, I think," she said.

"Yeah, me too," he said.

24

March/April 1984, Addis Ababa

The Buffet de la Gare was open every Sunday evening from six to ten to those who could afford the few Birr entrance. Ethiopian civil servants and trader families, NGO aid workers, ECA translators, international consultants, street girls, embassy staff, Senegalese, Nigerians, Dutch, Americans, Brits, Malawians, French, people from all over the world, crammed into the old railway cafe, to dance to the live band.

Izzie, Moe and Leila had curled themselves into the 2CV, windows and roof shut down against the cool dusk, and rumbled down the steep Churchill road. It always made her think of a helter-skelter, the way it swept steeply down and curved into a long straight, past the National Theatre. Right at the very end, they drew up in the railway station forecourt, its chunky Lion of Judah statue on a tall concrete plinth overseeing the passing of time. A brilliant show of stars and a slither of moon hung over them in the cold kereumt[72] night sky.

They had queued for their tickets under the tunnel awning, reminiscent of a classic hotel entrance in downtown Manhattan, before plunging into the mayhem of people and sound, their eyes alert for familiar faces.

"Darlings!" Alessandro called out over the noise, lifting his bottle when he saw them coming. His eyes shone. "Izzie, Moe, Leila!"

The South American Charge d'Affaires was an elegant man, in middle age. He sported a fine haircut, courtesy of the Hilton salon, where he went on the first Saturday of every month. He wore a jacket, regardless of the occasion, cut from expensive merino wool or a cotton mix cloth and tailored either in Madrid or Paris. He had a collection of colourful silk pocket-spares, one of which was tucked into his breast pocket. It gave him additional flair. He talked animatedly with people, who came

---

[72] Winter season.

and went around him like a flurry of starlings. In one hand, more accustomed to holding a glass of good Spanish wine, he held a bottle of beer, and in his other a cigarette, which he used for emphasis with small flourishes.

"Alessandro," Izzie's spirits lifted as soon as she spotted him. "It's a bright red one today I see," she patted his top pocket as she kissed him on either cheek.

"Hey," Moe said, smiling broadly and holding out his hand. "Good to see you."

"And the beautiful Leila," Alessandro said, leaning forward to kiss her. "How are you all this dreadful evening?"

The air, laced with cigarette smoke, sharp smelling perspiration, was thicker than the clear fresh evening air outside. Glasses and bottles chinked from the bar at the back. The music from the adjoining dance floor, a Congolese kwasa-kwasa, roused them to move to its beat.

"Dreadful?" Leila said, speaking loudly over the ruckus. "But you are looking your usual calm, suave self, Alessandro."

"We should have started doing something a year ago," he said. "Not waited until the rumours became their horrific reality, Leila darling."

"What have you heard?" Izzie said. As if things were not already bad enough.

"I'll get us some beers," Moe said, disappearing through the crowd.

"Yes, please," Izzie said, trying to conjure up a smile for him.

Moe's face looked drawn beneath the deep tan. Wax and Gold, she thought. They were both exhausted. From work, from each other, from the constant grim news. Yes, it was a 'dreadful' evening like every other. Not for them dreadful. They had the luxuries. A roof over their heads and full bellies, friends and laughter, music and dance. Alessandro was right. The interminable 'dreadful' of others. There was a real war, a real famine, going on out there. Everyone knew about the catastrophic backdrop to their lives. They could no longer say, 'it's in the making', it was actually happening. Even the streets of Addis were filling with more and more beggars, disabled and destitute families. A growing state of paralysis seemed to be seeping through the sinews of both the ministries and the international organisations. It was as if everyone was walking through black treacle.

"Where have you two been hiding?" Alessandro said, interrupting her thoughts.

"I wish I could say, 'We've been camping on the beach near Malindi, cooking fresh crabs over a fire,'" Izzie said. "That we've been sunbathing and drinking cocktails."

"Oh don't," Alessandro said, with an exaggerated toss of his head. "That sounds like a dream." He laughed.

"No, I have been down in Nazareth at the factory a lot. We've been producing uniforms to order. All in preparation for the big day in September," she said. "And I went to Tibila Farm, in Arussi. They need a wofchobate."

"A wofchobate?" Alessandro laughed. "What a wonderful word and what on earth is that?"

"A grinding mill," Izzie said. "We wrote up a funding request for one of the international NGOs. And Moe, he's been trying to get a permit to go up north. They really need to see for themselves what is going on."

"I bet he didn't have any luck with that. They don't want any of us to see anything," Alessandro said. "Oh, this place. We have to rely on a hotbed of rumours, confusion and God knows." He took a long drag on his cigarette and blew a stream of smoke up toward the ceiling.

"What have you been hearing?" Moe came up behind them with beers.

"Thank you, honey," Izzie said. Suddenly feeling weird. She never called him honey.

"Wondwossen, from the Relief Council, called us all to another meeting," Alessandro said, taking a bottle from Moe and chinking 'cheers' all round. "Ambassadors, charge d'affaires, international organisations. Your Mr Robert Riley Jnr was there, Moe. It was at the Ghion Hotel. Marvellous buffet. I couldn't swallow a mouthful. It somehow felt inappropriate."

"They've just produced their Ten Year Plan," Moe said. "Not an extra cent for the famine. How can he persuade you lot, any of us, to contribute if his own government isn't behind him? If we can't even go and do an assessment for ourselves."

"I just told Alessandro you have been trying to get up north to no avail," Izzie said.

"Wondwossen said an estimated 5.2 million people are affected, 40% of them under-five. They need 450,000 tons of grain from us," Alessandro said, leaning forward and mouthing the number. "It's only the Americans and the large international organisations who can come up with those quantities."

"That's the sort of figure we've been hearing," Moe said. "It would be a logistical nightmare to get that amount of grain through the port in Massawa though. We have a consultant from UK here to look into all that. In fact, I told him to join us here tonight." Moe looked around as if the man might appear as he spoke.

Duncan, Izzie thought. What a creep. She did not like the way he ogled Ethiopian women, any women. She bit her lip to stop herself from commenting. She and Moe had already crossed swords over him.

"The anti-American slogans don't help any," Leila said. "It's gotten real bad in Debre Berhan. The main road is lined with small groups of very sick, hungry, people. It's heart-breaking. We really have to do something."

"The Derg only wants to hear about success, not failures," Moe said. "The Ministry is struggling to come up with agricultural output stats which will satisfy them."

"At work the only talk seems to be about the 10th Anniversary of the Revolution and the coming elections for the Marxist-Leninist Party, " Izzie said. "We can't get much done. No decision-maker is available to sign off on a single bit of paper, or to meet to discuss anything else."

"Not even your wofchobate?"

"Alessandro!" Izzie punched him gently. "But fast learner, hey."

"The literacy campaign has been a great success," a voice behind them said. It was Hiwot. She was smiling broadly. "Increased from 10% to 60% since the Revolution."

"Hey Hiwot," Izzie said, kissing her on both cheeks. "Did Booker come too? That would be a first."

"No, I came with some other friends. We are over there, dancing. I just spotted you all. Why aren't you dancing?" She leant in, "And by the way, you guys are talking too loudly."

"God, I wasn't thinking," Izzie said. She was usually so careful.

Hiwot was always upbeat, laughing and chatting, but she was as worried as they were about the situation. She had applied to join the Relief Council Health Team in Gondar, and was waiting to hear back. She had worked with the Red Cross as a student nurse on the border with Somalia during the Somali war. She appeared light-hearted, but she was not to be underestimated.

"We should know better," Leila said.

"Hey guys! Can't you hear the music?" Tom ran his fingers through his damp locks. "I could do with a cold beer."

"Hi Tom," Izzie said.

"Hi buddy," Moe said.

"Your new friend Duncan is here. He's making a right nuisance of himself on the dance floor," Tom said. "He was drinking all day in the sun by the pool at the Hilton."

Izzie's heart sank. "Where's Aster? I thought she would be here?" she said.

"No sooner mentioned than appeared," Alessandro said. "Hello, gorgeous."

They only ever saw Aster on a Sunday at the Buffet and afterwards at The Cottage. She lived in a small villa, its wooden veranda fringed with ivy and bougainvillea, somewhere in the depths of Casanches. She was an exotic concoction of rural development consultant, Tarot card reader and hairdresser; never short of a way to earn her living. She had taken in three of her siblings' children to put through school in Addis, like so many of them did. There was no formal adoption procedure. The children seemed to end up belonging to their city relatives for life.

"Hi there ennante," Aster said, grinning warmly. She was a little out of breath. "What are you all doing standing around, enday?"

"I love that dress," Izzie said. It was a long white cotton-spun kaftan with bright traditional embroidery down the front.

"Let's go girls. Innihid," Aster said, laughing. She took Izzie's hand, and Leila's and nodded at Hiwot. Swaying her hips to the music, she made her way under the arch into the next-door room where the music hit them full on.

The seven-man band was all Ethiopian. They played eskista, funk and reggae fusion, and Congolese kwasa-kwasa. A rhythm familiar from the bars in Lilongwe and Nkotakota. The saxophonist was phenomenal. They played from a slightly raised platform. In the corner beside the stage sat two elderly men, one Italian, one Armenian, each with an accordion on their lap. Two glasses and a jug of water stood on the small round table between them. Izzie fancied they drank anis. The piano stood silent. A Finnish aid worker, a pale-skinned young man with white blonde hair, appeared some Sundays and banged out honky-tonk on it. It seemed he had to be drunk to do it.

They danced in a small group close to the band. It was loud, loud and packed. Familiar faces laughed and smiled greetings. Heaving, dancing, exuberant bodies. Izzie danced, eyes closed, inviting the rhythm into her body, wishing the longing, the pain and tiredness away.

**

The city was being renovated, streets tidied up and painted, corrugated iron fencing erected along the main boulevards to hide the slum-dwellings behind. National flags hung on every lamp post, while the poverty and hunger on the streets increased.

'Abate, abate,' the wailing funerals, crying out from the dark alleyways below, provided a macabre backdrop to the fights with Moe. They had no time for themselves, to think, to listen and care, to understand each other. And they had had too many visitors. Oh God, that couple from Italy he went to University with. Even Moe had been glad to see the back of them. Nothing had been good enough. Everything was too shocking, too dirty, too dangerous. So many questions and precautions. It had been draining. Negisst had been wonderful, sending them off with packed lunches and filtered water.

Earlier on that evening, Leila had inadvertently rescued them from one such row, by calling with the idea of going out to the Buffet de la Gare.

"You think yourself a Feminist," he had said, his eyes shining with disdain.

"So tell me. You tell me what a feminist is. Then I'll tell you yes or no, if that's me or not."

"She's independent. She looks after herself. Doesn't need a man to pay the bills, put a roof over her head."

"What?" she had shouted. "I pay my way. And this flat. You get that 'free-bee' with your job. Using up a chunk of development aid meant for Ethiopia, by the way, just like the rest of them."

"So it's OK you sponging off my good fortune, huh?"

"I can move out tomorrow, Moe. No worries," she had said, wondering when she would finally go a step too far. It had been drummed into her not to sponge. What was this sponging. They were living together. But she could pack a bag and leave. She was capable of that. "And if I did? Poor you Moe, who would do the shopping and cooking, looking after Negisst? Paying Negisst? Who would do all that? You do fuck all round here."

"I dare you to move out, Izzie, I dare you," he had said. "And needy. A feminist isn't so needy. 'Love me, love me, you never spend time with me,'" he mimicked in a high whining voice. His face red under that mop of sandy blonde hair, his blue eyes dark.

"Who decreed that women do the clean, shop and cook. Huh? Where did that come from? It seems to just happen. Time and a-boring-gain. You think I was trained for it? You think I took a degree in Home Economics? Well I didn't."

"Typical," he said. "Run away when it gets tough, why don't you?"

"All I want to know is whether we will be together a year from now. In ten years from now. What's wrong with that? That's got nothing to do with feminism, Moe. That's called being together, loving each other. Look at us. What happened? I have to just keep on taking it. Your silence, seeing the back of your head reading, you cheering up the minute anyone, anyone else, steps in the room. And that, that thing with Almaz. You know how humiliating that was?"

"Oh for God's sake, Izzie. You and these Ethiopian women you think are your friends. Almaz. She runs a bar, a brothel, a khat house."

"Exactly," Izzie spat back at him. "So what were you doing with her on your knee?"

"We've been through this."

"And that consultant from London. Be careful with him."

"Duncan? What are you on about?"

"He's a creep. He may be handsome, but he's a creep. The way he gives women the once over."

"You are ridiculous."

Her eyes had burned with tears. She'd felt the hysteria rising like venom in her throat with dread. Like a snake but faster, a whiplash, she could become uncontrollable. "I hate you!" she'd yelled. "I just want to know if you want to be with me. For the long run, Moe? What's wrong with wanting to know that?"

"Calm down, will you?" he had said, his eyes glistening with anger, fear, confusion. "You have to wait and see. Take a day at a time. That's all I can say."

Was he going to cry? She had stopped, taken a deep breath. "We are both exhausted," she'd said.

"I am sick of this. I can't give you what you need. I feel like I'm being sucked into your bottomless pit. There's a famine going on out there and no one's fucking listening. And I get your endless, hysterical, 'you don't love me anymore,' like a needle stuck in a groove, over and over."

She looked at him and felt mortified. Sorry for him, sorry for herself. She felt sick in the pit of her stomach and wanted a way out of this. "I'm sorry, Moe."

"You're a damn yo-yo," he said. "Up, down, one minute laughing, next minute weeping. I can't do it."

"I'm sorry." She had moved towards him. "I feel sorry for both of us."

He'd put out a hand to stop her. "Don't touch. Not now."

**

She danced, eyes shut, allowing the music in until it was vibrating through all her muscles and lifting her heart until the tears came. She didn't stop. She let it happen. Her friends around her.

**

They had been interrupted by the phone ringing.

"Hi there Leila," Moe had said. "Yes. OK, u-huh." He had stood slightly bent over the phone, running his hand through his hair. He turned with his hand over the mouthpiece. "It's Leila wanting to know if we want to go together to the Buffet?"

"Good idea," Izzie said. "Maybe that will cheer us out of this."

He turned back to the phone. "That's a great idea, Leila. You'll head for ours? Yeah sure. We'll be down in about ten minutes."

Izzie had gone to the bathroom. Washed her face in cold water and put on some mascara. How was it possible. One minute shrieking, next minute calm. There seemed to be a deep pool of misery and tears in the pit of her stomach, welling up from time to time, spoiling everything.

"Izzie?"

He was outside the door.

"Yeah," she had said, trying not to cry. It would smudge her mascara. "I'm just getting ready."

He had come in. Wrapped his arms around her and sunk his face in the crook of her neck. He mumbled something.

She looked at them both in the mirror and lifted her hand to stroke his head.

**

She felt his arms come around her and turned. They danced. They danced. She and Moe, Hiwot, Tom, Aster, Leila. And Duncan. Tom had been right, Duncan was drunk. He made a bee-line for them as soon as he saw them and danced too close to Hiwot.

Alessandro didn't dance. He held court, listened out for rumours. "Where there are rumours, something is going on."

Two trains had been blown up near Dire Dawa. Was it the rebels? Or was it contrabandists? Someone said it was the contrabandists. But they ply their trade between Djibouti, Dire Dawa and Addis, another said. Why would they want to blow it up? Like biting off their own faces, they wouldn't do that. It must have been the rebels from Tigray, another said. The freedom fighters.

"Those poor people," Alessandro said. "Esa pobre gente."

"Who? The freedom fighters?"

"No. They seem to be well organised and they have an aim, a reason to live and die," Alessandro said. "I mean the people of Tigray, the farming families. The women and children sneak into Korem looking for food, and the menfolk creep over the border into Sudan, looking for work. Work? What work will they find there?"

And in the big cities, Addis, Asmara, Mekele, the continued wariness and disturbances. Rumours of incidents, arrests and deaths in custody. When did it happen? How many? Individuals, family members, dealt with in 'the usual way'.

"Who?" Izzie joined Alessandro in his circle of gossip. "What happened?"

"We think, mi amiga, we are not sure," Alessandro said. "It was last week. I can't say who."

"Enday, you all talking too much again," Hiwot said, coming off the dance floor behind Izzie.

"Who's up for an Irish at The Cottage?" Moe said. "Leila, you're with us and we have room for one more."

"Sounds like a good idea," Aster said.

"Matt's here somewhere," Tom said. "I can go with him."

"Come on then, Duncan," Moe said. "You come with us, we can drop you at the Hilton after."

"Brilliant," Duncan said. "Brilliant."

Izzie stared at Moe trying to say, What? Really? with her eyes. "And what about Hiwot?" she said out loud.

"No worries, yeney konjo," Hiwot said. "I am making my way home. Early shift tomorrow. Alessandro said he would give me a lift."

They spilled out into the chill mountain air, still sweaty from dancing. Izzie climbed into the passenger seat. She felt Leila squeeze her shoulder from behind. She turned and smiled.

25

March/April 1984, Addis Ababa

Izzie's head still felt the effects of the night before. As soon as she opened the office door she knew something was up and could not quite get her mind around it.

"Come, Izzie, let's go," Simaynesh said. "I've been waiting for you." She had dark rings under her eyes and wore a black shawl over her head and shoulders.

"What happened?"

"Elsabet's brother," Simaynesh said. She went over and closed the office door.

Izzie's eyes filled with tears. "Oh God."

"You heard about it?" Simaynesh said. "He's dead."

"The one who's in prison?"

"It's hard. Betam kebad. Brutal. So final. Unnecessary." Simaynesh's voice was strained, rasping. As if there was no air in her windpipe.

Izzie had not even put her bag down. The car keys were still in her hand.

"The others are at Elsabet's house. At the Lekeso bate."

"I don't have anything to cover my head."

Simaynesh pulled a black shawl from her bag.

"You think of everything," Izzie said. "So kind to me." She took it and laid it across her head and shoulders and wrapped herself in it. "Thank you."

Monday morning.

She had had a couple of Irish coffees after the beers at the Buffet. She had laughed, chatted, drunk and danced. She had tried to drown out the fighting with Moe, the confusion and pain it caused her. And all the while something horrible, something agonising, had happened to their friend Elsabet's brother.

They got into the car and drove out of the office compound. The zabanya nodded his head and raised a hand as they went under the archway to the road. They both bowed their heads in return. He was a kind man.

Elsabet lived in a neighbourhood behind the Bole Road, at one end of which was the enormous statue of Lenin striding out, and at the other the airport, a few kilometres down. She lived with her husband and their two daughters. He managed a garage repair shop run by an Italian family. She always spoke proudly of him, and loved telling stories about her girls.

"Turn in here," Simaynesh said, pointing to a narrow dirt road going up a hill to the left.

They could hear the wailing already.

"Oh God," Izzie said.

Simaynesh sucked her teeth.

Izzie parked right up against the fence opposite Elsabet's to allow space for other cars to pass. There was a deep gulley all the way up the other side of the road to take rain water away. It was bone dry. Wooden planks lay across it at intervals to allow access to the houses set back along a stony pathway. Elsabet's bungalow crouched behind corrugated iron fencing. The gate was open. Thin strands of young eucalyptus bowed over the top of the fence, their leaves glistening silver and green in the sun.

There was a humming and sobbing, punctuated by loud, high-pitched, sing-song wailing.

"That's Elsabet," Simaynesh said.

They picked their way over the stones and potholes in the road, across the makeshift bridge and into the compound. The small front garden was overwhelmed by the white tarpaulin tent erected for the lekeso. Chairs and benches were lined up opposite each other around the house under the tarpaulin, their occupants wrapped in white shawls, black scarves around their heads. Some rocked back and forth, crying softly. Others sat quietly. Two women came out of the dark interior and down the wooden steps from the veranda carrying trays of food and cups of coffee. As they were served, each mourning visitor took the offering in two hands and bowed their head in thanks.

Izzie spotted Gezahegn, Wozeiro Meheret, Ato Embaye, Genet and Ato Solomon. Comrade Adugna was not there. Of course he wasn't. Elsabet's brother was a traitor, a counter-revolutionary. Comrade Adugna could not be there. Izzie followed Simaynesh towards their colleagues. They went between the rows of mourners, shaking hands and bowing their heads.

Seeing Genet and hearing the wailing she was reminded of Kidane Meheret church. Thank goodness Genet had recovered. She had become even more pious since her illness. But they worked together as effectively and with the same warmth and laughter as before. There was an empty chair between Genet and Wozeiro Meheret. Genet motioned Izzie to come sit.

Elsabet's wailing became louder. She stood pounding her chest and chanting, lifting her hands to the sky and weeping.

Izzie took the seat between Wozeiro Meheret and Genet. They wriggled room for her, touching her hands and smiling sadly.

Simaynesh did not sit. "Mindin neouw?" she said. "How long has she been like this?"

"Since early morning, and all last night," a woman said.

The air around the house was filled with the smell of woodsmoke from the outdoor kitchen; berberri spices, roasting coffee and the sweet pungent smell of burning itan. It infused the walls, their shawls, their hair, and cloaked them all in an ancient certainty. The certainty of living and dying, reminiscent of their forefathers and mothers, of past wars and struggles. This was a well-known pain, the wailing rising into the surrounding hillside, past the tops of the eucalyptus, juniper and warka trees and into the stark blue sky. God knew best, it was in His hands. Izzie struggled with that. If there was a God, where was he now?

Elsabet's anguished cries were penetrating. In Elsabet's tormented wailing Izzie could feel the cold shock, the deep loss, the brutality of it all deep in her bones.

"What is she saying?" Izzie whispered.

"She's remembering the days they played in the compound as children," Wozeiro Meheret whispered, her hand on Izzie's knee. "Shimayless was his name, she says. Remember him and his many kindnesses, she says. He died for love. For his love of Ethiopia, for justice. Instead of his coming home… He was to come, she says. We were expecting him. We were ready with injera and kitfo for him to eat. Instead they got rid of him. Our dear brother. Where is our God when we need Him? That is what she is saying, Izzie." Wozeiro Meheret cried softly. "Weyne, Weyne! Egziyabher inya gar yihun. God save us. God stay by us."

"Aysosh, aysosh," Izzie whispered, holding her colleague's hand.

Simaynesh was holding Elsabet trying to calm her. "It's enough, sister, it's enough." She kept saying. "Yibakal. It's enough. You will make yourself sick."

Other women got up too, surrounding Elsabet like turtle doves, cooing and fluttering. "Aysosh, aysosh, " they said. "It's enough, it's enough."

A young girl came with a tray of coffee and Ambasha dabbo cut into squares. Izzie looked at Gezahegn.

He nodded encouragement, Yes, take some.

She didn't know why, but she needed his say-so. She took a small cup of coffee and a square of bread, bowing her head slightly, "Egziersteling," she said.

The girl smiled and moved on with her tray.

The coffee was hot, thick and dark.

Simaynesh and the women surrounded Elsabet and moved slowly with her towards the veranda. Elsabet was shuddering from the intense sobbing. They went with her up the steps and disappeared into the darkness of the bungalow.

Izzie looked at the earth between her feet, and at the shawl-clad figures sitting around her. The murmuring, sniffing and weeping continued, finding a fresh wave when someone new arrived in their midst. A raven, balancing on the fence, cawed loudly, its beak wide open, eyes black and piercing. Its head cocked to one side and then the other. Did ravens come to collect our souls, she wondered. Surely there would be a more amicable companion when the time came.

Ato Embaye sat opposite her. So skinny. He sat with his hands tucked between his knees, his shoulders hunched. He looked awkward on his low stool. She could feel Wozeiro Meheret's body against hers. They were all huddled up together, against this enormity that had hit their friend. And still more people came. Izzie was not sure how long they would sit there.

Gezahegn was looking up at the blue sky between the edge of the tarpaulin and the trees. His eyes squinting, as if trying to see some very tiny particle, his jaw tight. He was a handsome man. What could be going through his head, she wondered. She realised how little she knew about his life beyond their office, apart from the odd coffee at Enricho's, or his favourite lunchtime zilzil tibs with injera at Oroscopo's. What had these people lived through while she was drinking pints of beer from plastic cups at a City Poly disco, cycling home to Dalston, drunk, concentrating on the yellow parking lines so as not to fall off her bike. What had they seen and done while she worked night shifts in the

Matchbox toy car factory to earn enough to hitchhike through France and Spain to Morocco? Their student years had been so different to hers. And they must all have friends or relatives, who had died, or gone missing, or who had left the country. And still there seemed no end to it.

She sat. Feeling the sun. There was some comfort in being together. A strong sense of here and now. She felt a deep admiration for these people. There was something about them beyond her reach. She could never quite get inside their shoes, walk along the paths they walked. And yet she was there. Amongst them. Sharing some of their pain.

26

He sat on the edge of his cot. A strip of pale morning light fell through the darkness across the floor from the open door. It was quiet outside. No birdsong. No comforting scratching sounds and whirring clucks from the neighbours' chicken. The fire was cold. Small lumps of charred wood and a pile of grey ashes. He stared at it until he conjured up a flash of light igniting the wood, turning it into coals burning red, edged with tiny flames. He watched as his pot bubbled with tea and spices, the water turning orange, the colour of dried flame tree petals.

Zewdie came through the door, shattering his dream. "We'll have tea this evening," she said. "There's none left. I will buy some when I sell the firewood today, Egziyabher sifeked."

"Ishi," he said, rubbing his eyes. He yawned, his mouth open wide, and got up. He wished his goats were still in the beret behind their house. Lakew had sold them when he came that time, and given the money to Zewdie. He'd left for work further south, not knowing when he would be back.

"Temima wants you to take their animals today, Ashebir. Mohamed Abdu has to pull the oxen. His father wants to plough in case the rain comes."

"Ishi, Zewdie," he said quietly. Poor Mohamed Abdu, he thought. It was exhausting work. The soil was too hard for Ahmed to drive the oxen on his own. It was a long time since any rain had softened the soil.

They went outside. Zewdie bent over a large pile of firewood, coughing. He helped her tie it up with a long string of sisal, so she could strap it to her back. It was their last hope. Collecting wood in the ravines and selling it in the market for a few centimes.

"I'll go to Mohamed Abdu's then," he said.

"Tell Temima I am leaving for the market soon."

"Ishi," he said, and walked towards their gate.

He walked up the path looking into the trees for small birds, just in case. He had his slingshot in his bag; maybe he would get one or two today.

When he reached Mohamed Abdu's compound he called out, "Tenasteling."

His friend's mother, Temima came out. "Tenasteling, Ashebir. How are you and your mother today?"

"We are fine, thank you. How is everyone at home? Is Mohamed Abdu there?"

"We are fine too, Allah be praised," Temima said. "Mohamed Abdu and Mohamed Ahmed just left."

"Zewdie said to tell you she is leaving for the market soon."

"Here," she said, "it's not much, but take it with you." She gave him a small piece of ki'ta bread.

He hesitated. "Maybe give it to Zewdie," he said, even though he was hungry.

"I have some for your mother too, Ashebir. Don't worry. Allah is with us." Temima smiled at him, her head on one side. She was a kind woman.

She had a large pile of firewood on the ground ready to go to the market. The sheep and goats were bleating and bumping around him, eager to get out. There were three sheep and two goats left. He jumped aside to keep away from their horns. They too looked skinny.

He held out both hands and bowing his head took the bread from her. "Thank you, Temima," he said putting it in his bag. It was still warm and smelt good, she must have just made it. Having land and a father made a difference, he thought.

He whistled at the animals and they took off up the path. He would go to the flat pastures of Upper Ataye to the north; maybe there would be some grazing there. He hoped he would find Ali on the way.

In a clearing on the mountainside, he sat and ate Temima's bread. He took small mouthfuls, chewing over and over to make it last. His grandmother Emet Hawa had sometimes given him caramella. He would suck the sweet for a while and then put it back in his pocket in the wrapper for later. This way the sweet lasted a few days. He was so hungry he could not leave any of the bread for later.

It was quiet. Just the flies buzzed. Flies. They do well while everyone else is suffering, he thought. They eat and drink anything; cow dung, carcasses, any rotting stinking thing, the filthiest water. They even drink the water in small children's eyes. Five or ten at a time they would huddle in the corner, drinking.

The animals snuffled around in the short dry stubble. He got up and walked after them, throwing pebbles at their rumps, calling the strays to come back. Any movement and shouting tired him. He crouched on his haunches to catch his breath, dull pains shooting through his stomach. The air was still. The sky a deep blue. He looked up at his beloved Muletta, and begged the mountain to make it rain. He longed to see clouds again, their darkness filling the sky on the horizon. And when they rained in the distance, the wind would carry the strong sweet smell of wet grasses and of dust turning to mud. He and his friends would breathe it in, knowing the downpour would reach them soon and that the season for planting had come. There would be green shoots and new leaves on the bushes for the animals. But despite all their prayers, their faith in Allah, in God and the heavenly good, the rain did not come and did not come. He could not understand it.

Some of the adults said: 'It's a punishment for our sins.'

The thought of God's anger, of His enormous power, made him afraid. What could they have done to deserve this? They lived peacefully together. His Uncle Mohamed Shinkurt could be harsh, but Zewdie said he was a 'big man' with worries in his head.

Even the Ataye River was just a trickle of water now. They couldn't swim in it anymore. The elders in the village said it might dry up altogether, like in Haile Selassie's time.

"Will it dry up, Zewdie? Will it?" he had asked his mother, terrified at the idea. Where would they wash? Where would they get water?

"Egziyabher yawkal," she said. "Only God knows."

The talking made him angry. What if God didn't know? What if he was so angry, he didn't care? What then? The tears stung hot in his eyes. He kept his mouth shut in those moments.

If only the rain would come. Bring a harvest. He and Zewdie would get a share. She could brew tella beer again or bake her famous injera to sell. But now they were among the poorest in their village. He knew that. A few families still had a little grain in their gurgwad underground stores, but they didn't have enough to share.

Kites circled high above, their wings spread wide, floating on the hot air. He wondered if they could see him down there, whether they could see the suffering. He looked closer for a moment, shading his eyes from the sun. Or were they vultures? It was only the vultures, the hyenas and the flies that could eat their fill. He remembered the animal carcasses scattered across the plain on the way to Senbatey market, the flies buzzing loudly in swarms and the vultures hopping around, their necks stretched out and ugly.

The sun burnt down on his head. He pulled on his straw hat. He sat on the boulder to throw pebbles at a large rock. He hoped half-heartedly to hear that old sharp Clack! sound. It wasn't happening, his arms had become weaker.

After a while he got up and moved on slowly, putting two dried cow pats into his bag as he went. Zewdie could use them for the fire. He whistled softly, imitating birdsong, to stop from feeling alone. The animals had scattered in search of food, the goats stretching their front legs high into the bushes. He bent to pick up pebbles and threw them at their rumps, calling out, "Innihid." They trotted slowly on. "Let's go," he called again. He took the path which led down to the river. Maybe Ali would be there to cheer him up.

He scoured the bushes for berries. Mohamed Abdu and Ali had shown him which wild fruits were edible; enkoy, sholla, kulkwal. But the bushes were bare. The birds had already been.

He reached an expanse of rough ground covered in grey rocks and boulders. Towering cactus plants stood in clumps surrounded by thick prickly bushes. 'Maybe there's fruit on the cactus,' he thought, his mouth watering. The cactus had bright yellow flowers and sweet fruits, which were hard to reach especially through the prickly bushes. 'Fruit guards,' Ali called them. The fruits were about the size of an egg and covered in tiny bristles. They were soft inside.

Ashebir had often struggled through the bush around the tall cactus to reach the fruits with Mohamed Abdu and Ali, the thorns clinging to their clothes, holding them back and scratching their skin. They would use their sticks to knock the fruit off.

As Ashebir got closer, he saw the baboons. They obviously had the same idea as he. They moved closer, looking from him to the cactus. The males had huge teeth and great lions' manes, which shook and shone in the sun. They were determined, and they were strong. His heart pounding, he slowly laid his sickle and bag on the ground. He put a handful of stones in his pocket. With his arms high in the air, he pushed his way through the spiky bushes towards the cactus, waving his stick, trying to shout. A thin sound came out of his mouth, like a kite's cry as it circled high in the blue. He stopped. Pinned to the spot. He clenched his fists and bit hard on his upper lip not to whimper. He took one stone at a time from his pocket and threw them at the baboons. Not one of them hit its target. The large animals just looked at him and darted at the cactus. They plucked the fruits and ran off, their hands full. He wiped his tears away angrily with the back of his arm. The baboons sat on the hillside above him, alternately eating and looking down at him.

He slowly unpicked himself from the bushes, walking backwards. He rounded up the animals and continued towards the river. He had walked in a large pointless circle. The grinding pain in his belly made waves into his legs and chest.

As he went down the mountainside, he could see the grey tarmac road winding its way up from Addis Ababa and Debre Berhan like a snake. It went north to Kombolcha, Dessie and Korem before reaching Mekele in Tigray. Places he had heard about but never been to. It was the road Mohamed Hussein had cycled down; the road that took young soldiers to war in the back of open trucks. "Wotaderoch! Wotaderoch!" He and his friends used to run after them, shouting, 'Soldiers! Soldiers!' before they bent over, exhausted and panting. That was before they understood that many of those young men would die. It was the road that had taken boys from the village, including his cousin Yimam. Zewdie always shook her head when she talked about Yimam. She loved him. He had helped her build their house. She liked the way he laughed and joked with her. But he had been too loud, too political, she would say, tutting with worry. Comrade Abebe had finally come to call on Mohamed Shinkurt. It was time Yimam did something for the revolution, time for him to join the army, fight for the Motherland, he had said.

And now it was the road The Hungry walked down from the north. They came every day in search of food. Women, men and children, the elderly, carrying a few things on their backs, walking with the help of a prayer stick, with a continuous low murmur of voices, like the river running over rocks. Some stopped, sat on the side of the road in silence, and never stood up again.

"Please God, save us from joining them," Ashebir whispered, his mouth dry, fear swirling around with the pain in his belly.

Mohamed Abdu's father, Mohamed Ahmed, told them that anyone with a vehicle, a bus, a pick-up, a Land Rover, or a car, was doing good business. While most people went on foot, there were others who had saved a little money to pay for transport. They were all heading for Addis Ababa, he said.

Their parents, talking quietly in the evening light, would say, surely the Derg, the makers of the revolution, the men who had sent the Zemecha students to educate them, would not let them down? Not like their Emperor, who, they bowed their heads whispering, 'Forgive him, bless his soul, may he rest in peace,' had forgotten them before? But they were puzzled. The Kebele did not give them bags of grain, like they did to their own. Comrade Abebe's belly was still round.

Ashebir reached the river. There was a trickle under the Ataye Bridge. The animals drank. He stood watching. Ali was not there. Women and girls from the village were washing clothes, scrubbing them against the rocks with endod leaves, making foam. No one bought the thick white bricks of soap any more.

He took off his clothes and, cupping his hands, collected water to splash over his head and back, and down his chest. He rubbed the cool water over his arms and legs. He drank. The rocks stuck out above the shallow water. He found a place where the stones were smooth and he could lie on the river bed. Above him, a bus passed over the bridge, leaving a trail of black smoke and strains of music hovering in the air behind it. The traffic was different from before. Sometimes open-backed trucks rumbled past, heading north, carrying sacks of grain, crates of Coca Cola, soldiers with guns. He was too tired to run after them anymore. The only time he would still try to reach the road in time was if a white Toyota or Land Rover passed with foreigners inside. It did not happen often any more. He and his friends used to shout, "Farenj! Farenj!" waving and running after them, until they ran out of breath, or the vehicle turned a bend.

He had never seen a farenj close up. Their blank pink faces stared out of the windows, their hair the colour of faded grass. He wondered if they were ill. People who had been close to them said their shirts got wet with sweat and they smelt like plucked chickens. People said they came from countries where everyone could work and eat as much as they wanted. They laughed and smiled a lot, shaking hands and speaking in the farenj language, which had been on his t-shirt but now faded to a hole. Sometimes they would wave from their vehicles. He and the other children would wave back, then fall over laughing. Farenj were strange. He was secretly glad they did not stop and get out. That would be terrifying.

He tossed more water over his head to cool himself, then lay on the bank to dry off. From where he was, he could see the small groups of people walking over the bridge. From their hairstyles and traditional clothes he knew they were from the highlands further north. The women carried bundles on their heads, and their babies in smooth dark leather pouches on their backs.

A group of women sat together on the shore, shading their eyes from the sun to watch their children who they let wander and splash in the water. The smallest were naked, their bellies swollen, their legs spindly like the branches he chopped for firewood near Gidim.

Three Degenya boys they used to play with came to join him.

"Tadias," Ashebir said, looking up. "How are you?"

"We are fine, Egziyabher yimesgen. Only sad we can't swim," the smallest said smiling shyly. His two front teeth looked too big for his face. He sat down next to Ashebir. He picked up a pebble, threw it in the air and caught it again, over and over.

"Look at those people," Ashebir said nodding his head towards the travellers.

"They pass every day," an older boy said, "looking for food before they die."

"Your fathers can't fish anymore," Ashebir said.

"It's too shallow," the older boy said.

His legs were skinny too. Ashebir looked down to compare them with his own.

The boy wore a thin jumper with large holes under each arm. There was a faded picture of a mouse wearing red shorts on the front. He sat on a boulder, dabbling his feet in a puddle of water.

"We have students in our village," the little boy said proudly.

"They were sent from Addis," the boy with the mouse on his jumper said.

"What are they doing?" Ashebir asked, pulling his shorts on again.

"They say we have to celebrate. They say it's the Tenth Anniversary of the Revolution," the boy said.

Ashebir wondered what there was to celebrate.

"They called everyone to a meeting in the village," the older boy said. "They said we have to follow Marxism-Leninism."

"We were all there. Everyone just sat quietly and looked," the boy with the mouse on his jumper said.

"Everyone is hungry," the little boy lisped through his large teeth. "Afterwards my mother said, 'How can we celebrate when we can't feed our children once a day?'"

"Then my grandfather got up," the older boy said. "He started shouting, 'We want food. Not Marxism. Bring us food, and then we'll celebrate.'"

"My mother said he better keep quiet," the little boy said, shrugging his shoulders.

"But his granddad just started shouting again," the boy with the mouse jumper said.

"Yes. He shouted out, 'In the Emperor's time it was peaceful. We worked for the landlord and ate. There were no wars. No vagabonds. No political meetings.'"

"The Emperor," the small boy giggled.

Something about this little boy's giggle made them all laugh.

"I like hearing the old people in my village tell stories about the Emperor's time," Ashebir said. "They say it was better in his day. Until the famine came."

"You're not allowed to talk about the Emperor," the older boy said.

"Did your grandfather get in trouble?" Ashebir asked him.

"Someone from the Kebele came and took him out of the way, under the trees. The grownups were all going, 'tut, tut'. They knew he was right, but everyone was afraid."

"No one has been to our village to talk about the celebration," Ashebir said. "But I have seen them practicing in Ataye. They wear green uniforms and march up and down behind the red flag."

"And the Ethiopian flag," the little boy said, puffing his chest out. Ashebir could see each rib, like a skinny zebu calf.

"Mohamed Abdu's animals," Ashebir said, getting up. He looked around and saw they had scattered over the stony river bed and along the path. "I better go round them up."

As he walked away he heard them chanting, "Marxism! Leninism! Is our guiding light!"

He turned to see the small boy shrieking as the others splashed him. He waved and they waved back, smiling in the sun. "Don't disappear," they called out. "We will see you again soon."

**

When he reached the path near their home, it was almost dark. A thin line of smoke made its way into the darkness from the small black chimney on top of their gojo-bate. Zewdie must have bought some flour in the market. She was cooking. He almost wept for joy and walked a bit faster. As he got nearer he could hear her cough.

"Tenasteling, Zewdie," he said as he came in the door. The room was full of smoke. It stung his eyes. He coughed. The coals burnt deep red and blue, like in his morning dream, and the tea bubbled orange.

"Tenasteling, my child," she said. "How are you?"

"I am fine, Egziyabher yimesgen," he said. "And you?" He put the cow pats he had collected by a small pile of kindling.

"Thank you," she said.

He went to sit by her while she cooked, picking up a twig to poke the embers.

"We'll have tea and bread soon," Zewdie said, turning the thin flat bread over to cook on the other side.

"It smells good," he smiled at her. "I'm hungry."

They bowed their heads and thanked God from their hearts for their meal. The kerosene lamp hung on its hook unlit. The price of kerosene had gone up. They sat and ate by the light of the fire.

"I saw more people walking today," he said.

"They are walking every day. More and more of us with little or no food."

"We will be alright, though, won't we, Zewdie?"

"I think we have to sell a few things," she said. "We don't need the lamp anymore and there are Hawa's old cooking pots and tea glasses."

Ashebir slurped his tea. "What will we use to drink from then?" he asked, looking up at her.

"We have two enamel mugs. They will do us," she said. "Eat slowly or the pains will come."

He lifted the plate towards her. "Zewdie, you are not eating," he said. "Take some. It's good for you."

Her smile was tired and he noticed her sunken cheeks and the dark shadows under her eyes. She suddenly looked like the women by the river.

"Please eat," he said again, the fear fluttering up in his stomach. He was relieved when she broke off a piece of bread and put it in her mouth. She sighed, and chewed slowly.

Before they had finished, and while the hunger still gnawed in his stomach, she took the remaining ki'ta bread and wrapped it in a cloth. "We'll keep this for tomorrow," she said. "I am not well Ashebir. I need to rest for a day or two. I want you to collect firewood tomorrow and sell it in the market. You can take a piece of this bread with you."

"Ishi," he said quietly.

**

He left early, his bag and tillik'o over his shoulder. He had woken with a sore throat and now he was coughing. Maybe he had Zewdie's coughing sickness.

The gorge near Gidim was on the other side of the main Dessie Road. He would find firewood there. The road was empty except for a thin train of camels going north, swaying one behind the other, their heads held high. He took the path into the valley, leaving the river behind him. He felt small surrounded by tall, dark mountains. The gorge fell away, thick with brush and trees on his left. He looked to find an opening in the bush and saw a narrow track leading down the steep slope. He secured his bag and tillik'o on his shoulder and climbed down backwards, his face to the mountainside, making sure he had a strong foothold. Many people had fallen here. If he fell and broke a bone, he might not survive. With every step he looked below him for a rock or root to hold or place his foot on. The soil was dry and crumbled away easily. Each time he jiggled hard to make sure it would hold him. He climbed down slowly, coughing into his shoulder.

He stopped on a wide ledge and started chopping. Each slice into the wood echoed in the valley. Muffled voices on the other side of the gorge, and the sound of chopping, reached him. It was comforting to know he was not alone.

After cutting as many branches as he thought he could carry, he bound them together and secured the bundle across his back. His heart pounding, he climbed slowly up the gorge, seeking out rocks and roots with his hands. Terrified that if he lost his grip, he would tumble all the way down. It was a relief to reach the top.

He walked at a slow and steady pace, the firewood balanced on his head. The sun sank, turning the day into late afternoon, sending his shadow out along the path beside him. I'm walking with my soul shadow, he thought, looking at his shadow. The idea made him uneasy. Zewdie said they all had souls. He tried to concentrate on his feet moving forward. His shadow stayed with him, one step after the next.

The market was not as busy as he had hoped. He was not the only one who had firewood to sell. He joined the row of firewood sellers, sitting beside his pile to wait. No one even came to ask the price. Soon it would be getting dark. He looked around feeling helpless. He would not be able to buy their supper unless he sold the wood.

"How much for that pile?" he heard a voice above him. He stood up slowly, feeling dizzy.

"Five Birr," he said.

"Five Birr?" the man repeated. "I can get three bundles for that."

Ashebir coughed into his t-shirt then looked at the man again. "Ishi, three," he said, his voice barely a whisper.

"I will give you two and that's the end of it," the man said gruffly.

"Thank you sir," Ashebir said, knowing the man had taken pity. Two Birr, he thought, relieved. Zewdie will be happy.

He asked for a cup of water at one of the kiosks which lined the edge of the market. Those shops always had food and drink, salt and sugar, oil, tea and green coffee beans. They would never go hungry if they had a shop. The young man gave him a glass of water from a large jerry can. Ashebir bought a piece of flatbread for 25 cents. It was very thin and did nothing to sate his hunger.

He took the path along the road leading out of Ataye. He leant against the stone wall which ran beside the path. He didn't know if he would make it home. Suddenly, everything swirled into darkness. He was in a deep sleep, his soul shadow lying next to him. He was far away, relieved not to have to struggle any more. In his dreaming he heard voices.

"Someone bring water."

"Weyne, miskin, poor boy."

He tried to lift his head. He was lying on the path surrounded by women, muttering and calling for help.

"He's very sick."

"I have water." A woman lifted his head and made him sip. She put her hand on his forehead. It felt strong and comforting.

"He's got fever," she said.

"Where is his mother?"

"At home," he managed to whisper. His body felt heavy and aching. He turned on his side and curled up. He coughed. It sent pains through his head.

"Where are you from?"

"I have seen him before. He's from a nearby village," one woman said.

"Rest here a while and then go home," the woman with the water told him. "We can't stay with you. We have our own children at home."

He lay there for some time after the women left. He sat up and leant against the wall, his head hurting. People came and went along the path, Ataye townspeople. He wished someone from his village would pass.

Finally, he managed to stand. He went slowly towards a nearby kiosk, his head and bones aching. He bought two pieces of bread. Zewdie would be worrying, he thought, it was already dark. He walked looking at his feet, his soul shadow no longer there. He would reach home. He could walk that path with his eyes closed.

27

July 1984, Ataye

Zewdie had made a small fire. A pot of water was bubbling on it.

"Temima gave us tea and bread," she said. She did not turn and look at him as was her habit.

She had something on her mind. He sat quietly beside her until the tea was ready and knew that only then would she speak. When she bent her head, he lowered his head, waiting for her prayer, his eyes shut.

"Egziyabher yimesgen, for this food and drink, and for our friends and family," she whispered. "And be with us in the days to come, Amen."

"Amen," he whispered.

He watched her pour the steaming tea. He waited.

"Mindin neouw, Zewdie?" he said finally. "What is wrong?"

"We have to leave," she said in a quiet voice. "We have to go back to Alem Tena." She covered her mouth with her shawl and coughed.

"But this is our home now," he said. "And you are not well." He stood up, his legs shaking. Were they going to join the people walking down the grey snake of the Dessie Road?

"Please, Ashebir."

He sniffed hard. "No. I have to go outside." He went as fast as he could to the spot he always used on the hill behind their house and threw up into the bushes. There was hardly anything there. He coughed and retched, feeling pain in his guts. He sat down, hugging himself and rocked back and forth, a whining noise coming from his throat.

Zewdie came towards him. "Come home," she said.

She seemed far away, as if she were on the other side of the ravine.

"We have no choice Ashebir." She sat beside him and put her arm around his shoulders.

He leant against her, breathing in her familiar smell.

"Let's go back to the house," she said.

He got up with her and they walked down the hill.

"I wish Lakew was here," he said, and started crying.

"I know, I know."

He followed her through the door.

"Come and sit by the fire. Eat something," she said. "Drink your tea."

He felt the tears coming again and drank, trying to swallow them away. He put a small piece of bread in his mouth and chewed. His throat almost too tight to swallow.

"We can't go," he said. "Zewdie, please." He felt ashamed of his sobbing but could not stop himself.

"Yeney lij, can you remember when we came with my mother, Emet Hawa?"

"Yes," he said, wiping his eyes and sniffing into his t-shirt. "A little." He shivered. His mother laid a gabi round his shoulders.

"We came by bus from a small town south of Addis. Hawa was sick and wanted to die here, near her home."

"I remember her ram," he said. He could not help a small smile, still shuddering from the crying. "He was as fat as two goats. He used to come up behind her, and knock her right over."

"You were about five then."

He saw the tears in her eyes.

"Why do we have to go back?" he said, wiping his nose on the gabi.

"Things will get even worse if we stay," she said. She smiled, wiping her eyes with the thin black scarf, which lay lightly round her shoulders. It was becoming frayed and looked like the long soot-covered spiders' webs which hung from the rafters above the fire, floating in the heat. He looked up at the ceiling.

She took his hand in hers and he held on tightly.

"We know people in Alem Tena. Things may be better down there. We may find food and work. Maybe you can even go to school."

"But I want to stay here with Mohamed Abdu and Ali." He put his head in her lap and cried. His world was falling apart. His soul shadow appeared more often, frightening him and haunting his dreams at night. It might get him on the open road.

She stroked his head. "Come on now, that's enough," she said after a while, ruffling his hair. "My brother, Mohamed Shinkurt, and our friends all agree it is time for us to leave. They can't help us anymore."

He understood there was no arguing. "How will we go? Will we walk? Like the other people?" He started crying again.

"Aysoh, aysoh," she said quietly, stroking his face. "We can pay for transport if we leave now. I sold our last things today, and kept a few Birr from the sale of the goats."

"But you are sick."

"I will be fine," she said, smiling at him. "I'll have you with me, won't I? Now eat your bread. Then we will get ready. We are leaving early in the morning."

"Tomorrow? Already?"

"Yes, we have to go before our transport money runs out."

He finished his bread and tea in silence, struggling to swallow. It was as if Emet Hawa's ram had run hard into his belly, leaving him with no air in his lungs.

"I have packed our cooking pot, the small jerry can, our dish for making ki'ta bread, our plate and mugs, and a few clothes. It is all wrapped in the old gabi," she said, pointing at the bundle by the door.

"Ishi Zewdie," he whispered.

"Now let's sleep. We leave very early."

**

It was dark when she woke him. Ashebir rose slowly. He wrapped his gabi around himself, rolled up his ox-skin, and picked up his sickle and bag. Zewdie threw a cup of water over the last embers and there was a low hiss. The gojo-bate was empty. He followed her out. Zewdie clicked the padlock shut.

"Who will have the key?" he asked.

"Mohamed Shinkurt."

There was a half-moon in the sky. He could make out the dark shape of the other half. Maybe that's how it will be, he thought. I will be on the dark side and Mohamed Abdu on the light side. But we will still both be there even if we cannot see each other.

Zewdie closed the gate behind them, its rattle echoing in the silence. He felt her hand on his shoulder. Her eyes were not good in the dark. A small group was waiting, wrapped in their shawls, to say goodbye. They were weeping, soft moaning sounds like the wind through the eaves, like a lekeso. The fear running through his veins buckled his knees and he stumbled. The tears poured down his face.

Temima's voice rose above the others, "Let Allah look on us with mercy," she said.

"Ashebir," it was Mohamed Ahmed, Mohamed Abdu's father.

"Look after your mother. And don't forget, praise Allah at all times, even when life is hard."

"We'll pray to Allah you reach safely," Temima said, hugging him and then Zewdie. "You will come home when things are better, Insha'Allah."

The two women held each other, crying softly. Ashebir turned away. They had been friends since they were children, just like he and Mohamed Abdu. His stomach was tied in knots to his throat. He could barely swallow.

Mohamed Abdu was standing quietly on one side. Ashebir went over to him and stood by him, just touching fingers.

"Let's go," he heard his uncle Mohamed Shinkurt's voice. "Come Zewdie, let Nuru Ahmed carry your bundle. Ashebir walk with your mother."

Nuru Ahmed now did everything his brother Yimam would have done. No one spoke of the older brother, in case it brought bad luck. It was some months since he had left for the war up north.

"Ashebir," Temima said, tapping his shoulder. "Put this in your bag. It's food for the journey."

"Thank you, Temima," he whispered, taking the food wrapped in a cloth and bowing his head in thanks.

"Berta, Ashebir." He heard his friend's quiet voice nearby. "Be strong."

"Ishi," he whispered. He put the food in his bag and went to help his mother along the path. He felt her hand on his shoulder. It gave him comfort.

"Let's go," Mohamed Shinkurt said again. "The light is coming up."

The old man started down the path leading them to the Ataye Bridge and the main road. His son followed, carrying Zewdie's bundle across his shoulders, his head bent forward. Zewdie walked behind Ashebir. It felt like a funeral procession.

"Ashebir, Ashebir," he heard his friend calling.

He turned round still trying to keep pace with his uncle in front.

"Have you got your slingshot?"

Ashebir smiled and patted the bag hanging by his side. "It's in here," he said.

Zewdie squeezed his shoulder gently.

"Goodbye Mohamed Abdu," he called back quietly.

"Goodbye wendimey, my brother."

The air was misty with smoke from the small fires on the river bank below. They glowed, dots of red in the dark, groups of women and children huddled round. People, like ghosts floating in the early morning haze, were already on the road, walking south. Village men and women surrounded the vehicle owners, townspeople wearing jackets under their white gabis, on the road by the bridge. They were talking intently in low voices, discussing distance, stopping places, and prices. The vehicle owners decided the price and who could travel. It was always like that. The man with the vehicle had the last word. That's what Lakew had told him and it was true.

Mohamed Shinkurt had disappeared. Nuru Ahmed waited with them, Zewdie's bundle on the ground between his feet. They stood waiting in silence.

"Come," his uncle's voice called urgently. "Come."

Ashebir walked in the direction of Mohamed Shinkurt's voice, his mother still holding onto his shoulder.

"Zewdie, I got you two places in this Land Rover," his uncle said.

The Land Rover was old and battered. It was open at the back with a tarpaulin cover tied loosely over the top.

"Get in, get in," he said. "Don't lose your places. Sit here near the opening at the back, Zewdie, so you get more air." He helped Zewdie in. "Come on boy," he said. "Nuru Ahmed, wake up. Pass the bundle up to your aunt."

Zewdie sat, looking at her brother. She had never looked so sad and alone.

"I'm sorry Zewdie," Mohamed Shinkurt said. "We are all poor now."

His uncle was upset. It was new for Ashebir to see this. He was a 'big man', an elder of the village, a member of the Peasant Association, Zewdie always told him. 'He has a lot on his head,' she always said, trying to excuse his harshness.

His mother coughed heavily into her gabi. The dark shadows under her eyes seemed to have grown deeper overnight. The black cloth wound tightly round her head made her cheek bones even more pronounced. She pulled her gabi over her head and wrapped it tightly around her. She looked like The Hungry, he thought, all huddled up. He bit down hard on his lip.

"Don't worry, wendimey, my dear brother," she said. "You have helped us as best you could. God is with us now."

His uncle turned to look at him. Ashebir was shaken to see the man's eyes watering. "Praise Allah," Mohamed Shinkurt said. "I was hard on you, Ashebir, but I see you are a good boy, you work hard. Look after your mother."

It was the first time his uncle had spoken to him with any affection. The man took him in his arms. "We belong to Allah. He is with us," he said.

Ashebir found himself weeping into the old man's thick gabi. He buried his face in the soft woven cloth, feeling the loss of something he never had until this moment.

"Ayezoh, calm yourself," his uncle said.

Ashebir looked up at him. "I am afraid, uncle," he said quietly. "We will be alone."

"Be strong, berta, Ashebir," Mohamed Shinkurt said. "You will come back, Insha'Allah."

Ashebir passed his bundle and his stick to his mother and turned to shake hands with Nuru Ahmed and his uncle. They looked at him kindly.

"Go in peace," his uncle said.

He climbed in and sat next to Zewdie. The hard metal bench ran the length of the vehicle to the cab where the driver sat. On the other side, the bench was already full. As more people climbed in, he shuffled closer and closer to his mother. The women talked in low voices, sucking their teeth.

A man raised his voice at another, "Move over will you? I have paid for a place on the bench."

The other looked up and said in a quiet voice, "Egziyabher yawkal, we have all paid the same, sir. Take a seat where you can, like the rest of us."

The man with the loud voice pulled his gabi closer round himself and sat down right on top of all the bundles. The women's voices rose a little to object and fell again, like the wind through their gojo-bate chimney. None of them had the energy to argue.

"This one will take you to Robit, Zewdie," Mohamed Shinkurt called out. "You will have to pick another vehicle from there to Debre Berhan."

"Ishi," his mother whispered, nodding her head a little.

Other vehicles were filling up too. There were two pick-ups and another Land Rover, its panels dented like the many beatings on a donkey's backside. One of its front lights was an orange-brown rusty hole.

"Ataye. Senbatey. Robit," the ticket tout called out in a sing-song voice. He was not any older than Nuru Ahmed, still a boy.

Ashebir wondered what it might be like to work like him, instead of looking after animals. He preferred animals, their warm snuffly noses, the long, thick, soft skin hanging under the zebu's chin, how he and his friends had to skip out of the way of the goats' sharp horns. He hugged himself.

"Innihid!" the tout shouted. "Let's go. We're full." He held a fat wad of Birr notes tightly in his fist, as he walked past the back of the Land Rover.

Maybe he made a lot of money, Ashebir thought. Maybe it was a good job after all. That boy would not have to leave home in search of food.

By now men, women and children were packed in on both sides of the Land Rover and on top of the bundles in the middle. The loud man had settled down. Ashebir covered his nose and mouth with his gabi. The smell was strong with so many people. Warm sweat on unwashed clothes and, he thought, diarrhoea.

He peered out looking for Mohamed Shinkurt and Nuru Ahmed in the small crowd gathered behind the vehicle. The dawn was coming up pink over the mountains. The boy banged the backside of the vehicle and it took off. Ashebir watched as the boy ran alongside to jump in the front. He heard the door slam with a clatter. They chugged away, everything rattling, a puff of black smoke spurted out behind them. Ashebir raised his hand to wave at Mohamed Shinkurt and Nuru Ahmed, watching them until the vehicle turned a corner. He watched until they disappeared behind a hillside of dried earth and rocks crumbling into the road.

28

The engine whined as it strained up and down the hills and round the tight bends. The vehicle bumped and jarred along the road. It was only because they were so tightly packed in that they weren't thrown from one side to the other. Zewdie was looking across the hills and back along the road. Her eyes were dry. He put his head on her shoulder, not sure whether it was to comfort her or himself. He could not cry any more. He could not sleep. His eyes were wide open. He stared at the bundles at his feet, at the others in the Land Rover, at the country passing by, without really seeing.

He looked up hearing children's voices shouting. They were running after the car waving their sticks in the air. He could see their goats scattered on the side of the road and up the rocky slopes. Ashebir felt a moment of excitement. He sat up and waved at them. Then they were gone. He leant his head on Zewdie's shoulder and watched the road disappear behind them. It was getting hot.

They came to the flat lands of the valley bottom. He recognised it. He and Zewdie had walked that dry place many times.

"Look Zewdie," he said, talking loudly over the noise of the car, nudging her to get her attention

"Mmm," she said, her eyes peering out of the back, over her gabi, which she held tightly over her mouth and nose.

The remains of oxen and goats lay scattered in the dust between scrub bushes.

She shook her head and he knew she would be tutting under her shawl and saying a prayer.

"Look, the vultures," he said.

They hopped around the carcasses and circled in the blue sky, their wings open wide.

"I don't like vultures, Zewdie. Or hyenas."

She nodded again.

The vehicle bumped on over the road throwing up dust behind.

"Look, Zewdie," Ashebir said.

She peered out and nodded.

"It's Senbatey market," he said.

The vehicle stopped. "Senbatey, Senbatey," the tout sang out. "All for Senbatey get down."

The air was hot and still.

"How fast we came. It takes so long to walk, you know?" Ashebir said, leaning out over Zewdie to look for the place where the goats and sheep were sold. The market was busy with people but not as full as he remembered it. He watched a train of camels treading the road carefully, rocking slowly from side to side as they went. "It's so fast in a car, Zewdie," he said again.

"You're right," she said.

He sat back pulling his gabi round his nose. The stench in the vehicle was too much. He was glad uncle Mohamed had got them a place near the opening at the back.

"When will we get there?"

"I don't know, Ashebir. It is still a long way."

One woman holding her baby, its mouth still hanging onto her breast, climbed down from the back and onto the tarmac. Her breast was long and flat and Ashebir wondered if she had any milk at all. Someone passed her bundle and Ashebir stood up to hand it down to her.

"Egziersteling," she said. "God be with you."

He bowed his head.

No one else got out. The boy banged the side of the car, ran alongside to jump in the front and slammed the door. The Land Rover took off chugging as before, letting out a large cloud of black smoke. Ashebir covered his mouth and tried not to breathe in.

The woman opposite them leaned forward. "Where are you coming from?" she asked.

"Ataye," Zewdie said.

The woman's face was thin. She had Zewdie's black rings under her eyes. Her sandaled feet rested on a large bundle on the floor between them.

"And you?" Zewdie said.

"Werey Ilu," she said.

"You had to travel far to reach Ataye then," Zewdie said.

"Yes. This is my daughter, Feker," she said, touching the slim girl next to her. She was fast asleep against her mother.

Something moved under the woman's gabi.

"My son is sick," she said, pulling back her gabi. A small boy lay curled up on her lap.

"Weyne," Zewdie said. "What happened?"

The boy looked slowly towards them. Ashebir had never seen such a sick child. The skin on his face was drawn tight over his cheeks. His eyes sat in hollows, the corners full of yellow pus. His mother took the edge of her shawl and wiped it away tutting. His mouth opened slowly and then closed again. It was cracked and dry. It reminded Ashebir of a nest of baby birds he and Mohamed Abdu had once disturbed. Their beaks opened and closed without a sound, they were naked and skinny. One lay dead on the ground covered in ants.

"I don't know. First we did not have enough to eat and then he got diarrhoea and every time I gave him something it just came out again," the woman said, tears in her eyes. She covered the boy up again, patting his body through her gabi.

"Be Egziyabher, oh God," Zewdie whispered. "What to do? Weyne, Min yishallal?"

"I am going to my brother's place near Robit," the woman said. "I hope he can help us."

An old man at the back started coughing. It sounded even worse than Emet Fahte's. Ashebir wondered where he was going to spit it out, feeling disgusted.

It was too hot and cramped in the car. He tried to find new places for his legs and feet. He was not used to sitting for so long and his body ached.

"It's like Lakew said, Zewdie, those people just want to make money," he said. "It's too crowded back here."

"I know, I know," she sighed.

"Shall I give the boy a piece of bread, Zewdie?"

"Ask his mother."

"Would he like some of our ki'ta bread?" Ashebir asked the woman.

"Thank you, yeney konjo. God bless you," she said. "He cannot eat. He will only vomit. I hope my brother can take him to the hospital. Egziyabher sifeked," her eyes rolled up to the heavens above the tarpaulin.

"What about Feker? Maybe she wants some?" he asked, looking at the sleeping girl.

"I am sure she will. Give me a little for when she wakes."

Ashebir pulled the bread Temima had given him out of his bag. It was wrapped in a piece of cloth. He broke a bit off and reached it over to the woman with two hands, giving a small nod of his head.

"God bless you," she said, taking it, bowing her head in return.

He felt pleased for the first time that day.

The canvas cover flapped against the sides as they rattled along. Ashebir was glad of the shelter from the burning sun. He leant against Zewdie once more and closed his eyes. He did not want to look at the boy, or the vultures hopping around the dead oxen any more.

**

A loud clanging woke Zewdie. It sounded like the harsh echoes ricocheting from the corner of Ataye market where they turned metal into buckets and cans. It was the ticket tout banging the side of the vehicle.

"Robit, Robit, Robit," he called out in his sing-song voice. "Woradjey alle. Robit, Robit. Everyone get out here."

She felt hot and sweaty under her gabi, which she had pulled over herself and Ashebir to sleep. His head lay heavy against her. She gently ruffled his hair. It was longer than usual and thick with dust from the road.

He slowly stretched his body and groaned, his eyes still closed.

She did not want to get up either. Her mouth was dry. Her left leg had gone dead. Her stomach gnawed and ached. It was the hunger living in her. She had not eaten much for some time. Her chest felt tight and she hoped the coughing would not start again. She leaned out. "What is it?" she called to the boy. "Can't you take us to Debre Berhan?"

"Everyone out at Robit," the boy called out, as if to remind everyone, not just her.

"God help us," she muttered, wondering if her money would last the journey. On the road, there was an ebb and flow of people on the move. So many of them. "Come on Ashebir, we have to get out."

"Ishi," the boy mumbled, rubbing his eyes.

"Make way," the man from Ataye with the gruff voice said, looking straight at Zewdie. "We all have to get out here."

"Ashebir," she nudged him. "We have to get out."

He rubbed his eyes trying to stir himself.

Others in the back were sorting their bundles and shaking their sleepy children.

"How is your boy doing?" Zewdie asked Feker's mother.

"The same, the same," the woman said, sighing. "Thank God we will be at my brother's soon." She was holding the child under her gabi with one hand, and pulling at a dusty black bag from the pile on the floor with the other. It was held together with sisal rope, the was zip broken.

"Here, you get out first," Zewdie said to the woman. "Ashebir will pass your bag to you."

"Really? He is a good boy," the mother said. "Come on Feker, let's get down."

Ashebir passed the bag to them without a word.

Feker was standing by her mother, nibbling at Ashebir's bread. She had large soft eyes and reminded Zewdie of Temima's daughter. She smiled and the girl smiled shyly back before disappearing behind her mother's skirts.

"God be with you and your son," the woman said.

"And with you," Zewdie said. "I'll pray for your boy."

"Zewdie," Ashebir said. "We have to get out now. You go first and I will pass our things to you."

"Alright," she said, trying to feel the strength in her legs before standing. She got up, stumbled and felt Ashebir's hand catch her arm. She started coughing. The pains in her chest worried her. She sat again and coughed into her gabi.

"Please help my mother get down," she heard Ashebir calling out. "Come Zewdie, we are in the way here." He put his hand out to help her stand.

She looked at Ashebir and wondered when he had grown up. She stood slowly, shaking her head. Maybe it was somewhere between Ataye and Senbatey? Or had it happened before, without her noticing?

A youth was looking up at her from the road. He was wearing a woollen hat and a bright red cotton jacket rolled up at the sleeves. He smiled, encouraging her. His face was clean. He must have washed that morning.

"Come Enatey, let me help you," he said stretching his arms towards her.

With Ashebir holding her from behind, and the youth on the road in front, she managed to get down onto the tarmac. She felt its heat through her black plastic shoes. They had worn thin. The right one was split open at the top. She had not wanted to do the journey bare foot. "Thank you," she said and walked slowly to the side of the road to find somewhere to sit.

"I'll bring your things," the youth said, catching her bundle from Ashebir. He carried it over and put it on the ground beside her.

"You are kind," she said. "Your mother must be proud."

Ashebir dropped his ox-skin roll and stick onto the ground from the back of the Land Rover and climbed down after them. She watched as he chatted with the youth with the red jacket and clean face. He was looking up at the boy who patted him on the shoulder. Then he walked over and put his bundle next to hers.

"What shall we do now, Zewdie?" he said, suddenly looking lost and small again. "There are so many people."

"Yes, so many people," she said. Zewdie looked around them, wishing Lakew was with them. "Oh God," she whispered. "What is happening to us all?"

Some sat along the roadside like her for a rest. Others walked as if in a trance, even their children were silent, their eyes staring at the ground beneath their bare feet.

Ashebir sat close to her leaning his head on her arm. She looked around to a group of women from Wollo sitting nearby. "Do you know where we can get transport to Debre Berhan?" she asked.

"You have money for transport?"

"Yes, thanks to God, I have a little."

"We have no Birr left."

Zewdie looked at the woman with no money left. One child was crawling over her lap. The other sat cross-legged on the ground beside her, flies crawling in the corners of her eyes. They were naked except for a thin black thread which hung round their necks holding a small pouch of medicine. Their bodies were dusty, their bellies slightly swollen. She could see the tell-tale white crusts of scabies in between their fingers. The woman waved her hand above the children to keep the flies away. Zewdie did not know what to say. She wondered how long her money would last. She coughed into her shawl again.

"You can ask over there," the woman said motioning her head towards a small group of men. "They will take you for a price."

"What will you do?" Zewdie asked her.

"Rest a while and then try walking a little further," she said. "Egziyabher yawkal. We will reach somewhere where they will give us food and water. We have faith in God."

"Ashebir," she said. "You stay with our things. I will see if I can get us transport to Debre Berhan."

"No one will take you that far," another woman said. "Ask for Debre Sina."

"They won't take us to Debre Berhan?" Zewdie said.

The two women looked at each other and then at Zewdie.

"Petrol rationing," the one with no money said.

Zewdie got up. She would try.

**

She found a pick-up truck that would take them. The Wollo women on the roadside had been right. The driver would only take them as far as Debre Sina. She could get a bus to Debre Berhan from there, he said. She was surprised at the price but had to accept. They sat on the hard metal floor under the torn canvas awning which was loosely tacked onto a rusty frame. Once more they were tightly packed in.

Zewdie held on tightly to her bundle as the truck took off. She felt Ashebir's head leaning against her and was comforted by the boy. She stared at the road passing quickly beneath them, looking up every now and then at the dry fields. How did things get so bad? She did not know what they would do. Their money would only get them as far as Debre Berhan. It was a week's walk to Addis from Debre Berhan, and she did not have the strength.

She felt a nudge.

"Look Zewdie," he whispered.

Everyone's eyes were on a little girl opposite them. She was lying under a faded cotton shema on her mother's lap. Her rib bones stuck out and her belly swollen. Her mother held her close. The girl's legs were like long skinny twigs. Zewdie's eyes filled with tears as she watched the woman rocking back and forth, moaning softly and kissing the child's forehead. The little girl wore round metal earrings and a dirty bead necklace.

"She's got 'swollen belly' Zewdie," Ashebir whispered.

Zewdie nodded and said a quick prayer.

The girl's skin was like old leather. The child was dying. Her eyes, deep in their sockets. Her lips the colour of ash. Zewdie put her arm around Ashebir, pulling him closer. Oh my dear God, she thought. Please have mercy on us.

Everyone was silent, watching. One woman began whispering prayers.

Zewdie had known things were bad but had not expected this. To find

351

so many people on the road. Every vehicle full, and small groups of sickly, hungry families walking together. They came down the hillsides and climbed up out of the valleys, all heading south. Even in the pick-up, her travelling companions were thin; their bodies gave off a thick sickly smell, not the healthy odour of working country folk. The sight of all these people, in their worn out grey clothing, leaving their homes, their fields, their animals, shook her. She looked down at Ashebir, patting his face and hair gently. They were in God's hands now.

Every time the pick-up hit a pot-hole they were lifted off the hard floor and bumped back down again. They held onto each other and the sides of the truck. One woman vomited over the edge and another passed her a sip of water. We have become like neighbours in a short space of time, Zewdie thought.

The little girl's mother suddenly wailed, "Weyne! Weyne!" and buried her face in the child's still body.

"Zim-bey, zim-bey, hush, hush, my sister," an older woman whispered urgently. "If they hear you they will stop and put you and the child on the road." She motioned her head towards the driver and his mate in the cab at the front. They had music on and were chatting loudly over the noise of the engine.

"They won't carry a dead body in their truck."

The woman looked around the other passengers, wiping the tears from her face with a dirty shawl.

"Hush, hush, my dear, be Egziyabher," the older woman whispered.

Zewdie felt the tears run down her cheeks. The sobs stuck painfully in her chest. She started coughing again. The others in the truck, even the men, cried softly into their shawls, muffling the sound. They motioned to each other to keep the noise low. The road ran fast behind them and the wind blew through the open back.

The mother covered the little girl with her gabi, her hands moving constantly as if wrapping the child back inside herself again. She rocked back and forth moaning softly.

The woman's misery was unbearable. Zewdie felt Ashebir move even closer to her. He turned and buried his face in the bundle on her knees and sobbed quietly. She held him and their few belongings, the bundle that had stood by the door to their gojo-bate just the night before. Her world on her lap. An uneasy feeling crept over her. Maybe they should have stayed in the village. Too late, too late, she thought. Better not to think about it.

When they reached Debre Sina, the sun was high in the sky. The women in the truck helped the bereaved mother get down with the little girl's body. They had gently wrapped it in a cloth and secured it to her back, covering it with her shawl, which she pulled up over her head. The woman walked away, her eyes dazed.

Zewdie wondered where she would go. She watched her disappear into the throngs of similar looking people with tired faces. There was a hum of noise, someone calling a name, touts calling out destinations in sing-song voices from better times, selling their tickets, wads of Birr in their hands; crying babies, frightened children wailing.

Once on the tarmac, Zewdie found herself in the midst of the commotion. She looked down at Ashebir. "Hold on to my skirt, tight, so we don't lose each other," she said. "Don't let go." Her gaze followed the woman. *At least the little girl's suffering is over.* She felt guilty the instant the thought came to mind. She knew very well that the mother's had just begun.

The driver of their pick-up was oblivious to the death in the back of his truck. His ticket tout was already looking for passengers to take back to Robit. "Robit. Robit. Robit," he called out. "Robit, Robit, Robit."

"He won't get many going that way," she heard one of their fellow passengers mutter as he climbed down. "Most of us want to get to Addis."

"Addis?" A man standing on the tarmac watching them said, with a sharp short laugh. "You won't get to Addis. Miskin. They are not letting peasants into the city. They won't let The Hungry in."

"Enday? Haven't you heard about the road blocks?" A man standing next to him said.

Zewdie moved closer to hear what they were saying.

"What do you mean?" her neighbour from the pick-up truck said.

"I am sorry, comrade," the local man said, a little more politely. His shirt hung loosely over his trousers, and he wore barabasso sandals.

He did not look like one of The Hungry filling the road, but he was skinny and his face sharp and ruddy like the country people, 'the peasants', as he called them. *He must be a 'political' from Debre Sina,* she thought.

"Have you not heard? They are preparing to celebrate the tenth anniversary of the Revolution. No duriyey , vagabonds, thieves, or hungry are allowed into the city," he said.

"But we are going to Alem Tena, south of Addis," Zewdie said.

She could see from their eyes that she would not get there.

"Miskin," a woman muttered and sucked her teeth. "Egziyabher anchee gar yihun. God be with you."

"Get yourself to Debre Berhan," the 'political' from Debre Sina said. "Maybe someone will help you there."

Zewdie decided not to talk with the men any more. She bowed her head slightly, "Egziersteling," she said and moved on. "Hold on to me, Ashebir," she said, terrified of losing him, and wove her way slowly in and out of the people, The Hungry, the peasants, on the road. "Excuse me," she said, moving past an old man and his grandchild. "Sorry," she said, putting her hand on a woman's shoulder to get by. "Egziersteling," she said, as she made her way through these people, who were becoming familiar to her, her heart softening towards them, her new neighbours.

She looked up at the mountain which towered over the small town. A slow stream of thinly clad people was making its way up the steep road, snaking up the mountainside in the heat. She headed towards the groups sitting along the roadside and around the square near the bus depot. She needed to sit and think.

Still more people were on the move around her. They walked past the tin-roofed buna bate with metal tables and chairs set outside, past the men slurping at glasses of hot tea and coffee; they walked past kiosks selling caramella, Coca Cola, Omo powder, yellow tins of baby milk powder and bright coloured plastic toys. They walked past and walked past, along the road heading south to Debre Berhan. Ethiopian flags, hung limply in the heat from single storey buildings, bright green, yellow, red. Hawker-boys stood around, trays of cigarettes and sweets around their necks, watching in bewilderment as the people passed. Other boys held up bunches of small sweet bananas, to no avail. How she wished she had a few coins to spare to buy one for Ashebir. Some had woven sheep's wool hats for sale, stacked high on their heads. No one had any money.

Zewdie looked around to see where they could sit quietly. Ashebir was silent by her side. "Let's sit over there and eat a piece of Temima's bread, Ashebir," she said, trying to sound tempting, as if she were offering him a slice of sweet papaya. He must be tired she thought. She tutted.

He nodded, looking up at her, his eyes glazed. He lifted her bundle onto his shoulders and walked in the direction she had pointed.

They sat among the others on the rough stones and dry stubble that made a path along the verge. Zewdie shaded her eyes from the sunlight. Her scarf had become loose in the wind in the back of the pick-up. She took it off, shook out the red dust and wound it back round her head again.

"Your ears are so small, Zewdie," Ashebir said.

"Just like Lakew's" she said smiling at him. "You have the bread. Are you going to share a piece with your mother?"

"Where is Lakew?" Ashebir asked.

"I don't know," she said. "He will find us, he always does. Don't worry. Come, let's eat."

Ashebir took some bread and chewed. "Zewdie?"

"Yes, what is it?"

"Where will we sleep tonight?"

She felt fear fluttering inside her. She sighed. They would be sleeping by the roadside tonight, where else? "I don't know. Egziyabher yawkal," she said, not wanting to tell him just yet.

"Let's see if we can get transport to Debre Berhan. We don't want to stay here tonight."

"We'll keep this bread for later, Zewdie," he said, wrapping the remaining bread into the cloth again.

"Turu neow, good idea," she said, knowing he was still hungry. "Look after the cloth, it's Temima's. We will keep it to remember her."

"I'll take your bundle, Zewdie."

She picked up his ox-skin and watched as he lifted her bundle onto the back of his neck, across his shoulders. The weight pressed his chin forward onto his chest so he had to look up at an awkward angle to see where he was going. There were two small country buses. One was nearly full. A boy was climbing over the top, securing luggage. Another stood in front of the open door calling out, "Debre Berhan, Ch'ach'a, Sembo. Debre Berhan, Ch'ach'a, Sembo."

"There are two of us," she said, turning away to cough into her shawl.

"Where to? Where are you going?"

She motioned at Ashebir to answer, unable to speak with the coughing.

"Debre Berhan," she heard Ashebir's small voice. He had put her bundle on the ground between his legs.

Zewdie put her hand on her chest. "How much?" she asked. She unwrapped the remaining notes she had knotted into the top of her skirt for safe keeping, and showed the tout the Birr in her hand.

"You are one Birr short," the tout said and walked past her.

"Please, my boy, yeney lij," she said, catching hold of his arm. "I am asking you, be enateh, in your mother's name, be Egziyabher, take us to Debre Berhan, ebakeh, be enateh."

At that moment the driver came round the side of the bus scratching himself. "What's the matter?" he asked, still adjusting his pants. She saw the green traces of khat round his teeth.

"She's one Birr short," the boy said.

"How many are you?" the driver asked her.

"We are two. Just me and my boy," she said. "Please sir. Be Egziyabher, be enateh, help us if you can."

"Let them on," the driver said and carried on to a small shack by the side of the road, towards the strong smell of coffee drifting from within.

The tout took Zewdie's last Birr. She felt suddenly naked. That was it. Not one centime left. Only Temima's bread. She muttered a prayer and gave Ashebir a gentle push to get on the bus. He picked up her bundle and climbed up the metal steps in front of her.

When the bus drew out of Debre Sina the driver pushed a cassette into his player. The words, 'come, come, my love, come, come,' brought tears to Zewdie's eyes. She wondered if Kassahun could see her from his life beyond hers. She had already sold his ring some time ago. She looked down at her finger and remembered the day he had pushed it on over her knuckle, laughing at her hard, working hands. He had been proud of her. The thought made her feel warm inside for a moment and she smiled a little. Love. The songs were all about love. The pain of love lost, the joy of loving and the hope of being together. She wiped her face with her shawl and looked down at Ashebir who had leant against her. He was already asleep.

29

July 1984, Addis Ababa

It was Saturday evening. She was expecting him back. The flat was quiet apart from the soft whirr of the oven roasting the poor chicken, that had been strutting about under the kitchen table only hours before. She popped open a beer from the fridge. The first sip hit the back of her throat, cold and fresh. She inched a cigarette out of the full packet, flicked open her old flint lighter, took a long drag, and went out onto the terrace. Dusk had fallen over the rooftops on the hillside opposite, and met the glow of Piazza's shop lights below. She peered over the balustrade. Taxis passed by slowly down below, tired and hopeful. Outside the African Bookshop a small group of students talked, laughed and tussled with each other, the anxiety and excitement of first flirtatious encounters. Izzie was glad she had all that behind her.

The boys were down there as usual. One foot propped against the wall of the Blue Nile Bar, as if it were the cool thing to do, chatting. Shoeshine boxes ready. They stepped out in front of couples walking past arm in arm, holding out packets of Winston and Marlborough. Piazza, a road snaking its way through temptations. Bars and cafes offering food, cakes, teas, coffees, whiskey and beer. And one jeweller after the next displaying sumptuous gold and silver behind glass windows. It was all too expensive for her.

A plaintiff cry in the sky made her look up. The kites. Circling high above it all. What she would give to be one of them for a moment.

She thought of the night she and Moe had spent in a small guesthouse overlooking the escarpment at Debre Libanos. Just the two of them, a rare event. The enormous, overwhelming landscape seemed to have the effect of unifying them for once. It shrank their existence into perspective. The night's deep black silence, broken by the occasional cry from a bird of prey, had induced a mystical softness and whispering between them.

"Do you think Tekle Himanot really stood on one leg for seven years?"

"Impossible," Moe had whispered back. "And why seven?"

"He's a saint. Saints can do anything."

"What would you do?" he had said after a pause, his breath soft in her ear. "I mean, if you could do anything."

"I would take off from the edge of that incredible escarpment," she'd said, her voice low, her body tingling, "and fly, spread my wings, the morning sun on my back."

He had wrapped himself around her.

"What about you?"

"I would sail, sail away into the sunset," he'd said, laughing softly. "With a picnic basket packed with a fresh cottage loaf, cheddar cheese, tomatoes, cheese and onion crisps, oh and one fresh jam donut," he'd whispered. "And six cans of Green King."

They had giggled quietly.

"Alone?"

"Alone." He'd kissed her nose. "There's only one donut."

They had laughed.

"You can watch me from up there in the sky."

The Piazza lights suddenly became a blur through her tears. Her heart felt heavy. She didn't trust what was going on, what she felt might be going on. Her throat felt like a clenched fist. She took another swig of the sharp, cold beer to loosen it. It was ridiculous, the way Moe behaved when he was with that Duncan, especially around women. And now they had spent a whole week together in Harar. Something must be going wrong with them for her to feel this suspicious. Moe was often distracted these days. Doing things with other people, or reading, buried away from her in a book.

And what about her? As long as she was working, or with friends, she was okay. When she was with Moe, she felt awkward, maybe even trapped. She longed for their old love. If she was honest, the time she and Moe spent in each other's company was probably trying for both of them. She wanted him to want the things she wanted. She wanted to absorb everything around her, understand it, be part of it. She wanted to travel with him through the enormous Ethiopian landscapes. Even with the travel restrictions, they could surely explore more of Shewa region. But Moe seemed happy with the British Club barbecues and Hash runs. And now there was talk of another theatre performance.

Maybe her yo-yo bouts of melancholy and random exuberance were too much for him.

She needed to get out of the city. It was suffocating her.

'Where is the old man to untangle the riddle?' Gezahegn would say when they all fell silent in the office.

Angels passing.

She shivered.

A car drew up outside the building. A door clunked shut. Her heart stopped. She peered over. The vehicle moved on. It wasn't him.

The food was ready, plates laid out in the kitchen. A bottle of red Gouder, open to 'breathe'.

If only she could breathe. Find relief from her fluttering belly.

Duncan. Smooth-talking, self-serving, Duncan. He had dark-haired, bright-eyed, confident, good looks, but she didn't like him. Didn't trust him.

**

A week or so before Moe and Duncan had left for Harar, she and Moe had been chatting over breakfast. She had not expected him to go anywhere. There was tight security. The Ministry for Public Security was not issuing travel permits to foreigners. Even in her office, some of the cadres were accusing the farenj of making up famine stories. All efforts were on getting the city ready to celebrate the 10th Anniversary of the Revolution. Nothing should divert attention from that.

"I can't believe I'm working in the Ministry responsible for clearing the streets of 'undesirables', Moe," she'd started. "We round them up and dump them in a so-called 'Reception Centre' on the Gojjam road."

"Well you're not exactly doing that, Izzie, are you?"

"You know the old fellow with leprosy outside the China Bar, the one that looks after our car? You know he's disappeared?"

"I know, you said. Pass me the bread, honey?"

"Here," she'd held out the finely woven basket. "Negisst waited in a queue for an hour to buy that bread." She'd taken a sip of hot coffee.

"Someone got out of bed on the wrong side," Moe had muttered, as he dipped his bread into the honey on his plate and took a large bite.

"For 'undesirables', read disabled, street children, beggars, homeless, prostitutes. Prostitutes, huh. They've already got the project for three hundred of them up and running. Tehadso it's called. They are sewing. What is it with all this sewing?"

"I know, honey, you've said."

"And you know, it's as if a giant hoover is passing through Addis, clearing up the unsavoury debris. An army of little men, and women following in their broad sun hats, carrying pots of paint, corrugated iron sheets for fencing and plants for roundabouts, sprucing it all up."

"Honey, I'm going on a field trip. Just waiting for the permit," he'd said. "Probably leave Saturday." He'd slurped loudly on his coffee. "Mmmm… that's good."

"Do you hear anything I say?" She remembered saying.

"Yes, honey, I do. But what can I say. What can I do?" He'd run his fingers though his hair. "I need a haircut."

"I can do it if you like."

He'd laughed. "Not after the last time, you won't!" He gave her a peck on the cheek. "Honey, they've been preparing for the 10th Anniversary for months. I know the amount of effort and money they are putting into it at a time like this is grotesque. You know it's grotesque. But I can't be talking about it day in day out."

"I know," she'd sighed. He had a point. "But I feel like a collaborator, you know?"

"Your department is doing good stuff. Hang onto that, huh?"

"Yeah, you're right, I suppose," she'd said, not convinced. She didn't feel she was doing enough.

"And, by the way, Izzie, I could say the same. Did you hear what I said? I am going to Harar at the weekend. For a week, maybe ten days."

"Yes I did hear. Sorry. I thought there was a ban on foreigners' travel?"

"It mostly affects NGOs and journalists. Mengistu doesn't want them poking their noses in. We are going with the Ministry. Maybe they think they can control us better."

"He's choosing to call it a 'natural disaster', not a famine," Izzie said.

"It's depressing."

"Fasika said Wondwassen's appeal to foreign donors fell flat on its face. That they, like Alessandro said, continue to be unconvinced."

"By the way, to change the subject, I'm going with your best mate," Moe had grinned, like he'd scored a point in an ongoing competition.

"Who? Duncan? He's not coming back, is he?" she'd pulled a face. "You know he's bad news, don't you? You know he asked me to 'fix him up' with Hiwot?"

"Don't take any notice. He was probably just trying to wind you up. He's not that bad." Moe had got up from the table, bent down to give her a kiss and pushed his chair in. "I have to go."

"Yes me too," she'd said. "And he is that bad."

**

"Izzie!" She heard a call from the street below.

Mekonnen and Hailu had spotted her. She leant over and waved. They jumped up and down, laughing. She relaxed a little and smiled.

Three men came out of the Blue Nile Bar. Mekonnen and Hailu dashed to the roadside, flapping hands, flagging down a taxi for them. Making wide gestures, Hailu ushered the men towards the taxi, while Mekonnen held the cab door open, bowing slightly. Little performers. She shook her head, smiling.

A white Toyota pulled up in front of their building. Her stomach turned. Hailu and Mekonnen left the taxi and ran across the road, joined by Biniam and a boy they all called Moshe Dyan, though she never knew why. They were like bees to honey. They ran to the side doors, and hovered around the boot. There were coins to be made here.

"Moe!" they called out.

She watched the scene, with growing, sixth sense, unease. Unwanted suspicions and imaginings. Something about Duncan. They will have been up to no good, she felt sure.

She saw Moe's straw blonde head of hair appear from the vehicle, lit by the Piazza evening street lights, as he climbed down.

He turned to reach inside and passed two bags back to the boys. He ruffled their heads.

Mekonnen pulled at his sleeve and pointed up.

Moe turned his face up and waved. One hand high in the air. "Hi!"

She waved back, feeling a bit caught out, as if she were spying.

The boys surrounded him, talking, gesticulating, and laughing, shuffling him, like ants round their prey, towards the main door of the building. The zabanya came forward and bowed slightly. They all disappeared, swallowed up by the entrance.

It was chilly. She rubbed her arms and went inside, shutting the terrace door behind her. She lit the candle on the dining table. She must baste the chicken. Heat up Negisst's vegetables. Do something practical. Take the freshly cut pineapple out of the fridge. All so well organised. She took a deep breath to calm herself and got busy. Was she building herself up for nothing?

The bell startled her.

They were already there. Muffled laughter, voices, scuffling, knocks on the hard wood door. "Izzie!"

She took a handful of centimes from the basket on the shelf, and opened the door to a blaze of cheerful, expectant faces, and small upturned hands. "Hey," she said, smiling at them all.

Moe pushed his bags over the threshold with his old suede boots and came through the door bringing warm on-the-road smells with him. Miles and miles of tarmac and dirt, traces of his familiar sweat, laced with cigarettes and beer. His being filled the hallway. The boys danced around him.

She shared the money out, received by the boys like gold coins from the bottom of a Christmas stocking. She looked up at Moe. "Hi there," she managed.

He turned to the boys, 'Ciao, ciao," he said, "see you tomorrow."

"Goodie night, Moe"

"Ciao, Izzie."

"Bye!"

The boys waved, tumbling around each other, and disappeared down the stairs, echoes floating up behind them.

Moe shut the door. He stood tall, brown, grinning. "Hey, honey."

She looked up at him, noticing how handsome he was. "Hey," she said again, hesitant, trying to take a breath.

"Smells good in here," he laughed, taking his jacket off. He was beaming. Eyes shining with unusual excitement, it seemed. Something different about him.

"You had a good trip," she said, trying to smile. She backed away.

"Yes," he said, "very." He opened his arms, "Come here, I missed you."

She folded into him. Breathing him in. Hoping. She looked up at him. "Did you? I missed you too. It's been long this time."

"Yup," he smiled down at her. "So what's cooking?"

"Chicken," she said, dismayed that her eyes had filled with tears. She didn't want him to see. "Woops. I better get it out of the oven. Heat up the veg. Beer?" She disappeared into the kitchen.

He was lifting his things to take through to the bedroom. "I just had one. A glass of wine, maybe?"

"Help yourself, it's on the dining table," she called out. So they had stopped at a bar on the way for a last one before home, she thought. She took the chicken out of the oven. It had a nice brown crust and steamed, warm delicious flavours. Her mouth watered. She covered it to rest before they carved it up. Everything was laid out on the side table in the kitchen, ready to take through.

Wine's breathing, chicken's resting, she thought. She almost giggled at herself, slight hysteria rising through her throat. I'm being ridiculous. He's home safe. All is well.

"I've poured you one too," he said, coming through to the kitchen, already carrying two full glasses.

"Thanks," she said, taking one from him. They went into the sitting room.

"Cheers," he said, standing in front of her.

As they lifted and clinked their glasses, she looked into his eyes. She saw it. She looked at him, her heart beating.

"What?" he said.

She stood looking at him.

"What's the matter?" he said, taking a sip, peering at her over the rim of his glass. "Honey."

"Did you?" she said. She couldn't stop herself. It was too soon, too early, they hadn't even eaten.

"Did I what?"

"With Duncan. Did you?"

"Honey, what's going on?" He took a step back. He looked uncomfortable. "You OK?"

Her heart was beating too fast. Too loud. She swallowed. "I'm fine." She took a sip of wine. "Just wondering. You know. Going to bars – with Duncan."

"Of course we did, Izzie," he said, relaxing a little. "You know us, you and me, we love a bop, a drink. No harm, huh?"

"Yes, but Duncan likes the girls, doesn't he? Did he get up to anything?" She looked up at him, took a sip of wine, wishing her hand would stay steady. "You know, while you two were out there doing your bit to save the world. There is a famine going on after all."

They stood face to face. Burning.

She could feel the panic rising. Give anything not to be standing here, she thought. If only Leila were here, even Booker, someone solid who knew them both.

He took a large gulp of wine and put the glass down on the mantlepiece above the fire. "We could put a fire on," he said, his voice low. He coughed and turned away, running a hand through his hair. He picked up some logs from the pile and started stacking them in the fireplace. He was sitting on his haunches with his back to her, his blue jeans tight across his backside. He had broad shoulders, wearing his father's old black sailing jumper with the worn grey leather patches at the elbows. She liked him in it.

Anger shot through her stomach. She managed to stop the urge to push him over. "Moe," she said, tight and careful. "I am asking you a question." Before she knew it she'd grabbed at his jumper with both hands. Her wine glass shattering on the floor spilling red. She pulled hard. "Did. You?"

"Hey," he put one hand out behind him to stop from falling over, the other swung round to shake her off.

She stumbled.

He stood up facing her. His face red, eyes dark. "What's going on?"

She grabbed at his jumper again shaking him.

"Stop this," he said. "What's got into you?"

"He goes with prostitutes. Did you?" she said, loud, angry. Furious to feel the tears in her eyes. "Did you?" She pushed at him. He didn't budge.

"Of course not, Izzie. What are you thinking?" His voice was hoarse. He stepped back. "What the fuck is going on?"

She'd caught him out.

"Don't lie to me Moe. I know you too well. I can see it in your eyes. I can almost smell it on you," she said through her teeth.

"Don't be ridiculous," his voice low, hoarse.

"How many times? Once or more? Every night? On your way home? After that beer you just had, or before?" The words rattled out one after the next.

Disbelief was written all over his face. A child caught out. He opened his arms, shrugging. An 'I own up' gesture of old. Maybe he wouldn't get in too much trouble. "OK. I did, we did, just once."

She stared at him.

"Just once," she said. "Really. Is that how it works. Just?" She let out a joyless laugh. A short sharp Uschi 'Ha!' "I love the idea of 'just', Moe."

"I..."

"How much did you pay her, Moe?"

"I don't know," he said, running his fingers back and forth through his hair.

"You can't remember how much you paid, that 'just' one time?" She pushed him with each word she spoke. "Sure about that Moe? Cos she deserves a hellova lot more, than, 'I don't know'."

He stood firm. "Izzie," he said. "Stop this, for fuck's sake."

She stared at him.

"I'm not the only one," he said.

"Don't give me that," she said. "You are my only one. Were." She wanted to tear him apart. She wanted this to stop. "These women, Moe. These girls. Girls. Christ. How old was she?"

"I don't know."

"Fuck's sake. You sound pathetic. Woman or child, Moe?"

"A young woman," he mumbled. "They were young women. Not girls, for God's sake."

"'They', you say. So it wasn't 'just once'. It was more than once. Don't think I'm going to believe that you tried it out once, and then stood at the bar while old Duncan went back for more."

Moe turned away.

"It's all about you, isn't it. You guys. Your pleasure. You actually believe, in that moment, that they like you. Well let me tell you something. They don't. They fucking don't." Tears welled in her eyes. "They are human beings, Moe. They have feelings. Dammit. How could you?" Her hands in tight fists. "Dammit."

"Izzie," he said.

"And by the way. You know there's an AIDS epidemic?" she said. "You've probably picked it up and passed it on, knowing you." She stopped. It suddenly struck her. "Fuck it, Moe. You haven't done this before, have you?" She felt sick. "And then come back to me? Would you have slept with me tonight?" She backed away shaking her head. "No, you wouldn't. You wouldn't."

"Izzie, I…"

"How much did you pay them Moe?" She couldn't let go. "That's what I want to know. What's the going rate for a farenj? Huh?"

He had both hands held straight out in front of him. "Izzie, stop."

"I hope you paid two hundred and fifty dollars US minimum, at the very least. Or do you pay thirty Birr and think you're being generous? God I hate you. All of you."

She knew the feeling. She needed to smash something, hit the wall, break something. She turned, stormed into the kitchen, frustration coursing from her belly into her arms. She saw the food all neatly laid out, the plates, the chicken, the vegetables. She swiped her arm across the whole lot, sent it flying across the kitchen. The chicken hit the wall and fell to the floor. Its juices left a running smear down the green paint. She'd never liked that green. Carrots, potatoes, scattered everywhere. Smashed plates, forks and knives across the floor. She let out a roar. "How dare you, Moe!"

She held her head in her hands, standing in the midst of the carnage. Her body at once tingling with the exertion and deflated. A homemade rag doll, the stitches round its red cloth heart unpicked. Its cheeks blush red.

There was silence in the sitting room and then a low voice. She wondered who he might be talking to. Wasn't he ashamed?

She wept. A loud howling noise came out.

"Shhhhh, Izzie," he said, coming up behind her.

"Worried about the fucking neighbours are you? The East German spies downstairs? They will be hearing it all, won't they?"

He took hold of her. "Hush, quiet. Hush, Izzie," he said. He wrapped his arms around her, held her tight into him, burying her face into his chest.

She couldn't breathe. She jiggled her legs, wriggled and pushed. "Let go," she shouted into his jumper. His Dad's old fishing jumper. "It's over. Let me go. Fuck it." She could hear herself screaming, "Let go. Let go." She knew this feeling. She had lost it.

He held her and rocked from side to side. "Hush Izzie, hush. Calm yourself. Hush."

She took a deep breath. Smelling him. It's over. She couldn't stay with him after this. An affair, maybe she could cope with. She hadn't always been an angel either after all. But this. No going back from this, no.

"That's right," he said. "Just breathe. Slow."

He started walking slowly with her, lifting, pushing gently, towards the sitting room. He sat her on the sofa.

She pulled her feet up, hugging her knees, head down, rocking back and forth.

"Here," he said. "I got you a shot of whiskey. Drink up."

She cupped it in two hands like a mug of tea. She took a gulp and coughed at the sharpness. She started crying. "You bastard, Moe. You miserable bastard. This is it now. You know that don't you? It's over."

"I'm sorry, Izzie." He was sitting on the floor beside her. "I'm sorry. What an idiot."

A shot of anger sprang through her again. "Sorry!" She shrieked, flinging the glass of whiskey across the floor. "Idiot? Is that it? 'I'm an idiot'?" she mimicked.

Moe got to his feet. "Izzie. Calm down, hey?"

"Not me you have to apologise to, Moe. It's those girls you take advantage of. Tell them you're sorry, Moe. Not me." She laughed.

The front door bell rang.

"What's that?" she said, looking towards the door.

Moe looked sheepish, ran a hand across his mouth. "Booker," he said.

"Booker? What's he doing here?" She looked at him closer. "It was him you called? You fucking coward." She got up off the sofa.

"You were going crazy, Izzie."

The bell rang again.

"I better get it," he said.

"You damn coward," she said to herself, heading quickly to the bathroom. She locked the door. She heard their voices in the corridor. Men's voices, surveying the kitchen and disappearing into the sitting room.

She looked at herself. The bathroom mirror was old, pockmarked with black dots and cracked in the top right corner. How many faces had it seen? And now hers, in this moment. Dishevelled, distraught, a thirty-year-old woman, about to be alone again. How did that work? Where would she go? Her mascara (of course she had made herself look good for him) had become two dark circles under her eyes. She had been yelling at him looking like that? Oh God. Her face screwed up to cry, the tears came pouring down again. Why do we look so ugly when we cry? she thought. She ran the hot tap until it almost burned her fingers. She held a flannel under it. Wrung it out, took a long deep breath and covered her whole face in the steaming cloth. She breathed out. She did the whole process again. And again. She sat on the edge of the bath. She would run a bath later if she had the energy. Her body ached.

There was a knock at the bathroom door.

"Izzie?"

It was Booker. She froze.

"Izzie?"

"Yes," she barely whispered.

"You OK?"

She started crying again. "No."

"Let me in?"

"I look a wreck."

"Come on, Izzie. Open up."

She got up, took a look at herself in the bathroom mirror, wiped a finger under each eye and went to the door. She unlocked it.

"Oh dear," he said.

"I told you," she said, managing a small smile and shrugging. "It's over. You know?"

"I know," he said. "I'm sorry."

"Yeah."

"Let's get out of here, shall we?"

"What?" she took a step back. "I'm not going anywhere tonight. You are kidding me, right? Is that what he wants?" She pushed past Booker. "Moe," she said. "What the fuck? Booker says I'm going with him? What's going on here?"

"Izzie," Moe came towards her, his arms open, shrugging again. "It's better. If I go, you would be here on your own. Better if you're with someone."

"Come back with me, Izzie, sweetheart," Booker said. "You can have a hot bath, a drink. We can have a chat."

"Don't patronise me, OK?"

"I didn't mean to," Booker said, raising his hands. "Sorry."

"OK, and thanks, but I don't want to. This is my place too. Moe?" She looked between them. Of course it would be Moe that stayed in the flat. It came with his job. "Oh God, this is awful." She put her hands over her face, holding it. It felt like a breaker wave was crashing over her head, salt water flooding up her nostrils. She couldn't breathe. She put a hand out against the wall.

**

She didn't know how it happened but she found herself in Booker's car, wrapped in the warmest gabi they had, hugging a holdall. She had no idea what was inside it. Elton John was on the cassette player. She looked out onto the passing lit-up jewellers shops, last orders in the cafes, going home people. The sky was pitch black. Must be nearing the midnight curfew.

She felt numb. That's how it feels when everything comes to an end. Everything else whittles down to insignificance. Izzie and Moe. It was over. She loved him. She couldn't bear it. It felt completely unreal. This sudden confusion, emptiness, void. He could have done almost anything else. But prostitutes. Nothing worse than these white men, so full of themselves, highly paid white men, using those poor girls and women for their own self-indulgent, momentary, pleasure. Not 'poor them' poor, but poverty stricken poor, no other choices poor. Those men use them and throw them, like a soggy condom; worthless and instantly forgotten. Did he use a condom? There was no going back. Ironic. She glanced at Booker. Here she was being 'rescued' by

Booker, the infamous womaniser.

He looked at her, gave her a brief smile, and looked back at the road.

He was tall and lanky, and had smile wrinkles around his eyes. His hair was dark and slightly greying. He was a bit older than them.

"Is your new girlfriend at home, Booker?" she said.

"No, we haven't seen each other for a bit. Nothing bad happened. Quite amicable really."

"You miss being with Leila, don't you?"

"Hmmm…" he shrugged and chuckled softly.

He wasn't going to admit it.

**

Booker lived in a small bungalow on the hillside just below the English School. Izzie had been there a few times; for a play reading, or a film. It was a cosy place full of books, videos and music. He had Ethiopian furniture; chunky, beautifully carved hardwood chairs, and ox-skin lampshades, hand painted with rural scenes. He liked to think of himself as cultured, a cut above the rest. Compared to some of the ex-pats, maybe he was.

The last stretch was dark. No street lamps, just the headlights seeking out the way home.

He stopped outside a tall corrugated iron fence covered in ivy, and hooted once. "Here we are."

His zabanya opened up. The gate scraped and clanked open.

Booker swept the car through and stopped. Killed the engine. Silence.

The zabanya opened the door for her.

She bowed her head, nodding. "Egziersteling," she said. She felt tired. As she climbed out, the old zabanya put out a hand to hold her elbow, steadying her. He must have noticed.

"Come on," Booker said. "Let's get you inside." He took her bag from her.

She almost stumbled, losing the only thing she had to hold on to.

"Steady," he said.

They walked into the warm living room, glowing red from the blazing fire.

"I just want to go to bed," she said.

"OK. As you like," Booker said. "I can't get you a drink? Take it with you?"

"Thanks."

"Whiskey?"

"Yes, please."

"Bedroom's through there. First on the left. Bed's made up."

"You were expecting me?"

"It's always made up," he laughed. "You know what it's like. Stream of unexpected visitors."

"True," she smiled, accepting the tumbler of whiskey, and headed for the 'first on the left' with her holdall under her arm. She shut the door behind her. The lamp was on. There was a white, handwoven bedcover with a brightly coloured Lalibela cross embroidered on it. It was one from the Alert project. Beautiful. She lay back on it, curling herself into her gabi, and the tears came. She wept into the cloth, crying and crying. That familiar, night-time, heart-wrenching, silent crying. The holdall stood by the bed unopened. She saw Moe's shocked face, the chicken fat on the wall. She wondered if he would eat the chicken, if he would pick the potatoes and carrots off the floor. Knowing him he would.

What would Negisst say?

Why had she let Booker take her away from home? Moe should have left. Not her. Every thought brought a new wave of tears. She sat up and took a sip of the whiskey, like medicine. It 'hit the right spot,' as Dad would say. He loved his whiskey. The thought of him brought on another wave of crying. She curled up into herself.

**

The cockerel woke her. The room was bright with sunshine through the light cotton curtains. Water gushed from a standpipe, hitting the insides of a metal bucket outside her window. She took a moment to realise where she was. To remember what had happened. Where that feeling of dread came from. She shuffled herself back down under the bedcovers, still wrapped in her gabi, and wept. The misery and anger coursed through her like poison. The crying kept coming. It was too much. She couldn't stop it. She saw him. Saw them, dancing together. His warm smile on her face, and their laughter. They were planning to go to Langano with Shirley and Brian again soon. What would they say? What was she going to do. She had nowhere to live. She would leave. She couldn't do this. She would leave Ethiopia. Go home.

There was a knock at the door.

She shrank into the bedclothes. Stayed quiet, her heart beating, hoping whoever it was would go away.

"It's me," came Booker's voice.

She lent on one elbow, wiping her eyes and face with the gabi.

The door opened slowly. "Tea and toast," he said, putting a tray on the bedside table.

"Gosh," she said. "Thanks."

"We can't have you lying in bed all day, miserable," he said.

"You're not going to work?" she said, shuffling herself up to sitting, she took the tea, cupping it in both hands. Hot steam in her face. She sipped. It was just what she needed, black and finely laced with spices.

"Not on a Sunday," he smiled and lowered himself slowly to sit at the end of the bed, as if half-expecting a rebuffal.

"Ah, yes." She was surprised how comfortable she felt with him. They had never really been friends as such. "You're being very kind," she said.

"You're surprised," he laughed.

That's where he got those friendly wrinkles. He laughed easily. Like he didn't have a care.

"I am sorry though, Izzie. Honestly. I like you and Moe. I got a feeling something like this might happen."

"You knew?"

"We'd been talking."

"Do other people know?" her voice became louder.

"No, just me. We talked a couple of times. That's all. I thought you knew." His voice was soft, calming.

"No."

What now? Her eyes welled up again.

"This is the worst part, Izzie. It will get better, I promise."

"I'm thirty," she started crying again.

"Come on Izzie," Booker patted her leg.

"I'll have to go home," she said. "I don't have anywhere to live here. I don't have an international salary and benefits like you lot."

"For God's sake, Izzie. You aren't going anywhere. We'll work something out. In the meantime you can stay here. We'll go and get your stuff."

"I don't want to see him right now."

"We'll go when he's not there."

"I can't go in to work tomorrow."

"Just take a day at a time," he said, getting up. "You'll be alright."

**

She could hear Booker's maid talking on the phone outside her door. There was a soft knock. "Here, Izzie, it's for you."

"Farenj, mindin neouw? What are you doing?" It was Fasika. "Booker says you've been in bed crying for three days."

Izzie felt the tears welling up again. "I can't stop, Fasika. I can't stop."

"Go take a shower. Put on some clothes, and get yourself over to our office."

"I can't," Izzie said.

"You can. He's just a man. That's what men do. Just pull yourself together. Come on over here. We'll have lunch."

"Ishi," she said. "OK."

"Good. I'll see you in an hour or so, OK?"

"OK."

The phone clicked shut. Dial tone.

**

"Eat," Fasika said. "You have to eat."

"Ishi," Izzie said. "I am eating, look."

"You like Chinese, I know you do. So eat, ishi?"

"Ishi." Izzie looked at Fasika. So elegant. So beautiful. Her face perfectly made up. She wore a smart navy blue jacket over her bright yellow frock. It was a frock. It had that 1940's look. How did she get to have a friend like Fasika, she wondered.

"It's good, Fasika," she said. "Thank you, really." Hot rice with chicken and cashew nuts. She took a spring roll and dipped it into the sweet chilli sauce.

"A friend of ours from the ECA has just moved into a flat with her boyfriend. Well, her husband now. They met here. So they are living together and her flat is empty. She says you can have it."

"Really?" Izzie stopped chewing. "How much is the rent. You know I don't earn that much. It is, or rather was, enough, but to pay rent on top... I just don't know." Izzie could feel the tears coming again.

Fasika put a hand over hers, quite firmly. "This has to stop, Izzie. Pull yourself together. Berchi. No one has died."

Izzie breathed in deep. "Where is the flat?

"Arat Kilo, it's perfect for you, right?"

"Yes, perfect."

"That's more like it."

She looked at Fasika.

Fasika was smiling warmly at her. "You'll be alright, yeney konjo. You have us."

**

Negisst opened the door to their flat. "Izzie," she said, opening her arms.

"Don't you start crying, Negisst," Izzie said. "I've only just managed to stop."

"But you have to come back, Izzieye. Mr Moe can't be here without you."

"He doesn't want me here, Negisst. And I don't want to be with him any more either." She wanted to add, 'shit happens,' but didn't.

"Mr Booker," Negisst said, sniffing and wiping her eyes on her shema. "How are you?" She shook hands with him bowing slightly.

"Fine, fine, Negisst," he said.

Izzie was already in the bedroom folding clothes on her bed.

"I can help," Negisst said, taking over.

"Ishi, thank you. I will look around for other bits and pieces." Izzie took her books off the shelves, her photos from home and the lamp with village women spinning cotton, painted on one of the sides of stretched ox-skin. She went through the cassettes and took hers, and one of the cushions from the sofa.

From the kitchen she took cups, plates, knives and forks for two. Hiwot, Simaynesh or Leila would definitely come to visit her. She looked at the wall, half hoping that the chicken fat would still be splattered down it. It was gone. The green wall was clean again.

She kept going, collecting and putting things that were hers, or that she needed, into the bags she had brought from Booker's.

"Nearly done?" he said.

"Just let me have one more look around?"

Negisst had packed the suitcase. Izzie didn't have many clothes.

The boys stood at the open door.

"Izzie, Moe not coming. It's OK." Mekonnen said.

Hailu bobbed about. "We take those bags?"

"Where you live, Izzie?" Mekonnen said.

"Arat Kilo. Not far," she said.

She gave Negisst directions where to come and find her. "I coming one day here, one day to you," Negisst said.

"OK, Negisst, that would be lovely. But my place is too small. You can come once a week. It's enough, ishi?"

"Two times, then?"

Somehow they got her things and the boys out of the flat and down the stairs. The door shut with a loud bang. There was, as always, that familiar echo on the stairs.

**

It was a small bedsit with a large French window down one side. She pulled it back and walked out onto a wide terrace overlooking the city. "Wow," she said, shielding her eyes from the sun. "This is amazing."

It was a large airy room, a bed at one end and a kitchen at the other. Fasika's friend had left her furniture there. Apparently she didn't need it. And she didn't want any rent either. She said it was in her 'package' anyway. She didn't want to make money out of it. Izzie couldn't believe her luck.

They had brought her bags up in the tiny lift, bit by bit.

"I haven't even got anything to make you a coffee, Booker," she said. "I don't know how to thank you."

"Another time," he said. "And you're welcome. It's good to see you looking better."

There was a commotion outside the open door.

"I don't believe it!"

It was Mekonnen, Hailu, Biniam and Moshe Dyan.

"You won't be getting rid of that lot so fast," Booker said, smiling.

"Mindin neouw?" she said, laughing. "What are you all doing here so soon?"

"Negisst, she giving address," Hailu was out of breath and smiling broadly. "Here, she giving food." He handed her a basket with fruits and vegetables and a loaf of precious bread on top.

"Egziersteling, yeney konjo," she said. "Thank you so much."

"Well, you are certainly not alone in this city, Izzie," Booker said.

"No, it seems not," she looked at the boys and around at her new home. "I really can't believe my luck. I think I'm going to be fine." Her voice was slightly thinner than usual. The heavy feeling was still in her belly. What had Moe expected her to do? How long had he been waiting for this moment. He must have known it would end. Maybe he'd wanted it for a while. Part of her couldn't wait for all of them to leave so she could just cry.

30

August 1984, On the Roadside Debre Berhan

"Debre Berhan. Debre Berhan," their tout shouted. "All for Debre Berhan get off here. Next stop Ch'ach'a." He walked past Ashebir, a wad of Birr notes in his fist, a pencil stuck behind his ear, and disappeared round the front of the bus.

The sun sent shadows across the ground, creating a shadow-shape of the bus and the luggage piled up on top, and a boy crawling over it, hunting for someone's bag.

A man was looking up, shading his eyes. His face wore the lines of his smiles and the highland weather. "No, not that one," he called out. "Yes, that's it. That's it. Good boy."

He was just like Mohamed Abdu's father,

Zewdie stood near the bottom of the steps holding Ashebir's rolled up ox-skin.

"Here Zewdie, give it to me," Ashebir said.

"This is the bus station," she said. "Debre Berhan bus station."

"Zewdie? Are you alright?" he said. He looked up at her face. "Zewdie, what are we going to do now?"

She stood motionless.

"Let's stay on the bus and go to Ch'ach'a, Zewdie?"

"I have to rest," she said. She lifted her chin in the direction of a space under a nearby bus shelter.

Ashebir picked up their bundle and went as fast as he could to get that space before someone else did. He sat down out of breath, put his arms round the bundle and waited.

She made her way slowly to him, and sat down beside him with a grunt. Her face had lost its softness. Her eyes stared without really seeing.

"Zewdie, look," he said, tugging her sleeve. He wanted her to be, look and talk like she was before. "They are all living here."

She sucked her teeth and sighed.

He moved closer to her. Goats rummaged in the rubbish, bleating, reminding him of home. That already felt so far away.

Women walked past, skinny ankles sticking out under dusty skirts, their bare feet dry, ashen and cracked from long walking. Most of them were in traditional dress, turned grey-brown from the lack of washing, and torn. They carried their babies on their backs in soft ox-skins, but there was no movement or crying. Ashebir peered to get a closer look. He wondered if the babies inside were still alive. He covered his head with his hands and buried his face in the bundle. He could not believe what he was seeing and half hoped it would be gone when he looked up again. But the murmur of voices was all around him.

He looked at Zewdie. "Maybe we can get a bus when we've rested?" When he got no reaction he looked around to see where he was. He would ask her again when she had rested.

There was a large market behind the bus station. Local village women were heading away from there towards the road and onto paths leading across the fields on the other side. They carried small bundles on their backs, baskets on their heads. They passed the weak and hungry, their eyes to the ground, as if they did not want to see the suffering. Some held up large black umbrellas against the sun.

Traders, he thought. Just like Zewdie and Temima.

Men wrapped in thick white gabis walked alongside small flocks of jiggling, trotting goats and sheep. They kept them close with the tip of their long sticks, the animals bleating a familiar, Bleh-eh-eh-eh! Their tongues sticking out.

He wondered what Mohamed Abdu was doing now.

"Caramella. Caramella. Winis-ton. Winis-ton," a small boy went past shouting, a box hung round his neck. A man in a jacket and polished shoes bought a single cigarette. The boy lit it with a bright red lighter which dangled on a string from his box.

Ashebir watched children run after their mothers. The small ones were naked; others wore shirts which hung from their shoulders in shreds with nothing underneath. Wood smoke hung in the air, as people began to light small fires. He wondered if this was where they would sleep tonight.

"Zewdie."

"Yes."

He looked at her for a while. She was still tired. "Will we get a bus a little later?"

She sucked her teeth and shook her head slowly.

"Will we, Zewdie?"

A small group of people next to them crouched around their fire. The woman was making thin ki'ta bread on a blackened metal dish over the flames.

"Look," he whispered. "They are cooking their supper."

"They've probably run out of money for transport," she sighed. "They probably can't go back and they can't go on."

More of The Hungry, were arriving over the fields, and along the track by the tarmac.

The Kebele school teacher had taught them about 'one hundred', but Ashebir could not count that far. If he started counting the people on the road, he thought, he would have to count for a long, long, time. Maybe it would be more than that number 'one hundred'.

"Zewdie," he tapped her gently. "What will we do now?"

"I don't know," she said. She pulled a thin blanket out of their bundle and spread it on the ground. She curled up on it, drawing her gabi tight around her. "Let me rest," she said and closed her eyes.

He looked from her to the people around them. He was thirsty. "Shall I look for water, Zewdie?"

She lifted her head a little. "Take the small jerry can. Ask at a kiosk, ishi? Can you manage?"

He pulled out the yellow plastic container he used to take to the river. It was the same as everyone had. All the soldiers carried them. Zewdie had bought it in Ataye market from a large pile tied together with string.

"Was it this morning we left, Zewdie?"

She smiled. "It seems so long ago, doesn't it?"

He pushed the bundle close to her. "I'll go and get some water."

"Ishi," he heard her whisper.

The bus station covered a wide area. There were several bus shelters. They all looked the same. He walked slowly, looking over his shoulder, making sure not to lose his way back. The sky was a deep blue. Below, the haze from the fires made the people moving about take on soul shadow shapes in their greying clothes. He turned, hearing a red and yellow Anbessa bus, honking at everyone to clear a path. It stopped with a loud sigh and waited for passengers to climb off before loading up again. He wished they could get on it.

He passed a group of people sitting round a fire. A woman was making ki'ta bread.

"There's a feeding centre further south," the man with her was saying.

He tried to hear more. What did he mean, 'a feeding centre'?

"My father can't walk any further," one woman said.

An old man, wrapped in a thin grey blanket, sat near her. He looked up at Ashebir without a word. His pale brown eyes were sad and watery, clouded in a film of grey.

"At least the Women's Association come with food sometimes," another woman said. She stood by the fire, a child on her hip. The little boy's skin was a pale yellow, his head had been shaved bald.

"They should open a feeding centre here," the man said.

"My baby needs milk," a younger woman sitting on the ground said. "I can't feed my baby." Her breast hung flat and empty. The child lay asleep cradled in her lap.

Ashebir stood listening. The empty can hung from his hand. Egziyabher yet alle? he wondered. Where was God now, where was Allah? He cleared his throat. "Tenasteling," he said, bowing his head slightly. "I am looking for water?"

The woman making bread looked up at him. "Go over to those houses and ask. Maybe someone there will give you."

He looked where her finger was pointing. Set back from the road was a row of chikka[73] houses and coffee shops. Some, built from stone, were two stories high, the lower part painted yellow or pale blue. He had never seen a house one built on top of the other before.

"Just ask the people standing around outside," the woman said.

He nodded. He and Zewdie used to ask for a drink at the kiosks and neighbouring houses near the market in Ataye. The place and the people were familiar. This was different.

He stopped at a coffee house. Tables and chairs were set out under a blue plastic awning held up by wooden poles. A man sat with a glass of tea and a newspaper. He was cleaning his teeth with a wooden tooth-stick, like the mefakia the Afar use.

Ashebir went closer, his heart pounding, then backed away again, hoping the man had not seen him. He looked over his shoulder at the road behind him. A constant murmur rose with the wood smoke from the people settled all along the roadside. A horse-drawn gari jingled past. He moved towards the man again.

"Excuse me," he said. "Tenasteling."

The man slurped his tea noisily and picked up his paper.

Ashebir coughed to clear the tightness in his throat. "Tenasteling," he

---

[73] Mud.

said again, as loudly as he could.

The man looked up.

"Excuse me. Can I get water here?" He lifted his plastic container.

"Where are you from, my boy?" the man asked.

"Ataye."

"What is your name?"

"Ashebir."

"Are you alone?"

"My mother is over there," he said, looking at the bus shelter where his mother lay. "She is sick."

"They won't give you water here. Too many people asking."

Ashebir nodded and turned to go.

"Wait," the man said. "You can come with me. Just wait a little."

"Ishi," Ashebir said. "Thank you." He squatted on the ground.

The man carried on reading.

Ashebir could hear his slurping. How he would love just one sip of that hot tea. One sip. He rocked from side to side, trying to shift the paining hunger in his belly. He stood and stretched, rubbing his tummy.

Finally, the man waved to the girl inside. She came out of the dark interior with a metal tray. She took the man's glass and the coin he had left. She sniffed, wiped the table once round with a dirty cloth, glanced at Ashebir and went back inside.

"We filled our water drum this morning," the man said. "Come."

Ashebir followed the man along a dusty path. On one side were the coffee shops and houses, on the other, an open ditch. Ashebir looked from the man ahead of him, to the bus station behind him, so he would find his way back. A wooden plank lay over the ditch. The man crossed it and disappeared behind a kiosk on the other side. The ditch was full of stinking rubbish. Two dead rats lay side by side as if they had been chatting until the last moment. Flies buzzed around their bared teeth. Ashebir crossed carefully, not to fall in.

He hurried down the path after the man. He was a little way ahead. The huts and houses were crammed on either side of the alley making it dark and shadowy. Narrow pathways went off to the left and right. He could hear the hollow thudding sound of someone pounding.

A woman appeared from a doorway. She wore a long white traditional dress. He had not seen such white cloth for a while. It was embroidered green, yellow and red round the neck and down the front, just like the national flag.

"Worku," the woman said. "Where have you been? The Kebele

Chairman is looking for you."

The man looked at his watch. "I didn't realise it was so late."

"And who have we here?" she asked, looking at Ashebir.

"This is Ashebir. The boy needs water. His mother is sick. Can you look after him? I better get going." The man hurried on up the path between the houses.

"You better be quick, or you'll be in trouble," the woman called after him. "Here, yeney lij, give me your jerry can and I'll fill it for you." She took it and went inside.

Someone was frying garlic and onions. The smell was delicious and unbearable. His stomach gnawed and his mouth watered. Strains of music and the clatter of pans came from nearby houses.

A man walked up the path with a sack over his shoulder. "Scraps, metal, plastic? Scraps, metal, plastic?" His sing-song was different from the ticket tout's. The man stopped and stared at Ashebir.

To Ashebir's relief, the woman came out with his yellow jerry can.

"Here you are," she said. "And take this, it's some bread I just baked." She gave him a small package.

Ashebir could not believe the woman's generosity. He took the bread, bowing his head, trying to smile. He lifted the now heavy jerry can onto his shoulder. "Egziyabheresteling," he said. "Thanks be to God."

"Where is he from?" the rag-and-metal collector asked.

"From the countryside, like the rest of them," the woman said. "Yifat na Timooga maybe?"

The man sucked his teeth, tutted and moved on.

Ashebir gritted his teeth, trying to hold back the tears. He and Zewdie were not like the rest of them.

Ashebir turned and walked back along the dim alleyway, trying to go faster, wanting to reach the bus shelter before nightfall. The full can on his shoulder slowed him. When he came out into the open, the sun had gone down, leaving the sky swept in broad brushes of deep pink. He passed the kiosk. Ashebir crossed the plank carefully, thinking of the two rats in deathly conversation down below. They were no longer visible in the dimming light. He could see the outlines of the bus shelters in the distance. Small fires glowed red all along the roadside, small dots of hope. He felt the cold through his t-shirt and shivered.

He looked under the first shelter. Zewdie was not there. He walked on a little further to the next.

Two buses were getting ready to leave. A man was arguing loudly with the driver, a small boy crying at his side. The tout swung from the door, "Debre Sina, Debre Sina, Robit, Robit, Ataye, Ataye. Leaving now. Innihid!" He called out. "Let's go!"

Ashebir froze on hearing, 'Ataye!' Tears blurred the scene in front of him. He rubbed his eyes with his free hand, sniffed hard and carried on. He looked under the next shelter. There she was, curled up just as he had left her.

She lifted her head, "There you are poor boy. I was getting worried."

"Are you alright?" he said, putting the can down. "Look. I got water. A man helped me and his wife filled the container."

"Good boy. Gobez. That should last us a few days," she said.

"The woman gave me fresh bread." He put the bread on the blanket and poured her a cup of water.

She sat up, took the cup in both hands and drank in small sips. "Thank you," she said, looking up at him, smiling.

He was glad the strange empty look had gone. "Let's eat, Zewdie," he said.

"Get your gabi, Ashebir. It's cold."

He sucked his teeth, as he wrapped his gabi round his whole body. He shivered. "Are we staying the night? It's very cold here."

Zewdie was quiet.

"A bus just left for Ataye," he said, as he sat down close to her, drawing his knees up to his chin.

"Let's eat," she said. She prayed quietly and broke the bread, giving some to him. She ate, chewing and chewing.

The neighbours' small fire glowed orange and looked warm.

"We will think again in the morning, Ashebir. I cannot go anywhere today."

"Me too," he said. After they ate, he curled himself up next to her and pulled his ox-skin over them. He just wanted to sleep.

**

Ashebir woke to the moaning. It was dark under the ox-skin. He held his breath to listen to the sound. The moaning went on. His heart beat fast. Where was he? Then he remembered. They had slept under the bus shelter. He felt like crying. The moaning and wailing went on. Someone had died.

He pulled the gabi away from his face and peered out. The town was hidden in mist. There was a strong smell of damp burnt-out firewood.

The wailing became louder, "Aaa-yeee. Aaa-yeee."

He could make out the shapes of people moving, hear their low voices, and the wailing. "Weyne, Be-Egziyabher." He thought of soul shadows. If only he had a handful of fluffy white fendisha he could throw to the edge of the shelter, to pacify the spirits like Emet Hawa used to do.

Zewdie lay still beside him. He listened. He sat up and shook her. "Zewdie, Zewdie," he said loudly.

She moved slightly under his shaking hand.

"Wake up, Zewdie. Wake up," he cried.

Zewdie pulled the gabi away from her face. "Be Egziyabher. Mindin neouw?" She lifted herself onto her elbow. "What in God's name is the matter?"

He cried, clenching his teeth not to make a noise. Pulling his knees up to his chest, he held his head in his hands, rocking himself back and forth.

"What is it?"

He took in a deep breath and sighed. "Nothing," he said. "It's nothing."

Zewdie pulled her gabi around her. "This is hard," she said. "I'm sorry, my child."

"Somebody died," he said. He sniffed and scratched his head. For a moment he was distracted. The scratching made the itch worse and better at the same time.

"You must have lice," she said.

"Maybe," he scratched again.

The wailing continued. "Weyne, Be-Egziyabher."

"God help us," Zewdie said.

"Aaa-yeee. Aaa-yeee, yeney lij."

They huddled together, looking around them.

"The mist will clear once the sun is up," she said after a while.

"I've got a cold," he said and sniffed, wiping his nose on his gabi.

"Sorry, really. Aysoh, yeney lij. It will get warm soon." Her coughing started again.

It sounded worse this morning.

"It's too cold for you here," he said. "We should leave today."

Finally, the coughing stopped. She breathed deep and slow, her hand on her breast, liquid gurgling in her lungs.

He pulled his gabi up over his head and round his shoulders. His stomach griped and grumbled, complained and pained him. "We are not like these people, Zewdie," he said quietly, his body tight with anger. "We are on our way to Alem Tena, to people who know us. You said."

Zewdie mumbled.

He thought she was praying.

She cleared her throat in the way she had when she had something important to say. He looked at her.

"We don't have any money left," she said.

He looked at her. He felt winded, like the time when he fell, running along the edge of the ravine. He hugged himself tighter, not knowing what to say.

"You said we were going to friends," he whispered.

Zewdie was crying softly. "Yes, but we have no money left."

He looked at her. He put a hand on her shoulder

"Zewdie, don't cry," he said. "It's alright. Egziyabher alle. Insha'Allah."

She smiled at him. "Yeney lij. You are growing up fast. You are looking after your mother."

He patted her, wanting her pain and worry to go away. "Remember what Mohamed Abdu's father says, Zewdie?" he said. "He says, 'Praise Allah at all times, even when life is hard.'" Mohamed Ahmed's words brought tears to his eyes.

"You are right," she said. "But the people with transport are asking too much money," she said. "It costs more than Mohamed Shinkurt and I thought."

He sat quietly beside her.

She cried.

He never saw her cry. Only tears of happiness.

They should never have left Ataye. Any hardship with their friends and neighbours would have been better than this.

"Look at us crying." Zewdie wiped her face with her gabi, and smiled. "Let's have breakfast."

"Breakfast?"

"We have the last of Temima's bread, and a cup of water. Don't we?"

"Ishi," he said, wiping his nose with the back of his hand. He stood up and pulled the enamel mug from Zewdie's bundle. He poured fresh water into it from the yellow jerry can. He took a sip before passing it to her. The water was cold and made him cough.

The sun shone white through the mist. Their neighbours had already lit a fire. They greeted Zewdie and Ashebir, getting up slightly and bowing their heads before sitting on their haunches again. "Tenasteling," the woman said. "How are you? Are you alright?"

Zewdie bowed her head, "We are fine, Egziyabher yimesgen," she said. "How are you and your family?"

"We are fine, Egziyabher yimesgen," the woman said. "God knows we are struggling. But we are here this morning."

"Listen to the people mourning," Zewdie said, sucking her teeth.

"So many die every night," the woman said, shaking her head. "Mostly children and old people. They are so sick. The cold out here in the open takes them."

Zewdie frowned. "Where do they bury them?" she asked the woman.

"A large white municipal truck comes every morning to collect the bodies," the woman said. "Sometimes, if it's only one or two, they take them away on stretchers." She poked the fire with a stick and blew on the cinders to get the flames going. The smoke blew into her face. She wiped the tears from her eyes and moved round to the other side.

"Where do they take them?" Zewdie said.

"They bury them somewhere in the hills. God help us all."

Ashebir gave the bread to Zewdie.

"Will you and your husband share our bread?" Zewdie asked the woman.

The woman sucked her teeth. "I think it's your last bread, but let me have a small piece for my daughter." The woman got up. "We don't know each other but you are already my neighbour. My name is Wozeiro Tsehai." She bent towards Zewdie with her hands outstretched and bowed her head slightly. "Egziersteling," she whispered, as Zewdie broke a piece of Temima's bread and gave it to her.

Ashebir watched and listened. He sat as close to Zewdie as he could. Then he and Zewdie bent their heads together. She said thanks to God for the food and water, and that they were alive. They ate in silence. Zewdie did not take much.

"Eat, Zewdie," he whispered.

"I am eating," she said.

"You arrived yesterday afternoon," the woman said.

He could tell from her accent she was from Wollo. Her traditional dress was the same brown-grey colour as the others. The green and black embroidery round the edges had faded. The sleeves and bottom of her dress were torn and hung in pieces. Ashebir watched her as he chewed. He wondered whether he and Zewdie would stay long enough to make a fire and bake ki'ta bread too.

"Yes," Zewdie said. "How long have you been here?"

"Maybe two weeks, I don't know," the woman said. She turned to the man next to her. "How long have we been here?" she asked him. Then she looked at Zewdie again. "This is my husband."

"Maybe two weeks, maybe three. I don't know," he said and coughed like the old man in the Land Rover.

Ashebir thought he must have been handsome once but now his face was thin and frowning. He was sitting on his haunches next to the woman, resting his elbows on his knees, his hands hanging over the fire, a gabi hung over his shoulders.

"Where do you get food?" Zewdie asked the woman.

The woman placed a soot-blackened flat dish on three large grey stones over the flames.

Ashebir nearly asked for the soot to make ink. Then realised it would be of no use to him in a place like this.

"The Women's Association comes with food sometimes," the woman said. "They gave me this flour two days ago. I am using it a little at a time." She mixed the flour and water in a plastic jug with her hand. Two children, two or three years old, stood near the fire and watched. They both had a tuft of hair in the middle of their otherwise bald heads and wore thin grey smocks. One wore a red bead necklace. Their noses were running. One of them coughed and looked shyly at Ashebir.

He nodded at the child and tried to smile. In their village he would have waved for him to come sit and would have chatted with him. But he didn't know what to say to this child. Everything was so strange. So he looked away and carried on watching the woman. He took a sip of cold water and wished it was a glass of hot tea.

"The people in Debre Berhan are good to us," the woman said.

"Do you have other children?" Zewdie asked.

"My little boy died on the road coming here," she said, wiping her eyes with the back of her hand. She looked down and carried on working. She scooped up a little of the grey watery mixture and let it fall through her fingers onto the hot plate, round and round in a circle, starting in the centre and working to the edge. "My girl has gone with a mug to the coffee houses to see if she can get tea."

Ashebir glanced quickly at Zewdie. "Let me try?"

Zewdie coughed into her gabi.

He had finished his bread. The sun was spreading warmth on this unhappy place. Local villagers walked from the fields on the other side of the road with their sheep and donkeys to the market. Buses arrived and left. The ebb and flow, the talking and murmuring, the weeping, and the rising strong smells of yesterday were there all over again.

He got up. "I want to look around," he said.

Zewdie curled up in her gabi again.

"Ishi," she whispered. "Don't stay too long."

He was about to put the mug away, then thought better. He would try and fill it with tea. "I'll come soon," he said. He walked away, his gabi round his shoulders, the empty mug dangling in his hand. His heart beat faster as he walked towards the row of coffee houses, where the man who helped him with water had been drinking tea the day before.

The girl was wiping the tables with the same dirty cloth. She looked up at him, finished wiping and went inside without a word. He was not the only one. There were other children. Some with their hands out, begging passers-by for a centime.

He suddenly felt ashamed.

He watched as one little girl followed a man close behind. "One centime, please sir, be Egziyabher, just one centime," she whined in a high voice. She wore a dirty torn dress and had bare feet. Her hair was long and matted. She reminded him of Yishaereg.

He walked back to the bus shelter and sat next to Zewdie, not knowing what to do. They had nothing left to eat. He closed his eyes and saw the Ataye River. He was swimming in his mind with Mohamed Abdu and Ali and the Degenya children. He cried quietly, not wanting to disturb his mother.

**

The next day he had to do something. He went to the coffee house again. An old man sat at a table with a glass of coffee, the steam rising. He was reading. Ashebir went nearer, shaking his hand up and down like he had seen the other children do. "Can you give me one centime?" he whispered.

A woman came out. "Enday! What is this?" she said. "Mindin neouw? Can't my customers drink their coffee in peace?"

The man looked at her and shook his head. "Here," he said, reaching into his pocket. He held out twenty-five cents.

Ashebir looked at the woman and then at the man's hand. He took the coin and bowed his head. "Egziersteling," he said softly. He walked as fast as he could back to the bus shelter and sat down out of breath, a smile on his lips. He put the coin in his bag and sat in the warmth of the sun, listening to his heart beating.

When he had calmed down, he got up and went to the market. There were large piles of wool for sale. In a far corner, skinny animals were bleating and shuffling against each other, stumbling on the rocky ground. A woman had arranged her pottery on the ground; black earthenware cooking pots, jabena coffee pots, and small ornaments made from clay, lions and cockerels. A row of women sat under black umbrellas, selling onions and red and green chilli peppers; like Zewdie and Wozeiro Etalem used to do. Wozeiro Etalem, who had lost both sons in the fighting, and nearly lost her mind, Zewdie had said.

One woman sat behind a large bowl of groundnuts.

"Please, be Egziyabher," he said, putting out a cupped hand he shook it up and down. He glanced over his shoulder towards the bus shelter.

The woman looked at him. She shook her head and sucked her teeth. "Come," she said.

He went closer, his hand outstretched.

She scooped the nuts up in a small tin cup and tipped the contents into a twisted newspaper cone. "Here," she said.

He was so surprised he barely found his voice to whisper, "Egziersteling."

He went back to fetch the twenty-five cents and went to a kiosk selling bread. "How much is one bread?" he said, standing on tip-toe to look over the counter.

"Twenty five cents," the boy said.

"Give me one, please," Ashebir said, pushing his coin across the wooden counter.

He took the thin bread and walked back to Zewdie, slightly apprehensive. He felt as if he had stolen the food.

"Zewdie," he said quietly, shaking her gently. "Look. A woman in the market gave me a handful of groundnuts."

Zewdie looked up at him with sad eyes. "My boy," she said.

"And a man at the coffee house gave me twenty five cents."

"Yeney lij," she said.

"I bought bread with the money. We can eat."

She let out a groan as she sat up.

"Are you angry with me?"

"Endaye, how can I be angry?" she said.

He lay Temima's cloth on the ground and put the bread and nuts on it. They prayed together giving thanks for the food.

Ashebir tore off a piece of bread and ate one of the groundnuts.

"Chew slowly," Zewdie told him. "One thing is," she paused, "if you eat fast, you will get stomach pains."

"Ishi," he said and chewed slowly. "Zewdie, eat, please."

She broke off a small piece of bread and took a groundnut. "I am eating, I am eating," she said.

That night he thought of his village, his friends Mohamed Abdu and Ali, and wept. Even though Zewdie was not angry with him for begging, he felt ashamed. He cried quietly, so she would not hear. He could not believe they were like The Hungry. So poor that he had to beg for food. He wished he was still the Ashebir who ran home to his gojo-bate in the late afternoons. He wished he could hear his mother pounding coffee and laughing with the neighbours. That was a long time ago.

31

August/September 1984, On the Roadside Debre Berhan

Every morning he lay listening to the wailing. Every morning he was afraid he might find her dead beside him. If they died under the bus shelter, no one would know who they were or where they came from.

In the middle of the previous night, he woke to a familiar sound and the ground rumbled beneath him. He saw the dark shapes of army lorries going past one after the next. They looked threatening, their large headlights shining through the night mist. Their engines grumbled loudly. For the first time he was afraid of them. No children ran shouting, "Soldiers! Soldiers!" in excitement. Nor did any young soldiers shout out, "Etiopia Tikdem! Ethiopia First!" They went by, a long line of large ominous shapes. The soldiers must be inside, he thought, sitting in the back, holding onto their rifles. He pulled his gabi over his head to muffle the droning noise and tried to sleep with the earth shuddering beneath him.

He woke again in a sweat. His fists and teeth clenched. He dreamt the white truck had come to take them away. He was shouting at it, "We are not The Hungry. We are not The Hungry." Men in khaki were throwing bodies into a dark hole. One after the next. Bodies dressed in shabby, grey-brown, traditional Wollo dress. Zewdie's mother, Emet Hawa sat by the edge of the dark hole, spinning cotton. Now and then she stopped spinning and threw popcorn into the hole, to pacify the spirits. The dream was so vivid he could not get it out of his head.

In the morning lament, women cried out, "Why has God forsaken us? Where is He now?"

He took a deep breath and shook Zewdie. "Wake up," he said. "Zewdie, wake up."

She moved and her face appeared. "What is it, Ashebir?"

He scratched his head to hide his relief. "Did you hear the lorries in the night?"

"Morning Ashebir, are you alright?" she said.

"Did you hear the lorries last night?"

"No. I didn't. Did they pass by again?"

"Yes, so many. They kept me awake for a long time." He could not tell her about the dream that still lurked in his mind. He curled up close to her against the chill.

Once the sun's warmth came through his gabi, it was time to get up. "I'll look for breakfast, Zewdie," he said. "Egziyabher sifeked I'll get a mug of tea."

"Aysoh," she said. "God is with us."

He crouched beside her and patted her gently. "Don't worry, Zewdie. Don't worry," he said, trying to smile.

"Ishi," she whispered, and closed her eyes.

"I'll come quickly," he said.

The market was getting busier. He looked up into strangers' faces. "Please just a few centimes for bread. My mother is sick. We have no food."

He cupped his hand and tried again: "Be enatesh. In your mother's name, please. A few centimes for one bread?"

His voice was drowned in the murmuring of so many people, the touts calling out destinations, the traders sing-song-selling their produce, the sheep and goats bleating. He felt small. He coughed. Bending low, he blew the snot from his nose onto the soil. He tried again, "Please, a few centimes for a cup of tea?" His eyes filled with tears. He looked up at the passers-by. "Please, my mother is sick," he said to himself, feeling hopeless. "My mother is sick," he heard himself whining.

Someone tapped his shoulder. "Take this," a woman said. She pressed a coin into his hand.

"Thank you," he said, surprised. He closed his hand tightly round it. He sniffed and wiped his nose. He couldn't see who had taken pity. Whoever it was had vanished into the crowd.

When he coughed. His chest hurt. His head hurt. He knew he was dirty, his hair thick and matted, his hands and nails grubby. He started again, "Can you spare a coin?" He needed just one more coin.

"Be Egziyabher," he coughed and tried to call out louder, "one centime, please?"

"Don't I know you?" a woman said.

He knew her face. Maybe she was one of the Association women that gave out flour and milk powder.

"Are you here alone?" she said.

He pointed towards the bus shelter behind him. "My mother is over there," he said, crying. "I think she is dying." The truth came out. He wiped his face with his t-shirt, wishing he had not burst out like that in front of a stranger. But now the crying had started he could not stop it. "I'm sorry," he wept. "I'm sorry." He turned away, wanting to disappear.

The woman took his hand. "Come," she said, and led him to a kiosk. She bought two bread rolls.

The boy behind the counter wrapped them in a sheet of newspaper and pushed them across to her.

"There you are," she said. "Take them to your mother."

"Thank you," he whispered, bowing his head slightly, his breath still shuddering from the crying. He held tightly to his coin and with the bread pressed to his chest, he walked back to Zewdie. He was afraid that someone might grab their breakfast, or that he would drop it in the dirt. He walked faster, crying all the way.

As he came near to their bus shelter, he tried to stop his crying. He put the bread in his bag and took the coin and a mug to the coffee house.

The girl was standing outside with her tray, the dirty cloth hanging from her skirt. There were no customers. His head began to throb as he got nearer.

"Ebakish," he said. "Please. I have a coin. Be enatesh, please fill my mug with tea?"

She looked at him, and didn't move. Music crackled out from inside. A man sang, "Mela, Mela." Ashebir recognised the song. It always made Zewdie smile.

"Please," he said. She made him feel ashamed. He swallowed hard. His throat dry. He licked his lips, "Please, for my mother."

She peered back into the coffee house, looked at him, tutted and took the mug.

He stood waiting, hearing the music, seeing the people huddled together around their fires along the roadside under a blanket of smoke. It was strange. This mix of townspeople going about their business and The Hungry lining the road in all their misery. Waiting to die. Was no one going to help them? His eyes filled with tears again.

She came back with the mug full of steaming tea. He could smell the spices in it. His mouth watered and he wiped his eyes. She put the mug down next to a bowl of sugar.

"Put sugar if you want."

He hesitated and looked at her.

"Go on," she said more kindly. She meant it.

"Thank you," he said. He put two spoons of sugar into the mug and stirred. He put the coin on the table

She waved a hand over the coin, "Go," she said. "Quickly. Hid. Take your money." She looked over her shoulder again.

Ashebir was so thankful. The girl was not a lot older than him.

He walked over to Zewdie, carefully holding the mug of steaming tea. He smiled at the thought of how pleased she would be. It was the first tea they had had in days.

**

"Wubit! Ashebir! The Association women are there. Quickly." Wozeiro Tsehai suddenly called out, making him jump.

He picked up their bowl and ran.

"Where is that girl?" He could hear Wozeiro Tsehai calling out, "Wubit!"

He had to get to the front of the queue. Everyone did. There were more people than food.

Within moments a large throng of mostly women, rushed towards the Association women, who stood in a row behind their sacks of flour. Zabanyas in khaki shirts were shouting and waving their sticks in the air, trying to control the mass of people.

Ashebir ran, his heart pounding, his legs aching. He weaved his way in and out of the women, dipping his head and pushing to get as close to the front as he could. People were calling out, hands grasping and clutching their way forward, some women were weeping. He saw one woman fall over, but he kept going through the thick smell of bodies unwashed and hot foul breath.

"Stand in line," he heard one zabanya shout as he got closer. "Make a line." Ashebir recognised him from his soldiers' boots tied with string round the top. They were too big for him. He lifted his feet awkwardly over the uneven ground like Comrade Abebe in Ataye market. People used to laugh at Comrade Abebe, even though he was a powerful man. The zabanya tapped the women's sides and ankles with his stick as if they were sheep.

The children's tearful hunger, day and night, made the women frantic. They pushed and shouted around him. Whenever food or thin grey army blankets were handed out, they lost their customary reserve and politeness. Ashebir wriggled through their wiry bodies and sharp elbows.

He was small, but had to fight to keep his place.

"No one will get any food if you don't line up," the zabanya shouted over the hubbub as he walked up and down, swinging his stick in the air. Then he stopped. "You. Boy. You here again?" He grabbed Ashebir tightly by the arm. It hurt. Ashebir tried to pull away, afraid he might get a beating. To his surprise the man pushed him firmly forward and right into the midst of the heaving mass. "Get in. Stay close behind this woman and keep moving so no one takes your place," he said. Then he turned and went off, marching down the line, shouting and waving his stick. "Enday! No pushing, stay in line."

Ashebir was stunned by the man's kindness. He muttered, "Egziyanheresteling, thanks be to God," rubbing his sore arm. He was carried along by the thronging bodies, struggling to keep his feet on the ground. It was like swimming in the Ataye River in the rainy season. Holding his bowl tightly with one hand he used the other to clutch and push the people around him. He was pinched and shoved all over. His feet trampled and trodden on. He could not cover his nose against the smell of heavy sweat and sickly disease that filled his lungs. This must be how it felt to be a sheep in the middle of a flock being driven to market. He had a strong urge to bleat with his tongue hanging out.

The women scooped flour into outstretched containers asking each time, "How many family members?"

He became more and more anxious as he got closer.

When he reached the front, a woman said, "How many are you?"

"Two, my mother and me."

The woman looked at him with kind eyes. She shook her head and tutted.

He lifted his bowl, trying to hold it firmly in place. He could feel bodies squeezing him and hard bones poking on either side and from behind. It was hard to stand still. He was afraid he might lose some of his flour. The woman held his bowl still and scooped the grey flour in.

He bowed his head, "Egziersteling," he said, and squeezed himself out backwards holding the bowl tightly to his chest, covering the top with his hand.

Zewdie was sitting up when he got back.

"Look," he said. "I got it back without spilling. And that zabanya helped me."

She looked at him, curious. "Who?"

"The one that walks like Comrade Abebe," he said. "He got hold of me and pushed me forward in the queue."

Zewdie smiled at him.

"How are you, Zewdie?" he said.

"I am proud of you."

He gave the flour to their neighbour, Wozeiro Tsehai. "I will collect firewood for you later," he said rubbing his arm. He was exhausted. Ashebir and Wozeiro Tsehai had come to an agreement. The first time he ran to get flour from the Women's Association, he had come back proudly clutching his bowl. "Look Zewdie. Look," he had said. "I got us some flour." It was only then that he realised she would not be able to prepare it. He'd sat down utterly miserable, holding the bowl to his chest.

Wozeiro Tsehai had come to his rescue. "Ashebir, whenever you get flour I will prepare ki'ta bread for you. In return you can collect kindling, and fetch water for me."

He'd nodded his head, relieved and handed his first bowl of flour over to her.

"I have firewood and water, enough for today," Wozeiro Tsehai said, as she took the bowl from him. "You can collect some tomorrow with my little Wubit," she said, trying to smile. It was never a real smile.

This place took the real smiles and laughter out of everyone. The children who could still play didn't laugh from their bellies like he used to with Mohamed Abdu and Ali. Many children sat quietly beside their mothers, flies crawling in their eyes and round their mouths, or lay breathing under old rags, their legs sticking out skinny like the little girl's in the pick-up.

"Ishi, Wozeiro Tsehai," he said, sitting down close to Zewdie, his legs aching.

"Ashebir," Zewdie suddenly gasped, making his stomach leap.

"What is it?"

"Look over there," she said, pulling him closer, leaning forward and pointing.

"Where? What?"

"Over there," she said.

All he could see were more people getting off buses. The same bustle and murmuring, the whining children; the touts calling out destinations, places he and Zewdie could not go on to, nor return to.

"What is it?" his voice sounded more irritable than he meant.

"That man, near the blue taxi-bus, the small bus. There, where the people are just getting off. You see?

He stood, putting a hand on her shoulder and looked harder. "Yes," he said, still doubtful.

"You see the man with the red cloth round his head?"

There were several men wearing the traditional red cloth wrapped round their heads to protect them from the harsh highland sun. Then he saw him. Ashebir looked closely as the man bent to pick his bundle from the ground. He lifted it onto his shoulder and looked around as though hoping to see a familiar face.

"Lakew!" Ashebir shouted. He ran, hitching his shorts up as he went.

Even though he was slim, he looked stronger than many. He walked with his slight bounce. Ashebir always thought he looked as if he was about to run.

"Ashebir, my boy. What are you doing here?" Lakew dropped the bundle and opened his arms.

Ashebir ran and buried his face in Lakew's chest, breathing in the warm earthy smell of him. "Abaye," he said, looking up, relieved to see a familiar smiling face. There was something like Zewdie around his eyes and in his high cheek bones. Lakew's face glowed, his hair was cropped and he wore a beard. It had two small grey flecks in it, although he was not an old man. Lakew always said the grey patches saved him from conscription. He did not want to fight his brothers in the north. He wanted the wars to stop. "Don't ever join the army, Ashebir," Lakew told him every time. "Fighting brings more fighting, death and sorrow. Nothing grows strong and healthy on fields of spilt blood."

"Weyne, look at you, so skinny," Lakew muttered.

"I am fine. I am fine," Ashebir said, not liking his father's worried sadness. "Really, I am."

"Where's your mother?"

"Over there. Under that bus shelter," Ashebir pointed. He looked up at Lakew and laughed. It was a strange feeling. He had not laughed from his stomach for so long.

"Let's go," Lakew said, ruffling Ashebir's hair. "Enday, thick as sheepskin."

Ashebir scratched his head.

Lakew looked in the direction of the bus shelter, his eyes squinting slightly in the sun.

"Yes, that one there," Ashebir said.

Lakew frowned. "How long have you been here?"

"I don't know. A long time maybe. The transport was too expensive. We ran out of money." He felt excitement rising in his chest, telling

Lakew the story. He half skipped alongside his father, and got quickly out of breath from the effort. "It's good you have your gabi," he told Lakew. "It is cold here at night."

Zewdie was waiting for them in tears.

"Lakew, it is you. I can't believe you have found us. Thank God you are here." She started coughing again, covering her mouth with her gabi.

"What happened to you?" Lakew said. "Be Egziyabher, look at you my lovely, yeney konjo. And look at the boy."

Ashebir looked on while Lakew embraced Zewdie and her coughing slowly stopped. They kissed on either cheek over and over. They were both crying. Zewdie stroked Lakew's cheeks. Ashebir's joy suddenly left him. Fear clutched his stomach as he stood watching. What if Lakew had no money, too?

"Come, come, Ashebir," Lakew held out an arm to gather him closer. "Don't stand there alone and sad."

Zewdie started coughing again.

Ashebir poured water into their mug and gave it to her.

"Thank you," she said. "Egziyabheresteling. See how he cares for his mother? "Gobez lij," Lakew said. "He was always a good boy. Strong, hard worker like his mother."

Zewdie wiped her face with her black shawl. "How did you find us?" she said.

"I went to our village and met with our brother, Mohamed Shinkurt," Lakew said.

"How are they? Are they alright?" She looked worried.

Seeing Lakew, Ashebir realised his mother had become thinner and older since they left the village. There were more lines on her forehead and round her eyes. The skin was drawn thin across her cheek bones. As he moved closer to her, the frown on her face moved to cloud his face too.

"You both look so worried," Lakew said. "You both lost weight. You are too thin."

"How are they, Lakew?" she asked again.

"It's hard and there is little food but they are still there."

"And Temima and Mohamed Ahmed, did you see them?"

"They are also still there, Zewdie. Egziyabher yimesgen. They said if I found you to send greetings. So many people are lost, you know." Lakew bit his lip. "Life is hard for everyone. What to do. We have to keep our faith in God's will. He knows best."

"God help us. Lakew. Tell me, did the Meher rains come?" Zewdie asked. "They say there was a little rain here last month but there has been none since we came."

"There has been no rain in Ataye. They are all looking into the sky and praying to Allah. People have eaten the seeds they were going to plant."

"Maybe the government will give them more for planting?" Zewdie said.

Lakew shook his head, passing his fingers back and forth over the dry crumbling earth they sat on. "Mohamed Ahmed said even if Mengistu gave them more seeds and they planted now, the land would not give grain. It is certainly too late."

Zewdie sucked her teeth. "Then they are living from hand to mouth, ke ij wadde af," she said. "Just like us." She patted Ashebir's shoulder.

"Now the rich, like Mohamed Ahmed, Mohamed Bilal from Albuko and Mohamed Shinkurt, are poor. They have already sold most of the livestock they had left, in order to buy food," Lakew said. "So many oxen, cows, goats and sheep have died."

Ashebir looked and listened. His unease spreading.

"What are we going to do?" Zewdie said. "Look at the people, Lakew. Look at us."

"God only knows, Zewdie. God only knows."

They sat; the voices and movement around them filling their silence. Ashebir stared at the ground, waiting for them to speak again. He wanted to know about his friend. Finally, he looked up and said, "Lakew?"

"What is it my child?" Lakew put a hand on his shoulder.

"Did you see Mohamed Abdu?"

"No, he is working as an erregnya somewhere on Muletta mountain. His mother says he is alright but missing his friend," Lakew smiled a real smile. "His friend Ashebir."

Ashebir tried to smile back, but Zewdie's frown sat on his head like crows' feet on the bus shelter roof, and his tearful eyes made everything a blur. He wiped his eyes and sniffed hard, brushing the back of his hand across his nose. It ran all the time.

"They told me you were going to our friends in Alem Tena. I decided to follow you. But it is expensive. I only have a few Birr left."

"What are you going to do?" Zewdie asked.

"I have to go back and find work. There is food for work terracing further north. If I am lucky they will hire me. There are so many of us though. Not just men; women are out there digging the terraces too, and carrying rocks."

Ashebir held his breath. He tried to hide his face. Lakew would leave. He knew it. He stayed quiet not knowing what to say, wishing the heavy feeling in his head and stomach would go away.

"Tenasteling." It was Wozeiro Tsehai.

Ashebir's heart sank. She always joined their talking.

"Lakew, this is our neighbour, Wozeiro Tsehai," Zewdie said. "She has helped us so much."

Lakew took her hand in both of his, "Tenasteling, Wozeiro Tsehai," he said.

"Your Ashebir is a good boy. He went to fetch flour just now. I am making ki'ta bread," she said. "You must be hungry."

She was a good woman, she almost made it feel as if they were in the village.

"Yes, Wozeiro Tsehai, you are right," Lakew said. "I am hungry."

"We can all eat together," Zewdie said.

They sat closer around Wozeiro Tsehai's small fire and watched as she made the bread. Ashebir stared at the flames, covering his eyes when the smoke rose in his direction. He had had a brief moment of joy thinking they would leave this place with Lakew. Now everything seemed worse than before. He let the tears fall behind his hand, hoping the others would think it was the smoke making his eyes water.

Lakew put an arm round his shoulder.

"I will come back, Ashebir," Lakew whispered in his ear. "I will go and work and then come."

"Ishi," Ashebir whispered. He wiped his face again. "You will stay tonight though?"

"Yes, I will sleep here and leave in the morning."

"Come, come, food is there. Eat, eat," Wozeiro Tsehai was saying.

Ashebir closed his eyes and bowed his head with them all. He whispered a prayer to God and then to Allah. He was so sad that his body felt limp. He pulled away a piece of the ki'ta bread and ate. It was hot from the pan. He was hungry and at the same time suddenly too weary to eat, exhausted, disappointed.

**

Lakew left early the following morning, before the sun lit up the mist. Ashebir felt Lakew's hand gently shaking him awake. He peered out. It was dark. Everything was still, just the odd cry from a baby, the coughing and the dogs barking at each other across town.

"Abaye," he whispered.

"I'm leaving now," Lakew said softly. "Stay warm under there. I will come soon. Look after yourself and your mother. My dear child, God is with you. Be strong."

Ashebir didn't know what to say. He didn't want his father to stay and suffer, but neither could he bear him leaving them. He wished he could say, 'Please take us with you.' But he knew there was not enough money for that. "Ishi," he said. He scratched his head. "When will you come?"

"Soon. I will come soon, God willing."

"Ishi," he said. His mouth felt dry. He moved to get up.

"No, stay warm. Go back to sleep."

"Ishi," he said, and laid his head back down again. "Lakew," he started, sitting up again, but Lakew was already walking away. He could make out the bounce in his step and the shape of his small bundle held up by his stick over his shoulder. "Good bye," he whispered.

**

It was another morning. He could smell his own sweat and dirt under the gabi. When did he last wash? His diarrhoea had come back. When he got that feeling, he had to go fast; trotting across the road, looking for a space in the field for boys and men, treading carefully in his bare feet between the muck. He had to crouch, watching their watery yellow stuff come out, seeing his own; his stomach aching to be rid of the poison. Only poison could be that painful, he thought.

Still he could hear the sounds of mourning, the muffled voices of the neighbours. Still more people arrived from highland villages every day. The bus station and the whole length of roadside was getting fuller.

Zewdie did not move about much. He would walk her slowly to the women's field across the road for the toilet, wait for her and walk her back. He didn't know what to do to get her better.

The wailing was very close this morning. Someone's child. It sounded as if the old man with the watery eyes had died as well. The one who sat all day looking out from under his thin grey blanket, never speaking.

He sat up and pulled the gabi over his head, wrapping it round himself. He sat hugging himself, watching. His gabi had become that grey-brown colour. He used to wash it white in the river, scrubbing it with endod leaves against the rocks. He sniffed in hard and wiped his nose on it, then turned to look at the place where the old man always sat. He was no longer sitting up. The women stood around what looked like small mounds of soil under a gabi, wailing. Ashebir clenched his teeth and felt hot tears in his eyes. It was not fair. He put his forehead on his knees and sobbed quietly, not wanting to worry Zewdie.

Zewdie. His stomach turned like it did every morning. He whispered a short prayer, then he shook her gently. "Zewdie," he said. "Zewdie."

He heard her mumble and her head appeared.

"Zewdie, the old man's gone."

"Wey, sorry really," she said and started coughing.

"There is no food left," he said, when the coughing stopped. "Zewdie. We have no food."

32

August 1984, Addis Ababa

Booker was an anomaly. He had really helped her out. When she asked, "Why are you doing this?" he said he liked the two of them and was sorry about the break-up. Moe, with whom he worked closely on and off, was an idiot. It was the least he could do, he said. That sort of thing. He, among others, had got her on her feet again the moment it all went wrong. And to her surprise, Booker was much less 'interesting' than people wanted to believe. Izzie hadn't known him particularly well and had taken his 'womanising' reputation at face value, because of his tumultuous relationship with Leila. He was in fact not a bad guy. She was beginning to understand why Leila liked him. But he was not her type, nor she his. They had unanimously agreed on that.

He was making his way across the restaurant ahead of her, tall and lanky with dangling arms. She was surprised he didn't sweep salts and peppers and the little posies of flowers off the tables in his wake. He had the clumsy gait of a teenager, falling over his feet after a growth spurt. He turned and pointed at the corner table, a question mark in his raised eyebrows.

She nodded. Perfect.

She sat down opposite him with her back to the restaurant.

No sooner were they sitting, than the waiter came with a bottle of red, and a bottle of Ambo water.

"Ah, Solomon," Booker said. "Brilliant."

Solomon opened the wine and poured a taster into Booker's glass.

"Tenasteling," Izzie said. "How are you?"

Solomon looked surprised and smiled. "You speak Amharic?"

"Tinnish, tinnish," she said. "A little. Enough to get by."

Booker pushed the glass across the white tablecloth towards her. "You taste it," he said. "I hear you are a bit of a connoisseur."

"Not really," she said, a little embarrassed. It was funny to hear the sort of things Moe must have told others about her. Her throat tightened at the thought of him. "My grandfather owned a wine store with his two brothers. We grew up tasting different wines, that's all."

She swirled the red liquid round the glass and sniffed long and slow. "Hmmm. Gouder, nice little wine from the hills around Ambo, I believe." She smiled at her own theatrics and took a sip which she swilled round her mouth before swallowing. "It's great, Solomon, thank you. Very Gouder."

"And tej?" Solomon said. "You like our Ethiopian honey wine?"

"Yes I do indeed," she said. "But not with pasta."

"Turu neouw,[74]" Solomon said as he poured them each a glass. He flicked open the Ambo water with a fizz, put it on the table between them, turned on his heel and left.

"They obviously know you, Booker."

"I like the atmosphere and the food. Castelli's is obviously the best Italian in Addis but that's for special occasions."

Solomon was back with a plate of anti-pasti and two large menus.

"Oh, that looks delicious," she said, smiling up at him. "Egziersteling."

"I hope you don't mind," Booker said. "I always start with this."

"Perfect," she said, spreading the white linen napkin across her lap.

"Their ravioli is good," he said.

"I'll have that then," she said. She was happy not to have to look through the menu and think. It always took her forever.

Booker looked at Solomon. "Two ravioli please, Solomon. Thanks."

Solomon smiled, "Ishi," he said, and took the menus away.

"I'm curious," she said. "Moe said you were born in Malawi?"

"To be exact, I was born in Nyasaland," he said. "It only became Malawi in '64 at independence."

"What were your parents doing there?"

"My father was a District Commissioner for the Colonial Office. I don't know if that or being a missionary in those days was worse or better. For us it was idyllic. He was based in Salima on the shores of Lake Nyasa. My mother did all sorts of small projects with local women, like making jams and pickles for sale in the market, that kind of thing. She still does."

His eyes lit up as he spoke about his mother.

---

[74] Very good.

"What's she like?" Izzie said.

"Short, warm, round, sun-tanned, classic sun-bleached hair and blue eyes. My father is the dark-haired, tall, lanky one. They make quite a pair," he chuckled and took a sip of wine. "They live in Monkey Bay now. They couldn't leave when they retired. It's home."

"You were sent to boarding school, Moe said."

"The abrupt end to an idyllic childhood," Booker took a gulp of red wine and sighed. "To be honest, I felt betrayed," he said. "By my mother especially. I couldn't understand how she could do that to us."

Izzie was surprised to see Booker shift uncomfortably in his seat. He was quite moved. He didn't belong in her, 'emotional type', category. She should change the subject, but couldn't help herself asking more. "You didn't go back in the holidays then?" she said.

"Once a year in summer."

"Gosh."

"The first time, I was sat with a coke at Lilongwe Airport, mother wearing dark glasses, waiting for the plane to England. It was a shock to land in that drizzly grey country. My Aunt Clara kitted me out with a grey flannel uniform and deposited me, holding a tuck box, outside an imposing grey brick building. Aged nine."

"You flew all that way on your own at nine?"

"Yup," Booker wiped his mouth needlessly with the pristine napkin. "When I got back after the first year, I thought that was it. I was home and dry. Such a surprise to find myself on the plane again at the end of the holidays. I simply couldn't believe it."

"Gosh," Izzie said again. "That's really tough." She could almost see the nine year old's desperation and bewilderment in Booker's grey eyes.

"Cheers," he said, lifting his glass.

They clinked glasses.

"So what took you to Malawi?" he said.

"Love, of course," she said laughing.

"Aha," he said.

"I was with Sam. He got the job in Malawi and we decided to marry and go together. I had No. Idea. Honestly. I didn't have a clue what I wanted to do with my life. Had little knowledge of Africa, let alone Malawi. Of course I knew there were lots of poor people and assumed, without thinking, that people like Sam went to 'help'. That I would also 'help'." She laughed in a slightly despairing way. "Awful, isn't it? I was twenty-three. What on earth did I know?"

"So what did you do?"

"I learnt Chichewa with a school teacher in the old town who wanted to supplement his income. I taught English to some cloistered nuns. They spent all day praying for the world. So strange. They were really very lively and quite fun. Then I got a job in the administration at Likuni Hospital. As a volunteer, mind you. I wasn't allowed to work, as I was an accompanying spouse. You know the rules. And most of all, I learnt that I had a lot to learn," she said, biting her lip and nodding her head.

"You and Sam never came to the Club."

"No, it was, 'Whites Only', right?" she said. "You didn't mind that?"

"I did, but I liked the atmosphere at the clubhouse, old colonial, you know. And the classic G&T at sundown. Tennis courts."

"Exactly," she said. "Wonderful and appalling. I quickly realised, here too, just how privileged we are. We ex-pats, even as a woman, are treated differently. You live with a sense that nothing can happen to you. And at the end of every hot, sweaty day, there's a cold beer, in a comfortable bungalow or flat with hot running water and good food in the fridge, waiting for you. It's all very well us trying to understand 'the poor'. We don't know the half."

"And just look at us now," Booker said, smiling at her and looking round the restaurant.

"I know," she said, glancing behind her, she pulled a sheepish face. "I always loved a good meal. By the way this is delicious. I've never tried roasting peppers and aubergines. I must give it a go." Talking cooking and homey things gave her a pang. She took a sip of wine. She had literally been wrenched out of her life. She missed it. Or did she? Some things were better. Far better. She felt freer.

"You OK?" Booker said.

"Yup. Fine thanks. And thank you, Booker." She felt the tears well up in her eyes. "Woops. Don't want this. Deep breath." She rummaged for a hanky in her cavernous bag, and gave her nose a resounding blow. Moe had always said she sounded like a fog horn.

Booker topped up her wine.

"Negisst said Moe is seeing someone," she said.

"Well that doesn't surprise me. You?"

"I guess not."

"Anyone we know?"

"I don't think so," she shrugged. "Mekonnen says they try to chase her off when she comes." She laughed. Mekonnen was often waiting for her outside the flats at Arat Kilo in the evenings. He would exchange a few words and then take off again. He wanted to check if she was alright.

"They are funny. Mekonnen says even the zabanya gives her a hard time. He won't let her into the building."

"Poor woman," Booker said, helping himself to an assortment from the anti- pasti platter.

"Negisst told me she hides sachets of herbs under the sofa and under the mattress. Apparently it's magic to make him love her." Izzie took a piece of the soft white bread to mop up some olive oil speckled with green herbs. She stopped when Booker threw his head back and laughed.

He cut a funny figure with his long legs and arms around the table, and then this laugh, like a gurgling drain getting louder and louder.

Izzie had to laugh. "What?" she said.

"It happened to me. Don't tell me, Negisst runs cold water over it to kill its powers."

"So, did it work?" Izzie said, her eyes laughing at him. "Did it break the spell over you?"

"In a jiffy. Dumped the woman right away," Booker said.

"Did you?" Izzie said, a bit surprised. Booker was surely too cynical to believe in such things.

"Of course I didn't," Booker said. "What is Negisst doing anyway, hunting round the place?"

"I guess she's suspicious. Trying to protect us. And she's right. I believe in that sort of thing. It's not safe." Izzie said. "Anyway Negisst keeps saying she wants me to come back, you know. She wants Moe and me to be together again. I don't want to tell her what actually happened. That there is no way I can or want to go back."

"It's over, Izzie," Booker said, sobering up.

"Yup. It's nearly six weeks now."

"So, tell me, what's going on, what's new?"

"I sometimes spend the weekends with Leila at the Livestock Research Institute compound, when she's not in Debre Berhan," she said, hoping he didn't mind her mentioning Leila. "You know hyenas slouch about on the road up to the Institute's gates? I've seen them there at dusk a couple of times now. Funny creatures."

"The drought brings them closer to Addis. They're looking for food of course."

"The guy from the International NGO supporting the Nazareth project, Anthony, asked us to help out with a boy who had his face almost bitten off by a hyena. He's only fifteen. He said the lad needed a job. He couldn't live with his family anymore."

"And?"

"We've taken him on, in one of our carpet making workshops. They are mostly leprosy patients there. He seems to like it." Izzie nodded her head. "Good for him really. Anthony and his wife are paying for the boy's night school."

"His face must be quite a mess. Blimey. What a thing to happen," Booker said.

"They did their best to patch him up at St Paul's Hospital."

"The medical staff there are really good," Booker said. "Look at Hiwot. She's amazing."

"And she's been a really good friend to me too. She often stays over with me at Arat Kilo. We still go dancing. You know? At the Munich Bar on the Debre Zeit road? Music and dance does you good. Well it does me, anyway."

He raised an eyebrow. "No, I don't know," he said. "Give me Vivaldi any day."

"Hey," she heard a familiar voice behind her. "It's you."

She turned round. It was Ingo. "Hi there," she said. "What a surprise." She was genuinely taken aback.

"Booker, you know Ingo? He works at the Livestock Research Institute too.

"Hiya," a young woman peered over Ingo's shoulder. A mop of golden-brown curls.

"Hi, Susan," Izzie said. "How lovely to see you both. Venturing out into the big bad city on a Friday night?"

"Absolutely," Susan said. She had a broad open face, with a wonderful smile. She was fit, a good tennis player. Izzie had watched her. She was one of the reasons Izzie had politely turned down the several invitations to join in. She had never been much good at tennis.

"Yes, we know Booker, who doesn't?" she laughed.

Booker raised a hand, "Hi there, you two," and turned to Izzie with raised eyebrows.

Izzie shrugged and nodded agreement, amused by Booker's eyebrow-communication.

"Come," Booker said. "Pull up some chairs if you like."

"Yes, come on, join us," Izzie said.

"Love to," Susan said. "Ingo, what about you?"

"Perfect," Ingo said. "If we're not interrupting anything?" As he spoke he saw to it that Susan had a chair and was pulling one up for himself next to Izzie.

The chivalrous type, Izzie thought, looking up at him, knowing her eyes were smiling warmly. Her feminist soul, habitually fighting all that door-opening and chair-pulling, couldn't help melting just a little. There was something so relaxed about him. Lucky chap, she thought, he was obviously comfortable in his own skin. As he sat, she took a sideways glance. He was handsome, with a classic square jaw and thick dark blonde hair, slightly bleached by the sun. She had seen Ingo at the Institute a few times. He was always smiling and joking. He sometimes played tennis in the group with Susan. For his Friday night out he was clean-shaven and wore a fresh shirt. She could smell his aftershave. It made her slightly heady. She found herself wondering if he and Susan were together.

Solomon appeared as if by magic, holding another bottle of wine and two menus.

"Ha, well done Solomon," Booker said. "Fill them all up."

"Sure we're not interrupting?" Ingo asked her again. He had a twinkle in his eye. He turned to thank Solomon, who gave him a menu and had filled his glass.

"Not at all," she said. "We're just catching up. Booker is my saviour, my friend in need, if you like," Izzie laughed.

Booker raised hands, claiming innocence.

"Well, you are," she said.

"Battle of Adwa," Susan said, turning the illustration on the menu round to show them.

"That's what I like about this place," Booker said. "The Ethiopians roundly defeated the Italians in 1896. A fact they proudly display on their menu. And here we have the mingling of worlds, an Ethio-Italian restaurant serving spaghetti to the haunting sounds of Tilahun Gessesse. Just Ethiopian wine, not a drop of Valpolicella or Chianti in sight."

"Is that his name? The musician singing?" Ingo said. "Seem to hear him everywhere."

"He's hugely popular," Booker said. "Hugely." He waved his arms about expansively, as if everyone should know this fact.

Izzie turned to Susan, who was still looking at the artwork on her menu. "There's a small art gallery and souvenir shop down one of the backstreets in Piazza," she said. "You can find all those classic paintings there, mostly on parchment. The owner himself is an artist. He says he learnt from his father. He claims his grandfather, Belachew, I think his name was, was one of the first Ethiopian artists who painted in that way. He did a famous one of the battle of Adwa. Maybe that's a copy of it?"

Susan looked more closely. "Doesn't seem to have a name on it. And if it does I can't read Amharic, anyway."

"I wouldn't mind having a look in that shop," Ingo said. "It's my cousin's wedding at the end of the month. Maybe I can find something for them there?"

"It's near Taitu's Hotel, if you know that," Izzie said. "Would be a really original gift."

"Maybe I should hire you as my personal guide?" Ingo said. "You seem to know your way around."

Izzie felt her face flush and took another slice of aubergine to distract herself. "I ought to," she said, chewing. "Piazza is my neighbourhood. Well it was." she added quickly, with a sinking feeling in her stomach. She took a large sip of wine and looked across at Booker.

He smiled and raised his glass, with a look at Ingo.

She glared back, trying to conjure a determined, I am not interested in him, look on her face.

"I'd be happy to take you round Piazza," she said, sitting up, trying to regain her ease and confidence. "The art gallery, the fruit and veg stalls, the crazy people, Mahmoud's Music shop on the corner opposite Castelli's? We could see all that. You know Castelli's?"

"Of course I do," he said.

"Booker saves Castelli's for 'best'," Izzie said. "And you?"

"You have a birthday coming up?" he said, his eyes smiling amusement. "Or shall we celebrate mine in retrospect?"

"Ha-ha, we'll see about that," Izzie said, feeling drawn to this guy. It was too soon. He was flirting with her. So he and Susan were not, 'an item', as Mum would say.

"How's it going, Izzie?" Susan said, her head cocked to one side, a sympathetic look on her face.

Izzie didn't want pity. "I'm fine," she said. "Totally."

"I hear you have a lovely flat in Arat Kilo," Susan went on.

"It's great," Izzie said. "Cosy. It's got a balcony overlooking the city." She picked a red pepper from the plate she was sharing with Booker, and popped it in her mouth, chewing and smiling. "You should come over sometime, Susan."

"I'd love to," Susan said. "A city sleep-over. Cool."

"Shall we share an anti-pasti, Suz?" Ingo said. "It looks really good."

"That will do me," Susan said.

"Me too," Ingo said. "That's us then."

They waved at Solomon who came over and took their order, removing the empty Ambo bottle.

Booker nodded for him to bring one more.

"Well, this is very nice," Ingo said, taking the large linen napkin and laying it across his knees.

She noticed he was wearing khaki trousers, not jeans like most of them.

"You like the zabanyas' uniform then?" Izzie said, tempted to tease him.

"Oh yes," he said, grinning. "I'm actually very fond of these. I had them tailor-made in Bamako, in 1978, as it happens."

"Bamako, hey?"

"I suppose you're mostly in Debre Zeit now, Susan?" Booker said.

"Yes, I am. I'm staying in a lovely bungalow belonging to the Institute, not far from Lake Bishoftu. It's so beautiful with the surrounding hills and mountains. I sometimes go swimming in the evenings after work. And it's a hellova lot warmer than Debre Berhan."

"The ponds in Debre Berhan are finished?" Ingo said.

"Yes, well, we handed them over to the Peasant Association, and just go to check on them now and then."

"Ponds?" Izzie said. "What are you doing?" She had only seen Susan on the tennis court or for a brief chat at the Buffet de la Gare on a Sunday night. So they hadn't ever really talked work.

"It's a water resources meets livestock part of the Institute's work," Susan said, suddenly looking serious. "Obviously we all know there are water shortages. Clear." She rolled her eyes. "The Institute has designed an ox-drawn scoop for excavating ponds."

"Wow," Izzie said.

"It's brilliant," Susan leant forward on her elbows and shuffled her bum in her seat, getting into her subject. "We work with the Peasant Associations and local farmers who bring their teams of oxen. We supply the scoops. You should come sometime, Izzie, and take a look."

"I'd love to," Izzie said. "I've never stopped in Debre Zeit, always gone straight through on the way to Nazareth, or Langano."

Susan and Ingo leaned back, smiling as Solomon laid a plate of antipasti between them and a basket of fresh bread.

"That looks delicious," Ingo said.

A smaller waiter stood beside Solomon with two plates of ravioli.

Izzie was already full, but it looked good, served in a sauce of butter and sage. "Do you have a pepper mill?"

The smaller waiter nodded and was back in an instant with pepper and parmesan.

"Bliss," Izzie said.

Silence fell as they ate and sipped at their wine. She could hear people on the tables behind her. A constant hum, murmur and chat, and clink of cutlery on china plates. A raised voice and laughter. It was mostly Ethiopians eating there, and a few Koreans, in Addis to assist with the preparations for the 10th Anniversary. So much pomp and pizazz; banners with slogans: 'Long Live Proletarian Internationalism!'; billboards with classic communist art, bold blocks of colour depicting the farmers, the workers, the soldiers, the cadres, all marching forward. Tight security, in anticipation of the event, was already in place. It was all the talk at work.

"A few of us are planning to climb Mount Zukwala next Sunday, right Suz?" Ingo said. "You should both come."

Booker waved his arms in the air as if he might do the hokey cokey. "I'll be transporting beers for the Hash next Sunday," he said. "I won't be coming. Too much like hard work, climbing mountains." He lowered his arms again reaching for his wine. "Those ravioli were good, eh?"

"You finished already?" Izzie said, peering across at his plate.

"Why don't you come, Izzie?" Susan said. "And you know what, Ingo, you should all come down to Debre Zeit on Saturday. Sleep over. Make a weekend of it. It will be a blast."

"I would love to," Izzie said, "but I don't have a car right now."

"That's no problem, we can pick you up in Arat Kilo on our way through," Ingo said. "That's easy enough."

She was surprised how quickly her sore heart warmed to him.

"Thank you," she said. "Do you think I can walk it in my pumps, Susan? I don't have any boots."

"Of course you can," Susan said. "It's not much climbing. It will be great. Early start on Sunday morning, while it's still cool."

"Makes sense for us to stay over, if you've got room for us all, Suz," he said. "We'll be four with Izzie."

"Looks like we've got a plan," Susan said. "Shame you can't join us, Booker."

"Don't you worry about me," Booker said. "I'm not too keen on spending a whole day walking in the sun. I'll be happy in the shade, by the car, with the cold beers waiting for them all to finish running."

"You don't run the Hash?"

"Can you see me running, Izzie, really?" Booker laughed.

"You're right, I can't."

"And the sun is pretty relentless these days."

"Yes, it sure is. Not a drop of rain, it seems like forever," Izzie said.

There they were eating their fill, while a famine raged around them. She wondered whether it really mattered where one was. Whether it was just as bad to eat your fill in London, Hertfordshire, Surrey, Norfolk, or anywhere come to that, with a famine going on, as it was to eat your fill right there in Addis, with the famine right under your nose? She looked at Ingo, who was slowly shaking his head. He took a glug of wine. Maybe he was having similar thoughts.

"How long have you been at the Institute? What are you working on?" Izzie rattled out, anxious to move her thoughts on.

"Actually, I just got back from Mali today," he said.

"Made a visit to your tailor, did you?" Booker said and laughed.

Izzie sighed with relief at him. "Your laugh, Booker!"

"Yes, that's right. I had a shirt made this time. Also in khaki. Just like Izzie's jacket," Ingo raised his eyebrows at Izzie and smiled at Booker. "Actually, I'm working on some research there," he said. "Impact of imported food aid on local dairy markets." He said it quickly as if to get it out of the way.

"Wow," Izzie said. "I wasn't expecting that."

"It's fascinating," Susan said. "The Common Market exports their excess milk and butter to West Africa as 'food aid', and thereby undercuts the prices of local milk producers."

"So, unsurprisingly, local dairy farmers in Mali are going out of business. Everyone buys the cheaper imported milk from the Common Market, of course," Ingo said.

"They still have to buy it? Even though it's food aid?" Izzie said.

"Absolutely," Ingo said.

"It's ironic, isn't it?" Booker said, filling everyone's wine glasses. "The EEC has mountains of grain, milk, butter, beef and wine. We have this massive famine here, and little or no food aid coming in."

"The roadside in Debre Berhan is filling up with families from northern Shewa and Wollo," Susan said. "Leila is in tears every time she passes them. They're dying like flies up there, she says."

"Its cold war politics," Ingo said. "Pretty disgusting."

"That's right. The Americans and Brits apparently don't want to provide food aid where the Russians are in residence," Izzie said. "Wondwossen is urgently trying to persuade the international community to step up with grains supplies. They need millions of tons." She'd heard Moe on about it, and Fasika too.

"Wondwossen?" Ingo said.

"Head of the Relief Council," Izzie said. "You know him, don't you Booker?"

Booker nodded. "The latest is that a 'National Disaster' has been declared, not a famine; and all roads into Addis have been blocked. They don't want starving people in the capital in the run up to the anniversary celebrations."

Izzie pushed the last piece of ravioli round her plate. "Maybe we have to wait until the 10th Anniversary is over," she said. "But honestly, if Wondwossen can't do anything, who can? He is part of the government. And Fasika says he has done the rounds of European capitals. No one is listening, inside or outside. And no journalists or NGOs are allowed to travel out of Addis. No one is allowed to see and record what is going on."

"We have been collecting data on rainfall and harvests across Africa, and at our stations in Ethiopia of course, for years," Ingo said. "We raised the alert with international aid agencies and embassies here a year ago. We were met with silence, apparently."

"And things have become steadily worse," Booker said.

They sat in front of their plates.

"Come on," Susan said. "Let's finish up here and go for an Irish at The Cottage? How about that?"

"I could do with a whiskey," Izzie said.

"Ingo?" Susan said. "One for the road?" They still had to drive out to the Institute compound.

"Perfect," Ingo said. "But just to say something. I don't think the effort is over. We will do something, I am sure of it."

"It's going to be too late," Izzie said. "It is too late."

"You just can't imagine what it must be like," Susan said.

Ney ney ney…

Her favourite song played in the background. She turned to look around the restaurant behind her, caught Solomon looking at her, and smiled. She looked at her new friends. Their faces flushed with wine and shadowed by the thoughts they shared. It was such a strange situation to be in. The contrast between their comfort and the famine. And for her, she was already a step away from her life with Moe. And so far from her old life, from the fish and chip shop on Dalston Lane, ice cream vans on Hyde Park, London pubs and a pint of beer. And so far from the Much Hadham village fete on August bank holiday. They would be gathering stuff for the bric-a-brac stall, baking amazing cakes, making sure there were enough prizes for the tombola. Fund-raising. That's what they were good at. She sighed. She wasn't doing anything.

"A penny for them?" Susan said.

"Ha," Izzie said. "Another time."

"Let's get the bill?" Ingo said.

Solomon was already there. They rummaged in back pockets and bags for wallets, dividing 'the damage' by four.

Booker needed to get home. Izzie went with Ingo and Susan. She had spent many an evening with Moe at The Cottage. It would be strange to be there without him.

The old man stood in the carpark, wrapped in his gabi from head to foot, and waved them into a space. He greeted them, smiling his usual friendly smile, and nodding reassurance that the car would still be there after they had had their fill inside.

"What did you say you call her?" Izzie said.

"Lucille," Ingo said, slamming the driver's door shut with a clunk. It was a second-hand pale yellow Renault 16. "You must know the song? Kenny Rogers? She left me stranded on the road from Langano to Addis one hot Sunday afternoon. Not to be trusted."

Izzie laughed. "I like that."

"What? That I was stranded?"

"No. Her name, her character."

Izzie walked in first. The restaurant and bar were busy. Loud. Chat and laughter. The air warm, welcoming, a fug from the smell of hot food, alcohol and cigarette smoke.

"Hey! Yeshi Emebate," she called out, seeing a tall dark woman. She was standing a few people back from the bar, obviously waiting for someone. She was well made up and wore tight jeans with a loose white cheesecloth shirt on top. Simple but stunning, Izzie thought. Some women just had the knack.

The two greeted each other, exchanging cheeks. Izzie noticed her strong sweet perfume. Even after she drew away it clung to her cheeks and her khaki jacket.

"What are you doing here, yeney konjo?" Yeshi Emebate said. She looked ruffled for a moment.

Izzie shrugged a 'why not'? "Just a last drink with friends," she said. "You?"

"Here you go," Moe came up behind Yeshi Emebate with two Irish coffees and then saw Izzie. "You two know each other?"

"I thought you said you were going to Langano," she said, her voice choked. "And I thought you said you don't drink, Yeshi," Izzie said, trying to gather her thoughts.

"Well, I do sometimes," Yeshi said, taking her drink from Moe. She'd regained her composure and smiled undeterred as she moved up against him so the length of her body was touching his.

"How do you know each other?" Moe said, moving a little away from Yeshi.

"More to the point, Yeshi, how did you, you know, how did you work, this... huh?" Izzie's finger pointed from Moe to Yeshi, one to the other, like she was stirring something.

Yeshi Emebate stood tall, cool, in command. "Well you did tell me a lot about him. It was easy..."

Izzie felt a hand slip round her waist and turned. "Ingo," she said. "I..."

"What am I getting you?" he said.

"Hi there, Moe," Susan said. "How are you doing?" She laughed a slightly higher note than usual. "Lots of coincidences tonight."

"I'd love an Irish coffee with an extra shot if that's OK," Izzie said. She managed to smile at Ingo.

"You and Susan go get a table, I've got this," Ingo said. He headed for the bar.

Moe smiled one of his hopeless, lopsided, smiles. "You're looking amazing, Izzie," he said, like it might help him get away with murder. He headed off towards an empty cubicle at the back. Yeshi Emebate sauntered behind him.

"That smile is not going to get you anywhere," Izzie called after him. She could feel her temper rising. "What was that about us women sticking together, eh Yeshi?" she called after Yeshi in Amharic. "And your stupid magic won't work on him."

"Enough," Susan pulled Izzie towards a cubicle out of the way. "Come on love, I don't know what you were saying, but that's enough."

Some Ethiopians sitting nearby laughed. "Enday, yigirmal," one said. "You speak really good Amharic," he smiled at her, nodding his approval. He looked over his shoulder at Moe and Yeshi Emebate, still smiling.

It was embarrassing. Izzie let Susan steer her towards an empty table. Her legs had gone to jelly. She slid across the bench to lean her head against the wall. "Oh God," she sighed.

"How do you know her, anyway?" Susan whispered loudly.

Ingo arrived with three Irish coffees in tall glasses, a thick layer of white whipped cream on top of the dark black coffee. "Here we go," he said, his eyes sparkling. He put them on the table and sat in beside Izzie. "You alright? Take a sip of that – you'll soon feel a lot better."

The Cottage had a cosy atmosphere with its dark wood cubicles and tables, and small lamps with red shades. The sounds of chat, laughter and chinking glass flowed around her like waves on a shore. She lit a cigarette, offering them around. No one else smoked. She shrugged. They raised their glasses. She took a sip. "Hmmm, you're right, just what I needed," she murmured. "Thank you, Ingo. And for what just happened there."

"What did happen?" he said.

"I think you kind of tried to help me out."

Ingo looked pleased with himself. "I'm glad if I did," he grinned. "It looked like it was getting awkward."

"So, how do you know her?" Susan persisted, still speaking in a stage whisper.

"I knew that he was with an Ethiopian woman. My maid Negisst told me. And that she's leaving black magic around our flat to entice Moe. To make him love her. That's what Negisst says anyway." She still thought of it as 'their' flat. She sighed and took another sip of the strong dark liquid, softened by the cream. She licked her lips.

"Black magic woman," Ingo said. "Intriguing lives you city folk lead."

"You are not taking this serious," Izzie said, nudging him with her elbow.

"But how do you know her?" Susan said. "That's what I want to know."

"She lives in the flat above me in Arat Kilo."

"You are kidding me," Susan said, flopping back into her seat.

"The boys, the Piazza street boys, made such a rumpus when they first came to visit, when I moved in, that she came down to see what was going on."

"So how did she get to be with Moe?" Susan said, her eyes sparkling.

"Exactly my point," Izzie said. "How the fuck did she wriggle that one?" Her Irish coffee was much depleted. She lit another cigarette and blew the smoke at the rafters. "She's got a baby with this German guy." She looked at Ingo. "I doubt you know him."

"Me too," Ingo said.

"He's paying her rent," Izzie said. "Poor little thing. That babe. So tiny and pale. I don't think it's very well. You know, she has this photo album. It's full of photos of herself with different farenj guys. I didn't recognise any of them, I hasten to add."

"I wonder if Moe knows what he's getting himself into?" Susan said.

"What should I care? But Yeshi Emebate really pulled one on me there. Clever girl, hey?

"What a life," Ingo said. This time he looked genuinely sorry.

"Enough of my stuff," Izzie said. "Let me get another round, and we'll drink to that mountain."

"Zukwala," Susan and Ingo said unanimously.

"Yes, to Zukwala," Izzie said. "What a beautiful name."

33

September 1984, On the Roadside Debre Berhan

The sun sent long shadows across the dust; the earth under his feet still warm from the day. The scrap of newspaper the boy at the kiosk had wrapped round his bread was almost new, not wrinkled and dirty as usual. He could practice reading.

A large red Anbessa bus, its painted yellow lion fading into the side, honked as it pulled in to the depot, leaning heavily on one side. It was on its way north, past their home. Ashebir stood and looked.

When he got back to their bus shelter he unwrapped the bread and put it straight in his bag. They had agreed to eat after sunset. He had to wait.

"Zewdie look, I got a newspaper," he said. "It is almost new. Shall we read it?"

She sat up with a low grunt, "Ishi, let's see."

He sat down next to her, shuffling the dirt and small sharp stones with his bottom to get comfortable.

"You can read?" The mocking voice stood between him and the sun.

His heart sank. Wubit. She was older than him. Her skinny legs poked out under her long skirt showing the tillik'o scars on her shins.

"You went to school?"

"I went to the Kebele school in the evenings."

"'Literacy'?" she said.

He looked at Zewdie.

"Yes, you went to 'Literacy' in Ataye," Zewdie said.

"We don't have a school, or 'Literacy', in our village," Wubit said. "Anyway, I had to help my mother."

"Girls don't need school," Ashebir said, a sharp tongue spitting out from his empty belly.

"Ashebir," Zewdie chided. "Of course girls need school. Even Mengistu says so."

Of course there were girls and women in his Kebele 'Literacy' class.

Aminat used to come with him and Mohamed Abdu. Of course they should go to school. But his spiteful jab was for Wubit alone.

"He's right," Wozeiro Tsehai said. "What do girls want with reading and writing when they are going to cook, collect firewood and have babies?"

"Boys and girls both need school," Zewdie said.

"That's right," Wubit said, kicking Ashebir, looking pleased.

"Ow-waa," Ashebir rubbed his ankle.

"A lot of good school is for any of us," Wozeiro Tsehai said. "You can't eat Ha Hu Hee."

"I can," Ashebir said, taking letters off the newspaper here and there, as if he were picking tasty bits of zilzil tibs from a plate of injera. He put them in his mouth, stuck his tongue in his cheek to make it look full, and chewed.

He looked at Zewdie and Wozeiro Tsehai smiling at their laughter, his mouth still closed and chewing.

He felt a hard slap across his head. "Goat," Wubit said, laughing.

"Hey," he said, raising a hand to shield himself. He could not hit back, even in play. She was a girl. He rubbed his head, his ear buzzing.

"Ishi, let's see what you can do, schoolboy," Wubit said, sneering. She squatted between him and his mother and peered forward over his shoulder.

Her breath smelt bad. He shrugged his shoulder to get her away, and spread the paper out. She poked him in the back. He cleared his throat and started, "Ga Ze Ta." His dirty finger traced the line of letters. "Gazeta," he said. It was an effort.

"Good boy," Zewdie said.

"And this is, Ah Mu Ts Uh." He looked at Zewdie. "Amutsuh?"

"Rebel," Wubit said. "Must be about the war."

"What does it say?" Wozeiro Tsehai asked.

He looked at the mystery of black letters. They had not reached the end of the alphabet in his class.

"I don't know," he said, deflated.

"'Literacy'," Wubit said, as if she was spitting.

To his relief she got up and left.

"Zewdie," he said. "Did you hear the army trucks again last night?"

"Yes, I did. It's too bad."

"They will kill the rebels," he said, lifting an imaginary rifle. He closed one eye and aimed it at the crowd gathered around the Anbessa bus. "Ktsch. Ktsch. Ktsch."

"They are people, like us," Zewdie said. "They are mothers and sons."

He lowered his rifle. He wondered what it was like, sitting in the back of an army truck, clutching a gun between his knees, the dark sky above. He was sure the soldiers got to eat. "Some of the trucks were going back to Addis," he said.

"Maybe they were taking the wounded to the army hospital," she said, putting a hand on her chest and coughing.

"There's a hospital just for soldiers?"

"There is, God have mercy." Zewdie sniffed into her shawl. She curled up on the ground, resting her head on her arm.

She knows so many things, he thought. Her face was pale and drawn. His smiling, laughing, strong mother was fading before his eyes.

A crow peered over the shelter, its claws curled round the edge of the corrugated roof. It cawed at him.

Ashebir jumped up and flapped the paper at it. "Hid, hid!" he shouted. "Go away!" Hot tears shot into his eyes.

The large bird cocked its head to one side, stared at him for a moment, then flew off slow and heavy.

Crows and ravens carried away the spirits of the dead. That's what he had heard. They hovered over dead creatures, picked the flesh from their bones. He had seen them.

"They are evil," he said, the bird's black eyes preying on his mind. "Do they take away people's spirits, Zewdie?"

"No. Aysoh," she said, her voice raspy. "They just feed on rubbish and carcasses. They clean everything up."

"I don't like them," he said. He wondered what would happen to the spirit inside the crow if he killed it with his wenchef.[75] Zewdie did not let him use it here. There were too many people, she said. If he missed his target someone could get hurt. He went back to his paper, randomly sounding out the letters he recognised, "Ki Be Leh Ha," he whispered, "Bu Dee La."

"They aren't going to hospital," Wozeiro Tsehai said. "They are taking them to march in Addis."

Ashebir looked up.

Zewdie turned towards their neighbour. "For the 10th Anniversary?"

"Do you think they will celebrate the revolution in Debre Berhan with all of us here, living under the open sky?" Wozeiro Tsehai said. She smiled one of her God help us smiles, looking up to heaven.

---

[75] Slingshot.

"I saw people practicing further up the road," Ashebir said. "They were marching behind the Ethiopian flag."

Zewdie sucked her teeth. Then, to his surprise, she muttered, "Revolutionary Motherland or Death."

The two women laughed until Zewdie started coughing again.

"They were clearing young pickpockets off the streets yesterday," Wozeiro Tsehai said.

"You hear that, Ashebir?" Zewdie said. "You be careful. They might think you are a dooriyey, and take you away with those bad boys."

He looked at the two women, huddled next to each other, wrapped in their shawls against the creeping evening cool, their clothes the colour of the grey dirt around them. He shivered and pulled his own gabi round his shoulders. Too tired to read any more, he used the paper to keep the flies away from his face. "Zewdie, can we eat now?" he said.

"When the sun has gone down," she said.

"I am hungry."

"We agreed."

He gritted his teeth and tried to think of something to ask her.

"Zewdie, what is the 10th Anniversary?"

"Ten years since the revolution. Since they got rid of the Emperor," she said.

"While we are sick and hungry they are marching and putting up flags."

"Was he a bad man?" he asked Zewdie.

"Some say it was better in his time," Wozeiro Tsehai said.

He missed the chatting, just him and Zewdie; the evenings by the hearth in their own home. He suddenly wanted to be back with Mohamed Abdu and Ali; on Muletta mountain with the animals. He even wanted to go to the ravine and collect firewood again, then fall asleep, exhausted, under their thatch roof beside the fire. He wondered if the smoke-blackened cobweb still hung from the rafters.

"There was hunger in the Emperor's time too. Egziyabher yawkal," Zewdie said.

Wozeiro Tsehai shook her head. "Many, many people died at that time. But this time it seems even worse."

"But we will be alright, Zewdie, won't we?"

"Maybe it is time we eat, Ashebir?" Zewdie said.

He got the bread from his bag and laid it on Temima's cloth. It looked very little for two. One bread roll. His heart sank when his mother nudged Wozeiro Tsehai.

"Eat a little with us, Wozeiro Tsehai?" she said.

He looked to see what Wozeiro Tsehai would do.

"No, you eat. I will eat later."

He sighed, relieved. Just a little bread without sauce, he thought. Not enough for three. He looked up and saw Wozeiro Tsehai's sad face and suddenly felt bad.

"What? You have to eat with us," Zewdie said.

"Ishi, I will have a little. God bless you, Zewdie."

"Let us pray," Zewdie said.

He closed his eyes.

"Thanks to God for this bread. Thanks to God for our kind neighbour, Wozeiro Tsehai. God bless Lakew, God bless us. Amen."

"Amen," he whispered. He waited for Zewdie to take some bread first.

"Eat, Wozeiro Tsehai," she said. "Ashebir, eat."

"Ishi," he said, and broke a piece off. "Eat, Mama Tsehai," he said quietly.

"Ishi," Wozeiro Tsehai said, bowing her head politely. She pulled a small piece away from the bread and put it in her mouth.

He ate, watching Zewdie chew. She frowned each time she swallowed as if it hurt, and took sips of water. She looked as though she would lie down again without eating more.

"Eat, Zewdie," he said, pushing the bread towards her, brushing the flies away.

"Ishi," she said, and pulled another small piece away with her fingers.

When the bread was gone, the hunger pains were still there. He sat back and sighed, wishing he could have a plate of injera with sherro, or a handful of fendisha.[76] The cool of the evening crept through his clothes. He wrapped his gabi around, hugging himself and rocked back and forth. He watched as smoke from the small fires along the roadside filled the air and became one long, low-hanging mist. The sun went down, burning the sky a deep pink red, like a huge fire in heaven. Maybe God was angry with them. The people in their village had said The Hunger was a punishment from God. He still did not understand what they had done wrong.

**

The next morning he was squatting in the field where the boys and men

---

[76] Popcorn.

went. All around him small piles of excrement sent up a nasty thick smell. The place was buzzing with flies; around his face, in his ears, up his nose. They bit. He swatted them with his hands, kept his mouth shut tight, and blew out through his nose to get them away. He tried to finish quickly. He got up and pulled up his shorts, wiping his hands on them. He picked his way back towards the road, anxious to wash.

The early morning mist had already lifted. It was market day again. People were heading into town along the main road, coming down the paths between the fields with their donkeys, women holding up black umbrellas, old men on their mules. A small flock of sheep strayed haphazardly across the road, bleating. A boy whirled his whip in the air and slapped it down on the tarmac with a loud crack. The sheep hurried closer together. Ashebir remembered playing a game with his friends: whose whip cracked the loudest. He was good at it, but Mohamed Abdu was better.

"I never wanted you to suffer like this," Zewdie said as he winced, washing his hands. The scabies between his fingers was painful. "You need medicine," she said.

"At least we are not like them," he said, looking at The Hungry around them.

No one had medicine for diarrhoea, or for the coughing and running noses. All they could do was beg and wait, or lie on the ground under dirty rags until the crows came.

"What is everyone waiting for, Zewdie?"

"For the government to come and help," she said.

The air smelt of sweat and sickness, of damp burnt out wood from the night before. The white truck was there. A scavenging hyena. Two men moved from one small wailing group to the next with their wooden stretcher. The white truck frightened him. He thought of the deep black hole in his dream. His grandmother throwing fendisha into the endless darkness.

He heard Zewdie suck her teeth and sigh.

"What is it?" he said.

"We are like them," she said. "We are just like them, The Hungry, Ashebir."

Her words made him angry. He turned away. "We are not like them," he said between gritted teeth. He hated this place. It smelt like rotten meat in the market on a hot day. The crows cawing, the wailing. He longed for home. His throat felt blocked. He tried to swallow. He wiped his nose on his gabi, leaving a shiny trail on the dirty cloth.

No, he and Zewdie were not like those people. When they had left the village, he thought that it was only a few people who were in difficulty. On their journey to Debre Berhan, he had been shocked to see so many Hungry on the road, their empty eyes and bony faces, the children's skinny legs like kindling. He and Zewdie were in trouble, but they were not like them.

"I am hungry, Zewdie," he managed to say. "You too?"

"Yes, me too," Zewdie said.

"I'll go to the market, see what I can find."

**

A row of women sat behind their onions, tomatoes and dried chillies. He lingered over the sweet smell and deep red colour. Maybe he could stoop as if his foot hurt and slip a tomato into his hand. He looked around. Even the thought of it made his heart beat fast. If only he were braver.

Women sat under their umbrellas behind large sacks of red and yellow lentils. Zewdie used to make a good sherro sauce with lentils, sprinkling dark red chilli spices through her fingers over the bubbling pot. His stomach grumbled, he pressed his hand in deep, bending over to stop the aching. A pain shot into his chest. He gasped. Thinking he might vomit, he squatted down, holding onto his stomach. He let people brush past until the pain eased.

Smelling something warm and sweet, like fresh bread, his mouth watered. A woman sat behind a charcoal brazier on a low stool. She wore a shawl over her shoulders, and a long skirt which sat in the dust around her feet. A black umbrella shaded her from the sun. He wondered what she was roasting. He stood up and stretched, rubbing his stomach and chest to relieve the cramps.

"Tenasteling." Someone gripped his shoulder hard.

The boy was taller than Ashebir, filthy and in rags. His dark-skinned cheeks were marked with the scars rough town boys wore. His bushy hair was caked with dirt, his eyes bloodshot.

Ashebir looked about him in despair.

"I've seen you before," the boy smiled, his teeth stained green from khat. His breath smelt of cigarettes.

Ashebir nodded.

"What's your name?" the boy said. His hand still holding Ashebir's shoulder.

"Ashebir," he said, looking away.

Zewdie said to stay away from boys like that. They are bad, very bad.

"Let's go," the dooriyey said, laughing. "My friends are over there." He pointed his chin to the far end of the market.

Ashebir held back, digging his toes into the earth. He wanted to see what the woman was cooking. He needed to eat. And if he went with this boy, he might be rounded up. They would think he was a dooriyey too.

The woman carried on roasting the food, turning it swiftly with the tips of her fingers as it went black on the underside. Her hands were strong like Zewdie's, the nails cracked and dirty.

He caught her eye and quickly looked away. If she thought he was with this boy, his chance of getting any food was gone. He shook his shoulders angrily to loosen the tight grip.

"What's the matter?" the boy sneered. "You after the corn cob?"

"Corn cob?" Ashebir said.

"You don't know? You a miserable Hungry and you haven't eaten donkey food yet?"

Ashebir tried to wriggle away.

"Little snake," the boy laughed. He put his arm round Ashebir's shoulders and started walking with him. "Don't worry, Ashebir, I will show you how to get rid of the hunger pains."

"Stop," Ashebir said. "No."

"We are not going far. Look, over there." The boy pointed to a row of corrugated iron shacks at the edge of the market.

Ashebir had been there exploring once. Some of the rooms were gloomy khat dens, others housed butchers. Carcasses buzzing with flies, hung on metal hooks, the bones white. Pools of blood-stained water congealed with the mud outside the open doors. Even though the thick stench had made him feel sick, he had stared at the pink and dark red flesh, wishing he knew how to pinch a piece to roast on Mama Tsehai's fire.

As they got closer, he could see more boys hanging around a dark entrance.

"We'll eat with them," the dooriyey said, pushing Ashebir towards the small group.

They were all bigger than him. They would tease him, punch him, make him steal, get him in trouble. He had seen them with other small boys. He tried to slow down, searching all the time for somewhere to dart away between the people. He could feel the boy's arm, heavy round his shoulder. With his stomach churning, he took a deep breath, struck his elbow hard under the boy's ribs and ducked away.

The boy doubled up. "Filthy rat," Ashebir heard him shout. "I'll get you."

Ashebir moved as quickly as he could between the people. Their soft gabis brushed his cheeks as he squeezed through. He kept going until the stitch in his side forced him to stop. He was panting heavily. There was no sign of the boy.

"What is it, yeney lij?" a woman said.

He shook his head to say don't worry about me.

"He's one of those Hungry," another voice said.

"Miskin, poor boy."

He clenched his teeth. When the pain eased a little he got up slowly and headed for the corner of the market where the donkeys were tethered. He sat on the ground, his head in his hands. A donkey snuffled near his feet, nibbling and searching for food. Ashebir felt its soft muzzle and warm breath against his shin. He stroked its neck.

The fear and exertion had brought on the diarrhoea feeling. He looked to see if anyone was watching, pulled down his shorts and let it out. Like water, yellow. When he was finished he pulled on his shorts again and stood up, steadying himself against the donkey. He had to go back to that woman and get one of those corn cobs. Keeping his eye open for the dooriyey boys, he went up to a group of men.

They were arguing angrily over the price of wool. "No, it's too low," they said.

He put a hand out and whined, "One centime, in God's name, one centime."

Out of nowhere, a hard cuff smacked his head and sent him flying. "Dooriyey," a man growled.

Without a word for his misery, Ashebir scrambled to his feet. He walked on shaky legs, towards the more familiar territory of women selling vegetables.

"One centime for food," he whined. "In the name of God, one centime," he said, "Be Egziyabher." He held out his cupped hand. When he got no response, he turned away.

"Wey-guud," one woman exclaimed. "Look at the poor boy."

"God have mercy," her neighbour said.

"Let's give him something."

He could not believe it. The women were collecting coins between them.

"There you are, God bless you, child," one said, placing the coins in his upturned hand.

"Thank you, Emayey," he said. He opened his hand and counted three five centimes coins. He wondered if it would be enough for a corn cob.

Suddenly there was a commotion near the butchers shops and khat dens.

Ashebir got on tip-toes to see what was going on. Young men and boys stumbled out of the darkness of the den, straight into the hands of three Kebele guards holding rifles. He could not see his particular 'friend'.

"Weyne," a woman near him cried out.

"They are dooriyey," an old man said. "Get them," he shouted to the uniformed men.

Ashebir crouched low, clutching the coins tightly in his fist.

"Those miserable thieves won't be any good to the revolutionary army."

"You think that's where they are taking them?" a woman, sitting behind her piles of onions, said, sucking her teeth loudly. She covered her face with her shawl and put her head down on her knees as if to hide from whatever was going on around her.

A loudspeaker crackled and whined into life. "This is Debre Berhan Council," a voice announced. "Citizens, brothers and sisters, do not be afraid. This is your Kebele. We are rounding up dooriyey for your safety. Long live the Revolution."

Ashebir looked up, his heart pounding. He had to get to the corn cobs. He counted the coins in his hand again. He might have enough for one. He crept through the murmuring people towards the woman turning her cobs on the hot coals.

The loudspeaker crackled again. He froze. He had never been afraid of the Kebele in Ataye. They had taught him to read and write. He listened, feeling sick with hunger and fear. Suddenly his head felt light. He thought the blackness would come and take him, like the day he passed out in Ataye. He sat on the ground, looking through a forest of legs and feet, still holding onto his coins.

"This is your Kebele," the man on the loudspeaker shouted again. "Stay calm. We are nearly finished. Etiopia Tikdem! Ethiopia First!" His tannoy let out a shrill squeak.

Ashebir winced. He cautiously stood up to see if they had caught that dooriyey. A small gang of boys and young men stood by a lorry surrounded by a group of soldiers. The tailgate was hanging down.

Ashebir saw his dooriyey climbing in with the others. He squeezed his hand round his coins. He thanked God for taking the boy away. Staying low, he continued in the direction of the woman cooking the cobs.

There were still plenty left.

"What do you want?" the woman said.

"Please, how much is one corn cob?"

"Twenty centimes."

He opened his hand. "I have fifteen," he said.

She looked as poor as he and Zewdie. She needed the money.

He could see she felt sorry. 'Please, be Egziyabher, just one.'

She held out one corn. It was the shortest.

"Here," she said. "Give me your centimes."

He gave her his coins, not daring to ask for the one he had had his eye on. He took the corn cob from her and almost as quickly dropped it. It was hot. He picked it up, sucking in short breaths, 'ow, ow.' He squatted, holding the corn with the tips of his fingers blowing it and brushing the dirt away. It smelt sweet. His mouth watered. He tried to take a bite. It was too hot. It even burnt his teeth. He had never eaten anything that was too hot for his teeth.

He saw someone breaking the bits off, and popping them into his mouth. He copied the man, tearing off a few bits into his cupped hand. He blew on them and put them in his mouth. They were a little hard on the outside, but burst hot and sweet in his mouth when he chewed, the soil gritty. It was the best thing he had ever tasted, even better than Zewdie's sherro. He chewed and chewed to make each mouthful last.

Two little boys watched him, whispering in each others ears.

He picked more seeds off his cob and ate. He looked at the small boys. "Go, get lost," he said, bending as if to pick a stone to fling at them. "Hid!"

They jumped up and ran off giggling.

No one was going to stop him enjoying this food. Then he remembered Zewdie and felt bad. He would save some for her. Maybe after he finished he would go begging and buy another one. Maybe the woman would have too many left at the end of the day and give him one. He carried on eating, chewing slowly, starting to feel better.

The tannoy squealed again.

Ashebir's heart jumped.

"You people living on the roadside, come and listen," a man shouted through the speaker. "The revolutionary government will not abandon you. Comrades, there is work for you. Work and food."

People gathered to listen to the men in khaki.

He got up, still chewing on his cob, and went to have a look.

"Comrades," a woman nearby muttered with disgust.

An elderly man in a khaki jacket walked about waving papers in the air. "Does anyone want work for their boys?" he called out, looking to the left and right.

Ashebir shrank behind the woman. His mouth was dry. What sort of work? His legs felt weak. He waved the flies away from his face.

"How old are you?" the old man with the papers poked Ashebir's shoulder, giving him a fright.

"I don't know," he said, wondering where the man had appeared from so suddenly.

"He looks like eight or nine," the woman said.

"You can eat if you go and work for one of these farmers. They are looking for erregnya," the old man said. He tapped a man behind him with his papers. "This is Comrade Tadesse. See? He needs a boy like you to look after his cattle."

He did not look like a Comrade, he looked like an ordinary farmer. A little older than Lakew, maybe Uncle Mohamed Chinkurt's age. He wore a thick white cotton gabi wrapped round his shoulders over a woollen jacket.

"Can you herd animals?" the man called Comrade Tadesse asked him.

"Yes," Ashebir mumbled.

The man's eyes were watery, his skin wrinkled and hard.

"Where is your mother?"

Ashebir pointed towards the bus shelter.

"What is your name?" the man in khaki appeared with his papers again.

"Ashebir."

"Ishi," the man in khaki said, shrugging his jacket onto his shoulders. He wrote on a piece of paper and nodded at Comrade Tadesse. "You can take him."

Comrade Tadesse signalled to Ashebir to start walking.

Ashebir looked up at the two men. They could just decide like that? He turned and went towards the bus shelter, the corn cob still in his hand. Fear fluttered in his stomach. Zewdie would know what to do. He turned to look at Comrade Tadesse walking behind him, leading his mule. The animal had a beautiful silver and black speckled coat, a black mane and tail. Its hooves clicked against the stones on the ground. It snorted and shook its head making the bells on the reins jingle. A small cloud of flies rose and fell.

34

September 1984, The Road to Ankober

Zewdie looked up at the farmer, shading her eyes from the sharp sunlight.

Ashebir picked a bit of corn off his cob and chewed, watching them. She would not want him to go with this man. She needed him to look after her.

"My name is Ato Tadesse," he was saying. "I live near Ankober with my wife."

"Look how we are living," Zewdie said.

Ato Tadesse looked at his feet and sucked his teeth.

"Ankober is far from here," she said.

A small group of women and children had gathered to listen. Ashebir brushed the flies from his face.

"It's a day's ride," Ato Tadesse looked over his shoulder, indicating the direction.

"How is it with you? Do you have enough food?" Zewdie asked. "Enough to feed him?" She indicated Ashebir with her chin.

"We have enough, thanks to God," he said, looking up in the sky. "And we have started harvesting, Egziyabher alle."

There were green pastures on the other side of the road. God was not angry with the people here. Ashebir looked at Ato Tadesse. He was like most country people of a certain age. Skinny, with a brow of deep furrowed lines. But he did not seem unkind. He talked respectfully with Zewdie, all the while holding the mule's reins firmly in one hand.

The animal smelt warm. A dark red cloth, bordered with yellow and green stitching, hung down on either side under its leather saddle. Ashebir put a hand on the mule's soft coat. It twitched under his touch.

"And your children?" Zewdie was saying.

"I have two sons and three daughters still living, thanks to God," he said. "My sons were taken by the army. My daughters are married."

She turned to Ashebir, clicking her tongue. "Maybe you should go," she said.

Ashebir stopped stroking the mule and stared at Zewdie.

"You will get food." She coughed. It gurgled in her chest.

"Zewdie, wait," he said, crouching in front of her so their foreheads almost touched. "I can't leave you."

"My child," she said. "Go for a short while."

He clenched his teeth to stop the tears. "How will you eat if I am not here?" He held out the half eaten cob. "Look. I bought you a corn cob."

"Bless you, my beautiful, thank you," she said, taking the corn from him with both hands and bowing her head. "I want you to go. You will eat. Mama Tsehai and the others are here. I will be alright."

Ashebir scratched his fingers nervously through his thick hair. He stood up, his back to Ato Tadesse. "Uncle said to look after you, Lakew said to look after you," he said in a whisper just for her. He clasped his hands behind his head, jutting his stomach out, his mouth turned down, waiting for her to say something.

The mule snorted.

Ashebir turned to Ato Tadesse. He could not decide if he liked the man.

"Go," Mama Tsehai said. "There's no food here, Egziyabher yawkal."

What was it to Mama Tsehai? But she had to have her say, he thought angrily.

"We are all in God's hands," another woman said, clicking her tongue.

"If you don't come, I will find another boy," Ato Tadesse said, starting to move away.

"He can go with you," Zewdie said, grunting with the effort of getting up. "But look after him and bring him soon."

Ashebir felt her hand on his shoulder, leaning on him.

"Zewdie, please," Ashebir said. All of a sudden the dark shadows under his mother's eyes looked almost black.

"I am here every Saturday for the market," the farmer said. "I can bring you news."

Ashebir panicked. A day's ride.

"Come here, sweet Ashebir," Zewdie said. "Yeney lij."

He felt her hands on his cheeks. Rough and skinny. Not as strong as before.

"God is with you, child of my soul, my only boy," she said, her eyes sad and smiling. She kissed him. He felt her hard cheek bone against his, on one cheek then the other, over and over. The hurt inside filled him.

He held on to her, not wanting to let go. He heard hooves clicking against the hard ground behind him.

Ato Tadesse had mounted the silver speckled mule, and was pulling its head round towards the main road.

"Go, Ashebir, go," Zewdie said, "Before he takes another boy."

He stepped back, almost losing his balance. He wrapped his gabi round his shoulders, and, not looking at anyone, picked up his bag with his wenchef inside. His breath shuddered through his body, his stomach tight from the effort of hiding his crying. "Ishi, Zewdie," he whispered. He turned and walked away.

"Ashebir," Zewdie called after him. "I love you."

He looked back. Through his tears she was an uncertain shape under the bus shelter. He tried to smile.

"God go with you," she said. "Egziyabher ante gar yihun."

He wiped his eyes and lifted a hand to wave. He could not speak. His misery had filled his throat and wrapped itself round his tongue. He fixed his eyes on the mule's skinny hind legs. His feet felt the pebbles and dust of the track. They crossed the tarmac, warm from the sun, onto the rough path which lead across the fields on the other side. All the time a low whining, like mourning, hummed in his ears.

"You, boy," Ato Tadesse said, pulling on the reins. The mule snorted loudly and flicked its tail. "You can stop your crying. God is watching over you. You are luckier than the others."

Ashebir looked up at the man, bundled thickly in his gabi. The soft wailing was his own crying. He fell to his knees. This was his luck? Hungry and alone without Zewdie?

"Come," Ato Tadesse said, dismounting the mule. "Get up here."

Ashebir took the man's outstretched hand. It was strong and rough. Ashebir's nose and empty stomach filled with the smell of the man's sweat and tella beer, which hovered about him like a fine mist. It made him nauseous. The few bites of corn cob had not been enough. Zewdie would finish it off. At the thought of her, his eyes filled with tears again. He brushed them away with the back of his hand. He did not want this man to think he was weak.

Ato Tadesse said nothing. Nor did his face soften.

The man held out cupped hands. Ashebir scrambled up onto the mule. His guardian climbed into the saddle behind him and kicked the mule into a trot. Unsure of this man whose full body pressed on him, and with the heavy smell of tella in his nostrils, Ashebir began his journey.

The mule made a loud sneezing sound and shook its head; a soft jingle rang out in the quiet countryside.

Ashebir held onto the saddle with both hands, fearful of falling. The path beneath his dangling feet was uneven and rocky. The mule moved with jerking movements. Ashebir could feel the bones in his bottom rubbing his skin sore against the hard leather saddle.

The sun was high in the sky. It burnt down on his head. He squinted into the deep blue sky. A few large birds circled above, their piercing cries echoed from way up there, far away. The wide pastures spread around him, dotted with sheep and cattle grazing peacefully. It was a wonderful sight, even for his unhappy eyes. The vastness of the land tumbling and stretching out around him made him feel small.

Ato Tadesse kicked and steered the mule towards the foot of a hillside, on top of which sat a few dwellings surrounded by spindly eucalyptus trees. They skirted the edge of the slope and rode into a valley where a stream shone in the sunlight.

At the water's edge, Ato Tadesse pulled on the reins and swung down.

The mule moved about restlessly, trampling its feet.

"Woa!" Ato Tadesse growled.

Ashebir was anxious to get off but could not feel his legs.

Ato Tadesse held the agitated animal firmly, "Get down boy in Heaven's name," he said.

"Ishi," Ashebir whispered. He leant over and fell to the side. He clutched at the man's jacket as he came down. He landed awkwardly on the hard ground. He sat up, trying to rub life into his legs, "Sorry, Sir, sorry," he said.

The mule took off for the river, kicking up its hind legs.

Ato Tadesse walked away towards the stream shaking his head and looking up into the blue sky.

As Ashebir pulled his cloth bag towards him, the half eaten corn cob rolled out. His eyes clouded with tears. When had Zewdie put it there? He picked it up, brushed the dirt off and bit into it, chewing hungrily. It was almost as good cold. Better maybe. He closed his eyes and turned his face to the sun, breathing deeply, smelling the eucalyptus and gorse. Flies buzzed loudly over a dried cow pat, the smells and sounds of home. He stretched himself up as he ate and rubbed at the pain in his stomach.

The stream ran along the valley. He wondered where it came from and where it ended. Were the hot springs and Afar warriors at the end of this river? Tree roots snaked out of the banks on the other side where the dry earth had crumbled away. He wished he felt strong enough to jump in splashing and laughing. He got up and walked to the river, stumbling like a new-born calf. On the banks his feet sank into the dark mud, the water lapped at his feet. He dropped onto his haunches sighing, almost smiling, as he felt the soft wet earth ooze between his toes. He cupped his hands and drank, closing his eyes to throw water over his face and head, down his neck.

Peering over the bushes he could see Ato Tadesse further down the river. He quickly took off his clothes and went slowly into the middle of the stream. It came to his waist. He ducked down. Its cold took his breath away. He stood up and splashed water all over himself, gasping and almost laughing.

"You, boy," Ato Tadesse called out. "We don't have time for that."

"Ishi," Ashebir said. Looking to see if the man was still watching, he ducked under once more before going ashore. He pulled on his clothes and wrapped himself in his gabi. Picking up his bag, he hobbled back as fast as he could, his hair dripping wet. He was still shaky but his body tingled and felt alive.

Ato Tadesse was filling an old leather container with water.

Ashebir squatted nearby scratching his head. It was full of bugs. He prayed Ato Tadesse had something to eat. He cleared his throat to speak and started coughing. It hurt. He hoped it was not his mother's cough.

"What is it? " Ato Tadesse said. "Are you sick?"

Ashebir shook his head and tried to keep the cough inside. He cleared his throat. "Are we nearly there?" His voice came out a rough whisper.

"What's that, nearly there?" Ato Tadesse said with a short laugh, his face still frowning. "The eagle owl will be out hunting by the time we reach."

"The brown one?" Ashebir said. "The one that calls out toooot-toot?"

"That's the one, boy. Now let's go."

**

By the time they reached the man's home Ashebir was shivering all over. It was cold and damp, the sky dark, a thin moon amongst the faraway stars. It hurt when he swallowed. They rode slowly into the compound and the mule came to a halt.

A woman's voice came out of the darkness. "Hello, Tadesse, is that you?"

"Hello, it is us," Ato Tadesse said. "How are you?"

"I am fine, Egziyabheresteling," she said. "Welcome home after the long road."

"Thank you," he said.

"So you sold the sheep and found a boy."

"That's right." He untied a small bundle from the mule and started removing the saddle. "Take him inside."

Ashebir could barely stand for cold and aching.

"What is your name?" The woman pushed him towards the low entrance under the thatch.

"Ashebir," he whispered.

"Don't be afraid," she said, sounding more impatient than kind.

A kerosene lamp hissed, lighting parts of the room between dark shadows.

"Sit there," she said, nodding to a corner.

He sat, feeling a worn sheepskin under him, most of the softness gone. The room had a familiar smell of animal hides, wood smoke and burnt coffee beans. He pulled his gabi round him to try and stop the shivering.

"Here," she said giving him a small cup of milk and a piece of ki'ta bread.

He took the food with both hands bowing his head slightly. "Egziersteling," he mumbled. When he finished he curled up on the ground. His head itched. He scratched. It felt better and worse at the same time. He cradled his head in his hands, gritting his teeth and drew his knees in. When he closed his eyes he saw Zewdie under the bus shelter with all The Hungry, the white truck standing nearby. He bit his lip and tried not to cry.

Ato Tadesse said something in his gruff voice. Someone turned down the lamp. The hissing stopped. A door closed.

Ashebir felt his body sink away, disappearing into the earth.

The room was dark and quiet except for the rustling sound of nighttime creatures. Ato Tadesse and his wife must be asleep. Ashebir woke, itching all over. How had it spread from his head to his body? He scratched through his clothes, then pulled his gabi tighter round and fell asleep again. He spent the night like that, waking and itching, feeling the cold again and falling into another sleep.

**

The cock crowing woke him. For a moment he thought he was home. But when he opened his eyes he was far from Zewdie and the bus shelter, far from their village. He bit his lip. These people would not stand for crying. He sat up and coughed. The light in the room was still dim, but the woman had already made a fire and a blackened pot sat on it. He hoped she was making tea.

"Why did you bring a sick one home?" he heard the woman muttering.

"He was not sick when I found him, Turunesh," Ato Tadesse said. "Anyway they are all sick." He bent his head down and went out through the door.

Turunesh, Ashebir thought. That is her name.

"Come, eat," Turunesh said. She was making bread. The thick creamy liquid poured from her fingers and sizzled as it hit the flat earthen plate on the fire.

Ashebir sat on the floor near the fire. The fire cracked as a twig burst. It was good to feel the warmth. He coughed and it hurt in his chest.

"Here," Turunesh said, clicking her tongue. She passed him a glass of steaming tea and a piece of bread.

"Thank you," he said quietly, his heart lifting a little. He looked at her expecting a smile, but she turned to make another flatbread without looking at him. The liquid sizzled against the plate again.

He sipped the tea loudly. It burnt his tongue. He bit into the bread feeling wretched. He could barely swallow for the effort not to cry. He put down the bread and tea and got up.

She turned briefly from her baking. "It's round the back," she said.

There was a small shed with a rusted corrugated iron door. He cranked it open to a loud buzzing. Flies. It stank. He stepped in and peed into the hole. The flies rose in a cloud. He cried, sobbing to let out his pain before going back to the woman.

His breakfast was still there on the floor, the tea steaming. A small pile of round flat breads lay on a metal plate next to Turunesh. She got up to drink a cup of water from the large gourd by the door, her wide flat feet moving quietly over the dirt floor. Then she tucked her skirts in between her legs and sat at the fire again, letting out a small grunt. She flipped the bread over with her fingers to cook on the other side.

"Eat quickly," she said, her eyes on the bread. "You have to take the animals out." Her head motioned in the direction of the door.

He nodded and tried to eat faster. He blew over the tea and drank tiny sips with loud slurps. It eased his throat. He finished the food, bowed his head a little and said, "Egziersteling," took his bag, and went out.

The animals were kept in a large room dug into the hillside under the hut, not in a pen round the back like at home. Ato Tadesse and

Turunesh's house was square. They must be rich.

Ato Tadesse nodded at Ashebir. Like Mohamed Abdu's father, the man only said as much as he needed. As he herded the animals into the open, Ato Tadesse made deep guttural noises. The sheep and goats were bleating, stumbling against each other. Ashebir liked their strong smell. He joined in, shoo-ing them out, but the animals buffeted him. Afraid he might fall and get trampled, he crept out of the way. He stood by the entrance, his gabi pulled over his head and round his shoulders against the cold.

"Don't just stand there. Move them out." Ato Tadesse shouted, coming towards him with a long whip.

Ashebir shrank back.

"Here, take this." Ato Tadesse handed him the whip.

Ashebir took it from him, relieved, his heart beating fast.

"Take them that way," Ato Tadesse said, pointing across the open pasture and to the brow of a hill.

"Ishi," Ashebir said, coughing into his gabi.

The animals were already heading off. He followed. The sun was coming up, a deep orange. Ashebir looked around, noting the small copse of trees near the homestead, the dip in the hill and the large pile of boulders. The animals would know the way back. They always did. He looked at the whip in his hand and wondered if he could still make it crack like a gun shot. The boy in Debre Berhan had cracked his loud against the black tarmac. Black tarmac. Trucks rumbling through the night. Soldiers driving to the fighting. Marching banners. The white truck. Zewdie shading her eyes, surrounded by The Hungry. He shivered.

The oxen went slowly; the sheep and goats scattered. Ashebir brought his arm up and snapped it down again, flicking his wrist to make the whip snap. Nothing. There was no strength in his arm. His body ached with the effort of walking. He would get to the other side of the hill and then find a place to sit in the sun and rest. How many animals did he have? He started counting, "One, two, three sheep. One, two goats. Only two? There's one more. Three goats. Two cows and one oxen." One of the goats had a large belly. She must be having kids soon.

Looks like two, he could hear Mohamed Abdu saying. Looks like two in there.

**

Cold misty mornings and long hungry days tired him. Nights interrupted by bugs biting and the itching. His coughing was worse and some days he thought he had fever. He pictured Zewdie's face every night before sleeping, and prayed he could go to her soon. Sometimes her face was as it used to be, round and smiling, talking with her friend Temima, her gold tooth shining in the sun. Sometimes it was her face under the bus shelter, drawn and thin, resting in a frown. It must be weeks since he'd left her. Ato Tadesse had been to the market in Debre Berhan several times. He never brought news of Zewdie.

Ashebir took the animals to a clear stream nearby. It trickled over the stones down the middle of a wide river bed. He liked to sit in the warmth of the sun, watching the women and girls washing clothes in the icy water. He could not wash his; it was too cold and he had no others to put on while they dried.

Other children came with their animals. "Ashebir, Ashebir," they called out to him. "Come. We are making a fire."

He went to squat beside the smallest. He was called Tirs,[77] because he had lost his two front teeth top and bottom. Tirs was either lively and laughing, or running, mouth open wide, crying to his big sister. The other boys laughed at his small backside, bare through the holes in his shorts.

The children's fire crackled and smoked on the river bank. Tirs' brother had a metal pan and a stick. He poured seeds onto the pan and moved them round and round roasting them.

"It smells good," Ashebir said.

"It's barley," Tirs explained, putting his hand on Ashebir's knee.

Ashebir put his hand on the little boy's shoulder and so they were friends.

"Roasted barley," Tirs' brother said.

Ashebir's mouth watered.

The boy swept the barley seeds back and forth across the pan until they were dark brown. It was like roasting coffee beans except it smelt different.

When it was done, the boy poured the roasted barley into a basket to cool. Then each boy got a handful, including Ashebir. In that moment, chewing the hot nutty seeds with Tirs and the boys by the stream, Ashebir forgot everything. He smiled and laughed with his new friends.

But when they were not there, when he sat in the sun alone, the flea-bites on his body and the sores on his hands itched and hurt even more. He would cry, aching to be home with Zewdie.

---

[77] Tooth.

35

September 1984, Addis Ababa

It was early. The sky was clear, not a whisp of cloud to be seen. She opened her French windows, filling the room with the deep blue, fresh morning air. Kites circled way up above, too far away to hear their mournful cries. The city, muffled in an unusual quietness, was waking to the 10th Anniversary of the Revolution. She was excited. The day had finally arrived. Leila would be there soon and they would walk down to Revolution Square to watch the parades. She put on the water to make coffee.

The main roads would be closed to traffic, and lined with soldiers; young men, their uniforms sharply pressed, boots shining, weapons at the ready. Security was on high alert.

She was learning what the physical power of state could mean. The military and security arm of the state infiltrated everything and played with the mind. The potential for consequences was enough to silence. Power had been vested in individuals who took up the uniform; a zabanya, the Kebele, a soldier. The baton, the uniformed individual standing inside heavy black boots, the holder of the old Italian carcano rifle, the Kalashnikov, symbolised the full power of the state. Given that, the people's daily acts of silent resistance fascinated and impressed her.

Their spirit found its way into everyday things. Just the act of appearing day in day out, with small piles of vegetables to sell in Mercato, of pressing those black trousers for work to a shine, of carefully looking after that jacket and skirt, the fresh hospital uniform. The fact that so many sought out night school, that shoeshine boys made sure to attend their shift at school to learn. They drove taxis and buses, they brushed their children's hair and tied it up in bows for school, they stood in churches to sing and hum, to pray, even when it was frowned upon by the Derg. They kept the city fed and on the move. They gathered their neighbours around dark clay, pot-bellied jabenas filled with fresh roasted coffee, balanced on red hot coals, chunks of itan burning fragrant on the side, white popcorn piled in brightly woven baskets, fresh grass strewn on the floor, to chat, gossip, laugh and cry. That very ceremony, evocative in its mix of flavours and aromas as it was, demonstrated their pride and determination. Had that ceremony become an act of defiance in itself? A way of coming together when a little too much curiosity, a wrong word here or there, and suspicion could prove so dangerous? And they laughed, despite it all. She was watching, trying to learn from them.

A couple of Sundays ago, Negisst had invited her and Hiwot to come for coffee. They had worn their long white traditional dresses. The cloth and embroidery were beautiful but Izzie never felt quite comfortable in hers. She thought farenj looked clumsy in traditional dress. Negisst lived down an alleyway behind the Cuban quarters, amidst a warren of small houses under korkorro roofs. When the rain came down it clattered like a cavalry galloping overhead. A sound they had not heard in a long while. Inside was cosy and functional. A large sofa filled one length of the room. Small stools and the odd chair were scattered to sit on. The concrete floor had been swept and spread with fresh green grass. Two of Negisst's neighbours were already there. Her 'girl' sat on a low stool behind the small metal stove, moving the green coffee beans across the metal plate, turning them dark brown, sounds of the sea's ebb and flow. Kish-kish, kish-kish. The itan burned from its own red clay pot, filling the room with its smoky incense, mingling with the sharp smell of the freshly roasted coffee.

They exchanged greetings with a familiar warmth, which belied the more often than not distant servant-madam relationships.

"Eska sorstenya," Negisst had said, laughing, covering her mouth. "We'll drink three rounds. It will bring us luck."

They had talked about their children, the ever-increasing price of a quintal of teff and a kilo of onions, how everything was getting expensive, and they'd talked about men.

"You see my neighbour here?" Negisst had put a firm hand on her friend's arm as if to hold her down while she told the story. "Her husband came late every night, creeping past our front doors. We decided to tease him. One night we left a metal chair outside each door. You should have heard the clatter when he stumbled past." She laughed, her eyes sparkling mischievously.

"Poor man," Izzie had said, smiling.

The women laughed. "Poor man? He was tenquolenya.[78] Telling so many stories of this and that and how, be Egziyabher. We all knew he was going to the bar every night to see this woman."

"She was using magic on him," the neighbour said.

"Don't make excuses for him," the other said.

"They get tired of us, Egziyabher yawkal," Negisst had said, rolling her eyes up to the Lord who saw and knew everything. "Their eyes and minds follow their you- know-whats." She covered her mouth and laughed.

Her neighbours laughed with her about their men, as if they were kids who didn't know better. Negisst and her neighbours thought Izzie should go back to Moe.

Izzie exchanged glances with Hiwot, who nodded her head as if to say, They've got a point? with an amused smile.

Izzie frowned at her. It was clear that if she were one of Negisst's neighbours, she would still be with Moe, come what may.

"All men are like that," the neighbour said. "What to do."

"We don't leave our men after one mishap," the other said.

"He's a good man, Izzie," Negisst had said. "Befitsum, honestly, that woman is spoiling him. He doesn't really like her. Not yet. You need to get back home soon."

"No," Izzie had said. "It's over, Negisst. Finished." And she knew it was. Any small corner of hope and longing to rekindle feelings at all belonged to a relationship that had happened in a more distant past. She knew that. She had nudged Hiwot. "Help me out here."

"Izzie has been to a fortune-teller," Hiwot said, her eyes smiling over her coffee cup as she took a sip.

"Hiwot!" Izzie said.

The women looked at Izzie, their eyes wide with curiosity.

"Enday?" Negisst said, turning herself round in her stool to face Izzie.

"It's true, she is a friend of ours," Hiwot said. "She's a hairdresser in Casanches, isn't she Izzie?"

Izzie was not prepared for this. That had been an extraordinary evening. They knew Aster from the Buffet de la Gare on a Sunday night. She was an old friend of Hiwot's. She was good. Too good.

"Does she use cards?" the neighbour asked.

"You want to go?" Negisst said, pushing her neighbour's knee. "You want to find out what that husband of yours is up to?"

---

[78] Scheming, manipulative, like a snake.

The neighbour wiped her face with her shema and sucked her teeth, smiling uncertainly.

"Tarot cards," Hiwot said. "She knew everything about Izzie." Hiwot had laughed. "Isn't that right, Izzieye?"

Izzie looked at her friend, shaking her head and smiling. Hiwot always threw her head back when she was totally at ease, laughing. It was a loud, guttural, dirty, laugh. It didn't match the innocent look she sometimes wore when her face was resting, when she was just there, listening. It always came unexpected. Izzie loved her for that.

"Your face was quite red Izzie, yeney konjo."

"She told us about the woman Moe is seeing," Izzie said, trying to regain control of the story. Aster had known a lot about Izzie's escapades, which she did not particularly want aired here. And those truths had given weight to the woman's predictions. "She said he was seeing a dark Ethiopian woman. Obviously Yeshi Emebate."

"Definitely," Negisst had said, nodding. "Tekur sou nat,[79]" she confirmed, nodding at her friends.

"And that I would meet a handsome farenj; unpredictable, a traveller. And we would have one child."

"Ingo," Hiwot said.

"Izzieye," Negisst said. "Mindin neouw? You met someone?"

"No, Negisst, I haven't. Hiwot is teasing." She looked at Hiwot. "Anchee!"

Negisst was sitting behind the jabena by now. She lifted the clay pot off the coals and poured the last round of coffee into the small white cups. The girl came with a basket of fresh hot fendisha. She offered it round to each in turn. They all dug a hand in and took a fistful.

"You have to admit, he's nice. And I think he likes you," Hiwot had said.

"The cards don't lie," Negisst said. "Egziyabher yawkal."

"How much did you pay?" the neighbour asked.

"Oh, I don't know, five Birr maybe?" Izzie had said. "She didn't really want to take money from us." It was always about money in the end.

**

She shook her head, remembering. Took the coffee off the stove and poured herself a mug. She was wearing her red t-shirt and silver Lalibela

---

[79] She's dark-skinned.

earrings for the 10th Anniversary and had wrapped a white shema round her head against the sun. Her face smelt of Ambre Solaire and sandy beach holidays.

She went out onto the terrace with her coffee and lit a cigarette. Drawing on it deeply, she lifted her face to the sun. She couldn't help wondering what Moe would be doing today. Whether he had woken in their bed with Yeshi Emebate beside him. She winced. It was not supposed to affect her any more, but it did.

Yeshi's girlfriends popped in from time to time to see if she was alright, and to apologise again and again for what Yeshi Emebate had done. "Don't tell Yeshi we came, OK?" they would say, smiling conspiratorially. They were obviously afraid of her. Maybe Yeshi was their 'Madam'.

"She phones him all the time, saying, 'I love you, I love you,'" they said, with worried looks on their faces. Like small sweet birds.

"Don't worry," she told them time over. "She's welcome to him. I'm done." Still, she avoided Yeshi Emebate.

She had quickly made acquaintance with a number of others in the building, including two very tall guys from Senegal, who shared the flat next door. They were translators at the ECA, charming and easy company. She'd had a beer with them on the terrace the night before. It was a wide bare terrace which extended across her side of the building, with a concrete wall just high enough not to fall over. There was nothing there to make it cosily appealing, no potted plants or wicker chairs. The open sky above and splendid view across the city made up for that. They had agreed it was best not to go out on the eve of the 10th Anniversary celebrations. The heavily armed soldiers, the underlying tension in the city. It was best to stay home.

**

There was a knock on the door. "Izzie, Izzie," she heard Leila's voice.

"Coming!" she called as she went to pull the door open.

They hugged.

"Good to see you," Izzie said. "Come in, come in."

"You look great, by the way," Leila said.

"Thanks, you too. Actually you do, what's going on? Was it easy to get here from the Institute? The roads into town will be closed."

"I, well, I stayed over at Booker's last night," Leila said, blushing and grinning. "So I came from his. Not so far. The roads were clear."

"Aha, aha, aha," Izzie said. "That wry fox. I tell you. I knew it. So hard to get him to say a word about you. I knew he was pining. I'm so glad Leila."

All the while, Izzie was looking for her keys and putting a few Birr into the white leather bag slung over her shoulder.

"Ah, there they are," she said, throwing the keys up in the air and catching them. "We can go. Guess I better not take a camera, hey?"

"Better not," Leila said.

The walk down to Revolution Square was easy. It was strangely quiet without traffic. By contrast, continuous rumbling and throbbing sounds came up from further south. As they got nearer and the noise became louder, the tension rose in Izzie's chest. She almost felt giddy. It was a once in a lifetime event. She was in this incredible city, the centre of so much controversy and tragedy on the day of this huge celebration. The concrete grey and yellowing buildings had been adorned from their rooftops in gigantic extravagant decoration, under Korean direction. A lot of dragon-red, gold and glitzy tassels, red stars, hammers and sickles, and loud slogans in Amharic and English. Revolutionary Motherland or Death! declared one of the banners which had been strung up across the junction on the Bole road leading into the expansive Revolution Square. Too true.

There were so many people there already. A hubbub. Izzie could not quite gauge the mood. It was undoubtedly an awesome event. But people were suffering after all. Some were there because they wanted to be. And some were there because they had to be. The Kebeles had been at work making sure everyone attended. For the majority, she could only surmise, being there was the result of some form of coercion. Something as simple as cutting Kebele store rations, which everyone depended on.

"Yigirta, yigirta," she said. "Sorry, sorry, can we get through?" She held on tight to Leila's hand as they made their way through the crowd.

Bodies packed together, jostling to keep their place, people calling over their shoulders to each other, the hot odour of sweat, perfume and kebey;[80] gabis washed white in the sweet scent of Omo powder. They could see the heads of soldiers marching past on the main road, hear their boots on the tarmac and the military bands playing. The noise was deafening.

---

[80] Butter used to oil hair.

They sneaked and ducked and wriggled their way to the front. Izzie felt a bit guilty but she just had to see. No one seemed to mind.

**

"You're not going are you farenj?" Fasika had said, laughing in disbelief.

"We have to be there," Izzie said. "Anyway, don't you have to march with the Women's Association, Fasika? I thought you've been secretly practicing in your back yard?"

"I will be safely indoors," Fasika had said. "I might put the television on. Make buna."

"Me too," Mulu had said. "Nothing for us to celebrate there."

"I just need to see it. I want to see what's going on," Izzie had said. "Fidel Castro is going to be there."

"Ibd nesh,[81]" Fasika had said, laughing. "You think you are going to meet him?"

"I wouldn't put it past her," Mulu had said.

**

"We made it," she squeezed Leila's hand.

They were right up front. At intervals, all along the road, soldiers and police stood to attention, legs planted firmly apart, heads high. Some with a rifle, some with a long stick, at the ready to push straying members of the public back into the crowd.

Opposite, way on the other side of Revolution Square, was a vast bank of students, hundreds of them, each holding a large card up high. With immaculate synchronisation, they turned the cards to form messages and pictures against a white or red background. WELCOME one read, then they switched and an Amharic slogan came up, then communist emblems and figures. Behind them stood the massive billboards – the trio – Marx, Lenin and Engels. And beside them, a new one, a fourth – Mengistu Haile Mariam.

Izzie was high with the atmosphere. It was all she could do to stop herself from shouting out loud. Whatever the revolution had brought these people, this was an incredible display.

"Madness!" Izzie shouted in Leila's ear.

---

[81] You're crazy.

Leila nodded, her eyes shining.

Soldiers in green, frog-marched past, legs kicking high. Absolutely in time. Why did they do that? How did those young men and women keep it up? Their faces stoic, emotionless, stern. She wondered where they had marched from and where they would go to? Where did they get to stop? Somewhere way up the Debre Zeit Road? There were so many of them. They were followed by rolling tanks, and artillery mounted on enormous carriers. Soviet equipment. The loud rumbling machinery of war just kept on going by. This was the largest army in Africa. And with all this lot, as well as the contingent up north and in the Ogaden, it was easy to believe.

Long Live Proletarian Internationalism, read a massive banner carried by yet more troops, this time in khaki. A brilliant army band marched behind them, drums beating and trilling, cymbals echoing loudly and vibrating, brass instruments, trumpets and French horns, glistened in the sun. They played well. They were followed by the Navy in white. Perfectly in time. It was impressive. The numbers, the noise, the synchronicity. Then came the Youth Association. They paraded in blocks of colour, carrying ten foot tall green, yellow and red flags. They wore white shirts and their ties matched the flags they carried. They turned to the crowds, "Wadde fite![82]" they shouted.

"Wadde fite!" the crowds shouted back in one voice.

Izzie kept her mouth closed.

Then came the ordinary folk, dressed in their daywear, women and men of all ages. Their walk, their pace, while quite normal, looked sloppy compared to the perfectioned drill of the other sections that had marched past. They smiled, chatted and waved to the crowds. People called out, whistled, waved back.

"That must be the Women's Association behind them," Leila pointed. A section of women, dressed in long green skirts, white shirts and red neck scarves marched past. Again came the: "Wadde fite!"

"Wadde fite!" the crowd around them shouted back, some raised their fists in the air.

It was hot. They must already have been there more than an hour. "You don't have any water do you, Leila?"

"Ha-ha! Of course I do," Leila pulled a bottle from her large bag. "Here."

"You saviour, thank you," Izzie said. She drank. "Are you holding

---

[82] 'Forward!'

445

out? This will take at least another hour or two." She looked up at the sun.

"I'm fine," Leila said. "It will take time to get away from here, mind you." She nodded over her shoulder. The crowd had become denser all around and behind them. They would not get back as easily as they had come.

"Cross that when we get to it, eh?"

"Have to," Leila shrugged. She seemed uncertain.

"Just say, OK?" Izzie turned to the parade again.

Women in beautiful white cotton dresses, with fine yellow, green and red embroidered borders, were now marching past. Their gait was not as harsh and formal as the others but they still walked to time. Walking, walking.

"Look, maybe they are the Women's Association," Izzie said. "Not the others before them."

"Actually Izzie, I can't watch this any more," Leila said.

"You alright, Leila? You feel dizzy? Maybe the sun?"

Leila's dark eyes were full of tears.

"Sure, honey, let's go." Izzie took Leila's hand. "Come."

The women around them, patted Leila's back, "Aysosh, aysosh," they said, and made way for them to pass.

Izzie headed through the throng, up the road towards Stadium and the Red Cross offices, keeping hold of Leila's hand.

Dotted along the road were soldiers on guard. It looked like they were starting to wilt. It was too hot. They shifted from one foot to the other. Called out to each other. Some were mere boys.

Clear of the crowds and with the noise from the parade still vibrating in her ears, Izzie stopped. There was something awesome and terrible about raw, male, military power. Even with women soldiers, the concept of army, the military, was essentially an overpowering one of masculine might. The beating drums, the black boots on tarmac. Izzie put a hand on her chest as if they were drumming on inside her.

Leila was crying.

"Oh Leila," she said, putting her arms around her. "Come, let's see if we can find a cold drink? Maybe the Ras Hotel is open. I am sure it will be, with farenj staying there for the celebrations."

"It's just all that money," Leila said. "That they don't care at all. Those people, hundreds and hundreds of them, walking and walking down from Ifat ena Timooga, looking for food, dying on the roadside. How can they be so thoughtless, so cruel?"

"I know, I know," Izzie said. "If they can organise all this... The practice, the perfection, the money, they can organise anything."

"You know Debre Berhan council has opened up a shelter?" Leila gathered herself. "The Relief Council has sent two guys to run it, and some supplies."

"No, I hadn't heard. That's really good news, at least."

"It's miserable," Leila said. "We've started a massive fund-raising campaign."

"Leila," Izzie said, putting a hand on her friend's arm. "Let's get ourselves to the Ras Hotel, or anywhere on the way where we can sit with a cold drink. OK? Then we can talk."

"OK," Leila said. "That's a good idea. Let's do that."

**

They sat at a small metal table outside the Ras Hotel at the bottom of Churchill Avenue. They ordered a cold coke each and a piece of dry cake. Most places were closed, but as Izzie had guessed, since a number of foreigners were staying at the hotel, the café was open.

"Tell me, Leila," Izzie said. "What are you doing at the camp in Debre Berhan?"

"It's a combination of things. First of all we have a massive fund-raising campaign. Everyone is contacting everyone they know to raise funds. By the way, your Ingo has raised a huge amount."

"My Ingo?" Izzie laughed. "That's new."

"Come on, Izzie, we can all see what's coming."

"We'll see," Izzie said. "Anyway you say he's raised a lot."

"Amazing amount. All his German friends and family."

"He's a bit of a dark horse, really."

"He's a typical Leo – charming, fun, outgoing, quite a big ego, maybe?" Leila said, smiling as if to say, you should know. "And then this modest side of him popped up. Raised all this money and doesn't want to talk about it."

"Pretty impressive," Izzie said, thinking she had not raised any money for the famine. "But tell me what you're doing with the funds?"

"You know the Livestock Research Institute has a station in Debre Berhan, where we have a small herd of cross-breed cattle. So we are giving the feeding centre milk from our cows. We have been to talk to the Relief Council guys there to see what they need. So we've given them blankets, flour, milk powder, fuel and cooking utensils so far."

"How many people are there?"

"I think anywhere between two and four thousand at any one time. They were camped all along the roadside. Now they are all in the camp. And there are still people coming. Every day."

"What is it like?"

"At the camp?" Leila looked at Izzie. "It's a nightmare, Izzie. All these people with nothing. Imagine, you need water, you need the toilet, you need to cook something, you need shelter, you need to put a jumper on, or a warm jacket. They don't have any of that. They are dying at night. They are so cold. You know how cold it can get in Debre Berhan? Its like north European winters. It gets below eight degrees. And they just have their cotton clothing and are sleeping out in the open. They can't fit them all into the tents."

Izzie didn't know what to say.

"And this. This display they are putting on. I really don't understand it. The whole point of the revolution was for a better life for the people. The masses." Leila drank from her bottle of coke, and broke off a bit of cake. "You should come, Izzie."

"Yes, I will, I want to. Even just to see if I can do anything," Izzie said. "There are two RC guys there, you say?"

"Yes, they're amazing. Two young guys absolutely working their butts off. They have help from the local Women's Association who come every day. The local bakers bake masses of small loaves every day, to hand out. I think there are some youth volunteers too, I'm not sure. Maybe you could do something?"

"I still have to work my contract through. I don't have any holiday time left."

"You aren't really going to leave, are you Izzie?"

"I don't want to, but I need a job, right? I've been to the UN offices. The NGOs all hire from their home countries, not from in-country. And if they do hire here, they hire locals. Fair enough, of course."

"Maybe you can get an extension in your current job?"

"We are talking about it. I think they want me to stay. I am increasingly doing project proposals for different projects. It feels useful and basically I don't want to leave yet. I really like working there."

"And then there's Ingo," Leila's dark eyes sparkled for the first time that afternoon.

"And?"

"Well you like him don't you?"

"Yes, Hmm. I do, but it's not long since all the drama with Moe, you know. I'm not ready for anything serious." Izzie cleared her throat. "By the way – quick change of subject -" she laughed. "We are going to Susan's at the week-end and hiking up Yerer from there. We went up Zukwala a few weeks ago. It was amazing. You should come."

"I think I'll be with Booker. I'll run the Hash. I always feel good after that. I know you don't like it. But it's not bad, Izzie. And it's one way of keeping fit."

"I'm glad you and Booker are together again, Leila. He has been a good friend to me these past weeks. I hardly knew him before. It's surprising really."

The waiter came to see if they needed anything. "We are closing early," he said and shrugged. His eyes glanced at the military presence all the way up Churchill Avenue. Soldiers were standing at intervals all the way to the top. "Min yishallal?[83]"

"No, I think we are fine now, thanks," Leila said. "You can bring the hissab, please?"

"Next bit of exercise is the walk up Churchill. I wonder whether the taxis will have started moving around Piazza by the time we get there," Izzie said.

"Let's go," Leila said. "This was a good idea, thanks Izzie. I feel better now. And we'll fix a time for us to go to Debre Berhan, OK?"

**

Regular as clockwork, night fell like a proverbial blanket around six. The golden rule was no driving after nightfall. That's when accidents happened. It only needed one isolated, invisible, broken down lorry on a dark long narrow country road, and it was too late. So they had arrived back in town from Debre Zeit in good time, had taken a shower at hers and were ready to eat. It was Sunday evening. They'd had an early start that morning and spent the day walking up Mount Yerer as it got hotter, and walking down it again as it cooled off. Because of the time, they had left Susan, not even accepting the cup of tea and slice of banana bread she'd offered. "It's got groundnuts in it!" she'd called after them, laughing.

Izzie's feet ached. She looked up at the large red dragon suspended over the main entrance and let Ingo open the door for

---

[83] What to do?

her. The China Bar restaurant was an old haunt. She and Moe had gone there often. The waiters had known them. She nodded at the two waiters standing watch at the door, noted that three tables were already occupied, and let the third waiter usher them to a table in the corner. She was somehow relieved that there was no one there she knew.

"You order," Ingo said, shutting his menu.

"Why?"

"You know the food better. I haven't eaten much Chinese."

"All that heavy German stuff, hey?"

"Yeah, knusprig gebratene Schweinshaxen,[84]" he said, his eyes twinkling. "Every day for breakfast."

"What a mouthful. I'm not even going to try to repeat that," she said. "Schwein is pig, right? You eat pork for breakfast?"

"Every day."

"Nah, you don't," she said. "You'd be fatter." She lit a cigarette, blowing a string of smoke towards the ceiling. "You don't mind do you?"

"Go ahead," he said. "You've already lit it."

She chose to ignore the slight jibe and raised her hand towards the waiter. He was tall for an Ethiopian and round-faced with a comfortable body, the buttons on his red waistcoat only just doing up.

He smiled and walked over. She could tell he was trying to keep the curiosity off his face. Moe must definitely have been here with Yeshi Emebate and now here she was with this new farenj guy.

"Tenasteling," she said.

He bowed slightly. They exchanged the customary greetings, establishing that they, and their families, were fine.

She included all her favourites in their order: sweet and sour spare ribs, chicken and peanuts, veg spring rolls, stir fry vegetables, and fluffy white rice. "And a bottle of Gouder, please?" The question was aimed at Ingo, who nodded his head in approval.

The waiter nodded and gathered up their menus.

"Must be strange for you living in Ethiopia and working elsewhere?" she said. "You don't really get to know the country."

"In some ways you're right, especially living on the edge of the city at the Institute. Weekends like these I get to know the place better. But I do like the travel. I get to know Mali, and Rwanda, as well as Ethiopia," he said. "I'll never be as immersed as you are. But maybe

---

[84] Crispy roast pork.

that's who you are, and I am not?"

"I feel really at home here," she said. "And my job keeps on expanding and changing."

"Your Amharic is impressive," he said. "The way you were chatting with those kids on the mountainside. I gave up on Amharic classes. I was not using it much."

"I learnt it in Piazza with the street boys and zabanyas, and I do need it for my job. When I'm at the factory in Nazareth, or at the carpet workshops here in Addis. You know? I need to talk to the people working there. The machinists and carpet weavers."

The waiter bought the wine and starters.

"Thank you," she said. "It looks great." She smiled up at him, and immediately couldn't help wondering what he thought of people like her, coming in and stuffing their faces while the country starved. The contradiction never escaped her. And still she ate.

"And your life too?" Ingo said, picking up a spring roll in his fingers and dipping it into the dish of soy sauce. "Expanding and changing?"

"You mean the break-up with Moe? My new flat?"

"I guess," he smiled.

His face was tanned from the sun, making his eyes even bluer. Hiwot was right, he was a handsome fellow. She could feel the heat of the day in her cheeks and hoped they were not a startling pink. She ruffled her hands through her hair.

"You look lovely," he said, as if reading her mind.

"Oh I'm always a bit of a mess," she said, now her cheeks really did feel hot. "And just to say, it's over with Moe. I'm past it. I just want to have some fun now. Today was perfect. We never really did anything like climbing Zukwala, or Yerer. We'd got into a bit of a rut." It all came tumbling out with a sudden attack of nerves. "That's all. Best not to talk about it."

"OK, OK, I hear you," he said. "Let's drink to that." He raised his glass.

They clinked glasses, smiling. He feels it too, she thought, the shiver inside, and wondered if he would lean across the table and kiss her. He didn't. Once more, the gentleman. She drank. "I'm not up for anything serious," she said.

"Suits me," he said, taking a large sip of wine and popping the rest of the spring roll into his mouth.

"You're looking pleased with yourself," she said.

"I am!" He grinned.

The waiter came with more bowls of steaming food.

"This looks good," Ingo said.

"My favourite food, Chinese," she said. "And Italian, and Ethiopian, especially beye aynetu."

"Beye aynetu?"

"Fasting food, no meat, just an assortment of tasty vegetables, lentil sauce, you know sherro, and mustard sauce. It's really good. It's what I choose if I can."

"And English food?" he said. "I have experience of that."

"Experience of it?" she said, helping herself to rice and a few pieces of spare rib with a slice of pineapple on top.

"I was on a school exchange. The mother put a pot of meat and vegetables in the oven in the morning and took it out to feed us when we came in from school in the evening."

Izzie turned up her nose. "Irish stew?"

"I never tasted anything so awful."

"Sorry," she said. "Is that why your English is so good? I mean, going on school exchanges?"

"I doubt it. I was only there for two weeks, thank goodness." His eyes twinkled, softening the mild attack. "You seem to have spent a lot of time away from home? Australia, Malawi, here? Anything to do with the food at home?"

"I never thought of it like that. Maybe you're right, I just needed to get away from over-cooked vegetables," she laughed. "But seriously for a minute, talking about food, Leila told me that the Livestock Research Institute is fundraising for the feeding centre that's opened in Debre Berhan. She said you raised a lot of money."

"Yes, my family and friends in Germany. I don't know what I expected but they've all been incredibly generous. I'm quite overwhelmed," he said, his eyes reddening. He cleared his throat.

"Hey," she said, putting a hand gently on his arm. "It's fantastic, Ingo."

"I think people were relieved to finally be able to do something. And so directly. It's been all over the news. The famine in Ethiopia."

"They've probably seen more than we have," Izzie said. "I feel so useless. I love my work, but I am not doing anything about the famine. That's the big issue right now. Leila said the situation is grim."

"That's what I hear too. Though I haven't been up to Debre Berhan myself yet. At least they are not camped along the roadside any more. Apart from the two Relief Council guys who work there, I think there's a small clinic and a local doctor who visits too."

"They must be totally overwhelmed. Leila said there are at least two to four thousand people there at any one time."

He raised his eyebrows and shrugged, looking at the remaining food. "We eat out and talk about the famine. Come on, let's finish up." He helped himself to rice and vegetables, and pushed the bowl of spare ribs towards her. "I like your choice, except for the pork."

"OK," she said. "I'll bear that in mind. No Schwein."

He was quite direct. Reminded her of her Dutch friends in Lilongwe. Ethiopians were the same, they just said what they thought. Came right out with it. It had shocked her at first, but it made things easier. Maybe that's why she felt she could be straight forward with him.

They sat in silence. She felt uneasy about the situation. The famine. They lived on the edge of it. Since the 10th Anniversary its victims had begun to seep through the cracks into the city. There was more talk, more recognition in government circles, more people understood that there was a real disaster, a real famine.

"You're pretty good with chopsticks for someone who doesn't eat Chinese," she said finally.

He tapped the side of his nose, and winked. "Fast on the uptake."

"Tell me what you really love doing above all else," she said.

"Skiing," he said without hesitation.

"Ha! You won't be doing much of that here."

"I used to ski in the Black Forest with my Grandmother. And more recently I've been going with friends. We go to the mountains, several of us together, hire a chalet, buy beers and noodles, stuff for breakfast, and we're off. Nothing better than an early start and a whole day out there on the slopes. We get back as it's getting dark. You get warm, drink a few beers, put on a pot of spaghetti and sleep like a log. Today is not far off that, now I come to think of it."

"You could say that," she laughed. "It has been a good day. I really enjoyed it. Pity about Susan's banana bread though, hey?"

"'With groundnuts!'" he mimicked. "That's very East Africa. 'Groundnuts'. She was in Malawi too. I wonder why you all go to Malawi. One of your old colonies I suppose."

"Did Germany have any colonies?" Izzie wondered out loud.

"Yes, we had what was called German East Africa, which included Tanganyika, and what is now Rwanda and Burundi. And German South West Africa, which is now Namibia. We lost all of it after the

First World War. It was taken over by South Africa. There are still German descendants in Namibia."

"Have you ever been? You have any relatives there?"

"No. Funny question. Why would I?" he said. "Do you have relatives in any of the old colonies?"

"My Grandpa and my Dad were both in India, and I have cousins in South Africa, but that's not really an old colony of ours. Both my parents have cousins who emigrated there some time back."

"Huh, interesting," he said. "Well, in southern Africa I have been to Botswana and Kenya, and as you know, I now go to Rwanda and Mali. But where I work has nothing to do with a colonial past. It's just where the work is."

"Seeing all those places, I mean, working in so many different places, must be amazing," Izzie said. "I think I prefer to get stuck in, in one place though. You think of yourself as a traveller? A wanderer?"

He laughed. "Not really. I don't think of myself like that. I don't know." He shrugged and poured them the last of the wine.

"You have a girlfriend in Germany?" The question just came out.

"I thought this was 'having fun', no back stories, no complications. Hmm?" He signalled between them. "Goes both ways, right?" To her relief he was still smiling. He didn't seem to take anything, apart from the famine situation, very seriously.

"Right," she said. "I take it back. I don't really need or want to know."

"We split up," he said. "That's all there is to know."

"Right," she said again. "You finish the chicken? I finish the spare ribs?"

"Sounds like a plan."

"Talking of plans, Leila asked if I want to go with her to Debre Berhan sometime. Are you planning to go?"

"Yes, I need to, so I can write to the people who donated about how their money is being spent. But I leave for Mali next week."

"Oh, that's a shame," she said, without thinking.

He looked up at her quizzically.

"I was thinking of going with her in a week or so, that's all. In case we thought of going at the same time." she said quickly.

"I know it sounds crazy but there's the Hilton ball when I get back. You know, they're fundraising. Shall I get two tickets? Would you like to come?"

"It feels so extravagant," Izzie said. "A ball. I don't know. So incongruous. It might be fun. I obviously don't have an evening dress.

'A backless evening strap.'"

"A what?" he leant forward, smiling.

"A backless evening strap. That's what Dad calls an evening dress. I guess I can find one somewhere." Who on earth had a ball gown in Addis, she wondered.

36

October 1984, Ankober to Debre Berhan

In the evenings, the damp mist moved through the mountains, chilling him to the bone. Every night he sat in the corner, eating his share of bread, before curling up to sleep, bitten by the bugs that crawled in the oily sheepskin and under his clothes. His cough sounded like Zewdie's, rasping and gurgling in his chest. He was afraid for himself and longed for her.

One night he woke shivering, his body wet, his throat burning. He curled up tight pulling his gabi close round him, but couldn't get warm.

He called out, "Zewdie, Zewdie."

He moved from one side to the other, itching all over. He sat up and scratched, lay down again and groaned. He heard voices murmuring, shapes moving around him. Every part of his body ached. There was no way to lie in comfort.

"Zewdie," he called. "It's the evil eye. The buda has come. Call Emet Fahte."

"What is it, boy?" A woman's voice said. "Who is this Emet Fahte?"

"The buda," he whispered. "Don't let the white truck take me away?"

"You have fever. It's not the evil eye."

"Zewdie, is that you?" He tried to sit up.

"No. It is I, Turunesh," the woman said, putting a hand on his shoulder, she pushed him gently down again.

He felt a blanket over him. It made him hot. He threw the blanket and his gabi to one side. "God is angry with us, you know?"

The chill returned, and his body shook so much he was sure the devil had entered him. "Throw fendisha! Throw fendisha!" he called out. "Protect us from the evil spirits!" He fell into a deep sleep. The crow was perched on the bus shelter, its black eyes staring at him. He hit out to send it away. "Go away. Go away," he shouted. "Leave me alone."

"You brought a sick one. I knew it from the start," he heard the woman saying.

"What is it, woman?" A gruff voice filled the room.

"You have to take him back to his mother," the woman said.

Ashebir tried to sit up. "Take me to my mother," he whispered. "Please take me."

"You're telling me to take him back?" the man's voice said.

Ashebir looked up, not sure if the words came in his dreaming. It was dark and smoky, but he could smell the sweat of a working man, and arake.[85] It was Ato Tadesse.

"I don't want him to die here," Turunesh said. "God will punish us. There is enough death, enough dying. Egziyabher yawkal."

"Mama Turunesh?" Ashebir said, struggling to sit up.

"Wait until the morning and we'll put him out," Ato Tadesse said.

"God save us. How can we do that?" Turunesh said.

"He is not going to die," Ato Tadesse said. "He will be fine in the morning. He can walk back to Debre Berhan."

"Be Egziyabher. He can't walk that far. Take him on the mule."

"Are you arguing with me?"

"No, Tadesse, no. Just as you wish. We will do as you wish," she said with a sigh.

Ashebir heard a door shut. The man was gone. Did he say they should put him out? "Mama Turunesh," he whispered.

"Hush," she said. "I've made a tea for you. It will take the fever and pains away."

Her hand was trembling as she held the cup to his lips. He took a sip. It was thick like Emet Fahte's herbal mixtures. He shrank back as his mouth filled with its sour taste.

"Drink, it will make you better," she said, holding his head up, tipping the cup between his lips. "Drink, child. Drink."

He shook his head.

"Drink, it is good for you."

When the cup was empty, he lay back and fell asleep. He was sitting outside their house in their village, old Emet Fahte's toothless face appeared. As her face came closer to his it took on the black features and dark shining eyes of a crow, its beak hovering over his right eye socket. He turned away quickly before it could peck, shouting out for Zewdie. She was not there. The house was empty, the compound brushed clean.

---

[85] Locally made schnapps.

In the distance, the white truck drove across the steam to the other side and he knew she was in it. He ran after it, plunging into the water, struggling to cross, as it turned into thick mud. Little Tirs was running away, his mouth wide open, crying for his sister.

**

Ato Tadesse shook him from his sleep. "Come on," he said, pulling Ashebir to his feet. "Out with you, boy."

"What is it?" Ashebir said, raising a hand in front of his head, terrified. "Please, Ato Tadesse."

A thick smell of arake poured from Ato Tadesse's mouth, making Ashebir feel sick. "Mama Turunesh," Ashebir wailed, struggling to get free. But he hung from the man's hands like the hide of a skinned lamb, the legs and hooves still intact, dangling.

"I have had enough," Ato Tadesse said. "You are no good to us lying here. Keeping her busy with her teas; eating our food." He dragged Ashebir to the door, opened it and flung him out into the still dark early hours.

Ashebir fell to the ground, grazing his hands and knees. He turned to sit, brushing the dirt away. "Please don't," he cried. "Be Egziyabher."

Ato Tadesse disappeared inside.

Ashebir wanted to shout, but was afraid the man would come back with his switch. He rubbed himself, shivering. He only had his filthy shorts and a t-shirt on.

The trees around the compound loomed tall and still. The morning mist hung low and quiet. He listened for the crack of a twig. It was still the time of hyenas prowling. He got to his feet, shivering cold, and went back to the house.

"In God's name, please, Ato Tadesse," he said through the open door. "I am better today. I can take the animals out." He did feel a bit better. Mama Turunesh's sour medicine must have worked on him in the night. She knew as much as Emet Fahte about leaves and herbs. People from the surrounding villages came with an egg or a small dish of honey when she made them better.

Ato Tadesse appeared again. He threw Ashebir's bag and gabi on the ground and went back inside. The metal door rattled loudly as he slammed it shut behind him.

Mama Turunesh's complaining noises seeped out under the entrance. This could end in a thrashing. He had once hit her so hard she fell across the room, almost into the fire.

Ashebir went to the door and tried to hit it with his hand. The noise it made would not wake a mouse. He sank to the ground. He knew it. The buda had been and sucked out all his strength.

The door flew open. Ato Tadesse looked taller and louder than Ashebir had ever seen him before.

"You know the path," he said. "Hid! Go. Go on. Out of here!"

Ashebir crawled backwards away from the door and threw up. The liquid was dark. Mama Turunesh's tea. His gabi lay on the ground. He imagined a soul slipping out from under it into the mist. He hesitated to pull it towards him in case he uncovered a skeleton. His bag lay nearby. Shivering, he got up and lifted the gabi slowly, only breathing again when he saw the ground beneath was bare.

The door slammed shut. Ato Tadesse had gone inside. How could he be so cruel? Ashebir had worked hard every day from sunrise to sunset. It was the drink. Drink takes away a man's fear of God, Zewdie used to say. A drunkard can do many things without feeling sorry.

"But God will punish you," Ashebir whispered through his teeth at the door. "I know He will." He stopped for a moment to listen. He heard his heart beating. The arguing inside the house had stopped. He put his bag over his shoulder. It was heavier than usual. He peered inside and saw some bread. Mama Turunesh. She must have put it in when Ato Tadesse was not looking. She had never said much, but she had fed him, however little, and when he got sick, she had looked after him. The bread was her way of getting him home.

He decided to walk. He would go back to Zewdie. He went looking for the path on which he had first come. It lead through pastures now partially hidden by the morning fog. His heart lifted when he saw the wide rocky path winding like a black crocodile in and out of the mist. He found a sheltered spot amongst the roots of a tall warka tree and sat down to eat one of Mama Turunesh's breads. As he ate, he couldn't help but cry. Trembling with cold. So alone. He sniffed in hard and wiped his eyes. Poor Mama Turunesh, living in fear with that man. When a man was angry, a woman could do nothing.

There had been a few evenings when their daughters' children had come and Ato Tadesse had told them stories by the fire. Ashebir had sat in the shadows, listening. Stories of old times, of battles against the Italianoch, he called them, and of passing traders dressed in long cloaks from Arab lands.

Ashebir chewed on his bread. This was the very path, Ato Tadesse had said, which had been used since the olden days. It had taken traders from the highlands over the ravines and down to the hot plains of Harar in the east. And he had told them how, in their turn, the Arabs had come with goods from a place called the Red Sea. Ashebir had imagined a wide river of blood.

He finished his bread. Wrapping his gabi around him and over his head, he got up. Unsteady. He better keep moving. He tried to picture Zewdie but kept seeing Mama Turunesh or the wrinkled face of Emet Fahte. It was quiet. He could hardly see anything through the fog. He stopped and listened. He could hear voices and the faint click-clack of hooves. He hid behind the tree and peered into the mist behind him. After some moments he made out the shapes of two, no three, women, bent low, carrying large bundles of firewood on their backs. A man, walking alongside his heavily-laden donkey, emerged behind them. He carried a long stick across his shoulders. Another man came behind him, wearing a cap under his gabi. All of them were wrapped up against the cold.

They almost walked past him, when one of the women stopped. "What is this? Are you all alone?" she said.

He looked into her soft face.

"Be Egziyabher," she said. "Look at you."

"What is it sister? We have no time to stop," a woman said, turning awkwardly towards Ashebir. She was bent double under her load. She wore a thick woollen shawl round her head, her face drawn in a frown.

The woman with the soft face looked into his eyes. "Why are you alone? What happened?" She turned to the others looking distressed. "In God's name, just wait a moment. Look. The boy is sick, can't you see? He is starving."

They all stopped and came as close as their burdens would allow, gathering around clicking their tongues. "Poor child, in heaven's name," they mumbled.

In their sympathy and kindness, Ashebir saw the miserable state he was in, and how badly he had been treated. He started to cry. He told them about Zewdie under the bus shelter, about his fever and the bug-ridden sheepskin, and how Ato Tadesse had thrown him out. He wanted to say more, about the buda, about Mama Turunesh's bread and her bitter medicine tea, and the mist, and the soul that had slithered into the woods from under his gabi, about the hyenas and how afraid he was. But his voice had dried up.

"He should come with us," the women agreed.

"What is your name?" the man with the cap said. It had a dark red revolutionary badge on it with a yellow hammer and sickle. He looked at Ashebir with a slight squint through a pair of large black rimmed glasses.

"Ashebir," he said.

"Thanks to God we found him, Comrade," one woman said.

"Ashebir," the Comrade said. "You walk with us. We'll help you find your mother."

"Ishi," he whispered.

The Comrade put his hand on Ashebir's shoulder, "Come, let's go," he said.

"Let's go," another woman said, walking on with small stiff steps, swaying from side to side under her load. "We have to get to market."

Ashebir picked his way over the sharp stones, glad of the Comrade's comforting hand. Seeing the women with their heavy loads of firewood made him think of Zewdie rubbing Emet Fahte's eucalyptus oil into her legs at night. He so wanted to be by her side.

**

When they reached Debre Berhan, Ashebir looked about uneasily.

The women walked on to the market, waving, calling that they did not want to stop, "God's blessings, Ashebir," they said one after the other.

"Make sure he finds his mother, Comrade."

Passengers sat with their luggage where Zewdie once lay. Zewdie, Mama Tsehai, her husband, Wubit, the silent old man's family, all had vanished. Everyone was gone.

"I know where they are," a voice said.

Ashebir looked down. A man with skinny stumps where his legs had been, sat on a wooden trolley. He wore a dirty earth-brown t-shirt which hung in shreds about his shoulders.

"I know you," the man said, smiling up at Ashebir with black teeth and swollen gums.

The man tugged at Ashebir's shorts. "I saw you with your mother, and then you left." He cocked his head to one side, smiling, "I see everything here."

Ashebir was not sure if he could believe him. "Where did my mother go? Is she alright?"

The Comrade rummaged in his jacket pocket. "Here," he said, holding out a coin.

"God bless you," the man said, holding out both hands. He took the coin, bowing his head. "They took her to the hospital. She was very sick. If God is merciful, you will still find her there." He raised a small wooden cross to his lips. It hung on a single black thread round his neck.

37

Ashebir had never been to a hospital before. He felt more tired and alone than ever. He made his way to the large main doors.

People were going in and out. Beggars, their feet bound in soiled rags, sat in the entrance holding out stumpy fingers. Zewdie told him not to go near people like that, they had a terrible disease. He kept his eyes averted to the worn stone-grey steps as he climbed them one at a time. Once inside, he stood in the confusion. People brushed past him, voices murmuring, a baby's cry echoed from further down the corridor. The air was heavy with the familiar smell of The Hungry, their unwashed clothes and hair, their sweat, the pungent smell of vomit and diarrhoea. Zewdie was here somewhere.

A woman with kind eyes and a gap between her front teeth put a hand on his shoulder. "You, child," she said. "What is it?"

"My mother," he said.

"She's a patient? She's sick?"

"Yes," he said. He felt light-headed, his legs barely held him up.

She sucked her teeth and shook her head. "Go ask over there, behind the counter. She will tell you."

A young woman sat behind a glass window.

"Her?" he said.

She nodded and gave him a gentle push in that direction.

He stood up on his tip-toes, peering through the glass window. "I am looking for my mother," he said.

"What is her name?" The young woman put her ear to the glass. She was wearing a soft white shawl over her hair and across her shoulders.

"Zewdie. Zewdie Tamru," he whispered, his eyes filling with tears.

Her finger, orange-brown with henna, stopped half way down a sheet of paper. "Zewdie Tamru?" she said, looking at him. She had beautiful eyes.

He nodded. Zewdie was there. He held on tight to the counter.

"Ward six. First floor."

"First floor?"

She looked down at him and smiled.

He could see the pity in her eyes.

"Go up the steps over there," she said. "Follow that nurse, see?"

"Nurse?"

"The woman in the blue uniform with the hat on?"

He nodded, swallowing hard.

"And look for the number six. Ishi?" she said. "You will see it written over the door."

"Egziersteling," he said, bowing his head a little. "Six." Zewdie was there.

"Aysoh," the woman in the glass box said. "It's alright. Don't worry."

He whispered, "One, two, three, four, five, six."

He stopped on each step to take a breath. At the top, there was a long corridor full of people, some lying on the floor, their relatives squatting next to them. The roof above him was lit by strips of sunlight trapped behind glass and buzzing like Uncle Ahmed's bees. A man in a white coat walked past, followed by a flock of country women like tiny birds on an ox's back.

Ashebir looked through a wide entrance. Above the door he saw the number '4'. People lay on beds and on the floor. A woman was wailing softly. He walked on, trying not to step on anyone, feeling the strange cold smoothness of the ground under his feet. He searched women's faces in case he missed her passing by. 'Four, five, six. Where was six?' He held his bag tighter. There it was, '6'. He went inside, his heart beating faster. The stench was stronger than in the corridor. He gagged and pulled his gabi up over his nose.

There was a row of metal beds on either side of the long room, green walls halfway down, pale yellow halfway up. There was a continuous murmur of voices. The sun blazed though the window onto a group of people sitting on the floor. A woman groaned and cried out from a far corner. He looked into each bed and at the faces of those lying on the floor. His heart jumped each time he thought it was Zewdie. No, no, not that one. He went on to the end of the room and had not seen her. He turned back. Maybe that one was her?

He went to a bed by a window. A woman lay there, eyes closed deep inside their sockets, her high cheek bones stuck out above her hollowed cheeks, her brow drawn into a worried frown. Her corn row plaited hair was turning grey. It was messy and the black scarf she always wore was missing.

"Zewdie?" he whispered, shocked. He could not believe what had happened to her.

Zewdie's hand lay pale and bony across her chest. She took short shallow breaths.

"Zewdie," he whispered. He put his hand lightly on hers.

Her eyes did not open but she smiled. "Ashebir," she mouthed, barely a sound. A tear ran down the side of her cheek onto the sheet.

His head throbbed like it might burst. He fell forward onto her bed, crying. He quickly stood up again, afraid he might break her.

He touched her hair, stroked it. It was as soft as ever.

"What is this?"

Ashebir looked round. A nurse in a blue uniform came up behind him.

"She is very weak. Behaving like that will not help."

He stepped back, sniffing the tears away, tripping over someone lying on the floor under a soiled cloth. The old woman looked up at him with watery eyes.

The nurse picked up Zewdie's wrist and stood holding it, looking at her watch. "She is very sick," she said. "She came here too late. There is not much we can do."

"What shall I do?" he whispered.

"You can sit in that chair and look after her until her time comes," the nurse said.

An old wooden chair stood there as if it had been waiting for him. He pulled it close to Zewdie's bed. He watched the nurse as she wrote on a piece of paper. Her eyebrows, thin black lines, had been painted on.

Without another word, she went to the next bed. She wore black shoes and walked a town walk, her bottom swinging briskly from side to side.

He imagined she wrote down names for the men in the white trucks. People they had to collect. He took a deep breath and coughed to get rid of the stench that filled his lungs. They were all dying in here. Emet Fahte would never have said there was nothing she could do. She would brew one of her bitter medicine teas or get her razor and cut. Then he realised what Emet Fahte did. She gave people hope. Now he understood. He blew his nose on his gabi and wiped his eyes.

"Zewdie?"

She turned and looked at him. Her eyes saying, "How are you, yeney konjo?" Her mouth slightly open, a small smile, no sound. He came closer. Her breath smelled foul, not sweet like it used to. Was she rotting inside? How could he stop 'her time' coming?

"Do you hurt, Zewdie?" he said.

She raised her eyebrows to say, yes. Yes, she did.

"Where? Where do you hurt?"

Lifting her hand, she slowly pointed round her body. Her head, her stomach, her chest, her back.

"Do you want some water?"

She clicked her tongue. No, she didn't.

Ashebir sat on the old chair by Zewdie's bed that night and the next days. He covered himself with his old ox-skin. He tried not to look at the old woman with the watery eyes on the floor beside them. One morning two men came. They wrapped her up in her rags and carried her away on a stretcher. No one said anything. Ashebir sat and looked. His head empty. He felt nothing.

He never got used to the smell in that place. Nor the discomfort of sitting on that chair. The floor was too hard and cold. He was still weak and his hands and body itched. He had sores between his fingers where he had scratched too hard. So he spent the nights sitting on his chair, trying to keep his eyes open, trying not to scratch, watching Zewdie.

They bought pasta for her. He tried to tempt her with small mouthfuls. The first day she ate a little, then motioned to him to eat the rest. He ate and was glad of the food. After three days she could not eat. Each time he put a little in her mouth, she slowly pushed it out again with her tongue. She could not swallow.

"Eat, Zewdie, eat," he said. "Please, take something."

But she could not.

He wiped her face and hands with a wet cloth and dropped water on her lips. He stroked her hair. He thought of things to tell her. He wanted to remind her that Lakew would come for them soon. He wanted to ask her where Mama Tsehai was, and Wubit. But Zewdie did not talk, only her eyes told him she was still there, that she loved him, that she was sad, very sad.

"Don't be sad, Zewdie," he said. "It will be alright. Egziyabher alle. You are in hospital. You will be alright." But was God there? It seemed He had left them all. His people. The very people who ploughed His fields and scattered His seeds, who looked after the cattle and took them to the meadows, and down to the river to drink. It seemed He had deserted them all.

When she was awake, she did not take her eyes off him.

"I am here, Zewdie," he said, getting up to stroke her hand.

She smiled with her eyes on him.

So he stayed by her and watched. When she slept, she was not in pain or coughing. It was as if she was in another place, a stranger, as if she had already gone. He wanted to find the man in the white coat, the doctor. Wanted to ask him to make her better. But he was a big man, and Ashebir did not dare.

They stayed like that for days and nights. He wanted to tell her how he had missed her, about the bugs at night, the Ankober early morning mist, and how cold it had been. About the clear stream that had reminded him of home, and his little friend, Tirs. He wanted to say, 'You will be better soon, Zewdie, then we can go home.' But he knew it was not true, so he kept quiet. In some way he knew Zewdie did not want to hear any of these things, about life. She was leaving it. Was that possible? His eyes were heavy. His head sank. Now and then he would fall asleep and wake with a jolt to see her still lying there.

Zewdie sank into her body more and more each day. She frowned in pain when she moved. It scared him to watch her. When she smiled at him, his heart lifted. For a moment she was with him again.

One morning he sat up from his sleep. His body stiff. She was still asleep. He drew the pale green sheet up around her shoulders. He went to fetch water to wash her face and hands as he did every morning before breakfast, the breakfast for her which he ate.

He went outside to the tap and waited in the queue. It was misty and cold. He shivered. He went back up the steps one at a time, still tired from the night, his bare feet padding along the hard concrete. He walked past empty faces until he reached room '6'. He walked back to Zewdie's bed with his tin of water. She was still asleep. He sat on his chair waiting for her to wake. It was good for her to sleep.

The nurse came. It was the one with the glasses, the older one.

Ashebir stood up. "My mother is asleep," he said.

The nurse picked up Zewdie's hand by the wrist. She put Zewdie's hand back down.

Ashebir looked at the nurse, trying to see what her eyes said behind the glasses.

"Dear child, your mother will not wake today. God rest her soul." The nurse started to pull the sheet over Zewdie's face.

"Wait," he said. "She is asleep."

The nurse sniffed and pushed her glasses up her nose. "Ishi, I will give you a few minutes," she said. She walked to the next patient, lifted the woman's hand and looked at her watch.

Zewdie lay with the pale green sheet pulled up around her neck, her face the colour of dried earth, her hair still plaited, untidy in wisps. She was strangely still. She was not frowning any more. He touched her cheek. It was cold.

"Zewdie?" he whispered. His legs gave way, he crumpled forwards and lay with his head on her chest. It was hard, not full and soft like it used to be. He let out a loud cry. He stood up. Looked at her. Shook her shoulder. "Zewdie," he said. "Wake up. I got water for us," he shouted. "Please don't leave me, Zewdie. Please don't go. Don't go, Zewdie. I will wash your face," he sobbed. " Zewdie," he called again. Fear, like iced-water rushed through his bones. "Don't leave me alone, Zewdie," he shouted. "Please." He gritted his teeth. All he could see was her grey face and the pale green sheet.

Some women started wailing and he felt arms around him.

"Zewdie," he shouted. "Zewdie, don't leave me."

"What's going on? Mindin neouw?" the nurse said. It was the one with the painted eyebrows. "Stop this noise."

"Don't let the men come and take her away, please," he shouted.

"Stop this noise. What about the other patients? It's not good for them to hear all this. Go outside and cry," the nurse said. She pulled him away from the bed.

He struggled. "Let go. Let go," he shouted. "Zewdie."

The nurse pulled the sheet over Zewdie's face. "Get your things," she said. "Stop this noise."

"I want to stay with her," he shouted. "Leave me alone."

The nurse grabbed his ox-skin, took hold of his arm and dragged him out of the room.

He shouted all the way. "My mother died. Leave me. Let go. Let go. Zewdie, Zewdie."

The nurse took him down the stairs, holding him in a tight grip all the way. It hurt. They got to the doors that opened onto the veranda at the back.

He could feel her fury running through him.

"Go. Go outside. Cry and shout there," she said. She pushed him from the veranda onto the wasteland below.

He fell onto the hard ground. He sat up, his knees and hands hurting, surrounded by tall grass. The sky a dark blue above. His crying came out in shudders, his chest heaving. He could hardly breathe. He rubbed his arm. How could they treat him like this. He was a human being, wasn't he? Don't they mourn the dead in hospital? He cried and cried, trying to get air, his mouth open. He was so far from home. So alone, and filled with disbelief. Where would he go? What would he do?

Suddenly the sky rumbled, louder and louder, until it was over his head. So loud he covered his ears. Stopped his crying. What was it? He looked up terrified, his heart beating painfully. An enormous machine, green like the army trucks, hovered above him like an eagle over its prey. Great big blades whirling round and round above it. Flattening the grasses with the wind it created. He lay looking up. He could not breathe, or run. There were soldiers inside peering out.

People ran away in all directions, shouting, ducking from the whirlwind of flying rubbish and dust. After some moments, the machine, a huge bird-like vehicle, lifted into the air and flew away, taking its noise with it. Ashebir watched until it was a small dot. What was it? He turned round and vomited, again and again, until he could no more.

He moved round the outside of the building and found a place to sit, his back against the wall, as if leaning on Zewdie. She was still in there. "Zewdie," he whispered, his chest still shuddering from the sobbing. "Zewdie."

The morning moved on, the sun burnt down from the dry blue sky. He leant into the shade of the stone hospital wall, feeling it hard against his back. He heard a vehicle hooting its horn and looked up. His heart jumped and the nausea rose in his throat again.

The white truck stood at the gates. It drove into the compound, turned and reversed towards the hospital side entrance, further down. Two men jumped down, opened the back doors wide, and went inside. They came out again, carrying a body on a wooden stretcher. It was wrapped in a pale green sheet. They climbed awkwardly with it into the back of the lorry.

Ashebir tried to call out to her, but his voice had left him and he could not move. The men jumped down again, the stretcher now empty. Other bodies followed, two in white sheets, three in thin grey blankets and two very small ones wrapped in rags.

"Where are you taking her? Let me come with you." He wanted to shout. "Zewdie, don't leave me alone. What am I going to do?"

He heard the sound of her voice, This is our life, Ashebir. My beautiful child. It is God's will. He saw her in the forest, cutting firewood. It is a hard life. It is our life.

There were loud clanks, the doors at the back of the truck were slammed shut. The driver jumped in the cab and started up the engine. He pulled out of the compound, waving to the guard holding the hospital gates open.

The guard called out and waved back. He closed the gates behind the truck. They grated along the ground.

38

October 1984, Debre Berhan

He saw their feet, bare, cracked and dry. Feet in worn-out sandals, in torn black plastic slippers like Zewdie's, in townspeople shoes. People coming and going from the hospital. Some walked slow and careful, a few in a hurry, children ran to keep up. He looked up, watched them pass. He heard the sound of voices, but not a word. They passed him by. He sat, his back against the stone wall, as if leaning on Zewdie.

He scratched his head until the itching got worse. He scratched the sores between his fingers, that Zewdie had no money to buy ointment for, until they bled. He pulled his knees up to his chest and wrapped his arms around himself to stop the pains in his stomach. He coughed and spat out the phlegm. He hung his head and let the tears fall.

I thought it was you. He heard the sound of Zewdie's voice at their gate. Put the animals away and come inside to eat.

He saw the goats' hooves kicking up dust, and himself running behind, throwing pebbles at their rumps to keep them on the path. He heard the low bellow of oxen lumbering home in the late afternoon, the long soft skin under their necks swinging back and forth, their horns piercing the evening sky.

He heard himself laugh. We chased the monkeys from the cactus fruits today, Zewdie. He saw her smile.

He covered his ears and shut his eyes tight. Where had the men in the white truck taken her? He pulled his rolled up ox-skin closer. It was all he had. It was his bed, his home, his village.

"Child, yeney lij," a gruff voice said. "Listen to me."

Ashebir looked up. The figure in front of him, a dark shadow against the sun. He looked more closely. It was the guard from the hospital gates.

"You can't stay here. You have to go to the camp," he said. "See? See those people? Go. Go walk with them and you will reach the camp."

Ashebir looked through the open hospital gates and saw them. The Hungry, walking.

"Ishi," he said, putting a hand against the wall to heave himself to his feet. He had no words or questions, no tears or shouts left.

"See? Go that way," the old man said. "With them. You will get food there."

The road was crowded. Ordinary farmers, from Northern Shewa, Wollo and Tigray, walking with their families. He picked up his ox-skin and walked slowly towards the gates and onto the road to join them, as the man had said to do. They mostly walked in silence. When they spoke, it was Orominya or Tigrinya. He was different from them. There was no one that looked like the people of his area. He was alone, but he was one of them. He was like them. He walked with them.

The afternoon was drawing in. It was the time to be heading homeward. He felt like an ox, lumbering slowly along with the herd. The people around him must have trodden the road for days now, losing a child, a father, a mother, on the way. He walked with them, one foot after the other. They reached a river which they crossed by foot. It was a trickle of water. He wanted to bend to wash his face, take a drink, just for a moment, but the flow of walking people did not allow for that. He kept going.

There was a small hill to climb and then on the other side, he saw it down below, the camp. The whole area was milling with people. He caught his breath. He could hear their murmuring in the distance, on and on like worker bees. The cries of their babies and children echoed up the hillside. To the right was a wide open field, where people were squatting, doing their toilet. A bit further on, huge white tents loomed around a square of low brick buildings. The camp was in a valley with hills climbing up on the other side. The man had said he would get food there. He kept walking. Having lost faith in God for that day, he for some reason had faith in the old man. His voice had not been unkind. A man who spent his days opening and closing the gates of the hospital for the white trucks that came and went.

It looked like market day. The place was full of farmers, men, women and children, but there were no animals. No oxen, no goats or donkeys. No sound of outraged chickens squawking from wooden cages. No piles of dark green chillies, no onions and tomatoes, no sacks of grain or spices, no deep red berberri, no orange and yellow lentils.

He walked with the people until he reached the compound. It was a long single storey building with outhouses on either end. A wide veranda linked all the rooms. He sat down where he arrived, not knowing what else to do. The other children had families, a mother, or a father, a leg to stand by, a hand to hang on to. Women sat, kutch-kutch,[86] around small fires and cooked ki'ta bread like Mama Tsehai had done under the bus shelter. He wondered if she was here.

A girl about his age lay curled up on her side not far from where he sat. She looked as though she was watching him but he could not be sure. Her eyes had sunk into their sockets. Her mouth was dry and cracked. She opened it a little. Was she trying to say something? The skin on her cheeks was thin. Flies crawled over her teeth, and in her eyes. She looked like a skeleton. She slowly lifted a hand as if to brush the flies away, but did not seem to have the strength. The skin on her arm was grey and scaly like a lizard's. A woman sat next to the girl staring at nothing. She looked as if her mind had left her. Maybe a crow had plucked it out of her head and flown away with it. A baby lay naked and crying in her lap like an abandoned new-born bird. The child's hand reached up to claw the cloth which barely covered his mother's breast.

He sat. Looked. His head empty. His tongue dry. The muscles in his belly contracted with pain, his chest and legs ached. He had not had one mouthful that day. He saw no one who could give him food. How would he eat without family? He sat and watched. He coughed as his lungs filled with the thick smoke from the small fires around him. The sun faded behind the hills, leaving a pale blue sky over their heads, as the chill set in.

People were going in and out of the rooms, whose doors opened onto the long veranda. He picked up the ox-skin. He walked up the few steps onto the veranda and squeezed past a man coming out of one of the rooms. No one noticed him. It was dim inside, warm, thick with the heat of bodies and human breath. The smell was worse than in the hospital. As his eyes became accustomed, the dark shapes became women with their children, huddled in small groups, men leaning against the walls, their heads in their hands. A child whined softly, the dry empty whine of a starving child. A sound he knew well. People coughed and spat. He could not bear it. The phlegm on the floor and the walls. No one took notice of him. No one greeted

---

[86] Sitting on their haunches.

him. His face felt heavy with sadness. His throat tight. He could not open his mouth to speak, to ask. He could not stay there. He went outside and found a piece of bare earth to lie on. He curled up and pulled his ox-skin over.

He woke up over and over all night. The chill pierced through his bones. He could not stop his body from shivering, however close he pulled his gabi and ox-skin around him. Had they already buried Zewdie in this cold, hard earth? This God forsaken place with no family, no friends and neighbours to mourn her, to remind the world what a good mother she was. Her love, her hard work, her laughter and stories. Her love for Lakew. Lakew. Where was he? Ashebir began to cry again. Would Lakew be able to find him? That seemed impossible. Fear crept through his belly into his chest.

He woke. The morning dew covered everything with its damp chill. A strange quietness shrouded the camp. The wailing that accompanies death started up. The wailing that seemed to have replaced the cock's crow. He could not stop his body trembling. He was cold and hungry. He sat up and looked. People stirred, waking, with a murmuring of voices. The air smelt of damp burnt wood. The girl and her mother were gone.

"Tenasteling," a man said. "Miskin. You are freezing." The man put a grey blanket around Ashebir's shoulders. "You here alone? Where's your family?"

Ashebir bowed his head and pulled the thin cloth around him.

"You have a bad cough," the man said. "Aysoh, it will get warm soon. Don't worry."

Ashebir gritted his teeth to stop the tears. The man's voice was kind.

"My name is Mesfin. I work here. We'll look after you. Aysoh, ishi?"

"Ishi," Ashebir whispered. He felt the tears run down his cheeks and sniffed into the new blanket.

"Come, let's get you breakfast."

Ashebir's throat felt dry and tight. "Ishi," he whispered and pushed himself to his feet. He staggered a little, his legs stiff.

The man caught him.

Women and children with small piles of firewood on their backs were coming to make their fires again.

"Let's go," the man said, keeping a hand around Ashebir's shoulders. "We'll get you a hot tea."

"Mesfin, ebakeh, be Egziyabher" a man said. "We need blankets too. It is too cold. Please."

"Ishi," Mesfin said. "I am coming. I will bring more blankets."

Another man joined in the plea.

Ashebir pulled his new blanket closer around himself and looked at the ground.

Mesfin nodded and smiled. Yes, he would bring them. Later. Later.

"It's always 'later'," a woman said.

"We are doing our best, my mother," Mesfin said. "The women from Ye Sate Mehaber[87] will be coming soon to give you flour and milk powder. Get yourselves ready. Make a line."

Tea. Ashebir could not remember when he last had tea. At Mama Turunesh's in Ankober? That felt long ago. He followed Mesfin up the steps, along the veranda and into one of the rooms. There were more people from the town there. They were clean and dressed against the cold.

A young woman with a round comfortable body came up to him. "Who have we here?" she said, smiling. She wore a red jumper and a long dark skirt. A thin white shema was thrown loosely over her head and shoulders. She had pale brown skin and pink cheeks. Her eyes shone. "What is your name, boy?"

"Ashebir," he whispered.

"Belaynesh," Mesfin said. "Let's give him some bread and tea. I found him all alone. He is freezing."

"Ishi, ishi," Belaynesh said. "Sit, yeney lij, sit down here." She motioned to a chair beside a desk. Within moments she had poured hot tea into a glass, put two teaspoons of sugar in it and placed it by him. She bustled off and came back with a fresh roll."

"Mesfin," an older woman said. "Give me the keys to the store, please. We'll start handing out the flour and milk."

"Here," Mesfin passed her a bunch of keys. "The women will be waiting for you. I told them you are coming."

"Ishi," the woman said. She left the room, followed by two young men and two girls from the town.

"Chew slowly, Ashebir," Mesfin said. "Alright?"

"Ishi," Ashebir said. As he bowed his head in thanks, a habitual gesture, his eyes filled with tears.

"What is it, child?" Belaynesh said. "Eat, eat."

---

[87] Women's Association.

Ashebir picked up the glass with two hands. The red-orange liquid shone and steamed. The glass was too hot to hold. He put it down. My mother died. She's dead. She's gone. He wanted to tell them. I don't know where to go, what to do.

"Let me give him some water," Mesfin said. "Maybe he needs some water first."

"Yes, yes," Belaynesh said.

Mesfin gave him a metal cup of cool water. "Here," he said. "Try and drink this, take small sips."

Mesfin and Belaynesh spoke an Amharic he could recognise. He felt a sense of relief.

"Egziersteling," Ashebir whispered. He drank. Mesfin's face was round and friendly.

"Ashebir, what happened to you?" Mesfin said. "Can you tell us?"

Ashebir lifted the blanket to cover his face. "My mother," he said. He rocked back and forth, humming a low wail, crying his misery. "She's gone. I am alone. Honetey neou.[88]"

"Oh no, no," Mesfin sucked his teeth. "Your mother died?"

"Yesterday. Before coming here," he cried. "I don't know what to do."

Belaynesh sucked her teeth and tutted. "Miskin lij," she said. "Wey, sorry really."

"They told me to stop shouting, to stop crying. They said, "She's dead. Stop making that noise." He took a breath. "I wanted to wash her face," he whispered.

"Who is 'they'? Where did she die?" Mesfin said.

"At the hospital. The nurse. She threw me out." Ashebir was talking and sobbing at the same time.

Belaynesh had tears in her eyes.

"Is it forbidden to mourn in the hospital?" Ashebir said.

"Of course it's not. Of course we mourn," Belaynesh said. "I'm sorry really," she said again.

"Aysoh, Ashebir. We are here." Mesfin had that sad look when he smiled. A look Ashebir was beginning to recognise. The guard at the hospital had had it too. They felt sorry for him.

After his breakfast, Ashebir went and sat in the sun. Mesfin and Belaynesh were busy all day. He sat. Later on, as the afternoon sun waned and the chill threatened to return, he went in search of Mesfin.

---

[88] I'm not lying.

To the room where he had been that morning.

He looked through the open door. "Do you have food for me?" he said.

"Ashebir," Mesfin said. "Just wait a moment, until the doctor and I are finished."

How long was a moment? He looked up. The eyes of the President were watching him from the pale green wall behind Mesfin's table. He wondered about Lakew. He had told Mesfin about Lakew and how he had said he would come for them. Ashebir was less and less certain that he would ever see Lakew again. When he closed his eyes, he saw Zewdie's grey face and shivered.

The men bade each other a good night.

The doctor touched Ashebir gently on the shoulder as he passed. "Goodnight Ashebir," he said. "Egziyabher ante gar yihun."

Ashebir nodded. "Ishi," he whispered.

Mesfin switched on a light. The bulb was immediately surrounded by insects. "We'll wash hands and eat," he said, going to a tap in the corner.

Ashebir followed. The water was icy cold. The soap stung the sores between his fingers. He gritted his teeth.

"That doesn't look good," Mesfin said. "The nurse will look at it tomorrow."

The nurse? Ashebir looked up at Mesfin.

"Don't be afraid," Mesfin laughed. "They are very kind nurses. That's called ekek on your hands. They will give you some ointment for it. It will get better."

"Ishi," Ashebir whispered.

Mesfin opened two containers. One tin had injera in it, and the other sherro wot.

Seeing the food made Ashebir's mouth water.

"Sit here," Mesfin said, patting a chair by the desk. "We will pray first."

"And for my mother?" Ashebir whispered.

"That's a good idea," Mesfin said, closing his eyes and folding his hands.

Ashebir did the same, and then looked up. Mengistu was still watching him. He shut his eyes quickly.

"Thank you Lord for keeping Ashebir safe," Mesfin said. "God bless Ashebir's Mami. Let her rest in peace, Amen"

"Amen," Ashebir whispered.

"Thanks to God for the food we are about to share, Amen."

"Amen," Ashebir whispered.

Mesfin pushed the plate closer to Ashebir. "Eat, eat," he said. "But small mouthfuls and chew slowly or your stomach will hurt."

Zewdie had always said that. "Do you know where they took my mother?" he asked. "I want to see her. To see the place."

"Listen, Ashebir. There is a place where they bury all the dead. It is behind the hill, on the other side of the camp. Too many die every day. It is impossible to do one burial at a time."

"Do they mourn? Like we do in the village?" Ashebir felt his lip tremble.

"A priest is always there with his large silver cross, incense and prayers. They will have buried her there. God rest her soul." Mesfin put his hand on Ashebir's shoulder. "I am really sorry."

Ashebir nodded.

"Take it easy," Mesfin said. "Try and eat a little. It is good for you."

Ashebir broke off a piece of injera and dipped it into the sherro sauce. He turned it round in his mouth slowly before chewing. He smiled. "It is too good," he said.

Mesfin laughed. "That's it, eat," he said, and put more injera on Ashebir's side of the plate.

Ashebir took another mouthful and another until his body began to feel heavy and his eyes began to close. He needed to sleep but he was afraid of the cold. That he might die in that cold.

"We will find you a corner in one of the rooms for the night." Mesfin said. "Let's go." He pulled a large bunch of keys from his pocket. They went out, padlocking the door behind them.

He followed Mesfin, carrying his ox-skin. He picked his way in and out of the families sitting and lying along the wide veranda.

"Mesfin, Mesfin, give me a blanket for my child," an old man begged, reaching up to hold Mesfin's arm.

Ashebir heard Mesfin's gentle voice, "Not tonight Baba, tomorrow, OK?"

More men came. "Hello Mesfin, how are you? God bless and keep us, we are fine but it is cold. Be Egziyabher, give us a blanket?"

The men pushed past Ashebir and grabbed at Mesfin.

Ashebir's heart beat faster.

Mesfin stopped. "Not tonight, friends," he said, "tomorrow."

The men continued to push and pull.

Ashebir stood with his back against the wall, trying to shrink away.

"We will hand out clothes and blankets when Daniel is here

tomorrow," Mesfin said. "Now go back to your families. Good night and God bless and keep us all."

Ashebir was relieved when the men gave up and slowly moved away into the darkness, their shoulders drooping. He felt sorry. Skinny men from the countryside with strong jaws and scrawny necks like vultures.

Ashebir followed Mesfin, looking at the women sitting kutch-kutch round their small fires in the compound, their children curled up under rags in the open. The rooms along the veranda were full. In some, a kerosene lamp hissed loudly, lighting parts of faces through the open doors. He could hear the grown-ups, talking softly inside.

People greeted Mesfin, "Tenasteling, Mesfin, how are you?"

Some spoke Amharic like Ashebir, but most sounded like the Oromos from around Ataye and Senbate market.

Mesfin disappeared into a room, "Tenasteling, yigirta," he said quietly, picking his way through sleeping bodies. "God bless you."

The air was thick with the smell of sickness. Ashebir covered his mouth and nose with his blanket, trying to ignore the nervous feeling in his stomach. At least it was warmer inside. He just wanted to lie down and sleep.

"Here Ashebir, you can sleep here," Mesfin said, pointing to a corner of the room. "I will see you in the morning, ishi? If you need anything, ask these people. Don't be afraid. They are good people." He turned to a young woman who was feeding her baby, "You are all from the same village near Ifat na Timooga, isn't it?"

"Yes," she said softly. "That's our home, and now we are under your roof, Egziyabher yibarkih."

"Good people," Mesfin said again quietly.

Ashebir put his ox-skin on the floor.

"Good night, Ashebir, God bless you."

"Good night," Ashebir whispered. "Egziyabheresteling."

He lay on his ox-skin, covered himself with his gabi and new blanket, curled up tight and closed his eyes. He saw Zewdie standing by their gate in the village, talking and laughing with her friends.

39

November 1984, Addis Ababa

Some of the RAF were billeted at the Livestock Research Institute. They had arrived with the first three Hercules C130s at the beginning of the month. Maggie Thatcher's 'Operation BUSHEL'. They did four or five sorties a day over the northern highlands. Goodness knows what the villagers made of those bulbous, low-flying aircraft. They must be incredibly loud. Instead of bombs, fat bags of grain fell out of the skies. Merciful Lord, finally some relief. But Maggie Thatcher doing good? Izzie wondered. It was incredible. What was her ulterior motive? This was the Prime Minister who had refused to take out sanctions against apartheid South Africa, who was a good friend of Pinochet, who set police on horseback against her own mining community in Rotherham.

It was Sunday and another endlessly sunny day, skies blue as ever. Fabulous if the need for rain were not so desperate. Izzie was just arriving to join Susan and Leila for a barbeque at the Livestock Research Institute Club. She had to give it to them. The expat community had got into gear with parties and barbeques to keep the lads from home happy. Ingo wouldn't be there. He was off again on one of his research missions. That was a disappointment, took the spark out of things. He was funny, unpredictable and outspoken. She liked the tension, the joking, his smile. Especially when he grinned at her. She shook her head and smiled as she switched off the cassette player. She had just blasted the rambling pastures and scrubland on the outskirts of Addis with Elton John's 'Nikita', singing her heart out. She pushed the car door shut with its familiar clunk.

As she walked towards the clubhouse, shrieks and splashes echoed from the pool, and she caught the warm, tempting smell of charcoal-grilled chicken legs, mutton and beef wafting across from the barbeque. Her mouth watered. The incongruities and contradictions of their lives in Addis constantly accompanied her. The buffet inside would be piled high with different salads and rice dishes to go with the barbequed meat. There would be plates and bowls of injera and wot, breads and Shola cheese, fruits and deserts. The LRI club excelled in its Sunday lunches, and especially now in honour of the RAF 'boys'.

She spotted Susan with a small group of them. In fact she had already heard Susan's laugh, obviously enjoying herself, and maybe the attention she undoubtedly drew. She was lovely. And looked relaxed in a faded pink t-shirt over pale blue jeans, a bottle of cold beer in her hand. "Hey, Izzie!" she called. "Over here." It was almost as if she was the hostess at a garden party.

Izzie laughed and waved, "Coming."

She liked the lads from England. Their raw London, Yorkshire, and Humberside accents reminded her of home. They referred to her and Susan and the other Brits as, 'You lot out 'ere!' and were full of enthusiasm for their mission.

"Sometimes we fly fifteen feet above the ground," one was saying as she came up to them. He skimmed his hand like a bird over water, his round cheeks bright red from too much sun and beer.

"The landscape is unbeleeeevable," another said. "You climb up over rugged mountains and reach these huge 'scarpments. We do four passes, dropping one pallet each time." He was a small, tightly built man they nicknamed Scud. Scud had a strong Cockney accent and took her straight back to Hackney. He turned when he saw her, "You alright, luv?"

"You remind me of hot chestnuts," Izzie said, putting out a hand automatically to greet them all and leant forward to give Susan a kiss on both cheeks.

"Cor! Scud mate, I think you just got a come-on there."

"Nah," Scud said. "Anyhow the Mrs wouldn't take kindly," he winked at Izzie. "No offence, luv."

Izzie blushed. These men certainly created an atmosphere.

"'ere you go luv," the one with the bright red cheeks said, handing her a beer.

"Oh cool, thanks," Izzie said, chinking the bottle against his and drinking down the first welcome mouthfuls of ice cold beer. "That's better."

She stood with them, listening, fascinated. Finally, huge quantities of grain were reaching people. Wondwossen at the Relief Counsel must be pleased, even if the Derg were apparently indignant, to say the least. Western forces on communist soil. It was tantamount to an invasion.

"Am sure we can take you girls up," the one called Andy said. He was tall and fit. Gym, basketball, squash written all over him. And unlike his red-faced colleague, his skin tanned evenly. A lucky, dark haired brown-eyed type. He'd obviously taken a fancy to Susan, the way he kept looking at her.

"That would be amazing," Susan said. "Right, Izzie?"

"Wow, yeah, we'd love that," Izzie said. She trod on Susan's foot.

Susan looked at her, her eyes laughing and bubbly.

"You know what, some of the bags burst open on the last drop," Scud said, his eyes tearing up. "We're really trying to get it right."

"Hey Scud," Andy clapped a hand on his back. "Easy goes."

"You know what gets me?" he went on. "People pick up every grain, every single grain, off the ground. You can see they're bloody starving." Scud wiped his nose on the back of his hand and took a few slugs of beer, his Adam's apple going up and down furiously.

Izzie looked at him. "You're doing a great job," she said. "Really. It will be such a relief to those people." Behind her there was another shriek and a splash as someone plunged into the pool.

"How long do you think you'll stay?" Susan said.

"As long as it takes, far as we know," Andy said. "And honest, I mean it, you girls should come up."

The lad with the red cheeks said, "You know what, I don't mind sayin' it. I'm really ravenous. Let's get us some of that grub, eh?"

**

The next morning she sat down behind her desk, letting out a long sigh. "The Boogie's been arrested again," she said.

Gezahegn came in behind her, murmured something and closed the door. He was holding a sheaf of papers.

"Is that, by any chance in heaven, my contract?" Izzie said, her mood lifting immediately. Her current contract ran out in two weeks time. The job hunt was not going too well, and in her heart of hearts she wanted to stay put, right where she was.

Simaynesh looked up from her desk by the window on the other side of the room. She was wearing a bright yellow jumper, no make-up, her Afro a halo round her head. She looked stunning. "Mindin neouw?" she said. "What happened this time?" She leant back and pushed the buzzer on the wall. "Did you hear that, Gezahegn? Her car has been detained again."

Gezahegn shook his head. "Where is it? Kebele Haya Hullet?" He sat down with a grunt opposite Izzie's desk and lit a cigarette. "Yes, they might be the papers you are waiting for. It's still a draft, I'm afraid to say. But we'll get it, don't worry."

"Hey, really?" Izzie clapped. "That's fantastic! Do I need to do anything?"

"We'll talk about that. But first, what happened to the car this time?" Gezahegn said. "Where is it?"

"I was driving back from friends on the Asmara road," Izzie said.

"Here we go," Gezahegn shook his head as if in despair.

"From seeing your new gwadenya?[89]" Simaynesh winked at Gezahegn.

"No, actually, he's in Mali, sadly." Izzie resisted the urge to stick her tongue out.

The door opened. Desta, slight, dressed in black, stood in the doorway, her metal tray in hand.

"Three tekur macchiato," Gezahegn said, leaning forward to tap the ash off his cigarette into Izzie's ashtray. He raised his eyebrows at Izzie and Simaynesh for confirmation.

They nodded simultaneously.

Desta smiled and left, shutting the door quietly behind her.

"She's so timid," Izzie said. "She always looks so sad."

"Of course," Simaynesh said. "To her we are tillik sou-woch."

"Even after the revolution?" Izzie said. "Things should change surely. No more 'big people' and 'little people'?"

"Some things never change," Gezahegn said and coughed.

"He is very traditional," Simaynesh said, pointing her chin towards Gezahegn. "I don't know what kind of revolution would make him change." She laughed. She enjoyed teasing him. Not many people would dare.

"All is well," Gezahegn said, clearing his throat and sighing. "Things have moved on. We have established the Workers Party and numerous committees. Comrade Adugna has the job he wanted, and we only have to tolerate political meetings once a month now."

"It's not great though. It's not the same working for him," Izzie said.

"Ishi, enough of that," Gezahegn said, stubbing out his cigarette. "We need to talk about the Tibila proposal, Izzie. But first the car."

---

[89] Friend.

He sat back, crossed his legs, folded his arms across his chest and looked at her, ready for the story.

"Yes, Tibila. I've nearly finished the proposal for the grinding mill at Tesfa Hiwot farm." She turned the black knob on her typewriter back and forth, so the last page of the report went up and down in front of her. It was as she had left it, Saturday lunchtime. "There are some things I need to ask you."

"The car," Simaynesh said.

"As I said, I was driving back from the Livestock Research Institute," she looked at Simaynesh. "They'd put on a barbeque for the RAF guys. Some friends invited me along. You know Susan and Leila. Anyway, it was getting dark. Well, not completely, but the street lights were on along the British Embassy Road. Basically the headlights only work on dim. Actually they start off bright enough and get dimmer and dimmer as you drive along."

She heard Gezahegn suck his teeth, and the beginnings of Simaynesh's laughter, a soft low-pitched giggle.

"There's something wrong with the battery, or the connection, I don't know. I thought I would just about make it home. In fact I was nearly there." She looked at Gezahegn in silent appeal, and shrugged her shoulders. "So they stopped me. Two police. I was just coming up to the Arat Kilo roundabout. They stepped out and waved me down."

Simaynesh, her head cupped in her hand, was looking sideways at Izzie. She was grinning, her eyes laughing. "Anchee."

"My heart sank. They were the same two as last time." Izzie play-acted the scene. She made as if to flip up the half window of the 2CV, and peered out and up.

"'Tenasteling,' I said, smiling, in the hopes they would wave me on. 'Anchee nesh, enday?[90]' one of them said."

Simaynesh's laughter burst out. "They recognised you, of course."

Gezahegn was shaking his head and smiling despite himself.

"'Be enateh,[91] let me go home,' I said, still peering out of the window at them. I didn't want to get out of the car. I thought that would be the end of it if I did."

Simaynesh let out a whine like she might cry, clutching her sides.

Izzie tried to stifle a laugh.

The door opened with a waft of coffee. Desta placed a glass in front of

---

[90] Is that you again?

[91] In your mother's name.

each of them. She must have heard them laughing from outside and was smiling shyly. They thanked her and she left, shutting the door quietly behind her.

"She must think we're crazy," Izzie said.

"You are," Gezahegn said. "Anchee, mindin nesh?[92]" He tutted and sighed.

Izzie knew he would scold her in the end.

"Ishi," Simaynesh said. "Then what?"

"They asked me to get out of the car. Oh no! I thought. I kind of stood in the door, half in and half out. One of them pointed at the lights and said something. The other got a pad out and started filling a form. 'Ebakachew,[93] let me go home? It's just over there,' I said. I pointed in the direction of the flats on the other side of the roundabout. 'I just want to get home,' I said again. 'Yes, we want to go home too,' the one filling the form said. 'But you are keeping us busy. Aydellem enday?' I could see he wanted to laugh but was trying to stay serious."

"Wey!" Simaynesh was holding her stomach for laughing.

Gezahegn was chuckling.

Izzie couldn't help laughing as she continued the story. Once Simaynesh got going it was hard not to laugh with her.

"By now," she went on, "people heading home along the roadside, started to gather around. They even stood in the road, holding up the traffic. I looked around at them and shouted out, 'Mindin neouw ennante? Yehey theatre aydellem![94]'"

Simaynesh was laughing so loud by now, Izzie thought there would be an incident in the office.

"The policeman holding the form looked at me and said, 'Anchee theatre nesh.' He told me to get back into the car. 'You know the place,' he said, and, would you believe it? They got into the car too. One in the front and one in the back."

"Wey guud," Simaynesh breathed out, holding her stomach.

"'Ishi,' I said. I got in and started the car. What could I do? We had a chat on the way. They asked how I was, how's work, whether I like eating injera, you know. That kind of thing."

Simaynesh was crying with laughter.

"I think basically, they wanted a lift back to the station."

---

[92] Who on earth are you?

[93] Please.

[94] What is it, all of you? This isn't a theatre performance!

"I am sure they did," Simaynesh said, wiping her eyes with a hanky.

The car had only been impounded two weeks earlier. She had gone across a red light that time. Very slowly. It was night time, not a soul around, no cars, she'd just crept across the lights to get home, and they'd appeared out of the dark and stopped her.

"So where is the car now?" Gezahegn said, looking at Simaynesh and chuckling despite himself.

"At Police Tabia Haya Hullet, like you said. And they took my driving licence."

Gezahegn sat up. "What?" he said, suddenly serious. "Chinklat yelleshim enday? Are you completely brainless?"

Simaynesh let out a whoop. "Wey! Stop it now. I can't breathe."

"Ishi, I know you're angry with me, Gezahegn," Izzie said, trying to suppress her laughter. "Why not drink your coffee, it's going cold." She got a cigarette out and offered one to him. A small peace offering. All the while laughter bubbling up in her chest.

He leant forward to take his coffee off her desk, waving a 'no thanks' to the cigarette.

"We have to go straight to the Police Tabia and get your driving licence," he said. "They are not allowed to hold it. It's one of your I.D.s. What if they lose it?"

"Sorry, Gezahegn," Izzie said. "You're right. I wasn't thinking."

"That's what I said. Chinklat yelleshim. Let's have our coffee and go."

"What about the Tibila proposal?"

"We can talk about it on the way, isn't it?" Gezahegn said. "You said you are nearly done. Right?"

"Right," she said. "And my contract?"

"We'll talk about that too. Innihid. Come on."

**

"I think Mengistu is nervous," Ato Embaye said, slurping at the hot tea Desta had just brought him. He had stirred it round and round to dissolve the three heaped spoons of sugar he had dropped in from the stainless steel bowl on Desta's tray. "All these farenj in town."

"Even I can't believe it," Izzie said. "And I am sure it's just the beginning. Oxfam, SCF, World Vision, UNICEF, who else? The World Food Programme. They are all sending people and planning to send more."

"So many white Toyotas," Simaynesh said, somewhat sceptically.

"Uncomfortable for a Soviet satellite," Ato Embaye said. "All you Westerners." He smiled at Izzie. "Present company excepted. You are almost an Habesha, Izzie."

"Why thank you, Ato Embaye," Izzie said, feeling chuffed. "So what are the Soviets doing about the famine?"

"They've sent in transporters, Antonovs, trucks, helicopters," Ato Embaye said.

"At least people are getting food now," Izzie said. "You must think that's good, Simiye?"

"Of course it is. We are just not particularly enjoying the farenj take-over, that's all. They are like that British expert of ours, high salaries, walking around making suggestions, eating in Castelli's, and talking as if they know everything."

"I was in Castelli's with Ingo the other night," Izzie said, feeling a little guilty. "There was a film crew there from London. They gave me a tin of baked beans. Army rations they'd been given in case they get belly-ache."

"So you are one of them," Simaynesh said. "I knew it." She narrowed her eyes at Izzie.

"Yes, I guess I am," she said. "Sometimes." The food was delicious.

"Only now, after those BBC reports and the international outcry..." Ato Embaye said. "At least now something is being done about it. Even in Addis people are hungry, you know?"

"Everyone gets subsidised food from the Kebele shops," Simaynesh said. "They try to keep us city people satisfied. But you're right. There has even been a shortage in the city now."

"Look at the queues for bread," Izzie said. She looked at Ato Embaye. He was surely one of the city's hungry. His long skinny wrists stuck out from his oversize jacket sleeves. He had ten children. How did he feed them and himself on that tiny salary?

"So it sounds like you're listening to your radio every night, Ato Embaye?" Simaynesh smiled at him.

"Of course," Ato Embaye said. "They talked about one film called 'Bitter Harvest'. What does that mean, Izzie? There was, 'No Harvest'."

"That film raised eight million pounds," Izzie said.

"Izzie, you said you're going to Debre Berhan?" Simaynesh said.

"Yes I might go at the weekend with Ingo and Leila. They are taking blankets and milk powder. Maybe I can raise some money in my parents' village."

"I don't understand you farenj. All this running about trying to solve other people's problems."

"I can't solve anything, Simiye," Izzie said, feeling a shot of anger and hurt. "But I am here and I want to do something. I feel a bit useless." She looked at Simaynesh. "You think I shouldn't do anything? We shouldn't?" Simaynesh had a point. What was she doing here anyway? Fate had brought her. And now she wanted to be here more than anywhere else.

"Aysosh," Simaynesh said. "You're not useless Izzie. And we want you here."

The door opened and Gezahegn came in.

"Izzie thinks she's useless unless she goes to feed the hungry," Simaynesh said.

"I've got your new contract here, Izzie. You don't want it? You got a job with World Vision now? Or maybe with the British RAF? You going to be a pilot?"

"Ha, Ha," Izzie said. "Of course not."

"So it's done? That's amazing," Simaynesh grinned. "When does it start?"

"After Christmas, and runs for six months, funding all approved," Gezahegn said.

"Oh my goodness," Izzie leant her chair back against the wall behind her, like she used to at school. "Let me take that in. Another six months. That's so brilliant I could cry. Thank you, thank you, Gezahegn." Izzie said, resisting the temptation to jump up and hug him.

40

The back of the station wagon, and the seat next to her were stuffed to the gunnels with blankets and large tins of Cerelac. She had squeezed in first and then Ingo beside her. She leant on his leg, cupping her hand round his knee and felt his arm across the back of the seat behind her. They had been on the road for at least an hour.

"You Ok?" he said.

"Yes. It feels a bit strange. Not sure what to expect," she said and then laughed. "And I've been sitting on half a butt all the way. It's numb."

He whispered in her ear. She laughed again.

Leila was driving, "What's going on, you two?"

Peter was in front with his rucksack between his knees. He had worked with the others at the Institute and then spent six months writing project proposals for Swedish SCF. He was an agronomist, but was more of a pontificating academic. Perhaps prompted by his own Scottish highlands heritage, he was deeply concerned and interested in the lives of the highland farmers, their familial and social systems. "We've left it a bit late, haven't we?" he said, his soft accent adding credence to his concern.

"It's OK, Peter. Relax," Leila said. "We're nearly there. I know this road like the back of my hand."

"You let the guesthouse know we're coming?" Ingo said, leaning forward over the seat.

"Yes, yes, why so nervous guys. It's all set up."

"Will we go straight to the camp?" Izzie said. "Or maybe a loo-stop first? I need a wazz."

"We'll dump our stuff at the guesthouse, let Solomon, the cook, know we are here, and then go on to the camp," Leila said. "Let me fill you in a bit. The place where the camp is was originally built as a shelter home for the 'dekuman' – the destitute, elderly and disabled, by one of the Princes in Haile Selassie's time."

"Dekuman dirigit," Izzie whispered. "We work with the dekuman; all the poorest people at the bottom of the pile. Funny we haven't made use of this place."

"He built a few, all to the same simple design, yeah? This one has been empty for some time. So when hundreds of people came into town looking for food, and settled along the roadside, the town administration decided to open up this place as a camp. It took some time to organise everything as they needed the Relief Council to be involved."

"Then you started fund raising," Izzie said. She looked at Ingo, smiled, and gave him a peck on the cheek.

"Well, with our research station right here, we had to do something," Ingo said. "There's a neighbouring Kebele we work with, right Leila?"

"Yes, just near the camp, one of the wealthier, better organized ones as it happens. They've got a grinding mill and bakery. So the Relief Council grain goes to the mill for grinding and then the flour goes to the bakery. They make literally thousands of bread rolls every day. Their Women's and Youth Associations are really active. That's where the camp recruits its volunteers. They distribute flour, milk and egg powder to the women who have cooking utensils, so they can make their own pancakes.

"Ki'ta bread," Izzie said.

"How many people are at the camp?" Peter said.

"About two to three thousand at the moment, with fifty to a hundred arriving each day."

"What about the people being re-settled from the north?" Ingo said.

"Yes, several thousand arrive some days, I've heard. Guys I don't know everything. I've only been once or twice. Just to deliver stuff, or to give them petty cash."

"Imagine, one bread roll to last you the whole journey from the highlands all the way down to some far off place in the south," Peter said. "Inconceivable, eh?"

With its broad brush-strokes of soft pale yellows, blues and oranges, the sky ahead of them gave the impression that the world was at peace. That there would be another bright day tomorrow. Nothing could be further from the truth.

On the outskirts of town, they turned down a rough narrow lane, lined by sisal and juniper. It was darkly overgrown.

"Here we are, the guesthouse," Leila said. "Let's not doo-lally. Just a quick turn-around?"

**

The track to the camp was rough and sandy white. It left the main road, passing under a half-moon archway. A revolutionary slogan in Amharic script was painted on it in large red letters. Soon they were bumping across a small stream, and a up an incline past a line of wispy eucalyptus on the other side. The sky was dramatic. The hazy blue above the watercolour wash starting to fill with stars. At the top of the hill was a gate. It was wide open, bordered by a flimsy, chicken-wire fence.

Leila stopped the car. She leaned out of the widow to talk to the zabanya. "Tenasteling," she said.

His rifle hung loosely over his shoulder. He smiled his greeting. "Tenasteling," he said, peering in through the windows.

"We've got blankets and milk in the back," she said. "They are still coming then?"

Small groups of people walked slowly past them in silence.

Izzie tingled with the frustration of being couped up in the back of the car. Not able to look out without bending and peering awkwardly. Doubt raced through her like dread. Was she here to observe other people's misery? Her curiosity getting the better of her?

"That's right," the zabanya said. "Every day. You will see." He sucked his teeth and muttered, "Egziyabher yawkal." His eyes rolled heavenwards.

A guard at the gates of hell. Izzie inched closer to Ingo if that was possible. "What are we doing here?" she whispered.

"You wanted to come. You wanted to see for yourself, to raise money at home, remember?"

"Right," she said. The village church came to mind. Sitting there in solid innocence amongst fallen autumn leaves. A chill November night. The sweet smell of bonfires in the air. The village women in their warm kitchens, aprons on, mixing dried and candied fruits, brown sugar and butter, brandy and nutmeg in large bowls. Christmas puddings for the elderly. They would give generously, if they were sure the money was going straight to the right place.

They drove on to the cusp of the hill.

"Let's get out," Izzie said. The angst was creeping up her throat. "I want to see."

Leila killed the engine. A strange silence hung over everything for a moment.

Izzie clambered out after Ingo. They stood overlooking a scene beyond their imagination. The wide valley below was teaming with people. Their murmur rose towards them. Six huge white marquees stood adjacent to a small compound, the Dekuman Leila had described. She counted at least thirty trucks and buses parked in rows, like toys. A soft blueish layer of woodsmoke hovered over the compound. The endlessly wide evening sky stretched to the hills on the other side. An other-worldly scene.

Country people continued to walk past them. Women and children passed, talking in quiet voices, carrying small bundles of firewood on their backs and heads.

"Tenasteling," Izzie whispered. Not expecting a reply.

Exhaustion was written in the slow tread of their feet, the bowed heads.

So I am here, she thought. I can reach out and touch the living, walking, famine. The tightness in her throat made it hard to swallow. Tears seemed pointless. Cynical even. They hadn't come here to cry.

Peter stood a few feet away in his slightly oversized jeans, with his wispy red-blonde hair and beard. She thought of him as one of those eccentric Brits in Africa. He was standing with one hand on his hip, the other over his mouth. He turned around. Eyes staring through dark-rimmed glasses. "Dante's Inferno," he said. His gentle Scottish lilt taking the sting out of his words. He was a reader of books she never touched. A proud descendant of Fergus the Great, he always boasted. No one knew whether to laugh or to believe him. He said many things.

"Let's get going," Leila said. "It will be dark in no time."

They drove slowly down the hillside, jolting and lurching along the dirt track, into the wide valley below. The pastures had lost their grace, become barren of trees, and been transformed into a vast open toilet. Those who needed firewood must have to walk much further afield. Another demand on the remaining fragments of strength.

Izzie leant over Ingo to peer out of the window. She felt the small comfort of his hand on her back. He was looking out too. They were all silent.

Leila circled the large marquees and came to a halt on the edge of the compound where the single-storey buildings created an open square.

This space under open skies was full of families squatting around small fires. Dark shapes in the dusk, made eerie by the grey-blue woodsmoke which hung in the chill. As soon as the car stopped they were surrounded.

"Farenj, farenj."

The flats of hands of all sizes banged against the windows, the doors and the bonnet. They could barely open the doors for the throng.

"Farenj, farenj."

Izzie suddenly felt claustrophobic. "Come on, let's get out," she said, wriggling against Ingo.

"OK, OK," he said, opening the door, his long legs seeking out room to put a foot down among the many feet. He stood, hands dug deep in his pockets, looking. His shoulders up round his ears.

"Sorry," she said. She stood behind him and put her hands on his back. "That was rude." She reached up and squeezed his shoulders briefly.

"It's OK," he said, turning round, tears in his eyes.

"Take a deep breath," she said.

Leila was already talking to a man with a friendly face. He wore a black cap and a dark green bomber jacket, zipped up to his neck. He was a good looking man with a quiet confident air.

Izzie and Ingo stepped forward to shake hands. The man's was firm and warm.

"Tenasteling," Izzie said. "Endate nachew? Dehenanachew?" Though what a silly question. They were obviously desperate here. How are you, indeed.

"Tenasteling," he said, smiling broadly. "You speak Amharic?"

"Tinnish, tinnish," she said. "Just a little."

"Not just a little. She actually speaks very well," Leila said. "Guys, this is Mesfin. He manages the camp. He's from the Relief Counsel. Mesfin, this is Izzie, Ingo and Peter. Ingo has raised a lot of money and wanted to come and see. Maybe he can raise some more?" She shrugged her shoulders and smiled at Ingo.

"Welcome," Mesfin said. "And thank you. We are grateful for your help, really." He seemed genuine.

"The car is full of blankets and tins of milk powder," Leila said. "What do you want us to do with them?"

"We can put them in the store for now," Mesfin said, pointing up towards the end of the veranda.

"It's freezing," Izzie said, buttoning up her khaki jacket. She shivered. It was never this cold in Addis. She looked at the people around her. A small child lay curled on the ground next to her mother, a thin mud-brown rag tucked over her. A boy, maybe her brother, stood beside her, watching them with large eyes. He wore a thin t-shirt and his shorts, held together round his waist with a piece of string, billowed round his stick-skinny legs. His head had been shaved except for a small knot on his crown. He chewed his finger. "Can't we give these people the blankets? They look so cold. This boy." She couldn't imagine. They were going to sleep out here in t-shirt and shorts?

"It's difficult," Mesfin said. "They will rush and grab, especially the men. And it's getting dark now. You can't control anything."

"We should maybe give it a go, no?" Peter said, stepping forward. He pointed behind them. "Over there, out in the open, people don't even have the shelter of this compound. We could distribute them over there?"

"I know. I'm sorry, really," Mesfin said. He sucked his teeth. "Let's just put everything in the store for now. I will sort it tomorrow."

"Come on guys, lets get the tins into the store at least and then we can see," Leila said.

They opened up the car. There was a flurry of movement. "Farenj, farenj."

Izzie felt hard fingers gripping and pulling at her. "Please," she said, peeling their grasp off. She resisted the urge to tell them to, 'go away', 'zorbellu!' She tried to smile as she walked firmly to the back of the car and took tins of Cerelac from Leila. "Give me one more," she said. "Pile it on top."

Peter stood, arms out wide beside the open boot, holding people back. It was like a small tidal wave.

Mesfin told the people to stand back, that nothing would be handed out tonight. "Please," he said. He lead the way up the steps to the veranda and the storeroom. He took a bunch of keys from his pocket and undid the large metal padlock.

Families sat, huddled up, along the veranda from where doors opened into rooms. Izzie could see the shapes of people moving around inside. There was a strong, thick odour; unwashed bodies and clothes, urine and more. Eyes watched her from finely chiselled, weather-worn faces. Hard-working highland people, uprooted, in shock. In the midst of disaster. And, most likely, she thought, avoidable. Where was their Egziyabher now? She thought of her Dad saying, "I think God needs a little help." He certainly needed some help here.

The door to the storeroom grated loudly across the rough concrete as Mesfin opened it. It hung badly on its hinges. A group of men appeared with complaining voices, sucking their teeth, their imploring becoming more insistent, more physical. Mesfin spoke to them, explaining and apologising. They were not convinced.

"What are they saying, Izzie?" Ingo said.

"They want him to give them clothes and blankets. They say they are freezing, that they will die of cold in the night. He is telling them tomorrow, when Daniel is here. I guess he works with him."

Something about Mesfin impressed her. He was quietly polite towards these people. He obviously cared. But she couldn't understand why he couldn't give them the blankets they so desperately needed.

"The store is full," Leila said, her voice cutting through all the others. "Mesfin, it's full of stuff. Why? All these bags of clothes, and the blankets I bought last time. Why? What's going on?"

Mesfin stood back. "I know," he said. "But there are just two of us."

"The store should be empty. Always empty," Leila said.

"I know," Mesfin said, "You are right. It's a problem."

"Leila," Izzie said, stepping forward. She wanted Leila to calm down. She was right but they had to hear him out.

"She's right, Izzie," Ingo said. "We can't justify raising money and bringing stuff if its not getting to the people. I can't anyway."

Mesfin moved forward and locked the door once the tins of Cerelac had been placed inside. "Let's go to my office," he said.

"No, sorry Mesfin," Leila said. "I want us to at least give out the blankets we brought tonight. Then we'll come to your office."

She spoke with authority. The donor. But Mesfin was the one in charge here. Izzie was torn. She did not want to defy Mesfin but Leila was right. It was freezing. They had to give out the blankets.

"It's really cold," Izzie said. "We can't just bring blankets and put them in the store. Right?"

"Ishi, ishi, I understand," he said. "Go ahead, try. You'll see."

Peter was already heading for the car. "Let's go," he said. "Let's do it. Come on Leila. You got the keys?"

Izzie followed the others to the car.

Peter was pulling blankets out of the back. He piled them up onto Ingo's and Izzie's outstretched arms.

"Come on, Izzie," Ingo said. "Let's go."

"Head over there where they are furthest from the shelter," Peter said.

Within seconds they were engulfed.

Women's voices cried out begging, "Be Egziyabher irridegne."

"Farenj."

"Ebakachew."

Sharp fingers clutched at Izzie. Bodies crammed, pushed and shoved against each other in their desperation to get closer, buffeting her. Their faces hopelessly contorted. They cried out, and groaned. The air was heavy with the smell of their long-worn clothes, their thick warm breath. It was all Izzie could do to keep her feet on the ground as wiry men snatched the blankets and disappeared into the dark.

"Hey," she found herself shouting. "Zorbellu, go away. Stop it." Suddenly outraged at the people she had come to help. The people she had been looking at with compassion moments before. What had she imagined? Handing a blanket out one at a time to the chosen few. Mothers taking them for their children with a look of warm gratitude on their faces?

The same was happening to Ingo, Peter and Leila. It was mayhem.

All the blankets disappeared from the car. Every last one. Vanished into the darkness. Heaven knows who got them. It was mostly men who grabbed them. Like Mesfin said.

"Yesus Kristos," Peter said. "A diabolical shambles."

"That was horrible," Izzie said. She felt shaken, pinched all over, grubby, mortified. She sat on the back seat of the car with the door open. She lit a cigarette, her hands shaking. "We should have listened to Mesfin." She could still feel the skinny, bony fingers grabbing at her, as if they had left imprints all over her body.

"Totally. Yes." Leila said, running her fingers through her dishevelled hair several times. "Give me one of those, Izzie?" She took a cigarette, lit it and inhaled deeply.

"Doesn't feel quite right to smoke here?" Ingo said. He looked ruffled.

Izzie took another drag, dropped the cigarette on the ground and twisted it under her boot. "True," she said. "Sorry." She looked up at the sky. A clear star-studded night. "I'm just thinking, I want to come and help them out. Just for a bit. My contract ends next week."

"You think you could?" Ingo said. "They need more hands. It's useless if we bring all this stuff and they can't hand it out. Such a tough job. And just two of them."

"I can come too," Peter said.

"Would you?" Izzie looked up at Peter, heartened, and at the same time wondering what it would be like to work with him.

"Sure I can. My contract has come to an end too. I was thinking of travelling, actually. But I can delay that."

"I'll supply the whiskey," Ingo said. "But not the cigarettes."

"Ha, ha," Izzie said, giving him a gentle kick.

"Let's talk to Mesfin. See what he thinks?" Leila said.

"I think we owe him an apology first," Peter said.

"Too right," Izzie said.

They went up the steps to Mesfin's office. He was standing at the door. He looked a bit sorry for them. "I tried to warn you," he said.

"Oh my God. That was awful," Leila said, her hand on her chest. "I am so sorry, Mesfin."

"Horrible," Izzie said. "We should have listened to you. Betam yigirta. Sorry really."

"Come on in." Mesfin went into his office. It suddenly looked warm and welcoming with the yellow glow of light from the one bulb hanging in the centre of the room.

"Oh, we interrupted your supper," Izzie said, seeing the plate with injera and sherro on the desk. "Sorry."

"It's OK," Mesfin took the plate to what looked like a makeshift kitchen corner at the back of the room, a table with a small gas stove, some glasses and plates on it. He came back, gesturing with his hands open, "So?" he said.

Ingo sat against the desk, hands in pockets, his blue eyes looking intensely at Mesfin. "We were thinking it's hopeless us bringing you stuff, if you can't hand it out. We were wondering what we could do."

"They basically overwhelmed us, snatched the blankets and vanished." Izzie rubbed her arms to smooth away the memory of pinching fingers.

"That's what happens," Mesfin said, smiling and shrugging his shoulders. He ran his hand across his mouth. "When Daniel and I have time, we get some of the volunteers from the local Youth Association and we try to give everything out in an orderly way."

"I was thinking, maybe I can come and help out?" Izzie said. "I mean, work out a system with you how to get stuff out to these people." She hesitated. "I can do anything you might need help with." She didn't know any better. It was overwhelming. She just wanted to come and do something useful. It would be a challenge. And she liked Mesfin. Wanted to help him if she could.

"That would be great," he said. "Of course."

"Peter has offered to come with Izzie," Leila said.

"Yes," Peter said. "I have a bit of time. I'd be happy to come too if that helps."

"Sure. You're both welcome," Mesfin said. He looked genuinely pleased with the idea. "When do you think you can start?"

"My contract ends next week. I can come then," Izzie said. She was starting to feel excited.

"You'll have to get permits, Izzie," Ingo said. "Maybe talk to your NGO, see if they can help at all."

"We can work all that out," Mesfin said. "I know the people at the city administration. That will be fine. You should definitely come."

"You know what, Ingo, you're right. I'm sure the international NGO that funds me would be interested in funding specific things for the camp. I'm sure of that," Izzie said, altogether warming to the idea. "While we are here, we can put together a list of things, Mesfin. Write up a brief funding proposal. Peter and I could do that."

"Great," Mesfin said, looking at Izzie and smiling.

Izzie looked at Leila. "What do you think? Could we stay at the LRI guest house?"

"I think everything is possible," Leila said. "Looks like we have a plan."

"We should let you get some shut-eye, Mesfin," Peter said. He reached out to shake hands.

"We could stop by in the morning, Mesfin, just to finalise things?" Leila said.

"Sure. And you can meet Daniel then too."

They all headed for the door. As Leila opened it, a shaft of pale yellow light fell across the veranda illuminating the people lying and huddled there. They went out into the cold from the relative warmth and normality of Mesfin's office with its small kitchen.

"Dehenader," Izzie said, turning back to shake Mesfin's hand. "Good night."

"Dehenaderi, Izzie," he said. "See you tomorrow."

The compound below sat in misty darkness, small fires glowing and crackling like a cigarette end, when the smoker takes a drag. Izzie could hear murmuring voices beneath the curtain of woodsmoke. As they went down the steps to the car, faces turned for a moment. She sighed as she climbed into the car next to Ingo, and shut the door. They could open and close doors on the nightmare. The people out there could not.

Leila turned the key and drove slowly away.

None of them said a word.

*

Mesfin had closed the door. One bulb hung from the ceiling surrounded by moths. It gave a dull light. They were sitting together by Mesfin's desk, sharing supper. Ashebir's feet did not touch the floor. He wriggled on the hard seat.

"Look at you with your melata," Mesfin laughed, running his hand over Ashebir's smooth head.

Belaynesh had shaved his hair and that of other children in the camp. They all had lice and scabies, she said, tutting as she held them still between her knees to do the job. "God knows you can do without lice feeding on you," she had said, chuckling like an auntie, dropping clumps of soapsuds and hair on the ground beside her. When it was his turn, he had lifted his face to the sun and closed his eyes. Zewdie had always talked and laughed as she shaved his head. He imagined the chickens whirring and scratching, rrr-kuk-kuk-rrrr, around them in the compound and the rhythmical sound of Yishaereg's mother grinding sorghum on the other side of the fence. "That's you done," Belaynesh had said, bringing him crashing back to reality with a sharp pat on his shoulder. "Next one, please." A line of children sat on the ground in front of her, waiting their turn.

Ashebir looked at Mesfin and pulled up the hood of the red coat Belaynesh had given him from the store, smiling. He liked Mesfin's attention. But the comforting feeling was quickly shadowed by the Worry. What would happen if Mesfin left? Who would look after him? What would become of him? Where would he go?

"Is this your home, Mesfin?" he said.

"No, it's not, Ashebir. My family is in Addis," Mesfin said. "I normally work in an office there. I was sent here to look after the camp."

"I was in Addis once," Ashebir said. "With my mother and grandmother." He turned his head away and coughed.

"Is that so?" Mesfin said, then sucked his teeth. "That cough isn't getting any better." He put more injera on Ashebir's side of the dish.

Ashebir hadn't told Mesfin that after two nights in the room full of the good people of Yifat na Timooga, he had gone outside to sleep. They had been kind to him but the phlegm on the floor, the heavy smells of vomit and shint, the thick coughing, was even worse for him to suffer than the cold. He had been taking his ox-skin and blanket outside at night to sleep on the bare earth. He almost felt closer to Zewdie there. But it froze his bones and his cough was getting worse. He bowed his head, giving thanks for the food. "I remember the bus station and the lights. So many lights," he said. "Do you have children, Mesfin?"

"I have a baby boy. I hope he grows strong and brave like you, Ashebir."

"I can teach him how to throw a sling, how to catch fish in the river," Ashebir said, his heart feeling lighter at the thought of it.

Mesfin laughed. "That I am sure you can. I don't think many boys in Addis know how to do that."

"I can show them all then," Ashebir said and laughed. The sound of laughter rose up to meet him from days spent with Mohamed Abdu and Ali in the pastures and by the river. Tears filled his eyes. "How long have I been here, Mesfin?"

"Maybe a week, yeney lij," Mesfin put a hand on his shoulder. "It's good to hear you laugh. But we have to do something about your cough. We will ask the doctor tomorrow."

The sun had gone down leaving the sky washed with colour. This time of day he would be coming home from the pastures with the animals. He closed his eyes not knowing what to think. Would Mesfin take him to Addis? Would he stay here? Before, before all this happened, he knew a whole village. Now, he knew no one. Just Mesfin and Belaynesh. Would he stay here, sleeping on the cold earth where Zewdie was buried? This was the Worry.

There was a sudden commotion outside the door.

"Mesfin, Mesfin," voices called. "Farenj have come."

"Ishi, ishi," Mesfin said. "I'm coming." He got up, put his black cap on, zipped up his dark green jacket and went outside. "What is it?" He went down the steps.

Ashebir slipped off the chair, hugged his coat around himself and followed. Farenj meant blankets, food, clothes. He was curious to see them close up. He had seen them at Senbate market when he went with Zewdie. But only from a distance.

A large white car had pulled up on the edge of the compound. It was already surrounded by people talking and pushing each other to get anything that might be given out. They reminded him of bees around a honeycomb or flies swarming over a carcass. A farenj woman with black hair stood by the open car door, looking towards Mesfin's office. The evening was drawing in fast. It would be dark very soon. Ashebir shivered in anticipation of another night in the cold.

"Tenasteling," Mesfin called, making his way through the milling crowd. "Sorry," he said. "Let me through."

Ashebir stayed close behind him. He heard him speak farenj language with the woman. A tall man and another woman got out of the back of the car. The woman stood close behind the farenj man. He was surprised that she wore a zabanya jacket. They both had blue eyes. He had never seen blue eyes before. The tall farenj looked around with that sad look Ashebir had seen. The sad look for The Hungry. Another man came round the front. He looked funny with his thin hair and beard and large black glasses. He was skinny like the farmers from Wollo. They all shook hands with Mesfin, smiling and talking. The car was packed full of things inside.

People pushed against each other to get closer to the farenj and whatever they might have in the car. They called out for blankets, for warm clothes. "Help us?"

It was difficult to stay steady on his feet. He wondered at them pushing the farenj like this. He moved away not to get crushed.

Mesfin was pointing at the store. The farenj opened the back of the car and took out large tins of baby milk. They followed him up the steps to the store.

Ashebir knew the store. That was where the piles of blankets, sacks of clothes and woollen jumpers, the grain and tins of milk powder were kept. It was in that store that Belaynesh had found his red coat with the hood, and new shorts and t-shirt with farenj writing on it.

He followed Belaynesh and Mesfin every day. That way they would not forget him. And the Worry would be less. He was used to having jobs to do at home. So he asked them every day what he could do? He asked for food, "Do you have breakfast for me, Mesfin?" He stayed close, so they knew he was still there. That he was still alive.

The idea that they might forget him terrified him. What would happen to him? How would he eat. This Worry filled his head every day. Looking up into the heavens and saying 'Egziyabher yawkal', like the people from Yifat na Timooga was too risky for him. He knew he had to do something to make sure he stayed alive, to make sure someone knew he, Ashebir, was There.

He saw Mesfin get the keys out of his pocket, unlock the padlock and unhook the door. It scratched and grated open along the concrete floor. Mesfin was always saying he would 'fix that door'. The light went on. One bulb, hanging from the ceiling, glowed, sending a circle of light into the darkness outside. It reminded him of Zewdie's lantern hanging from the central pole in their home. She had been so proud of it.

The farenj took turns to peer inside the store. The woman with the black hair and shiny dark eyes spoke loudly. Mesfin took a step back. Ashebir could see his friend explaining something to her. But the farenj were not pleased. They were pointing at the store and then to the people outside. Mesfin shook his head and talked, his hands explaining. Ashebir felt sorry. They did not understand his friend. Mesfin went back into the store. The light went out. The door grated shut under his hand and he padlocked it up again.

The farenj went back to their car and opened up the back. They were immediately surrounded by people pushing and shoving around each other for a place. Ashebir watched as the farenj took piles of blankets out. Those thin grey ones, like his. More men and women appeared out of nowhere and moved quickly towards them. The farenj were engulfed. There was a short, frenzied, commotion, like fish in the Ataye river when they threw a piece of ki'ta bread in to draw them to the surface.

He could hear the farenj shouting out, 'Hey!' One after the other, people grabbed at the precious blankets. They snatched and moved off into the dark, until there were none left.

It was bitterly, painfully, cold at night. Every day people complained. They begged Mesfin and Daniel, they begged Belaynesh and the women from the Women's Association for shelter, for blankets, for gabis, for clothes. Every night people died in that cold.

Ashebir, his heart beating fast, looked to see where Mesfin had gone.

There he was, standing by his office door, his hands in his jacket pockets, watching. The farenj sat in their car, talking. The women smoked. Then they came up the steps towards Mesfin. He stepped aside and let them into the office. Ashebir thought of his unfinished meal on the desk and waited. He did not dare to go near. He saw the light through the crack under the door. There was talking. After a while the door opened. He stood back.

The farenj shook hands with Mesfin. They were all smiling.

The woman with the blue eyes and zabanya jacket turned back and said, "Dehenader,[95] Mesfin."

"Dehenaderi, Izzie," Mesfin replied.

Ashebir waited until the farenj had driven off before going to stand quietly beside Mesfin. He felt the man's hand on his head.

"Come on my friend. Let's finish our meal, shall we?"

---

[95] Good night.

41

November/December 1984, Debre Berhan Camp

Trucks and buses, so full of people they could barely sit, had arrived the evening before from Tigray and Wollo. Ashebir watched them coming in the twilight. The peoples' voices, the traditional clothes, their hairstyles, the leather slings carrying their babies, told the tale of their homelands deep in the highlands. A few women had thrown their anguish and frustration in shrill voices at Mesfin, or anyone they could find who was dressed in townspeople clothes. But most just stayed quietly in the buses and in the backs of the open trucks and had slept the night where they sat. Staring, hopeless. Tired despair.

Belaynesh and the other women had handed out small loaves of bread, talking as they went. Clicking tongues, sucking teeth, shaking their heads and trying to smile kindness. But there was no hot tea against the bitter cold.

Ashebir had slept inside that night, squeezed between sleeping forms curled under grey blankets and ghee-infused, weather-worn, cloth.

The wailing came streaming in through the door with the morning light, looking for somewhere to go. It woke him and wrapped itself around his own sadness and filled his eyes with tears. He sat up wiping his face with the blanket and sniffed. The air in the room was thick. His back and tummy ached. When he breathed in, he felt the sharp pain in his chest. Was his heart hungry too, he wondered. He longed for Zewdie. The comfort of her voice, the touch of her hand. He watched as the good women from Yifat na Timooga moved about in the room, tutting and sucking their teeth. They gently shook the sleeping bodies around them, gingerly lifting cloth and blanket, checking. Every night people died.

Surely someone would do something. How long would this go on for? The Worry seeped into his misery with unanswered questions. He closed his eyes and let his mother's voice from the forest by Gemoj come to him, 'This is our life, Ashebir. It is a hard life, but this is our life.' He looked down at his shins and touched the scars he had collected chopping wood with her.

It was strange to be where not one face was familiar. He would even be happy to see Mama Tsehai and her unkind daughter Wubit, who had shared the bus shelter with them in town. The wailing outside got under his skin. He felt the pain, felt so alone it hurt in his belly. He pulled his hood over his head, hugged the thin grey blanket around himself and rocked slowly back and forth.

"Ashebir, are you there?"

Ashebir looked up.

"Ashebir?"

He heard his name again.

A tall dark shape stood in the open door, the white sunlight streaming behind him. Shadows of The Hungry passed behind along the veranda outside. It was Dawit. He could tell by his thick curly hair, and from the way he stood, legs apart. He was from the neighbouring Kebele. He said he had two meals a day and a mother and four sisters at home. He felt lucky. So he came to help.

"Come," Dawit said. "There's someone looking for you."

Ashebir's heart turned. He pushed himself up. "For me?" he said. "Who?" It could not be Lakew. He went out into the light, shading his eyes.

Dawit put a hand on Ashebir's head. "You OK little man?" he said.

Ashebir smiled, feeling awkward.

"What are you doing hiding away all alone?" Dawit said. "Look, over there, there's a man looking for you. Do you know him?"

The morning light turned all figures into dark shadows. Ashebir followed Dawit's pointing finger, squinting. Then he saw the old red shawl Lakew always wore loosely wound round his head against the sun.

"Lakew," Ashebir called out. He ran down the steps. He had come. He had come and found him. "Egziyabher alle, thanks to God, thanks to God," Ashebir whispered as he ran.

Lakew, his face a broad smile, eyes sparkling with his own mischief and joy, came towards him. He trod carefully through the family groups crouched around their cold, black fires, waiting for the next rations.

"Ashebir, is that you?"

"Abaye Lakew, Abaye Lakew." Ashebir buried his face in Lakew's gabi, breathing in the familiar smell of his labour's sweat, the heat of the sun and dark soil. "Abaye, it is you. It's you. You came," he wept.

"What is it?" Lakew said, holding Ashebir at arm's length, and frowning. "Where is your mother?" Lakew looked towards the door Ashebir had come from. His head bobbed back and forth from the door to Ashebir and back again like an anxious bird. "Is she in there? Is she sick?"

Ashebir looked at the ground.

"Ashebir?"

"She's not there," he said, dread creeping under his skin.

Lakew sank to the ground, holding his head in his hands. He took in short sharp breaths, "Be Egziyabher, God help us. No." He rocked back and forth. "No, No. Please. In God's name," he muttered.

Ashebir leant over Lakew, whining. He could sense people gathering around them, clicking their tongues and wailing softly like the wind. He felt their hands on his body, stroking him and patting.

Lakew sniffed hard into his gabi. He stood up. "Come," he said, putting his hand firmly on Ashebir's shoulder. "It is God's will," he said. But he sounded angry. "We have to trust in him."

"We are all in God's hands," a woman said, raising her eyes to heaven.

"You are right," Lakew said, looking over at the trucks and buses, at the miserable country people gathered around.

Ashebir saw the anger and pain in his eyes.

"Let's go where we can be alone, Ashebir," Lakew said. He picked up his stick and bundle. "We have to mourn for Zewdie properly," he said.

"Abaye, over there," Ashebir pointed to the hill in the distance. "I think she is buried over there, on the other side." He slipped his hand into Lakew's. It was good to feel it firmly around his.

They walked away from the compound, past the large white tents where so many people slept and died in the cold, past the trucks and buses parked in lines, past the muddy open fields where people did their toilet. They walked through the brush and spindly eucalyptus trees in the soft foothills and climbed up the steep hillside.

Ashebir was soon out of breath and coughing.

"Let's slow down," Lakew said.

They climbed one step at a time, pausing for breath, until they reached the top. They were not alone. Behind them to the right, women and children were scratching like guinea fowl in the dry bush, collecting firewood. The air was hot and still. The hollow echoes of branches cracking and voices calling out reminded him of collecting firewood on the mountainside at home.

They walked over the brow of the hill and looked down to where three white trucks were parked at odd angles around wide freshly dug graves.

"Why did we get so poor?" Ashebir turned to face Lakew as a bolt of anger shot through his body. "Why is God so angry with us? What did you and Zewdie do? We are good people aren't we?" He pummelled his fists against Lakew. "Why did you leave us?"

Lakew pulled him in and held him firmly. Hugging him and saying hush, in God's name quieten down, it's alright. "Aysoh, aysoh, aysoh," he kept repeating in a soft deep whisper.

Ashebir let out the whine that had been stuck behind his teeth, down his throat for so long. He wanted to be free of the pain and the Worry.

"It is not our fault, Ashebir," Lakew said. "No rains, no life."

"God gave rains to some and not to us. What did we do to make him angry?"

"God is not angry. He loves us. Our land is dry. I don't know why."

The sun was hot on their heads. A soft breeze carried the strong sickly smell of the rotting remains below. It rose and fell away, coming and going, like ghosts passing through. Ashebir sat down feeling sick.

Lakew disappeared and came back crushing eucalyptus leaves between his fingers. He put them in Ashebir's cupped hand. "Breathe it in," he said.

Ashebir closed his eyes, breathing the familiar scent in. 'This will stop your coughing,' she said. He saw Zewdie putting a steaming bowl of eucalyptus leaves on the floor beside his cot.

"It will take the smell away," Lakew said as he sat down beside Ashebir and drew his gabi over them both, making a roof. "Our mourning tent," he said. "Our own lekesobate."

Ashebir felt secure and miserable all at once. He leant on his father, the nearest to Zewdie he could be. The eucalyptus cleared his head. He stared at the black dots of birds hopping around the mounds of earth below and watched the kites circling in the deep blue sky, their forms making dark shadows on the ground beneath.

"What happened?" Lakew said quietly.

"She died in the hospital."

Lakew suddenly wailed, giving Ashebir a fright.

"My sweet Zewdie. God forgive me," Lakew cried. "Zewdie, I should never have left you alone. God knows you were good to me, my beautiful Zewdie." Lakew held his head in his hands sobbing. His body shook as if he were possessed by the Buda.

Lakew's despair frightened Ashebir's own to stillness. They had been close. Ashebir had never seen Lakew beat Zewdie once, not like other husbands.

"I wish it were me that died, Zewdie," Lakew wept. "You should be here for Ashebir, the son given to you. What will we do without you, Zewdie? God help us."

Ashebir shook Lakew's arm gently. "It's alright, Abaye, it's alright. Please stop."

"You worked so hard. You don't deserve this. My Zewdie."

Ashebir put a hand on his father's arm. "Please Abaye, calm yourself. Aysoh."

After a while Lakew became still.

"It's alright," he said. "It's alright. I'm done." Lakew held his head in his hands, taking short breaths. "Forgive me. The shock."

Ashebir picked up the fallen eucalyptus leaves, rubbed them between his fingers and breathed in. He held them under Lakew's nose. "Here," he said.

"God bless you, yeney lij."

He looked down to where the gravediggers were working. He could hear their shovels against the hard earth. One of the truck doors stood open. A cassette was playing a song Ashebir knew. When one of the kiosks played it in the market Zewdie used to laugh and say, 'Listen Ashebir, it's Gash Aberra singing the train song.' They would stand together listening and she would sing.

"She sometimes comes at night," Ashebir said in a low voice. "I see her smiling."

"That's good, Ashebir, that's good. Thanks to God."

Lakew was so like Zewdie, the high cheek bones and large gentle eyes. Ashebir snuggled closer. "They didn't let me mourn in the hospital," he said. "They put me outside the door." Ashebir clenched his teeth, tears pouring down his face. "They took her away in a white truck, like those down there, and left me behind."

A raven squawked loudly from the branches of a nearby tree. Ashebir picked up a pebble and flicked it at the bird. "I dreamt they threw her down a hole," he said.

The bird cocked its head sideways at him and flew off.

"You are right to be angry," Lakew said. "But her soul is at peace now, Ashebir. She is with the Lord, the Holy Trinity. You and I have to be strong, we have to survive and work hard for her sake."

Lakew passed his hand over Ashebir's bald head. "I can see they are looking after you, child," he said.

"An auntie did it."

"We should not stay in this place," Lakew said.

"Can we go home, Abaye? Please."

"No. Everyone is leaving the village, looking for food. We should go to the new settlements in the south. The government is taking people. We will find work there. Maybe you can go to school."

Mesfin had told Ashebir the people in the buses and trucks were going to the settlement areas. He had heard the adults telling stories of people being snatched from markets and forced at gunpoint onto trucks. They said they had no time to tell their families in the villages. Some did not even know where they were going until they were on the road. They looked lost and confused, as if just coming out of a deep sleep. In the early mornings, the trucks swayed away again, up the bumpy track and over the stream. Some of the people in the trucks had to leave their dead behind.

"No," Ashebir said quietly.

"No? What do you mean?" Lakew said.

Ashebir rolled crumbs of earth with his toes. "I am not leaving here," he said, praying his father would understand. "You stay here with me."

"In heaven's name, you don't want to come?"

"Please, Abaye. Zewdie and I were hungry for too long. You and I can eat here, sleep inside. We will get food every day, sometimes even twice. It's more than we ate for a long time in the village."

Ashebir was surprised when his father hugged him close. So tight it hurt. He thought Lakew would be angry.

"God save us, yigirmal, how you have grown up," Lakew said. "You know I can't stay Ashebir, don't you? I have to move and find work. I cannot sit and wait for someone to bring me food, for someone to decide when I can eat. You are a child. You need to be cared for. The camp has become your mother."

Ashebir's heart sank. Lakew could not stay in a place like this, and he, Ashebir, could not leave. The thought of being out there again, the two of them alone without a village, terrified him. Sleeping under the sky peppered with shining stars, waiting for the nights of full moon to see the way, begging for food, looking for transport. No, he could not face it again.

"Please stay, Lakew? Stay until it is alright to go home?"

Lakew got up with a grunt. He turned to walk back down the slope. "Come, let's go," he said, putting his arm around Ashebir.

We are even sadder than before, Ashebir thought. He saw the mass of people in the camp, coming and going like ants, squatting, walking, living and dying around the tents and in the small compound. From the top of the hill he could hear thin wafts of their talking and in the distance the sound of a bus honking.

"You know the birds don't sing here, Abaye? I don't see the dark red bulbul or the tiny yellow ones that fly in clouds."

"The countryside has been taken over by crows and vultures," Lakew said.

When they reached the compound Lakew stopped and looked at Ashebir long and hard, as if he was trying to memorize every curve, read into his very soul.

Ashebir looked back, his throat tight. He could only swallow with difficulty.

Lakew nodded, "God will be by your side."

"No, Abaye, please. Stay, even for a short while."

"You can come, Ashebir. But I cannot stay in this place."

"I am afraid to go out there."

"I will come back for you, don't worry. I know where you are," Lakew pulled Ashebir to him. "God will give you strength," he whispered. "You are a good boy. Your mother loved you and I am proud of you." He kissed Ashebir on each cheek so hard it hurt. "God willing, we will meet again," he said and began to wind the red shawl around his head. He wrapped his gabi around his shoulders and picked up his small bundle and stick. He turned and walked away with the familiar bounce he always had in his step.

Ashebir stood, not able to move. He watched Lakew go. He wanted to shout, "Wait," but no sound came. He watched until Lakew disappeared. He turned and went to his ox-skin in the room he shared with the good people from Ifat na Timooga. He lay down in the dark, pulling his grey blanket over his head. He wanted to close his eyes and sleep forever. He could see Zewdie. She was smiling, greeting Lakew outside their house in their village. In another place. In another life.

42

December 1984, Debre Berhan Camp

Before she could turn round, Izzie was there. Woodsmoke from hundreds of tiny fires stung her eyes and infused her home-knitted grey jumper with the strong smell of charred eucalyptus. It was one of Sam's old jumpers. She couldn't remember why she still had it. It was far too big and hung down over her jeans like a comfort blanket.

Countryside women sat kutch-kutch on their haunches over small fires, preparing ki'ta bread. There was a quiet defiance alongside their despair in this simple act.

She stopped to greet them. They took her hand. Theirs, strong and bony, put hers to shame. Their hands had worked hard. They had physically created sustenance for their families from the soil and vegetation in the highlands, day in and day out. They had lifted and carried water and heavy loads of firewood over miles. She had seen their kind on Entoto Mountain, and on the road to Nazareth. Their eyes held a depth of knowledge and being. She was drawn to them, wishing she could know more. At the same time she could see their pain. They had been uprooted from all they knew. Their homes and neighbours. But they were proud, not yet defeated, these country women. Their clothes were torn to shreds, grey and long unwashed, the cloth too thin for the climate. And still they looked dignified. They did not want her pity. She could see that. And they greeted her, nodding their heads.

"Izzie," Peter said, interrupting her. "Belaynesh wants us."

"We want to sort out the kitchen," Belaynesh said, flipping her white shema over her shoulder and heading off along the veranda. "There are not enough fireplaces. Come. I will show you the room." She was a younger version of Negisst with her slightly plump body and kind, round face. Like Negisst she wore a small wooden cross on a black thread around her neck, which she touched now and then when she spoke. A self-reassuring gesture.

Izzie followed her, carefully stepping in and out of people sitting and lying along the wide terrace, Peter close behind.

"Here," Belaynesh said. "Welcome to the kitchen." It was a large, dark, almost empty room with one fireplace. In it lay the blackened remains of firewood and grey ash, crisscross on the concrete floor, surrounded by a square of broken bricks. A makeshift fire pit. A tall oil drum stood beside it. "We need more fireplaces like this one. We need to make large quantities of fafa."

"There are more bricks and some old oil drums." It was Mesfin, talking as he appeared through the light of the open door. "They just need cleaning out."

"The boys from the Youth Association can help," Belaynesh said. "How many do you need? They are good boys."

"Tenasteling, Mesfin," Izzie said, turning to shake his hand. "How are you doing?"

"Fine thanks, Egziyabher yimesgen," Mesfin said, reaching out to shake her hand and Peter's. "And you? How are you both? I see Belaynesh has already got a job for you." He chuckled.

"And who have we here?" Izzie said, bending to peer behind Mesfin.

A child stood there, a small figure in a red coat. Izzie recognised it from a box of clothes they had collected from the Hilton Hotel some few weeks back.

"Tenasteling," she said, putting out a hand, wondering if he would take it. She looked into the small face under the hood. Some of the children were terrified of her and Peter. Their white faces. But the boy put out his hand. Such a skinny little wrist.

His hand was small and somehow strong in hers. "What's your name?"

The boy looked at her with large, inquisitive eyes. "Ashebir," he whispered.

Mesfin steered the boy around to his side, keeping a hand on his shoulder. "You'll have to give this little man a job. He likes to be busy, don't you?"

The child smiled up at Mesfin.

"Ashebir. His name means running here and there, disturbing everyone," Belaynesh said. She looked at him fondly. "But he is no trouble at all, miskin."

"He's on his own?" Izzie said, thinking he somehow looked lost. A child alone, in this overwhelming place?

"Yes," Mesfin said. "His mother died in the hospital. He says they came from Ataye up north. We do have a few other orphans, but this one," Mesfin nodded his head, smiling, "He likes to make sure we don't forget him. Aydellem enday?" He patted Ashebir's head.

"Ishi, Ashebir," Izzie said. "Don't worry, we won't forget you." She smiled at him. I'm really sorry about your mother, she wanted to say, but the words stuck in her throat. It was too big. Too overwhelming.

"Some kitchen," Peter said. He was already measuring the wall.

"We should be able to fit four more fireplaces along that wall," Mesfin said.

"That's about right," Peter said, snapping his measure back into its cannister. "We can get three more fireplaces along here." He pointed at the windowless wall behind him. "And one more over there, next to the one you already have. We need to repair that brick structure though." He looked at Izzie. "I can't believe this."

"None of us can," Mesfin said.

"How many people do you need to cook fafa for?" Izzie said. "We'll need a light bulb too. It's dark in here, even in the daylight."

Belaynesh tutted. "You won't believe it. Hundreds, thousands."

"I'll have to get permission," Mesfin said. "We have to check with the First Secretary at the Awraja before we do any alterations. It won't be a problem. Comrade Tadele is a good man."

"Can you do that today?" Izzie said.

"I'll go right away," Mesfin said. "You can start getting everything ready."

"And you'll stay with us, Ashebir?" Izzie said. He had such a fine small face with those large eyes. His skinny legs were scarred around his shins and his small feet had the wide toes and tell-tale cracked heels of going barefoot for miles.

"Ishi," the boy whispered. He looked up at Mesfin, and ran his hand over his hood keeping it in place.

"We can do with an extra pair of hands," Peter said, smiling at the boy. "Hey Daniel. How are you? We've just made a plan to renovate the kitchen."

Daniel was shorter and skinnier than Mesfin. His eyes were narrow, dark and bright. His face lined from sun and weather. He wore his gabi lightly thrown round his shoulders and over his head. He chewed on a wooden tooth stick, spitting tiny splinters of it on the ground behind him. "It's great to have you two here," he said. "I wondered what you were up to. I can get Dawit and a few other boys to come and help."

**

By the time Mesfin came with permission from the Awraja, the 'Kitchen' was already swept clean and bricks were piled up in squares in the four designated places.

"We got some cement in town, Mesfin," Peter said.

Dawit was mixing it in a large metal container. Ashebir was crouched beside him, dribbling water in under the bigger boy's instruction. They were a good team.

"You two have obviously worked together before," Izzie said.

"Did you get the go-ahead, Mesfin?" Peter said.

Mesfin waved a thin sheet of paper with blue typing on it. It was a carbon copy. "Let's do it."

Izzie raised a hand to do a high-five with Ashebir, who looked up from his work, obviously puzzled. Dawit raised a hand and clapped it against Izzie's. The small boy's face lit up. He raised his hand too. "You look beautiful when you smile, little Hilton boy," Izzie said, her eyes welling up. "Right, onwards and upwards." She left the boys to the cement-making and brick-laying.

"We need more firewood," Daniel said. "A lot more."

"The Research Institute's committee gave Mesfin petty cash," Izzie said. "We can use some to buy firewood. Can you get a receipt? Silly question."

"No chance," Daniel said.

"We'll work something out," Izzie took her car keys out of her shoulder bag and followed him out into the sun.

"You can let Belaynesh know that this kitchen will be up and running by late afternoon," Peter called after her. "When the firewood is delivered, she can start making her fafa."

"Ishi, I will," she called back and left with Daniel.

**

Early the next morning, Izzie did a round of the tents with Mesfin. There were many extreme cases. Those who never came near the compound, or to the small clinic attended by two nurses on a rota from the hospital. People lay on the ground and sat together in small groups. The tents were large, like wedding marquees. There was a subdued hum of voices.

An emaciated woman sat quietly beside a bundle on the ground. Izzie gently lifted the brown-grey cloth, thick with dirt, exposing the wracked old face of a child in the last moments of life. Its cage-like ribs heaved up and down uncontrollably. The child's eyes stared out from deep sockets, terrified. "Mesfin, look," she said.

"I know, I know," he said quietly. "There are too many of them."

"We could take them to the hall next to the kitchen, Mesfin. We can try feeding them there."

"We can do that. But I think it's too late for that little one."

Izzie nodded at the mother, her heart in her mouth, hoping her eyes spoke with understanding. But how facile. She would never know or understand what it was like for that mother, to sit over the heaving bundle, unable to do anything. Anything at all.

The mother's eyes looked up at Mesfin. Her mouth silent.

He muttered something and put a hand on her shoulder.

They moved around, looking, assessing, gauging the situation.

"These people are too sick to be moved to the settlement areas," Mesfin said.

"Is that what you're supposed to do?"

"Yes, they want to empty this place and move everyone south."

Izzie crouched beside a child, leaning against its mother's chest. Its eyes were completely crusted over. Closed. Such a simple thing to solve.

"Mesfin, let me come with water and cotton wool. I can clean these children's eyes. We can give them Vitamin A for as long as they are here."

"Are you a doctor too?" Mesfin smiled at her. "Sure that's a good idea."

"I'm not a doctor but I have this book called, 'Where There Is No Doctor'. I've read about this, the children's eyes, in there."

"Let's do it then."

"I think the nurses should come and see the people where they are, don't you? I mean they are too sick to come to the clinic."

"I agree, but they won't come. They are not used to it."

"And they're registering every patient. Seems such a waste of time. The whole process takes too long."

"I know, but they come with hospital procedures. They don't know anything else. Basically, Izzie, we don't have the means to help these people. They need so much more than we can give. And the hospital is full. So we only take the cases we think they can really help, like mothers who are about to give birth."

**

With Ashebir by her side, in his red coat and hood up, Izzie took a box filled with cotton wool, antiseptic wipes, and Vitamin A drops. Ideally they needed tetracycline ointment too. But there was none.

Ashebir carried a small bucket with water and a cup.

The boy just appeared to help them, whatever they were doing. Mesfin was right. It was as if the child wanted to make sure they knew he was there. That he wasn't forgotten. She was glad that at least she could communicate with him in his own language. Not everything, but enough.

They stopped at the first child whose eyes were crusted shut. Whenever the woman stopped waving her hand over the child's face, flies settled back to eat. Two rows of busy flies where the child's eyes should be. It was awful.

"Tell the mother, Ashebir, tell her we will clean the child's eyes." She stood by while Ashebir explained. He was so serious and sweet. She hoped he would be the softener to any fear they had of farenj. The mother looked up from where she sat. Looked from Ashebir to Izzie.

"Ishi," the mother said. "Ishi."

Izzie crouched down beside her. She dipped the cotton wool in the cup held out by Ashebir and gently dabbed away at the crust, softening it, until it came away.

Within minutes they were surrounded by curious people, leaning in close, their breath hot on her face.

"Please," Izzie said, raising a hand. "Stay back. Ashebir, ask them to stay back."

Her legs started to ache. She sat down, shuffling herself some room on the ground next to the mother. She thought of the Jane Fonda exercises with Fasika and Mulu in Robert Wiley Junior's office. That was a world away. She needed to get fitter. How did these women sit kutch-kutch for hours on end?

The child's eye popped open like a surprise. One bright little brown eye.

The mother smiled.

"Look, Ashebir," Izzie said. "Look. That's amazing."

"Yigirmal," he said, smiling. "Yigirmal."

The crowd gathered around them again closer, to look. "Wey, Enday!" some muttered.

Izzie gently touched the women and children, asking them to move back again. She turned her attention to the child's other eye. With soft, slow dab, dab, dabs and dipping the cotton into the cup of water, the second eye popped open. The child looked around in shock and burst into tears. The mother laughed, held it close and rocked back and forth, comforting. "Egziyabheresteling," she said, hugging the child to her. "Thank you."

Izzie clapped her hands, laughing. "You are welcome, you are welcome," she said. "Let me give the child some medicine," Izzie said to the mother. "Tell her Ashebir. It is good for the child's eyes."

Ashebir turned to the mother and explained what Izzie had said.

"I will put drops in the child's mouth, that's all," Izzie said.

The next mother was already by her side. She held her baby out towards Izzie.

Izzie shuffled round and started on the next child.

It was a small, small thing to do.

"Betam yigirmal," Ashebir said quietly each time it happened. "So surprising."

Izzie showed Dawit and two other boys what to do. From then on, if they were sitting doing nothing, she would send them off with a makeshift medical tray and a pail of water to treat the children's eyes. There beside them, holding the pail of water and a cup was, more often than not, a small figure wearing the red Hilton coat.

**

It was early morning. The camp had been cleared. Thirty to forty trucks had been filled up like so much cargo, each carrying about sixty people. The squat vehicles had lumbered off up the hill and onto the main road heading south towards Addis and beyond.

Izzie stood for a moment with Mesfin, watching. "Those poor people," she said.

"Hmmm," he replied. "Come on. We have work to do."

They cleared out the tents, made large bonfires of filthy mats, rubbish, the odd piece of cloth, a shoe.

Belaynesh and her women made fafa and ki'ta bread for the few people left behind. Young boys appeared from nowhere.

"Do you think they leave their children behind on purpose, Mesfin?" Izzie said.

"Maybe. Maybe they think we will look after them better. That they'll get food every day."

"They suddenly appeared after all the vehicles had gone," Izzie said. "They must have a good hiding place."

"By now people know they are not going home. They don't know where they are being taken. Maybe they want their boys to try and find their way home, to look after their homesteads."

"But imagine leaving your child behind," Izzie said. "And what about those three brothers. The ones who said their Dad had gone home to get the rest of the family? He never came back. They must have gone with the buses today. They'll never find each other again."

"I saw them getting on one of the buses," Daniel said. "Poor boys. They kept looking back, in case there was a chance to stay, I think. I felt sorry too, really."

They had moved some of the extreme cases, to the large room adjacent to the kitchen. Izzie walked through and found the mother with the baby and the two-year-old girl. The children were in a bad way but looked like they stood a chance. The mother sat, legs stretched out in front of her, staring at the floor. Eyes glazed.

"She's in shock," Daniel said. "Goodness knows what she has been through."

"She's exhausted," Izzie said. She and Daniel clothed each child in a bright knitted jumper and placed them in a cardboard box they had found. "Emayey," Izzie crouched next to the mother, her hand on the woman's arm. "We are going to put your children in the sun to warm up for a short while."

The woman did not move or look at Izzie.

They carried the box out into the sun. They sat and fed each child with rehydration fluid and runny fafa.

"That should do it," Daniel said, his small dark eyes smiling encouragement. "Let's put this blanket over the box to shade them. We can feed them once more and take them inside again before we go for our lunch."

**

It was late afternoon. They were sitting on the terrace of a small megib-bate.[96] They had just had injera. Peter had had an omelette filled with green chilli peppers and onions in a fresh roll, one of his favourites.

"You and your chillies," Izzie said.

"You like your 'karia," Mesfin laughed. "He's a real Ethiopian."

"My boss likes whole 'karia with chopped up green chillies and raw

---

[96] Local restaurant, sometimes a local resident's own home, serving food in a front room or on the front terrace.

onions stuffed inside," she said. "I tried it once. Phew!" It made her go red just thinking about it. She closed her eyes and lifted her face to the sun. The climate was harsh here. Scorching shards of sunlight in the day, extreme chill and cold at night.

"Well, that's something I have yet to try," Peter said. "You watch it there, Izzie. That sun burns." His face and arms were bright red and dotted with freckles. "Look what it's done to me."

Mesfin laughed. "Typical pink farenj."

"The sun feels good though," Izzie said, not moving.

The girl came to take their plates and was waiting to hear what more they wanted.

"Izzie?" Mesfin said.

"Yes, I'll have a buna," she said. "Thanks."

They all ordered coffee.

Izzie offered her pack of Winston around. No one else smoked. She lit a cigarette. She'd bought a few packets from the boys in Piazza before leaving. Mekonnen was happy for the windfall business and Hailu had given her a caramella for the road. Piazza felt far away. It was as if they were in a different country. She inhaled deeply. They had worked hard from early morning, ever since the trucks and buses had left.

"Those families were planning to go home again," Izzie said. "I feel so sorry for them."

"They didn't put up much fight," Peter said.

"They have no choice," Mesfin said. "They are all to go south. What to do?"

"Its good you kept an eye on Ashebir," Izzie said. "We don't want him disappearing." The lump was forming in her throat. She could feel the tears coming and took another deep drag on her cigarette. Thankfully the girl came with a tray of thick, dark coffee in small glasses, each with a layer of sugar at the bottom. "Lovely," she said. "Betam Egziersteling."

"Our little Hilton Boy," Mesfin said. "He really likes you, Izzie."

"He's your boy, Mesfin. He barely leaves your side." Izzie said. "What's going to happen to him?"

"You have to take him," Mesfin said. His eyes looked sad and smiling. He took a loud slurp of his coffee.

"What?" Izzie said. "How?"

"Why not," Daniel said, still stirring his coffee. "I think it's a good idea."

"But guys, I live on my own in a tiny place in the city. He's a country boy." She wondered. Could she? "I would have to have permission. I can't just drive off with a child in the back of the car."

"That didn't take long," Peter said. "I heard you were impulsive, but you should think about it, Izzie. What will you do with him? Will you adopt him?"

"I don't know, Peter. But he can't stay here and at some point they'll put him in a truck to Walkitey. That would be disastrous."

"No more disastrous than it is for all the other children," Peter said.

"But we're talking about Ashebir," Mesfin said. "Take him Izzie."

"Hey," Peter said. "Yesus Kristos. You see what I'm seeing?"

"Wow," Izzie said.

A long endless string of trucks and buses was driving one after the next down the main road. Packed full of people. Vomit streaked down the sides. The slow train of deathly humanity went past. Trails of black smoke shot out in great puffs from behind the old diesel buses.

"Must be a kerosene mix in there," Peter muttered.

"Hissab!" Mesfin called out, putting a hand in his back pocket for his wallet.

"I'll get this," Izzie said.

"They said that up to 7,000 people a day will pass through," Mesfin said. "But not today."

"They didn't tell you anything about people arriving today?" Daniel said. He was already on his feet.

Izzie paid the girl and rummaged for the car keys in her shoulder bag.

"Let's go," Daniel said. "Innihid."

They jogged down the steps onto the road, piled into Izzie's car and set off towards the convoy.

"They won't let me in," Izzie said, her indicator tick-tocking away.

"Just keep inching forward," Peter said.

"Put your hands out the windows," Izzie said.

They squeezed between an open truck, packed full of people standing and holding onto the sides, and a battered old VW taxi-bus.

"How many are they? Did they warn you?" Izzie said. "Mesfin?"

"No. This is the first I hear – I see."

"Be Egziyabher," Daniel said. "We don't have enough bread for them."

"Drop me at the Kebele office, Izzie," Mesfin said. "We'll get them to organize the flour for the bakery. They can start baking now."

"Ishi," Izzie said.

"We need to get the fires going for the fafa," Daniel said. "And we could cut the blankets in two so they'll go further."

"I'll grab Dawit. We can do that," Peter said.

"I'll help Belaynesh get the fires going," Izzie said. "OK?"

"Ishi, turu neouw," Mesfin said. "I'll be there as soon as I can."

**

"Where are they?" Ashebir wondered. He was sitting on the steps to the veranda, feeling the warmth of the sun on his face and body. He was trying to soak it in, to store it for the coming freezing night. He heard the rumbling, and saw them coming. One bus and truck after the next. They kept arriving. Mesfin and the others should be there, he thought. But they had gone and not come back. He stood to look harder from the safety of the veranda. They parked up in a long line one after another like at the bus station. More of The Hungry from the northern highlands.

Some of them climbed down, looking puzzled and expectant. They looked for someone who could give them answers to their questions.

Others sat deep in thought.

Some needed the toilet.

Ashebir recognised the Worry on their furrowed brows, in their pained eyes. There were so many of them suddenly. They reminded him of a large ants nest. Disturbed. Ants going frantically in every direction. Climbing over each other. To his relief he saw Izzie's funny car bouncing down the hill towards the camp. They would know what to do.

He went down one step, ready to greet them.

They jumped out of the car and took off in different directions. Izzie came towards him, Peter to the store, sweeping Dawit with him, and Daniel to the office. Mesfin wasn't there.

"Ashebir," Izzie said. "There you are. Did you eat? Here take this." She gave him a small package as she went past. "And then come and find me in the kitchen. We have work to do."

He opened the paper. An egg sandwich. He couldn't believe his luck. He sat down against the wall.

A small boy came and sat close by. Looking at him. At his sandwich.

"Here," Ashebir said, breaking his prize in two. "Eat, eat."

They sat like brothers, eating.

"Chew slowly," Ashebir said. "Or your stomach will hurt."

"Ishi," the boy whispered.

**

"There must be thousands of them," Peter said, coming into the kitchen. "Yesus Kristos, I can't count."

"Where is Ashebir?" Daniel said.

"I left the little Hilton boy eating a sandwich. He'll come in a minute," Izzie said.

Izzie, Belaynesh and the women from the Women's Association were already stoking the fires. They were used to it. Weddings, funerals, they knew how to work together making large quantities of food.

The energy, excitement and panic ran through her.

"I'll bring the bags of flour, milk powder and all to make the fafa," Daniel said heading out of the door with two of the boys. "I hope Mesfin's not too long."

"We won't have enough food for them all, Daniel," Peter called after him. Peter knew exactly how much of each ingredient they had, the exact quantities that had to go in the oil drum to make the fafa, and how much was left in the store. He liked numbers.

"Have you finished the blankets already, Peter?" Izzie said.

"Nearly done. I left the boys finishing off. Thought you could do with a hand here."

They piled wood in the fireplaces and lit them. Daniel came with the boys, carrying sacks full of flour, sugar, soy and milk powder from the store. The oil drums were set onto the bricks round the fire, filled with water and bag after bag of ingredients carefully measured and tipped in. The Youth Association boys took turns with the women to stand on the brick surrounds, each with a long eucalyptus pole, stirring and stirring the mixture. The fires crackled and spat under them, hot smoke burning their eyes.

"More milk powder, Ashebir," Izzie said, stirring. Her sleeves rolled up above her elbows, face burning. "Keep going until those bags are empty, yeney konjo."

Ashebir tipped more powder in, one bag after the next.

"Good boy," she called at him. "Now the sugar. You're doing a great job."

They had all the fires going. It was hot, smoky and loud in their makeshift kitchen.

"Dawit and the boys finished all the blankets, Izzie," Peter shouted behind her.

"Brilliant," Izzie called back without turning.

"The boys are handing them out now."

"That's great, Peter."

"You look knackered. You want me to take over for a bit?"

"Sure, here," Izzie said. "Thanks." She stepped down, wiping her face and neck. Through the door she could see the dusk falling. The night had crept up on them, stealthy, almost like a cheat, stealing the warmth of the day, giving nothing in exchange. She went to look out of the door and get some fresh air on her face.

Zabanyas were out there getting people, mostly women and children, to sit on the ground in long rows, lined up to wait for the fafa. The Kebele boys had already started taking long wooden planks lined with cups of the hot thick liquid and were giving them out, one to each mother.

She looked at Ashebir. He was still tipping ingredients into their oil drum. It wasn't thick enough yet. "You alright?" she said.

The boy smiled his wonderful bright smile at her.

"Yes," he said. He used his arm to wipe his eyes.

"The smoke?" she said.

"Yes, but I know it. I know this cooking smoke from home."

"This barrel is nearly ready," Peter said. "Let's fill the cups and get the boys to pass them round."

They worked like this, taking turns, into the night.

Finally, Mesfin said, "That's it. The store is empty. No more milk powder, no flour, not a jumper or blanket left."

"There must be so many people didn't get anything," Izzie said. Then an ice cold thought shot through her. "Oh my God."

"What?" Daniel said, coming up beside her.

"The box babies," she said and moved towards the next room. They had brought them back to their mother before going for lunch. She had had every intention of feeding them again when she came back from lunch. "We forgot them, Daniel." She made her way carefully across the large room full of sick people sitting and lying on the floor. It was dark and gloomy. The woman, the mother, was still there, sitting upright with a blanket over her shoulders. The children were fast asleep in the box, cosily wrapped in their knitted jumpers and covered with a blanket.

"Thank goodness," Izzie let out a sigh. She touched the mother's shoulder. "I'll just get a bottle for them," she said. The mother, like before, did not respond. Izzie went and got a bottle of rehydration fluid, some runny, warm fafa and a teaspoon.

She sat on the floor, sighed again, suddenly realising how tired she was. It had been a long day of overwhelming impressions, drama and physical exertion. Just this one last thing. She would do this one last thing and then go back to the guest house. Maybe Solomon would have prepared some supper for them. It was very late. He would have long gone to bed. Maybe she and Peter would just get a cold beer from the fridge.

She gently lifted the baby out of the box. "You first little one," she said softly. "Shh, come." She settled the child in the crook of her crossed legs, cradling its head in her arm. She took the bottle of fluid and lifted the teat to the child's lips. It was only then that she realised the child lay there like a wax doll. Izzie froze. The child lay motionless in her arms. It dawned on her. She was sitting on the concrete floor, in that large dim room, surrounded by the dark shapes of the hopeless, the smell of their vomit and sickly effluent thick in the air. She was sitting there, holding this woman's dead baby. She looked at the mother. Then sat staring at nothing in particular, as motionless as the mother now. She took a deep breath and lifted the child, laying it gently in the box next to its sister. "Aysoh," she whispered. "Egziyabher ante gar yihun." Gingerly, she touched the sister's cheek. It was still warm. She got up slowly, biting the tears back.

"What is it Izzie?"

It was Daniel. His eyes peering at her. He laid a hand on her shoulder. The tears ran down her cheeks. She clenched her jaw. She could not let it out now.

"The baby. Daniel. The baby's dead."

"Ishi," Daniel whispered. "Sorry, Izzie."

"What shall we do? The mother. Look at her. She hasn't moved."

"And the sister?" Daniel bent over the box and laid a hand on the older child. "She's still alive, thank God. We can't do anything about the mother. She is in a state of shock, Izzie. Just pick the baby up."

"Shall I?"

"Pick the baby up and follow me," Daniel said.

She stood by the mother for a moment with the stiff little body in her arms. Look. Look. I'm taking your little one away. We didn't look after him enough. I forgot him. I am so sorry. I'm sorry.

The mother did not stir.

Izzie could not breathe. She followed Daniel like a zombie to the makeshift mortuary. Her body felt like lead. Every step a miserable effort.

The mortuary was already full. Children and adults laid out in rows. Wrapped in cloth. She laid the child down next to another tiny form. "Tell them to leave the jumper on the little one, Daniel," she whispered.

"Ishi," he said.

"Let's get out of here." She felt sick.

"It's not your fault Izzie."

"I forgot them."

"We both did," he sucked his teeth. "We haven't stopped."

"The mother. She didn't even notice."

"She couldn't. She's gone too, Izzie. We will try and look after her and the little girl. I'll give them something now. You go get some rest."

"Ishi," she said. "Thanks Daniel."

Izzie turned to go in search of Peter. "Let's go, Peter," she said.

"You OK?" he said.

"Yes, let's just go."

"OK."

They drove in silence. Nothing but the hum of the engine in the headlights. Peter glanced at her now and then. She'd noticed he either spoke ten to the dozen about anything and everything when he was nervous, or said nothing at all.

When they arrived at the guest house and the engine died there was a strange, and sudden silence around them. A kerosene lamp burned in what was the sitting room, filling the one window with a warm orange glow. It did nothing to lift the heavy darkness of the rest of the house.

"It's so dark here," she said. "It's as if the whole world knows there's a catastrophe, and doesn't know what to do."

"How about a beer?" Peter ventured.

"Yes, let's," she said. "I don't think I can eat more than a snack though."

Inside, with a beer in hand and crunching on the homemade crisps Ingo had bought at the Stadium grocery for them, she curled her legs under on the hard sofa. "I think I will take Ashebir," she said. "He can't stay here."

"Really," Peter said slowly, nodding his head. "What will you do with him? Will you adopt him?"

"No, I don't think so. My life is so up and down. I only have another six months here for sure and then what? No, I think I'll look for an orphanage. Not one of the government ones if possible. He'll be with other children. He can start school."

Peter carried on nodding his head and drank, contemplating. She could tell he would not even think of taking the child. "Well, if you think you know what you're doing," he said. "I wish you luck."

"I think the boy has luck on his side," she said. "Everyone is drawn to him. His mother must have been quite a woman. She's given him this ability to work, to fight for his place, his survival. I wish I could have met her. I think we owe it to her to make sure he's alright, don't you?" She drank.

"You know it's not your fault what happened there tonight, don't you?"

Izzie put a hand up to stop him going on. It was all she could do to hold back the tears.

"He told me his mother's name," Izzie said. "She was called Zewdie."

43

December 1984, Debre Berhan Camp to Addis Ababa

Helping make fafa by the hot fires in the afternoons and evenings distracted him and kept him warm. Now he shivered through the night under his blanket, the cold biting painfully into his bones. His cough was getting worse. His chest hurt when he breathed in. He kept his breaths short, fearful of the sharp pain. He slept fitfully, waking anxiously, hoping that in the morning the zabanyas wouldn't notice him. Every morning he hoped he would reach Daniel, Mesfin or Belaynesh before anyone grabbed his arm and pulled him onto a bus with a tight grip.

The Worry gnawed at his mind. What if they were too busy and forgot about him? Every day there were so many people to look after and feed. He stayed close and worked beside Izzie. But the night before she had left suddenly without him seeing her go. Would she come this morning? Who would make sure he was not put on a bus? People were being taken to far away places in the south. Had Lakew gone there already? How would he ever find Lakew again? How would he get back home? They were rounding up children without families and putting them on the buses. Some of the boys hid in the early morning to avoid the zabanyas. Should he join them? But he was reminded of the dooriyey, the bad boys in the Debre Berhan market. How lucky he had been to escape them. How lucky he had not been rounded up with them.

With the movements around him before the first morning light, he woke and sat up. He looked around. Small mounds covered in cloth, or grey blankets, lay sleeping. Women sat beside blackened, cold hearths, their faces long and empty. Their small children climbed into their laps and clawed at breasts that hung empty. Would no one come to help them? People were afraid to go with the buses but they had no strength to resist. They wanted to wait in Debre Berhan and return home to their villages. But they had no choice. They shrugged when they were rounded up, and they went.

The compound was crowded every night. Many had to sleep out in the open. They woke to the sound of wailing for the dead. Last night had been a bad night, he heard the women say, sucking their teeth. A bad night.

The office door was still shut. He hoped Belaynesh would be there soon. He would go to her, make sure she knew he was still there. She would give him a cup of tea. If he was lucky.

As the sun rose, he picked up his ox-skin, pulled his blanket around him and went, expecting to sit by the office door and wait. There was no space to sit, the veranda was full. He stood, determined not to move until one of them arrived. This way the Worry was overcome by his wishing for a while.

**

Finally, he saw them. Belaynesh with her women from the Women's Association, Dawit, and some of the boys who worked with him. Ashebir's heart lifted. Seeing them he felt less afraid.

"Who have we here," Belaynesh said, unlocking the door to the office. "Come, come, Ashebir. You are one of our workers. Did you see how he worked last night, Dawit?"

Dawit patted Ashebir on the head. "How are you today, little man?" He looked at Belaynesh. "He doesn't look too good, enday."

"So many look bad today, Dawit. I worry for them having to travel so far in their state." Belaynesh sucked her teeth.

Ashebir followed them into the office.

"Sit, sit, we will make tea. Don't worry," Belaynesh said. She looked warm and well-fed, comfortable. She smelt of soap and fresh water. Her eyes shone with kindness. She bustled as usual, keeping busy and trying to be cheerful.

Ashebir sat on the stool by the desk. He could still feel the cold in his bones.

Belaynesh gave out instructions to the women. They were to hand out fresh rolls to as many people as possible. Dawit had already gone with the boys to see what they could do around the camp. They would also look for the orphan children to see if they were alright.

The sky was its deep blue. The earth slowly began to feel the heat of the sun. By midday even the shadows on the veranda would be hot.

Mesfin came into the room. "Tenasteling," he said. "How are we all today." His voice was heavy. "Did you hear, Belaynesh, fifty people died last night? This is terrible."

"Is it true that they will take as many as they can today?"

"Yes, everyone is to go south, to the settlement areas."

Ashebir listened intently.

"I am afraid many won't survive," Belaynesh said. "They are too sick. Too weak. How will they have the strength to farm?"

Ashebir watched them. He was still so cold, so fearful. He could not find the courage to say, 'Please don't let them take me.'

"Here," Belaynesh said, placing a glass of honey-coloured, steaming tea on the desk beside him and a fresh bread roll. He could see the layer of sugar at the bottom of the glass. She stirred it for him, talking. "He does not look well today, Mesfin." she said.

"Let him stay in the office," Mesfin said. "Izzie will be coming soon."

"She's leaving for Addis today, isn't she?"

"Yes," Mesfin said. "It's a pity but she has to go back to England. She wants to fund-raise and come back."

Ashebir had followed Izzie like a kitten, she was something new for him. She was funny. Her Amharic was funny. Why did she have to leave?

He heard the rumble of her car arriving. The door slamming with a familiar clunk.

"There she is now," Mesfin said.

"Did you tell Ashebir?" Belaynesh said.

"No, I told Izzie she should ask him herself."

"Ishi, turu neow," Belaynesh said. She smiled at Ashebir.

Ashebir tore a small piece of bread from the roll and put it in his mouth. He chewed slowly. He took a tiny slurp of the hot tea. It was good for his throat. How lucky he was. The people outside did not get a hot tea. If he had a family he would not get hot tea.

"I'm going to see what's going on," Belaynesh said. "When do we get another delivery of flour and milk powder, Mesfin? We used everything up again last night."

"I know. We should be getting a delivery today. I'll call the Relief Counsel now. Peter said that he and Leila will come at the weekend with more supplies."

"Ishi, turu neow," she said again as she bustled towards the door. On her way out she gave Ashebir another smile. "Aysoh," she said.

All he could do was look. He was so tired. He took another tiny sip of the hot tea.

Izzie came through the door. "Tenasteling," she said, her blue eyes shining like the blue skies outside. "Hey, Ashebir," she said, patting his head. "How is our Hilton boy today?"

Ashebir nodded. He tried a smile. He wished he could say how afraid he was, how much his cough hurt, how cold it was outside at night.

Mesfin greeted her warmly, shaking her hand. They drew close and touched shoulders. "Endate nesh?" he said.

"I am fine," she said. "And you?"

"We are fine, aren't we Ashebir?" Mesfin said.

Ashebir nodded again, adjusting the hood of his coat over his head. "I'm fine," he whispered. He tried to stop the tears in his eyes. Sometimes he cried until he was empty. He knew many others did the same. There was no end to the overwhelming loss, the extreme discomfort, the pain.

Izzie and Mesfin carried on talking in that farenj language he could not understand. They looked at him and he could see they were worried.

"Ashebir," Izzie pulled a chair to sit by him and put a hand on his arm. "I know you are not very well. I'm sorry. This is not the place for you."

Mesfin sat against the desk opposite, his arms folded across his chest, listening.

"I am leaving for Addis today, you know?" she said, taking her hand away and running it through her hair, as she often did.

"Ishi," Ashebir said. "I know." He took another sip of his tea. He looked at the engrained markings in the wooden desk and at his feet that barely touched the floor. He swung them for a moment.

"Do you want to come with me?" she said. "To Addis?"

He looked up and met her eyes. They were searching his face, large and worried.

"To Addis?" he said.

"Yes, Izzie wants to take you with her, Ashebir," Mesfin said. "What do you think?"

Ashebir's heart beat faster. He could not believe it. Go to Addis with Izzie? The darkness inside lifted. He smiled. "I can go," he said.

"We would get a fekad, a piece of paper," Izzie said. "We'd get permission. I can't just take you like that." She clicked her fingers.

A piece of paper, he thought. He did not know what that meant.

He looked at Mesfin who was smiling at him and nodding.

"Ishi," he whispered. He felt happy but could not say anything.

Izzie put her hands on his shoulders. He could see tears in her eyes, even though they were still smiling. "Turu neouw, turu neouw," she said. "Don't be afraid."

Maybe there would be a bright way ahead for him. Lightness in his life. He did not know what it meant. What would happen to him. But yes, he would go. He would take this chance.

Izzie and Mesfin talked some more.

"You stay here, Ashebir. Ishi?" Izzie said. "I have to go with Mesfin to see Gwad Tadele at the Awraja office in town. Ask his permission to take you. Then, Egziyabher sifeked, we will leave this afternoon."

Ashebir nodded. He would leave this afternoon. Where would he sleep that night? Not on the cold earth. He felt a lightness that he had not felt for a long time. Life here was taking more energy out of him than he had. He was getting weaker. He had no idea what would happen to him, but he knew that if he stayed here much longer he would not last long enough to see Lakew again, or he would be put on one of the buses going south. Then he would be lost forever.

**

The sun had moved around to its afternoon place. It stopped for a while before sinking, leaving the chill of the evening air behind, and the fear of another cold night in his mind. He had left his ox-skin, his old gabi and the blanket in the room where he had been with the good people of Ifat ena Timooga. It was empty now. They had all been taken away. He felt sorry. They had said, 'No, please. Let us stay here.' They had said, 'No, please. We want to go home.' The officials did not listen, and Mesfin and Daniel seemed powerless to do anything except to stand there trying to hide their deep discomfort.

The camp was almost empty again. A few orphan boys, some extremely sick people, and children left behind by their parents, were still there. Even really old people had been put on the buses. Ashebir heard Daniel wondering what those old people would do in the new settlement areas. Belaynesh sucked her teeth and tutted, saying she was sure they would not survive the journey.

He heard Izzie's car, like a large bumble bee coming towards the compound. This time the sound and the vehicle took on a different significance. It belonged to his destiny. It would transport him into the next phase of his life. He had reached Debre Berhan with Zewdie by various means, an old Land Rover and a bus or two. And now he would be taking this new journey alone in Izzie's funny car. He watched as she and Mesfin got out of the car. They waved at him, smiling. He realised he would have to say goodbye to Mesfin. Mesfin, who had looked after him, helped save him from the Worry. And Belaynesh too. She had given him some injera and wot in a small picnic box for the journey to Addis.

"Egziyabher ante gar yihun, Ashebir," she had said. "God go with you and protect you. Izzie will make sure you are alright. Don't be afraid." She had pulled him close to her briefly and let him go, tutting as she left. "I have to get home to my children now. Goodbye, Ashebir. Good luck!"

Izzie came up the steps onto the veranda. She sat on the ground beside him. "Look, Ashebir, I have the paper." She opened up a sheet of paper with black writing and a large stamp. "It's in Amharic. Can you read Amharic?"

Ashebir shook his head. "Only a little," he said.

"Me too. I know some of the letters but I can't read." She laughed. "Hopeless."

He looked at the sheet of paper and remembered how he had tried to read the newspaper to Zewdie under the bus shelter. Wozeiro Tsehai's daughter Wubit had called him a goat because he couldn't read. He felt a familiar stab of sadness in his belly. Zewdie. She would want him to go with this farenj woman, surely?

"Well it says your name and my name and it says we are allowed to go together," Izzie said. "Are you ready, Ashebir? You want to get your things and we can go?"

"Ishi," he said and got up to go to the room to collect his few things, his old ox-skin and the thin grey blanket Mesfin had given him.

Mesfin and Daniel came down the steps from the office to bid them a safe journey.

Izzie took his things and put them in the back of the car.

Ashebir looked up at Mesfin, holding onto the hood of his coat so it did not come off. His hair had grown again and with it small bugs that itched his scalp, especially at night.

"Ishi, Ashebir. Go well, stay safe and good luck," Mesfin said. "Izzie will take care of you. We will miss you but I am glad you are leaving this place. Egziyabher ante gar yihun."

Ashebir was not sure what to do so he put out his hand. Mesfin took it and drew him close. He had no idea where he was going, or where he would sleep that night. But he trusted Izzie, and he was filled with a brightness, a light. He was not going to walk away from that.

He went to Daniel and received another warm embrace. "Go well Ashebir," he said. "Take care."

"Come on," Izzie said. "Let's go. Innihid." She shook hands with the two men and embraced them like family. "Thank you, thank you," she said. "We will see each other, for sure. I will come when I am back from

England." She held the back door open. "You can travel in the back, Ashebir. It's safer for you."

Feeling slightly timid, Ashebir smiled at Mesfin and Daniel and climbed into the back of Izzie's car.

Izzie's face popped in through the door. "You alright there, yeney konjo?" she said.

"Yes," he said.

The door shut behind him with its familiar clunk. Izzie went round the other side. He could hear the keys jingling in her hand and her voice calling, "Bye!"

Through the window he could see Mesfin and Daniel waving. Izzie turned the key and the car set off, rumbling up the hill and out of the camp.

**

He must have slept. When he woke and looked out, it was already dark. He could see the lights of the city and the red lights of a car in front of them. He scratched his head and pulled his gabi around him. His mind was quiet. He sat and stared out of the window. It felt new for him. This city with its horns and its lights.

"Ashebir," he heard Izzie's voice. "Are you alright?"

"Yes," he said.

"I will take you to my mamita. Her name is Negisst. She has children the same age as you. She will look after you, OK? You will sleep at hers tonight and I will come in the morning."

"Ishi," he said.

"Don't worry, Ashebir. She is like Belaynesh. You will like her."

"Ishi," he said.

His mind was still. Izzie knew what to do. The Worry was almost gone.

The car turned off the main road and bumped from side to side down a path, lit up by the large lamps at the front of the car. They went over rocks and stones between small dwellings under korkorro roofs. Izzie stopped and switched the engine off. There was silence. He could hear water rushing into a pail and a woman calling out to a child who was crying.

"Wait there, Ashebir," Izzie said, getting out of the car.

"Ishi," he said.

A woman came towards them. "Izzie, How are you? Endemin nesh?"

The two women embraced each other.

"I am fine, Negisst. How are you?"

"We are fine, thanks to God," Negisst said.

"Negisst, there's a boy in the car," Izzie said.

Before Izzie could say more, the back door opened and Ashebir saw the round worried face of a woman just like Belaynesh. "Weyne, miskin," she said. "Come, come. Let's go inside." She motioned him to get out of the car.

He got his ox-skin and the blanket Mesfin had given him, and the picnic of injera and wot Belaynesh had prepared, and climbed out of the car. Immediately he felt a warm comforting hand on his shoulder.

"Let's go, my child," the woman called Negisst said. "Izzie, you go home. Take rest. We will see you in the morning."

In a daze, he was propelled towards one of the dwellings. They went through the door into the light of a large room where two children sat eating.

"You will eat too," Negisst said, smiling at him. "But first in a tub with you." She started removing his clothes almost before he had passed the threshold. The children giggled. He found himself laughing with them. Laughing with children for the first time in a long time.

"Wey miskin!" Negisst said.

Epilogue

The night dragged on. His body tingled with anticipation, butterflies fluttering in his belly. Night-time creatures scrabbled about in the eves. He could hear Tedi breathing evenly beside him, and the haunting bark of dogs in the neighbourhood. Were they afraid of ghosts or calling out to them? The air in the room was thick and airless. As Tedi had said, the whole family slept together in that room. It was incredible to think he had crossed the river and been at his old home that very afternoon. His mind jumped from his old friend, Mohamed Abdu, standing with the child on his hip by the door of his house, to Emet Temima and Mohamed Ahmed's familiar but now age-worn faces, their soft friendly eyes looking intently at him. They had said it was Mohamed Shinkurt, Zewdie's brother, who could tell him the story. What story? What story did he have to tell? What did he know?

The thought of all he had seen, and of meeting his uncle the next day, kept him awake. In his mind he walked every step of the way to his uncle's house.

His mind wandered to his home in Addis. The garden with the boulders he had painted, one with the bridge over the river, another with the gojo-bate and the warka tree in the village, another with Muletta mountain. He thought of his studies and his dream to open a small shop. He was no scholar. It was only thanks to Izzie's persistence that he had finally passed his Grade 12 exam and graduated. She had come for the ceremony. It was to her that he presented the lily every student gave to their parent. Her eyes had sparkled with tears and pride. They had hugged tightly and remembered Zewdie. He would talk with Izzie. Surely she would agree to his plan to open a small shop? When had he last seen her? He hoped she would come soon and ask him as she always did: "Min adis neger alle? What's new?"

Finally, the next-door's cockerel called out. He woke, wondering how and when he had fallen asleep. Tedi's mother was up and preparing tea. After a simple breakfast, he and Tedi took off. They walked up the path along the river until he saw the place. "It's that one, Tedi," he said. "That's Mohamed Shinkurt's house."

The path continued past the house on up the hill. The river flowed much closer to his uncle's house than he recalled. It looked as if it had taken part of the old vegetable patch with it. The neat fence Ashebir remembered now looked shabby. He knocked hesitatingly on the rusty old korkorro gate. It was just about attached to what was left of the wooden fencing, and shook when he knocked, sending out a familiar rattling clang, clang, sound. When there was no reply he knocked again, sending the gate into another fit of shaking. Eventually an elderly woman appeared.

"Emet Selam," Ashebir said, excitedly. Mohamed Shinkurt's wife. She had always tempered his uncle's ferocity with her kindness.

"Is it you, Ashebir?" she said. "I heard you had come. Zewdie's beloved child. How are you, Allah be praised. Come, come. We will tell Mohamed you are here."

They found Mohammed Shinkurt standing behind his gojo-bate, looking out over the river. He must have been waiting for them.

"Praise be to Allah," he said. "Ashebir, are you alive? Let me look at you, my boy."

Ashebir's childhood anxiety was suddenly there again. He hesitated for a moment. The man had not accepted him. Had even sent him away. But then he remembered the day they parted company. How his uncle had voiced regret.

"Come, come, boy, don't be afraid."

"Uncle," Ashebir said, stepping forward. "Yes, I am here. How are you? I see you are well and strong, Praise be to Allah."

"Yes we are well. Those days are behind us for now. But I heard of Zewdie's passing." The old man sucked his teeth and shook his head. "It pained me. She was my beloved sister. A tough woman, with her own will. But I loved her." The old man's eyes became watery. He wiped his face with his gabi. "I was hard on her and on you too. It was for her own good. I don't know. I only wish she were still here with us today."

"She always spoke well of you, uncle," Ashebir said. "She knew you had her best interests at heart. Tell me how is Yimam. I remember he went to the army?"

"My son is what they call a Hero. He never came back from the war. It was Allah's will. We only know he died. We don't know where or how. I often wish he would walk through that gate, just as you have done today. Insha'Allah."

"I am sorry really, uncle. I remember him," Ashebir said. "He was good to us."

"We are here today. Let us be happy with our luck," the old man said, pulling a stool into the shade of the house. "I hear you are looking for stories," Mohamed Shinkurt said, his eyes twinkling.

"Your uncle has become quite the story-teller in his old age," Emet Selam said. "You all sit. I will prepare coffee and we can hear the story."

Once they were sitting, the old man coughed and began:

The story begins in a village outside Tinsaye Berhan, in the months before the Emperor Haile Selassie was removed from his throne. The time of dissatisfaction and complaining, and when promises were made. It was a fertile area, in Arussi province, with a river running through and livestock aplenty. A woman, by the name of Elfinesh from Aleltu, came to settle with her husband. She gave birth to a boy and a girl. Her life changed when her husband was killed, pierced by a knife in a futile skirmish. She was left with her two children, a pair of oxen, some cows and a few sheep. More than sufficient for her livelihood, but she needed a helper.

Elfinesh met Ato Haile Tesfaye. He lived in a village not far from the Abune Teklehaymanot church, which, as is customary, sat atop a hill, some few hours on horseback from Tinsaye Berhan. Ato Haile had grown up in that area. He knew every bush, every blade of grass. They moved together and had two children they named Almaz and Genene. However, the couple did not live happily. They bickered, particularly over the children from her first marriage. Things became worse. Tragedy struck when the big rains were particularly heavy and by accident her first born son drowned in a flooded ditch. Elfinesh left for her sister's in Alem Tena. She took the youngest child, Genene, barely two years old, with her. There, overwhelmed by grief and from the long road, she fell fatally ill. While her sister tried to look after her, the small Genene took his first steps across the compound and into the neighbour's house. The kind neighbour picked up the child, cleaned off his hands and feet, kissed him, looked after him and carried him home in the evenings to his sick mother and aunty.

Ashebir nodded in thanks as Selam came round with the dish of dark roasted coffee beans for them to savour. The hot rich smell made his mouth water. He looked at Tedi, glad that his friend was there beside him.

"Your uncle is indeed a good story-teller," Tedi said. "But I wonder what this has to do with you, brother."

"Let's hear," Ashebir said, smiling at his uncle. "We won't stop you, uncle. We want to hear more."

Selam went to pound the roasted beans, a soft thud, thud, in the background.

Mohamed Shinkurt nodded, cleared his throat and went on:

In earlier years, maybe the 1950's, another brother and sister were born in a place called Albuko, in Ethiopia's northern highlands. They were named Ali and Aminat. They were as one. They loved each other, worked, played and laughed together and slept on the same cot. As children they were shepherds, and helped their older brother at harvest and threshing times. When Aminat was eighteen and Ali nineteen, she was given in marriage. It was a good, suitable marriage, but Aminat had a mind of her own and did not care for it. She ran away with Ali to Addis Ababa at the age of twenty-two and came to know city life for the first time. It was tough but she was a hard worker and learned to become a good trader. She met a tall, handsome man of light brown complexion, by the name of Kassahun. He was a Christian. To her family's utter dismay, she converted from Islam and took the name Zewdie, Zewdie Tamru.

Ashebir looked up. He had been listening in a dream to the old man's soft lilting voice, completely taken into the story. Hearing Zewdie's name sent a shock through his body. "My mother, Zewdie?" he said.

"Wait and listen," Mohamed Shinkurt said.

Emet Selam was gently shaking the ground coffee into the round bellied jabena coffee pot. She set it on the hot coals to simmer.

"But if she was married to Kassahun, how is it that Lakew is my father?" Ashebir could see his uncle enjoyed the hold of the story-teller over his listeners.

"Yes it is a surprising story, the one I have to tell. Let me continue." The old man cleared his throat:

> So this Kassahun, he was a driver in a government ministry. A good job. But the nature of his work imposed an unwanted physical distance between the two, as he was often away. But at least once or twice a week they met by telephone. For two and a half years they carried on this arrangement, living in a small place under a korkorro roof in the Casanches district of Addis Ababa. Finally, they agreed to move south to Alem Tena, next to Mojo. The town was a central market and also a transit point for Kassahun. This was altogether more convenient for both of them. Their love was beautiful. And even though Zewdie was sad not to have a child, she led a happy life and her business was good.

"But uncle," Ashebir said, standing up, beating his fist against his chest. "She had me. Look at me, her child. I am here, ye Zewdie lij." He felt angry, excited and afraid all at once. Was his uncle up to his old tricks, clothed in a love story? Was he trying to hurt him again?

"Aysoh," the old man said softly. "Sit down, kutchebel enday. Wait and see what the story will tell us. Nothing changes the love of a mother." He cleared his throat, motioning for Ashebir to sit. "Sit, sit."

"Let's drink coffee," Selam said. "The first round. Here, pass the basket of fendisha, will you Tedi?"

Ashebir looked up to take the hot cup of coffee from Emet Selam. He bowed his head, "Egziyabheresteling, Emet Selam."

Mohamed Shinkurt took the coffee in turn from his wife, nodding his thanks. He slurped loudly. He threw a few pieces of hot white fluffy fendisha in his mouth and chewed thoughtfully before continuing.

> You won't believe it, but tragedy struck once more. Zewdie's beloved husband, Kassahun, was killed by bandits, shiftas. A miserable, pointless attack. Beaten and left in a ditch to die. You cannot imagine the sorrow that filled the house. Mourning and loneliness broke her, and her business declined. So worried was her brother, that he sent for their mother,

Emet Hawa Jafer. She agreed to come from the northern highlands to live together with Zewdie.

"Uncle," Ashebir stood up again. "Emet Hawa was my grandmother." He could feel his legs trembling. His eyes blurred with tears; upset, angry, overwhelmed. "You know that." He stroked his head back and forth with both hands, agitated. "We came with Emet Hawa, here to this village, to this house, when she thought her time was come. She died here. You know she was my grandmother." Ashebir was in tears. "This is not true. Tell me the true story."

"Aysoh, aysoh," Selam said. "Calm yourself. Mohamed, tell him now. Weave the threads together. Don't let the boy suffer."

"Ishi, ishi, we are coming to the end now," the old man said. "Give us all another round of coffee, Selam. It is too good."

When Zewdie converted to Christianity, so did Ali. As I said they were very close. He also took a Christian name. He chose to be called Lakew.

"No," Ashebir said. "What are you saying? Lakew was Zewdie's brother?"

"Lakew was Zewdie's brother, my boy," Mohamed Shinkurt said, nodding. "My brother and sister, Ali and Aminat became Lakew and Zewdie."

Ashebir tried to absorb what Mohamed Shinkurt was telling him. He looked at his uncle.

The man seemed to have become less sure of himself. He suddenly looked old and tired, his face darkened with sadness. "It was a terrible day when I heard what they had done. That they had converted to Christianity. But they were my younger siblings. I loved them," he said.

"When I first went to school, in Debre Zeit. When I was at the orphanage," Ashebir found himself saying. "My first day. I could not say my name. I was puzzled. Why was my mother Zewdie Tamru and my father Lakew Tamru? It was not possible that they were both Tamru." He lowered his head, holding it in his hands.

Tedi sucked his teeth.

"Here, yeney lij," Selam said. "Have another coffee. Be strong. Aysoh."

"Ishi," he said, his head numb. "Egzierstelin, Emet Selam." He passed his cup for her to fill. He looked at the old man. "Please, finish the story, uncle."

"Here, let me give you some water, Abaye," Emet Selam said. She poured some from their gourd into a cup and handed it to the old man.

Mohamed Shinkurt took it, drank and cleared his throat again.

Zewdie undertook trips to Nazareth, Meki and Shashemene from Alem Tena. She bought and sold goods. You know, lentils, spices, onions, potatoes. But in bulk. She was really a tough woman. Lakew helped her from time to time. And with her mother, Hawa, by her side, her business picked up again. She was happy. She did not look for another companion.

When she heard that her neighbour's sister, Elfinesh, had come from the countryside, she went to visit. The poor woman was very ill. And to her delight the small boy, Genene, had the habit of coming into their compound, looking for distractions and to play. He spent his days there and when Zewdie was away, he was with Emet Hawa, playing at her feet while she spun her cotton. When Zewdie went to visit Elfinesh, the poor woman would say, 'Take care of my child, Zewdie, please take care of him.' Elfinesh knew her days were coming to an end. She called for Genene to be brought to her. She looked at him with longing, her eyes full of tears, as if praying to take the image of him with her. How hard for a mother to part from her small child.

"Ashebir," Tedi said. "Are you alright? Are you hearing what I am hearing? You sit there so still."

Ashebir nodded. His eyes full of tears.

The child Genene wept when the others wept. He was too small to understand the mystery of death. But his weeping intensified the weeping around him. Elfinesh was young, a good woman. The mother of four children, one of whom had already been taken from her. The pain of that loss had hastened her own death, and left her baby son in a strange place far from his home and his father.

"Weyne," Selam gasped. "It is a sad story and we are weeping again for that poor Elfinesh. Miskin."

"Uncle, tell me," Ashebir said. "Can you tell me." He hesitated. "What is my name?"

"My boy, your name is Ashebir Lakew Tamru. But you were once that small boy, Genene Haile Tesfaye."

Ashebir had an awful feeling in his belly. He got up and ran to the river's edge. He vomited, and vomited. He sank to his haunches and held the ground with his open hands, breathing, trying to steady himself. He waited and listened, to see what his body would do next.

"Ashebir," he heard Tedi calling. "Take it easy, brother."

Ashebir moved closer to the river's edge, and scooped up the river water. The Ataye river water. The water he had swum in, drunk from, washed his clothes in, Zewdie's clothes. He had led their animals to that water and let them drink their fill. He cupped the clear freshness in his hands and chucked it at his face, over and over. He sobbed as he did this. He could not stop. Was he mourning his mother? His real mother? It felt like it.

He felt Tedi's hand firmly on his shoulder. "Aysoh, Ashebir. It's enough. It's OK. Ishi? It's OK. Come, let's sit down."

They sat on the bank together, watching the river go by, as it had done for years and as it would for many more, Insha'Allah.

"You know it was almost empty when Zewdie and I left. It was so shallow. We could not swim in it. It came to our ankles," Ashebir said.

"And now look at it," Tedi said. "It is strong and full. Beautiful."

"I feel strange. Almost as if I am not in my body. As if I am a snake that shed its skin. Who am I, Tedi? And how can it be that my mother, Zewdie, is not my mother? She will always be my mother."

"You are Ashebir. And Zewdie is your mother. You are Ashebir who is about to discover who his father is. You have been alone all these years. This is amazing. Yigirmal. You will find your family, Ashebir." Then Tedi laughed and cuffed Ashebir gently across his head. "And you are Genene, Genene Haile."

"Hey," Ashebir jumped up and wrestled his friend.

They played like they used to as boys to help forget their worries, forget all the sadness.

"Who is that man? Genene Haile?" Tedi teased him. "Your father, Haile Tesfaye from that small town in Arussi? Who is he? Shall we find out the end of the story?"

"Innihid," Ashebir said, taking his friend's hand. "Let's go and find out."

They walked back to Mohamed Shinkurt's compound. The old man was standing by the fence. He pulled his gildim closer round his waist and threw his gabi around his shoulders. His face softened from the worried look as he saw them coming.

"Boys, come," he called. "We will eat together."

"Let us hear the story first, uncle," Tedi said.

"Ishi, sit down. We can continue while Selam prepares our food."

The smell of frying onions and garlic came from inside the gojo-bate, the smoke from the fire rose in a thin plume from the roof. Ashebir's mouth watered. His aunt would be preparing her renowned sherro.

"The mystery of your story, of love and loss, has given us an appetite, uncle," Tedi said, voicing Ashebir's thoughts. "Before we take food though, we need to know how it ends."

Ashebir could not speak. Sitting on the low stool before his uncle once more, all the emotions and doubts returned to freeze his tongue. He looked intently at Mohamed Shinkurt. He had been a Big Man in the village, a respected elder. Ashebir's eyes traced the man's familiar face, so like Zewdie and Lakew's, now aged by the years passing, by the strong sun and mountain air. The man's eyes were steady. There was no malice or forgery in his expression. He must be telling them the truth. It was clear Selam knew the story. He trusted she would not let Mohamed Shinkurt deceive him.

Mohamed Shinkurt took a sip from the cup of water and cleared his throat.

> News of the death of his young wife reached Ato Haile Tesfaye in their village in the mountains, some few hours by mule from Tinsaye Berhan. He left for Alem Tena as soon as he heard the news. Once there, however, he could not wait to attend the burial ceremony, being anxious to return home where he had left Genene's older sister in the care of a neighbour. While he was not a man of many words or emotions, he was deeply saddened by the early passing of Elfinesh. He had hoped for a reconciliation with the mother of his children. He stayed for four days of mourning. During that time, they discussed 'the future of Genene' together. Ato Haile Tesfaye worried about how he would take care of this small child. He had a farm and livestock to look after. His sister-in-law told him of Elfinesh's wish, that Genene should stay with Zewdie and her mother, Emet Hawa. The child had become accustomed to them, she said. It was as if the boy had chosen them himself. She

described how the boy went there every day to eat and play. She told him that Zewdie had no children of her own and was willing to adopt Genene. Haile listened quietly. He let the idea run through his thoughts and dreams at night. Finally, seeing that the child was truly loved and cared for by Zewdie and the elderly woman, he agreed. 'Ishi,' he said to them. 'If my boy is to stay with you, assure me that you will stay here in Alem Tena. So I will know where to find him. His aunt is here to watch over him too.' Zewdie, overjoyed, agreed wholeheartedly. She had grown to love Genene as her own. And that was how she and her mother came to take the child as their own and to give him a new name, Ashebir Lakew.

They sat in silence. Ashebir Lakew. The name seemed to have taken on a new meaning and lingered between them in the now hot mountain air.

"So that was why Zewdie wanted to leave me behind," Ashebir said. "I remember it well. Zewdie and Emet Hawa told me they were leaving and that I could not go with them. No wonder. She had made a promise. But I wept. I cried. I could not be without them. So they agreed to bring me here with them." He could not sort his feelings. The idea that Zewdie was not his mother, that she had known his true mother, had spoken with his father. These people he did not know. His parents. "My father," he suddenly realised. "All these years he could not find me." He looked up. "Is he still alive? My father? Haile Tesfaye? Is he alive?"

"I have no way of knowing, my boy," Mohamed Shinkurt said. "You will have to go to that village in the mountains of Arussi to ask for him. That is your country, your home. That is the place you were born. Not Alem Tena, not this village. You are not one of us."

"Come now, Mohamed," Selam said, carrying their mesob[97] out and setting it under the eaves. "You will always be one of us, Ashebir. You will always be Zewdie's son. She was your mother. She gave you all her love."

"True," the old man said, suddenly smiling. "This is true. Allah be praised. If ever a mother loved her son, it was she. Nothing changes the love of a mother."

"Will you go there?" Tedi said. "To look for Haile?"

---

[97] A woven basket table with conical shaped lid.

"I don't know," Ashebir said.

"Come, eat," Selam said. "This has been a shock. You will decide what to do in time. But now, let's try and calm down, let's give thanks and eat." She disappeared into their gojo-bate and returned with a red plastic bowl of water and a small piece of soap. She held it before her husband first. And then moved to Ashebir and Tedi. They washed hands in turn.

Each bowed their head and gave thanks. They moved to sit around the mesob. She laid out the injera and spooned the hot sherro into the middle. "Eat," she said. "Eat."

They ate in silence, Ashebir thinking he was feeding this new person he had become, he was feeding Genene. He was feeding Ashebir. He could not fathom what this all meant, and his body still felt as if it did not belong to him.

**

The days passed and became months. After they had eaten, Ashebir and Tedi had said farewell to Mohamed Shinkurt and his wife Selam, giving assurances they would return. As promised the day before, they had gone to visit Emet Temima and her husband, Mohamed Ahmed, and their friend, Mohamed Bilal from Albuko. They had taken coffee with Mohamed Abdu and his wife. It felt like one of his dreams. Ashebir heard the voices and breathed in the smells from his childhood. Familiar and far away. Much as he loved to be there, much as it soothed the longing, he wanted to return to the sanctuary of his home in Addis. He needed to think. He had thanked Tedi, who tried to persuade him to stay one more day, and had taken the bus home, reaching his own gate well into the night.

Some days he tried to forget he had ever heard Mohamed Shinkurt's story. But he could not unknow it and it lingered in a corner of his mind. On other days, the tension that precedes a difficult decision rose in his throat so that he could barely speak. Every day he woke and slept thinking of Zewdie. Missing her even more. Wishing he could sit and talk with her by the fire in their gojo-bate, feel her hand holding his, reassuring him, as she had always done. More than anything, he wished he could hear the story from her own lips.

You will always be my mother, he would tell her in his mind.

Soon a year was gone. The story of Genene and Ashebir did not sit easy with him. He was constantly troubled. His natural father was a man called Haile Tesfaye. His birth place, Tinsaye Berhan. Part of him wanted to go and find out if his father was still alive, see him face to face. Did he resemble him? Part of him wished he had never heard the story at all.

**

One night he woke. He pulled back the blind. The light on the veranda was on. One bulb and a sky full of stars lit up the compound. It was October and chilly. He wrapped up and went outside. He walked across the lawn to sit on the rock on which he had painted Muletta Mountain.

"Here I sit, on my mountain, looking up at the stars," he thought. The moon disappeared behind a cloud and reappeared again, as if it was playing with him. The dark and the light, the smile and the frown, a game he played with the neighbours' children, making them squeal with laughter.

"Shall I, shan't I," he thought. "What to do."

Sammy and Desalegn couldn't understand. "If your father, your father, Ashebir, might be there, might be alive, then why not go? What is stopping you?"

A mountain of reasons. A scattering of stars shedding points of light, then disappearing again behind clouds. He didn't know and couldn't explain.

So he had thrown his energy into opening a tiny shop with Desalegn's help. They had decided to start small-small to see what the demand for different products might be. Desalegn was the one who had stood up for him on that first day of school. They had been friends ever since. He was a bright boy. He had joined Ashebir at the school in Akaki, and gone from there to a business school in Addis. He was already working and earning a decent wage. He could invest in the business.

Starting the small shop had given Ashebir new life. He'd stopped his night school at Addis Ababa University and thrown all his energy into the business. His aim was to grow it into a proper roadside shop. He would sell everything people needed: fruit and vegetables, a twist of sugar to a half kilo, a cup full of cooking oil to a litre, enough green coffee beans for one jabena to a kilo or more, Omo soap powder, black plastic slippers, a packet of dry biscuits, baby milk powder, Coca Cola and Fanta. Their neighbourhood just had one or two 'hole in the wall' kiosks and a bottle store. There was definitely room for more.

He looked up into the night sky. Ishi, it's enough, he thought. I have to go. How would it be for Haile Tesfaye? If he was still alive. To suddenly see his son after all these years? He wondered if his father had come to visit him in Alem Tena after Elfinesh died and before they moved up to Ataye. Had he come looking for me?

Invigorated by his decision, he went back into the house to pack a small bag. He woke Sammy and Desalegn. "I've decided to go," he said.

"Finally," Sammy said, stretching sleepily. "Egziyabher ante gar yihun."

"Go well," Desalegn said. "We'll pray you return with good news."

The light was coming up. It was a fresh morning. He hailed a taxi to La Gare bus station where he would find transport to Nazareth.

**

The ticket tout shouted destinations, "Akaki, Dukem, Debre Zeit, Mojo, Nazareth! Innihid!" He collected fares as people climbed on board.

Ashebir took his chosen seat at the back by the window. He liked to watch the countryside pass by. The bus sweated out last night's onion, garlic and berbere, laced with the morning's soap and water, and fresh-washed gabis. There was an air of adventure and anticipation.

They stopped in Akaki where he had gone to school. He had been the first of the orphans to go there. His mind flashed with the alarm he had felt when the school emptied in a fit of panic, just six years before. Mengistu had fled to Zimbabwe as the EPRDF[98] descended from the north. They had invaded Addis from all sides. He bit his lip. No one looked out for the orphans. Teachers took off for their homes. Parents swept into the school, hastily packed bags into backs of cars and disappeared with their children. Like when they came with their picnics on Sundays, sitting out with their spread of food on the lawns surrounding the school. The Sunday picnics had always made him feel sad. He'd felt it. That he didn't have a family. That Zewdie was gone. That Izzie was no longer there.

So of course, on that day too, no one had come for them. He and Desalegn had made a run for the railway line. Like a pair of dooriyey, they had jumped the train. It had been pure desperation. They were terrified. It was the only way to get back to the one home they knew, the orphanage in Debre Zeit. They had climbed on top of the carriages,

---

[98] Ethiopian Peoples' Revolutionary Democratic Front.

and held on tight. The real dooriyey, who thought that he and Desalegn must have money on them, threatened them. Rough looking lads with green khat teeth and red eyes, who plied contraband between Addis Ababa and Dire Dawa. He and Desalegn had nothing to give them. At Debre Zeit they had jumped off and run, hearts pounding, out of breath, laughing their fear and excitement all the way up the narrow, dusty road to the orphanage. When they finally reached there, he heard that Izzie had been on the phone.

"Where is Ashebir?" they told him she'd said. "I called the school. They said no one is left. Where are the boys? Where is Ashebir? Is he OK?"

She had called from London, they said.

He had not been forgotten.

In the night, lying together in their dormitories at the orphanage, he and the boys had listened to the artillery pounding the Ethiopian Airforce headquarters only a few miles away. It had been the end of the Derg.

**

Arriving in Debre Zeit, the taxi-bus drove alongside the railway line, behind which lay the Girls' Home and beyond that, the open fields of maize. They stopped in this all too familiar place, where he had grown up and gone to his first school, and the place to which he had returned time and again. The boys and girls from the orphanage had become his family.

"Mojo, Mojo, Nazareth!" The tout called out in his sing-song voice, competing with others. There was no shortage of passengers. They were soon on the road again. They crossed the Mojo bridge, taking the fork to the south-east. The other fork, to the south-west, went past Koka Dam and on to Alem Tena. Zewdie would have been in Mojo many a time, and done her trading there.

And his mother, Elfinesh. That was difficult to take in. My mother, Elfinesh. She will have passed through Mojo with him on her back, on her way to her sister's in Alem Tena. Hard to imagine those lives gone by. How they felt, what they thought, the decisions they took then, that lead to him being in this place right here and now.

"Nazareth! Nazareth! Woradjey! Woradjey!" The tout called out. "We have arrived. Everyone get down. Woradjey! Woradjey!"

Ashebir climbed down into the heat.

"Sodere – Tinsaye Berhan!" The touts in the far corner of the bus station shouted. There were lines of small taxi-buses and a few large orange Anbessa coaches. And in the far corner, three battered old Land Rovers, clearly going to Tinsaye Berhan and on to Dire Dawa.

Nazareth was hot, hot, hot. He took off his jacket and stuffed it into his bag.

"Sodere – Tinsaye Berhan!" He heard the call again. It was time to go.

The hot springs at Sodere was one of the boys' favourite outings. The Awash river flowed nearby, full of hope, magic and crocodiles. The Afar lived in the dusty valley, moving their animals along its banks, taking their camel trains up north to the Danakil and past Ataye. The place where he and Mohamed Abdu had once so narrowly skimmed fate, rescued at the last minute by Wozeiro Zeineba. Those stories were vivid in his mind, like yesterday.

A boy stood next to one of the Land Rovers calling out, "Sodere – Dere – Tinsaye Berhan! Innihid!" He banged the side of the vehicle making it clang loudly.

It was an old model, battered and road-worn. Ashebir had no choice. Like the shattered Land Rover he had climbed into with Zewdie when they left Ataye, it would most likely get him there. He could still see his uncle, Mohamed Shinkurt, waving at them, until he became small. And then they had turned a corner and he disappeared.

Inside the open-backed vehicle there were metal benches on either side. The tattered awning would provide some protection from the sun. Ashebir paid his fare and climbed in, taking an inside seat, hoping it would be less dusty than the one over the back wheels by the tailgate.

"Tinsaye Berhan! Abomssa!" the boy called out, until he began to sound hoarse.

Two hours passed before all seats were taken and they were able to leave. It was one thirty in the afternoon when the vehicle finally shuddered into action, letting a large puff of black exhaust out the back. Ashebir prayed they would reach before nightfall. He did not want to look for somewhere to stay in the dark. Stories of dooriyey and shiftas made ordinary folk away from home nervous.

The other passengers were farmers, who had come to the market in Mojo. They mainly spoke Orominya. They filled the floor between the seats with hessian sacks full of produce. There was a warm congenial atmosphere amongst them. They had done good business.

The man opposite, however, stared at Ashebir with a discomforting intensity. Even though the days of the Derg were in the past, a sense of unease between strangers remained. Ashebir was aware he looked like a city boy, that he had a different accent, and was clearly not from these parts.

It was almost a relief when the man's face relaxed. "Where are you going?" he said.

"To Tinsaye Berhan," Ashebir replied.

They had to raise their voices over the noise of the engine, and the rattle of the chassis as they lurched and bumped over the uneven road. With every jolt, Ashebir landed painfully on the bones in his back-side as they met with the metal seat. He had grown taller and remained skinny.

"You have relatives there?"

"Yes," Ashebir said, hesitant to say more. He didn't even know if his father was alive. If he was, would his father welcome him? And what did he look like?

"What are their names?" the man said, leaning forward. "I am sure to know them." He might have been his father's age, somewhere in his forties, maybe. His face weather-beaten like Mohamed Shinkurt's.

"Woradjey for Sodere! Sodere! Sodere!" the boy called out as the vehicle drew into the roadside. He banged on the side of the car.

Ashebir peered down the road. They were in the Awash Valley. So hot that the air stood still. As if in shock.

"Don't worry, you can tell me," the man said. "In Tinsaye Berhan we all know one another."

"His name is Haile Tesfaye," Ashebir said.

"Haile Tesfaye?" the man said, the name obviously familiar.

Ashebir felt a jolt of excitement.

"Who is he to you?"

"He is my father."

"Befitsum? Honestly? I didn't know he had a grown son."

"Yes," Ashebir said, his heart lifting. His father was alive. "I am his son."

"I know him," the man went on. "He is a farmer in the hills above Tinsaye Berhan and a good carpenter."

The Land Rover took off with a jolt. It shuddered over the rutted, potholed road, whining and straining up the hillside past Tibila and the orange groves. It seemed happier on the plains. But the road to Tinsaye Berhan climbed steeply into the highlands, with wide open views over the valleys below and to the mountains further south. The old vehicle had to make an effort.

The man continued talking.

Ashebir's mind wandered. He peered out at the road. This was the road along which his mother Elfinesh must have carried him, the infant child, Genene. It was unbelievable. It was a long way from the village beyond Tinsaye Berhan to Alem Tena.

**

They finally arrived.

"Tinsaye Berhan! Tinsaye Berhan! Woradjey! Woradjey!" The tout banged the side of the vehicle.

The sun had gone down, leaving the sky washed pale dusty blue and orange. There was still just enough time for him to find shelter before dark. The man had to go far and regretted he could not offer Ashebir a place to stay. He wished him luck, they shook hands and bade each other farewell.

Ashebir started his search near the central square. Small eateries and coffee houses that might offer a bed for the night. But the places where he enquired were already full. He leant against a vehicle, slightly nervous, wondering what to do. He was an easy target for dooriyey.

A boy, his broad smile displaying a gap between his front teeth, came up to him with a bounce in his feet. He carried a tray of cigarettes and caramella. Ashebir put a hand up to indicate he was not buying.

"What is it?" the boy said. "What are you doing? It is late."

"I know," Ashebir said. "The hotels are full."

"Who are you looking for?"

"Do you know Ato Haile Tesfaye?"

"Yes, I know him. He lives far from here." The child pointed his chin upwards to the hills behind them. "It takes hours to reach that place."

"How do you know him?" Ashebir said, surprised.

"He comes to market every Saturday and drinks tella at our house."

"I see," Ashebir said. "Does your mother take guests?"

"Ishi, let's go," the boy said. "Innihid, let's ask her. Ade Senbeta is her name. Maybe you can stay the night with us."

The boy was a typical street boy, cheeky and bright. He took off with a skip in his step.

Ashebir walked alongside him as dusk fell and the evening became cooler. The small town was a mix of dwellings. Mostly traditional mud chikka-bate and others improved by korkorro roofs. His travelling companion had said something about a generator and electricity but there was none. No loud rumbling engine. A few places were lit inside by the warm orange glow of a kerosene lamp.

The boy's home was a simple place. He went inside, motioning Ashebir to wait by the door. He returned with his mother. She was older than Ashebir expected. She looked at him intensely, as if she might read his soul. A gift many mothers seem to possess.

"Tenasteling," she said. "My son says you just arrived in town."

She did not look on him unkindly, so he felt encouraged to speak. He repeated his tale and said he had no place to stay for the night. She was his only hope.

Behind him it was now dark. Stray dogs had taken up their watch, taking turns to bark at the possibility of danger lurking in the shadows. If Ade Senbeta did not take him in, he would have to sleep outside in the chill of the mountain air. He shivered involuntarily at the thought.

"Come in," she said. "It is too cold. You can stay here tonight."

Inside was gloomy. It was hard to see his way until his eyes had adjusted.

"The town generator broke six months ago and has not been fixed since," she said. She lit a lamp and showed him to a small raised platform in one corner, made of mud, with a grain sack for a pillow. That was to be his bed for the night.

"First show me your ID?" she said. "You look like a good man, but we have to be careful."

He pulled his wallet from his back pocket and showed her his ID with the grainy black and white photo he had had taken in Mercato. His face was distorted with the effort to stop laughing. Each time the photographer at the kiosk had asked him to sit still and look serious, Sammy had pulled a face.

"Ishi," she said, handing it back to him after she had peered at it for a while under the lamp. "You know, there's something about you that reminds me of Ato Haile. It certainly will be a surprise for him to find you here."

Her words sent a flutter of nerves through his stomach. This was real. He would see his father face to face the next day. He bowed his head and thanked her. He was grateful for her warmth and simple hospitality.

She placed a jabena on the fire and heated the remaining coffee. She gave him a cupful, bidding him good night. "Your father will be in the market tomorrow. My son will take you to meet him."

Despite Ade Senbeta's efforts, Ashebir could not sleep. His two beings seemed to be jostling for his mind. Genene and Ashebir. What would Genene have been like without Ashebir. How would it have been if he had grown up in the hills above Tinsaye Berhan? Would he have learnt to be a carpenter like his father? He would have stayed a real country boy and become a farmer. Maybe, like Mohamed Abdu, he would already be married with a child. Now and then he dropped off to sleep. Now and then he woke with his heart racing. How would he know it was his father? He calmed himself. He would be with Ade Senbeta's son. The boy would introduce them. Now that the time had come, it was hard to wait these few hours. He was eager for the day to start. The night seemed to have no end.

Finally, dawn came to transform the room. He could make out the round water gourd in the corner and a shelf on the wall with a row of plastic cups. He sat up, pulled on his jacket and drew his gabi round his shoulders. He went out of the house and found a boulder to sit on and contemplate.

Ade Senbeta came out looking for him. "There you are," she said. "How are you? Did you sleep?"

"Tenasteling," he said, going towards her. He had to lie of course. "I slept very well thank you, Ade Senbeta."

"What a blessing," she said. "A father will find his long lost son. It is as it was written in the Bible."

He laughed. "This is true," he said, quietly hoping that his father would be as overjoyed as the father in the parable.

"He will be the happiest man on earth today," she said. "Come drink tea and then my boy can take you to the market."

"Ishi," he said. "Betam Egziyabheresteling." She had rescued him. He was so very grateful to her, and to her boy, for not abandoning him the night before.

**

Ashebir and the boy took the main road out of town.

"The market is over there," the boy said, pointing. He carried his box of cigarettes, caramella, packets of tissues, the usual. "We will cross the river to reach it. See. People are already coming from the villages around here."

He obviously loved the market, as Ashebir had. So much going on, gossip and interesting characters.

It was a steep and clambering walk. Sometimes there was a path and sometimes not. He would have managed it easily as a boy. He put out a hand to steady himself, catching a branch to act as a helping hand.

The boy sprung on ahead like a mountain goat.

They stood and looked down the steep hillside to the river below. Women were washing clothes, spreading white gabis across the gorse bushes to dry in the sun. There was laughter and the echo of voices further downstream. Sounds from his past in Ataye. He wondered what had happened to Yishaereg, whether she was still alive.

"Innihid," the boy said, as if he knew he was interrupting Ashebir's dreaming.

Ashebir nodded, brought back to the moment.

They reached a spot from where they could see people coming down the slopes and through the bush, see them gathering in the open space with their produce and animals. There was something wonderful about watching the country folk making their way to market.

He would soon be standing in front of his father. He was slightly out of breath, not only from the exertion but with the tension, the anxiety.

"Look," the boy said, pointing to the hillside opposite.

There were four men walking in their direction.

"That one, the tall one, he is Ato Haile Tesfaye. That one is your father."

Ashebir stopped. His heart beat in his throat. Zewdie. Be with me, Zewdie. The thought of her brought tears to his eyes. He wiped his face with his gabi. His legs might give way. He must stay standing. He must move forward. He took a few steps.

"Boys, mindin neouw?" A woman said, trying to pass with her large bundle of firewood. "Why stop on the path? What is it?"

Ashebir and the boy moved to one side without speaking. They let her pass with her donkey, its hooves click-clacking.

Ashebir was looking directly into Ato Haile Tesfaye's eyes.

The man returned the look with a mixture of shock and recognition.

Yes, the man clearly knew who he was. Wey! Enday, Ashebir thought. What now?

The man was suddenly standing not an arm's length from him. "Genene. Genene. Is it you?"

"Yes, it is," Ashebir said, his legs shaking. "Eney negne. It's me."

He took a step towards the man, and felt his arms around him. He breathed in the strong country smell of his father's being and let out a sob. His face buried in his father's gabi, he could smell the morning woodsmoke, and the soft hide of zebu cows. All so familiar, reminding him of his village and Zewdie. He felt the man's strong arms around him. Could feel him shudder, hear his deep breathing.

The other men who had come with Ato Haile talked to each other in low voices.

"Betam yigirmal enday, betam yigirmal."

"It's surprising indeed. Where did he come from after all this time?"

"Maybe he was in the war?" one man said and tutted.

"He looks like Haile."

"Befitsum."

"It is his son. The one he thought was dead."

"Egziyabher alle."

"Haile, we should go. We need to get to the market."

Ato Haile drew away from Ashebir, still holding onto his shoulders as if to make sure he did not disappear. "Ishi, Ishi," he said. "I will come, I will see you there."

The men took turns to shake Ashebir by the hand, they held him and kissed him on each cheek several times. They blessed him and told him not to disappear, "At-taffa," they said. They turned and headed for the market, bending into each other, talking as they went.

"Let's sit under that tree," Ato Haile said. "It is famous in these parts. It's a meeting place and a resting place. Come."

It was a large old warka tree. Three log-shaped beehives hung at angles from the branches. Ashebir was familiar with these trees. It was under their warka tree in the village that he had seen the white hyena on his way to Emet Fahte's that night.

"Ishi," he said, and let himself be led by the man.

"When the tree flowers, it hums and sings and produces the best honey," Ato Haile said with a smile. "Let's sit."

They sat in silence for a while. Ato Haile took a piece of dried grass and drew patterns in the soil. "You know, last night, when I reached home late, I heard the news that you had arrived. 'Ato Haile Tesfaye's lost son is in town,' they were saying."

"How is that possible?" Ashebir said. But then he knew this village life.

"The man you met on the road sent a horseman with the news to my place."

Ashebir sat facing his father. He was a tall, skinny man, but strong. His was a thin, warm brown, face. His eyes sat deep in their sockets, looking worriedly onto the world. The endless worry of provision, survival and loss. But they smiled too, with warmth and humour. Ashebir realised he felt at ease with him, with his father!

"You are a grown man, taller and darker than I expected, Genene, but I know your face," Ato Haile said, his voice catching. "You have not changed. My child is still looking at me with those wide inquisitive eyes." He paused. "I looked for you. I came looking in Alem Tena, but could not find you. Where did they go? I wondered. Your mother's sister did not have an answer for me. 'They will come,' is all she said." He wiped his face with his gabi. "I prayed every night that my Creator should please help me, help me find my son." He raised both hands up to the sky, praised the Lord and gave thanks. "Egziyabher alle. He heard my prayers." He tutted, and sniffed into his gabi, wiping his eyes. "Such a long wait."

Ashebir sat silent, looking, listening, hardly breathing. He was a good man, his father. An honest man. What could he say to ease his pain?

Ato Haile reached out to touch Ashebir's face. He ran those hands, which knew how to carve a life, a livelihood, out of the harsh Ethiopian mountains, over Ashebir's face and shoulders. He patted Ashebir's chest, as if touching him would confirm his existence. "You are really here, my boy," he said, tears in his eyes.

Ashebir could see and feel the man's wound, the years of longing and worry he had endured. But maybe not until he had a child himself would he fully understand just how painful that wound was.

"My mother," Ashebir managed to say, his voice a whisper. "What about my mother?" Saying this hurt, after all the years believing Zewdie was his mother. He could not be disloyal to her. But Ato Haile, Elfinesh and Zewdie, had all met when he was too small to know anything. They had spoken and made decisions.

Ato Haile let go of Ashebir and bowed his head into his cupped hands. "Wey guud," he said, letting out a long deep sigh. "Your mother, Elfinesh Aboye died when you were an infant. You have a sister, an older sister she left behind. She is married now with children, thanks to God." He paused letting out a sigh. "Wey! I came so many times hoping to find you."

"I am sorry," Ashebir said quietly, laying a hand on the man's arm. "Azenalehu. I am sorry." He shifted uncomfortably. What could he do?

"I finally came to the conclusion that you had died. That they had taken you into the military and you had been killed. That was what I decided to believe."

They sat in silence, the air buzzing, insects filling the emptiness.

Ashebir had no words. He just felt stunned and sad. He waited.

"What happened?" Ato Haile said. "I heard you went with Zewdie and her mother. Somewhere up in northern Shewa, but they were not sure. They kept telling me, 'They will come.'"

"We went to their village, outside Ataye. Zewdie's mother Emet Hawa was very sick. She wanted to go home to die." Ashebir said, his voice croaky. "Until the hunger came, we lived there."

"So you were a country boy," Ato Haile said.

"I was," Ashebir smiled. "I was a shepherd boy with a sling shot."

"Ah, that is good to hear," Ato Haile managed to smile. "But not anymore. I can see that. Where are you living?"

"Addis Ababa, I live in Addis," he said. He wanted to tell Ato Haile about Zewdie. His heart beat faster.

"And Zewdie?" Ato Haile said. "Is she there with you?"

"She died. She died on the road," Ashebir said. "It's a long time back. I was small. I think she was trying to bring me back to you. The hunger. We had nothing more to eat. She got very sick."

"I am sorry," Ato Haile said, tutting and sighing. He put his arm around Ashebir.

They sat again in silence.

"How did you know where to find me?" Ato Haile said.

"I went home to Ataye. It was her brother, Mohamed Shinkurt, who told me the story from the beginning. He did not know if you were alive, but he said my mother had come from Tinsaye Berhan. That I might find you here."

"So will you come home now? Will you come and stay?"

"I will come," Ashebir said. "But not right away. Not now. I will come in a week or so."

"We have a lot to talk about," Ato Haile said. "Do you work in Addis?"

"Yes, I have a small shop," Ashebir felt proud to be able to say this. "We are starting small and hope to grow into a good business."

"But you will come home now? I need you here, Genene. I can do with another man at home."

Ashebir looked at the hope and expectation in the man's eyes. He did not want to disappoint him straight away. He was sure he could not live a village life again. He had been in the city for too long. "I will come and we can talk," he said.

"Ishi, ishi," Ato Haile said. "I understand." He drew lines in the soil with the long piece of dried grass. Then he said, "What happened to you after Zewdie passed? How did you survive alone?"

"It was a farenj woman, Izzie, who helped me, father. Shall I call you father? Ababa? Abaye?" He fell into the man's arms and wept. "I'm sorry. I'm sorry. This is too much."

They held each other. The shadows under the warka tree, the hum of bees making their honey and the murmur from the market enveloped them like a blanket.

"Come, Genene. Aysoh. We have found each other, finally. This is God's will. A miracle. We will take a coffee together. Then you will come back soon and stay with me." He started to get up. "Come I will walk with you to town."

"Ishi," Ashebir said, sniffing hard and wiping his face with his gabi. "That's good. Let's do that."

They stood together. Father and son, side by side. If only Zewdie could see this. What would she say?

"And then I will have to leave, to reach before dark." Ashebir said. He would have to stay over in Nazareth and travel on to Addis the following day.

"But you will come," Ato Haile said.

"I will come, Ababa," Ashebir said, suddenly feeling relief. "I feel free, like I have been born again." The cloud that had hung over his dreaming, the time of questions with no answers, had passed. He too knew where he came from. He too knew his story. The moon and the stars would shine light into his life again. "I will come back. I will come. We have so many things to tell each other."

Ato Haile put an arm around his shoulders.

They walked together.

A Note on the Author

Fra von Massow, born to Nod and Peter Bourne in 1954, Blackheath, London, is a mother, social development worker, youth and family support worker and writer. From 1977, and over a period of ten years, she lived and worked in Malawi, Ethiopia (1982-1986) and Zaire. Between 2000 and 2003, she lived and worked in India for three years with her husband and son. From 2011, she was proud to be part of the Kids Company, and then Corner House team in London for six years.

She has two sons whom she aims to visit in Ethiopia and Italy respectively whenever possible. She lives between London and a small village on the River Elbe in Germany, with her husband Valentin.

Acknowledgements

Grateful thanks to Bedilu Haile for entrusting me with his story and allowing me to weave a fictionalised thread through it.

Honing the craft of writing, an ongoing process, was initially influenced by a weekend workshop with Roselle Angwin. It was Roselle who suggested I add my side of the story to the book.

Gratitude to my creative writing teachers thereafter: Anne Aylor, a magical inspiration and wonderful teacher over many years, and Elise Valmorbida for her encouragement and vitality.

Appreciation to two special writers' groups for the many workshopping hours spent crafting our stories: *The Splinters* including Claud Devlin, Hekate Papadaki, Gerard Macdonald, Emma Healey, Ben Gardner Gray, Paula Brooke and Tray Morgen; and *The ZenAzzurrians* including Anne Aylor, Elise Valmorbida, Roger Levy, Anne Marie Neary, Aimee Hansen and Richard Simmons. Thank you all for your advice, comments, encouragement and friendship, and to Al Anderson for his support over the years.

Thank you to my first readers: Charlotte Uslar, Haneya Ahmed Bomba, Eloise Alanna and Maggie Davies, and to my final readers: Bedilu Haile, Asegid Alemayehu, Valentin von Massow, Sonia Bucci and Sally Bunning.

A big thank you to my editor, Sebastian von Massow, and to my amazing publishing team: Sebastian von Massow, Barnaby Dicker and Charlotte Uslar. And many thanks to Nadja von Massow for the final font and formatting fix!

For my wellbeing through the Covid months, love and appreciation to Lizzie Smosarski and Grace Robinson.

A quiet thanks to Theodros and Sileshi and to Airi Tuomi and Mami.

This has been a long project and I have my families in Ethiopia, England and Germany to thank for their continuous encouragement and support. A special thanks to Valentin, Bedilu and Sebastian for always believing!

Printed in Great Britain
by Amazon